P9-DHA-269

STEPHEN
KING

HEARTS IN ATLANTIS

SCRIBNER

SCRIBNER
1230 Avenue of the Americas
New York, NY 10020

This book is a work of fiction. Names, characters, places, and incidents either are products of the author's imagination or are used fictitiously. Any resemblance to actual events or locales or persons, living or dead, is entirely coincidental.

DESIGNED BY ERICH HOBBING

Set in Garamond No. 3

Manufactured in the United States of America

3 5 7 9 10 8 6 4 2

Library of Congress Cataloging-in-Publication Data
King, Stephen, 1947–
Hearts in Atlantis / Stephen King.
p. cm.
1. United States—Social life and customs—20th century Fiction.
2. Vietnamese Conflict, 1961–1975 Fiction. I. Title.
PS3561.I483H4 1999
813'.54—dc21 99-23889
CIP
ISBN 0-684-85351-5

A version of "Blind Willie" appeared in the final issue of *Antaeus,* Autumn 1994.

This is for Joseph and Leanora and Ethan:
I told you all that to tell you this.

Number 6: What do you want?
Number 2: Information.
Number 6: Whose side are you on?
Number 2: That would be telling. We want information.
Number 6: You won't get it!
Number 2: By hook or by crook . . . we will.

The Prisoner

Simon stayed where he was, a small brown image, concealed by the leaves. Even if he shut his eyes the sow's head still remained like an after-image. The half-shut eyes were dim with the infinite cynicism of adult life. They assured Simon that everything was a bad business.

WILLIAM GOLDING,
Lord of the Flies

"We blew it."

Easy Rider

1960: They had a stick sharpened at both ends.

1960

Low Men in Yellow Coats

I. A BOY AND HIS MOTHER. BOBBY'S BIRTHDAY. THE NEW ROOMER. OF TIME AND STRANGERS.

Bobby Garfield's father had been one of those fellows who start losing their hair in their twenties and are completely bald by the age of forty-five or so. Randall Garfield was spared this extremity by dying of a heart attack at thirty-six. He was a real-estate agent, and breathed his last on the kitchen floor of someone else's house. The potential buyer was in the living room, trying to call an ambulance on a disconnected phone, when Bobby's dad passed away. At this time Bobby was three. He had vague memories of a man tickling him and then kissing his cheeks and his forehead. He was pretty sure that man had been his dad. SADLY MISSED, it said on Randall Garfield's gravestone, but his mom never seemed all that sad, and as for Bobby himself . . . well, how could you miss a guy you could hardly remember?

Eight years after his father's death, Bobby fell violently in love with the twenty-six-inch Schwinn in the window of the Harwich Western Auto. He hinted to his mother about the Schwinn in every way he knew, and finally pointed it out to her one night when they were walking home from the movies (the show had been *The Dark at the Top of the Stairs,* which Bobby didn't understand but liked anyway, especially the part where Dorothy McGuire flopped back in a chair and showed off her long legs). As they passed the hardware store, Bobby mentioned casually that the bike in the window would sure make a great eleventh-birthday present for some lucky kid.

"Don't even think about it," she said. "I can't afford a bike for your birthday. Your father didn't exactly leave us well off, you know."

Although Randall had been dead ever since Truman was President and now Eisenhower was almost done with his eight-year cruise, *Your father didn't exactly leave us well off* was still his mother's most common response to anything Bobby suggested which might entail an expenditure of more than a dollar. Usually the comment was accompanied by a reproachful look, as if the man had run off rather than died.

No bike for his birthday. Bobby pondered this glumly on their walk home, his pleasure at the strange, muddled movie they had seen mostly gone. He didn't argue with his mother, or try to coax her—that would bring on a counterattack, and when Liz Garfield counterattacked she took no prisoners—but he brooded on the lost bike . . . and the lost father. Sometimes he almost hated his father. Sometimes all that kept him from doing so was the sense, unanchored but very strong, that his mother wanted him to. As they reached Commonwealth Park and walked along the side of it—two blocks up they would turn left onto Broad Street, where they lived—he went against his usual misgivings and asked a question about Randall Garfield.

"Didn't he leave anything, Mom? Anything at all?" A week or two before, he'd read a Nancy Drew mystery where some poor kid's inheritance had been hidden behind an old clock in an abandoned mansion. Bobby didn't really think his father had left gold coins or rare stamps stashed someplace, but if there was *something,* maybe they could sell it in Bridgeport. Possibly at one of the hockshops. Bobby didn't know exactly how hocking things worked, but he knew what the shops looked like—they had three gold balls hanging out front. And he was sure the hockshop guys would be happy to help them. Of course it was just a kid's dream, but Carol Gerber up the street had a whole set of dolls her father, who was in the Navy, had sent from overseas. If fathers *gave* things—which they did—it stood to reason that fathers sometimes *left* things.

When Bobby asked the question, they were passing one of the streetlamps which ran along this side of Commonwealth Park, and Bobby saw his mother's mouth change as it always did when he ventured a question about his late father. The change made him think of a purse she had: when you pulled on the drawstrings, the hole at the top got smaller.

"I'll tell you what he left," she said as they started up Broad Street

Hill. Bobby already wished he hadn't asked, but of course it was too late now. Once you got her started, you couldn't get her stopped, that was the thing. "He left a life insurance policy which lapsed the year before he died. Little did I know that until he was gone and everyone—including the undertaker—wanted their little piece of what I didn't have. He also left a large stack of unpaid bills, which I have now pretty much taken care of—people have been very understanding of my situation, Mr. Biderman in particular, and I'll never say they haven't been."

All this was old stuff, as boring as it was bitter, but then she told Bobby something new. "Your father," she said as they approached the apartment house which stood halfway up Broad Street Hill, "never met an inside straight he didn't like."

"What's an inside straight, Mom?"

"Never mind. But I'll tell you one thing, Bobby-O: you don't ever want to let me catch you playing cards for money. I've had enough of that to last me a lifetime."

Bobby wanted to enquire further, but knew better; more questions were apt to set off a tirade. It occurred to him that perhaps the movie, which had been about unhappy husbands and wives, had upset her in some way he could not, as a mere kid, understand. He would ask his friend John Sullivan about inside straights at school on Monday. Bobby thought it was poker, but wasn't completely sure.

"There are places in Bridgeport that take men's money," she said as they neared the apartment house where they lived. "Foolish men go to them. Foolish men make messes, and it's usually the women of the world that have to clean them up later on. Well . . ."

Bobby knew what was coming next; it was his mother's all-time favorite.

"Life isn't fair," said Liz Garfield as she took out her housekey and prepared to unlock the door of 149 Broad Street in the town of Harwich, Connecticut. It was April of 1960, the night breathed spring perfume, and standing beside her was a skinny boy with his dead father's risky red hair. She hardly ever touched his hair; on the infrequent occasions when she caressed him, it was usually his arm or his cheek which she touched.

"Life isn't fair," she repeated. She opened the door and they went in.

It was true that his mother had not been treated like a princess, and it was certainly too bad that her husband had expired on a linoleum floor in an empty house at the age of thirty-six, but Bobby sometimes thought that things could have been worse. There might have been two kids instead of just one, for instance. Or three. Hell, even four.

Or suppose she had to work some really hard job to support the two of them? Sully's mom worked at the Tip-Top Bakery downtown, and during the weeks when she had to light the ovens, Sully-John and his two older brothers hardly even saw her. Also Bobby had observed the women who came filing out of the Peerless Shoe Company when the three o'clock whistle blew (he himself got out of school at two-thirty), women who all seemed way too skinny or way too fat, women with pale faces and fingers stained a dreadful old-blood color, women with downcast eyes who carried their work shoes and pants in Total Grocery shopping bags. Last fall he'd seen men and women picking apples outside of town when he went to a church fair with Mrs. Gerber and Carol and little Ian (who Carol always called Ian-the-Snot). When he asked about them Mrs. Gerber said they were migrants, just like some kinds of birds—always on the move, picking whatever crops had just come ripe. Bobby's mother could have been one of those, but she wasn't.

What she *was* was Mr. Donald Biderman's secretary at Home Town Real Estate, the company Bobby's dad had been working for when he had his heart attack. Bobby guessed she might first have gotten the job because Donald Biderman liked Randall and felt sorry for her—widowed with a son barely out of diapers—but she was good at it and worked hard. Quite often she worked late. Bobby had been with his mother and Mr. Biderman together on a couple of occasions—the company picnic was the one he remembered most clearly, but there had also been the time Mr. Biderman had driven them to the dentist's in Bridgeport when Bobby had gotten a tooth knocked out during a recess game—and the two grownups had a way of looking at each other. Sometimes Mr. Biderman called her on the phone at night, and during those conversations she called him Don. But "Don" was old and Bobby didn't think about him much.

Bobby wasn't exactly sure what his mom did during her days (and her evenings) at the office, but he bet it beat making shoes or picking apples or lighting the Tip-Top Bakery ovens at four-thirty in the morning. Bobby bet it beat those jobs all to heck and gone. Also, when it came to his mom, if you asked about certain stuff you were asking for trouble. If you asked, for instance, how come she could afford three new dresses from Sears, one of them silk, but not three monthly payments of $11.50 on the Schwinn in the Western Auto window (it was red and silver, and just looking at it made Bobby's gut cramp with longing). Ask about stuff like that and you were asking for *real* trouble.

Bobby didn't. He simply set out to earn the price of the bike himself. It would take him until the fall, perhaps even until the winter, and that particular model might be gone from the Western Auto's window by then, but he would keep at it. You had to keep your nose to the grindstone and your shoulder to the wheel. Life wasn't easy, and life wasn't fair.

When Bobby's eleventh birthday rolled around on the last Tuesday of April, his mom gave him a small flat package wrapped in silver paper. Inside was an orange library card. An *adult* library card. Goodbye Nancy Drew, Hardy Boys, and Don Winslow of the Navy. Hello to all the rest of it, stories as full of mysterious muddled passion as *The Dark at the Top of the Stairs.* Not to mention bloody daggers in tower rooms. (There were mysteries and tower rooms in the stories about Nancy Drew and the Hardy Boys, but precious little blood and never any passion.)

"Just remember that Mrs. Kelton on the desk is a friend of mine," Mom said. She spoke in her accustomed dry tone of warning, but she was pleased by his pleasure—she could see it. "If you try to borrow anything racy like *Peyton Place* or *Kings Row,* I'll find out."

Bobby smiled. He knew she would.

"If it's that other one, Miss Busybody, and she asks what you're doing with an orange card, you tell her to turn it over. I've put written permission over my signature."

"Thanks, Mom. This is swell."

She smiled, bent, and put a quick dry swipe of the lips on his cheek, gone almost before it was there. "I'm glad you're happy. If I get home early enough, we'll go to the Colony for fried clams and ice cream. You'll have to wait for the weekend for your cake; I don't have time to bake until then. Now put on your coat and get moving, sonnyboy. You'll be late for school."

They went down the stairs and out onto the porch together. There was a Town Taxi at the curb. A man in a poplin jacket was leaning in the passenger window, paying the driver. Behind him was a little cluster of luggage and paper bags, the kind with handles.

"That must be the man who just rented the room on the third floor," Liz said. Her mouth had done its shrinking trick again. She stood on the top step of the porch, appraising the man's narrow fanny, which poked toward them as he finished his business with the taxi driver. "I don't trust people who move their things in paper bags. To me a person's things in a paper sack just looks *slutty.*"

"He has suitcases, too," Bobby said, but he didn't need his mother to point out that the new tenant's three little cases weren't such of a much. None matched; all looked as if they had been kicked here from California by someone in a bad mood.

Bobby and his mom walked down the cement path. The Town Taxi pulled away. The man in the poplin jacket turned around. To Bobby, people fell into three broad categories: kids, grownups, and old folks. Old folks were grownups with white hair. The new tenant was of this third sort. His face was thin and tired-looking, not wrinkled (except around his faded blue eyes) but deeply lined. His white hair was baby-fine and receding from a liverspotted brow. He was tall and stooped-over in a way that made Bobby think of Boris Karloff in the Shock Theater movies they showed Friday nights at 11:30 on WPIX. Beneath the poplin jacket were cheap workingman's clothes that looked too big for him. On his feet were scuffed cordovan shoes.

"Hello, folks," he said, and smiled with what looked like an effort. "My name's Theodore Brautigan. I guess I'm going to live here awhile."

He held out his hand to Bobby's mother, who touched it just briefly. "I'm Elizabeth Garfield. This is my son, Robert. You'll have to pardon us, Mr. Brattigan—"

"It's Brautigan, ma'am, but I'd be happy if you and your boy would just call me Ted."

"Yes, well, Robert's late for school and I'm late for work. Nice to meet you, Mr. Brattigan. Hurry on, Bobby. *Tempus fugit.*"

She began walking downhill toward town; Bobby began walking uphill (and at a slower pace) toward Harwich Elementary, on Asher Avenue. Three or four steps into this journey he stopped and looked back. He felt that his mom had been rude to Mr. Brautigan, that she had acted stuck-up. Being stuck-up was the worst of vices in his little circle of friends. Carol loathed a stuck-up person; so did Sully-John. Mr. Brautigan would probably be halfway up the walk by now, but if he wasn't, Bobby wanted to give him a smile so he'd know at least one member of the Garfield family wasn't stuck-up.

His mother had also stopped and was also looking back. Not because she wanted another look at Mr. Brautigan; that idea never crossed Bobby's mind. No, it was her son she had looked back at. She'd known he was going to turn around before Bobby knew it himself, and at this he felt a sudden darkening in his normally bright nature. She sometimes said it would be a snowy day in Sarasota before Bobby could put one over on her, and he supposed she was right about that. How old did you have to be to put one over on your mother, anyway? Twenty? Thirty? Or did you maybe have to wait until *she* got old and a little chicken-soupy in the head?

Mr. Brautigan hadn't started up the walk. He stood at its sidewalk end with a suitcase in each hand and the third one under his right arm (the three paper bags he had moved onto the grass of 149 Broad), more bent than ever under this weight. He was right between them, like a tollgate or something.

Liz Garfield's eyes flew past him to her son's. *Go,* they said. *Don't say a word. He's new, a man from anywhere or nowhere, and he's arrived here with half his things in shopping bags. Don't say a word, Bobby, just go.*

But he wouldn't. Perhaps because he had gotten a library card instead of a bike for his birthday. "It was nice to meet you, Mr. Brautigan," Bobby said. "Hope you like it here. Bye."

"Have a good day at school, son," Mr. Brautigan said. "Learn a lot. Your mother's right—*tempus fugit.*"

Bobby looked at his mother to see if his small rebellion might be forgiven in light of this equally small flattery, but Mom's mouth was ungiving. She turned and started down the hill without another word. Bobby went on his own way, glad he had spoken to the stranger even if his mother later made him regret it.

As he approached Carol Gerber's house, he took out the orange library card and looked at it. It wasn't a twenty-six-inch Schwinn, but it was still pretty good. Great, actually. A whole world of books to explore, and so what if it had only cost two or three rocks? Didn't they say it was the thought that counted?

Well . . . it was what his *mom* said, anyway.

He turned the card over. Written on the back in her strong hand was this message: "*To whom it may concern: This is my son's library card. He has my permission to take out three books a week from the adult section of the Harwich Public Library.*" It was signed *Elizabeth Penrose Garfield.*

Beneath her name, like a P.S., she had added this: *Robert will be responsible for his own overdue fines.*

"Birthday boy!" Carol Gerber cried, startling him, and rushed out from behind a tree where she had been lying in wait. She threw her arms around his neck and smacked him hard on the cheek. Bobby blushed, looking around to see if anyone was watching—God, it was hard enough to be friends with a girl without surprise kisses—but it was okay. The usual morning flood of students was moving schoolward along Asher Avenue at the top of the hill, but down here they were alone.

Bobby scrubbed at his cheek.

"Come on, you liked it," she said, laughing.

"Did not," said Bobby, although he had.

"What'd you get for your birthday?"

"A library card," Bobby said, and showed her. "An *adult* library card."

"Cool!" Was that sympathy he saw in her eyes? Probably not. And so what if it was? "Here. For you." She gave him a Hallmark envelope with his name printed on the front. She had also stuck on some hearts and teddy bears.

Bobby opened the envelope with mild trepidation, reminding himself that he could tuck the card deep into the back pocket of his chinos if it was gushy.

It wasn't, though. Maybe a little bit on the baby side (a kid in a Stetson on a horse, HAPPY BIRTHDAY BUCKAROO in letters that were supposed to look like wood on the inside), but not gushy. *Love, Carol* was a little gushy, but of course she was a girl, what could you do?

"Thanks."

"It's sort of a baby card, I know, but the others were even worse," Carol said matter-of-factly. A little farther up the hill Sully-John was waiting for them, working his Bo-lo Bouncer for all it was worth, going under his right arm, going under his left arm, going behind his back. He didn't try going between his legs anymore; he'd tried it once in the schoolyard and rapped himself a good one in the nuts. Sully had screamed. Bobby and a couple of other kids had laughed until they cried. Carol and three of her girlfriends had rushed over to ask what was wrong, and the boys all said nothing—Sully-John said the same, although he'd been pale and almost crying. *Boys are boogers,* Carol had said on that occasion, but Bobby didn't believe she really thought so. She wouldn't have jumped out and given him that kiss if she did, and it had been a good kiss, a smackeroo. Better than the one his mother had given him, actually.

"It's not a baby card," he said.

"No, but it *almost* is," she said. "I thought about getting you a grownup card, but man, they *are* gushy."

"I know," Bobby said.

"Are you going to be a gushy adult, Bobby?"

"I hope not," he said. "Are you?"

"No. I'm going to be like my mom's friend Rionda."

"Rionda's pretty fat," Bobby said doubtfully.

"Yeah, but she's cool. I'm going to go for the cool without the fat."

"There's a new guy moving into our building. The room on the third floor. My mom says it's really hot up there."

"Yeah? What's he like?" She giggled. "Is he ushy-gushy?"

"He's old," Bobby said, then paused to think. "But he had an interesting face. My mom didn't like him on sight because he had some of his stuff in shopping bags."

Sully-John joined them. "Happy birthday, you bastard," he said, and clapped Bobby on the back. *Bastard* was Sully-John's current favorite word; Carol's was *cool;* Bobby was currently between favorite words, although he thought *ripshit* had a certain ring to it.

"If you swear, I won't walk with you," Carol said.

"Okay," Sully-John said companionably. Carol was a fluffy blonde who looked like a Bobbsey Twin after some growing up; John Sullivan was tall, black-haired, and green-eyed. A Joe Hardy kind of boy. Bobby Garfield walked between them, his momentary depression forgotten. It was his birthday and he was with his friends and life was good. He tucked Carol's birthday card into his back pocket and his new library card down deep in his front pocket, where it could not fall out or be stolen. Carol started to skip. Sully-John told her to stop.

"Why?" Carol asked. "I *like* to skip."

"I like to say *bastard,* but I don't if you ask me," Sully-John replied reasonably.

Carol looked at Bobby.

"Skipping—at least without a rope—is a little on the baby side, Carol," Bobby said apologetically, then shrugged. "But you can if you want. We don't mind, do we, S-J?"

"Nope," Sully-John said, and got going with the Bo-lo Bouncer again. Back to front, up to down, whap-whap-whap.

Carol didn't skip. She walked between them and pretended she was Bobby Garfield's girlfriend, that Bobby had a driver's license and a Buick and they were going to Bridgeport to see the WKBW Rock and Roll Extravaganza. She thought Bobby was extremely cool. The coolest thing about him was that he didn't know it.

* * *

Bobby got home from school at three o'clock. He could have been there sooner, but picking up returnable bottles was part of his Get-a-Bike-by-Thanksgiving campaign, and he detoured through the brushy area just off Asher Avenue looking for them. He found three Rheingolds and a Nehi. Not much, but hey, eight cents was eight cents. "It all mounts up" was another of his mom's sayings.

Bobby washed his hands (a couple of those bottles had been pretty scurgy), got a snack out of the icebox, read a couple of old *Superman* comics, got another snack out of the icebox, then watched *American Bandstand.* He called Carol to tell her Bobby Darin was going to be on—she thought Bobby Darin was deeply cool, especially the way he snapped his fingers when he sang "Queen of the Hop"—but she already knew. She was watching with three or four of her numbskull girlfriends; they all giggled pretty much nonstop in the background. The sound made Bobby think of birds in a petshop. On TV, Dick Clark was currently showing how much pimple-grease *just one* Stri-Dex Medicated Pad could sop up.

Mom called at four o'clock. Mr. Biderman needed her to work late, she said. She was sorry, but birthday supper at the Colony was off. There was leftover beef stew in the fridge; he could have that and she would be home by eight to tuck him in. And for heaven's sake, Bobby, remember to turn off the gas-ring when you're done with the stove.

Bobby returned to the television feeling disappointed but not really surprised. On *Bandstand,* Dick was now announcing the Rate-a-Record panel. Bobby thought the guy in the middle looked as if he could use a lifetime supply of Stri-Dex pads.

He reached into his front pocket and drew out the new orange library card. His mood began to brighten again. He didn't need to sit here in front of the TV with a stack of old comic-books if he didn't want to. He could go down to the library and break in his new card—his new *adult* card. Miss Busybody would be on the desk, only her real name was Miss Harrington and Bobby thought she was beautiful. She wore perfume. He could always smell it on her skin and in her hair, faint and sweet, like a good memory. And although Sully-John would be at his trombone lesson right now, after the library Bobby could go up his house, maybe play some pass.

Also, he thought, *I can take those bottles to Spicer's—I've got a bike to earn this summer.*

All at once, life seemed very full.

Sully's mom invited Bobby to stay for supper, but he told her no thanks, I better get home. He would much have preferred Mrs. Sullivan's pot roast and crispy oven potatoes to what was waiting for him back at the apartment, but he knew that one of the first things his mother would do when she got back from the office was check in the fridge and see if the Tupperware with the leftover stew inside was gone. If it wasn't, she would ask Bobby what he'd had for supper. She would be calm about this question, even offhand. If he told her he'd eaten at Sully-John's she would nod, ask him what they'd had and if there had been dessert, also if he'd thanked Mrs. Sullivan; she might even sit on the couch with him and share a bowl of ice cream while they watched *Sugarfoot* on TV. Everything would be fine . . . except it wouldn't be. Eventually there would be a payback. It might not come for a day or two, even a week, but it *would* come. Bobby knew that almost without knowing he knew it. She undoubtedly *did* have to work late, but eating leftover stew by himself on his birthday was also punishment for talking to the new tenant when he wasn't supposed to. If he tried to duck that punishment, it would mount up just like money in a savings account.

When Bobby came back from Sully-John's it was quarter past six and getting dark. He had two new books to read, a Perry Mason called *The Case of the Velvet Claws* and a science-fiction novel by Clifford Simak called *Ring Around the Sun.* Both looked totally ripshit, and Miss Harrington hadn't given him a hard time at all. On the contrary: she told him he was reading above his level and to keep it up.

Walking home from S-J's, Bobby made up a story where he and Miss Harrington were on a cruise-boat that sank. They were the only two survivors, saved from drowning by finding a life preserver marked S.S. *LUSITANIC.* They washed up on a little island with palm trees and jungles and a volcano, and as they lay on the beach Miss Harrington was shivering and saying she was cold, so cold, couldn't he please hold her and warm her up, which he of course could and did, my pleasure, Miss Harrington, and then the natives came out of the jungle and at first they seemed friendly but it turned out they were cannibals who lived on the slopes of the volcano and killed their victims in a clearing ringed with skulls, so things looked bad but just as he and Miss Harrington were pulled toward the cooking pot the volcano started to rumble and—

"Hello, Robert."

Bobby looked up, even more startled than he'd been when Carol Gerber raced out from behind the tree to put a birthday smackeroo on his cheek. It was the new man in the house. He was sitting on the top porch step and smoking a cigarette. He had exchanged his old scuffed shoes for a pair of old scuffed slippers and had taken off his poplin jacket—the evening was warm. He looked at home, Bobby thought.

"Oh, Mr. Brautigan. Hi."

"I didn't mean to startle you."

"You didn't—"

"I think I did. You were a thousand miles away. And it's Ted. Please."

"Okay." But Bobby didn't know if he could stick to Ted. Calling a grownup (especially an *old* grownup) by his first name went against not only his mother's teaching but his own inclination.

"Was school good? You learned new things?"

"Yeah, fine." Bobby shifted from foot to foot; swapped his new books from hand to hand.

"Would you sit with me a minute?"

"Sure, but I can't for long. Stuff to do, you know." Supper to do, mostly—the leftover stew had grown quite attractive in his mind by now.

"Absolutely. Things to do and *tempus fugit.*"

As Bobby sat down next to Mr. Brautigan—Ted—on the wide

porch step, smelling the aroma of his Chesterfield, he thought he had never seen a man who looked as tired as this one. It couldn't be the moving in, could it? How worn out could you get when all you had to move in were three little suitcases and three carryhandle shopping bags? Bobby supposed there might be men coming later on with stuff in a truck, but he didn't really think so. It was just a room—a big one, but still just a single room with a kitchen on one side and everything else on the other. He and Sully-John had gone up there and looked around after old Miss Sidley had her stroke and went to live with her daughter.

"*Tempus fugit* means time flies," Bobby said. "Mom says it a lot. She also says time and tide wait for no man and time heals all wounds."

"Your mother is a woman of many sayings, is she?"

"Yeah," Bobby said, and suddenly the idea of all those sayings made him tired. "Many sayings."

"Ben Jonson called time the old bald cheater," Ted Brautigan said, drawing deeply on his cigarette and then exhaling twin streams through his nose. "And Boris Pasternak said we are time's captives, the hostages of eternity."

Bobby looked at him in fascination, his empty belly temporarily forgotten. He loved the idea of time as an old bald cheater—it was absolutely and completely right, although he couldn't have said why . . . and didn't that very inability to say why somehow add to the coolness? It was like a thing inside an egg, or a shadow behind pebbled glass.

"Who's Ben Jonson?"

"An Englishman, dead these many years," Mr. Brautigan said. "Self-centered and foolish about money, by all accounts; prone to flatulence as well. But—"

"What's that? Flatulence?"

Ted stuck his tongue between his lips and made a brief but very realistic farting sound. Bobby put his hands to his mouth and giggled into his cupped fingers.

"Kids think farts are funny," Ted Brautigan said, nodding. "Yeah. To a man my age, though, they're just part of life's increasingly strange business. Ben Jonson said a good many wise things between farts, by the way. Not so many as *Dr.* Johnson—Samuel Johnson, that would be—but still a good many."

"And Boris . . ."

"Pasternak. A Russian," Mr. Brautigan said dismissively. "Of no account, I think. May I see your books?"

Bobby handed them over. Mr. Brautigan (*Ted,* he reminded himself, *you're supposed to call him Ted*) passed the Perry Mason back after a cursory glance at the title. The Clifford Simak novel he held longer, at first squinting at the cover through the curls of cigarette smoke that rose past his eyes, then paging through it. He nodded as he did so.

"I have read this one," he said. "I had a lot of time to read previous to coming here."

"Yeah?" Bobby kindled. "Is it good?"

"One of his best," Mr. Brautigan—Ted—replied. He looked sideways at Bobby, one eye open, the other still squinted shut against the smoke. It gave him a look that was at once wise and mysterious, like a not-quite-trustworthy character in a detective movie. "But are you sure you can read this? You can't be much more than twelve."

"I'm eleven," Bobby said. He was delighted that Ted thought he might be as old as twelve. "Eleven today. I can read it. I won't be able to understand it all, but if it's a good story, I'll like it."

"Your birthday!" Ted said, looking impressed. He took a final drag on his cigarette, then flicked it away. It hit the cement walk and fountained sparks. "Happy birthday dear Robert, happy birthday to you!"

"Thanks. Only I like Bobby a lot better."

"Bobby, then. Are you going out to celebrate?"

"Nah, my mom's got to work late."

"Would you like to come up to my little place? I don't have much, but I know how to open a can. Also, I might have a pastry—"

"Thanks, but Mom left me some stuff. I should eat that."

"I understand." And, wonder of wonders, he looked as if he actually did. Ted returned Bobby's copy of *Ring Around the Sun.* "In this book," he said, "Mr. Simak postulates the idea that there are a number of worlds like ours. Not other planets but other Earths, *parallel* Earths, in a kind of ring around the sun. A fascinating idea."

"Yeah," Bobby said. He knew about parallel worlds from other books. From the comics, as well.

Ted Brautigan was now looking at him in a thoughtful, speculative way.

"What?" Bobby asked, feeling suddenly self-conscious. *See something green?* his mother might have said.

For a moment he thought Ted wasn't going to answer—he seemed to have fallen into some deep and dazing train of thought. Then he gave himself a little shake and sat up straighter. "Nothing," he said. "I have a little idea. Perhaps you'd like to earn some extra money? Not that I have much, but—"

"Yeah! Cripes, yeah!" *There's this bike,* he almost went on, then stopped himself. *Best keep yourself to yourself* was yet another of his mom's sayings. "I'd do just about anything you wanted!"

Ted Brautigan looked simultaneously alarmed and amused. It seemed to open a door to a different face, somehow, and Bobby could see that, yeah, the old guy had once been a young guy. One with a little sass to him, maybe. "That's a bad thing to tell a stranger," he said, "and although we've progressed to Bobby and Ted—a good start—we're still really strangers to each other."

"Did either of those Johnson guys say anything about strangers?"

"Not that I recall, but here's something on the subject from the Bible: 'For I am a stranger with thee, and a sojourner. Spare me, that I may recover strength, before I go hence . . .' " Ted trailed off for a moment. The fun had gone out of his face and he looked old again. Then his voice firmed and he finished. " '. . . before I go hence, and be no more.' Book of Psalms. I can't remember which one."

"Well," Bobby said, "I wouldn't kill or rob anyone, don't worry, but I'd sure like to earn some money."

"Let me think," Ted said. "Let me think a little."

"Sure. But if you've got chores or something, I'm your guy. Tell you that right now."

"Chores? Maybe. Although that's not the word I would have chosen." Ted clasped his bony arms around his even bonier knees and gazed across the lawn at Broad Street. It was growing dark now; Bobby's favorite part of the evening had arrived. The cars that passed had their parking lights on, and from somewhere on Asher Avenue Mrs. Sigsby was calling for her twins to come in and get their supper. At this time of day—and at dawn, as he stood in the bathroom, urinating into the bowl with sunshine falling through the little window and into his half-open eyes—Bobby felt like a dream in someone else's head.

"Where did you live before you came here, Mr. . . . Ted?"

"A place that wasn't as nice," he said. "Nowhere near as nice. How long have *you* lived here, Bobby?"

"Long as I can remember. Since my dad died, when I was three."

"And you know everyone on the street? On this block of the street, anyway?"

"Pretty much, yeah."

"You'd know strangers. Sojourners. Faces of those unknown."

Bobby smiled and nodded. "Uh-huh, I think so."

He waited to see where this would lead next—it was interesting—but apparently this was as far as it went. Ted stood up, slowly and carefully. Bobby could hear little bones creak in his back when he put his hands around there and stretched, grimacing.

"Come on," he said. "It's getting chilly. I'll go in with you. Your key or mine?"

Bobby smiled. "You better start breaking in your own, don't you think?"

Ted—it was getting easier to think of him as Ted—pulled a keyring from his pocket. The only keys on it were the one which opened the big front door and the one to his room. Both were shiny and new, the color of bandit gold. Bobby's own two keys were scratched and dull. How old was Ted? he wondered again. Sixty, at least. A sixty-year-old man with only two keys in his pocket. That was weird.

Ted opened the front door and they went into the big dark foyer with its umbrella stand and its old painting of Lewis and Clark looking out across the American West. Bobby went to the door of the

Garfield apartment and Ted went to the stairs. He paused there for a moment with his hand on the bannister. "The Simak book is a great story," he said. "Not such great writing, though. Not bad, I don't mean to say that, but take it from me, there is better."

Bobby waited.

"There are also books full of great writing that don't have very good stories. Read sometimes for the story, Bobby. Don't be like the book-snobs who won't do that. Read sometimes for the words—the language. Don't be like the play-it-safers that won't do *that.* But when you find a book that has both a good story and good words, treasure that book."

"Are there many of those, do you think?" Bobby asked.

"More than the book-snobs and play-it-safers think. Many more. Perhaps I'll give you one. A belated birthday present."

"You don't have to do that."

"No, but perhaps I will. And do have a happy birthday."

"Thanks. It's been a great one." Then Bobby went into the apartment, heated up the stew (remembering to turn off the gas-ring after the stew started to bubble, also remembering to put the pan in the sink to soak), and ate supper by himself, reading *Ring Around the Sun* with the TV on for company. He hardly heard Chet Huntley and David Brinkley gabbling the evening news. Ted was right about the book; it was a corker. The words seemed okay to him, too, although he supposed he didn't have a lot of experience just yet.

I'd like to write a story like this, he thought as he finally closed the book and flopped down on the couch to watch *Sugarfoot. I wonder if I ever could.*

Maybe. Maybe so. *Someone* had to write stories, after all, just like someone had to fix the pipes when they froze or change the street-lights in Commonwealth Park when they burned out.

An hour or so later, after Bobby had picked up *Ring Around the Sun* and begun reading again, his mother came in. Her lipstick was a bit smeared at one corner of her mouth and her slip was hanging a little. Bobby thought of pointing this out to her, then remembered how much she disliked it when someone told her it was "snowing down south." Besides, what did it matter? Her working day was over and, as she sometimes said, there was no one here but us chickens.

She checked the fridge to make sure the leftover stew was gone, checked the stove to make sure the gas-ring was off, checked the sink to make sure the pot and the Tupperware storage container were both soaking in soapy water. Then she kissed him on the temple, just a brush in passing, and went into her bedroom to change out of her office dress and hose. She seemed distant, preoccupied. She didn't ask if he'd had a happy birthday.

Later on he showed her Carol's card. His mom glanced at it, not really seeing it, pronounced it "cute," and handed it back. Then she told him to wash up, brush up, and go to bed. Bobby did so, not mentioning his interesting talk with Ted. In her current mood, that was apt to make her angry. The best thing was to let her be distant, let her keep to herself as long as she needed to, give her time to drift back to him. Yet he felt that sad mood settling over him again as he finished brushing his teeth and climbed into bed. Sometimes he felt almost hungry for her, and she didn't know.

He reached out of bed and closed the door, blocking off the sound of some old movie. He turned off the light. And then, just as he was starting to drift off, she came in, sat on the side of his bed, and said she was sorry she'd been so stand-offy tonight, but there had been a lot going on at the office and she was tired. Sometimes it was a madhouse, she said. She stroked a finger across his forehead and then kissed him there, making him shiver. He sat up and hugged her. She stiffened momentarily at his touch, then gave in to it. She even hugged him back briefly. He thought maybe it would now be all right to tell her about Ted. A little, anyway.

"I talked with Mr. Brautigan when I came home from the library," he said.

"Who?"

"The new man on the third floor. He asked me to call him Ted."

"You won't—I should say nitzy! You don't know him from Adam."

"He said giving a kid an adult library card was a great present."

Ted had said no such thing, but Bobby had lived with his mother long enough to know what worked and what didn't.

She relaxed a little. "Did he say where he came from?"

"A place not as nice as here, I think he said."

"Well, that doesn't tell us much, does it?" Bobby was still hugging her. He could have hugged her for another hour easily, smelling her White Rain shampoo and Aqua Net hold-spray and the pleasant odor of tobacco on her breath, but she disengaged from him and laid him back down. "I guess if he's going to be your friend—your *adult* friend—I'll have to get to know him a little."

"Well—"

"Maybe I'll like him better when he doesn't have shopping bags scattered all over the lawn." For Liz Garfield this was downright placatory, and Bobby was satisfied. The day had come to a very acceptable ending after all. "Goodnight, birthday boy."

"Goodnight, Mom."

She went out and closed the door. Later that night—much later—he thought he heard her crying in her room, but perhaps that was only a dream.

II. DOUBTS ABOUT TED. BOOKS ARE LIKE PUMPS. DON'T EVEN THINK ABOUT IT. SULLY WINS A PRIZE. BOBBY GETS A JOB. SIGNS OF THE LOW MEN.

During the next few weeks, as the weather warmed toward summer, Ted was usually on the porch smoking when Liz came home from work. Sometimes he was alone and sometimes Bobby was sitting with him, talking about books. Sometimes Carol and Sully-John were there, too, the three kids playing pass on the lawn while Ted smoked and watched them throw. Sometimes other kids came by—Denny Rivers with a taped-up balsa glider to throw, soft-headed Francis Utterson, always pushing along on his scooter with one overdeveloped leg, Angela Avery and Yvonne Loving to ask Carol if she wanted to go over Yvonne's and play dolls or a game called Hospital Nurse—but mostly it was just S-J and Carol, Bobby's special friends. All the kids called Mr. Brautigan Ted, but when Bobby explained why it would be better if they called him Mr. Brautigan when his mom was around, Ted agreed at once.

As for his mom, she couldn't seem to get *Brautigan* to come out of her mouth. What emerged was always *Brattigan.* That might not have been on purpose, however; Bobby was starting to feel a cautious sense of relief about his mother's view of Ted. He had been afraid that she might feel about Ted as she had about Mrs. Evers, his second-grade teacher. Mom had disliked Mrs. Evers on sight, disliked her *deeply,* for no reason at all Bobby could see or understand, and hadn't had a good word to say about her all year long—Mrs. Evers dressed like a frump, Mrs. Evers dyed her hair, Mrs. Evers wore too much makeup, Bobby had just better tell Mom if Mrs. Evers laid so much as *one finger* on him, because she looked like the kind of woman who would like to pinch and poke. All of this following a single parent-teacher conference in which Mrs. Evers had told Liz that Bobby was doing well in all his subjects. There had been four other parent-teacher conferences that year, and Bobby's mother had found reasons to duck every single one.

Liz's opinions of people hardened swiftly; when she wrote BAD under her mental picture of you, she almost always wrote in ink. If Mrs. Evers had saved six kids from a burning schoolbus, Liz Garfield might well have sniffed and said they probably owed the pop-eyed old cow two weeks' worth of milk-money.

Ted made every effort to be nice without actually sucking up to her (people *did* suck up to his mother, Bobby knew; hell, sometimes he did it himself), and it worked . . . but only to a degree. On one occasion Ted and Bobby's mom had talked for almost ten minutes about how awful it was that the Dodgers had moved to the other side of the country without so much as a faretheewell, but not even both of them being Ebbets Field Dodger fans could strike a real spark between them. They were never going to be pals. Mom didn't dislike Ted Brautigan the way she had disliked Mrs. Evers, but there was still something wrong. Bobby supposed he knew what it was; he had seen it in her eyes on the morning the new tenant had moved in. Liz didn't trust him.

Nor, it turned out, did Carol Gerber. "Sometimes I wonder if he's on the run from something," she said one evening as she and Bobby and S-J walked up the hill toward Asher Avenue.

They had been playing pass for an hour or so, talking off and on with Ted as they did, and were now heading to Moon's Roadside Happiness for ice cream cones. S-J had thirty cents and was treating. He also had his Bo-lo Bouncer, which he now took out of his back pocket. Pretty soon he had it going up and down and all around, whap-whap-whap.

"On the run? Are you kidding?" Bobby was startled by the idea. Yet Carol was sharp about people; even his mother had noticed it. *That girl's no beauty, but she doesn't miss much,* she'd said one night.

" 'Stick em up, McGarrigle!' " Sully-John cried. He tucked his Bo-lo Bouncer under his arm, dropped into a crouch, and fired an invisible tommygun, yanking down the right side of his mouth so he could make the proper sound to go with it, a kind of *eh-eh-eh* from deep in his throat. " 'You'll never take me alive, copper! Blast em, Muggsy! Nobody runs out on Rico! *Ah, jeez, they got me!*' " S-J clutched his chest, spun around, and fell dead on Mrs. Conlan's lawn.

That lady, a grumpy old rhymes-with-witch of seventy-five or so, cried: "Boy! *Youuu,* boy! Get off there! You'll mash my flowers!"

There wasn't a flowerbed within ten feet of where Sully-John had fallen, but he leaped up at once. "Sorry, Mrs. Conlan."

She flapped a hand at him, dismissing his apology without a word, and watched closely as the children went on their way.

"You don't really mean it, do you?" Bobby asked Carol. "About Ted?"

"No," she said, "I guess not. But . . . have you ever watched him watch the street?"

"Yeah. It's like he's looking for someone, isn't it?"

"Or looking *out* for them," Carol replied.

Sully-John resumed Bo-lo Bouncing. Pretty soon the red rubber ball was blurring back and forth again. Sully paused only when they passed the Asher Empire, where two Brigitte Bardot movies were playing, Adults Only, Must Have Driver's License or Birth Certificate, No Exceptions. One of the pictures was new; the other was that old standby *And God Created Woman,* which kept coming back to the Empire like a bad cough. On the posters, Brigitte was dressed in nothing but a towel and a smile.

"My mom says she's trashy," Carol said.

"If she's trash, I'd love to be the trashman," S-J said, and wiggled his eyebrows like Groucho.

"Do *you* think she's trashy?" Bobby asked Carol.

"I'm not sure what that means, even."

As they passed out from under the marquee (from within her glass ticket-booth beside the doors, Mrs. Godlow—known to the neighborhood kids as Mrs. Godzilla—watched them suspiciously), Carol looked back over her shoulder at Brigitte Bardot in her towel. Her expression was hard to read. Curiosity? Bobby couldn't tell. "But she's pretty, isn't she?"

"Yeah, I guess."

"And you'd have to be brave to let people look at you with nothing on but a towel. That's what I think, anyway."

Sully-John had no interest in *la femme Brigitte* now that she was behind them. "Where'd Ted come from, Bobby?"

"I don't know. He never talks about that."

Sully-John nodded as if he expected just that answer, and threw his Bo-lo Bouncer back into gear. Up and down, all around, whap-whap-whap.

In May Bobby's thoughts began turning to summer vacation. There was really nothing in the world better than what Sully called "the Big Vac." He would spend long hours goofing with his friends, both on Broad Street and down at Sterling House on the other side of the park—they had lots of good things to do in the summer at Sterling House, including baseball and weekly trips to Patagonia Beach in West Haven—and he would also have plenty of time for himself. Time to read, of course, but what he really wanted to do with some of that time was find a part-time job. He had a little over seven rocks in a jar marked BIKE FUND, and seven rocks was a start . . . but not what you'd call a *great* start. At this rate Nixon would have been President for two years before he was riding to school.

On one of these vacation's-almost-here days, Ted gave him a paperback book. "Remember I told you that some books have both a good story and good writing?" he asked. "This is one of that breed. A belated birthday present from a new friend. At least, I hope I am your friend."

"You are. Thanks a lot!" In spite of the enthusiasm in his voice, Bobby took the book a little doubtfully. He was accustomed to pocket books with bright, raucous covers and sexy come-on lines ("She hit the gutter . . . *AND BOUNCED LOWER!*"); this one had neither. The cover was mostly white. In one corner of it was sketched—*barely* sketched—a group of boys standing in a circle. The name of the book was *Lord of the Flies.* There was no come-on line above the title, not even a discreet one like "A story you will never forget." All in all, it had a forbidding, unwelcoming look, suggesting that the story lying beneath the cover would be hard. Bobby had nothing in particular against hard books, as long as they were a part of one's schoolwork. His view about reading for pleasure, however, was that such stories should be easy—that the writer should do everything except move your eyes back and forth for you. If not, how much pleasure could there be in it?

He started to turn the book over. Ted gently put his hand on Bobby's, stopping him. "Don't," he said. "As a personal favor to me, don't."

Bobby looked at him, not understanding.

"Come to the book as you would come to an unexplored land. Come without a map. Explore it and draw your own map."

"But what if I don't like it?"

Ted shrugged. "Then don't finish it. A book is like a pump. It gives nothing unless first you give to it. You prime a pump with your own water, you work the handle with your own strength. You do this because you expect to get back more than you give . . . eventually. Do you go along with that?"

Bobby nodded.

"How long would you prime a water-pump and flail the handle if nothing came out?"

"Not too long, I guess."

"This book is two hundred pages, give or take. You read the first ten per cent—twenty pages, that is, I know already your math isn't as good as your reading—and if you don't like it by then, if it isn't giving more than it's taking by then, put it aside."

"I wish they'd let you do that in school," Bobby said. He was thinking of a poem by Ralph Waldo Emerson which they were supposed to memorize. "By the rude bridge that arched the flood," it started. S-J called the poet Ralph Waldo Emerslop.

"School is different." They were sitting at Ted's kitchen table, looking out over the back yard, where everything was in bloom. On Colony Street, which was the next street over, Mrs. O'Hara's dog Bowser barked its endless *roop-roop-roop* into the mild spring air. Ted was smoking a Chesterfield. "And speaking of school, don't take this book there with you. There are things in it your teacher might not want you to read. There could be a brouhaha."

"A *what?*"

"An uproar. And if you get in trouble at school, you get in trouble at home—this I'm sure you don't need me to tell you. And your mother . . ." The hand not holding the cigarette made a little seesawing gesture which Bobby understood at once. *Your mother doesn't trust me.*

Bobby thought of Carol saying that maybe Ted was on the run from something, and remembered his mother saying Carol didn't miss much.

"What's in it that could get me in trouble?" He looked at *Lord of the Flies* with new fascination.

"Nothing to froth at the mouth about," Ted said dryly. He crushed his cigarette out in a tin ashtray, went to his little refrigerator, and took out two bottles of pop. There was no beer or wine in there, just pop and a glass bottle of cream. "Some talk of putting a spear up a wild pig's ass, I think that's the worst. Still, there is a certain kind of grownup who can only see the trees and never the forest. Read the first twenty pages, Bobby. You'll never look back. This I promise you."

Ted set the pop down on the table and lifted the caps with his churchkey. Then he lifted his bottle and clinked it against Bobby's. "To your new friends on the island."

"What island?"

Ted Brautigan smiled and shot the last cigarette out of a crumpled pack. "You'll find out," he said.

Bobby did find out, and it didn't take him twenty pages to also find out that *Lord of the Flies* was a hell of a book, maybe the best he'd ever read. Ten pages into it he was captivated; twenty pages and he was lost. He lived on the island with Ralph and Jack and Piggy and the littluns; he trembled at the Beast that turned out to be a rotting airplane pilot caught in his parachute; he watched first in dismay and then in horror as a bunch of harmless schoolboys descended into savagery, finally setting out to hunt down the only one of their number who had managed to remain halfway human.

He finished the book one Saturday the week before school ended for the year. When noon came and Bobby was still in his room—no friends over to play, no Saturday-morning cartoons, not even *Merrie Melodies* from ten to eleven—his mom looked in on him and told him to get off his bed, get his nose out of that book, and go on down to the park or something.

"Where's Sully?" she asked.

"Dalhouse Square. There's a school band concert." Bobby looked at his mother in the doorway and the ordinary stuff around her with dazed, perplexed eyes. The world of the story had become so vivid to him that this real one now seemed false and drab.

"What about your girlfriend? Take her down to the park with you."

"Carol's not my girlfriend, Mom."

"Well, whatever she is. Goodness sakes, Bobby, I wasn't suggesting the two of you were going to run off and elope."

"She and some other girls slept over Angie's house last night.

Carol says when they sleep over they stay up and hen-party practically all night long. I bet they're still in bed, or eating breakfast for lunch."

"Then go to the park by yourself. You're making me nervous. With the TV off on Saturday morning I keep thinking you're dead." She came into his room and plucked the book out of his hands. Bobby watched with a kind of numb fascination as she thumbed through the pages, reading random snatches here and there. Suppose she spotted the part where the boys talked about sticking their spears up the wild pig's ass (only they were English and said "arse," which sounded even dirtier to Bobby)? What would she make of it? He didn't know. All his life they had lived together, it had been just the two of them for most of it, and he still couldn't predict how she'd react to any given situation.

"Is this the one Brattigan gave you?"

"Yeah."

"As a birthday present?"

"Yeah."

"What's it about?"

"Boys marooned on an island. Their ship gets sunk. I think it's supposed to be after World War III or something. The guy who wrote it never says for sure."

"So it's science fiction."

"Yeah," Bobby said. He felt a little giddy. He thought *Lord of the Flies* was about as far from *Ring Around the Sun* as you could get, but his mom hated science fiction, and if anything would stop her potentially dangerous thumbing, that would.

She handed the book back and walked over to his window. "Bobby?" Not looking back at him, at least not at first. She was wearing an old shirt and her Saturday pants. The bright noonlight shone through the shirt; he could see her sides and noticed for the first time how thin she was, as if she was forgetting to eat or something. "What, Mom?"

"Has Mr. Brattigan given you any other presents?"

"It's *Brautigan,* Mom."

She frowned at her reflection in the window . . . or more likely it was his reflection she was frowning at. "Don't correct me, Bobby-O. Has he?"

Bobby considered. A few rootbeers, sometimes a tuna sandwich or a cruller from the bakery where Sully's mom worked, but no presents. Just the book, which was one of the best presents he had ever gotten. "Jeepers, no, why would he?"

"I don't know. But then, I don't know why a man you just met would give you a birthday present in the first place." She sighed, folded her arms under her small sharp breasts, and went on looking out Bobby's window. "He told me he used to work in a state job up in Hartford but now he's retired. Is that what he told you?"

"Something like that." In fact, Ted had never told Bobby anything about his working life, and asking had never crossed Bobby's mind.

"What kind of state job? What department? Health and Welfare? Transportation? Office of the Comptroller?"

Bobby shook his head. What in heck was a comptroller?

"I bet it was education," she said meditatively. "He talks like someone who used to be a teacher. Doesn't he?"

"Sort of, yeah."

"Does he have hobbies?"

"I don't know." There was reading, of course; two of the three bags which had so offended his mother were full of paperback books, most of which looked *very* hard.

The fact that Bobby knew nothing of the new man's pastimes for some reason seemed to ease her mind. She shrugged, and when she spoke again it seemed to be to herself rather than to Bobby. "Shoot, it's only a book. And a paperback, at that."

"He said he might have a job for me, but so far he hasn't come up with anything."

She turned around fast. "Any job he offers you, any chores he asks you to do, you talk to me about it first. Got that?"

"Sure, got it." Her intensity surprised him and made him a little uneasy.

"Promise."

"I promise."

"*Big* promise, Bobby."

He dutifully crossed his heart and said, "I promise my mother in the name of God."

That usually finished things, but this time she didn't look satisfied.

"Has he ever . . . does he ever . . ." There she stopped, looking uncharacteristically flustered. Kids sometimes looked that way when Mrs. Bramwell sent them to the blackboard to pick the nouns and verbs out of a sentence and they couldn't.

"Has he ever what, Mom?"

"Never mind!" she said crossly. "Get out of here, Bobby, go to the park or Sterling House, I'm tired of looking at you."

Why'd you come in, then? he thought (but of course did not say). *I wasn't bothering you, Mom. I wasn't bothering you.*

Bobby tucked *Lord of the Flies* into his back pocket and headed for the door. He turned back when he got there. She was still at the window, but now she was watching him again. He never surprised love on her face at such moments; at best he might see a kind of speculation, sometimes (but not always) affectionate.

"Hey Mom?" He was thinking of asking for fifty cents—half a rock. With that he could buy a soda and two hotdogs at the Colony Diner. He loved the Colony's hotdogs, which came in toasted buns with potato chips and pickle slices on the side.

Her mouth did its tightening trick, and he knew this wasn't his day for hotdogs. "Don't ask, Bobby, don't even think about it." *Don't even think about it*—one of her all-time faves. "I have a ton of bills this week, so get those dollar-signs out of your eyes."

She *didn't* have a ton of bills, though, that was the thing. Not this week she didn't. Bobby had seen both the electric bill and the check for the rent in its envelope marked *Mr. Monteleone* last Wednesday. And she couldn't claim he would soon need clothes because this was the end of the school-year, not the beginning. The only dough he'd asked for lately was five bucks for Sterling House—quarterly dues—and she had even been chintzy about that, although she knew it covered swimming and Wolves and Lions Baseball, plus the insurance. If it had been anyone but his mom, he would have thought of this as cheapskate behavior. He couldn't say anything about it to her, though; talking to her about money almost always turned into an argument, and disputing any part of her view on money matters, even in the most tiny particulars, was apt to send her into ranting hysterics. When she got like that she was scary.

Bobby smiled. "It's okay, Mom."

She smiled back and then nodded to the jar marked BIKE FUND. "Borrow a little from there, why don't you? Treat yourself. I'll never tell, and you can always put it back later."

He held onto his smile, but only with an effort. How easily she said that, never thinking of how furious she'd be if Bobby suggested she borrow a little from the electric money, or the phone money, or what she set aside to buy her "business clothes," just so he could get a couple of hotdogs and maybe a pie à la mode at the Colony. If he told her breezily that he'd never tell and she could always put it back later. Yeah, sure, and get his face smacked.

By the time he got to Commonwealth Park, Bobby's resentment had faded and the word *cheapskate* had left his brain. It was a beautiful day and he had a terrific book to finish; how could you be resentful and pissed off with stuff like that going for you? He found a secluded bench and reopened *Lord of the Flies.* He had to finish it today, had to find out what happened.

The last forty pages took him an hour, and during that time he was oblivious to everything around him. When he finally closed the book, he saw he had a lapful of little white flowers. His hair was full of them, too—he'd been sitting unaware in a storm of apple-blossoms.

He brushed them away, looking toward the playground as he did. Kids were teetertottering and swinging and batting the tetherball around its pole. Laughing, chasing each other, rolling in the grass. Could kids like that ever wind up going naked and worshipping a rotting pig's head? It was tempting to dismiss such ideas as the imaginings of a grownup who didn't like kids (there were lots who didn't, Bobby knew), but then Bobby glanced into the sandbox and saw a little boy sitting there and wailing as if his heart would break while another, bigger kid sat beside him, unconcernedly playing with the Tonka truck he had yanked out of his friend's hands.

And the book's ending—happy or not? Crazy as such a thing would have seemed a month ago, Bobby couldn't really tell. Never in his life had he read a book where he didn't know if the ending was good or bad, happy or sad. Ted would know, though. He would ask Ted.

Bobby was still on the bench fifteen minutes later when Sully came bopping into the park and saw him. "Say there, you old bastard!" Sully exclaimed. "I went by your place and your mom said you were down here, or maybe at Sterling House. Finally finish that book?"

"Yeah."

"Was it good?"

"Yeah."

S-J shook his head. "I never met a book I really liked, but I'll take your word for it."

"How was the concert?"

Sully shrugged. "We blew til everyone went away, so I guess it was good for us, anyway. And guess who won the week at Camp Winiwinaia?" Camp Winnie was the YMCA's co-ed camp on Lake George, up in the woods north of Storrs. Each year HAC—the Harwich Activities Committee—had a drawing and gave away a week there.

Bobby felt a stab of jealousy. "Don't tell me."

Sully-John grinned. "Yeah, man! Seventy names in the hat, seventy at *least,* and the one that bald old bastard Mr. Coughlin pulled out was John L. Sullivan, Junior, 93 Broad Street. My mother just about weewee'd her pants."

"When do you go?"

"Two weeks after school lets out. Mom's gonna try and get her week off from the bakery at the same time, so she can go see Gramma and Grampy in Wisconsin. She's gonna take the Big Gray Dog." The Big Vac was summer vacation; the Big Shew was *Ed Sullivan* on Sunday night; the Big Gray Dog was, of course, a Greyhound bus. The local depot was just up the street from the Asher Empire and the Colony Diner.

"Don't you wish you could go to Wisconsin with her?" Bobby asked, feeling a perverse desire to spoil his friend's happiness at his good fortune just a little.

"Sorta, but I'd rather go to camp and shoot arrows." He slung an arm around Bobby's shoulders. "I only wish you could come with me, you book-reading bastard."

That made Bobby feel mean-spirited. He looked down at *Lord of the Flies* again and knew he would be rereading it soon. Perhaps as early as August, if things got boring (by August they usually did, as hard as that was to believe in May). Then he looked up at Sully-John, smiled, and put his arm around S-J's shoulders. "Well, you're a lucky duck," he said.

"Just call me Donald," Sully-John agreed.

They sat on the bench that way for a little while, arms around each other's shoulders in those intermittent showers of apple-blossoms, watching the little kids play. Then Sully said he was going to the Saturday matinee at the Empire, and he'd better get moving if he didn't want to miss the previews.

"Why don't you come, Bobborino? *The Black Scorpion*'s playing. Monsters galore throughout the store."

"Can't, I'm broke," Bobby said. This was the truth (if you excluded the seven dollars in the Bike Fund jar, that was) and he didn't want to go to the movies today anyhow, even though he'd heard a kid at school say *The Black Scorpion* was really great, the scorpions poked their stingers right through people when they killed them and also mashed Mexico City flat.

What Bobby wanted to do was go back to the house and talk to Ted about *Lord of the Flies.*

"Broke," Sully said sadly. "That's a sad fact, Jack. I'd pay your way, but I've only got thirty-five cents myself."

"Don't sweat it. Hey—where's your Bo-lo Bouncer?"

Sully looked sadder than ever. "Rubber band snapped. Gone to Bo-lo Heaven, I guess."

Bobby snickered. Bo-lo Heaven, that was a pretty funny idea. "Gonna buy a new one?"

"I doubt it. There's a magic kit in Woolworth's that I want. Sixty different tricks, it says on the box. I wouldn't mind being a magician when I grow up, Bobby, you know it? Travel around with a carnival or a circus, wear a black suit and a top hat. I'd pull rabbits and shit out of the hat."

"The rabbits would probably shit *in* your hat," Bobby said.

Sully grinned. "But I'd be a cool bastard! Wouldn't I love to be! At anything!" He got up. "Sure you don't want to come along? You could probably sneak in past Godzilla."

Hundreds of kids showed up for the Saturday shows at the Empire, which usually consisted of a creature feature, eight or nine cartoons, Prevues of Coming Attractions, and the MovieTone News. Mrs. Godlow went nuts trying to get them to stand in line and shut up, not understanding that on Saturday afternoon you couldn't get even basically well-behaved kids to act like they were in school. She was also obsessed by the conviction that dozens of kids over twelve were trying to enter at the under-twelve rate; Mrs. G. would have demanded a birth certificate for the Saturday matinees as well as the Brigitte Bardot double features, had she been allowed. Lacking the authority to do that, she settled for barking "WHATYEARYABORN?" to any kid over five and a half feet tall. With all that going on you could sometimes sneak past her quite easily, and there was no ticket-ripper on Saturday afternoons. But Bobby didn't want giant scorpions today; he had spent the last week with more realistic monsters, many of whom had probably looked pretty much like him.

"Nah, I think I'll just hang around," Bobby said.

"Okay." Sully-John scrummed a few apple-blossoms out of his black hair, then looked solemnly at Bobby. "Call me a cool bastard, Big Bob."

"Sully, you're one cool bastard."

"Yes!" Sully-John leaped skyward, punching at the air and laughing. "Yes I am! A cool bastard today! A great big cool bastard of a magician tomorrow! Pow!"

Bobby collapsed against the back of the bench, legs outstretched, sneakers toed in, laughing hard. S-J was just so funny when he got going.

Sully started away, then turned back. "Man, you know what? I saw a couple of weird guys when I came into the park."

"What was weird about them?"

Sully-John shook his head, looking puzzled. "Don't know," he said. "Don't really know." Then he headed off, singing "At the Hop." It was one of his favorites. Bobby liked it, too. Danny and the Juniors were great.

Bobby opened the paperback Ted had given him (it was now looking exceedingly well thumbed) and read the last couple of pages again, the part where the adults finally showed up. He began to ponder it again—happy or sad?—and Sully-John slipped from his mind. It occurred to him later that if S-J had happened to mention that the weird guys he'd seen were wearing yellow coats, some things might have been quite different later on.

"William Golding wrote an interesting thing about that book, one which I think speaks to your concern about the ending . . . want another pop, Bobby?"

Bobby shook his head and said no thanks. He didn't like rootbeer all that much; he mostly drank it out of politeness when he was with Ted. They were sitting at Ted's kitchen table again, Mrs. O'Hara's dog was still barking (so far as Bobby could tell, Bowser *never* stopped barking), and Ted was still smoking Chesterfields. Bobby had peeked in at his mother when he came back from the park, saw she was napping on her bed, and then had hastened up to the third floor to ask Ted about the ending of *Lord of the Flies.*

Ted crossed to the refrigerator . . . and then stopped, standing there with his hand on the fridge door, staring off into space. Bobby would realize later that this was his first clear glimpse of something about Ted that wasn't right; that was in fact wrong and going wronger all the time.

"One feels them first in the back of one's eyes," he said in a conversational tone. He spoke clearly; Bobby heard every word.

"Feels what?"

"One feels them first in the back of one's eyes." Still staring into space with one hand curled around the handle of the refrigerator, and Bobby began to feel frightened. There seemed to be something in the air, something almost like pollen—it made the hairs inside his nose tingle, made the backs of his hands itch.

Then Ted opened the fridge door and bent in. "Sure you don't want one?" he asked. "It's good and cold."

"No . . . no, that's okay."

Ted came back to the table, and Bobby understood that he had either decided to ignore what had just happened, or didn't remember it. He also understood that Ted was okay now, and that was good enough for Bobby. Grownups were weird, that was all. Sometimes you just had to ignore the stuff they did.

"Tell me what he said about the ending. Mr. Golding."

"As best as I can remember, it was something like this: 'The boys are rescued by the crew of a battle-cruiser, and that is very well for them, but who will rescue the crew?' " Ted poured himself a glass of rootbeer, waited for the foam to subside, then poured a little more. "Does that help?"

Bobby turned it over in his mind the way he would a riddle. Hell, it *was* a riddle. "No," he said at last. "I still don't understand. They don't need to be rescued—the crew of the boat, I mean—because they're not on the island. Also . . ." He thought of the kids in the sandbox, one of them bawling his eyes out while the other played placidly with the stolen toy. "The guys on the cruiser are grownups. Grownups don't need to be rescued."

"No?"

"No."

"Never?"

Bobby suddenly thought of his mother and how she was about money. Then he remembered the night he had awakened and thought he heard her crying. He didn't answer.

"Consider it," Ted said. He drew deeply on his cigarette, then blew out a plume of smoke. "Good books are for consideration after, too."

"Okay."

"*Lord of the Flies* wasn't much like the Hardy Boys, was it?"

Bobby had a momentary image, very clear, of Frank and Joe Hardy running through the jungle with homemade spears, chanting that they'd kill the pig and stick their spears up her arse. He burst out laughing, and as Ted joined him he knew that he was done with the Hardy Boys, Tom Swift, Rick Brant, and Bomba the Jungle Boy. *Lord of the Flies* had finished them off. He was very glad he had an adult library card.

"No," he said, "it sure wasn't."

"And good books don't give up all their secrets at once. Will you remember that?"

"Yes."

"Terrific. Now tell me—would you like to earn a dollar a week from me?"

The change of direction was so abrupt that for a moment Bobby couldn't follow it. Then he grinned and said, "Cripes, yes!" Figures ran dizzily through his mind; Bobby was good enough at math to figure out a dollar a week added up to at least fifteen bucks by September. Put with what he already had, plus a reasonable harvest of returnable bottles and some summer lawn-mowing jobs on the street . . . jeepers, he might be riding a Schwinn by Labor Day. "What do you want me to do?"

"We have to be careful about that. Quite careful." Ted meditated quietly and for so long Bobby began to be afraid he was going to start talking about feeling stuff in the backs of his eyes again. But when Ted looked up, there was none of that strange emptiness in his gaze. His eyes were sharp, if a little rueful. "I would never ask a friend of mine—especially a young friend—to lie to his parents, Bobby, but in this case I'm going to ask you to join me in a little misdirection. Do you know what that is?"

"Sure." Bobby thought about Sully and his new ambition to travel around with the circus, wearing a black suit and pulling rabbits out of his hat. "It's what the magician does to fool you."

"Doesn't sound very nice when you put it that way, does it?"

Bobby shook his head. No, take away the spangles and the spotlights and it didn't sound very nice at all.

Ted drank a little rootbeer and wiped foam from his upper lip. "Your mother, Bobby. She doesn't quite dislike me, I don't think it would be fair to say that . . . but I think she *almost* dislikes me. Do you agree?"

"I guess. When I told her you might have a job for me, she got weird about it. Said I had to tell her about anything you wanted me to do before I could do it."

Ted Brautigan nodded.

"I think it all comes back to you having some of your stuff in paper bags when you moved in. I know that sounds nuts, but it's all I can figure."

He thought Ted might laugh, but he only nodded again. "Perhaps that's all it is. In any case, Bobby, I wouldn't want you to go against your mother's wishes."

That sounded good but Bobby Garfield didn't entirely believe it. If it was really true, there'd be no need for misdirection.

"Tell your mother that my eyes now grow tired quite easily. It's the truth." As if to prove it, Ted raised his right hand to his eyes and massaged the corners with his thumb and forefinger. "Tell her I'd like to hire you to read bits of the newspaper to me each day, and for this I will pay you a dollar a week—what your friend Sully calls a rock?"

Bobby nodded . . . but a buck a week for reading about how Kennedy was doing in the primaries and whether or not Floyd Patterson would win in June? With maybe *Blondie* and *Dick Tracy* thrown in for good measure? His mom or Mr. Biderman down at Home Town Real Estate might believe that, but Bobby didn't.

Ted was still rubbing his eyes, his hand hovering over his narrow nose like a spider.

"What else?" Bobby asked. His voice came out sounding strangely flat, like his mom's voice when he'd promised to pick up his room and she came in at the end of the day to find the job still undone. "What's the real job?"

"I want you to keep your eyes open, that's all," Ted said.

"For what?"

"Low men in yellow coats." Ted's fingers were still working the corners of his eyes. Bobby wished he'd stop; there was something creepy about it. Did he feel something behind them, was that why he kept rubbing and kneading that way? Something that broke his attention, interfered with his normally sane and well-ordered way of thinking?

"Lo *mein?*" It was what his mother ordered on the occasions when they went out to Sing Lu's on Barnum Avenue. Lo mein in yellow coats made no sense, but it was all he could think of.

Ted laughed, a sunny, genuine laugh that made Bobby aware of just how uneasy he'd been.

"Low *men,*" Ted said. "I use 'low' in the Dickensian sense, meaning fellows who look rather stupid . . . and rather dangerous as well. The sort of men who'd shoot craps in an alley, let's say, and pass around a bottle of liquor in a paper bag during the game. The sort who lean against telephone poles and whistle at women walking by on the other side of the street while they mop the backs of their necks with handkerchiefs that are never quite clean. Men who think hats with feathers in the brims are sophisticated. Men who look like they know all the right answers to all of life's stupid questions. I'm not being terribly clear, am I? Is any of this getting through to you, is any of it ringing a bell?"

Yeah, it was. In a way it was like hearing time described as the old bald cheater: a sense that the word or phrase was exactly right even though you couldn't say just why. It reminded him of how Mr. Biderman always looked unshaven even when you could still smell sweet aftershave drying on his cheeks, the way you somehow knew Mr. Biderman would pick his nose when he was alone in his car or check the coin return of any pay telephone he walked past without even thinking about it.

"I get you," he said.

"Good. I'd never in a hundred lifetimes ask you to speak to such men, or even approach them. But I *would* ask you to keep an eye out, make a circuit of the block once a day—Broad Street, Commonwealth Street, Colony Street, Asher Avenue, then back here to 149—and just see what you see."

It was starting to fit together in Bobby's mind. On his birthday—which had also been Ted's first day at 149—Ted had asked him if he knew everyone on the street, if he would recognize

(*sojourners faces of those unknown*)

strangers, if any strangers showed up. Not three weeks later Carol Gerber had made her comment about wondering sometimes if Ted was on the run from something.

"How many guys are there?" he asked.

"Three, five, perhaps more by now." Ted shrugged. "You'll know them by their long yellow coats and olive skin . . . although that darkish skin is just a disguise."

"What . . . you mean like Man-Tan, or something?"

"I suppose, yes. If they're driving, you'll know them by their cars."

"What makes? What models?" Bobby felt like Darren McGavin on *Mike Hammer* and warned himself not to get carried away. This wasn't TV. Still, it was exciting.

Ted was shaking his head. "I have no idea. But you'll know just the same, because their cars will be like their yellow coats and sharp shoes and the greasy perfumed stuff they use to slick back their hair: loud and vulgar."

"Low," Bobby said—it was not quite a question.

"Low," Ted repeated, and nodded emphatically. He sipped rootbeer, looked away toward the sound of the eternally barking Bowser . . . and remained that way for several moments, like a toy with a broken spring or a machine that has run out of gas. "They sense me," he said. "And I sense them, as well. Ah, what a world."

"What do they want?"

Ted turned back to him, appearing startled. It was as if he had forgotten Bobby was there . . . or had forgotten for a moment just who Bobby was. Then he smiled and reached out and put his hand over Bobby's. It was big and warm and comforting; a man's hand. At the feel of it Bobby's half-hearted reservations disappeared.

"A certain something I happen to have," Ted said. "Let's leave it at that."

"They're not cops, are they? Or government guys? Or—"

"Are you asking if I'm one of the FBI's Ten Most Wanted, or a communist agent like on *I Led Three Lives*? A bad guy?"

"I know you're not a bad guy," Bobby said, but the flush mounting into his cheeks suggested otherwise. Not that what he thought changed much. You could like or even love a bad guy; even Hitler had a mother, his own mom liked to say.

"I'm not a bad guy. Never robbed a bank or stole a military secret. I've spent too much of my life reading books and scamped on my share of fines—if there were Library Police, I'm afraid they'd be after me—but I'm not a bad guy like the ones you see on television."

"The men in yellow coats are, though."

Ted nodded. "Bad through and through. And, as I say, dangerous."

"Have you seen them?"

"Many times, but not here. And the chances are ninety-nine in a hundred that you won't, either. All I ask is that you keep an eye out for them. Could you do that?"

"Yes."

"Bobby? Is there a problem?"

"No." Yet something nagged at him for a moment—not a connection, only a momentary sense of groping toward one.

"Are you sure?"

"Uh-huh."

"All right. Now, here is the question: could you in good conscience—in *fair* conscience, at least—neglect to mention this part of your duty to your mother?"

"Yes," Bobby said at once, although he understood doing such a thing would mark a large change in his life . . . and would be risky. He was more than a little afraid of his mom, and this fear was only partly caused by how angry she could get and how long she could bear a grudge. Mostly it grew from an unhappy sense of being loved only a little, and needing to protect what love there was. But he liked Ted . . . and he had loved the feeling of Ted's hand lying over his own, the warm roughness of the big palm, the touch of the fingers, thickened almost into knots at the joints. And this wasn't lying, not really. It was leaving out.

"You're really sure?"

If you want to learn to lie, Bobby-O, I suppose leaving things out is as good a place to start as any, an interior voice whispered. Bobby ignored it. "Yes," he said, "really sure. Ted . . . are these guys just dangerous to you or to anybody?" He was thinking of his mom, but he was also thinking of himself.

"To me they could be very dangerous indeed. To other people—*most* other people—probably not. Do you want to know a funny thing?"

"Sure."

"The majority of people don't even see them unless they're very, very close. It's almost as if they have the power to cloud men's minds, like The Shadow on that old radio program."

"Do you mean they're . . . well . . ." He supposed *supernatural* was the word he wasn't quite able to say.

"No, no, not at all." Waving his question away before it could be fully articulated. Lying in bed that night and sleepless for longer than usual, Bobby thought that Ted had almost been afraid for it to be spoken aloud. "There are lots of people, quite ordinary ones, we don't see. The waitress walking home from work with her head down and her restaurant shoes in a paper bag. Old fellows out for their afternoon walks in the park. Teenage girls with their hair in rollers and their transistor radios playing Peter Tripp's countdown. But children see them. Children see them all. And Bobby, you are still a child."

"These guys don't sound exactly easy to miss."

"The coats, you mean. The shoes. The loud cars. But those are the very things which cause some people—many people, actually—to turn away. To erect little roadblocks between the eye and the brain. In any case, I won't have you taking chances. If you do see the men in the yellow coats, *don't approach them.* Don't speak to them even if they should speak to you. I can't think why they would, I don't believe they would even see you—just as most people don't really see them—but there are plenty of things I don't know about them. Now tell me what I just said. Repeat it back. It's important."

"Don't approach them and don't speak to them."

"Even if they speak to you." Rather impatiently.

"Even if they speak to me, right. What *should* I do?"

"Come back here and tell me they're about and where you saw them. Walk until you're certain you're out of their sight, then run. Run like the wind. Run like hell was after you."

"And what will you do?" Bobby asked, but of course he knew. Maybe he wasn't as sharp as Carol, but he wasn't a complete dodo, either. "You'll go away, won't you?"

Ted Brautigan shrugged and finished his glass of rootbeer without meeting Bobby's eyes. "I'll decide when that time comes. *If* it comes. If I'm lucky, the feelings I've had for the last few days—my sense of these men—will go away."

"Has that happened before?"

"Indeed it has. Now why don't we talk of more pleasant things?"

For the next half an hour they discussed baseball, then music (Bobby was startled to discover Ted not only knew the music of Elvis Presley but actually liked some of it), then Bobby's hopes and fears concerning the seventh grade in September. All this was pleasant enough, but behind each topic Bobby sensed the lurk of the low men. The low men were here in Ted's third-floor room like peculiar shadows which cannot quite be seen.

It wasn't until Bobby was getting ready to leave that Ted raised the subject of them again. "There are things you should look for," he said. "Signs that my . . . my old friends are about."

"What are they?"

"On your travels around town, keep an eye out for lost-pet posters on walls, in shop windows, stapled to telephone poles on residential streets. 'Lost, a gray tabby cat with black ears, a white bib, and a crooked tail. Call IRoquois 7-7661.' 'Lost, a small mongrel dog, part beagle, answers to the name of Trixie, loves children, ours want her to come home. Call IRoquois 7-0984 or bring to 77 Peabody Street.' That sort of thing."

"What are you saying? Jeepers, are you saying they kill people's *pets?* Do you think . . ."

"I think many of those animals don't exist at all," Ted said. He sounded weary and unhappy. "Even when there is a small, poorly reproduced photograph, I think most are pure fiction. I think such posters are a form of communication, although why the men who put them up shouldn't just go into the Colony Diner and do their communicating over pot roast and mashed potatoes I don't know.

"Where does your mother shop, Bobby?"

"Total Grocery. It's right next door to Mr. Biderman's real-estate agency."

"And do you go with her?"

"Sometimes." When he was younger he met her there every Friday, reading a *TV Guide* from the magazine rack until she showed up, loving Friday afternoons because it was the start of the weekend, because Mom let him push the cart and he always pretended it was a racing car, because he loved *her.* But he didn't tell Ted any of this. It was ancient history. Hell, he'd only been eight.

"Look on the bulletin board every supermarket puts up by the checkout registers," Ted said. "On it you'll see a number of little hand-printed notices that say things like CAR FOR SALE BY OWNER. Look for any such notices that have been thumbtacked to the board upside down. Is there another supermarket in town?"

"There's the A&P, down by the railroad overpass. My mom doesn't go there. She says the butcher's always giving her the glad-eye."

"Can you check the bulletin board there, as well?"

"Sure."

"Good so far, very good. Now—you know the hopscotch patterns kids are always drawing on the sidewalks?"

Bobby nodded.

"Look for ones with stars or moons or both chalked near them, usually in chalk of a different color. Look for kite tails hanging from telephone lines. Not the kites themselves, but only the tails. And . . ."

Ted paused, frowning, thinking. As he took a Chesterfield from the pack on the table and lit it, Bobby thought quite reasonably, quite clearly, and without the slightest shred of fear: *He's crazy, y'know. Crazy as a loon.*

Yes, of course, how could you doubt it? He only hoped Ted could be careful as well as crazy. Because if his mom heard Ted talking about stuff like this, she'd never let Bobby go near him again. In fact, she'd probably send for the guys with the butterfly nets . . . or ask good old Don Biderman to do it for her.

"You know the clock in the town square, Bobby?"

"Yeah, sure."

"It may begin ringing wrong hours, or between hours. Also, look for reports of minor church vandalism in the paper. My friends dislike churches, but they never do anything too outrageous; they like to keep a—pardon the pun—low profile. There are other signs that they're about, but there's no need to overload you. Personally I believe the posters are the surest clue."

" 'If you see Ginger, please bring her home.' "

"That's exactly r—"

"Bobby?" It was his mom's voice, followed by the ascending scuff of her Saturday sneakers. "Bobby, are you up there?"

III. A MOTHER'S POWER. BOBBY DOES HIS JOB. "DOES HE TOUCH YOU?" THE LAST DAY OF SCHOOL.

Bobby and Ted exchanged a guilty look. Both of them sat back on their respective sides of the table, as if they had been doing something crazy instead of just talking about crazy stuff.

She'll see we've been up to something, Bobby thought with dismay. *It's all over my face.*

"No," Ted said to him. "It is not. That is her power over you, that you believe it. It's a mother's power."

Bobby stared at him, amazed. *Did you read my mind? Did you read my mind just then?*

Now his mom was almost to the third-floor landing and there was no time for a reply even if Ted had wanted to make one. But there was no look on his face saying he *would* have replied if there had been time, either. And Bobby at once began to doubt what he had heard.

Then his mother was in the open doorway, looking from her son to Ted and back to her son again, her eyes assessing. "So here you are after all," she said. "My goodness, Bobby, didn't you hear me calling?"

"You were up here before I got a chance to say boo, Mom."

She snorted. Her mouth made a small, meaningless smile—her automatic social smile. Her eyes went back and forth between the two of them, back and forth, looking for something out of place, something she didn't like, something wrong. "I didn't hear you come in from outdoors."

"You were asleep on your bed."

"How are you today, Mrs. Garfield?" Ted asked.

"Fine as paint." Back and forth went her eyes. Bobby had no idea what she was looking for, but that expression of dismayed guilt must have left his face. If she had seen it, he would know already; would know that *she* knew.

"Would you like a bottle of pop?" Ted asked. "I have rootbeer. It's not much, but it's cold."

"That would be nice," Liz said. "Thanks." She came all the way in and sat down next to Bobby at the kitchen table. She patted him absently on the leg, watching Ted as he opened his little fridge and got out the rootbeer. "It's not hot up here yet, Mr. Brattigan, but I guarantee you it will be in another month. You want to get yourself a fan."

"There's an idea." Ted poured rootbeer into a clean glass, then stood in front of the fridge holding the glass up to the light, waiting for the foam to go down. To Bobby he looked like a scientist in a TV commercial, one of those guys obsessed with Brand X and Brand Y and how Rolaids consumed fifty-seven times its own weight in excess stomach acid, amazing but true.

"I don't need a full glass, that will be fine," she said a little impatiently. Ted brought the glass to her, and she raised it to him. "Here's how." She took a swallow and grimaced as if it had been rye instead of rootbeer. Then she watched over the top of the glass as Ted sat down, tapped the ash from his smoke, and tucked the stub of the cigarette back into the corner of his mouth.

"You two have gotten thicker than thieves," she remarked. "Sitting here at the kitchen table, drinking rootbeer—cozy, thinks I! What've you been talking about today?"

"The book Mr. Brautigan gave me," Bobby said. His voice sounded natural and calm, a voice with no secrets behind it. "*Lord of the Flies.* I couldn't figure out if the ending was happy or sad, so I thought I'd ask him."

"Oh? And what did he say?"

"That it was both. Then he told me to consider it."

Liz laughed without a great deal of humor. "I read mysteries, Mr. Brattigan, and save my consideration for real life. But of course I'm not retired."

"No," Ted said. "You are obviously in the very prime of life."

She gave him her *flattery-will-get-you-nowhere* look. Bobby knew it well.

"I also offered Bobby a small job," Ted told her. "He has agreed to take it . . . with your permission, of course."

Her brow furrowed at the mention of a job, smoothed at the mention of permission. She reached out and briefly touched Bobby's red hair, a gesture so unusual that Bobby's eyes widened a little. Her eyes never left Ted's face as she did it. Not only did she not trust the man, Bobby realized, she was likely *never* going to trust him. "What sort of job did you have in mind?"

"He wants me to—"

"Hush," she said, and still her eyes peered over the top of her glass, never leaving Ted.

"I'd like him to read me the paper, perhaps in the afternoons," Ted said, then explained how his eyes weren't what they used to be and how he had worse problems every day with the finer print. But he liked to keep up with the news—these were very interesting times, didn't Mrs. Garfield think so?—and he liked to keep up with the columns, as well, Stewart Alsop and Walter Winchell and such. Winchell was a gossip, of course, but an *interesting* gossip, didn't Mrs. Garfield agree?

Bobby listened, increasingly tense even though he could tell from his mother's face and posture—even from the way she sipped her rootbeer—that she believed what Ted was telling her. That part of it was all right, but what if Ted went blank again? Went blank and started babbling about low men in yellow coats or the tails of kites hanging from telephone wires, all the time gazing off into space?

But nothing like that happened. Ted finished by saying he also liked to know how the Dodgers were doing—Maury Wills, especially—even though they had gone to L.A. He said this with the air of one who is determined to tell the truth even if the truth is a bit shameful. Bobby thought it was a nice touch.

"I suppose that would be fine," his mother said (almost grudgingly, Bobby thought). "In fact it sounds like a plum. I wish *I* could have a plum job like that."

"I'll bet you're excellent at your job, Mrs. Garfield."

She flashed him her dry *flattery-won't-work-with-me* expression again. "You'll have to pay him extra to do the crossword for you," she said, getting up, and although Bobby didn't understand the remark, he was astonished by the cruelty he sensed in it, embedded like a piece of glass in a marshmallow. It was as if she wanted to make fun of Ted's failing eyesight and his intellect at the same time; as if she wanted to hurt him for being nice to her son. Bobby was still ashamed at deceiving her and frightened that she would find out, but now he was also glad . . . almost viciously glad. She deserved it. "He's good at the crossword, my Bobby."

Ted smiled. "I'm sure he is."

"Come on downstairs, Bob. It's time to give Mr. Brattigan a rest."

"But—"

"I think I *would* like to lie down awhile, Bobby. I've a little bit of a headache. I'm glad you liked *Lord of the Flies.* You can start your job tomorrow, if you like, with the feature section of the Sunday paper. I warn you it's apt to be a trial by fire."

"Okay."

Mom had reached the little landing outside of Ted's door. Bobby was behind her. Now she turned back and looked at Ted over Bobby's head. "Why not outside on the porch?" she asked. "The fresh air will be nice for both of you. Better than this stuffy room. And I'll be able to hear, too, if I'm in the living room."

Bobby thought some message was passing between them. Not via telepathy, exactly . . . only it *was* telepathy, in a way. The humdrum sort adults practiced.

"A fine idea," Ted said. "The front porch would be lovely. Good afternoon, Bobby. Good afternoon, Mrs. Garfield."

Bobby came very close to saying *Seeya, Ted* and substituted "See you, Mr. Brautigan" at the last moment. He moved toward the stairs, smiling vaguely, with the sweaty feeling of someone who has just avoided a nasty accident.

His mother lingered. "How long have you been retired, Mr. Brattigan? Or do you mind me asking?"

Bobby had almost decided she wasn't mispronouncing Ted's name deliberately; now he swung the other way. She was. Of course she was.

"Three years." He crushed his cigarette out in the brimming tin ashtray and immediately lit another.

"Which would make you . . . sixty-eight?"

"Sixty-six, actually." His voice continued mild and open, but Bobby had an idea he didn't much care for these questions. "I was granted retirement with full benefits two years early. Medical reasons."

Don't ask him what's wrong with him, Mom, Bobby moaned inside his own head. *Don't you dare.*

She didn't. She asked what he'd done in Hartford instead.

"Accounting. I was in the Office of the Comptroller."

"Bobby and I guessed something to do with education. Accounting! That sounds very responsible."

Ted smiled. Bobby thought there was something awful about it. "In twenty years I wore out three adding machines. If that is responsibility, Mrs. Garfield, why yes—I was responsible. Apeneck Sweeney spreads his knees; the typist puts a record on the gramophone with an automatic hand."

"I don't follow you."

"It's my way of saying that it was a lot of years in a job that never seemed to mean much."

"It might have meant a good deal if you'd had a child to feed, shelter, and raise." She looked at him with her chin slightly tilted, the look that meant if Ted wanted to discuss this, she was ready. That she would go to the mat with him on the subject if that was his pleasure.

Ted, Bobby was relieved to find, didn't want to go to the mat or anywhere near it. "I expect you're right, Mrs. Garfield. Entirely."

She gave him a moment more of the lifted chin, asking if he was sure, giving him time to change his mind. When Ted said nothing else, she smiled. It was her victory smile. Bobby loved her, but suddenly he was tired of her as well. Tired of knowing her looks, her sayings, and the adamant cast of her mind.

"Thank you for the rootbeer, Mr. Brattigan. It was very tasty." And with that she led her son downstairs. When they got to the second-floor landing she dropped his hand and went the rest of the way ahead of him.

Bobby thought they would discuss his new job further over supper, but they didn't. His mom seemed far away from him, her eyes distant. He had to ask her twice for a second slice of meatloaf and when later that evening the telephone rang, she jumped up from the couch where they had been watching TV to get it. She jumped for it the way Ricky Nelson did when it rang on the *Ozzie and Harriet* show. She listened, said something, then came back to the couch and sat down.

"Who was it?" Bobby asked.

"Wrong number," Liz said.

In that year of his life Bobby Garfield still waited for sleep with a child's welcoming confidence: on his back, heels spread to the corners of the bed, hands tucked into the cool under the pillow so his elbows stuck up. On the night after Ted spoke to him about the low men in their yellow coats (*and don't forget their cars,* he thought, *their big cars with the fancy paintjobs*), Bobby lay in this position with the sheet pushed down to his waist. Moonlight fell on his narrow child's chest, squared in four by the shadows of the window muntins.

If he had thought about it (he hadn't), he would have expected Ted's low men to become more real once he was alone in the dark, with only the tick of his wind-up Big Ben and the murmur of the late TV news from the other room to keep him company. That was the way it had always been with him—it was easy to laugh at Frankenstein on Shock Theater, to go fake-swoony and cry "Ohhh, *Frankie!*" when the monster showed up, especially if Sully-John was there for a sleepover. But in the dark, after S-J had started to snore (or worse, if Bobby was alone), Dr. Frankenstein's creature seemed a lot more . . . not real, exactly, but . . . *possible.*

That sense of possibility did not gather around Ted's low men. If anything, the idea that people would communicate with each other via lost-pet posters seemed even crazier in the dark. But not a dangerous crazy. Bobby didn't think Ted was really, deeply crazy, anyhow; just a bit too smart for his own good, especially since he had so few things with which to occupy his time. Ted was a little . . . well . . . cripes, a little *what?* Bobby couldn't express it. If the word *eccentric* had occurred to him he would have seized it with pleasure and relief.

But . . . it seemed like he read my mind. What about that?

Oh, he was wrong, that was all, mistaken about what he thought he'd heard. Or maybe Ted *had* read his mind, read it with that essentially uninteresting adult ESP, peeling guilt off his face like a wet decal off a piece of glass. God knew his mother could always do that . . . at least until today.

But—

But nothing. Ted was a nice guy who knew a lot about books, but he was no mind-reader. No more than Sully-John Sullivan was a magician, or ever would be.

"It's all misdirection," Bobby murmured. He slipped his hands out from under his pillow, crossed them at the wrists, wagged them. The shadow of a dove flew across the moonlight on his chest.

Bobby smiled, closed his eyes, and went to sleep.

The next morning he sat on the front porch and read several pieces aloud from the Harwich Sunday *Journal.* Ted perched on the porch glider, listening quietly and smoking Chesterfields. Behind him and to his left, the curtains flapped in and out of the open windows of the

Garfield front room. Bobby imagined his mom sitting in the chair where the light was best, sewing basket beside her, listening and hemming skirts (hemlines were going down again, she'd told him a week or two before; take them up one year, pick out the stitches the following spring and lower them again, all because a bunch of poofers in New York and London said to, and why she bothered she didn't know). Bobby had no idea if she really was there or not, the open windows and blowing curtains meant nothing by themselves, but he imagined it all the same. When he was a little older it would occur to him that he had *always* imagined her there—outside doors, in that part of the bleachers where the shadows were too thick to see properly, in the dark at the top of the stairs, he had always imagined she was there.

The sports pieces he read were interesting (Maury Wills was stealing up a storm), the feature articles less so, the opinion columns boring and long and incomprehensible, full of phrases like "fiscal responsibility" and "economic indicators of a recessionary nature." Even so, Bobby didn't mind reading them. He was doing a job, after all, earning dough, and a lot of jobs were boring at least some of the time. "You have to work for your Wheaties," his mother sometimes said after Mr. Biderman had kept her late. Bobby was proud just to be able to get a phrase like "economic indicators of a recessionary nature" to come off his tongue. Besides, the other job—the hidden job—arose from Ted's crazy idea that some men were out to get him, and Bobby would have felt weird taking money just for doing that one; would have felt like he was tricking Ted somehow even though it had been Ted's idea in the first place.

That was still part of his job, though, crazy or not, and he began doing it that Sunday afternoon. Bobby walked around the block while his mom was napping, looking for either low men in yellow coats or signs of them. He saw a number of interesting things—over on Colony Street a woman arguing with her husband about something, the two of them standing nose-to-nose like Gorgeous George and Haystacks Calhoun before the start of a rassling match; a little kid on Asher Avenue bashing caps with a smoke-blackened rock;

liplocked teenagers outside of Spicer's Variety Store on the corner of Commonwealth and Broad; a panel truck with the interesting slogan YUMMY FOR THE TUMMY written on the side—but he saw no yellow coats or lost-pet announcements on phone poles; not a single kite tail hung from a single telephone wire.

He stopped in at Spicer's for a penny gumball and gleeped the bulletin board, which was dominated by photos of this year's Miss Rheingold candidates. He saw two cards offering car for sale by owner, but neither was upside down. There was another one that said MUST SELL MY BACKYARD POOL, GOOD SHAPE, YOUR KIDS WILL LOVE IT, and that one was crooked, but Bobby didn't guess crooked counted.

On Asher Avenue he saw a whale of a Buick parked at a hydrant, but it was bottle-green, and Bobby didn't think it qualified as loud and vulgar in spite of the portholes up the sides of the hood and the grille, which looked like the sneery mouth of a chrome catfish.

On Monday he continued looking for low men on his way to and from school. He saw nothing . . . but Carol Gerber, who was walking with him and S-J, saw him looking. His mother was right, Carol was really sharp.

"Are the commie agents after the plans?" she asked.

"Huh?"

"You keep staring everywhere. Even behind you."

For a moment Bobby considered telling them what Ted had hired him to do, then decided it would be a bad idea. It might have been a good one if he believed there was really something to look for—three pairs of eyes instead of one, Carol's sharp little peepers included—but he didn't. Carol and Sully-John knew that he had a job reading Ted the paper every day, and that was all right. It was enough. If he told them about the low men, it would feel like making fun, somehow. A betrayal.

"Commie agents?" Sully asked, whirling around. "Yeah, I see em, I see em!" He drew down his mouth and made the *eh-eh-eh* noise again (it was his favorite). Then he staggered, dropped his invisible tommygun, clutched his chest. "They got me! I'm hit bad! Go on without me! Give my love to Rose!"

"I'll give it to my aunt's fat fanny," Carol said, and elbowed him.

"I'm looking for guys from St. Gabe's, that's all," Bobby said.

This was plausible; boys from St. Gabriel the Steadfast Upper and Secondary were always harassing the Harwich Elementary kids as the Elementary kids walked to school—buzzing them on their bikes, shouting that the boys were sissies, that the girls "put out" . . . which Bobby was pretty sure meant tongue-kissing and letting boys touch their titties.

"Nah, those dinkberries don't come along until later," Sully-John said. "Right now they're all still home puttin on their crosses and combin their hair back like Bobby Rydell."

"Don't swear," Carol said, and elbowed him again.

Sully-John looked wounded. "Who swore? I didn't swear."

"Yes you did."

"I did not, Carol."

"Did."

"No sir, did not."

"*Yes* sir, did too, you said dinkberries."

"That's not a swear! Dinkberries are *berries!*" S-J looked at Bobby for help, but Bobby was looking up at Asher Avenue, where a Cadillac was cruising slowly by. It was big, and he supposed it was a little flashy, but wasn't any Cadillac? This one was painted a conservative light brown and didn't look low to him. Besides, the person at the wheel was a woman.

"Yeah? Show me a picture of a dinkberry in the encyclopedia and maybe I'll believe you."

"I ought to poke you," Sully said amiably. "Show you who's boss. Me Tarzan, you Jane."

"Me Carol, you Jughead. Here." Carol thrust three books—arithmetic, *Adventures in Spelling,* and *The Little House on the Prairie*—into S-J's hands. "Carry my books cause you swore."

Sully-John looked more wounded than ever. "Why should I have to carry your stupid books even if I *did* swear, which I didn't?"

"It's pennants," Carol said.

"What the heck is pennants?"

"Making up for something you do wrong. If you swear or tell a lie, you have to do pennants. One of the St. Gabe's boys told me. Willie, his name is."

"You shouldn't hang around with them," Bobby said. "They can be mean." He knew this from personal experience. Just after Christmas vacation ended, three St. Gabe's boys had chased him down Broad Street, threatening to beat him up because he had "looked at them wrong." They would have done it, too, Bobby thought, if the one in the lead hadn't slipped in the slush and gone to his knees. The others had tripped over him, allowing Bobby just time enough to nip in through the big front door of 149 and turn the lock. The St. Gabe's boys had hung around outside for a little while, then had gone away after promising Bobby that they would "see him later."

"They're not all hoods, some of them are okay," Carol said. She looked at Sully-John, who was carrying her books, and hid a smile with one hand. You could get S-J to do anything if you talked fast and sounded sure of yourself. It would have been nicer to have Bobby carry her books, but it wouldn't have been any good unless he asked her. Someday he might; she was an optimist. In the meantime it was nice to be walking here between them in the morning sunshine. She stole a glance at Bobby, who was looking down at a hopscotch grid drawn on the sidewalk. He was so cute, and he didn't even know it. Somehow that was the cutest thing of all.

The last week of school passed as it always did, with a maddening, half-crippled slowness. On those early June days Bobby thought the smell of the paste in the library was almost strong enough to gag a maggot, and geography seemed to last ten thousand years. Who cared how much tin there was in Paraguay?

At recess Carol talked about how she was going to her aunt Cora and uncle Ray's farm in Pennsylvania for a week in July; S-J went on and on about the week of camp he'd won and how he was going to shoot arrows at targets and go out in a canoe every day he was there. Bobby, in turn, told them about the great Maury Wills, who might set a record for base-stealing that would never be broken in their lifetime.

His mom was increasingly preoccupied, jumping each time the telephone rang and then running for it, staying up past the late news (and sometimes, Bobby suspected, until the Nite-Owl Movie was over), and only picking at her meals. Sometimes she would have long, intense conversations on the phone with her back turned and her voice lowered (as if Bobby wanted to eavesdrop on her conversations, anyway). Sometimes she'd go to the telephone, start to dial it, then drop it back in its cradle and return to the couch.

On one of these occasions Bobby asked her if she had forgotten what number she wanted to call. "Seems like I've forgotten a lot of things," she muttered, and then: "Mind your beeswax, Bobby-O."

He might have noticed more and worried even more than he did—she was getting thin and had picked up the cigarette habit again after almost stopping for two years—if he hadn't had lots of stuff to occupy his own mind and time. The best thing was the adult library card, which seemed like a better gift, a more *inspired* gift, each time he used it. Bobby felt there were a billion science-fiction novels alone in the adult section that he wanted to read. Take Isaac Asimov, for instance. Under the name of Paul French, Mr. Asimov wrote science-fiction novels for kids about a space pilot named Lucky Starr, and they were pretty good. Under his own name he had written other novels, even better ones. At least three of them were about robots. Bobby loved robots. Robby the Robot in *Forbidden Planet* was one of the all-time great movie characters, in his opinion, totally rip-shit, and Mr. Asimov's were almost as good. Bobby thought he would be spending a lot of time with them in the summer ahead. (Sully called this great writer Isaac Ass-Move, but of course Sully was almost totally ignorant about books.)

Going to school he looked for the men in the yellow coats, or signs of them; going to the library after school he did the same. Because school and library were in opposite directions, Bobby felt he was covering a pretty good part of Harwich. He never expected to actually see any low men, of course. After supper, in the long light of evening, he would read the paper to Ted, either on the porch or in Ted's kitchen. Ted had followed Liz Garfield's advice and gotten a fan, and

Bobby's mom no longer seemed concerned that Bobby should read to "Mr. Brattigan" out on the porch. Some of this was her growing preoccupation with her own adult matters, Bobby felt, but perhaps she was also coming to trust Ted a little more. Not that trust was the same as liking. Not that it had come easily, either.

One night while they were on the couch watching *Wyatt Earp,* his mom turned to Bobby almost fiercely and said, "Does he ever touch you?"

Bobby understood what she was asking, but not why she was so wound up. "Well, sure," he said. "He claps me on the back sometimes, and once when I was reading the paper to him and screwed up some really long word three times in a row he gave me a Dutch rub, but he doesn't roughhouse or anything. I don't think he's strong enough for stuff like that. Why?"

"Never mind," she said. "He's fine, I guess. Got his head in the clouds, no question about it, but he doesn't seem like a . . ." She trailed off, watching the smoke from her Kool cigarette rise in the living-room air. It went up from the coal in a pale gray ribbon and then disappeared, making Bobby think of the way the characters in Mr. Simak's *Ring Around the Sun* followed the spiraling top into other worlds.

At last she turned to him again and said, "If he ever touches you in a way you don't like, you come and tell me. Right away. You hear?"

"Sure, Mom." There was something in her look that made him remember once when he'd asked her how a woman knew she was going to have a baby. *She bleeds every month,* his mom had said. *If there's no blood, she knows it's because the blood is going into a baby.* Bobby had wanted to ask where this blood came out when there was no baby being made (he remembered a nosebleed his mom had had once, but no other instances of maternal bleeding). The look on her face, however, had made him drop the subject. She wore the same look now.

Actually there *had* been other touches: Ted might run one of his big hands across Bobby's crewcut, kind of patting the bristles; he would sometimes gently catch Bobby's nose between his knuckles and intone *Sound it out!* if Bobby mispronounced a word; if they spoke at the same moment he would hook one of his little fingers around one of Bobby's little fingers and say *Good luck, good will, good fortune, not ill.* Soon Bobby was saying it with him, their little fingers locked, their voices as matter-of-fact as people saying pass the peas or how you doing.

Only once did Bobby feel uncomfortable when Ted touched him. Bobby had just finished the last newspaper piece Ted wanted to hear—some columnist blabbing on about how there was nothing wrong with Cuba that good old American free enterprise couldn't fix. Dusk was beginning to streak the sky. Back on Colony Street, Mrs. O'Hara's dog Bowser barked on and on, *roop-roop-roop,* the sound lost and somehow dreamy, seeming more like something remembered than something happening at that moment.

"Well," Bobby said, folding the paper and getting up, "I think I'll take a walk around the block and see what I see." He didn't want to come right out and say it, but he wanted Ted to know he was still looking for the low men in the yellow coats.

Ted also got up and approached him. Bobby was saddened to see the fear on Ted's face. He didn't want Ted to believe in the low men too much, didn't want Ted to be too crazy. "Be back before dark, Bobby. I'd never forgive myself if something happened to you."

"I'll be careful. And I'll be back years before dark."

Ted dropped to one knee (he was too old to just hunker, Bobby guessed) and took hold of Bobby's shoulders. He drew Bobby forward until their brows were almost bumping. Bobby could smell cigarettes on Ted's breath and ointment on his skin—he rubbed his joints with Musterole because they ached. These days they ached even in warm weather, he said.

Being this close to Ted wasn't scary, but it was sort of awful, just the same. You could see that even if Ted wasn't totally old now, he soon would be. He'd probably be sick, too. His eyes were watery. The corners of his mouth were trembling a little. It was too bad he had to be all alone up here on the third floor, Bobby thought. If he'd had a wife or something, he might never have gotten this bee in his bonnet about the low men. Of course if he'd had a wife, Bobby might never have read *Lord of the Flies.* A selfish way to think, but he couldn't help it.

"No sign of them, Bobby?"

Bobby shook his head.

"And you feel nothing? Nothing here?" He took his right hand from Bobby's left shoulder and tapped his own temple, where two blue veins nested, pulsing slightly. Bobby shook his head. "Or here?" Ted pulled down the corner of his right eye. Bobby shook his head again. "Or here?" Ted touched his stomach. Bobby shook his head a third time.

"Okay," Ted said, and smiled. He slipped his left hand up to the back of Bobby's neck. His right hand joined it. He looked solemnly into Bobby's eyes and Bobby looked solemnly back. "You'd tell me if you did, wouldn't you? You wouldn't try to . . . oh, I don't know . . . to spare my feelings?"

"No," Bobby said. He liked Ted's hands on the back of his neck and didn't like them at the same time. It was where a guy in a movie might put his hands just before he kissed the girl. "No, I'd tell, that's my job."

Ted nodded. He slowly unlaced his hands and let them drop. He got to his feet, using the table for support and grimacing when one knee popped loudly. "Yes, you'd tell me, you're a good kid. Go on, take your walk. But stay on the sidewalk, Bobby, and be home before dark. You have to be careful these days."

"I'll be careful." He started down the stairs.

"And if you see them—"

"I'll run."

"Yeah." In the fading light, Ted's face was grim. "Like hell was after you."

So there had been touching, and perhaps his mother's fears had been justified in a way—perhaps there had been too much touching and some of the wrong sort. Not wrong in whatever way she thought, maybe, but still wrong. Still dangerous.

On the Wednesday before school let out for the summer, Bobby saw a red strip of cloth hanging from somebody's TV antenna over on Colony Street. He couldn't tell for sure, but it looked remarkably like a kite tail. Bobby's feet stopped dead. At the same time his heart accelerated until it was hammering the way it did when he raced Sully-John home from school.

It's a coincidence even if it is a kite tail, he told himself. *Just a lousy coincidence. You know that, don't you?*

Maybe. Maybe he knew. He had almost come to believe it, anyway, when school let out for the summer on Friday. Bobby walked home by himself that day; Sully-John had volunteered to stay and help put books away in the storeroom and Carol was going over to Tina Lebel's for Tina's birthday party. Just before crossing Asher Avenue and starting down Broad Street Hill, he saw a hopscotch grid drawn on the sidewalk in purple chalk. It looked like this:

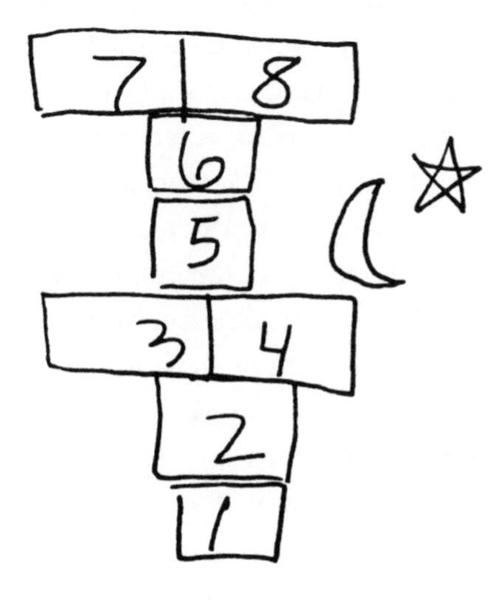

"Oh Christ no," Bobby whispered. "You gotta be kidding."

He dropped to one knee like a cavalry scout in a western movie, oblivious of the kids passing by him on their way home—some walking, some on bikes, a couple on roller skates, buck-toothed Francis Utterson on his rusty red scooter, honking laughter at the sky as he paddled along. They were almost as oblivious of him; the Big Vac had just started, and most were dazed by all the possibilities.

"Oh no, oh no, I don't believe it, you *gotta* be kidding." He reached out toward the star and the crescent moon—they were drawn in yellow chalk, not purple—almost touched them, then drew his hand back. A piece of red ribbon caught on a TV antenna didn't have to mean anything. When you added this, though, could it still be coincidence? Bobby didn't know. He was only eleven and there were a bazillion things he didn't know. But he was afraid . . . afraid that . . .

He got to his feet and looked around, half-expecting to see a whole line of long, overbright cars coming down Asher Avenue, rolling slow the way cars did when they were following a hearse to the graveyard, with their headlights on in the middle of the day. Half-expecting to see men in yellow coats standing beneath the marquee of the Asher Empire or out in front of Sukey's Tavern, smoking Camels and watching him.

No cars. No men. Just kids heading home from school. The first ones from St. Gabe's, conspicuous in their green uniform pants and skirts, were visible among them.

Bobby turned around and backtracked for three blocks up Asher Avenue, too worried about what he'd seen chalked on the sidewalk to concern himself about bad-tempered St. Gabe's boys. There was nothing on the Avenue telephone poles but a few posters advertising Bingo Nite at the St. Gabriel Parish Hall and one on the corner of Asher and Tacoma announcing a rock-and-roll show in Hartford starring Clyde McPhatter and Duane Eddy, the Man with the Twangy Guitar.

By the time he got to Asher Avenue News, which was almost all the way back to school, Bobby was starting to hope he had overreacted. Still, he went in to look at their bulletin board, then all the way down Broad Street to Spicer's Variety, where he bought another gumball and checked that bulletin board as well. Nothing suspicious on either one. In Spicer's the card advertising the backyard pool was gone, but so what? The guy had probably sold it. Why else had he put the card up in the first place, for God's sake?

Bobby left and stood on the corner, chewing his gumball and trying to make up his mind what to do next.

Adulthood is accretive by nature, a thing which arrives in ragged stages and uneven overlaps. Bobby Garfield made the first adult decision of his life on the day he finished the sixth grade, concluding it would be wrong to tell Ted about the stuff he had seen . . . at least for the time being.

His assumption that the low men didn't exist had been shaken, but Bobby wasn't ready to give it up. Not on the evidence he had so far. Ted would be upset if Bobby told him what he had seen, maybe upset enough to toss his stuff back into his suitcases (plus those carryhandle bags folded up behind his little fridge) and just take off. If there really were bad guys after him, flight would make sense, but Bobby didn't want to lose the only adult friend he'd ever had if there weren't. So he decided to wait and see what, if anything, happened next.

That night Bobby Garfield experienced another aspect of adulthood: he lay awake until well after his Big Ben alarm clock said it was two in the morning, looking up at the ceiling and wondering if he had done the right thing.

IV. TED GOES BLANK. BOBBY GOES TO THE BEACH. MCQUOWN. THE WINKLE.

The day after school ended, Carol Gerber's mom crammed her Ford Estate Wagon with kids and took them to Savin Rock, a seaside amusement park twenty miles from Harwich. Anita Gerber had done this three years running, which made it an ancient tradition to Bobby, S-J, Carol, Carol's little brother, and Carol's girlfriends, Yvonne, Angie, and Tina. Neither Sully-John nor Bobby would have gone anywhere with three girls on his own, but since they were together it was okay. Besides, the lure of Savin Rock was too strong to resist. It would still be too cold to do much more than wade in the ocean, but they could goof on the beach and all the rides would be open—the midway, too. The year before, Sully-John had knocked down three pyramids of wooden milk-bottles with just three baseballs, winning his mother a large pink teddy bear which still held pride of place on top of the Sullivan TV. Today S-J wanted to win it a mate.

For Bobby, just getting away from Harwich for a little while was an attraction. He had seen nothing suspicious since the star and the moon scribbled next to the hopscotch grid, but Ted gave him a bad scare while Bobby was reading him the Saturday newspaper, and hard on the heels of that came an ugly argument with his mother.

The thing with Ted happened while Bobby was reading an opinion piece scoffing at the idea that Mickey Mantle would ever break Babe Ruth's home-run record. He didn't have the stamina or the dedication, the columnist insisted. " 'Above all, the character of this man is wrong,' " Bobby read. " 'The so-called Mick is more interested in night-clubbing than—' "

Ted had blanked out again. Bobby knew this, felt it somehow, even before he looked up from the newspaper. Ted was staring emptily out his window toward Colony Street and the hoarse, monotonous barking of Mrs. O'Hara's dog. It was the second time he'd done it this morning, but the first lapse had lasted only a few seconds (Ted bent into the open refrigerator, eyes wide in the frosty light, not moving . . . then giving a jerk, a little shake, and reaching for the orange juice). This time he was totally gone. Wigsville, man, as Kookie might have said on 77 *Sunset Strip.* Bobby rattled the newspaper to see if he could wake him up that way. Nothing.

"Ted? Are you all r—" With sudden dawning horror, Bobby realized something was wrong with the pupils of Ted's eyes. They were growing and shrinking in his face as Bobby watched. It was as if Ted were plunging rapidly in and out of some abysmally black place . . . and yet all he was doing was sitting there in the sunshine.

"Ted?"

A cigarette was burning in the ashtray, except it was now nothing but stub and ash. Looking at it, Bobby realized Ted must have been out for almost the entire article on Mantle. And that thing his eyes were doing, the pupils swelling and contracting, swelling and contracting . . .

He's having an epilepsy attack or something. God, don't they sometimes swallow their tongues when that happens?

Ted's tongue looked to be where it belonged, but his eyes . . . his *eyes*—

"Ted! Ted, wake up!"

Bobby was around to Ted's side of the table before he was even aware he was moving. He grabbed Ted by the shoulders and shook him. It was like shaking a piece of wood carved to look like a man. Under his cotton pullover shirt Ted's shoulders were hard and scrawny and unyielding.

"Wake up! *Wake up!*"

"They draw west now." Ted continued to look out the window with his strange moving eyes. "That's good. But they may be back. They . . ."

Bobby stood with his hands on Ted's shoulders, frightened and awestruck. Ted's pupils expanded and contracted like a heartbeat you could see. "Ted, what's wrong?"

"I must be very still. I must be a hare in the bush. They may pass by. There will be water if God wills it, and they may pass by. All things serve . . ."

"Serve what?" Almost whispering now. "Serve what, Ted?"

"All things serve the Beam," Ted said, and suddenly his hands closed over Bobby's. They were very cold, those hands, and for a moment Bobby felt nightmarish, fainting terror. It was like being gripped by a corpse that could only move its hands and the pupils of its dead eyes.

Then Ted was looking at him, and although his eyes were frightened, they were almost normal again. Not dead at all.

"Bobby?"

Bobby pulled his hands free and put them around Ted's neck. He hugged him, and as he did Bobby heard a bell tolling in his head—this was very brief but very clear. He could even hear the pitch of the bell shift, the way the pitch of a train-whistle did if the train was moving fast. It was as if something inside his head were passing at high speed. He heard a rattle of hooves on some hard surface. Wood? No, metal. He smelled dust, dry and thundery in his nose. At the same moment the backs of his eyes began to itch.

"Shhh!" Ted's breath in his ear was as dry as the smell of that dust, and somehow intimate. His hands were on Bobby's back, cupping his shoulderblades and holding him still. "Not a word! Not a thought. Except . . . baseball! Yes, baseball, if you like!"

Bobby thought of Maury Wills getting his lead off first, a walking lead, measuring three steps . . . then four . . . Wills bent over at the waist, hands dangling, heels raised slightly off the dirt, he can go either way, it depends on what the pitcher does . . . and when the pitcher goes to the plate Wills heads for second in an explosion of speed and dust and—

Gone. Everything was gone. No bell ringing in his head, no sound of hooves, no smell of dust. No itching behind his eyes, either. Had that itching really ever been there? Or had he just made it up because Ted's eyes were scaring him?

"Bobby," Ted said, again directly into Bobby's ear. The movement of Ted's lips against his skin made him shiver. Then: "Good God, what am I doing?"

He pushed Bobby away, gently but firmly. His face looked dismayed and a little too pale, but his eyes were back to normal, his pupils holding steady. For the moment that was all Bobby cared about. He felt strange, though—muzzy in the head, as if he'd just woken up from a heavy nap. At the same time the world looked amazingly brilliant, every line and shape perfectly defined.

"Shazam," Bobby said, and laughed shakily. "What just happened?"

"Nothing to concern you." Ted reached for his cigarette and seemed surprised to see only a tiny smoldering scrap left in the groove where he had set it. He brushed it into the ashtray with his knuckle. "I went off again, didn't I?"

"Yeah, *way* off. I was scared. I thought you were having an epilepsy fit or something. Your eyes—"

"It's not epilepsy," Ted said. "And it's not dangerous. But if it happens again, it would be best if you didn't touch me."

"Why?"

Ted lit a fresh cigarette. "Just because. Will you promise?"

"Okay. What's the Beam?"

Ted gazed at him sharply. "I spoke of the Beam?"

"You said 'All things serve the Beam.' I think that was it."

"Perhaps sometime I'll tell you, but not today. Today you're going to the beach, aren't you?"

Bobby jumped, startled. He looked at Ted's clock and saw it was almost nine o'clock. "Yeah," he said. "Maybe I ought to start getting ready. I could finish reading you the paper when I get back."

"Yes, good. A fine idea. I have some letters to write."

No you don't, you just want to get rid of me before I ask any other questions you don't want to answer.

But if that was what Ted was doing it was all right. As Liz Garfield so often said, Bobby had his own fish to fry. Still, as he reached the door to Ted's room, the thought of the red scrap of cloth hanging from the TV aerial and the crescent moon and the star next to the hopscotch grid made him turn reluctantly back.

"Ted, there's something—"

"The low men, yes, I know." Ted smiled. "For now don't trouble yourself about them, Bobby. For now all is well. They aren't moving this way or even looking this way."

"They draw west," Bobby said.

Ted looked at him through a scurf of rising cigarette smoke, his blue eyes steady. "Yes," he said, "and with luck they'll *stay* west. Seattle would be fine with me. Have a good time at the seaside, Bobby."

"But I saw—"

"Perhaps you saw only shadows. In any case, this isn't the time to talk. Just remember what I said—if I should go blank like that again, just sit and wait for it to pass. If I should reach for you, stand back. If I should get up, tell me to sit down. In that state I will do as you say. It's like being hypnotized."

"Why do you—"

"No more questions, Bobby. Please."

"You're okay? Really okay?"

"In the pink. Now go. Enjoy your day."

Bobby hurried downstairs, again struck by how sharp everything seemed to be: the brilliance of the light slanting through the window on the second-floor landing, a ladybug crawling around the lip of an empty milk-bottle outside the door of the Proskys' apartment, a sweet high humming in his ears that was like the voice of the day—the first Saturday of summer vacation.

Back in the apartment, Bobby grabbed his toy cars and trucks from various stashes under his bed and at the back of his closet. A couple of these—a Matchbox Ford and a blue metal dumptruck Mr. Biderman had sent home with his mom a few days after Bobby's birthday—were pretty cool, but he had nothing to rival Sully's gasoline tanker or yellow Tonka bulldozer. The 'dozer was especially good to play with in the sand. Bobby was looking forward to at least an hour's serious roadbuilding while the waves broke nearby and his skin pinkened in the bright coastal sunshine. It occurred to him that he hadn't gathered up his trucks like this since sometime last winter, when he and S-J had spent a happy post-blizzard Saturday afternoon making a road-system in the fresh snow down in Commonwealth Park. He was old now, eleven, almost too old for stuff like this. There was something sad about that idea, but he didn't have to be sad right now, not if he didn't want to. His toy-truck days might be fast approaching their end, but that end wouldn't be today. Nope, not today.

His mother packed him a lunch for the trip, but she wouldn't give him any money when he asked—not even a nickel for one of the private changing-stalls which lined the ocean side of the midway. And almost before Bobby realized it was happening, they were having what he most dreaded: an argument about money.

"Fifty cents'd be enough," Bobby said. He heard the baby-whine in his voice, hated it, couldn't stop it. "Just half a rock. Come on, Mom, what do you say? Be a sport."

She lit a Kool, striking the match so hard it made a snapping sound, and looked at him through the smoke with her eyes narrowed. "You're earning your own money now, Bob. Most people pay three cents for the paper and you get paid for reading it. A dollar a week! My God! When I was a girl—"

"Mom, that money's for my bike! You know that."

She had turned to the mirror, frowning and fussing at the shoulders of her blouse—Mr. Biderman had asked her to come in for a few hours even though it was Saturday. Now she turned back, cigarette still clamped between her lips, and bent her frown on him.

"You're still asking me to buy you that bike, aren't you? *Still.* I told you I couldn't afford it but you're still asking."

"No, I'm not! I'm not either!" Bobby's eyes were wide with anger and hurt. "Just a lousy half a rock for the—"

"Half a buck here, two bits there—it all adds up, you know. What you want is for me to buy you that bike by handing you the money for everything else. Then you don't have to give up any of the *other* things you want."

"That's not fair!"

He knew what she would say before she said it, even had time to think that he had walked right into that one. "*Life's* not fair, Bobby-O." Turning back to the mirror for one final pluck at the ghost of a slip-strap hovering beneath the right shoulder of her blouse.

"A nickel for the changing-room?" Bobby asked. "Couldn't you at least—"

"Yes, probably, oh I imagine," she said, clipping off each word. She usually put rouge on her cheeks before going to work, but not all the color on her face this morning came out of a powderbox, and Bobby, angry as he was, knew he'd better be careful. If he lost his temper the way she was capable of losing hers, he'd be here in the hot empty apartment all day, forbidden to so much as step out into the hall.

His mother snatched her purse off the table by the end of the couch, butted out her cigarette hard enough to split the filter, then turned and looked at him. "If I said to you, 'Gee, we can't eat this week because I saw a pair of shoes at Hunsicker's that I just had to have,' what would you think?"

I'd think you were a liar, Bobby thought. *And I'd say if you're so broke, Mom, what about the Sears catalogue on the top shelf of your closet? The one with the dollar bills and the five-dollar bills—even a ten or two—taped to the underwear pages in the middle? What about the blue pitcher in the kitchen dish cabinet, the one tucked all the way in the back corner behind the gravy boat with the crack in it, the blue pitcher where you put your spare quarters, where you've been putting them ever since my father died? And when the pitcher's full you roll the quarters and take them to the bank and get bills, and the bills go into the catalogue, don't they? The bills get taped to the underwear pages of the wishbook.*

But he said none of this, only looked down at his sneakers with his eyes burning.

"I have to make choices," she said. "And if you're old enough to work, sonnyboy of mine, you'll have to make them, too. Do you think I like telling you no?"

Not exactly, Bobby thought, looking at his sneakers and biting at his lip, which wanted to loosen up and start letting out a bunch of blubbery baby-sounds. *Not exactly, but I don't think you really mind it, either.*

"If we were the Gotrocks, I'd give you five dollars to spend at the beach—hell, ten! You wouldn't have to borrow from your bike-jar if you wanted to take your little girlfriend on the Loop-the-Loop—"

She's not my girlfriend! Bobby screamed at his mother inside his head. *SHE IS NOT MY LITTLE GIRLFRIEND!*

"—or the Indian Railroad. But of course if we were the Gotrocks, you wouldn't need to save for a bike in the first place, would you?" Her voice rising, rising. Whatever had been troubling her over the last few months threatening to come rushing out, foaming like sodapop and biting like acid. "I don't know if you ever noticed this, but your father didn't exactly leave us well off, and I'm doing the best I can. I feed you, I put clothes on your back, I paid for you to go to Sterling House this summer and play baseball while I push paper in that hot office. You got invited to go to the beach with the other kids, I'm very happy for you, but how you finance your day off is your business. If you want to ride the rides, take some of the money you've got in that jar and ride them. If you don't, just play on the beach or stay home. Makes no difference to me. I just want you to stop whining. I hate it when you whine. It's like . . ." She stopped, sighed, opened her purse, took out her cigarettes. "I hate it when you whine," she repeated.

It's like your father. That was what she had stopped herself from saying.

"So what's the story, morning-glory?" she asked. "Are you finished?"

Bobby stood silent, cheeks burning, eyes burning, looking down at his sneakers and focusing all his will on not blubbering. At this point a single choked sob might be enough to get him grounded for the day; she was really mad, only looking for a reason to do it. And blubbering wasn't the only danger. He wanted to scream at her that he'd rather be like his father than like her, a skinflinty old cheapskate like her, not good for even a lousy nickel, and so what if the late not-so-great Randall Garfield hadn't left them well off? Why did she always make it sound like that was *his* fault? Who had married him?

"You sure, Bobby-O? No more smartass comebacks?" The most dangerous sound of all had come into her voice—a kind of brittle brightness. It sounded like good humor if you didn't know her.

Bobby looked at his sneakers and said nothing. Kept all the blubbering and all the angry words locked in his throat and said nothing. Silence spun out between them. He could smell her cigarette and all of last night's cigarettes behind this one, and those smoked on all the other nights when she didn't so much look at the TV as through it, waiting for the phone to ring.

"All right, I guess we've got ourselves straight," she said after giving him fifteen seconds or so to open his mouth and stick his big fat foot in it. "Have a nice day, Bobby." She went out without kissing him.

Bobby went to the open window (tears were running down his face now, but he hardly noticed them), drew aside the curtain, and watched her head toward Commonwealth, high heels tapping. He took a couple of big, watery breaths and then went into the kitchen. He looked across it at the cupboard where the blue pitcher hid behind the gravy boat. He could take some money out of it, she didn't keep any exact count of how much was in there and she'd never miss three or four quarters, but he wouldn't. Spending it would be joyless. He wasn't sure how he knew that, but he did; had known it even at nine, when he first discovered the pitcher of change hidden there. So, with feelings of regret rather than righteousness, he went into his bedroom and looked at the Bike Fund jar instead.

It occurred to him that she was right—he *could* take a little of his saved dough to spend at Savin Rock. It might take him an extra month to accumulate the price of the Schwinn, but at least spending this money would feel all right. And there was something else, as well. If he refused to take any money out of the jar, to do anything but hoard it and save it, he'd be like *her.*

That decided the matter. Bobby fished five dimes out of the Bike Fund, put them in his pocket, put a Kleenex on top of them to keep them from bouncing out if he ran somewhere, then finished collecting his stuff for the beach. Soon he was whistling, and Ted came downstairs to see what he was up to.

"Are you off, Captain Garfield?"

Bobby nodded. "Savin Rock's a pretty cool place. Rides and stuff, you know?"

"Indeed I do. Have a good time, Bobby, and don't fall out of anything."

Bobby started for the door, then looked back at Ted, who was standing on the bottom step of the stairs in his slippers. "Why don't you come out and sit on the porch?" Bobby asked. "It's gonna be hot in the house, I bet."

Ted smiled. "Perhaps. But I think I'll stay in."

"You okay?"

"Fine, Bobby. I'm fine."

As he crossed to the Gerbers' side of Broad Street, Bobby realized he felt sorry for Ted, hiding up in his hot room for no reason. And it *had* to be for no reason, didn't it? Sure it did. Even if there were low men out there, cruising around someplace (*in the west,* he thought, *they draw west*), what could they want of an old retired guy like Ted Brautigan?

At first the quarrel with his mother weighed him down a little (Mrs. Gerber's pudgy, pretty friend Rionda Hewson accused him of being "in a brown study," whatever that was, then began tickling him up the sides and in the armpits until Bobby laughed in self-defense), but after they had been on the beach a little while he began to feel better, more himself.

Although it was still early in the season, Savin Rock was full speed ahead—the merry-go-round turning, the Wild Mouse roaring, the little kids screaming, tinny rock and roll pouring from the speakers outside the funhouse, the barkers hollering from their booths. Sully-John didn't get the teddy bear he wanted, knocking over only two of the last three milk-bottles (Rionda claimed some of them had special weights in the bottom to keep them from going over unless you whacked them just right), but the guy in the baseball-toss booth awarded him a pretty neat prize anyway—a goofy-looking anteater covered with yellow plush. S-J impulsively gave it to Carol's mom. Anita laughed and hugged him and told him he was the best kid in the world, if he was fifteen years older she'd commit bigamy and marry him. Sully-John blushed until he was purple.

Bobby tried the ringtoss and missed with all three throws. At the Shooting Gallery he had better luck, breaking two plates and winning a small stuffed bear. He gave it to Ian-the-Snot, who had actually been good for a change—hadn't thrown any tantrums, wet his pants, or tried to sock either Sully or Bobby in the nuts. Ian hugged the bear and looked at Bobby as if Bobby were God.

"It's great and he loves it," Anita said, "but don't you want to take it home to your mother?"

"Nah—she's not much on stuff like that. I'd like to win her a bottle of perfume, though."

He and Sully-John dared each other to go on the Wild Mouse and finally went together, howling deliriously as their car plunged into each dip, simultaneously sure they were going to live forever and die immediately. They went on the Tilt-a-Whirl and the Krazy Kups. Down to his last fifteen cents, Bobby found himself on the Ferris wheel with Carol. Their car stopped at the top, rocking slightly, making him feel funny in his stomach. To his left the Atlantic stepped shoreward in a series of white-topped waves. The beach was just as white, the ocean an impossible shade of deep blue. Sunlight ran across it like silk. Below them was the midway. Rising up from the speakers came the sound of Freddy Cannon: she comes from Tallahassee, she's got a hi-fi chassis.

"Everything down there looks so little," Carol said. Her voice was also little—uncharacteristically so.

"Don't be scared, we're safe as can be. The Ferris wheel would be a kiddie-ride if it didn't go so high."

Carol was in many ways the oldest of the three of them—tough and sure of herself, as on the day she had made S-J carry her books for swearing—but now her face had almost become a baby's face again: round, a little bit pale, dominated by a pair of alarmed blue eyes. Without thinking Bobby leaned over, put his mouth on hers, and kissed her. When he drew back, her eyes were wider than ever.

"Safe as can be," he said, and grinned.

"Do it again!" It was her first real kiss, she had gotten it at Savin Rock on the first Saturday of summer vacation, and she hadn't been paying attention. That was what she was thinking, that was why she wanted him to do it again.

"I better not," Bobby said. Although . . . up here who was there to see and call him a sissy?

"I dare you, and don't say dares go first."

"Will you tell?"

"No, swear to God. Go on, hurry up! Before we go down!"

So he kissed her again. Her lips were smooth and closed, hot with the sun. Then the wheel began to move and he stopped. For just a moment Carol laid her head against his chest. "Thank you, Bobby," she said. "That was nice as could be."

"I thought so, too."

They drew apart from each other a little, and when their car stopped and the tattooed attendant swung the safety bar up, Bobby got out and ran without looking back at her to where S-J was standing. Yet he knew already that kissing Carol at the top of the Ferris wheel was going to be the best part of the day. It was his first real kiss, too, and Bobby never forgot the feel of her lips pressing on his—

dry and smooth and warmed by the sun. It was the kiss by which all the others of his life would be judged and found wanting.

Around three o'clock, Mrs. Gerber told them to start gathering their things; it was time to go home. Carol gave a token "Aw, Mom," and then started picking stuff up. Her girlfriends helped; even Ian helped a little (refusing even as he fetched and carried to let go of the sand-matted bear). Bobby had half-expected Carol to tag after him for the rest of the day, and he had been sure she'd tell her girlfriends about kissing on the Ferris wheel (he would know she had when he saw them in a little knot, giggling with their hands over their mouths, looking at him with their merry knowing eyes), but she had done neither. Several times he had caught her looking at him, though, and several times he had caught himself sneaking glances at her. He kept remembering her eyes up there. How big and worried they had been. And he had kissed her, just like that. Bingo.

Bobby and Sully toted most of the beachbags. "Good mules! Giddyap!" Rionda cried, laughing, as they mounted the steps between the beach and the boardwalk. She was lobster red under the cold-cream she had smeared over her face and shoulders, and she moaned to Anita Gerber that she wouldn't sleep a wink that night, that if the sunburn didn't keep her awake, the midway food would.

"Well, you didn't have to eat four wieners and two doughboys," Mrs. Gerber said, sounding more irritated than Bobby had ever heard her—she was tired, he reckoned. He felt a little dazed by the sun himself. His back prickled with sunburn and he had sand in his socks. The beachbags with which he was festooned swung and bounced against each other.

"But amusement park food's so *gooood,*" Rionda protested in a sad voice. Bobby laughed. He couldn't help it.

They walked slowly along the midway toward the dirt parking lot, paying no attention to the rides now. The barkers looked at them, then looked past them for fresh blood. Folks loaded down and trudging back to the parking lot were, by and large, lost causes.

At the very end of the midway, on the left, was a skinny man wearing baggy blue Bermuda shorts, a strap-style undershirt, and a bowler hat. The bowler was old and faded, but cocked at a rakish angle. Also, there was a plastic sunflower stuck in the brim. He was a funny guy, and the girls finally got their chance to put their hands over their mouths and giggle.

He looked at them with the air of a man who has been giggled at by experts and smiled back. This made Carol and her friends giggle harder. The man in the bowler hat, still smiling, spread his hands above the makeshift table behind which he was standing—a slab of fiberboard on two bright orange sawhorses. On the fiberboard were three redbacked Bicycle cards. He turned them over with quick, graceful gestures. His fingers were long and perfectly white, Bobby saw—not a bit of sun-color on them.

The card in the middle was the queen of hearts. The man in the bowler picked it up, showed it to them, walked it dextrously back and forth between his fingers. "Find the lady in red, *cherchez la femme rouge,* that's what it's all about and all you have to do," he said. "It's easy as can beezy, easy-Japaneezy, easy as knitting kitten-britches." He beckoned Yvonne Loving. "Come on over here, dollface, and show em how it's done."

Yvonne, still giggling and blushing to the roots of her black hair, shrank back against Rionda and murmured that she had no more money for games, it was all spent.

"Not a problem," the man in the bowler hat said. "It's just a demonstration, dollface—I want your mom and her pretty friend to see how easy it is."

"Neither one's my mom," Yvonne said, but she stepped forward.

"We really ought to get going if we're going to beat the traffic, Evvie," Mrs. Gerber said.

"No, wait a minute, this is fun," Rionda said. "It's three-card monte. Looks easy, just like he says, but if you're not careful you start chasing and go home dead broke."

The man in the bowler gave her a reproachful look, then a broad and engaging grin. It was the grin of a low man, Bobby thought suddenly. Not one of those Ted was afraid of, but a low man, just the same.

"It's obvious to me," said the man in the bowler, "that at some point in your past you have been the victim of a scoundrel. Although how anyone could be cruel enough to mistreat such a beautiful classy dame is beyond my ability to comprehend."

The beautiful classy dame—five-five or so, two hundred pounds or so, shoulders and face slathered with Pond's—laughed happily. "Stow the guff and show the child how it works. And are you really telling me this is legal?"

The man behind the table tossed his head back and also laughed. "At the ends of the midway everything's legal until they catch you and throw you out . . . as I think you probably know. Now . . . what's your name, dollface?"

"Yvonne," she said in a voice Bobby could barely hear. Beside him, Sully-John was watching with great interest. "Sometimes folks call me Evvie."

"Okay, Evvie, look right here, pretty baby. What do you see? Tell me their names—I know you can, a smart kid like you—and point when you tell. Don't be afraid to touch, either. There's nothing crooked here."

"This one on the end is the jack . . . this one on the other end is the king . . . and this is the queen. She's in the middle."

"That's it, dollface. In the cards as in life, there is so often a woman between two men. That's their power, and in another five or six years you'll find it out for yourself." His voice had fallen into a low, almost hypnotic chanting. "Now watch closely and never take your eyes from the cards." He turned them over so their backs showed. "Now, dollface, where's the queen?"

Yvonne Loving pointed at the red back in the middle.

"Is she right?" the man in the bowler asked the little party gathered around his table.

"So far," Rionda said, and laughed so hard her uncorseted belly jiggled under her sundress.

Smiling at her laughter, the low man in the bowler hat flicked one corner of the middle card, showing the red queen. "One hundred per cent keerect, sweetheart, so far so good. Now watch! Watch close!

It's a race between your eye and my hand! Which will win? That's the question of the day!"

He began to scramble the three cards rapidly about on his plank table, chanting as he did so.

"Up and down, all around, in and out, all about, to and fro, watch em go, now they're back, they're side by side, so tell me, dollface, where's she hide?"

As Yvonne studied the three cards, which were indeed once more lined up side by side, Sully leaned close to Bobby's ear and said, "You don't even have to watch him mix them around. The queen's got a bent corner. Do you see it?"

Bobby nodded, and thought *Good girl* when Yvonne pointed hesitantly to the card on the far left—the one with the bent corner. The man in the bowler turned it over and revealed the queen of hearts.

"Good job!" he said. "You've a sharp eye, dollface, a sharp eye indeed."

"Thank you," Yvonne said, blushing and looking almost as happy as Carol had looked when Bobby kissed her.

"If you'd bet me a dime on that go, I'd be giving you back twenty cents right now," the man in the bowler hat said. "Why, you ask? Because it's Saturday, and I call Saturday Twoferday! Now would one of you ladies like to risk a dime in a race between your young eyes and my tired old hands? You can tell your husbands—lucky fellas they are to have you, too, may I say—that Mr. Herb McQuown, the Monte Man at Savin Rock, paid for your day's parking. Or what about a quarter? Point out the queen of hearts and I give you back fifty cents."

"Half a rock, yeah!" Sully-John said. "I got a quarter, mister, and you're on."

"Johnny, it's gambling," Carol's mother said doubtfully. "I don't really think I should allow—"

"Go on, let the kid learn a lesson," Rionda said. "Besides, the guy may let him win. Suck the rest of us in." She made no effort to lower her voice, but the man in the bowler—Mr. McQuown—only looked at her and smiled. Then he returned his attention to S-J.

"Let's see your money, kid—come on, pony up."

Sully-John handed over his quarter. McQuown raised it into the afternoon sunlight for a moment, one eye closed.

"Yeh, looks like a good 'un to me," he said, and planked it down on the board to the left of the three-card lineup. He looked in both directions—for cops, maybe—then tipped the cynically smiling Rionda a wink before turning his attention back to Sully-John. "What's your name, fella?"

"John Sullivan."

McQuown widened his eyes and tipped his bowler to the other side of his head, making the plastic sunflower nod and bend comically. "A name of note! You know what I refer to?"

"Sure. Someday maybe I'll be a fighter, too," S-J said. He hooked a left and then a right at the air over McQuown's makeshift table. "Pow, pow!"

"Pow-pow indeed," said McQuown. "And how's your eyes, Master Sullivan?"

"Pretty good."

"Then get them ready, because the race is on! Yes it is! Your eyes against my hands! Up and down, all around, where'd she go, I don't know." The cards, which had moved much faster this time, slowed to a stop.

Sully started to point, then drew his hand back, frowning. Now there were *two* cards with little folds in the corner. Sully looked up at McQuown, whose arms were folded across his dingy undershirt. McQuown was smiling. "Take your time, son," he said. "The morning was whizbang, but it's been a slow afternoon."

Men who think hats with feathers in the brims are sophisticated, Bobby remembered Ted saying. *The sort of men who'd shoot craps in an alley and pass around a bottle of liquor in a paper bag during the game.* McQuown had a funny plastic flower in his hat instead of a feather, and there was no bottle in evidence . . . but there was one in his pocket. A little one. Bobby was sure of it. And toward the end of the day, as business wound down and totally sharp hand-eye coordination became less of a priority to him, McQuown would take more and more frequent nips from it.

Sully pointed to the card on the far right. *No, S-J,* Bobby thought, and when McQuown turned that card up, it was the king of spades. McQuown turned up the card on the far left and showed the jack of clubs. The queen was back in the middle. "Sorry, son, a little slow that time, it ain't no crime. Want to try again now that you're warmed up?"

"Gee, I . . . that was the last of my dough." Sully-John looked crestfallen.

"Just as well for you, kid," Rionda said. "He'd take you for everything you own and leave you standing here in your shortie-shorts." The girls giggled wildly at this; S-J blushed. Rionda took no notice of either. "I worked at Revere Beach for quite awhile when I lived in Mass," she said. "Let me show you kids how this works. Want to go for a buck, pal? Or is that too sweet for you?"

"In your presence everything would be sweet," McQuown said sentimentally, and snatched her dollar the moment it was out of her purse. He held it up to the light, examined it with a cold eye, then set it down to the left of the cards. "Looks like a good 'un," he said. "Let's play, darling. What's your name?"

"Pudd'ntane," Rionda said. "Ask me again and I'll tell you the same."

"Ree, don't you think—" Anita Gerber began.

"I told you, I'm wise to the gaff," Rionda said. "Run em, my pal."

"Without delay," McQuown agreed, and his hands blurred the three red-backed cards into motion (up and down, all around, to and fro, watch them go), finally settling them in a line of three again. And this time, Bobby observed with amazement, all three cards had those slightly bent corners.

Rionda's little smile had gone. She looked from the short row of cards to McQuown, then down at the cards again, and then at her dollar bill, lying off to one side and fluttering slightly in the little seabreeze that had come up. Finally she looked back at McQuown. "You suckered me, pally," she said. "Didn't you?"

"No," McQuown said. "I *raced* you. Now . . . what do you say?"

"I think I say that was a real good dollar that didn't make no trouble and I'm sorry to see it go," Rionda replied, and pointed to the middle card.

McQuown turned it over, revealed the king, and made Rionda's dollar disappear into his pocket. This time the queen was on the far left. McQuown, a dollar and a quarter richer, smiled at the folks from Harwich. The plastic flower tucked into the brim of his hat nodded to and fro in the salt-smelling air. "Who's next?" he asked. "Who wants to race his eye against my hand?"

"I think we're all raced out," Mrs. Gerber said. She gave the man behind the table a thin smile, then put one hand on her daughter's shoulder and the other on her sleepy-eyed son's, turning them away.

"Mrs. Gerber?" Bobby asked. For just a moment he considered how his mother, once married to a man who had never met an inside straight he didn't like, would feel if she could see her son standing here at Mr. McQuown's slapdash table with that risky Randy Garfield red hair gleaming in the sun. The thought made him smile a little. Bobby knew what an inside straight was now; flushes and full houses, too. He had made inquiries. "May I try?"

"Oh, Bobby, I really think we've had enough, don't you?"

Bobby reached under the Kleenex he had stuffed into his pocket and brought out his last three nickels. "All I have is this," he said, showing first Mrs. Gerber and then Mr. McQuown. "Is it enough?"

"Son," McQuown said, "I have played this game for pennies and enjoyed it."

Mrs. Gerber looked at Rionda.

"Ah, hell," Rionda said, and pinched Bobby's cheek. "It's the price of a haircut, for Christ's sake. Let him lose it and then we'll go home."

"All right, Bobby," Mrs. Gerber said, and sighed. "If you have to."

"Put those nickels down here, Bob, where we can all look at em," said McQuown. "They look like good 'uns to me, yes indeed. Are you ready?"

"I think so."

"Then here we go. Two boys and a girl go into hiding together. The boys are worthless. Find the girl and double your money."

The pale dextrous fingers turned the three cards over. McQuown spieled and the cards blurred. Bobby watched them move about the table but made no real effort to track the queen. That wasn't necessary.

"Now they go, now they slow, now they rest, here's the test." The three red-backed cards were in a line again. "Tell me, Bobby, where's she hide?"

"There," Bobby said, and pointed to the far left.

Sully groaned. "It's the *middle* card, you jerk. This time I never took my eye off it."

McQuown took no notice of Sully. He was looking at Bobby. Bobby looked back at him. After a moment McQuown reached out and turned over the card Bobby had pointed at. It was the queen of hearts.

"What the *heck?*" Sully cried.

Carol clapped excitedly and jumped up and down. Rionda Hewson squealed and smacked him on the back. "You took im to school that time, Bobby! Attaboy!"

McQuown gave Bobby a peculiar, thoughtful smile, then reached into his pocket and brought out a fistful of change. "Not bad, son. First time I've been beat all day. That I didn't *let* myself get beat, that is." He picked out a quarter and a nickel and put them down beside Bobby's fifteen cents. "Like to let it ride?" He saw Bobby didn't understand. "Like to go again?"

"May I?" Bobby asked Anita Gerber.

"Wouldn't you rather quit while you're ahead?" she asked, but her eyes were sparkling and she seemed to have forgotten all about beating the traffic home.

"I *am* going to quit while I'm ahead," he told her.

McQuown laughed. "A boasty boy! Won't be able to grow a single chin-whisker for another five years, but he's a boasty boy already. Well then, Boasty Bobby, what do you think? Are we on for the game?"

"Sure," Bobby said. If Carol or Sully-John had accused him of boasting, he would have protested strongly—all his heroes, from John Wayne to Lucky Starr of the Space Patrol, were modest fellows, the kind to say "Shucks" after saving a world or a wagon train. But he felt no need to defend himself to Mr. McQuown, who was a low man in blue shorts and maybe a card-cheater as well. Boasting had been the furthest thing from Bobby's mind. He didn't think this was much like his dad's inside straights, either. Inside straights were all hope and guesswork—"fool's poker," according to Charlie Yearman, the Harwich Elementary janitor, who had been happy to tell Bobby everything about the game that S-J and Denny Rivers hadn't known—but there was no guesswork about this.

Mr. McQuown looked at him a moment longer; Bobby's calm confidence seemed to trouble him. Then he reached up, adjusted the slant of his bowler, stretched out his arms, and wiggled his fingers like Bugs Bunny before he played the piano at Carnegie Hall in one of the Merrie Melodies. "Get on your mark, boasty boy. I'm giving you the whole business this time, from the soup to the nuts."

The cards blurred into a kind of pink film. From behind him Bobby heard Sully-John mutter "Holy crow!" Carol's friend Tina said "That's too *fast*" in an amusing tone of prim disapproval. Bobby again watched the cards move, but only because he felt it was expected of him. Mr. McQuown didn't bother with any patter this time, which was sort of a relief.

The cards settled. McQuown looked at Bobby with his eyebrows raised. There was a little smile on his mouth, but he was breathing fast and there were beads of sweat on his upper lip.

Bobby pointed immediately to the card on the right. "That's her."

"How do you know that?" Mr. McQuown asked, his smile fading. "How the hell do you know that?"

"I just do," Bobby said.

Instead of flipping the card, McQuown turned his head slightly and looked down the midway. The smile had been replaced by a petulant expression—downturned lips and a crease between his eyes. Even the plastic sunflower in his hat seemed displeased, its to-and-fro bob now sulky instead of jaunty. "No one beats that shuffle," he said. "No one has *ever* beaten that shuffle."

Rionda reached over Bobby's shoulder and flipped the card he had pointed at. It was the queen of hearts. This time all the kids clapped. The sound made the crease between Mr. McQuown's eyes deepen.

"The way I figure, you owe old Boasty Bobby here ninety cents," Rionda said. "Are you gonna pay?"

"Suppose I don't?" Mr. McQuown asked, turning his frown on Rionda. "What are you going to do, tubbo? Call a cop?"

"Maybe we ought to just go," Anita Gerber said, sounding nervous.

"Call a cop? Not me," Rionda said, ignoring Anita. She never took her eyes off McQuown. "A lousy ninety cents out of your pocket and you look like Baby Huey with a load in his pants. Jesus wept!"

Except, Bobby knew, it wasn't the money. Mr. McQuown had lost a lot more than this on occasion. Sometimes when he lost it was a "hustle"; sometimes it was an "out." What he was steamed about now was the *shuffle.* McQuown hadn't liked a kid beating his shuffle.

"What I'll do," Rionda continued, "is tell anybody on the midway who wants to know that you're a cheapskate. Ninety-Cent McQuown, I'll call you. Think that'll help your business?"

"I'd like to give *you* the business," Mr. McQuown growled, but he reached into his pocket, brought out another dip of change—a bigger one this time—and quickly counted out Bobby's winnings. "There," he said. "Ninety cents. Go buy yourself a martini."

"I really just guessed, you know," Bobby said as he swept the coins into his hand and then shoved them into his pocket, where they hung like a weight. The argument that morning with his mother now seemed exquisitely stupid. He was going home with more money than he had come with, and it meant nothing. Nothing. "I'm a good guesser."

Mr. McQuown relaxed. He wouldn't have hurt them in any case—he might be a low man but he wasn't the kind who hurt people; he'd never subject those clever long-fingered hands to the indignity of forming a fist—but Bobby didn't want to leave him unhappy. He wanted what Mr. McQuown himself would have called an "out."

"Yeah," McQuown said. "A good guesser is what you are. Like to try a third guess, Bobby? Riches await."

"We really have to be going," Mrs. Gerber said hastily.

"And if I tried again I'd lose," Bobby said. "Thank you, Mr. McQuown. It was a good game."

"Yeah, yeah. Get lost, kid." Mr. McQuown was like all the other midway barkers now, looking farther down the line. Looking for fresh blood.

Going home, Carol and her girlfriends kept looking at him with awe; Sully-John, with a kind of puzzled respect. It made Bobby feel uncomfortable. At one point Rionda turned around and regarded him closely. "You didn't just guess," she said.

Bobby looked at her cautiously, withholding comment.

"You had a winkle."

"What's a winkle?"

"My dad wasn't much of a betting man, but every now and then he'd get a hunch about a number. He called it a winkle. *Then* he'd bet. Once he won fifty dollars. Bought us groceries for a whole month. That's what happened to you, isn't it?"

"I guess so," Bobby said. "Maybe I had a winkle."

When he got home, his mom was sitting on the porch glider with her legs folded under her. She had changed into her Saturday pants and was looking moodily out at the street. She waved briefly to Carol's mom as she drove away; watched as Anita turned into her own driveway and Bobby trudged up the walk. He knew what his mom was thinking: Mrs. Gerber's husband was in the Navy, but at least she *had* a husband. Also, Anita Gerber had an Estate Wagon. Liz had shank's mare, the bus if she had to go a little farther, or a taxi if she needed to go into Bridgeport.

But Bobby didn't think she was angry at him anymore, and that was good.

"Did you have a nice time at Savin, Bobby?"

"Super time," he said, and thought: *What is it, Mom? You don't care what kind of time I had at the beach. What's really on your mind?* But he couldn't tell.

"Good. Listen, kiddo . . . I'm sorry we got into an argument this morning. I *hate* working on Saturdays." This last came out almost in a spit.

"It's okay, Mom."

She touched his cheek and shook her head. "That fair skin of yours! You'll never tan, Bobby-O. Not you. Come on in and I'll put some Baby Oil on that sunburn."

He followed her inside, took off his shirt, and stood in front of her as she sat on the couch and smeared the fragrant Baby Oil on his back and arms and neck—even on his cheeks. It felt good, and he thought again how much he loved her, how much he loved to be touched by her. He wondered what she would think if she knew he had kissed Carol on the Ferris wheel. Would she smile? Bobby didn't think she would smile. And if she knew about McQuown and the cards—

"I haven't seen your pal from upstairs," she said, recapping the Baby Oil bottle. "I know he's up there because I can hear the Yankees game on his radio, but wouldn't you think he'd go out on the porch where it's cool?"

"I guess he doesn't feel like it," Bobby said. "Mom, are you okay?"

She looked at him, startled. "Fine, Bobby." She smiled and Bobby smiled back. It took an effort, because he didn't think his mom was fine at all. In fact he was pretty sure she wasn't.

He just had a winkle.

That night Bobby lay on his back with his heels spread to the corners of the bed, eyes open and looking up at the ceiling. His window was open, too, the curtains drifting back and forth in a breath of a breeze, and from some other open window came the sound of The Platters: "Here, in the afterglow of day, We keep our rendezvous, beneath the blue." Farther away was the drone of an airplane, the honk of a horn.

Rionda's dad had called it a winkle, and once he'd hit the daily number for fifty dollars. Bobby had agreed with her—*a winkle, sure, I had a winkle*—but he couldn't have picked a lottery number to save his soul. The thing was . . .

The thing was Mr. McQuown knew where the queen ended up every time, and so I *knew.*

Once Bobby realized that, other things fell into place. Obvious stuff, really, but he'd been having fun, and . . . well . . . you didn't question what you knew, did you? You might question a winkle—a feeling that came to you right out of the blue—but you didn't question *knowing.*

Except how did he *know* his mother was taping money into the underwear pages of the Sears catalogue on the top shelf of her closet? How did he even know the catalogue was up there? She'd never told him about it. She'd never told him about the blue pitcher where she put her quarters, either, but of course he had known about that for years, he wasn't blind even though he had an idea she sometimes thought he was. But the catalogue? The quarters rolled and changed into bills, the bills then taped into the catalogue? There was no way he could know about a thing like that, but as he lay here in his bed, listening while "Earth Angel" replaced "Twilight Time," he knew that the catalogue was there. He knew because *she* knew, and it had crossed the front part of her mind. And on the Ferris wheel he had known Carol wanted him to kiss her again because it had been her first real kiss from a boy and she hadn't been paying enough attention; it had been over before she was completely aware it was happening. But knowing that wasn't knowing the future.

"No, it's just reading minds," he whispered, and then shivered all over as if his sunburn had turned to ice.

Watch out, Bobby-O—if you don't watch out you'll wind up as nuts as Ted with his low men.

Far off, in the town square, the clock began bonging the hour of ten. Bobby turned his head and looked at the alarm clock on his desk. Big Ben claimed it was only nine-fifty-two.

All right, so the clock downtown is a little fast or mine is a little slow. Big deal, McNeal. Go to sleep.

He didn't think he could do that for at least awhile, but it had been quite a day—arguments with mothers, money won from three-card monte dealers, kisses at the top of the Ferris wheel—and he began to drift in a pleasant fashion.

Maybe she is *my girlfriend,* Bobby thought. *Maybe she's my girlfriend after all.*

With the last premature bong of the town square clock still fading in the air, Bobby fell asleep.

V. BOBBY READS THE PAPER. BROWN, WITH A WHITE BIB. A BIG CHANCE FOR LIZ. CAMP BROAD STREET. AN UNEASY WEEK. OFF TO PROVIDENCE.

On Monday, after his mom had gone to work, Bobby went upstairs to read Ted the paper (although his eyes were actually good enough to do it himself, Ted said he had come to enjoy the sound of Bobby's voice and the luxury of being read to while he shaved). Ted stood in his little bathroom with the door open, scraping foam from his face, while Bobby tried him on various headlines from the various sections.

"VIET SKIRMISHES INTENSIFY?"

"Before breakfast? Thanks but no thanks."

"CARTS CORRALLED, LOCAL MAN ARRESTED?"

"First paragraph, Bobby."

" 'When police showed up at his Pond Lane residence late yesterday, John T. Anderson of Harwich told them all about his hobby, which he claims is collecting supermarket shopping carts. "He was very interesting on the subject," said Officer Kirby Malloy of the Harwich P.D., "but we weren't entirely satisfied that he'd come by some of the carts in his collection honestly." Turns out Malloy was "right with Eversharp." Of the more than fifty shopping carts in Mr. Anderson's back yard, at least twenty had been stolen from the Harwich A&P and Total Grocery. There were even a few carts from the IGA market in Stansbury.' "

"Enough," Ted said, rinsing his razor under hot water and then raising the blade to his lathered neck. "Galumphing small-town humor in response to pathetic acts of compulsive larceny."

"I don't understand you."

"Mr. Anderson sounds like a man suffering from a neurosis—a mental problem, in other words. Do you think mental problems are funny?"

"Gee, no. I feel bad for people with loose screws."

"I'm glad to hear you say so. I've known people whose screws were not just loose but entirely missing. A good many such people, in fact. They are often pathetic, sometimes awe-inspiring, and occasionally terrifying, but they are not funny. CARTS CORRALLED, indeed. What else is there?"

"STARLET KILLED IN EUROPEAN ROAD ACCIDENT?"

"Ugh, no."

"YANKEES ACQUIRE INFIELDER IN TRADE WITH SENATORS?"

"Nothing the Yankees do with the Senators interests me."

"ALBINI RELISHES UNDERDOG ROLE?"

"Yes, please read that."

Ted listened closely as he painstakingly shaved his throat. Bobby himself found the story less than riveting—it wasn't about Floyd Patterson or Ingemar Johansson, after all (Sully called the Swedish heavyweight "Ingie-Baby")—but he read it carefully, nevertheless. The twelve-rounder between Tommy "Hurricane" Haywood and Eddie Albini was scheduled for Madison Square Garden on Wednesday night of the following week. Both fighters had good records, but age was considered an important, perhaps telling factor: Haywood, twenty-three to Eddie Albini's thirty-six, and a heavy favorite. The winner might get a shot at the heavyweight title in the fall, probably around the time Richard Nixon won the Presidency (Bobby's mom said that was sure to happen, and a good thing—never mind that Kennedy was a Catholic, he was just too young, and apt to be a hothead).

In the article Albini said he could understand why he was the underdog—he was getting up in years a little and some folks thought he was past it because he'd lost by a TKO to Sugar Boy

Masters in his last fight. And sure, he knew that Haywood outreached him and was supposed to be mighty savvy for a younger fellow. But he'd been training hard, Albini said, skipping a lot of rope and sparring with a guy who moved and jabbed like Haywood. The article was full of words like *game* and *determined;* Albini was described as being "full of grit." Bobby could tell the writer thought Albini was going to get the stuffing knocked out of him and felt sorry for him. Hurricane Haywood hadn't been available to talk to the reporter, but his manager, a fellow named I. Kleindienst (Ted told Bobby how to pronounce the name), said it was likely to be Eddie Albini's last fight. "He had his day, but his day is over," I. Kleindienst said. "If Eddie goes six, I'm going to send my boy to bed without his supper."

"Irving Kleindienst's a *ka-mai,*" Ted said.

"A what?"

"A fool." Ted was looking out the window toward the sound of Mrs. O'Hara's dog. Not totally blank the way he sometimes went blank, but distant.

"You know him?" Bobby asked.

"No, no," Ted said. He seemed first startled by the idea, then amused. "Know *of* him."

"It sounds to me like this guy Albini's gonna get creamed."

"You never know. That's what makes it interesting."

"What do you mean?"

"Nothing. Go to the comics, Bobby. I want Flash Gordon. And be sure to tell me what Dale Arden's wearing."

"Why?"

"Because I think she's a real hotsy-totsy," Ted said, and Bobby burst out laughing. He couldn't help it. Sometimes Ted was a real card.

A day later, on his way back from Sterling House, where he had just filled out the rest of his forms for summer baseball, Bobby came upon a carefully printed poster thumbtacked to an elm in Commonwealth Park.

PLEASE HELP US FIND PHIL!
PHIL is our WELSH CORGI!
PHIL is 7 YRS. OLD!
PHIL is BROWN, with a WHITE BIB!
His EYES are BRIGHT & INTELLIGENT!
The TIPS OF HIS EARS are BLACK!
Will bring you a BALL if you say HURRY UP PHIL!
CALL HOusitonic 5-8337!
(OR)
BRING to 745 Highgate Avenue!
Home of THE SAGAMORE FAMILY!

There was no picture of Phil.

Bobby stood looking at the poster for a fair length of time. Part of him wanted to run home and tell Ted—not only about this but about the star and crescent moon he'd seen chalked beside the hopscotch grid. Another part pointed out that there was all sorts of stuff posted in the park—he could see a sign advertising a concert in the town square posted on another elm right across from where he was standing—and he would be *nuts* to get Ted going about this. These two thoughts contended with each other until they felt like two sticks rubbing together and his brain in danger of catching on fire.

I won't think about it, he told himself, stepping back from the poster. And when a voice from deep within his mind—a dangerously *adult* voice—protested that he was being *paid* to think about stuff like this, to *tell* about stuff like this, Bobby told the voice to just shut up. And the voice did.

When he got home, his mother was sitting on the porch glider again, this time mending the sleeve of a housedress. She looked up and Bobby saw the puffy skin beneath her eyes, the reddened lids. She had a Kleenex folded into one hand.

"Mom—?"

What's wrong? was how the thought finished . . . but finishing it would be unwise. Would likely cause trouble. Bobby had had no recurrence of his brilliant insights on the day of the trip to Savin

Rock, but he *knew* her—the way she looked at him when she was upset, the way the hand with the Kleenex in it tensed, almost becoming a fist, the way she drew in breath and sat up straighter, ready to give you a fight if you wanted to go against her.

"What?" she asked him. "Got something on your mind besides your hair?"

"No," he said. His voice sounded awkward and oddly shy to his own ears. "I was at Sterling House. The lists are up for baseball. I'm a Wolf again this summer."

She nodded and relaxed a little. "I'm sure you'll make the Lions next year." She moved her sewing basket from the glider to the porch floor, then patted the empty place. "Sit down here beside me a minute, Bobby. I've got something to tell you."

Bobby sat with a feeling of trepidation—she'd been crying, after all, and she sounded quite grave—but it turned out not to be a big deal, at least as far as he could see.

"Mr. Biderman—Don—has invited me to go with him and Mr. Cushman and Mr. Dean to a seminar in Providence. It's a big chance for me."

"What's a seminar?"

"A sort of conference—people get together to learn about a subject and discuss it. This one is Real Estate in the Sixties. I was very surprised that Don would invite me. Bill Cushman and Curtis Dean, of course I knew *they'd* be going, they're agents. But for Don to ask *me* . . ." She trailed off for a moment, then turned to Bobby and smiled. He thought it was a genuine smile, but it went oddly with her reddened lids. "I've wanted to become an agent myself for the longest time, and now this, right out of the blue . . . it's a big chance for me, Bobby, and it could mean a big change for us."

Bobby knew his mom wanted to sell real estate. She had books on the subject and read a little out of them almost every night, often underlining parts. But if it was such a big chance, why had it made her cry?

"Well, that's good," he said. "The ginchiest. I hope you learn a lot. When is it?"

"Next week. The four of us leave early Tuesday morning and get back Thursday night around eight o'clock. All the meetings are at the Warwick Hotel, and that's where we'll be staying—Don's booked the rooms. I haven't stayed in a hotel room for twelve years, I guess. I'm a little nervous."

Did nervous make you cry? Bobby wondered. Maybe so, if you were a grownup—especially a *female* grownup.

"I want you to ask S-J if you can stay with him Tuesday and Wednesday night. I'm sure Mrs. Sullivan—"

Bobby shook his head. "That won't work."

"Whyever *not?*" Liz bent a fierce look at him. "Mrs. Sullivan hasn't ever minded you staying over before. You haven't gotten into her bad books somehow, have you?"

"No, Mom. It's just that S-J won a week at Camp Winnie." The sound of all those *W*'s coming out of his mouth made him feel like smiling, but he held it in. His mother was still looking at him in that fierce way . . . and wasn't there a kind of panic in that look? Panic or something like it?

"What's Camp Winnie? What are you talking about?"

Bobby explained about S-J winning the free week at Camp Winiwinaia and how Mrs. Sullivan was going to visit her parents in Wisconsin at the same time—plans which had now been finalized, Big Gray Dog and all.

"Damn it, that's just my luck," his mom said. She almost never swore, said that cursing and what she called "dirty talk" was the language of the ignorant. Now she made a fist and struck the arm of the glider. "*God* damn it!"

She sat for a moment, thinking. Bobby thought, as well. His only other close friend on the street was Carol, and he doubted his mom would call Anita Gerber and ask if he could stay over there. Carol was a girl, and somehow that made a difference when it came to sleepovers. One of his mother's friends? The thing was she didn't really *have* any . . . except for Don Biderman (and maybe the other two that were going to the seminar in Providence). Plenty of acquaintances, people she said hi to if they were walking back from the supermarket or going to a Friday-night movie downtown, but no one she could call up and ask to keep her eleven-year-old son for a couple of nights; no relatives, either, at least none that Bobby knew of.

Like people travelling on converging roads, Bobby and his mother gradually drew toward the same point. Bobby got there first, if only by a second or two.

"What about Ted?" he asked, then almost clapped his hand over his mouth. It actually rose out of his lap a little.

His mother watched the hand settle back with a return of her old cynical half-smile, the one she wore when dispensing sayings like *You have to eat a peck of dirt before you die* and *Two men looked out through prison bars, one saw the mud and one saw the stars* and of course that all-time favorite, *Life's not fair.*

"You think I don't know you call him Ted when the two of you are together?" she asked. "You must think I've been taking stupid-pills, Bobby-O." She sat and looked out at the street. A Chrysler New Yorker slid slowly past—finny, fenderskirted, and highlighted with chrome. Bobby watched it go by. The man behind the wheel was elderly and white-haired and wearing a blue jacket. Bobby thought he was probably all right. Old but not low.

"Maybe it'd work," Liz said at last. She spoke musingly, more to herself than to her son. "Let's go talk to Brautigan and see."

Following her up the stairs to the third floor, Bobby wondered how long she had known how to say Ted's name correctly. A week? A month?

From the start, Dumbo, he thought. *From the very first day.*

Bobby's initial idea was that Ted could stay in his own room on the third floor while Bobby stayed in the apartment on the first floor; they'd both keep their doors open, and if either of them needed anything, they could call.

"I don't believe the Kilgallens or the Proskys would enjoy you yelling up to Mr. Brautigan at three o'clock in the morning that you'd had a nightmare," Liz said tartly. The Kilgallens and the

Proskys had the two small second-floor apartments; Liz and Bobby were friendly with neither of them.

"I won't have any nightmares," Bobby said, deeply humiliated to be treated like a little kid. "I mean *jeepers.*"

"Keep it to yourself," his mom said. They were sitting at Ted's kitchen table, the two adults smoking, Bobby with a rootbeer in front of him.

"It's just not the right idea," Ted told him. "You're a good kid, Bobby, responsible and levelheaded, but eleven's too young to be on your own, I think."

Bobby found it easier to be called too young by his friend than by his mother. Also he had to admit that it might be spooky to wake up in one of those little hours after midnight and go to the bathroom knowing he was the only person in the apartment. He could do it, he had no doubt he could do it, but yeah, it would be spooky.

"What about the couch?" he asked. "It pulls out and makes a bed, doesn't it?" They had never used it that way, but Bobby was sure she'd told him once that it did. He was right, and it solved the problem. She probably hadn't wanted Bobby in her bed (let alone "Brattigan"), and she *really* hadn't wanted Bobby up here in this hot third-floor room—that he was sure of. He figured she'd been looking so hard for a solution that she'd looked right past the obvious one.

So it was decided that Ted would spend Tuesday and Wednesday nights of the following week on the pull-out couch in the Garfields' living room. Bobby was excited by the prospect: he would have two days on his own—three, counting Thursday—and there would be someone with him at night, when things could get spooky. Not a babysitter, either, but a grownup friend. It wasn't the same as Sully-John going to Camp Winnie for a week, but in a way it was. *Camp Broad Street,* Bobby thought, and almost laughed out loud.

"We'll have fun," Ted said. "I'll make my famous beans-and-franks casserole." He reached over and ruffled Bobby's crewcut.

"If you're going to have beans and franks, it might be wise to bring *that* down," his mom said, and pointed the fingers holding her cigarette at Ted's fan.

Ted and Bobby laughed. Liz Garfield smiled her cynical half-smile, finished her cigarette, and put it out in Ted's ashtray. When she did, Bobby again noticed the puffiness of her eyelids.

As Bobby and his mother went back down the stairs, Bobby remembered the poster he had seen in the park—the missing Corgi who would bring you a BALL if you said HURRY UP PHIL. He should tell Ted about the poster. He should tell Ted about everything. But if he did that and Ted left 149, who would stay with him next week? What would happen to Camp Broad Street, two fellows eating Ted's famous beans-and-franks casserole for supper (maybe in front of the TV, which his mom rarely allowed) and then staying up as late as they wanted?

Bobby made a promise to himself: he would tell Ted everything next Friday, after his mother was back from her conference or seminar or whatever it was. He would make a complete report and Ted could do whatever he needed to do. He might even stick around.

With this decision Bobby's mind cleared amazingly, and when he saw an upside-down FOR SALE card on the Total Grocery bulletin board two days later—it was for a washer-dryer set—he was able to put it out of his thoughts almost immediately.

That was nevertheless an uneasy week for Bobby Garfield, very uneasy indeed. He saw two more lost-pet posters, one downtown and one out on Asher Avenue, half a mile beyond the Asher Empire (the block he lived on was no longer enough; he found himself going farther and farther afield in his daily scouting trips). And Ted began to have those weird blank periods with greater frequency. They lasted longer when they came, too. Sometimes he spoke when he was in that distant state of mind, and not always in English. When he did speak in English, what he said did not always make sense. Most of the time Bobby thought Ted was one of the sanest, smartest, *neatest* guys he had ever met. When he went away, though, it was scary. At least his mom didn't know. Bobby didn't think she'd be too cool on the idea of leaving him with a guy who sometimes flipped out and started talking nonsense in English or gibberish in some other language.

After one of these lapses, when Ted did nothing for almost a minute and a half but stare blankly off into space, making no response to Bobby's increasingly agitated questions, it occurred to Bobby that perhaps Ted wasn't in his own head at all but in some other world—that he had left Earth as surely as those people in *Ring Around the Sun* who discovered they could follow the spirals on a child's top to just about anywhere.

Ted had been holding a Chesterfield between his fingers when he went blank; the ash grew long and eventually dropped off onto the table. When the coal grew unnervingly close to Ted's bunchy knuckles, Bobby pulled it gently free and was putting it out in the overflowing ashtray when Ted finally came back.

"Smoking?" he asked with a frown. "Hell, Bobby, you're too young to smoke."

"I was just putting it out for you. I thought . . ." Bobby shrugged, suddenly shy.

Ted looked at the first two fingers of his right hand, where there was a permanent yellow nicotine stain. He laughed—a short bark with absolutely no humor in it. "Thought I was going to burn myself, did you?"

Bobby nodded. "What do you think about when you go off like that? Where do you go?"

"That's hard to explain," Ted replied, and then asked Bobby to read him his horoscope.

Thinking about Ted's trances was distracting. Not talking about the things Ted was paying him to look for was even more distracting. As a result, Bobby—ordinarily a pretty good hitter—struck out four times in an afternoon game for the Wolves at Sterling House. He also lost four straight Battleship games to Sully at S-J's house on Friday, when it rained.

"What the heck's wrong with you?" Sully asked. "That's the third time you called out squares you already called out before. Also, I have to practically holler in your ear before you answer me. What's up?"

"Nothing." That was what he said. *Everything.* That was what he felt.

Carol also asked Bobby a couple of times that week if he was okay; Mrs. Gerber asked if he was "off his feed"; Yvonne Loving wanted to know if he had mono, and then giggled until she seemed in danger of exploding.

The only person who didn't notice Bobby's odd behavior was his mom. Liz Garfield was increasingly preoccupied with her trip to Providence, talking on the phone in the evenings with Mr. Biderman or one of the other two who were going (Bill Cushman was one of them; Bobby couldn't exactly remember the name of the other guy), laying clothes out on her bed until the spread was almost covered, then shaking her head over them angrily and returning them to the closet, making an appointment to get her hair done and then calling the lady back and asking if she could add a manicure. Bobby wasn't even sure what a manicure was. He had to ask Ted.

She seemed excited by her preparations, but there was also a kind of grimness to her. She was like a soldier about to storm an enemy beach, or a paratrooper who would soon be jumping out of a plane and landing behind enemy lines. One of her evening telephone conversations seemed to be a whispered argument—Bobby had an idea it was with Mr. Biderman, but he wasn't sure. On Saturday, Bobby came into her bedroom and saw her looking at two new dresses—*dressy* dresses, one with thin little shoulder straps and one with no straps at all, just a top like a bathing suit. The boxes they had come in lay tumbled on the floor with tissue paper foaming out of them. His mom was standing over the dresses, looking down at them with an expression Bobby had never seen before: big eyes, drawn-together brows, taut white cheeks which flared with spots of rouge. One hand was at her mouth, and he could hear bonelike clittering sounds as she bit at her nails. A Kool smoldered in an ashtray on the bureau, apparently forgotten. Her big eyes shuttled back and forth between the two dresses.

"Mom?" Bobby asked, and she jumped—literally jumped into the air. Then she whirled on him, her mouth drawn down in a grimace.

"Jesus *Christ!*" she almost snarled. "Do you *knock?*"

"I'm sorry," he said, and began to back out of the room. His mother had never said anything about knocking before. "Mom, are you all right?"

"Fine!" She spied the cigarette, grabbed it, smoked furiously. She exhaled with such force that Bobby almost expected to see smoke come from her ears as well as her nose and mouth. "I'd be finer if I could find a cocktail dress that didn't make me look like Elsie the Cow. Once I was a size six, do you know that? Before I married your father I was a size six. Now look at me! Elsie the Cow! Moby-damn-*Dick!*"

"Mom, you're not big. In fact just lately you look—"

"Get out, Bobby. Please let Mother alone. I have a headache."

That night he heard her crying again. The following day he saw her carefully packing one of the dresses into her luggage—the one with the thin straps. The other went back into its store-box: GOWNS BY LUCIE OF BRIDGEPORT was written across the front in elegant maroon script.

On Monday night, Liz invited Ted Brautigan down to have dinner with them. Bobby loved his mother's meatloaf and usually asked for seconds, but on this occasion he had to work hard to stuff down a single piece. He was terrified that Ted would trance out and his mother would pitch a fit over it.

His fear proved groundless. Ted spoke pleasantly of his childhood in New Jersey and, when Bobby's mom asked him, of his job in Hartford. To Bobby he seemed less comfortable talking about accounting than he did reminiscing about sleighing as a kid, but his mom didn't appear to notice. Ted *did* ask for a second slice of meatloaf.

When the meal was over and the table cleared, Liz gave Ted a list of telephone numbers, including those of Dr. Gordon, the Sterling House Summer Rec office, and the Warwick Hotel. "If there are any problems, I want to hear from you. Okay?"

Ted nodded. "Okay."

"Bobby? No big worries?" She put her hand briefly on his forehead, the way she used to do when he complained of feeling feverish.

"Nope. We'll have a blast. Won't we, Mr. Brautigan?"

"Oh, call him Ted," Liz almost snapped. "If he's going to be sleeping in our living room, I guess I better call him Ted, too. May I?"

"Indeed you may. Let it be Ted from this moment on."

He smiled. Bobby thought it was a sweet smile, open and friendly. He didn't understand how anyone could resist it. But his mother could and did. Even now, while she was returning Ted's smile, he saw the hand with the Kleenex in it tightening and loosening in its old familiar gesture of anxious displeasure. One of her absolute favorite sayings now came to Bobby's mind: *I'd trust him* (or her) *as far as I could sling a piano.*

"And from now on I'm Liz." She held out a hand across the table and they shook like people meeting for the first time . . . except Bobby knew his mother's mind was already made up on the subject of Ted Brautigan. If her back hadn't been against the wall, she never would have trusted Bobby with him. Not in a million years.

She opened her purse and took out a plain white envelope. "There's ten dollars in here," she said, handing the envelope to Ted. "You boys will want to eat out at least one night, I expect—Bobby likes the Colony Diner, if that's all right with you—and you may want to take in a movie, as well. I don't know what else there might be, but it's best to have a little cushion, don't you think?"

"Always better safe than sorry," Ted agreed, tucking the envelope carefully into the front pocket of his slacks, "but I don't expect we'll go through anything like ten dollars in three days. Will we, Bobby?"

"Gee, no, I don't see how we could."

"Waste not, want not," Liz said—it was another of her favorites, right up there with *the fool and his money soon parted.* She plucked a cigarette out of the pack on the table beside the sofa and lit it with a hand which was not quite steady. "You boys will be fine. Probably have a better time than I will."

Looking at her ragged, bitten fingernails, Bobby thought, *That's for sure.*

His mom and the others were going to Providence in Mr. Biderman's car, and the next morning at seven o'clock Liz and Bobby Garfield stood on the porch, waiting for it to show up. The air had that early hazy hush that meant the hot days of summer had arrived. From Asher Avenue came the hoot and rumble of heavy going-to-work traffic, but down here on Broad there was only the occasional passing car or delivery truck. Bobby could hear the *hisha-hisha* of lawn-sprinklers, and, from the other side of the block, the endless *roop-roop-roop* of Bowser. Bowser sounded the same whether it was June or January; to Bobby Garfield, Bowser seemed as changeless as God.

"You don't have to wait out here with me, you know," Liz said. She was wearing a light coat and smoking a cigarette. She had on a little more makeup than usual, but Bobby thought he could still detect shadows under her eyes—she had passed another restless night.

"I don't mind."

"I hope it's all right, leaving you with him."

"I wish you wouldn't worry. Ted's a good guy, Mom."

She made a little hmphing noise.

There was a twinkle of chrome from the bottom of the hill as Mr. Biderman's Mercury (not vulgar, exactly, but a boat of a car all the same) turned onto their street from Commonwealth and came up the hill toward 149.

"There he is, there he is," his mom said, sounding nervous and excited. She bent down. "Give me a little smooch, Bobby. I don't want to kiss you and smear my lipstick."

Bobby put his hand on her arm and lightly kissed her cheek. He smelled her hair, the perfume she was wearing, her face-powder. He would never kiss her with that same unshadowed love again.

She gave him a vague little smile, not looking at him, looking instead at Mr. Biderman's boat of a Merc, which swerved gracefully across the street and pulled up at the curb in front of the house. She reached for her two suitcases (two seemed a lot for two days, Bobby thought, although he supposed the fancy dress took up a good deal of space in one of them), but he already had them by the handles.

"Those are too heavy, Bobby—you'll trip on the steps."

"No," he said. "I won't."

She gave him a distracted look, then waved to Mr. Biderman and went toward the car, high heels clacking. Bobby followed, trying not to grimace at the weight of the suitcases . . . what had she put in them, clothes or bricks?

He got them down to the sidewalk without having to stop and rest, at least. Mr. Biderman was out of the car by then, first putting a casual kiss on his mother's cheek, then shaking out the key that opened the trunk.

"Howya doin, Sport, howza boy?" Mr. Biderman always called Bobby Sport. "Lug em around back and I'll slide em in. Women always hafta bring the farm, don't they? Well, you know the old saying—can't live with em, can't shoot em outside the state of Montana." He bared his teeth in a grin that made Bobby think of Jack in *Lord of the Flies.* "Want me to take one?"

"I've got em," Bobby said. He trudged grimly in Mr. Biderman's wake, shoulders aching, the back of his neck hot and starting to sweat.

Mr. Biderman opened the trunk, plucked the suitcases from Bobby's hands, and slid them in with the rest of the luggage. Behind them, his mom was looking in the back window and talking with the other two men who were going. She laughed at something one of them said. To Bobby the laugh sounded about as real as a wooden leg.

Mr. Biderman closed the trunk and looked down at Bobby. He was a narrow man with a wide face. His cheeks were always flushed. You could see his pink scalp in the tracks left by the teeth of his comb. He wore little round glasses with gold rims. To Bobby his smile looked as real as his mother's laugh had sounded.

"Gonna play some baseball this summer, Sport?" Don Biderman bent his knees a little and cocked an imaginary bat. Bobby thought he looked like a dope.

"Yes, sir. I'm on the Wolves at Sterling House. I was hoping to make the Lions, but . . ."

"Good. Good." Mr. Biderman made a big deal of looking at his watch—the wide gold Twist-O-Flex band was dazzling in the early sunshine—and then patted Bobby's cheek. Bobby had to make a conscious effort not to cringe from his touch. "Say, we gotta get this wagon-train rolling! Shake her easy, Sport. Thanks for the loan of your mother."

He turned away and escorted Liz around the Mercury to the passenger side. He did this with a hand pressed to her back. Bobby liked that even less than watching the guy smooch her cheek. He glanced at the well-padded, business-suited men in the rear seat—Dean was the other guy's name, he remembered—just in time to see them elbowing each other. Both were grinning.

Something's wrong here, Bobby thought, and as Mr. Biderman opened the passenger door for his mother, as she murmured her thanks and slid in, gathering her dress a little so it wouldn't wrinkle, he had an urge to tell her not to go, Rhode Island was too far away, *Bridgeport* would be too far away, she needed to stay home.

He said nothing, though, only stood on the curb as Mr. Biderman closed her door and walked back around to the driver's side. He opened that door, paused, and then did his stupid little batter-up pantomime again. This time he added an asinine fanny-wiggle. *What a nimrod,* Bobby thought.

"Don't do anything I wouldn't do, Sport," he said.

"But if you do, name it after me," Cushman called from the back seat. Bobby didn't know exactly what that meant but it must have been funny because Dean laughed and Mr. Biderman tipped him one of those just-between-us-guys winks.

His mother was leaning in his direction. "You be a good boy, Bobby," she said. "I'll be back around eight on Thursday night—no later than ten. You're sure you're fine with that?"

No, I'm not fine with it at all. Don't go off with them, Mom, don't go off with Mr. Biderman and those two grinning dopes sitting behind you. Those two nimrods. Please don't.

"Sure he is," Mr. Biderman said. "He's a sport. Ain't you, Sport?"

"Bobby?" she asked, not looking at Mr. Biderman. "Are you all set?"

"Yeah," he said. "I'm a sport."

Mr. Biderman bellowed ferocious laughter—*Kill the pig, cut his throat,* Bobby thought—and dropped the Mercury into gear. "Providence or bust!" he cried, and the car rolled away from the curb, swerving across to the other side of Broad Street and heading up toward Asher. Bobby stood on the sidewalk, waving as the Merc passed Carol's house and Sully-John's. He felt as if he had a bone in his heart. If this was some sort of premonition—a winkle—he never wanted to have another one.

A hand fell on his shoulder. He looked around and saw Ted standing there in his bathrobe and slippers, smoking a cigarette. His hair, which had yet to make its morning acquaintance with the brush, stood up around his ears in comical sprays of white.

"So that was the boss," he said. "Mr. . . . Bidermeyer, is it?"

"Bider*man.*"

"And how do you like him, Bobby?"

Speaking with a low, bitter clarity, Bobby said, "I trust him about as far as I could sling a piano."

VI. A DIRTY OLD MAN. TED'S CASSEROLE. A BAD DREAM. *VILLAGE OF THE DAMNED.* DOWN THERE.

An hour or so after seeing his mother off, Bobby went down to Field B behind Sterling House. There were no real games until afternoon, nothing but three-flies-six-grounders or rolly-bat, but even rolly-bat was better than nothing. On Field A, to the north, the little kids were futzing away at a game that vaguely resembled baseball; on Field C, to the south, some high-school kids were playing what was almost the real thing.

Shortly after the town square clock had bonged noon and the boys broke to go in search of the hotdog wagon, Bill Pratt asked, "Who's that weird guy over there?"

He was pointing to a bench in the shade, and although Ted was wearing a trenchcoat, an old fedora hat, and dark glasses, Bobby recognized him at once. He guessed S-J would've, too, if S-J hadn't been at Camp Winnie. Bobby almost raised one hand in a wave, then didn't, because Ted was in disguise. Still, he'd come out to watch his downstairs friend play ball. Even though it wasn't a real game, Bobby felt an absurdly large lump rise in his throat. His mom had only come to watch him once in the two years he'd been playing—last August, when his team had been in the Tri-Town Championships—and even then she'd left in the fourth inning, before Bobby connected for what proved to be the game-winning triple. *Somebody has to work around here, Bobby-O,* she would have replied had he dared reproach her for that. *Your father didn't exactly leave us well off, you know.* It was true, of course—she had to work and Ted was retired. Except Ted had to stay clear of the low men in the yellow coats, and that was a full-time job. The fact that they didn't exist wasn't the point. Ted *believed* they did . . . but had come out to see him play just the same.

"Probably some dirty old man wanting to put a suckjob on one of the little kids," Harry Shaw said. Harry was small and tough, a boy going through life with his chin stuck out a mile. Being with Bill and Harry suddenly made Bobby homesick for Sully-John, who had left on the Camp Winnie bus Monday morning (at the brain-numbing hour of five A.M.). S-J didn't have much of a temper and he was kind. Sometimes Bobby thought that was the best thing about Sully—he was kind.

From Field C there came the hefty crack of a bat—an authoritative full-contact sound which none of the Field B boys could yet produce. It was followed by savage roars of approval that made Bill, Harry, and Bobby look a little nervously in that direction.

"St. Gabe's boys," Bill said. "They think they own Field C."

"Cruddy Catlicks," Harry said. "Catlicks are sissies—I could take any one of them."

"How about fifteen or twenty?" Bill asked, and Harry was silent. Up ahead, glittering like a mirror, was the hotdog wagon. Bobby touched the buck in his pocket. Ted had given it to him out of the envelope his mother had left, then had put the envelope itself behind the toaster, telling Bobby to take what he needed when he needed it. Bobby was almost exalted by this level of trust.

"Look on the bright side," Bill said. "Maybe those St. Gabe's boys will beat up the dirty old man."

When they got to the wagon, Bobby bought only one hotdog instead of the two he had been planning on. His appetite seemed to have shrunk. When they got back to Field B, where the Wolves' coaches had now appeared with the equipment cart, the bench Ted had been sitting on was empty.

"Come on, come on!" Coach Terrell called, clapping his hands. "Who wants to play some baseball here?"

That night Ted cooked his famous casserole in the Garfields' oven. It meant more hotdogs, but in the summer of 1960 Bobby Garfield could have eaten hotdogs three times a day and had another at bedtime.

He read stuff to Ted out of the newspaper while Ted put their dinner together. Ted only wanted to hear a couple of paragraphs about the impending Patterson–Johansson rematch, the one everybody was calling the fight of the century, but he wanted to hear every word of the article about tomorrow night's Albini–Haywood tilt at The Garden in New York. Bobby thought this moderately weird, but he was too happy to even comment on it, let alone complain.

He couldn't remember ever having spent an evening without his mother, and he missed her, yet he was also relieved to have her gone for a little while. There had been a queer sort of tension running through the apartment for weeks now, maybe even for months. It was like an electrical hum so constant that you got used to it and didn't realize how much a part of your life it had become until it was gone. That thought brought another of his mother's sayings to mind.

"What are you thinking?" Ted asked as Bobby came over to get the plates.

"That a change is as good as a rest," Bobby replied. "It's something my mom says. I hope she's having as good a time as I am."

"So do I, Bobby," Ted said. He bent, opened the oven, checked their dinner. "So do I."

The casserole was terrific, with canned B&M beans—the only kind Bobby really liked—and exotic spicy hotdogs not from the supermarket but from the butcher just off the town square. (Bobby assumed Ted had bought these while wearing his "disguise.") All this came in a horseradish sauce that zinged in your mouth and then made you feel sort of sweaty in the face. Ted had two helpings; Bobby had three, washing them down with glass after glass of grape Kool-Aid.

Ted blanked out once during the meal, first saying that he could feel *them* in the backs of his eyeballs, then lapsing either into some foreign language or outright gibberish, but the incident was brief and didn't cut into Bobby's appetite in the slightest. The blank-outs were part of Ted, that was all, like his scuffling walk and the nicotine stains between the first two fingers of his right hand.

They cleaned up together, Ted stowing the leftover casserole in the fridge and washing the dishes, Bobby drying and putting things away because he knew where everything went.

"Interested in taking a ride to Bridgeport with me tomorrow?" Ted asked as they worked. "We could go to the movies—the early matinee—and then I have to do an errand."

"Gosh, yeah!" Bobby said. "What do you want to see?"

"I'm open to suggestions, but I was thinking perhaps *Village of the Damned,* a British film. It's based on a very fine science-fiction novel by John Wyndham. Would that suit?"

At first Bobby was so excited he couldn't speak. He had seen the ads for *Village of the Damned* in the newspaper—all those spooky-looking kids with the glowing eyes—but hadn't thought he would ever actually get to *see* it. It sure wasn't the sort of Saturday-matinee movie that would ever play at Harwich on the Square or the Asher Empire. Matinees in those theaters consisted mostly of big-bug monster shows, westerns, or Audie Murphy war movies. And although his mother usually took him if she went to an evening show, she didn't like science fiction (Liz liked moody love stories like *The Dark at the Top of the Stairs*). Also the theaters in Bridgeport weren't like the antiquey old Harwich or the somehow businesslike Empire, with its plain, undecorated marquee. The theaters in Bridgeport were like fairy castles—they had huge screens (swag upon swag of velvety curtains covered them between shows), ceilings where tiny lights twinkled in galactic profusion, brilliant electric wall-sconces . . . and *two* balconies.

"Bobby?"

"You bet!" he said at last, thinking he probably wouldn't sleep tonight. "I'd love it. But aren't you afraid of . . . you know . . ."

"We'll take a taxi instead of the bus. I can phone for another taxi to take us back home later. We'll be fine. I think they're moving away now, anyway. I don't sense them so clearly."

Yet Ted glanced away when he said this, and to Bobby he looked like a man trying to tell himself a story he can't quite believe. If the increasing frequency of his blank-outs meant anything, Bobby thought, he had good reason to look that way.

Stop it, the low men don't exist, they're no more real than Flash Gordon and Dale Arden. The things he asked you to look for are just . . . just things. *Remember that, Bobby-O: just ordinary* things.

With dinner cleared away, the two of them sat down to watch *Bronco,* with Ty Hardin. Not among the best of the so-called "adult westerns" (*Cheyenne* and *Maverick* were the best), but not bad, either. Halfway through the show, Bobby let out a moderately loud fart. Ted's casserole had begun its work. He snuck a sideways glance to make sure Ted wasn't holding his nose and grimacing. Nope, just watching the television, seemingly absorbed.

When a commercial came on (some actress selling refrigerators), Ted asked if Bobby would like a glass of rootbeer. Bobby said okay. "I thought I might help myself to one of the Alka-Seltzers I saw in the bathroom, Bobby. I may have eaten a bit too much."

As he got up, Ted let out a long, sonorous fart that sounded like a trombone. Bobby put his hands to his mouth and giggled. Ted gave him a rueful smile and left the room. Bobby's giggling forced out more farts, a little tooting stream of them, and when Ted came back with a fizzy glass of Alka-Seltzer in one hand and a foamy glass of Hires rootbeer in the other, Bobby was laughing so hard that tears streamed down his cheeks and hung off his jawline like raindrops.

"This should help fix us up," Ted said, and when he bent to hand Bobby his rootbeer, a loud honk came from behind him. "Goose just flew out of my ass," he added matter-of-factly, and Bobby laughed so hard that he could no longer sit in his chair. He slithered out of it and lay in a boneless heap on the floor.

"I'll be right back," Ted told him. "There's something else we need."

He left open the door between the apartment and the foyer, so Bobby could hear him going up the stairs. By the time Ted got to the third floor, Bobby had managed to crawl into his chair again. He didn't think he'd ever laughed so hard in his life. He drank some of his rootbeer, then farted again. "Goose just flew . . . flew out . . ." But he couldn't finish. He flopped back in his chair and howled, shaking his head from side to side.

The stairs creaked as Ted came back down. When he reentered the apartment he had his fan, with the electric cord looped neatly around the base, under one arm. "Your mother was right about this," he said. When he bent to plug it in, another goose flew out of his ass.

"She usually is," Bobby said, and that struck them both funny. They sat in the living room with the fan rotating back and forth, stirring the increasingly fragrant air. Bobby thought if he didn't stop laughing soon his head would pop.

When *Bronco* was over (by then Bobby had lost all track of the story), he helped Ted pull out the couch. The bed which had been hiding inside it didn't look all that great, but Liz had made it up with some spare sheets and blankets and Ted said it would be fine. Bobby brushed his teeth, then looked out from the door of his bedroom at Ted, who was sitting on the end of the sofa-bed and watching the news.

"Goodnight," Bobby said.

Ted looked over to him, and for a moment Bobby thought Ted would get up, cross the room, give him a hug and maybe a kiss. Instead of that, he sketched a funny, awkward little salute. "Sleep well, Bobby."

"Thanks."

Bobby closed his bedroom door, turned off the light, got into bed, and spread his heels to the corners of the mattress. As he looked up into the dark he remembered the morning Ted had taken hold of his shoulders, then laced his bunchy old hands together behind his neck. Their faces that day had been almost as close as his and Carol's had been on the Ferris wheel just before they kissed. The day he had argued with his mother. The day he had known about the money taped in the catalogue. Also the day he had won ninety cents from Mr. McQuown. *Go buy yourself a martini,* Mr. McQuown had said.

Had it come from Ted? Had the winkle come from Ted touching him?

"Yeah," Bobby whispered in the dark. "Yeah, I think it probably did."

What if he touches me again that way?

Bobby was still considering this idea when he fell asleep.

He dreamed that people were chasing his mother through the jungle—Jack and Piggy, the littluns, and Don Biderman, Cushman, and Dean. His mother was wearing her new dress from Gowns by Lucie, the black one with the thin straps, only it had been torn in places by thorns and branches. Her stockings were in tatters. They looked like strips of dead skin hanging off her legs. Her eyes were deep sweatholes gleaming with terror. The boys chasing her were naked. Biderman and the other two were wearing their business suits. All of them had alternating streaks of red and white paint on their faces; all were brandishing spears and shouting *Kill the pig, slit her throat! Kill the pig, drink her blood! Kill the pig, strew her guts!*

He woke in the gray light of dawn, shivering, and got up to use the bathroom. By the time he went back to bed he could no longer remember precisely what he had dreamed. He slept for another two hours, and woke up to the good smells of bacon and eggs. Bright summer sunshine was slanting in his bedroom window and Ted was making breakfast.

Village of the Damned was the last and greatest movie of Bobby Garfield's childhood; it was the first and greatest movie of what came after childhood—a dark period when he was often bad and always confused, a Bobby Garfield he felt he didn't really know. The cop who arrested him for the first time had blond hair, and what came to Bobby's mind as the cop led him away from the mom 'n pop store Bobby had broken into (by then he and his mother were living in a suburb north of Boston) were all those blond kids in *Village of the Damned.* The cop could have been one of them all grown up.

The movie was playing at the Criterion, the very avatar of those Bridgeport dream-palaces Bobby had been thinking about the night before. It was in black and white, but the contrasts were sharp, not all fuzzy like on the Zenith back in the apartment, and the images were *enormous.* So were the sounds, especially the shivery theremin music that played when the Midwich children really started to use their power.

Bobby was enthralled by the story, understanding even before the first five minutes were over that it was a *real* story, the way *Lord of the Flies* had been a real story. The people seemed like real people, which made the make-believe parts scarier. He guessed that Sully-John would have been bored with it, except for the ending. S-J liked to see giant scorpions crushing Mexico City or Rodan stomping Tokyo; beyond that his interest in what he called "creature features" was limited. But Sully wasn't here, and for the first time since he'd left, Bobby was glad.

They were in time for the one o'clock matinee, and the theater was almost deserted. Ted (wearing his fedora and with his dark glasses folded into the breast pocket of his shirt) bought a big bag of popcorn, a box of Dots, a Coke for Bobby, and a rootbeer (of course!) for himself. Every now and then he would pass Bobby the popcorn or the candy and Bobby would take some, but he was hardly aware that he was eating, let alone of *what* he was eating.

The movie began with everyone in the British village of Midwich falling asleep (a man who was driving a tractor at the time of the event was killed; so was a woman who fell face-first onto a lighted stove burner). The military was notified, and they sent a reconnaissance plane to take a look. The pilot fell asleep as soon as he was over Midwich airspace; the plane crashed. A soldier with a rope around his middle walked ten or twelve paces into the village, then swooned into a deep sleep. When he was dragged back, he awakened as soon as he was hauled over the "sleep-line" that had been painted across the highway.

Everyone in Midwich woke up eventually, and everything seemed to be all right . . . until, a few weeks later, the women in town discovered they were pregnant. Old women, young women, even girls Carol Gerber's age, all pregnant, and the children they gave birth to were those spooky kids from the poster, the ones with the blond hair and the glowing eyes.

Although the movie never said, Bobby figured the Children of the Damned must have been caused by some sort of outer-space phenomenon, like the pod-people in *Invasion of the Body Snatchers.* In any case, they grew up faster than normal kids, they were super-smart, they could make people do what they wanted . . . and they were ruthless. When one father tried to discipline his particular Child of the Damned, all the kids clubbed together and directed their thoughts at the offending grownup (their eyes glowing, that theremin music so pulsing and strange that Bobby's arms broke out in goosebumps as he drank his Coke) until the guy put a shotgun to his head and killed himself (that part wasn't shown, and Bobby was glad).

The hero was George Sanders. His wife gave birth to one of the blond children. S-J would have scoffed at George, called him a "queer bastard" or a "golden oldie," but Bobby found him a welcome change from heroes like Randolph Scott, Richard Carlson, and the inevitable Audie Murphy. George was really sort of ripshit, in a weird English way. In the words of Denny Rivers, old George knew how to lay chilly. He wore special cool ties and combed his hair back tight to his skull. He didn't look as though he could beat up a bunch of saloon baddies or anything, but he was the only guy from Midwich the Children of the Damned would have anything to do with; in fact they drafted him to be their teacher. Bobby couldn't imagine Randolph Scott or Audie Murphy teaching a bunch of super-smart kids from outer space *anything.*

In the end, George Sanders was also the one who got rid of them. He had discovered he could keep the Children from reading his mind—for a little while, anyway—if he imagined a brick wall in his head, with all his most secret thoughts behind it. And after everyone had decided the Children must go (you could teach them math, but not why it was bad to punish someone by making him drive over a cliff), Sanders put a time-bomb into his briefcase and took it into the schoolroom. That was the only place where the Children—Bobby understood in some vague way that they were only supernatural versions of Jack Merridew and his hunters in *Lord of the Flies*—were all together.

They sensed that Sanders was hiding something from them. In the movie's final excruciating sequence, you could see bricks flying out of the wall Sanders had constructed in his head, flying faster and faster as the Children of the Damned pried into him, trying to find out what he was concealing. At last they uncovered the image of the bomb in the briefcase—eight or nine sticks of dynamite wired up to an alarm clock. You saw their creepy golden eyes widen with understanding, but they didn't have time to do anything. The bomb exploded. Bobby was shocked that the hero died—Randolph Scott never died in the Saturday-matinee movies at the Empire, neither did Audie Murphy or Richard Carlson—but he understood that George Sanders had given his life For the Greater Good of All. He thought he understood something else, as well: Ted's blank-outs.

While Ted and Bobby had been visiting Midwich, the day in southern Connecticut had turned hot and glaring. Bobby didn't like the world much after a really good movie in any case; for a little while it felt like an unfair joke, full of people with dull eyes, small plans, and facial blemishes. He sometimes thought if the world had a *plot* it would be so much better.

"Brautigan and Garfield hit the bricks!" Ted exclaimed as they stepped from beneath the marquee (a banner reading **COME IN IT'S KOOL INSIDE** hung from the marquee's front). "What did you think? Did you enjoy it?"

"It was great," Bobby said. "Fantabulous. Thanks for taking me. It was practically the best movie I ever saw. How about when he had the dynamite? Did you think he'd be able to fool them?"

"Well . . . I'd read the book, remember. Will *you* read it, do you think?"

"Yes!" Bobby felt, in fact, a sudden urge to bolt back to Harwich, running the whole distance down the Connecticut Pike and Asher Avenue in the hot sunshine so he could borrow *The Midwich Cuckoos* with his new adult library card at once. "Did he write any other science-fiction stories?"

"John Wyndham? Oh yes, quite a few. And will no doubt write more. One nice thing about science-fiction and mystery writers is that they rarely dither five years between books. That is the prerogative of serious writers who drink whiskey and have affairs."

"Are the others as good as the one we just saw?"

"*The Day of the Triffids* is as good. *The Kraken Wakes* is even better."

"What's a kraken?"

They had reached a streetcorner and were waiting for the light to change. Ted made a spooky, big-eyed face and bent down toward Bobby with his hands on his knees. "It's a *monstah,*" he said, doing a pretty good Boris Karloff imitation.

They walked on, talking first about the movie and then about whether or not there really might be life in outer space, and then on to the special cool ties George Sanders had worn in the movie (Ted told him that kind of tie was called an ascot). When Bobby next took notice of their surroundings they had come to a part of Bridgeport he had never been in before—when he came to the city with his mom, they stuck to downtown, where the big stores were. The stores here were small and crammed together. None sold what the big department stores did: clothes and appliances and shoes and toys. Bobby saw signs for locksmiths, check-cashing services, used books. ROD'S GUNS, read one sign. WO FAT NOODLE CO., read another. FOTO FINISHING, read a third. Next to WO FAT was a shop selling SPECIAL SOUVENIRS. There was something weirdly like the Savin Rock midway about this street, so much so that Bobby almost expected to see the Monte Man standing on a streetcorner with his makeshift table and his lobsterback playing cards.

Bobby tried to peer through the SPECIAL SOUVENIRS window when they passed, but it was covered by a big bamboo blind. He'd never heard of a store covering their show window during business hours. "Who'd want a special souvenir of Bridgeport, do you think?"

"Well, I don't think they really sell souvenirs," Ted said. "I'd guess they sell items of a sexual nature, few of them strictly legal."

Bobby had questions about that—a billion or so—but felt it best to be quiet. Outside a pawnshop with three golden balls hanging over the door he paused to look at a dozen straight-razors which had been laid out on velvet with their blades partly open. They'd been arranged in a circle and the result was strange and (to Bobby) beautiful: looking at them was like looking at something removed from a deadly piece of machinery. The razors' handles were much more exotic than the handle of the one Ted used, too. One looked like ivory, another like ruby etched with thin gold lines, a third like crystal.

"If you bought one of those you'd be shaving in style, wouldn't you?" Bobby asked.

He thought Ted would smile, but he didn't. "When people buy razors like that, they don't shave with them, Bobby."

"What do you mean?"

Ted wouldn't tell him, but he did buy him a sandwich called a gyro in a Greek delicatessen. It came in a folded-over piece of homemade bread and was oozing a dubious white sauce which to Bobby looked quite a lot like pimple-pus. He forced himself to try it because Ted said they were good. It turned out to be the best sandwich he'd ever eaten, as meaty as a hotdog or a hamburger from the Colony Diner but with an exotic taste that no hamburger or hotdog had ever had. And it was great to be eating on the sidewalk, strolling along with his friend, looking and being looked at.

"What do they call this part of town?" Bobby asked. "Does it have a name?"

"These days, who knows?" Ted said, and shrugged. "They used to call it Greektown. Then the Italians came, the Puerto Ricans, and now the Negroes. There's a novelist named David Goodis—the kind the college teachers never read, a genius of the drugstore paperback displays—who calls it 'down there.' He says every city has a neighborhood like this one, where you can buy sex or marijuana or a parrot that talks dirty, where the men sit talking on stoops like those men across the street, where the women always seem to be yelling for their kids to come in unless they want a whipping, and where the wine always comes in a paper sack." Ted pointed into the gutter, where the neck of a Thunderbird bottle did indeed poke out of a brown bag. "It's just down there, that's what David Goodis says, the place where you don't have any use for your last name and you can buy almost anything if you have cash in your pocket."

Down there, Bobby thought, watching a trio of olive-skinned teenagers in gang jackets watch them as they passed. *This is the land of straight-razors and special souvenirs.*

The Criterion and Muncie's Department Store had never seemed so far away. And Broad Street? That and all of Harwich could have been in another solar system.

At last they came to a place called The Corner Pocket, Pool and Billiards, Automatic Games, Rheingold on Tap. There was also one of those banners reading **COME IN IT'S KOOL INSIDE**. As Bobby and Ted passed beneath it, a young man in a strappy tee-shirt and a chocolate-colored stingybrim like the kind Frank Sinatra wore came out the door. He had a long, thin case in one hand. *That's his pool-cue,* Bobby thought with fright and amazement. *He's got his pool-cue in that case like it was a guitar or something.*

"Who a hip cat, Daddy-O?" he asked Bobby, then grinned. Bobby grinned back. The kid with the pool-cue case made a gun with his finger and pointed at Bobby. Bobby made a gun with his own finger and pointed it back. The kid nodded as if to say *Yeah, okay, you hip, we both hip* and crossed the street, snapping the fingers of his free hand and bopping to the music in his head.

Ted looked up the street in one direction, then down in the other. Ahead of them, three Negro children were capering in the spray of a partly opened hydrant. Back the way they had come, two young men—one white, the other maybe Puerto Rican—were taking the hubcaps off an old Ford, working with the rapid seriousness of doctors performing an operation. Ted looked at them, sighed, then looked at Bobby. "The Pocket's no place for a kid, even in the middle of the day, but I'm not going to leave you out on the street. Come on." He took Bobby by the hand and led him inside.

VII. IN THE POCKET. THE SHIRT RIGHT OFF HIS BACK. OUTSIDE THE WILLIAM PENN. THE FRENCH SEX-KITTEN.

What struck Bobby first was the smell of beer. It was impacted, as if folks had been drinking in here since the days when the pyramids were still in the planning stages. Next was the sound of a TV, not turned to *Bandstand* but to one of the late-afternoon soap operas ("Oh John, oh Marsha" shows was what his mother called them), and the click of pool-balls. Only after these things had registered did his eyes chip in their own input, because they'd needed to adjust. The place was very dim.

And it was long, Bobby saw. To their right was an archway, and beyond it a room that appeared almost endless. Most of the pool-tables were covered, but a few stood in brilliant islands of light where men strolled languidly about, pausing every now and then to bend and shoot. Other men, hardly visible, sat in high seats along the wall, watching. One was getting his shoes shined. He looked about a thousand.

Straight ahead was a big room filled with Gottlieb pinball machines: a billion red and orange lights stuttered stomachache colors off a large sign which read IF YOU TILT THE SAME MACHINE TWICE YOU WILL BE ASKED TO LEAVE. A young man wearing another stingy-brim hat—apparently the approved headgear for the bad motorscooters residing down there—was bent over Frontier Patrol, working the flippers frantically. A cigarette hung off his lower lip, the smoke rising past his face and the whorls of his combed-back hair. He was wearing a jacket tied around his waist and turned inside-out.

To the left of the lobby was a bar. It was from here that the sound of the TV and the smell of beer was coming. Three men sat there, each surrounded by empty stools, hunched over pilsner glasses. They didn't look like the happy beer-drinkers you saw in the ads; to Bobby they looked the loneliest people on earth. He wondered why they didn't at least huddle up and talk a little.

Closer by them was a desk. A fat man came rolling through the door behind it, and for a moment Bobby could hear the low sound of a radio playing. The fat man had a cigar in his mouth and was wearing a shirt covered with palm trees. He was snapping his fingers like the cool cat with the pool-cue case, and under his breath he was singing like this: "Choo-choo-*chow,* choo-choo-ka-chow-chow, choo-choo-*chow-chow!*" Bobby recognized the tune: "Tequila," by The Champs.

"Who you, buddy?" the fat man asked Ted. "I don't know you. And he can't be in here, anyway. Can'tcha read?" He jerked a fat thumb with a dirty nail at another sign, this one posted on the desk: B-21 OR B-GONE!

"You don't know me, but I think you know Jimmy Girardi," Ted said politely. "He told me you were the man to see . . . if you're Len Files, that is."

"I'm Len," the man said. All at once he seemed considerably warmer. He held out a hand so white and pudgy that it looked like the gloves Mickey and Donald and Goofy wore in the cartoons. "You know Jimmy Gee, huh? Goddam Jimmy Gee! Why, his grampa's back there getting a shine. He gets 'is boats shined a lot these days." Len Files tipped Ted a wink. Ted smiled and shook the guy's hand.

"That your kid?" Len Files asked, bending over his desk to get a closer look at Bobby. Bobby could smell Sen-Sen mints and cigars on his breath, sweat on his body. The collar of his shirt was speckled with dandruff.

"He's a friend," Ted said, and Bobby thought he might actually explode with happiness. "I didn't want to leave him on the street."

"Yeah, unless you're willing to have to pay to get im back," Len Files agreed. "You remind me of somebody, kid. Now why is that?"

Bobby shook his head, a little frightened to think he looked like anybody Len Files might know.

The fat man barely paid attention to Bobby's head-shake. He had straightened and was looking at Ted again. "I can't be having kids in here, Mr. . . . ?"

"Ted Brautigan." He offered his hand. Len Files shook it.

"You know how it is, Ted. People in a business like mine, the cops keep tabs."

"Of course. But he'll stand right here—won't you, Bobby?"

"Sure," Bobby said.

"And our business won't take long. But it's a good little bit of business, Mr. Files—"

"Len."

Len, of course, Bobby thought. Just Len. Because in here was down there.

"As I say, Len, this is a good piece of business I want to do. I think you'll agree."

"If you know Jimmy Gee, you know I don't do the nickels and dimes," Len said. "I leave the nickels and dimes to the niggers. What are we talking here? Patterson–Johansson?"

"Albini–Haywood. At The Garden tomorrow night?"

Len's eyes widened. Then his fat and unshaven cheeks spread in a smile. "Man oh man oh Manischewitz. We need to explore this."

"We certainly do."

Len Files came out from around the desk, took Ted by the arm, and started to lead him toward the poolroom. Then he stopped and swung back. "Is it Bobby when you're home and got your feet up, pal?"

"Yes, sir." *Yes sir, Bobby Garfield,* he would have said anywhere else . . . but this was down there and he thought just plain Bobby would suffice.

"Well, Bobby, I know those pinball machines prolly look good to ya, and you prolly got a quarter or two in your pocket, but do what Adam dint and resist the temptation. Can you do that?"

"Yes, sir."

"I won't be long," Ted told him, and then allowed Len Files to lead him through the arch and into the poolroom. They walked past the men in the high chairs, and Ted stopped to speak to the one getting his shoes shined. Next to Jimmy Gee's grandfather, Ted Brautigan looked young. The old man peered up and Ted said something; the two men laughed into each other's faces. Jimmy Gee's grandfather had a good strong laugh for an old fellow. Ted reached out both hands and patted his sallow cheeks with gentle affection. That made Jimmy Gee's grandfather laugh again. Then Ted let Len draw him into a curtained alcove past the other men in the other chairs.

Bobby stood by the desk as if rooted, but Len hadn't said anything about not looking around, and so he did—in all directions. The walls were covered with beer signs and calendars that showed girls with most of their clothes off. One was climbing over a fence in the country. Another was getting out of a Packard with most of her skirt in her lap and her garters showing. Behind the desk were more signs, most expressing some negative concept (IF YOU DON'T LIKE OUR TOWN LOOK FOR A TIMETABLE, DON'T SEND A BOY TO DO A MAN'S JOB, THERE'S NO SUCH THING AS A FREE LUNCH, NO CHECKS ACCEPTED, NO CREDIT, CRYING TOWELS ARE NOT PROVIDED BY THE MANAGEMENT) and a big red button marked **POLICE CALL.** Suspended from the ceiling on a loop of dusty wire were cellophane packages, some marked GINSENG ORIENTAL LOVE ROOT and others SPANISH DELITE. Bobby wondered if they were vitamins of some kind. Why would they sell vitamins in a place like this?

The young guy in the roomful of automatic games whapped the side of Frontier Patrol, stepped back, gave the machine the finger. Then he strolled into the lobby area adjusting his hat. Bobby made his finger into a gun and pointed it at him. The young man looked surprised, then grinned and pointed back as he headed for the door. He loosened the tied arms of his jacket as he went.

"Can't wear no club jacket in here," he said, noting Bobby's wide-eyed curiosity. "Can't even show your fuckin colors. Rules of the house."

"Oh."

The young guy smiled and raised his hand. Traced in blue ink on the back was a devil's pitchfork. "But I got the sign, little brother. See it?"

"Heck, yeah." A tattoo. Bobby was faint with envy. The kid saw it; his smile widened into a grin full of white teeth.

"Fuckin Diablos, *'mano.* Best club. Fuckin Diablos rule the streets. All others are pussy."

"The streets down here."

"Fuckin right down here, where else is there? Rock on, baby brother. I like you. You got a good look on you. Fuckin crewcut sucks, though." The door opened, there was a gasp of hot air and streetlife noise, and the guy was gone.

A little wicker basket on the desk caught Bobby's eye. He tilted it so he could see in. It was full of keyrings with plastic fobs—red and blue and green. Bobby picked one out so he could read the gold printing: THE CORNER POCKET BILLIARDS, POOL, AUTO. GAMES. KENMORE 8-2127.

"Go on, kid, take it."

Bobby was so startled he almost knocked the basket of keyrings to the floor. The woman had come through the same door as Len Files, and she was even bigger—almost as big as the circus fat lady—but she was as light on her feet as a ballerina; Bobby looked up and she was just there, looming over him. She was Len's sister, had to be.

"I'm sorry," Bobby muttered, returning the keyring he'd picked up and pushing the basket back from the edge of the desk with little pats of his fingers. He might have succeeded in pushing it right over the far side if the fat woman hadn't stopped it with one hand. She was smiling and didn't look a bit mad, which to Bobby was a tremendous relief.

"Really, I'm not being sarcastic, you should take one." She held out one of the keyrings. It had a green fob. "They're just cheap little things, but they're free. We give em away for the advertising. Like matches, you know, although I wouldn't give a pack of matches to a kid. Don't smoke, do you?"

"No, ma'am."

"That's making a good start. Stay away from the booze, too. Here. Take. Don't turn down for free in this world, kid, there isn't much of it going around."

Bobby took the keyring with the green fob. "Thank you, ma'am. It's neat." He put the keyring in his pocket, knowing he would have to get rid of it—if his mother found such an item, she wouldn't be happy. She'd have twenty questions, as Sully would say. Maybe even thirty.

"What's your name?"

"Bobby."

He waited to see if she would ask for his last name and was secretly delighted when she didn't. "I'm Alanna." She held out a hand crusted with rings. They twinkled like the pinball lights. "You here with your dad?"

"With my *friend,*" Bobby said. "I think he's making a bet on the Haywood–Albini prizefight."

Alanna looked alarmed and amused at the same time. She leaned forward with one finger to her red lips. She made a *Shhh* sound at Bobby, and blew out a strong liquory smell with it.

"Don't say 'bet' in here," she cautioned him. "This is a billiard parlor. Always remember that and you'll always be fine."

"Okay."

"You're a handsome little devil, Bobby. And you look . . ." She paused. "Do I know your father, maybe? Is that possible?"

Bobby shook his head, but doubtfully—he had reminded Len of someone, too. "My dad's dead. He died a long time ago." He always added this so people wouldn't get all gushy.

"What was his name?" But before he could say, Alanna Files said it herself—it came out of her painted mouth like a magic word. "Was it Randy? Randy Garrett, Randy Greer, something like that?"

For a moment Bobby was so flabbergasted he couldn't speak. It felt as if all the breath had been sucked out of his lungs. "Randall Garfield. But how . . ."

She laughed, delighted. Her bosom heaved. "Well mostly your *hair.* But also the freckles . . . and this here ski-jump . . ." She bent forward and Bobby could see the tops of smooth white breasts that looked as big as waterbarrels. She skidded one finger lightly down his nose.

"He came in here to play pool?"

"Nah. Said he wasn't much of a stick. He'd drink a beer. Also sometimes . . ." She made a quick gesture then—dealing from an invisible deck. It made Bobby think of McQuown.

"Yeah," Bobby said. "He never met an inside straight he didn't like, that's what I heard."

"I don't know about that, but he was a nice guy. He could come in here on a Monday night, when the place is always like a grave, and in half an hour or so he'd have everybody laughing. He'd play that song by Jo Stafford, I can't remember the name, and make Lennie turn up the jukebox. A real sweetie, kid, that's mostly why I remember him; a sweetie with red hair is a rare commodity. He wouldn't buy a drunk a drink, he had a thing about that, but otherwise he'd give you the shirt right off his back. All you had to do was ask."

"But he lost a lot of money, I guess," Bobby said. He couldn't believe he was having this conversation—that he had met someone who had known his father. Yet he supposed a lot of finding out happened like this, completely by accident. You were just going along, minding your own business, and all at once the past sideswiped you.

"Randy?" She looked surprised. "Nah. He'd come in for a drink maybe three times a week—you know, if he happened to be in the neighborhood. He was in real estate or insurance or selling or some one of those—"

"Real estate," Bobby said. "It was real estate."

"—and there was an office down here he'd visit. For the industrial properties, I guess, if it was real estate. You sure it wasn't medical supplies?"

"No, real estate."

"Funny how your memory works," she said. "Some things stay clear, but mostly time goes by and green turns blue. All of the suit-n-tie businesses are gone down here now, anyway." She shook her head sadly.

Bobby wasn't interested in how the neighborhood had gone to blazes. "But when he *did* play, he lost. He was always trying to fill inside straights and stuff."

"Did your mother tell you that?"

Bobby was silent.

Alanna shrugged. Interesting things happened all up and down her front when she did. "Well, that's between you and her . . . and hey, maybe your dad threw his dough around in other places. All I know is that in here he'd just sit in once or twice a month with guys he knew, play until maybe midnight, then go home. If he left a big winner or a big loser, I'd probably remember. I don't, so he probably broke even most nights he played. Which, by the way, makes him a pretty good poker-player. Better than most back there." She rolled her eyes in the direction Ted and her brother had gone.

Bobby looked at her with growing confusion. *Your father didn't exactly leave us well off,* his mother liked to say. There was the lapsed life insurance policy, the stack of unpaid bills; *Little did I know,* his mother had said just this spring, and Bobby was beginning to think that fit him, as well: *Little did I know.*

"He was such a good-looking guy, your dad," Alanna said, "Bob Hope nose and all. I'd guess you got that to look forward to—you favor him. Got a girlfriend?"

"Yes, ma'am."

Were the unpaid bills a fiction? Was that possible? Had the life insurance policy actually been cashed and socked away, maybe in a bank account instead of between the pages of the Sears catalogue? It was a horrible thought, somehow. Bobby couldn't imagine why his mother would want him to think his dad was

(*a low man, a low man with red hair*)

a bad guy if he really wasn't, but there was something about the idea that felt . . . true. She could get mad, that was the thing about his mother. She could get *so* mad. And then she might say anything. It was possible that his father—who his mother had never once in Bobby's memory called "Randy"—had given too many people too many shirts right off his back, and consequently made Liz Garfield mad. Liz Garfield didn't give away shirts, not off her back or from anywhere else. You had to save your shirts in this world, because life wasn't fair.

"What's her name?"

"Liz." He felt dazed, the way he'd felt coming out of the dark theater into the bright light.

"Like Liz Taylor." Alanna looked pleased. "That's a nice name for a girlfriend."

Bobby laughed, a little embarrassed. "No, my *mother's* Liz. My girlfriend's name is Carol."

"She pretty?"

"A real hotsy-totsy," he said, grinning and wiggling one hand from side to side. He was delighted when Alanna roared with laughter. She reached over the desk, the flesh of her upper arm hanging like some fantastic wad of dough, and pinched his cheek. It hurt a little but he liked it.

"Cute kid! Can I tell you something?"

"Sure, what?"

"Just because a man likes to play a little cards, that doesn't make him Attila the Hun. You know that, don't you?"

Bobby nodded hesitantly, then more firmly.

"Your ma's your ma, I don't say nothing against anybody's ma because I loved my own, but not everybody's ma approves of cards or pool or . . . places like this. It's a point of view, but that's all it is. Get the picture?"

"Yes," Bobby said. He did. He got the picture. He felt very strange, like laughing and crying at the same time. *My dad was here,* he thought. This seemed, at least for the time being, much more important than any lies his mother might have told about him. *My dad was here, he might have stood right where I'm standing now.* "I'm glad I look like him," he blurted.

Alanna nodded, smiling. "You coming in here like that, just walking in off the street. What are the odds?"

"I don't know. But thanks for telling me about him. Thanks a lot."

"He'd play that Jo Stafford song all night, if you'd let him," Alanna said. "Now don't you go wandering off."

"No, ma'am."

"No, *Alanna.*"

Bobby grinned. "*Alanna.*"

She blew him a kiss as his mother sometimes did, and laughed when Bobby pretended to catch it. Then she went back through the door. Bobby could see what looked like a living room beyond it. There was a big cross on one wall.

He reached into his pocket, hooked a finger through the keyring (it was, he thought, a special souvenir of his visit down there), and imagined himself riding down Broad Street on the Schwinn from the Western Auto. He was heading for the park. He was wearing a chocolate-colored stingybrim hat cocked back on his head. His hair was long and combed in a duck's ass—no more crewcut, later for you, Jack. Tied around his waist was a jacket with his colors on it; riding the back of his hand was a blue tattoo, stamped deep and forever. Outside Field B Carol would be waiting for him. She'd be watching him ride up, she'd be thinking *Oh you crazy boy* as he swung the Schwinn around in a tight circle, spraying gravel toward (but not on) her white sneakers. Crazy, yes. A bad motorscooter and a mean go-getter.

Len Files and Ted were coming back now, both of them looking happy. Len, in fact, looked like the cat that ate the canary (as Bobby's mother often said). Ted paused to pass another, briefer, word with the old guy, who nodded and smiled. When Ted and Len got back to the lobby area, Ted started toward the telephone booth just inside the door. Len took his arm and steered him toward the desk instead.

As Ted stepped behind it, Len ruffled Bobby's hair. "I know who you look like," he said. "It come to me while I was in the back room. Your dad was—"

"Garfield. Randy Garfield." Bobby looked up at Len, who so resembled his sister, and thought how odd and sort of wonderful it was to be linked that way to your own blood kin. Linked so closely people who didn't even know you could sometimes pick you out of a crowd. "Did you like him, Mr. Files?"

"Who, Randy? Sure, he was a helluva gizmo." But Len Files seemed a little vague. He hadn't noticed Bobby's father in the same way his sister had, Bobby decided; Len probably wouldn't remember about the Jo Stafford song or how Randy Garfield would give you the shirt right off his back. He wouldn't give a drunk a drink, though; he wouldn't do that. "Your pal's all right, too," Len went on, more enthusiastic now. "I like the high class and the high class likes me, but I don't get real shooters like him in here often." He turned to Ted, who was hunting nearsightedly through the phonebook. "Try Circle Taxi. KEnmore 6-7400."

"Thanks," Ted said.

"Don't mention it." Len brushed past Ted and went through the door behind the desk. Bobby caught another brief glimpse of the living room and the big cross. When the door shut, Ted looked over at Bobby and said: "You bet five hundred bucks on a prizefight and you don't have to use the pay phone like the rest of the shmucks. Such a deal, huh?"

Bobby felt as if all the wind had been sucked out of him. "You bet *five hundred dollars* on Hurricane Haywood?"

Ted shook a Chesterfield out of his pack, put it in his mouth, lit it around a grin. "Good God, no," he said. "On Albini."

After he called the cab, Ted took Bobby over to the bar and ordered them both rootbeers. *He doesn't know I don't really like rootbeer,* Bobby thought. It seemed another piece in the puzzle, somehow—the puzzle of Ted. Len served them himself, saying nothing about how Bobby shouldn't be sitting at the bar, he was a nice kid but just stinking the place up with his under-twenty-oneness; apparently a free phone call wasn't all you got when you bet five hundred dollars on a prizefight. And not even the excitement of the bet could long distract Bobby from a certain dull certainty which stole much of his pleasure in hearing that his father hadn't been such a bad guy, after all. The bet had been made to earn some runout money. Ted was leaving.

The taxi was a Checker with a huge back seat. The driver was deeply involved in the Yankees game on the radio, to the point where he sometimes talked back to the announcers.

"Files and his sister knew your father, didn't they?" It wasn't really a question.

"Yeah. Alanna especially. She thought he was a real nice guy." Bobby paused. "But that's not what my mother thinks."

"I imagine your mother saw a side of him Alanna Files never did," Ted replied. "More than one. People are like diamonds in that way, Bobby. They have many sides."

"But Mom said . . ." It was too complicated. She'd never exactly said *anything,* really, only sort of suggested stuff. He didn't know how to tell Ted that his mother had sides, too, and some of them made it hard to believe those things she never quite came out and said. And when you got right down to it, how much did he really want to know? His father was dead, after all. His mother wasn't, and he had to live with her . . . and he had to love her. He had no one else to love, not even Ted. Because—

"When you going?" Bobby asked in a low voice.

"After your mother gets back." Ted sighed, glanced out the window, then looked down at his hands, which were folded on one crossed knee. He didn't look at Bobby, not yet. "Probably Friday morning. I can't collect my money until tomorrow night. I got four to one on Albini; that's two grand. My good pal Lennie will have to phone New York to make the cover."

They crossed a canal bridge, and down there was back there. Now they were in the part of the city Bobby had travelled with his mother. The men on the street wore coats and ties. The women wore hose instead of bobbysocks. None of them looked like Alanna Files, and Bobby didn't think many of them would smell of liquor if they went "Shhh," either. Not at four o'clock in the afternoon.

"I know why you didn't bet on Patterson–Johansson," Bobby said. "It's because you don't know who'll win."

"I *think* Patterson will this time," Ted said, "because this time he's prepared for Johansson. I might flutter two dollars on Floyd Patterson, but five hundred? To bet five hundred you must either know or be crazy."

"The Albini–Haywood fight is fixed, isn't it?"

Ted nodded. "I knew when you read that Kleindienst was involved, and I guessed that Albini was supposed to win."

"You've made other bets on boxing matches where Mr. Kleindienst was a manager."

Ted said nothing for a moment, only looked out the window. On the radio, someone hit a comebacker to Whitey Ford. Ford fielded the ball and threw to Moose Skowron at first. Now there were two down in the top of the eighth. At last Ted said, "It *could* have been

Haywood. It wasn't likely, but it could have been. Then . . . did you see the old man back there? The one in the shoeshine chair?"

"Sure, you patted him on the cheeks."

"That's Arthur Girardi. Files lets him hang around because he used to be connected. That's what Files thinks—*used* to be. Now he's just some old fellow who comes in to get his shoes shined at ten and then forgets and comes in to get them shined again at three. Files thinks he's just an old fellow who don't know from nothing, as they say. Girardi lets him think whatever he wants to think. If Files said the moon was green cheese, Girardi wouldn't say boo. Old Gee, he comes in for the air conditioning. And he's still connected."

"Connected to Jimmy Gee."

"To all sorts of guys."

"Mr. Files didn't know the fight was fixed?"

"No, not for sure. I thought he would."

"But old Gee knew. And he knew which one's supposed to take the dive."

"Yes. That was my luck. Hurricane Haywood goes down in the eighth round. Then, next year when the odds are better, the Hurricane gets his payday."

"Would you have bet if Mr. Girardi hadn't been there?"

"No," Ted replied immediately.

"Then what would you have done for money? When you go away?"

Ted looked depressed at those words—*When you go away.* He made as if to put an arm around Bobby's shoulders, then stopped himself.

"There's always someone who knows something," he said.

They were on Asher Avenue now, still in Bridgeport but only a mile or so from the Harwich town line. Knowing what would happen, Bobby reached for Ted's big, nicotine-stained hand.

Ted swivelled his knees toward the door, taking his hands with them. "Better not."

Bobby didn't need to ask why. People put up signs that said WET PAINT DO NOT TOUCH because if you put your hand on something newly painted, the stuff would get on your skin. You could wash it off, or it would wear off by itself in time, but for awhile it would be there.

"Where will you go?"

"I don't know."

"I feel bad," Bobby said. He could feel tears prickling at the corners of his eyes. "If something happens to you, it's my fault. I saw things, the things you told me to look out for, but I didn't say anything. I didn't want you to go. So I told myself you were crazy—not about everything, just about the low men you thought were chasing you—and I didn't say anything. You gave me a job and I muffed it."

Ted's arm rose again. He lowered it and settled for giving Bobby a quick pat on the leg instead. At Yankee Stadium Tony Kubek had just doubled home two runs. The crowd was going wild.

"But I knew," Ted said mildly.

Bobby stared at him. "What? I don't get you."

"I felt them getting closer. That's why my trances have grown so frequent. Yet I lied to myself, just as you did. For the same reasons, too. Do you think I want to leave you now, Bobby? When your mother is so confused and unhappy? In all honesty I don't care so much for her sake, we don't get along, from the first second we laid eyes on each other we didn't get along, but she is your mother, and—"

"What's wrong with her?" Bobby asked. He remembered to keep his voice low, but he took Ted's arm and shook it. "Tell me! You know, I know you do! Is it Mr. Biderman? Is it something about Mr. Biderman?"

Ted looked out the window, brow furrowed, lips drawn down tightly. At last he sighed, pulled out his cigarettes, and lit one. "Bobby," he said, "Mr. Biderman is not a nice man. Your mother knows it, but she also knows that sometimes we have to go along with people who are not nice. Go along to get along, she thinks, and she has done this. She's done things over the last year that she's not proud of, but she has been careful. In some ways she has needed to be as careful as I have, and whether I like her or not, I admire her for that."

"What did she do? What did he make her do?" Something cold

moved in Bobby's chest. "Why did Mr. Biderman take her to Providence?"

"For the real-estate conference."

"Is that all? Is that *all?*"

"I don't know. *She* didn't know. Or perhaps she has covered over what she knows and what she fears with what she hopes. I can't say. Sometimes I can—sometimes I know things very directly and clearly. The first moment I saw you I knew that you wanted a bicycle, that getting one was very important to you, and you meant to earn the money for one this summer if you could. I admired your determination."

"You touched me on purpose, didn't you?"

"Yes indeed. The first time, anyway. I did it to know you a little. But friends don't spy; true friendship is about privacy, too. Besides, when I touch, I pass on a kind of—well, a kind of window. I think you know that. The second time I touched you . . . really touching, holding on, you know what I mean . . . that was a mistake, but not such an awful one; for a little while you knew more than you should, but it wore off, didn't it? If I'd gone on, though . . . touching and touching, the way people do when they're close . . . there'd come a point where things would change. Where it wouldn't wear off." He raised his mostly smoked cigarette and looked at it distastefully. "The way you smoke one too many of these and you're hooked for life."

"Is my mother all right now?" Bobby asked, knowing that Ted couldn't tell him that; Ted's gift, whatever it was, didn't stretch that far.

"I don't know. I—"

Ted suddenly stiffened. He was looking out the window at something up ahead. He smashed his cigarette into the armrest ashtray, doing it hard enough to send sparks scattering across the back of his hand. He didn't seem to feel them. "Christ," he said. "Oh Christ, Bobby, we're in for it."

Bobby leaned across his lap to look out the window, thinking in the back of his mind about what Ted had just been saying—*touching and touching, the way people do when they're close*—even as he peered up Asher Avenue.

Ahead was a three-way intersection, Asher Avenue, Bridgeport Avenue, and the Connecticut Pike all coming together at a place known as Puritan Square. Trolley-tracks gleamed in the afternoon sun; delivery trucks honked impatiently as they waited their turns to dart through the crush. A sweating policeman with a whistle in his mouth and white gloves on his hands was directing traffic. Off to the left was the William Penn Grille, a famous restaurant which was supposed to have the best steaks in Connecticut (Mr. Biderman had taken the whole office staff there after the agency sold the Waverley Estate, and Bobby's mom had come home with about a dozen William Penn Grille books of matches). Its main claim to fame, his mom had once told Bobby, was that the bar was over the Harwich town line, but the restaurant proper was in Bridgeport.

Parked in front, on the very edge of Puritan Square, was a DeSoto automobile of a purple Bobby had never seen before—had never even *suspected.* The color was so bright it hurt his eyes to look at it. It hurt his whole *head.*

Their cars will be like their yellow coats and sharp shoes and the greasy perfumed stuff they use to slick back their hair: loud and vulgar.

The purple car was loaded with swoops and darts of chrome. It had fenderskirts. The hood ornament was huge; Chief DeSoto's head glittered in the hazy light like a fake jewel. The tires were fat whitewalls and the hubcaps were spinners. There was a whip antenna on the back. From its tip there hung a raccoon tail.

"The low men," Bobby whispered. There was really no question. It was a DeSoto, but at the same time it was like no car he had ever seen in his life, something as alien as an asteroid. As they drew closer to the clogged three-way intersection, Bobby saw the upholstery was a metallic dragonfly-green—the color nearly howled in contrast to the car's purple skin. There was white fur around the steering wheel. "Holy crow, it's them!"

"You have to take your mind away," Ted said. He grabbed Bobby by the shoulders (up front the Yankees blared on and on, the driver paying his two fares in the back seat no attention whatsoever, thank God for that much, at least) and shook him once, hard, before letting him go. "You have to take your mind *away,* do you understand?"

He did. George Sanders had built a brick wall behind which to hide his thoughts and plans from the Children. Bobby had used Maury Wills once before, but he didn't think baseball was going to cut it this time. What would?

Bobby could see the Asher Empire's marquee jutting out over the sidewalk, three or four blocks beyond Puritan Square, and suddenly he could hear the sound of Sully-John's Bo-lo Bouncer: whap-whap-whap. *If she's trash,* S-J had said, *I'd love to be the trashman.*

The poster they'd seen that day filled Bobby's mind: Brigitte Bardot (*the French sex-kitten* was what the papers called her) dressed only in a towel and a smile. She looked a little like the woman getting out of the car on one of the calendars back at The Corner Pocket, the one with most of her skirt in her lap and her garters showing. Brigitte Bardot was prettier, though. And she was *real.* She was too old for the likes of Bobby Garfield, of course

(*I'm so young and you're so old,* Paul Anka singing from a thousand transistor radios, *this my darling I've been told*)

but she was still beautiful, and a cat could look at a queen, his mother always said that, too: a cat could look at a queen. Bobby saw her more and more clearly as he settled back against the seat, his eyes taking on that drifty, far-off look Ted's eyes got when he had one of his blank-outs; Bobby saw her shower-damp puff of blond hair, the slope of her breasts into the towel, her long thighs, her painted toenails standing over the words Adults Only, Must Have Driver's License or Birth Certificate. He could smell her soap—something light and flowery. He could smell

(*Nuit en Paris*)

her perfume and he could hear her radio in the next room. It was Freddy Cannon, that bebop summertime avatar of Savin Rock: "She's dancin to the drag, the cha-cha rag-a-mop, she's stompin to the shag, *rocks* the bunny hop . . ."

He was aware—faintly, far away, in another world farther up along the swirls of the spinning top—that the cab in which they were riding had come to a stop right next to the William Penn Grille, right next to that purple bruise of a DeSoto. Bobby could almost hear the car in his head; if it had had a voice it would have screamed *Shoot me, I'm too purple! Shoot me, I'm too purple!* And not far beyond it he could sense *them.* They were in the restaurant, having an early steak. Both of them ate it the same way, bloody-rare. Before they left they might put up a lost-pet poster in the telephone lounge or a hand-printed CAR FOR SALE BY OWNER card: upside-down, of course. They were in there, low men in yellow coats and white shoes drinking martinis between bites of nearly raw steer, and if they turned their minds out this way . . .

Steam was drifting out of the shower. B.B. raised herself on her bare painted toes and opened her towel, turning it into brief wings before letting it fall. And Bobby saw it wasn't Brigitte Bardot at all. It was Carol Gerber. *You'd have to be brave to let people look at you with nothing on but a towel,* she had said, and now she had let even the towel fall away. He was seeing her as she would look eight or ten years from now.

Bobby looked at her, helpless to look away, helpless in love, lost in the smells of her soap and her perfume, the sound of her radio (Freddy Cannon had given way to The Platters—*heavenly shades of night are falling*), the sight of her small painted toenails. His heart spun as a top did, with its lines rising and disappearing into other worlds. Other worlds than this.

The taxi began creeping forward. The four-door purple horror parked next to the restaurant (parked in a loading zone, Bobby saw, but what did *they* care?) began to slide to the rear. The cab jolted to a stop again and the driver cursed mildly as a trolley rushed clang-a-lang through Puritan Square. The low DeSoto was behind them now, but reflections from its chrome filled the cab with erratic dancing minnows of light. And suddenly Bobby felt a savage itching attack the backs of his eyeballs. This was followed by a fall of twisting black threads across his field of vision. He was able to hold onto Carol, but he now seemed to be looking at her through a field of interference.

They sense us . . . or they sense something. Please God, get us out of here. Please get us out.

The cabbie saw a hole in the traffic and squirted through it. A moment later they were rolling up Asher Avenue at a good pace. That itching sensation behind Bobby's eyes began to recede. The black threads across his field of interior vision cleared away, and when they did he saw that the naked girl wasn't Carol at all (not anymore, at least), not even Brigitte Bardot, but only the calendar-girl from The Corner Pocket, stripped mother-naked by Bobby's imagination. The music from her radio was gone. The smells of soap and perfume were gone. The life had gone out of her; she was just a . . . a . . .

"She's just a picture painted on a brick wall," Bobby said. He sat up.

"Say what, kid?" the driver asked, and snapped off the radio. The game was over. Mel Allen was selling cigarettes.

"Nothing," Bobby said.

"Guess youse dozed off, huh? Slow traffic, hot day . . . they'll do it every time, just like Hatlo says. Looks like your pal's still out."

"No," Ted said, straightening. "The doctor is in." He stretched his back and winced when it crackled. "I did doze a little, though." He glanced out the back window, but the William Penn Grille was out of sight now. "The Yankees won, I suppose?"

"Gahdam Injuns, they roont em," the cabbie said, and laughed. "Don't see how youse could sleep with the Yankees playing."

They turned onto Broad Street; two minutes later the cab pulled up in front of 149. Bobby looked at it as if expecting to see a different color paint or perhaps an added wing. He felt like he'd been gone ten years. In a way he supposed he had been—hadn't he seen Carol Gerber all grown up?

I'm going to marry her, Bobby decided as he got out of the cab. Over on Colony Street, Mrs. O'Hara's dog barked on and on, as if denying this and all human aspirations: *roop-roop, roop-roop-roop.*

Ted bent down to the driver's-side window with his wallet in his hand. He plucked out two singles, considered, then added a third. "Keep the change."

"You're a gent," the cabbie said.

"He's a *shooter,*" Bobby corrected, and grinned as the cab pulled away.

"Let's get inside," Ted said. "It's not safe for me to be out here."

They went up the porch steps and Bobby used his key to open the door to the foyer. He kept thinking about that weird itching behind his eyes, and the black threads. The threads had been particularly horrible, as if he'd been on the verge of going blind. "Did they see us, Ted? Or sense us, or whatever they do?"

"You know they did . . . but I don't think they knew how close we were." As they went into the Garfield apartment, Ted took off his sunglasses and tucked them into his shirt pocket. "You must have covered up well. Whooo! Hot in here!"

"What makes you think they didn't know we were close?"

Ted paused in the act of opening a window, giving Bobby a level look back over his shoulder. "If they'd known, that purple car would have been right behind us when we pulled up here."

"It wasn't a car," Bobby said, beginning to open windows himself. It didn't help much; the air that came in, lifting the curtains in listless little flaps, felt almost as hot as the air which had been trapped inside the apartment all day. "I don't know what it was, but it only *looked* like a car. And what I felt of *them*—" Even in the heat, Bobby shivered.

Ted got his fan, crossed to the window by Liz's shelf of knickknacks, and set it on the sill. "They camouflage themselves as best they can, but we still feel them. Even people who don't know what they are often feel them. A little of what's under the camouflage seeps through, and what's underneath is ugly. I hope you never know how ugly."

Bobby hoped so, too. "Where do they come from, Ted?"

"A dark place."

Ted knelt, plugged in his fan, flipped it on. The air it pulled into the room was a little cooler, but not so cool as The Corner Pocket had been, or the Criterion.

"Is it in another world, like in *Ring Around the Sun*? It is, isn't it?"

Ted was still on his knees by the electrical plug. He looked as if he were praying. To Bobby he also looked exhausted—done almost to death. How could he run from the low men? He didn't look as if he could make it as far as Spicer's Variety Store without stumbling.

"Yes," he said at last. "They come from another world. Another where and another when. That's all I can tell you. It's not safe for you to know more."

But Bobby had to ask one other question. "Did you come from one of those other worlds?"

Ted looked at him solemnly. "I came from Teaneck."

Bobby gaped at him for a moment, then began to laugh. Ted, still kneeling by the fan, joined him.

"What did you think of in the cab, Bobby?" Ted asked when they were finally able to stop. "Where did you go when the trouble started?" He paused. "What did you see?"

Bobby thought of Carol at twenty with her toenails painted pink, Carol standing naked with the towel at her feet and steam rising around her. Adults Only. Must Have Driver's License. No Exceptions.

"I can't tell," he said at last. "Because . . . well . . ."

"Because some things are private. I understand." Ted got to his feet. Bobby stepped forward to help him but Ted waved him away. "Perhaps you'd like to go out and play for a little while," he said. "Later on—around six, shall we say?—I'll put on my dark glasses again and we'll go around the block, have a bite of dinner at the Colony Diner."

"But no beans."

The corners of Ted's mouth twitched in the ghost of a smile. "Absolutely no beans, beans *verboten.* At ten o'clock I'll call my friend Len and see how the fight went. Eh?"

"The low men . . . will they be looking for me now, too?"

"I'd never let you step out the door if I thought that," Ted replied, looking surprised. "You're fine, and I'm going to make sure you *stay* fine. Go on now. Play some catch or ring-a-levio or whatever it is you like. I have some things to do. Only be back by six so I don't worry."

"Okay."

Bobby went into his room and dumped the four quarters he'd taken to Bridgeport back into the Bike Fund jar. He looked around his room, seeing things with new eyes: the cowboy bedspread, the picture of his mother on one wall and the signed photo—obtained by saving cereal boxtops—of Clayton Moore in his mask on another, his roller skates (one with a broken strap) in the corner, his desk against the wall. The room looked smaller now—not so much a place to come to as a place to leave. He realized he was growing into his orange library card, and some bitter voice inside cried out against it. Cried no, no, no.

VIII. BOBBY MAKES A CONFESSION. THE GERBER BABY AND THE MALTEX BABY. RIONDA. TED MAKES A CALL. CRY OF THE HUNTERS.

In Commonwealth Park the little kids were playing ticky-ball. Field B was empty; on Field C a few teenagers in orange St. Gabriel's tee-shirts were playing scrub. Carol Gerber was sitting on a bench with her jump-rope in her lap, watching them. She saw Bobby coming and began to smile. Then the smile went away.

"Bobby, what's wrong with you?"

Bobby hadn't been precisely aware that *anything* was wrong with him until Carol said that, but the look of concern on her face brought everything home and undid him. It was the reality of the low men and the fright of the close call they'd had on their way back from Bridgeport; it was his concern over his mother; mostly it was Ted. He knew perfectly well why Ted had shooed him out of the house, and what Ted was doing right now: filling his little suitcases and those carryhandle paper bags. His friend was going away.

Bobby began to cry. He didn't want to go all ushy-gushy in front of a girl, particularly *this* girl, but he couldn't help it.

Carol looked stunned for a moment—scared. Then she got off the bench, came to him, and put her arms around him. "That's all right," she said. "That's all right, Bobby, don't cry, everything's all right."

Almost blinded by tears and crying harder than ever—it was as if there were a violent summer storm going on in his head—Bobby let her lead him into a copse of trees where they would be hidden from the baseball fields and the main paths. She sat down on the grass, still holding him, brushing one hand through the sweaty bristles of his crewcut. For a little while she said nothing at all, and Bobby was incapable of speaking; he could only sob until his throat ached and his eyeballs throbbed in their sockets.

At last the intervals between sobs became longer. He sat up and wiped his face with his arm, horrified and ashamed of what he felt: not just tears but snot and spit as well. He must have covered her with mung.

Carol didn't seem to care. She touched his wet face. Bobby pulled back from her fingers, uttering another sob, and looked down at the grass. His eyesight, freshly washed by his tears, seemed almost preternaturally keen; he could see every blade and dandelion.

"It's all right," she said, but Bobby was still too ashamed to look at her.

They sat quietly for a little while and then Carol said, "Bobby, I'll be your girlfriend, if you want."

"You *are* my girlfriend," Bobby said.

"Then tell me what's wrong."

And Bobby heard himself telling her everything, starting with the day Ted had moved in and how his mother had taken an instant dislike to him. He told her about the first of Ted's blank-outs, about the low men, about the signs of the low men. When he got to that part, Carol touched him on the arm.

"What?" he asked. "You don't believe me?" His throat still had that achy too-full feeling it got after a crying fit, but he was getting better. If she didn't believe him, he wouldn't be mad at her. Wouldn't blame her a bit, in fact. It was just an enormous relief to get it off his chest. "That's okay. I know how crazy it must—"

"I've seen those funny hopscotches all over town," she said. "So has Yvonne and Angie. We talked about them. They have little stars and moons drawn next to them. Sometimes comets, too."

He gaped at her. "Are you kidding?"

"No. Girls always look at hopscotches, I don't know why. Close your mouth before a bug flies in."

He closed his mouth.

Carol nodded, satisfied, then took his hand in hers and laced her fingers through his. Bobby was amazed at what a perfect fit all those fingers made. "Now tell me the rest."

He did, finishing with the amazing day he'd just put in: the movie, the trip to The Corner Pocket, how Alanna had recognized his father in him, the close call on the way home. He tried to explain how the purple DeSoto hadn't seemed like a real car at all, that it only looked like a car. The closest he could come was to say it had felt *alive* somehow, like an evil version of the ostrich Dr. Dolittle sometimes rode in that series of talking-animal books they'd all gone crazy for in the second grade. The only thing Bobby didn't confess was where he'd hidden his thoughts when the cab passed the William Penn Grille and the backs of his eyes began to itch.

He struggled, then blurted the worst as a coda: he was afraid that his mother going to Providence with Mr. Biderman and those other men had been a mistake. A *bad* mistake.

"Do you think Mr. Biderman's sweet on her?" Carol asked. By then they were walking back to the bench where she had left her jump-rope. Bobby picked it up and handed it to her. They began walking out of the park and toward Broad Street.

"Yeah, maybe," Bobby said glumly. "Or at least . . ." And here was part of what he was afraid of, although it had no name or real shape; it was like something ominous covered with a piece of canvas. "At least *she* thinks he is."

"Is he going to ask her to marry him? If he did he'd be your stepdad."

"God!" Bobby hadn't considered the idea of having Don Biderman as a stepfather, and he wished with all his might that Carol hadn't brought such a thing up. It was an awful thought.

"If she loves him you just better get used to the idea." Carol spoke in an older-woman, worldly-wise fashion that Bobby could have done without; he guessed she had already spent too much time this summer watching the oh John, oh Marsha shows on TV with her mom. And in a weird way he wouldn't have cared if his mom loved Mr. Biderman and that was all. It would be wretched, certainly, because Mr. Biderman was a creep, but it would have been understandable. More was going on, though. His mother's miserliness about money—her *cheapskatiness*—was a part of it, and so was whatever had made her start smoking again and caused her to cry in the night sometimes. The difference between his mother's Randall Garfield, the untrustworthy man who left the unpaid bills, and Alanna's Randy Garfield, the nice guy who liked the jukebox turned up loud . . . even that might be a part of it. (Had there really been unpaid bills? Had there really been a lapsed insurance policy? Why would his mother lie about such things?) This was stuff he couldn't talk about to Carol. It wasn't reticence; it was that he didn't know *how.*

They started up the hill. Bobby took one end of her rope and they walked side by side, dragging it between them on the sidewalk. Suddenly Bobby stopped and pointed. "Look."

There was a yellow length of kite tail hanging from one of the electrical wires crossing the street farther up. It dangled in a curve that looked sort of like a question mark.

"Yeah, I see it," Carol said, sounding subdued. They began to walk again. "He should go today, Bobby."

"He can't. The fight's tonight. If Albini wins Ted's got to get his dough at the billiard parlor tomorrow night. I think he needs it pretty bad."

"Sure he does," Carol said. "You only have to look at his clothes to see he's almost broke. What he bet was probably the last money he had."

His clothes—that's something only a girl would notice, Bobby thought, and opened his mouth to tell her so. Before he could, someone behind them said, "Oh looka this. It's the Gerber Baby and the Maltex Baby. Howya doin, babies?"

They looked around. Biking slowly up the hill toward them were three St. Gabe's boys in orange shirts. Piled in their bike-baskets was an assortment of baseball gear. One of the boys, a pimply galoot with a silver cross dangling from his neck on a chain, had a baseball bat in a homemade sling on his back. *Thinks he's Robin Hood,* Bobby thought, but he was scared. They were big boys, high-school boys, *parochial school* boys, and if they decided they wanted to put him in the hospital, then to the hospital he would go. *Low boys in orange shirts,* he thought.

"Hi, Willie," Carol said to one of them—not the galoot with the bat slung on his back. She sounded calm, even cheery, but Bobby could hear fright fluttering underneath like a bird's wing. "I watched you play. You made a good catch."

The one she spoke to had an ugly, half-formed face below a mass of combed-back auburn hair and above a man's body. The Huffy bike beneath him was ridiculously small. Bobby thought he looked like a troll in a fairy-tale. "What's it to you, Gerber Baby?" he asked.

The three St. Gabe's boys pulled up even with them. Then two of them—the one with the dangling cross and the one Carol had called Willie—came a little farther, standing around the forks of their bikes now, walking them. With mounting dismay Bobby realized he and Carol had been surrounded. He could smell a mixture of sweat and Vitalis coming from the boys in the orange shirts.

"Who are you, Maltex Baby?" the third St. Gabe's boy asked Bobby. He leaned over the handlebars of his bike for a better look. "Are you Garfield? You are, ain'tcha? Billy Donahue's still lookin for you from that time last winter. He wants to knock your teeth out. Maybe I ought to knock one or two of em out right here, give im a head start."

Bobby felt a wretched crawling sensation begin in his stomach—something like snakes in a basket. *I won't cry again,* he told himself. *Whatever happens I won't cry again even if they send me to the hospital. And I'll try to protect her.*

Protect her from big kids like this? It was a joke.

"Why are you being so mean, Willie?" Carol asked. She spoke solely to the boy with the auburn hair. "You're not mean when you're by yourself. Why do you have to be mean now?"

Willie flushed. That, coupled with his dark red hair—much darker than Bobby's—made him look on fire from the neck up. Bobby guessed he didn't like his friends knowing he could act like a human being when they weren't around.

"Shut up, Gerber Baby!" he snarled. "Why don't you just shut up and kiss your boyfriend while he's still got all his teeth?"

The third boy was wearing a motorcycle belt cinched on the side and ancient Snap-Jack shoes covered with dirt from the baseball field. He was behind Carol. Now he moved in closer, still walking his bike, and grabbed her ponytail with both hands. He pulled it.

"*Ow!*" Carol almost screamed. She sounded surprised as well as hurt. She pulled away so hard that she almost fell down. Bobby caught her and Willie—who could be nice when he wasn't with his pals, according to Carol—laughed.

"Why'd you do that?" Bobby yelled at the boy in the motorcycle belt, and as the words came out of his mouth it was as if he had heard them a thousand times before. All of this was like a ritual, the stuff that got said before the *real* yanks and pushes began and the fists began to fly. He thought of *Lord of the Flies* again—Ralph running from Jack and the others. At least on Golding's island there had been jungle. He and Carol had nowhere to run.

He says "Because I felt like it." That's what comes next.

But before the boy with the side-cinched belt could say it, Robin Hood with the homemade bat-sling on his back said it for him. "Because he felt like it. Whatcha gonna do about it, Maltex Baby?" He suddenly flicked out one hand, snake-quick, and slapped Bobby across the face. Willie laughed again.

Carol started toward him. "Willie, please don't—"

Robin Hood reached out, grabbed the front of Carol's shirt, and squeezed. "Got any titties yet? Nah, not much. You ain't nothing but a Gerber Baby." He pushed her. Bobby, his head still ringing from the slap, caught her and for the second time kept her from falling down.

"Let's beat this queer up," the kid in the motorcycle belt said. "I hate his face."

They moved in, the wheels of their bikes squeaking solemnly. Then Willie let his drop on its side like a dead pony and reached for Bobby. Bobby raised his fists in a feeble imitation of Floyd Patterson.

"Say, boys, what's going on?" someone asked from behind them.

Willie had drawn one of his own fists back. Still holding it cocked, he looked over his shoulder. So did Robin Hood and the boy with the motorcycle belt. Parked at the curb was an old blue Studebaker with rusty rocker panels and a magnetic Jesus on the dashboard. Standing in front of it, looking extremely busty in the chest and extremely wide in the hip, was Anita Gerber's friend Rionda. Summer clothes were never going to be her friends (even at eleven Bobby understood this), but at that moment she looked like a goddess in pedal pushers.

"Rionda!" Carol yelled—not crying, but almost. She pushed past Willie and the boy in the motorcycle belt. Neither made any effort to stop her. All three of the St. Gabe's boys were staring at Rionda. Bobby found himself looking at Willie's cocked fist. Sometimes Bobby woke up in the morning with his peter just as hard as a rock, standing straight up like a moon rocket or something. As he went into the bathroom to pee, it would soften and wilt. Willie's cocked arm was wilting like that now, the fist at the end of it relaxing back into fingers, and the comparison made Bobby want to smile. He resisted the urge. If they saw him smiling now, they could do nothing. Later, however . . . on another day . . .

Rionda put her arms around Carol and hugged the girl to her large bosom. She surveyed the boys in the orange shirts and *she* was smiling. Smiling and making no effort to hide it.

"Willie Shearman, isn't it?"

The formerly cocked-back arm dropped to Willie's side. Muttering, he bent to pick up his bike.

"Richie O'Meara?"

The boy in the motorcycle belt looked at the toes of his dusty Snap-Jacks and also muttered something. His cheeks burned with color.

"*One* of the O'Meara boys, anyway, there's so damned many of you now I can't keep track." Her eyes shifted to Robin Hood. "And who are you, big boy? Are you a Dedham? You look a little bit like a Dedham."

Robin Hood looked at his hands. He wore a class ring on one of his fingers and now he began to twist it.

Rionda still had an arm around Carol's shoulders. Carol had one of her own arms as far around Rionda's waist as she could manage. She walked with Rionda, not looking at the boys, as Rionda stepped up from the street onto the little strip of grass between the curb and the sidewalk. She was still looking at Robin Hood. "You better answer me when I talk to you, sonny. Won't be hard to find your mother if I want to try. All I have to do is ask Father Fitzgerald."

"Harry Doolin, that's me," the boy said at last. He was twirling his class ring faster than ever.

"Well, but I was close, wasn't I?" Rionda asked pleasantly, taking another two or three steps forward. They put her on the sidewalk. Carol, afraid to be so close to the boys, tried to hold her back, but Rionda would have none of it. "Dedhams and Doolins, all married together. Right back to County Cork, tra-la-tra-lee."

Not Robin Hood but a kid named Harry Doolin with a stupid homemade bat-sling strapped to his back. Not Marlon Brando from *The Wild One* but a kid named Richie O'Meara, who wouldn't have a Harley to go with his motorcycle belt for another five years . . . if ever. And Willie Shearman, who didn't dare to be nice to a girl when he was with his friends. All it took to shrink them back to their proper size was one overweight woman in pedal pushers and a shell top, who had ridden to the rescue not on a white stallion but in a 1954 Studebaker. The thought should have comforted Bobby but it didn't. He found himself thinking of what William Golding had said, that the boys on the island were rescued by the crew of a battle-cruiser and good for them . . . but who would rescue the crew?

That was stupid, no one ever looked less in need of rescuing than Rionda Hewson did at that moment, but the words still haunted Bobby. What if there *were* no grownups? Suppose the whole idea of grownups was an illusion? What if their money was really just play-ground marbles, their business deals no more than baseball-card trades, their wars only games of guns in the park? What if they were all still snotty-nosed kids inside their suits and dresses? Christ, that couldn't be, could it? It was too horrible to think about.

Rionda was still looking at the St. Gabe's boys with her hard and rather dangerous smile. "You three fellas wouldn't've been picking on kids younger and smaller than yourselves, would you? One of them a girl like your own little sisters?"

They were silent, not even muttering now. They only shuffled their feet.

"I'm sure you weren't, because that would be a cowardly thing to do, now wouldn't it?"

Again she gave them a chance to reply and plenty of time to hear their own silence.

"Willie? Richie? Harry? You weren't picking on them, were you?"

"Course not," Harry said. Bobby thought that if he spun that ring of his much faster, his finger would probably catch fire.

"If I thought a thing like that," Rionda said, still smiling her dangerous smile, "I'd have to go talk to Father Fitzgerald, wouldn't I? And the Father, he'd probably feel he had to talk to your folks, and *your* fathers'd probably feel obliged to warm your asses for you . . . and you'd deserve it, boys, wouldn't you? For picking on the weak and small."

Continued silence from the three boys, all now astride their ridiculously undersized bikes again.

"Did they pick on you, Bobby?" Rionda asked.

"No," Bobby said at once.

Rionda put a finger under Carol's chin and turned her face up. "Did they pick on *you,* lovey?"

"No, Rionda."

Rionda smiled down at her, and although there were tears standing in Carol's eyes, she smiled back.

"Well, boys, I guess you're off the hook," Rionda said. "They say you haven't done nothing that'll cause you a single extra uncomfy minute in the confessional. I'd say that you owe them a vote of thanks, don't you?"

Mutter-mutter-mutter from the St. Gabe's boys. *Please let it go at that,* Bobby pleaded silently. *Don't make them actually thank us. Don't rub their noses in it.*

Perhaps Rionda heard his thought (Bobby now had good reason to believe such things were possible). "Well," she said, "maybe we can skip that part. Get along home, boys. And Harry, when you see Moira Dedham, tell her Rionda says she still goes to the Bingo over in Bridgeport every week, if she ever wants a ride."

"I will, sure," Harry said. He mounted his bike and rode away up the hill, eyes still on the sidewalk. Had there been pedestrians coming the other way, he would likely have run them over. His two friends followed him, standing on their pedals to catch up.

Rionda watched them go, her smile slowly fading. "Shanty Irish," she said at last, "just trouble waiting to happen. Bah, good riddance to em. Carol, are you really all right?"

Carol said she really was.

"Bobby?"

"Sure, I'm fine." It was taking him all the discipline he could manage not to start shaking right in front of her like a bowl of cranberry jelly, but if Carol could keep from falling apart, he guessed he could.

"Get in the car," Rionda said to Carol. "I'll give you a lift up to your house. You move along yourself, Bobby—scoot across the street and go inside. Those boys will have forgotten all about you and my Carol-girl by tomorrow, but tonight it might be smart for both of you to stay inside."

"Okay," Bobby said, knowing they wouldn't have forgotten by tomorrow, nor by the end of the week, nor by the end of the summer. He and Carol were going to have to watch out for Harry and his friends for a long time. "Bye, Carol."

"Bye."

Bobby trotted across Broad Street. On the other side he stood watching Rionda's old car go up to the apartment house where the Gerbers lived. When Carol got out she looked back down the hill and waved. Bobby waved back, then walked up the porch steps of 149 and went inside.

Ted was sitting in the living room, smoking a cigarette and reading *Life* magazine. Anita Ekberg was on the cover. Bobby had no doubt that Ted's suitcases and the paper bags were packed, but there was no sign of them; he must have left them upstairs in his room.

Bobby was glad. He didn't want to look at them. It was bad enough just knowing they were there.

"What did you do?" Ted asked.

"Not much," Bobby said. "I think I'll lie down on my bed and read until supper."

He went into his room. Stacked on the floor by his bed were three books from the adult section of the Harwich Public Library—*Cosmic Engineers,* by Clifford D. Simak; *The Roman Hat Mystery,* by Ellery Queen; and *The Inheritors,* by William Golding. Bobby chose *The Inheritors* and lay down with his head at the foot of his bed and his stocking feet on his pillow. There were cave people on the book's cover, but they were drawn in a way that was almost abstract—you'd never see cave people like that on the cover of a kids' book. Having an adult library card was very neat . . . but somehow not as neat as it had seemed at first.

Hawaiian Eye was on at nine o'clock, and Bobby ordinarily would have been mesmerized (his mother claimed that shows like *Hawaiian Eye* and *The Untouchables* were too violent for children and ordinarily would not let him watch them), but tonight his mind kept wandering from the story. Less than sixty miles from here Eddie Albini and Hurricane Haywood would be mixing it up; the Gillette Blue Blades Girl, dressed in a blue bathing suit and blue high heels, would be parading around the ring before the start of every round and holding up a sign with a blue number on it. 1 . . . 2 . . . 3 . . . 4 . . .

By nine-thirty Bobby couldn't have picked out the private eye on the TV show, let alone guessed who had murdered the blond socialite. *Hurricane Haywood goes down in the eighth round,* Ted had told him; Old Gee knew it. But what if something went wrong? He didn't want Ted to go, but if he had to, Bobby couldn't bear the thought of him going with an empty wallet. Surely that couldn't happen, though . . . or could it? Bobby had seen a TV show where a fighter was supposed to take a dive and then changed his mind. What if that happened tonight? Taking a dive was bad, it was cheating—no shit, Sherlock, what was your first clue?—but if Hurricane

Haywood *didn't* cheat, Ted would be in a lot of trouble; "hurtin for certain" was how Sully-John would have put it.

Nine-thirty according to the sunburst clock on the living-room wall. If Bobby's math was right, the crucial eighth round was now underway.

"How do you like *The Inheritors?*"

Bobby was so deep into his own thoughts that Ted's voice made him jump. On TV, Keenan Wynn was standing in front of a bulldozer and saying he'd walk a mile for a Camel.

"It's a lot harder than *Lord of the Flies,*" he said. "It seems like there are these two little families of cave people wandering around, and one family is smarter. But the other family, the dumb family, they're the heroes. I almost gave up, but now it's getting more interesting. I guess I'll stick with it."

"The family you meet first, the one with the little girl, they're Neanderthals. The second family—only that one's really a tribe, Golding and his tribes—are Cro-Magnons. The Cro-Magnons are the inheritors. What happens between the two groups satisfies the definition of tragedy: events tending toward an unhappy outcome which cannot be avoided."

Ted went on, talking about plays by Shakespeare and poems by Poe and novels by a guy named Theodore Dreiser. Ordinarily Bobby would have been interested, but tonight his mind kept going to Madison Square Garden. He could see the ring, lit as savagely as the few working pool-tables in The Corner Pocket had been. He could hear the crowd screaming as Haywood poured it on, smacking the surprised Eddie Albini with lefts and rights. Haywood wasn't going to tank the fight; like the boxer in the TV show, he was going to show the other guy a serious world of hurt instead. Bobby could smell sweat and hear the heavy biff and baff of gloves on flesh. Eddie Albini's eyes came up double zeros . . . his knees buckled . . . the crowd was on its feet, screaming . . .

"—the idea of fate as a force which can't be escaped seems to start with the Greeks. There was a playwright named Euripides who—"

"Call," Bobby said, and although he'd never had a cigarette in his life (by 1964 he would be smoking over a carton a week), his voice sounded as harsh as Ted's did late at night, after a day's worth of Chesterfields.

"Beg your pardon, Bobby?"

"Call Mr. Files and see about the fight." Bobby looked at the sunburst clock. Nine-forty-nine. "If it only went eight, it'll be over now."

"I agree that the fight is over, but if I call Files so soon he may suspect I knew something," Ted said. "Not from the radio, either—this one isn't on the radio, as we both know. It's better to wait. Safer. Let him believe I am a man of inspired hunches. I'll call at ten, as if I expected the result to be a decision instead of a knockout. And in the meantime, Bobby, don't worry. I tell you it's a stroll on the boardwalk."

Bobby gave up trying to follow *Hawaiian Eye* at all; he just sat on the couch and listened to the actors quack. A man shouted at a fat Hawaiian cop. A woman in a white bathing suit ran into the surf. One car chased another while drums throbbed on the soundtrack. The hands on the sunburst clock crawled, struggling toward the ten and the twelve like climbers negotiating the last few hundred feet of Mount Everest. The man who'd murdered the socialite was killed himself as he ran around in a pineapple field and *Hawaiian Eye* finally ended.

Bobby didn't wait for the previews of next week's show; he snapped off the TV and said, "Call, okay? *Please* call."

"In a moment," Ted said. "I think I went one rootbeer over my limit. My holding-tanks seem to have shrunk with age."

He shuffled into the bathroom. There was an interminable pause, and then the sound of pee splashing into the bowl. "Aaah!" Ted said. There was considerable satisfaction in his voice.

Bobby could no longer sit. He got up and began pacing around the living room. He was sure that Tommy "Hurricane" Haywood was right now being photographed in his corner at The Garden, bruised but beaming as the flashbulbs splashed white light over his face. The Gillette Blue Blades Girl would be there with him, her arm around his shoulders, his hand around her waist as Eddie Albini slumped forgotten in his own corner, dazed eyes puffed almost shut, still not completely conscious from the pounding he had taken.

By the time Ted returned, Bobby was in despair. He *knew* that Albini had lost the fight and his friend had lost his five hundred dollars. Would Ted stay when he found out he was broke? He might . . . but if he did and the low men came . . .

Bobby watched, fists clenching and unclenching, as Ted picked up the telephone and dialed.

"Relax, Bobby," Ted told him. "It's going to be okay."

But Bobby couldn't relax. His guts felt full of wires. Ted held the phone to his ear without saying anything for what seemed like forever.

"Why don't they *answer?*" Bobby whispered fiercely.

"It's only rung twice, Bobby. Why don't you—hello? This is Mr. Brautigan calling. Ted Brautigan? Yes, ma'am, from this afternoon." Incredibly, Ted tipped Bobby a wink. How could he be so cool? Bobby didn't think he himself would have been capable of holding the phone up to his ear if he'd been in Ted's position, let alone winking. "Yes, ma'am, he is." Ted turned to Bobby and said, without covering the mouthpiece of the phone, "Alanna wants to know how is your girlfriend."

Bobby tried to speak and could only wheeze.

"Bobby says she's fine," Ted told Alanna, "pretty as a summer day. May I speak to Len? Yes, I can wait. But please tell me about the fight." There was a pause which seemed to go on forever. Ted was expressionless now. And this time when he turned to Bobby he covered the mouthpiece. "She says Albini got knocked around pretty good in the first five, held his own in six and seven, then threw a right hook out of nowhere and put Haywood on the canvas in the eighth. Lights out for the Hurricane. What a surprise, eh?"

"Yes," Bobby said. His lips felt numb. It was true, all of it. By this time Friday night Ted would be gone. With two thousand rocks in your pocket you could do a lot of running from a lot of low men; with two thousand rocks in your pocket you could ride the Big Gray Dog from sea to shining sea.

Bobby went into the bathroom and squirted Ipana on his toothbrush. His terror that Ted had bet on the wrong fighter was gone, but the sadness of approaching loss was still there, and still growing.

He never would have guessed that something that hadn't even happened could hurt so much. *A week from now I won't remember what was so neat about him. A year from now I'll hardly remember him at all.*

Was that true? God, was that true?

No, Bobby thought. *No way. I won't let it be.*

In the other room Ted was conversing with Len Files. It seemed to be a friendly enough palaver, going just as Ted had expected it would . . . and yes, here was Ted saying he'd just played a hunch, a good strong one, the kind you had to bet if you wanted to think of yourself as a sport. Sure, nine-thirty tomorrow night would be fine for the payout, assuming his friend's mother was back by eight; if she was a little late, Len would see him around ten or ten-thirty. Did that suit? More laughter from Ted, so it seemed that it suited fat Lennie Files right down to the ground.

Bobby put his toothbrush back in the glass on the shelf below the mirror, then reached into his pants pocket. There was something in there his fingers didn't recognize, not a part of the usual pocket-litter. He pulled out the keyring with the green fob, his special souvenir of a part of Bridgeport his mother knew nothing about. The part that was down there. THE CORNER POCKET BILLIARDS, POOL, AUTO. GAMES. KENMORE 8-2127.

He probably should have hidden it already (or gotten rid of it entirely), and suddenly an idea came to him. Nothing could have really cheered Bobby Garfield up that night, but this at least came close: he would give the keyring to Carol Gerber, after cautioning her never to tell his mom where she'd gotten it. He knew that Carol had at least two keys she could put on it—her apartment key and the key to the diary Rionda had given her for her birthday. (Carol was three months older than Bobby, but she never lorded it over him on this account.) Giving her the keyring would be a little like asking her to go steady. He wouldn't have to get all gushy and embarrass himself by saying so, either; Carol would know. It was part of what made her cool.

Bobby laid the keyring on the shelf, next to the toothglass, then went into his bedroom to put on his pj's. When he came out, Ted was sitting on the couch, smoking a cigarette and looking at him.

"Bobby, are you all right?"

"I guess so. I guess I have to be, don't I?"

Ted nodded. "I guess we both have to be."

"Will I ever see you again?" Bobby asked, pleading in his mind for Ted not to sound like the Lone Ranger, not to start talking any of that corny *we'll meet again pard* stuff . . . because it wasn't *stuff,* that word was too kind. Shit was what it was. He didn't think Ted had ever lied to him, and he didn't want him to start now that they were near the end.

"I don't know." Ted studied the coal of his cigarette, and when he looked up, Bobby saw that his eyes were swimming with tears. "I don't think so."

Those tears undid Bobby. He ran across the room, wanting to hug Ted, *needing* to hug him. He stopped when Ted lifted his arms and crossed them over the chest of his baggy old man's shirt, his expression a kind of horrified surprise.

Bobby stood where he was, his arms still held out to hug. Slowly he lowered them. No hugging, no touching. It was the rule, but the rule was mean. The rule was wrong.

"Will you write?" he asked.

"I will send you postcards," Ted replied after a moment's thought. "Not directly to you, though—that might be dangerous for both of us. What shall I do? Any ideas?"

"Send them to Carol," Bobby said. He didn't even stop to think.

"When did you tell her about the low men, Bobby?" There was no reproach in Ted's voice. Why would there be? He was going, wasn't he? For all the difference it made, the guy who did the story on the shopping-cart thief could write it up for the paper: CRAZY OLD MAN RUNS FROM INVADING ALIENS. People would read it to each other over their coffee and breakfast cereal and laugh. What had Ted called it that day? Galumphing small-town humor, hadn't that been it? But if it was so funny, why did it hurt? Why did it hurt so much?

"Today," he said in a small voice. "I saw her in the park and everything just kind of . . . came out."

"That can happen," Ted said gravely. "I know it well; sometimes the dam just bursts. And perhaps it's for the best. You'll tell her I may want to get in touch with you through her?"

"Yeah."

Ted tapped a finger against his lips, thinking. Then he nodded. "At the top, the cards I send will say *Dear C.* instead of *Dear Carol.* At the bottom I'll sign *A Friend.* That way you'll both know who writes. Okay?"

"Yeah," Bobby said. "Cool." It wasn't cool, none of this was cool, but it would do.

He suddenly lifted his hand, kissed the fingers, and blew across them. Ted, sitting on the couch, smiled, caught the kiss, and put it on his lined cheek. "You better go to bed now, Bobby. It's been a big day and it's late."

Bobby went to bed.

At first he thought it was the same dream as before—Biderman, Cushman, and Dean chasing his mom through the jungle of William Golding's island. Then Bobby realized the trees and vines were part of the wallpaper, and that the path under his mother's flying feet was brown carpet. Not a jungle but a hotel corridor. This was his mind's version of the Warwick Hotel.

Mr. Biderman and the other two nimrods were still chasing her, though. And now so were the boys from St. Gabe's—Willie and Richie and Harry Doolin. All of them were wearing those streaks of red and white paint on their faces. And all of them were wearing bright yellow doublets upon which was drawn a brilliant red eye:

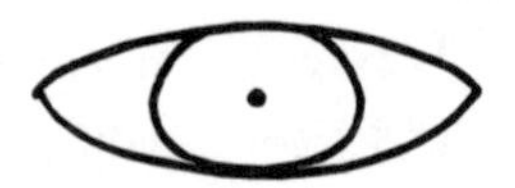

Other than the doublets they were naked. Their privates flopped and bobbed in bushy nests of pubic hair. All save Harry Doolin brandished spears; he had his baseball bat. It had been sharpened to a point on both ends.

"Kill the bitch!" Cushman yelled.

"Drink her blood!" Don Biderman cried, and threw his spear at Liz Garfield just as she darted around a corner. The spear stuck, quivering, into one of the jungle-painted walls.

"Stick it up her dirty cunt!" cried Willie—Willie who could be nice when he wasn't with his friends. The red eye on his chest stared. Below it, his penis also seemed to stare.

Run, Mom! Bobby tried to scream, but no words came out. He had no mouth, no body. He was here and yet he wasn't. He flew beside his mother like her own shadow. He heard her gasping for breath, saw her trembling, terrified mouth and her torn stockings. Her fancy dress was also torn. One of her breasts was scratched and bleeding. One of her eyes was almost closed. She looked as if she had gone a few rounds with Eddie Albini or Hurricane Haywood . . . maybe both at the same time.

"Gonna split you open!" Richie hollered.

"Eat you alive!" agreed Curtis Dean (and at top volume). "Drink your blood, strew your guts!"

His mom looked back at them and her feet (she had lost her shoes somewhere) stuttered against each other. *Don't do that, Mom,* Bobby moaned. *For cripe's sake don't do that.*

As if she had heard him, Liz faced forward again and tried to run faster. She passed a poster on the wall:

PLEASE HELP US FIND OUR PET PIG?
LIZ is our MASCOT!
LIZ IS 34 YRS. OLD!
She is a BAD-TEMPERED SOW but WE LOVE HER!
Will do what you want if you say "I PROMISE"
(OR)
"THERE'S MONEY IN IT"!
CALL HOusitonic 5-8337
(OR)
BRING to THE WILLIAM PENN GRILLE!
Ask for THE LOW MEN IN THE YELLOW COATS!
Motto: "WE EAT IT **RARE!**"

His mom saw the poster, too, and this time when her ankles banged together she *did* fall.

Get up, Mom! Bobby screamed, but she didn't—perhaps couldn't. She crawled along the brown carpet instead, looking over her shoulder as she went, her hair hanging across her cheeks and forehead in sweaty clumps. The back of her dress had been torn away, and Bobby could see her bare bum—her underpants were gone. Worse, the backs of her thighs were splashed with blood. What had they done to her? Dear God, what had they done to his mother?

Don Biderman came around the corner *ahead* of her—he had found a shortcut and cut her off. The others were right behind him. Now Mr. Biderman's prick was standing straight up the way Bobby's sometimes did in the morning before he got out of bed and went to the bathroom. Only Mr. Biderman's prick was *huge,* it looked like a kraken, a triffid, a *monstah,* and Bobby thought he understood the blood on his mother's legs. He didn't want to but he thought he did.

Leave her alone! he tried to scream at Mr. Biderman. *Leave her alone, haven't you done enough?*

The scarlet eye on Mr. Biderman's yellow doublet suddenly opened wider . . . and slithered to one side. Bobby was invisible, his body one world farther down the spinning top from this one . . . but the red eye saw him. The red eye saw *everything.*

"Kill the pig, drink her blood," Mr. Biderman said in a thick, almost unrecognizable voice, and started forward.

"Kill the pig, drink her blood," Bill Cushman and Curtis Dean chimed in.

"Kill the pig, strew her guts, eat her flesh," chanted Willie and Richie, falling in behind the nimrods. Like those of the men, their pricks had turned into spears.

"Eat her, drink her, strew her, *screw* her," Harry chimed in.

Get up, Mom! Run! Don't let them!

She tried. But even as she struggled from her knees to her feet, Biderman leaped at her. The others followed, closing in, and as their hands began to tear the tatters of her clothes from her body Bobby thought: *I want to get out of here, I want to go back down the top to my own world, make it stop and spin it the other way so I can go back down to my own room in my own world . . .*

Except it wasn't a top, and even as the images of the dream began to break up and go dark, Bobby knew it. It wasn't a top but a tower, a still spindle upon which all of existence moved and spun. Then it was gone and for a little while there was a merciful nothingness. When he opened his eyes, his bedroom was full of sunshine—summer sunshine on a Thursday morning in the last June of the Eisenhower Presidency.

IX. UGLY THURSDAY.

One thing you could say about Ted Brautigan: he knew how to cook. The breakfast he slid in front of Bobby—lightly scrambled eggs, toast, crisp bacon—was a lot better than anything his mother ever made for breakfast (her specialty was huge, tasteless pancakes which the two of them drowned in Aunt Jemima's syrup), and as good as anything you could get at the Colony Diner or the Harwich. The only problem was that Bobby didn't feel like eating. He couldn't remember the details of his dream, but he knew it had been a nightmare, and that he must have cried at some point while it was going on—when he woke up, his pillow had been damp. Yet the dream wasn't the only reason he felt flat and depressed this morning; dreams, after all, weren't real. Ted's going away would be real. And would be forever.

"Are you leaving right from The Corner Pocket?" Bobby asked as Ted sat down across from him with his own plate of eggs and bacon. "You are, aren't you?"

"Yes, that will be safest." He began to eat, but slowly and with no apparent enjoyment. So he was feeling bad, too. Bobby was glad. "I'll say to your mother that my brother in Illinois is ill. That's all she needs to know."

"Are you going to take the Big Gray Dog?"

Ted smiled briefly. "Probably the train. I'm quite the wealthy man, remember."

"Which train?"

"It's better if you don't know the details, Bobby. What you don't know you can't tell. Or be made to tell."

Bobby considered this briefly, then asked, "You'll remember the postcards?"

Ted picked up a piece of bacon, then put it down again. "Postcards, plenty of postcards. I promise. Now don't let's talk about it anymore."

"What should we talk about, then?"

Ted thought about it, then smiled. His smile was sweet and open; when he smiled, Bobby could see what he must have looked like when he was twenty, and strong.

"Books, of course," Ted said. "We'll talk about books."

It was going to be a crushingly hot day, that was clear by nine o'clock. Bobby helped with the dishes, drying and putting away, and then they sat in the living room, where Ted's fan did its best to circulate the already tired air, and they talked about books . . . or rather *Ted* talked about books. And this morning, without the distraction of the Albini–Haywood fight, Bobby listened hungrily. He didn't understand all of what Ted was saying, but he understood enough to realize that books made their own world, and that the Harwich Public Library wasn't it. The library was nothing but the doorway to that world.

Ted talked of William Golding and what he called "dystopian fantasy," went on to H. G. Wells's *The Time Machine,* suggesting a link between the Morlocks and the Eloi and Jack and Ralph on Golding's island; he talked about what he called "literature's only excuses," which he said were exploring the questions of innocence and experience, good and evil. Near the end of this impromptu lecture he mentioned a novel called *The Exorcist,* which dealt with both these questions ("in the popular context"), and then stopped abruptly. He shook his head as if to clear it.

"What's wrong?" Bobby took a sip of his rootbeer. He still didn't like it much but it was the only soft drink in the fridge. Besides, it was cold.

"What am I thinking?" Ted passed a hand over his brow, as if he'd suddenly developed a headache. "That one hasn't been written yet."

"What do you mean?"

"Nothing. I'm rambling. Why don't you go out for awhile? Stretch your legs? I might lie down for a bit. I didn't sleep very well last night."

"Okay." Bobby guessed a little fresh air—even if it was *hot* fresh air—might do him good. And while it was interesting to listen to Ted talk, he had started to feel as if the apartment walls were closing in on him. It was knowing Ted was going, Bobby supposed. Now there was a sad little rhyme for you: knowing he was going.

For a moment, as he went back into his room to get his baseball glove, the keyring from The Corner Pocket crossed his mind—he was going to give it to Carol so she'd know they were going steady. Then he remembered Harry Doolin, Richie O'Meara, and Willie Shearman. They were out there someplace, sure they were, and if they caught him by himself they'd probably beat the crap out of him. For the first time in two or three days, Bobby found himself wishing for Sully. Sully was a little kid like him, but he was tough. Doolin and his friends might beat him up, but Sully-John would make them pay for the privilege. S-J was at camp, though, and that was that.

Bobby never considered staying in—he couldn't hide all summer from the likes of Willie Shearman, that would be buggy—but as he went outside he reminded himself that he had to be careful, had to be on the lookout for them. As long as he saw them coming, there would be no problem.

With the St. Gabe's boys on his mind, Bobby left 149 with no further thought of the keyfob, his special souvenir of down there. It lay on the bathroom shelf next to the toothglass, right where he had left it the night before.

*   *   *

He tramped all over Harwich, it seemed—from Broad Street to Commonwealth Park (no St. Gabe's boys on Field C today; the American Legion team was there, taking batting practice and shagging flies in the hot sun), from the park to the town square, from the town square to the railway station. As he stood in the little newsstand kiosk beneath the railway overpass, looking at paperbacks (Mr. Burton, who ran the place, would let you look for awhile as long as you didn't handle what he called "the moichandise"), the town whistle went off, startling them both.

"Mothera God, what's up widdat?" Mr. Burton asked indignantly. He had spilled packs of gum all over the floor and now stooped to pick them up, his gray change-apron hanging down. "It ain't but quarter past eleven!"

"It's early, all right," Bobby agreed, and left the newsstand soon after. Browsing had lost its charms for him. He walked out to River Avenue, stopping at the Tip-Top Bakery to buy half a loaf of day-old bread (two cents) and to ask Georgie Sullivan how S-J was.

"He's fine," S-J's oldest brother said. "We got a postcard on Tuesday says he misses the fambly and wantsa come home. We get one Wednesday says he's learning how to dive. The one this morning says he's having the time of his life, he wantsa stay forever." He laughed, a big Irish boy of twenty with big Irish arms and shoulders. "He may wanta stay forever, but Ma'd miss im like hell if he stayed up there. You gonna feed the ducks with some of that?"

"Yeah, like always."

"Don't let em nibble your fingers. Those damned river ducks carry diseases. They—"

In the town square the Municipal Building clock began to chime noon, although it was still only quarter of.

"What's going on today?" Georgie asked. "First the whistle blows early, now the damned town clock's off-course."

"Maybe it's the heat," Bobby said.

Georgie looked at Bobby doubtfully. "Well . . . it's as good an explanation as any."

Yeah, Bobby thought, going out. *And quite a bit safer than some.*

* * *

Bobby went down River Avenue, munching his bread as he walked. By the time he found a bench near the Housatonic River, most of the half-loaf had disappeared down his own throat. Ducks came waddling eagerly out of the reeds and Bobby began to scatter the remaining bread for them, amused as always by the greedy way they ran for the chunks and the way they threw their heads back to eat them.

After awhile he began to grow drowsy. He looked out over the river, at the nets of reflected light shimmering on its surface, and grew drowsier still. He had slept the previous night but his sleep hadn't been restful. Now he dozed off with his hands full of bread-crumbs. The ducks finished with what was on the grass and then drew closer to him, quacking in low, ruminative tones. The clock in the town square bonged the hour of two at twelve-twenty, causing people downtown to shake their heads and ask each other what the world was coming to. Bobby's doze deepened by degrees, and when a shadow fell over him, he didn't see or sense it.

"Hey. Kid."

The voice was quiet and intense. Bobby sat up with a gasp and a jerk, his hands opening and spilling out the remaining bread. Those snakes began to crawl around in his belly again. It wasn't Willie Shearman or Richie O'Meara or Harry Doolin—even coming out of a doze he knew that—but Bobby almost wished it had been one of them. Even all three. A beating wasn't the worst thing that could happen to you. No, not the worst. Cripes, why did he have to go and fall *asleep?*

"Kid."

The ducks were stepping on Bobby's feet, squabbling over the unexpected windfall. Their wings were fluttering against his ankles and his shins, but the feeling was far away, far away. He could see the shadow of a man's head on the grass ahead of him. The man was standing behind him.

"Kid."

Slowly and creakily, Bobby turned. The man's coat would be yellow and somewhere on it would be an eye, a staring red eye.

But the man who stood there was wearing a tan summer suit, the jacket pooched out by a little stomach that was starting to grow into a big stomach, and Bobby knew at once it wasn't one of *them,* after all. There was no itching behind his eyes, no black threads across his field of vision . . . but the major thing was that this wasn't some *creature* just pretending to be a person; it *was* a person.

"What?" Bobby asked, his voice low and muzzy. He still couldn't believe he'd gone to sleep like that, blanked out like that. "What do you want?"

"I'll give you two bucks to let me blow you," the man in the tan suit said. He reached into the pocket of his jacket and brought out his wallet. "We can go behind that tree over there. No one'll see us. And you'll like it."

"No," Bobby said, getting up. He wasn't completely sure what the man in the tan suit was talking about, but he had a pretty good idea. The ducks scattered backward, but the bread was too tempting to resist and they returned, pecking and dancing around Bobby's sneakers. "I have to go home now. My mother—"

The man came closer, still holding out his wallet. It was as if he'd decided to give the whole thing to Bobby, never mind the two lousy dollars. "You don't have to do it to me, I'll just do it to you. Come on, what do you say? I'll make it three dollars." The man's voice was trembling now, jigging and jagging up and down the scale, at one moment seeming to laugh, at the next almost to weep. "You can go to the movies for a month on three dollars."

"No, really, I—"

"You'll like it, all my boys like it." He reached out for Bobby and suddenly Bobby thought of Ted taking hold of his shoulders, Ted putting his hands behind his neck, Ted pulling him closer until they were almost close enough to kiss. That wasn't like this . . . and yet it was. Somehow it was.

Without thinking about what he was doing, Bobby bent and grabbed one of the ducks. He lifted it in a surprised squawking flurry of beak and wings and paddling feet, had just a glimpse of one black bead of an eye, and then threw it at the man in the tan suit.

The man yelled and put his hands up to shield his face, dropping his wallet.

Bobby ran.

He was passing through the square, headed back home, when he saw a poster on a telephone pole outside the candy store. He walked over to it and read it with silent horror. He couldn't remember his dream of the night before, but something like this had been in it. He was positive.

HAVE YOU SEEN BRAUTIGAN!
He is an OLD MONGREL but WE LOVE HIM!
BRAUTIGAN has WHITE FUR and BLUE EYES!
He is FRIENDLY!
Will EAT SCRAPS FROM YOUR HAND!
We will pay A VERY LARGE REWARD
($ $ $ $)
IF YOU HAVE SEEN BRAUTIGAN!
CALL HOusitonic 5-8337!
(OR)
BRING BRAUTIGAN to 745 Highgate Avenue!
Home of the SAGAMORE FAMILY!

This isn't a good day, Bobby thought, watching his hand reach out and pull the poster off the telephone pole. Beyond it, hanging from a bulb on the marquee of the Harwich Theater, he saw a dangling blue kite tail. *This isn't a good day at all. I never should have gone out of the apartment. In fact, I should have stayed in bed.*

HOusitonic 5-8337, just like on the poster about Phil the Welsh Corgi . . . except if there was a HOusitonic exchange in Harwich, Bobby had never heard of it. Some of the numbers were on the HArwich exchange. Others were COmmonwealth. But HOusitonic? No. Not here, not in Bridgeport, either.

He crumpled the poster up and threw it in the KEEP OUR TOWN CLEAN N GREEN basket on the corner, but on the other side of the street he found another just like it. Farther along he found a third pasted to a corner mailbox. He tore these down, as well. The low men were either closing in or desperate. Maybe both. Ted couldn't go out at all today—Bobby would have to tell him that. And he'd have to be ready to run. He'd tell him that, too.

Bobby cut through the park, almost running himself in his hurry to get home, and he barely heard the small, gasping cry which came from his left as he passed the baseball fields: "Bobby . . ."

He stopped and looked toward the grove of trees where Carol had taken him the day before when he started to bawl. And when the gasping cry came again, he realized it was *her.*

"Bobby if it's you please help me . . ."

He turned off the cement path and ducked into the copse of trees. What he saw there made him drop his baseball glove on the ground. It was an Alvin Dark model, that glove, and later it was gone. Someone came along and just kifed it, he supposed, and so what? As that day wore on, his lousy baseball glove was the very least of his concerns.

Carol sat beneath the same elm tree where she had comforted him. Her knees were drawn up to her chest. Her face was ashy gray. Black shock-circles ringed her eyes, giving her a raccoony look. A thread of blood trickled from one of her nostrils. Her left arm lay across her midriff, pulling her shirt tight against the beginning nubs of what would be breasts in another year or two. She held the elbow of that arm cupped in her right hand.

She was wearing shorts and a smock-type blouse with long sleeves—the kind of thing you just slipped on over your head. Later, Bobby would lay much of the blame for what happened on that stupid shirt of hers. She must have worn it to protect against sunburn; it was the only reason he could think of to wear long sleeves on such a murderously hot day. Had she picked it out herself or had Mrs. Gerber forced her into it? And did it matter? *Yes,* Bobby would think when there was time to think. *It mattered, you're damned right it mattered.*

But for now the blouse with its long sleeves was peripheral. The only thing he noticed in that first instant was Carol's upper left arm. It seemed to have not one shoulder but two.

"Bobby," she said, looking at him with shining dazed eyes. "They hurt me."

She was in shock, of course. He was in shock himself by then, running on instinct. He tried to pick her up and she screamed in pain—dear God, what a sound.

"I'll run and get help," he said, lowering her back. "You just sit there and try not to move."

She was shaking her head—carefully, so as not to joggle her arm. Her blue eyes were nearly black with pain and terror. "No, Bobby, no, don't leave me here, what if they come back? What if they come back and hurt me worse?" Parts of what happened on that long hot Thursday were lost to him, lost in the shockwave, but that part always stood clear: Carol looking up at him and saying *What if they come back and hurt me worse?*

"But . . . Carol . . ."

"I can walk. If you help me, I can walk."

Bobby put a tentative arm around her waist, hoping she wouldn't scream again. That had been bad.

Carol got slowly to her feet, using the trunk of the tree to support her back. Her left arm moved a little as she rose. That grotesque double shoulder bulged and flexed. She moaned but didn't scream, thank God.

"You better stop," Bobby said.

"No, I want to get out of here. Help me. Oh God, it hurts."

Once she was all the way up it seemed a little better. They made their way out of the grove with the slow side-by-side solemnity of a couple about to be married. Beyond the shade of the trees the day seemed even hotter than before and blindingly bright. Bobby looked around and saw no one. Somewhere, deeper in the park, a bunch of little kids (probably Sparrows or Robins from Sterling House) were singing a song, but the area around the baseball fields was utterly deserted: no kids, no mothers wheeling baby carriages, no sign of Officer Raymer, the local cop who would sometimes buy you an ice cream or a bag of peanuts if he was in a good mood. Everyone was inside, hiding from the heat.

Still moving slowly, Bobby with his arm around Carol's waist, they walked along the path which came out on the corner of Commonwealth and Broad. Broad Street Hill was as deserted as the park; the paving shimmered like the air over an incinerator. There wasn't a single pedestrian or moving car in sight.

They stepped onto the sidewalk and Bobby was about to ask if she could make it across the street when Carol said in a high, whispery voice: "Oh Bobby I'm fainting."

He looked at her in alarm and saw her eyes roll up to glistening whites. She swayed back and forth like a tree which has been cut almost all the way through. Bobby bent, moving without thinking, catching her around the thighs and the back as her knees unlocked. He had been standing to her right and was able to do this without hurting her left arm any more than it already had been hurt; also, even in her faint, Carol kept her right hand cupped over her left elbow, holding the arm mostly steady.

Carol Gerber was Bobby's height, perhaps even a little taller, and close to his weight. He should have been incapable of even staggering up Broad Street with her in his arms, but people in shock are capable of amazing bursts of strength. Bobby carried her, and not at a stagger; under that burning June sun he ran. No one stopped him, no one asked him what was wrong with the little girl, no one offered to help. He could hear cars on Asher Avenue, but this part of the world seemed eerily like Midwich, where everyone had gone to sleep at once.

Taking Carol to her mother never crossed his mind. The Gerber apartment was farther up the hill, but that wasn't the reason. Ted was all Bobby could think of. He had to take her to Ted. Ted would know what to do.

His preternatural strength began to give out as he climbed the steps to the front porch of his building. He staggered, and Carol's grotesque double shoulder bumped against the railing. She stiffened in his arms and cried out, her half-lidded eyes opening wide.

"Almost there," he told her in a panting whisper that didn't sound much like his own voice. "Almost there, I'm sorry I bumped you but we're almost—"

The door opened and Ted came out. He was wearing gray suit pants and a strap-style undershirt. Suspenders hung down to his knees in swinging loops. He looked surprised and concerned but not frightened.

Bobby managed the last porch step and then swayed backward. For one terrible moment he thought he was going to go crashing down, maybe splitting his skull on the cement walk. Then Ted grabbed him and steadied him.

"Give her to me," he said.

"Get over on her other side first," Bobby panted. His arms were twanging like guitar strings and his shoulders seemed to be on fire. "That's the bad side."

Ted came around and stood next to Bobby. Carol was looking up at them, her sandy-blond hair hanging down over Bobby's wrist. "They hurt me," she whispered to Ted. "Willie . . . I asked him to make them stop but he wouldn't."

"Don't talk," Ted said. "You're going to be all right."

He took her from Bobby as gently as he could, but they couldn't help joggling her left arm a little. The double shoulder moved under the white smock. Carol moaned, then began to cry. Fresh blood trickled from her right nostril, one brilliant red drop against her skin. Bobby had a momentary flash from his dream of the night before: the eye. The red eye.

"Hold the door for me, Bobby."

Bobby held it wide. Ted carried Carol through the foyer and into the Garfield apartment. At that same moment Liz Garfield was descending the iron steps leading from the Harwich stop of the New York, New Haven & Hartford Railroad to Main Street, where there was a taxi stand. She moved with the slow deliberation of a chronic invalid. A suitcase dangled from each hand. Mr. Burton, proprietor of the newsstand kiosk, happened to be standing in his doorway and having a smoke. He watched Liz reach the bottom of the steps, turn back the veil of her little hat, and gingerly dab at her face with a bit of handkerchief. She winced at each touch. She was wearing makeup, a lot, but the makeup didn't help. The makeup only drew attention to what had happened to her. The veil was better, even though it only covered the upper part of her face, and now she lowered it again. She approached the first of three idling taxis, and the driver got out to help her with her bags.

Burton wondered who had given her the business. He hoped whoever it had been was currently getting his head massaged by big cops with hard hickories. A person who would do something like that to a woman deserved no better. A person who would do something like that to a woman had no business running around loose. That was Burton's opinion.

Bobby thought Ted would put Carol on the couch, but he didn't. There was one straight-backed chair in the living room and that was where he sat, holding her on his lap. He held her the way the Grant's department store Santa Claus held the little kids who came up to him as he sat on his throne.

"Where else are you hurt? Besides the shoulder?"

"They hit me in the stomach. And on my side."

"Which side?"

"The right one."

Ted gently pulled her blouse up on that side. Bobby hissed in air over his lower lip when he saw the bruise which lay diagonally across her ribcage. He recognized the baseball-bat shape of it at once. He knew whose bat it had been: Harry Doolin's, the pimply galoot who saw himself as Robin Hood in whatever stunted landscape passed for his imagination. He and Richie O'Meara and Willie Shearman had come upon her in the park and Harry had worked her over with his ball-bat while Richie and Willie held her. All three of them laughing and calling her the Gerber Baby. Maybe it had started as a joke and gotten out of hand. Wasn't that pretty much what had happened in *Lord of the Flies*? Things had just gotten a little out of hand?

Ted touched Carol's waist; his bunchy fingers spread and then slowly slid up her side. He did this with his head cocked, as if he were listening rather than touching. Maybe he was. Carol gasped when he reached the bruise.

"Hurt?" Ted asked.

"A little. Not as bad as my sh-shoulder. They broke my arm, didn't they?"

"No, I don't think so," Ted replied.

"I heard it pop. So did they. That's when they ran."

"I'm sure you did hear it. Yes indeed."

Tears were running down her cheeks and her face was still ashy, but Carol seemed calmer now. Ted held her blouse up against her armpit and looked at the bruise. *He knows what that shape is just as well as I do,* Bobby thought.

"How many were there, Carol?"

Three, Bobby thought.

"Th-three."

"Three boys?"

She nodded.

"Three boys against one little girl. They must have been afraid of you. They must have thought you were a lion. Are you a lion, Carol?"

"I wish I was," Carol said. She tried to smile. "I wish I could have roared and made them go away. They h-h-*hurt* me."

"I know they did. I know." His hand slid down her side and cupped the bat-bruise on her ribcage. "Breathe in."

The bruise swelled against Ted's hand; Bobby could see its purple shape between his nicotine-stained fingers. "Does *that* hurt?"

She shook her head.

"Not to breathe?"

"No."

"And not when your ribs go against my hand?"

"No. Only sore. What hurts is . . ." She glanced quickly at the terrible shape of her double shoulder, then away.

"I know. Poor Carol. Poor darling. We'll get to that. Where else did they hit you? In the stomach, you said?"

"Yes."

Ted pulled her blouse up in front. There was another bruise, but this one didn't look so deep or so angry. He prodded gently with his fingers, first above her bellybutton and then below it. She said there was no pain like in her shoulder, that her belly was only sore like her ribs were sore.

"They didn't hit you in your back?"

"N-no."

"In your head or your neck?"

"Uh-uh, just my side and my stomach and then they hit me in the shoulder and there was that pop and they heard it and they ran. I used to think Willie Shearman was nice." She gave Ted a woeful look.

"Turn your head for me, Carol . . . good . . . now the other way. It doesn't hurt when you turn it?"

"No."

"And you're sure they never hit your head."

"No. I mean yes, I'm sure."

"Lucky girl."

Bobby wondered how in the hell Ted could think Carol was *lucky.* Her left arm didn't look just broken to him; it looked half torn off. He suddenly thought of a roast-chicken Sunday dinner, and the sound the drumstick made when you pulled it loose. His stomach knotted. For a moment he thought he was going to vomit up his breakfast and the day-old bread which had been his only lunch.

No, he told himself. *Not now, you can't. Ted's got enough problems without adding you to the list.*

"Bobby?" Ted's voice was clear and sharp. He sounded like a guy with more solutions than problems, and what a relief that was. "Are you all right?"

"Yeah." And he thought it was true. His stomach was starting to settle.

"Good. You did well to get her up here. Can you do well a little longer?"

"Yeah."

"I need a pair of scissors. Can you find one?"

Bobby went into his mother's bedroom, opened the top drawer of her dresser, and got out her wicker sewing basket. Inside was a medium-sized pair of shears. He hurried back into the living room with them and showed them to Ted. "Are these all right?"

"Fine," he said, taking them. Then, to Carol: "I'm going to spoil your blouse, Carol. I'm sorry, but I have to look at your shoulder now and I don't want to hurt you any more than I can help."

"That's okay," she said, and again tried to smile. Bobby was a little in awe of her bravery; if *his* shoulder had looked like that, he probably would have been blatting like a sheep caught in a barbed-wire fence.

"You can wear one of Bobby's shirts home. Can't she, Bobby?"

"Sure, I don't mind a few cooties."

"Fun-*nee,*" Carol said.

Working carefully, Ted cut the smock up the back and then up the front. With that done he pulled the two pieces off like the shell of an egg. He was very careful on the left side, but Carol uttered a hoarse scream when Ted's fingers brushed her shoulder. Bobby jumped and his heart, which had been slowing down, began to race again.

"I'm sorry," Ted murmured. "Oh my. Look at this."

Carol's shoulder was ugly, but not as bad as Bobby had feared—perhaps few things were once you were looking right at them. The second shoulder was higher than the normal one, and the skin there was stretched so tight that Bobby didn't understand why it didn't just split open. It had gone a peculiar lilac color, as well.

"How bad is it?" Carol asked. She was looking in the other direction, across the room. Her small face had the pinched, starved look of a UNICEF child. So far as Bobby knew she never looked at her hurt shoulder after that single quick peek. "I'll be in a cast all summer, won't I?"

"I don't think you're going to be in a cast at all."

Carol looked up into Ted's face wonderingly.

"It's not broken, child, only dislocated. Someone hit you on the shoulder—"

"Harry Doolin—"

"—and hard enough to knock the top of the bone in your upper left arm out of its socket. I can put it back in, I think. Can you stand one or two moments of quite bad pain if you know things may be all right again afterward?"

"Yes," she said at once. "Fix it, Mr. Brautigan. Please fix it."

Bobby looked at him a little doubtfully. "Can you really do that?"

"Yes. Give me your belt."

"*Huh?*"

"Your belt. Give it to me."

Bobby slipped his belt—a fairly new one he'd gotten for Christmas—out of its loops and handed it to Ted, who took it without ever shifting his eyes from Carol's. "What's your last name, honey?"

"Gerber. They called me the Gerber Baby, but I'm not a baby."

"I'm sure you're not. And this is where you prove it." He got up, settled her in the chair, then knelt before her like a guy in some old movie getting ready to propose. He folded Bobby's belt over twice in his big hands, then poked it at her good hand until she let go of her elbow and closed her fingers over the loops. "Good. Now put it in your mouth."

"Put Bobby's *belt* in my *mouth?*"

Ted's gaze never left her. He began stroking her unhurt arm from the elbow to the wrist. His fingers trailed down her forearm . . . stopped . . . rose and went back to her elbow . . . trailed down her forearm again. *It's like he's hypnotizing her,* Bobby thought, but there was really no "like" about it; Ted *was* hypnotizing her. His pupils had begun to do that weird thing again, growing and shrinking . . . growing and shrinking . . . growing and shrinking. Their movement and the movement of his fingers were exactly in rhythm. Carol stared into his face, her lips parted.

"Ted . . . your *eyes* . . ."

"Yes, yes." He sounded impatient, not very interested in what his eyes were doing. "Pain rises, Carol, did you know that?"

"No . . ."

Her eyes on his. His fingers on her arm, going down and rising. Going down . . . and rising. His pupils like a slow heartbeat. Bobby could see Carol relaxing in the chair. She was still holding the belt, and when Ted stopped his finger-stroking long enough to touch the back of her hand, she lifted it toward her face with no protest.

"Oh yes," he said, "pain rises from its source to the brain. When I put your shoulder back in its socket, there will be a lot of pain—but you'll catch most of it in your mouth as it rises toward your brain. You will bite it with your teeth and hold it against Bobby's belt so that only a little of it can get into your head, which is where things hurt the most. Do you understand me, Carol?"

"Yes . . ." Her voice had grown distant. She looked very small sitting there in the straight-backed chair, wearing only her shorts and her sneakers. The pupils of Ted's eyes, Bobby noticed, had grown steady again.

"Put the belt in your mouth."

She put it between her lips.

"Bite when it hurts."

"When it hurts."

"Catch the pain."

"I'll catch it."

Ted gave a final stroke of his big forefinger from her elbow to her wrist, then looked at Bobby. "Wish me luck," he said.

"Luck," Bobby replied fervently.

Distant, dreaming, Carol Gerber said: "Bobby threw a duck at a man."

"Did he?" Ted asked. Very, very gently he closed his left hand around Carol's left wrist.

"Bobby thought the man was a low man."

Ted glanced at Bobby.

"Not that kind of low man," Bobby said. "Just . . . oh, never mind."

"All the same," Ted said, "they are very close. The town clock, the town whistle—"

"I heard," Bobby said grimly.

"I'm not going to wait until your mother comes back tonight—I don't dare. I'll spend the day in a movie or a park or somewhere else. If all else fails, there are flophouses in Bridgeport. Carol, are you ready?"

"Ready."

"When the pain rises, what will you do?"

"Catch it. Bite it into Bobby's belt."

"Good girl. Ten seconds and you are going to feel a lot better."

Ted drew in a deep breath. Then he reached out with his right hand until it hovered just above the lilac-colored bulge in Carol's shoulder. "Here comes the pain, darling. Be brave."

It wasn't ten seconds; not even five. To Bobby it seemed to happen in an instant. The heel of Ted's right hand pressed directly against that knob rising out of Carol's stretched flesh. At the same time he pulled sharply on her wrist. Carol's jaws flexed as she clamped down on Bobby's belt. Bobby heard a brief creaking sound, like the one his neck sometimes made when it was stiff and he turned his head. And then the bulge in Carol's arm was gone.

"Bingo!" Ted cried. "Looks good! Carol?"

She opened her mouth. Bobby's belt fell out of it and onto her lap. Bobby saw a line of tiny points embedded in the leather; she had bitten nearly all the way through.

"It doesn't hurt anymore," she said wonderingly. She ran her right hand up to where the skin was now turning a darker purple, touched the bruise, winced.

"That'll be sore for a week or so," Ted warned her. "And you mustn't throw or lift with that arm for at least two weeks. If you do, it may pop out again."

"I'll be careful." Now Carol could look at her arm. She kept touching the bruise with light, testing fingers.

"How much of the pain did you catch?" Ted asked her, and although his face was still grave, Bobby thought he could hear a little smile in his voice.

"Most of it," she said. "It hardly hurt at all." As soon as these words were out, however, she slumped back in the chair. Her eyes were open but unfocused. Carol had fainted for the second time.

Ted told Bobby to wet a cloth and bring it to him. "Cold water," he said. "Wring it out, but not too much."

Bobby ran into the bathroom, got a facecloth from the shelf by the tub, and wet it in cold water. The bottom half of the bathroom window was frosted glass, but if he had looked out the top half he would have seen his mother's taxi pulling up out front. Bobby didn't look; he was concentrating on his chore. He never thought of the green keyfob, either, although it was lying on the shelf right in front of his eyes.

When Bobby came back into the living room, Ted was sitting in the straight-backed chair with Carol in his lap again. Bobby noticed how tanned her arms had already become compared to the rest of her skin, which was a pure, smooth white (except for where the bruises stood out). *She looks like she's wearing nylon stockings on her arms,* he thought, a little amused. Her eyes had begun to clear and they tracked Bobby when he moved toward her, but Carol still didn't look exactly great—her hair was mussed, her face was all sweaty, and there was that drying trickle of blood between her nostril and the corner of her mouth.

Ted took the cloth and began to wipe her cheeks and forehead with it. Bobby knelt by the arm of the chair. Carol sat up a little, raising her face gratefully against the cool and the wet. Ted wiped away the blood under her nose, then put the facecloth aside on the end-table. He brushed Carol's sweaty hair off her brow. When some of it flopped back, he moved his hand to brush it away again.

Before he could, the door to the porch banged open. Footfalls crossed the foyer. The hand on Carol's damp forehead froze. Bobby's eyes met Ted's and a single thought flowed between them, strong telepathy consisting of a single word: *Them.*

"*No,*" Carol said, "*not* them, Bobby, it's your m—"

The apartment door opened and Liz stood there with her key in one hand and her hat—the one with the veil on it—in the other. Behind her and beyond the foyer the door to all the hot outside world stood open. Side by side on the porch welcome mat were her two suitcases, where the cab driver had put them.

"Bobby, how many times have I told you to lock this damn—"

She got that far, then stopped. In later years Bobby would replay that moment again and again, seeing more and more of what his mother had seen when she came back from her disastrous trip to

Providence: her son kneeling by the chair where the old man she had never liked or really trusted sat with the little girl in his lap. The little girl looked dazed. Her hair was in sweaty clumps. Her blouse had been torn off—it lay in pieces on the floor—and even with her own eyes puffed mostly shut, Liz would have seen Carol's bruises: one on the shoulder, one on the ribs, one on the stomach.

And Carol and Bobby and Ted Brautigan saw her with that same amazed stop-time clarity: the two black eyes (Liz's right eye was really nothing but a glitter deep in a puffball of discolored flesh); the lower lip which was swelled and split in two places and still wearing flecks of dried blood like old ugly lipstick; the nose which lay askew and had grown a misbegotten hook, making it almost into a caricature Witch Hazel nose.

Silence, a moment's considering silence on a hot summer afternoon. Somewhere a car backfired. Somewhere a kid shouted "*Come on, you guys!*" And from behind them on Colony Street came the sound Bobby would identify most strongly with his childhood in general and that Thursday in particular: Mrs. O'Hara's Bowser barking his way ever deeper into the twentieth century: *roop-roop, roop-roop-roop.*

Jack got her, Bobby thought. *Jack Merridew and his nimrod friends.*

"Oh jeez, what happened?" he asked her, breaking the silence. He didn't want to know; he had to know. He ran to her, starting to cry out of fright but also out of grief: her face, her poor face. She didn't look like his mom at all. She looked like some old woman who belonged not on shady Broad Street but down there, where people drank wine out of bottles in paper sacks and had no last names. "What did he do? What did that bastard do to you?"

She paid no attention, seemed not to hear him at all. She laid hold of him, though; laid hold of his shoulders hard enough for him to feel her fingers sinking into his flesh, hard enough to hurt. She laid hold and then set him aside without a single look. "Let her go, you filthy man," she said in a low and rusty voice. "Let her go right now."

"Mrs. Garfield, please don't misunderstand." Ted lifted Carol off his lap—careful even now to keep his hand well away from her hurt shoulder—and then stood up himself. He shook out the legs of his pants, a fussy little gesture that was all Ted. "She was hurt, you see. Bobby found her—"

"*BASTARD!*" Liz screamed. To her right was a table with a vase on it. She grabbed the vase and threw it at him. Ted ducked, but too slowly to avoid it completely; the bottom of the vase struck the top of his head, skipped like a stone on a pond, hit the wall and shattered.

Carol screamed.

"Mom, no!" Bobby shouted. "He didn't do anything bad! He didn't do anything bad!"

Liz took no notice. "How dare you touch her? Have you been touching my son the same way? You have, haven't you? You don't care which flavor they are, just as long as they're *young!*"

Ted took a step toward her. The empty loops of his suspenders swung back and forth beside his legs. Bobby could see blooms of blood in the scant hair on top of his head where the vase had clipped him.

"Mrs. Garfield, I assure you—"

"*Assure this, you dirty bastard!*" With the vase gone, there was nothing left on the table and so she picked up the table itself and threw it. It struck Ted in the chest and drove him backward; would have floored him if not for the straight-backed chair. Ted flopped into it, looking at her with wide, incredulous eyes. His mouth was trembling.

"Was he helping you?" Liz asked. Her face was dead white. The bruises on it stood out like birthmarks. "*Did you teach my son to help?*"

"Mom, he didn't hurt her!" Bobby shouted. He grabbed her around the waist. "He didn't hurt her, he—"

She picked him up like the vase, like the table, and he would think later she had been as strong as he had been, carrying Carol up the hill from the park. She threw him across the room. Bobby struck the wall. His head snapped back and connected with the sunburst clock, knocking it to the floor and stopping it forever. Black dots flocked across his vision, making him think briefly and confusedly

(*coming closing in now the posters have his name on them*)

of the low men. Then he slid to the floor. He tried to stop himself but his knees wouldn't lock.

Liz looked at him, seemingly without much interest, then back at Ted, who sat in the straight-backed chair with the table in his lap and the legs poking at his face. Blood was dripping down one of his cheeks now, and his hair was more red than white. He tried to speak and what came out instead was a dry and flailing old man's cigarette cough.

"Filthy man. Filthy filthy man. For two cents I'd pull your pants down and yank that filthy thing right off you." She turned and looked at her huddled son again, and the expression Bobby now saw in the one eye he could really see—the contempt, the accusation—made him cry harder. She didn't say *You too,* but he saw it in her eye. Then she turned back to Ted.

"Know what? You're going to jail." She pointed a finger at him, and even through his tears Bobby saw the nail that had been on it when she left in Mr. Biderman's Merc was gone; there was a bloody-ragged weal where it had been. Her voice was mushy, seeming to spread out somehow as it crossed her oversized lower lip. "I'm going to call the police now. If you're wise you'll sit still while I do it. Just keep your mouth shut and sit still." Her voice was rising, rising. Her hands, scratched and swelled at the knuckles as well as broken at the nails, curled into fists which she shook at him. "If you run I'll chase you and carve you up with my longest butcher knife. See if I don't. I'll do it right on the street for everyone to see, and I'll start with the part of you that seems to give you . . . you *boys* . . . so much trouble. So sit still, *Brattigan.* If you want to live long enough to go to jail, don't you move."

The phone was on the table by the couch. She went to it. Ted sat with the table in his lap and blood flowing down his cheek. Bobby huddled next to the fallen clock, the one his mother had gotten with trading stamps. Drifting in the window on the breeze of Ted's fan came Bowser's cry: *roop-roop-roop.*

"You don't know what happened here, Mrs. Garfield. What happened to you was terrible and you have all my sympathy . . . but what happened to you is not what happened to Carol."

"Shut up." She wasn't listening, didn't even look in his direction.

Carol ran to Liz, reached out for her, then stopped. Her eyes grew large in her pale face. Her mouth dropped open. "They pulled your dress off?" It was half a whisper, half a moan. Liz stopped dialing and turned slowly to look at her. "Why did they pull your dress off?"

Liz seemed to think about how to answer. She seemed to think hard. "Shut up," she said at last. "Just shut up, okay?"

"Why did they chase you? Who's hitting?" Carol's voice had become uneven. "Who's *hitting?*"

"*Shut up!*" Liz dropped the telephone and put her hands to her ears. Bobby looked at her with growing horror.

Carol turned to him. Fresh tears were rolling down her cheeks. There was knowing in her eyes—*knowing.* The kind, Bobby thought, that he had felt while Mr. McQuown had been trying to fool him.

"They chased her," Carol said. "When she tried to leave they chased her and made her come back."

Bobby knew. They had chased her down a hotel corridor. He had seen it. He couldn't remember where, but he had.

"*Make them stop doing it! Make me stop seeing it!*" Carol screamed. "*She's hitting them but she can't get away! She's hitting them but she can't get away!*"

Ted tipped the table out of his lap and struggled to his feet. His eyes were blazing. "Hug her, Carol! Hug her tight! That will make it stop!"

Carol threw her good arm around Bobby's mother. Liz staggered backward a step, almost falling when one of her shoes hooked the leg of the sofa. She stayed up but the telephone tumbled to the rug beside one of Bobby's outstretched sneakers, burring harshly.

For a moment things stayed that way—it was as if they were playing Statues and "it" had just yelled *Freeze!* It was Carol who moved first, releasing Liz Garfield's waist and stepping back. Her sweaty hair hung in her eyes. Ted went toward her and reached out to put a hand on her shoulder.

"Don't touch her," Liz said, but she spoke mechanically, without force. Whatever had flashed inside her at the sight of the child on Ted

Brautigan's lap had faded a little, at least temporarily. She looked exhausted.

Nonetheless, Ted dropped his hand. "You're right," he said.

Liz took a deep breath, held it, let it out. She looked at Bobby, then away. Bobby wished with all his heart that she would put her hand out to him, help him a little, help him get up, just that, but she turned to Carol instead. Bobby got to his feet on his own.

"What happened here?" Liz asked Carol.

Although she was still crying and her words kept hitching as she struggled for breath, Carol told Bobby's mom about how the three big boys had found her in the park, and how at first it had seemed like just another one of their jokes, a bit meaner than most but still just a joke. Then Harry had really started hitting her while the others held her. The popping sound in her shoulder scared them and they ran away. She told Liz how Bobby had found her five or ten minutes later—she didn't know how long because the pain had been so bad—and carried her up here. And how Ted had fixed her arm, after giving her Bobby's belt to catch the pain with. She bent, picked up the belt, and showed Liz the tiny tooth-marks in it with a mixture of pride and embarrassment. "I didn't catch all of it, but I caught a lot."

Liz only glanced at the belt before turning to Ted. "Why'd you tear her top off, chief?"

"It's *not* torn!" Bobby cried. He was suddenly furious with her. "He *cut* it off so he could look at her shoulder and fix it without hurting her! I brought him the scissors, for cripe's sake! Why are you so stupid, Mom? Why can't you see—"

She swung without turning, catching Bobby completely by surprise. The back of her open hand connected with the side of his face; her forefinger actually poked into his eye, sending a zag of pain deep into his head. His tears stopped as if the pump controlling them had suddenly shorted out.

"Don't you call me stupid, Bobby-O," she said. "Not on your ever-loving tintype."

Carol was looking fearfully at the hook-nosed witch who had come back in a taxi wearing Mrs. Garfield's clothes. Mrs. Garfield who had run and who had fought when she couldn't run anymore. But in the end they had taken what they wanted from her.

"You shouldn't hit Bobby," Carol said. "He's not like those men."

"Is he your boyfriend?" She laughed. "Yeah? Good for you! But I'll let you in on a secret, sweetheart—he's just like his daddy and your daddy and all the rest of them. Go in the bathroom. I'll clean you up and find something for you to wear. *Christ* what a mess!"

Carol looked at her a moment longer, then turned and went into the bathroom. Her bare back looked small and vulnerable. And white. So white in contrast to her brown arms.

"Carol!" Ted called after her. "Is it better now?" Bobby didn't think he was talking about her arm. Not this time.

"Yes," she said without turning. "But I can still hear her, far away. She's screaming."

"Who's screaming?" Liz asked. Carol didn't answer her. She went into the bathroom and closed the door. Liz looked at it for a moment, as if to make sure Carol wasn't going to pop back out again, then turned to Ted. "Who's screaming?"

Ted only looked at her warily, as if expecting another ICBM attack at any moment.

Liz began to smile. It was a smile Bobby knew: her I'm-losing-my-temper smile. Was it possible she had any left to lose? With her black eyes, broken nose, and swollen lip, the smile made her look horrid: not his mother but some lunatic.

"Quite the Good Samaritan, aren't you? How many feels did you cop while you were fixing her up? She hasn't got much, but I bet you checked what you could, didn't you? Never miss an opportunity, right? Come on and fess up to your mamma."

Bobby looked at her with growing despair. Carol had told her everything—all of the truth—*and it made no difference.* No difference! God!

"There is a dangerous adult in this room," Ted said, "but it isn't me."

She looked first uncomprehending, then incredulous, then furious. "How dare you? *How dare you?*"

"*He didn't do anything!*" Bobby screamed. "*Didn't you hear what Carol said? Didn't you—*"

"Shut your mouth," she said, not looking at him. She looked only at Ted. "The cops are going to be very interested in you, I think. Don called Hartford on Friday, before . . . before. I asked him to. He has friends there. You never worked for the State of Connecticut, not in the Office of the Comptroller, not anywhere else. You were in jail, weren't you?"

"In a way I suppose I was," Ted said. He seemed calmer now in spite of the blood flowing down the side of his face. He took the cigarettes out of his shirt pocket, looked at them, put them back. "But not the kind you're thinking of."

And not in this world, Bobby thought.

"What was it for?" she asked. "Making little girls feel better in the first degree?"

"I have something valuable," Ted said. He reached up and tapped his temple. The finger he tapped with came away dotted with blood. "There are others like me. And there are people whose job it is to catch us, keep us, and use us for . . . well, use us, leave it at that. I and two others escaped. One was caught, one was killed. Only I remain free. If, that is . . ." He looked around. ". . . you call this freedom."

"You're crazy. Crazy old Brattigan, nuttier than a holiday fruitcake. I'm calling the police. Let them decide if they want to put you back in the jail you broke out of or in Danbury Asylum." She bent, reached for the spilled phone.

"No, Mom!" Bobby said, and reached for her. "Don't—"

"*Bobby, no!*" Ted said sharply.

Bobby pulled back, looking first at his mom as she scooped up the phone, then at Ted.

"Not as she is now," Ted told him. "As she is now, she can't stop biting."

Liz Garfield gave Ted a brilliant, almost unspeakable smile—*Good try, you bastard*—and took the receiver off the cradle.

"What's happening?" Carol cried from the bathroom. "Can I come out now?"

"Not yet, darling," Ted called back. "A little longer."

Liz poked the telephone's cutoff buttons up and down. She stopped, listened, seemed satisfied. She began to dial. "We're going to find out who you are," she said. She spoke in a strange, confiding tone. "That should be pretty interesting. And what you've done. That might be even more interesting."

"If you call the police, they'll also find out who *you* are and what *you've* done," Ted said.

She stopped dialing and looked at him. It was a cunning sideways stare Bobby had never seen before. "What in God's name are you talking about?"

"A foolish woman who should have chosen better. A foolish woman who had seen enough of her boss to know better—who had overheard him and his cronies often enough to know better, to know that any 'seminar' they attended mostly had to do with booze and sex-parties. Maybe a little reefer, as well. A foolish woman who let her greed overwhelm her good sense—"

"What do you know about being alone?" she cried. "*I have a son to raise!*" She looked at Bobby, as if remembering the son she had to raise for the first time in a little while.

"How much of this do you want him to hear?" Ted asked.

"You don't know anything. You can't."

"I know *everything.* The question is, how much do you want Bobby to know? How much do you want your neighbors to know? If the police come and take me, they'll know what I know, that I promise you." He paused. His pupils remained steady but his eyes seemed to grow. "I know *everything.* Believe me—don't put it to the test."

"Why would you hurt me that way?"

"Given a choice I wouldn't. You have been hurt enough, by yourself as well as by others. Let me leave, that's all I'm asking you to do. I was leaving anyway. Let me leave. I did nothing but try to help."

"Oh yes," she said, and laughed. "*Help.* Her sitting on you practically naked. *Help.*"

"I would help *you* if I—"

"Oh yeah, and I know how." She laughed again.

Bobby started to speak and saw Ted's eyes warning him not to. Behind the bathroom door, water was now running into the sink. Liz lowered her head, thinking. At last she raised it again.

"All right," she said, "here's what I'm going to do. I'll help Bobby's little *girlfriend* get cleaned up. I'll give her an aspirin and find something for her to wear home. While I'm doing those things, I'll ask her a few questions. If the answers are the right answers, you can go. Good riddance to bad rubbish."

"Mom—"

Liz held up a hand like a traffic cop, silencing him. She was staring at Ted, who was looking back at her.

"I'll walk her home, I'll watch her go through her front door. What she decides to tell her mother is between the two of them. My job is to see her home safe, that's all. When it's done I'll walk down to the park and sit in the shade for a little while. I had a rough night last night." She drew in breath and let it out in a dry and rueful sigh. "Very rough. So I'll go to the park and sit in the shade and think about what comes next. How I'm going to keep him and me out of the poorhouse.

"If I find you still here when I get back from the park, sweetheart, I *will* call the police . . . and don't you put *that* to the test. Say whatever you want. None of it's going to matter much to anyone if I say I walked into my apartment a few hours sooner than you expected and found you with your hand inside an eleven-year-old girl's shorts."

Bobby stared at his mother in silent shock. She didn't see the stare; she was still looking at Ted, her swollen eyes fixed on him intently.

"If, on the other hand, I came back and you're gone, bag and baggage, I won't have to call anyone or say anything. *Tout fini.*"

I'll go with you! Bobby thought at Ted. *I don't care about the low men. I'd rather have a thousand low men in yellow coats looking for me—a* million—*than have to live with* her *anymore. I hate her!*

"Well?" Liz asked.

"It's a deal. I'll be gone in an hour. Probably less."

"No!" Bobby cried. When he'd awakened this morning he had

been resigned to Ted's going—sad but resigned. Now it hurt all over again. Worse than before, even. "No!"

"Be quiet," his mother said, still not looking at him.

"It's the only way, Bobby. You know that." Ted looked up at Liz. "Take care of Carol. I'll talk to Bobby."

"You're in no position to give orders," Liz said, but she went. As she crossed to the bathroom, Bobby saw she was limping. A heel had broken off one of her shoes, but he didn't think that was the only reason she couldn't walk right. She knocked briefly on the bathroom door and then, without waiting for a response, slipped inside.

Bobby ran across the room, but when he tried to put his arms around Ted, the old man took his hands, squeezed them once briefly, then put them against Bobby's chest and let go.

"Take me with you," Bobby said fiercely. "I'll help you look for them. Two sets of eyes are better than one. Take me with you!"

"I can't do that, but you can come with me as far as the kitchen, Bobby. Carol isn't the only one who needs to do some cleaning up."

Ted rose from the chair and swayed on his feet for a moment. Bobby reached out to steady him and Ted once more pushed his hand gently but firmly away. It hurt. Not as much as his mother's failure to help him up (or even look at him) after she had thrown him against the wall, but enough.

He walked with Ted to the kitchen, not touching him but close enough to grab him if he fell. Ted didn't fall. He looked at the hazy reflection of himself in the window over the sink, sighed, then turned on the water. He wet the dishcloth and began to wipe the blood off his cheek, checking his window-reflection every now and then for reference.

"Your mother needs you more now than she ever has before," he said. "She needs someone she can trust."

"She doesn't trust me. I don't think she even likes me."

Ted's mouth tightened, and Bobby understood he had struck upon some truth Ted had seen in his mother's mind. Bobby *knew* she didn't like him, he *knew* that, so why were the tears threatening again?

Ted reached out for him, seemed to remember that was a bad idea, and went back to work with the dishcloth instead. "All right," he said. "Perhaps she *doesn't* like you. If that's true, it isn't because of anything you did. It's because of what you *are.*"

"A boy," he said bitterly. "A fucking *boy.*"

"And your father's son, don't forget that. But Bobby . . . whether she likes you or not, she loves you. Such a greeting-card that sounds, I know, but it's true. She loves you and she needs you. You're what she has. She's badly hurt right now—"

"Getting hurt was her own fault!" he burst out. "She knew something was wrong! You said so yourself! She's known for weeks! *Months!* But she wouldn't leave that job! She knew and she still went with them to Providence! *She went with them anyway!*"

"A lion-tamer knows, but he still goes into the cage. He goes in because that's where his paycheck is."

"She's got money," Bobby almost spat.

"Not enough, apparently."

"She'll never have enough," Bobby said, and knew it was the truth as soon as it was out of his mouth.

"She loves you."

"I don't care! I don't love her!"

"But you do. You will. You must. It is *ka.*"

"*Ka?* What's that?"

"Destiny." Ted had gotten most of the blood out of his hair. He turned off the water and made one final check of his ghost-image in the window. Beyond it lay all of that hot summer, younger than Ted Brautigan would ever be again. Younger than Bobby would ever be again, for that matter. "*Ka* is destiny. Do you care for me, Bobby?"

"You know I do," Bobby said, beginning to cry again. Lately crying was all he seemed to do. His eyes ached from it. "Lots and lots."

"Then try to be your mother's friend. For my sake if not your own. Stay with her and help this hurt of hers to heal. And every now and then I'll send you a postcard."

They were walking back into the living room again. Bobby was starting to feel a little bit better, but he wished Ted could have put his arm around him. He wished that more than anything.

The bathroom door opened. Carol came out first, looking down at her own feet with uncharacteristic shyness. Her hair had been wetted, combed back, and rubber-banded into a ponytail. She was wearing one of Bobby's mother's old blouses; it was so big it came almost down to her knees, like a dress. You couldn't see her red shorts at all.

"Go out on the porch and wait," Liz said.

"Okay."

"You won't go walking home without me, will you?"

"No!" Carol said, and her downcast face filled with alarm.

"Good. Stand right by my suitcases."

Carol started out to the foyer, then turned back. "Thanks for fixing my arm, Ted. I hope you don't get in trouble for it. I didn't want—"

"Go out on the damned *porch,*" Liz snapped.

"—anyone to get in trouble," Carol finished in a tiny voice, almost the whisper of a mouse in a cartoon. Then she went out, Liz's blouse flapping around her in a way that would have been comical on another day. Liz turned to Bobby and when he got a good look at her, his heart sank. Her fury had been refreshed. A bright red flush had spread over her bruised face and down her neck.

Oh cripes, what now? Bobby thought. Then she held up the green keyfob, and he knew.

"Where did you get this, Bobby-O?"

"I . . . it . . ." But he could think of nothing to say: no fib, no outright lie, not even the truth. Suddenly Bobby felt very tired. The only thing in the world he wanted to do was creep into his bedroom and hide under the covers of his bed and go to sleep.

"I gave it to him," Ted said mildly. "Yesterday."

"You took my son to a bookie joint in Bridgeport? A *poker-parlor* in Bridgeport?"

It doesn't say bookie joint on the keyfob, Bobby thought. *It doesn't say poker-parlor, either . . . because those things are against the law. She knows what goes on there because my father went there. And like father like son. That's what they say, like father like son.*

"I took him to a movie," Ted said. "*Village of the Damned,* at the Criterion. While he was watching, I went to The Corner Pocket to do an errand."

"What sort of errand?"

"I placed a bet on a prizefight." For a moment Bobby's heart sank even lower and he thought, *What's wrong with you? Why didn't you lie? If you knew how she felt about stuff like that—*

But he *did* know. Of course he did.

"A bet on a prizefight." She nodded. "Uh-huh. You left my son alone in a Bridgeport movie theater so you could go make a bet on a prizefight." She laughed wildly. "Oh well, I suppose I should be grateful, shouldn't I? You brought him such a nice souvenir. If he decides to ever make a bet himself, or lose his money playing poker like his father did, he'll know where to go."

"I left him for two hours in a movie theater," Ted said. "You left him with me. He seems to have survived both, hasn't he?"

Liz looked for a moment as if she had been slapped, then for a moment as if she would cry. Then her face smoothed out and became expressionless. She curled her fist around the green keyfob and slipped it into her dress pocket. Bobby knew he would never see it again. He didn't mind. He didn't *want* to see it again.

"Bobby, go in your room," she said.

"No."

"*Bobby, go in your room!*"

"No! I won't!"

Standing in a bar of sunlight on the welcome mat by Liz Garfield's suitcases, floating in Liz Garfield's old blouse, Carol began to cry at the sound of the raised voices.

"Go in your room, Bobby," Ted said quietly. "I have enjoyed meeting you and knowing you."

"*Knowing* you," Bobby's mom said in an angry, insinuating voice, but Bobby didn't understand her and Ted took no notice of her.

"Go in your room," he repeated.

"Will you be all right? You know what I mean."

"Yes." Ted smiled, kissed his fingers, and blew the kiss toward Bobby. Bobby caught it and made a fist around it, holding it tight. "I'm going to be just fine."

Bobby walked slowly toward his bedroom door, his head down

and his eyes on the toes of his sneakers. He was almost there when he thought *I can't do this, I can't let him go like this.*

He ran to Ted, threw his arms around him, and covered his face with kisses—forehead, cheeks, chin, lips, the thin and silky lids of his eyes. "Ted, I love you!"

Ted gave up and hugged him tight. Bobby could smell a ghost of the lather he shaved with, and the stronger aroma of his Chesterfield cigarettes. They were smells he would carry with him a long time, as he would the memories of Ted's big hands touching him, stroking his back, cupping the curve of his skull. "Bobby, I love you too," he said.

"Oh for *Christ's sake!*" Liz nearly screamed. Bobby turned toward her and what he saw was Don Biderman pushing her into a corner. Somewhere the Benny Goodman Orchestra was playing "One O'Clock Jump" on a hi-fi turned all the way up. Mr. Biderman had his hand out as if to slap. Mr. Biderman was asking her if she wanted a little more, was that the way she liked it, she could have a little more if that was the way she liked it. Bobby could almost taste her horrified understanding.

"You really *didn't* know, did you?" he said. "At least not all of it, all they wanted. They thought you did, but you didn't."

"Go in your room right now or I'm calling the police and telling them to send a squad-car," his mother said. "I'm not joking, Bobby-O."

"I know you're not," Bobby said. He went into his bedroom and closed the door. He thought at first he was all right and then he thought that he was going to throw up, or faint, or do both. He walked across to his bed on tottery, unstable legs. He only meant to sit on it but he lay back on it crosswise instead, as if all the muscles had gone out of his stomach and back. He tried to lift his feet up but his legs only lay there, the muscles gone from them, too. He had a sudden image of Sully-John in his bathing suit, climbing the ladder of a swimming float, running to the end of the board, diving off. He wished he was with S-J now. Anywhere but here. Anywhere but here. Anywhere at all but here.

When Bobby woke up, the light in his room had grown dim and when he looked at the floor he could barely see the shadow of the tree outside his window. He had been out—asleep or unconscious—for three hours, maybe four. He was covered with sweat and his legs were numb; he had never pulled them up onto the bed.

Now he tried, and the burst of pins and needles which resulted almost made him scream. He slid onto the floor instead, and the pins and needles ran up his thighs to his crotch. He sat with his knees up around his ears, his back throbbing, his legs buzzing, his head cottony. Something terrible had happened, but at first he couldn't remember what. As he sat there propped against the bed, looking across at Clayton Moore in his Lone Ranger mask, it began to come back. Carol's arm dislocated, his mother beaten up and half-crazy as well, shaking that green keyfob in his face, furious with him. And Ted . . .

Ted would be gone by now, and that was probably for the best, but how it hurt to think of.

He got to his feet and walked twice around the room. The second time he stopped at the window and looked out, rubbing his hands together at the back of his neck, which was stiff and sweaty. A little way down the street the Sigsby twins, Dina and Dianne, were jumping rope, but the other kids had gone in, either for supper or for the night. A car slid by, showing its parking lights. It was even later than he had at first thought; heavenly shades of night were falling.

He made another circuit of his room, working the tingles out of his legs, feeling like a prisoner pacing his cell. The door had no lock on it—no more than his mom's did—but he felt like a jailbird just the same. He was afraid to go out. She hadn't called him for supper, and although he was hungry—a little, anyway—he was afraid to go out. He was afraid of how he might find her . . . or of not finding her at all. Suppose she had decided she'd finally had enough of Bobby-O, stupid lying little Bobby-O, his father's son? Even if she was here, and seemingly back to normal . . . was there even such a thing as normal? People had terrible things behind their faces sometimes. He knew that now.

When he reached the closed door of his room, he stopped. There was a scrap of paper lying there. He bent and picked it up. There was still plenty of light and he could read it easily.

Dear Bobby—

By the time you read this, I'll be gone . . . but I'll take you with me in my thoughts. Please love your mother and remember that she loves you. She was afraid and hurt and ashamed this afternoon, and when we see people that way, we see them at their worst. I have left you something in my room. I will remember my promise.

All my love,

Ted

The postcards, that's what he promised. To send me postcards.

Feeling better, Bobby folded up the note Ted had slipped into his room before leaving and opened his bedroom door.

The living room was empty, but it had been set to rights. It looked almost okay if you didn't know there was supposed to be a sunburst clock on the wall beside the TV; now there was just the little screw where it had hung, jutting out and holding nothing.

Bobby realized he could hear his mother snoring in her room. She always snored, but this was a heavy snore, like an old person or a drunk snoring in a movie. *That's because they hurt her,* Bobby thought, and for a moment he thought of

(*Howya doin Sport howza boy*)

Mr. Biderman and the two nimrods elbowing each other in the back seat and grinning. *Kill the pig, cut her throat,* Bobby thought. He didn't want to think it but he did.

He tiptoed across the living room as quietly as Jack in the giant's castle, opened the door to the foyer, and went out. He tiptoed up the first flight of stairs (walking on the bannister side, because he'd read in one of the Hardy Boys mysteries that if you walked that way the stairs didn't creak so much), and ran up the second.

Ted's door stood open; the room beyond it was almost empty. The few things of his own he'd put up—a picture of a man fishing at sunset, a picture of Mary Magdalene washing Jesus' feet, a calendar—were gone. The ashtray on the table was empty, but sitting beside it was one of Ted's carryhandle bags. Inside it were four paperback books: *Animal Farm, The Night of the Hunter, Treasure Island,* and *Of Mice and Men.* Written on the side of the paper bag in Ted's shaky but completely legible handwriting was: *Read the Steinbeck first. "Guys like us," George says when he tells Lennie the story Lennie always wants to hear. Who are guys like us? Who were they to Steinbeck? Who are they to you? Ask yourself this.*

Bobby took the paperbacks but left the bag—he was afraid that if his mom saw one of Ted's carryhandle bags she would go crazy all over again. He looked in the refrigerator and saw nothing but a bottle of French's mustard and a box of baking soda. He closed the fridge again and looked around. It was as if no one had ever lived here at all. Except—

He went to the ashtray, held it to his nose, and breathed in deeply. The smell of Chesterfields was strong, and it brought Ted back completely, Ted sitting here at his table and talking about *Lord of the Flies,* Ted standing at his bathroom mirror, shaving with that scary razor of his, listening through the open door as Bobby read him opinion pieces Bobby himself didn't understand.

Ted leaving one final question on the side of a paper bag: Guys like us. Who are guys like us?

Bobby breathed in again, sucking up little flakes of ash and fighting back the urge to sneeze, holding the smell in, fixing it in his memory as best he could, closing his eyes, and in through the window came the endless ineluctable cry of Bowser, now calling down the dark like a dream: *roop-roop-roop, roop-roop-roop.*

He put the ashtray down again. The urge to sneeze had passed. *I'm going to smoke Chesterfields,* he decided. *I'm going to smoke them all my life.*

He went back downstairs, holding the paperbacks in front of him and walking on the outside of the staircase again as he went from the second floor to the foyer. He slipped into the apartment, tiptoed across the living room (his mother was still snoring, louder than ever), and into his bedroom. He put the books under his bed—*deep* under. If his mom found them he would say Mr. Burton had given them to him. That was a lie, but if he told the truth she'd take the books away. Besides, lying no longer seemed so bad. Lying might become a necessity. In time it might even become a pleasure.

What next? The rumble in his stomach decided him. A couple of peanut butter and jelly sandwiches were next.

He started for the kitchen, tiptoeing past his mother's partly open bedroom door without even thinking about it, then paused. She was shifting around on her bed. Her snores had become ragged and she was talking in her sleep. It was a low, moaning talk Bobby couldn't make out, but he realized he didn't *have* to make it out. He could hear her anyway. And he could see stuff. Her thoughts? Her dreams? Whatever it was, it was awful.

He managed three more steps toward the kitchen, then caught a glimpse of something so terrible his breath froze in his throat like ice: HAVE YOU SEEN BRAUTIGAN! He is an OLD MONGREL but WE LOVE HIM!

"No," he whispered. "Oh Mom, no."

He didn't want to go in there where she was, but his feet turned in that direction anyway. He went with them like a hostage. He watched his hand reach out, the fingers spread, and push her bedroom door open all the way.

Her bed was still made. She lay on top of the coverlet in her dress, one leg drawn up so her knee almost touched her chest. He could see the top of her stocking and her garter, and that made him think of the lady in the calendar picture at The Corner Pocket, the one getting out of the car with most of her skirt in her lap . . . except the lady getting out of the Packard hadn't had ugly bruises above the top of her stocking.

Liz's face was flushed where it wasn't bruised; her hair was matted with sweat; her cheeks were smeary with tears and gooey with makeup. A board creaked under Bobby's foot as he stepped into the room. She cried out and he froze, sure her eyes would open.

Instead of awakening she rolled away from him toward the wall. Here, in her room, the jumble of thoughts and images coming out of her was no clearer but ranker and more pungent, like sweat pouring off a sick person. Running through everything was the sound of

Benny Goodman playing "One O'Clock Jump" and the taste of blood running down the back of her throat.

Have you seen Brautigan, Bobby thought. *He is an old mongrel but we love him. Have you seen . . .*

She had pulled her shades before lying down and the room was very dark. He took another step, then stopped again by the table with the mirror where she sometimes sat to do her makeup. Her purse was there. Bobby thought of Ted hugging him—the hug Bobby had wanted, needed, so badly. Ted stroking his back, cupping the curve of his skull. *When I touch, I pass on a kind of window,* Ted had told him while they were coming back from Bridgeport in the cab. And now, standing by his mother's makeup table with his fists clenched, Bobby looked tentatively through that window into his mother's mind.

He caught a glimpse of her coming home on the train, huddling by herself, looking into ten thousand back yards between Providence and Harwich so as few people as possible would see her face; he saw her spying the bright green keyfob on the shelf by the toothglass as Carol slipped into her old blouse; saw her walking Carol home, asking her questions the whole way, one after another, firing them like bullets out of a machine-gun. Carol, too shaken and worn out to dissemble, had answered them all. Bobby saw his mother walking—*limping*—down to Commonwealth Park, heard her thinking *If only some good could be salvaged from this nightmare, if only some good,* anything *good—*

He saw her sit on a bench in the shade and then get up after awhile, walking toward Spicer's for a headache powder and a Nehi to wash it down with before going back home. And then, just before leaving the park, Bobby saw her spy something tacked to a tree. These somethings were tacked up all over town; she might have passed a couple on her way to the park, so lost in thought she never noticed.

Once again Bobby felt like a passenger in his own body, no more than that. He watched his hand reach out, saw two fingers (the ones that would bear the yellow smudges of the heavy smoker in another few years) make a scissoring motion and catch what was protruding from the mouth of her purse. Bobby pulled the paper free, unfolded it, and read the first two lines in the faint light from the bedroom doorway:

HAVE YOU SEEN BRAUTIGAN!
He is an OLD MONGREL but WE LOVE HIM!

His eyes skipped halfway down to the lines that had no doubt riveted his mother and driven every other thought from her head:

We will pay A VERY LARGE REWARD
($ $ $ $)

Here was the something good she had been wishing for, hoping for, praying for; here was A VERY LARGE REWARD.

And had she hesitated? Had the thought "Wait a minute, my kid loves that old bastard-ball!" even crossed her mind?

Nah.

You *couldn't* hesitate. Because life was full of Don Bidermans, and life wasn't fair.

Bobby left the room on tiptoe with the poster still in his hand, mincing away from her in big soft steps, freezing when a board creaked under his feet, then moving on. Behind him his mom's muttering talk had subsided into low snores again. Bobby made it into the living room and closed her door behind him, holding the knob at full cock until the door was shut tight, not wanting the latch to click. Then he hurried across to the phone, aware only now that he was away from her that his heart was racing and his throat was lined with a taste like old pennies. Any vestige of hunger had vanished.

He picked up the telephone's handset, looked around quickly and narrowly to make sure his mom's door was still shut, then dialed without referring to the poster. The number was burned into his mind: HOusitonic 5-8337.

There was only silence when he finished dialing. That wasn't surprising, either, because there was no HOusitonic exchange in Harwich. And if he felt cold all over (except for his balls and the soles of his feet, which were strangely hot), that was just because he was afraid for Ted. That was all. Just—

There was a stonelike click as Bobby was about to put the handset down. And then a voice said, "Yeah?"

It's Biderman! Bobby thought wildly. *Cripes, it's Biderman!*

"Yeah?" the voice said again. No, not Biderman's. Too low for Biderman's. But it was a nimrod voice, no doubt about that, and as his skin temperature continued to plummet toward absolute zero, Bobby knew that the man on the other end of the line had some sort of yellow coat in his wardrobe.

Suddenly his eyes grew hot and the backs of them began itching. *Is this the Sagamore Family?* was what he'd meant to ask, and if whoever answered the phone said yes, he'd meant to beg them to leave Ted alone. To tell them he, Bobby Garfield, would do something for them if they'd just leave Ted be—he'd do anything they asked. But now that his chance had arrived he could say nothing. Until this moment he still hadn't completely believed in the low men. Now something was on the other end of the line, something that had nothing in common with life as Bobby Garfield understood it.

"Bobby?" the voice said, and there was a kind of insinuate pleasure in the voice, a sensuous recognition. "Bobby," it said again, this time without the question-mark. The flecks began to stream across Bobby's vision; the living room of the apartment suddenly filled with black snow.

"Please . . ." Bobby whispered. He gathered all of his will and forced himself to finish. "Please let him go."

"No can do," the voice from the void told him. "He belongs to the King. Stay away, Bobby. Don't interfere. Ted's our dog. If you don't want to be our dog, too, stay away."

Click.

Bobby held the telephone to his ear a moment longer, needing to tremble and too cold to do it. The itching behind his eyes began to fade, though, and the threads falling across his vision began to merge into the general murk. At last he took the phone away from the side of his head, started to put it down, then paused. There were dozens of little red circles on the handset's perforated earpiece. It was as if the voice of the thing on the other end had caused the telephone to bleed.

Panting in soft and rapid little whimpers, Bobby put it back in its cradle and went into his room. *Don't interfere,* the man at the Sagamore Family number had told him. *Ted's our dog.* But Ted wasn't a dog. He was a man, and he was Bobby's friend.

She could have told them where he'll be tonight, Bobby thought. *I think Carol knew. If she did, and if she told Mom—*

Bobby grabbed the Bike Fund jar. He took all the money out of it and left the apartment. He considered leaving his mother a note but didn't. She might call HOusitonic 5-8337 again if he did, and tell the nimrod with the low voice what her Bobby-O was doing. That was one reason for not leaving a note. The other was that if he could warn Ted in time, he'd go with him. Now Ted would *have* to let him come. And if the low men killed him or kidnapped him? Well, those things were almost the same as running away, weren't they?

Bobby took a final look around the apartment, and as he listened to his mother snore he felt an involuntary tugging at his heart and mind. Ted was right: in spite of everything, he loved her still. If there was *ka,* then loving her was part of his.

Still, he hoped to never see her again.

"Bye, Mom," Bobby whispered. A minute later he was running down Broad Street Hill into the deepening gloom, one hand wrapped around the wad of money in his pocket so none of it would bounce out.

X. DOWN THERE AGAIN. CORNER BOYS. LOW MEN IN YELLOW COATS. THE PAYOUT.

He called a cab from the pay telephone at Spicer's, and while he waited for his ride he took down a BRAUTIGAN lost-pet poster from the outside bulletin board. He also removed an upside-down file-card advertising a '57 Rambler for sale by the owner. He crumpled them up and threw them in the trash barrel by the door, not even bothering to look back over his shoulder to see if old man Spicer, whose foul temper was legendary among the kids on the west side of Harwich, had seen him do it.

The Sigsby twins were down here now, their jump-ropes put aside so they could play hopscotch. Bobby walked over to them and observed the shapes—

—drawn beside the grid. He got down on his knees, and Dina Sigsby, who had been about to toss her stone at the 7, stopped to watch him. Dianne put her grimy fingers over her mouth and giggled. Ignoring them, Bobby used both of his hands to sweep the shapes into chalk blurs. When he was done he stood up and dusted his hands off. The pole-light in Spicer's tiny three-car parking lot came on; Bobby and the girls grew sudden shadows much longer than they were.

"Why'd you do that, stupid old Bobby Garfield?" Dina asked. "They were pretty."

"They're bad luck," Bobby said. "Why aren't you at home?" Not that he didn't have a good idea; it was flashing in their heads like the beer-signs in Spicer's window.

"Mumma-Daddy havin a fight," Dianne said. "She says he got a girlfriend." She laughed and her sister joined in, but their eyes were frightened. They reminded Bobby of the littluns in *Lord of the Flies.*

"Go home before it gets all the way dark," he said.

"Mumma said stay out," Dina told him.

"Then she's stupid and so is your father. Go on!"

They exchanged a glance and Bobby understood that he had

scared them even more. He didn't care. He watched them grab their jump-ropes and go running up the hill. Five minutes later the cab he'd called pulled into the parking area beside the store, its headlights fanning the gravel.

"Huh," the cabbie said. "I dunno about taking any little kid to Bridgeport after dark, even if you do got the fare."

"It's okay," Bobby said, getting in back. If the cabbie meant to throw him out now, he'd better have a crowbar in the trunk to do it with. "My grandfather will meet me." But not at The Corner Pocket, Bobby had already decided; he wasn't going to pull up to the place in a Checker. Someone might be watching for him. "At the Wo Fat Noodle Company. That's on Narragansett Avenue." The Corner Pocket was also on Narragansett. He hadn't remembered the street-name but had found it easily enough in the Yellow Pages after calling the cab.

The driver had started to back out into the street. Now he paused again. "Nasty Gansett Street? Christ, that's no part of town for a kid. Not even in broad daylight."

"My grandfather's meeting me," Bobby repeated. "He said to tip you half a rock. You know, fifty cents."

For a moment the cabbie teetered. Bobby tried to think of some other way to persuade him and couldn't think of a thing. Then the cabbie sighed, dropped his flag, and got rolling. As they passed his building, Bobby looked to see if there were any lights on in their apartment. There weren't, not yet. He sat back and waited for Harwich to drop behind them.

The cabbie's name was Roy DeLois, it was on his taxi-meter. He didn't say a word on the ride to Bridgeport. He was sad because he'd had to take Pete to the vet and have him put down. Pete had been fourteen. That was old for a Collie. He had been Roy DeLois's only real friend. *Go on, big boy, eat up, it's on me,* Roy DeLois would say when he fed Pete. He said the same thing every night. Roy DeLois was divorced. Sometimes he went to a stripper club in Hartford. Bobby could see ghost-images of the dancers, most of whom wore feathers and long white gloves. The image of Pete was sharper. Roy DeLois had been okay coming back from the vet's, but when he saw Pete's empty dish in the pantry at home, he had broken down crying.

They passed The William Penn Grille. Bright light streamed from every window and the street was lined with cars on both sides for three blocks, but Bobby saw no crazy DeSotos or other cars that felt like thinly disguised living creatures. The backs of his eyes didn't itch; there were no black threads.

The cab crossed the canal bridge and then they were down there. Loud Spanish-sounding music played from apartment houses with fire escapes zig-zagging up the sides like iron lightning. Clusters of young men with gleaming combed-back hair stood on some street-corners; clusters of laughing girls stood on others. When the Checker stopped at a red light, a brown-skinned man sauntered over, hips seeming to roll like oil in gabardine slacks that hung below the waist-band of his bright white underwear shorts, and offered to wash the cabbie's windshield with a filthy rag he held. Roy DeLois shook his head curtly and squirted away the instant the light changed.

"Goddam spics," he said. "They should be barred from the country. Ain't we got enough niggers of our own?"

Narragansett Street looked different at night—slightly scarier, slightly more fabulous as well. Locksmiths . . . check-cashing services . . . a couple of bars spilling out laughter and jukebox music and guys with beer bottles in their hands . . . ROD'S GUNS . . . and yes, just beyond Rod's and next to the shop selling SPECIAL SOUVENIRS, the WO FAT NOODLE CO. From here it couldn't be more than four blocks to The Corner Pocket. It was only eight o'clock. Bobby was in plenty of time.

When Roy DeLois pulled up to the curb, there was eighty cents on his meter. Add in a fifty-cent tip and you were talking about a big hole in the old Bike Fund, but Bobby didn't care. He was never going to make a big deal out of money the way *she* did. If he could warn Ted before the low men could grab him, Bobby would be content to walk forever.

"I don't like leaving you off here," Roy DeLois said. "Where's your grandpa?"

"Oh, he'll be right along," Bobby said, striving for a cheerful tone and almost making it. It was really amazing what you could do when your back was against the wall.

He held out the money. For a moment Roy DeLois hesitated instead of taking the dough; thought about driving him back to Spicer's, but *if the kid's not telling the truth about his grandpa what's he doing down here?* Roy DeLois thought. *He's too young to want to get laid.*

I'm fine, Bobby sent back . . . and yes, he thought he could do that, too—a little, anyway. *Go on, stop worrying, I'm fine.*

Roy DeLois finally took the crumpled dollar and the trio of dimes. "This is really too much," he said.

"My grandpa told me to never be stingy like some people are," Bobby said, getting out of the cab. "Maybe you ought to get a new dog. You know, a puppy."

Roy DeLois was maybe fifty, but surprise made him look much younger. "How . . ."

Then Bobby heard him decide he didn't care how. Roy DeLois put his cab in gear and drove away, leaving Bobby in front of the Wo Fat Noodle Company.

He stood there until the cab's taillights disappeared, then began walking slowly in the direction of The Corner Pocket, pausing long enough to look through the dusty window of SPECIAL SOUVENIRS. The bamboo blind was up but the only special souvenir on display was a ceramic ashtray in the shape of a toilet. There was a groove for a cigarette in the seat. PARK YOUR BUTT was written on the tank. Bobby considered this quite witty but not much of a window display; he had sort of been hoping for items of a sexual nature. Especially now that the sun had gone down.

He walked on, past B'PORT PRINTING and SHOES REPAIRED WHILE U WAIT and SNAPPY KARDS FOR ALL OKASIONS. Up ahead was another bar, more young men on the corner, and the sound of The Cadillacs: *Brrrrr, black slacks, make ya cool, Daddy-O, when ya put em on you're a-rarin to go.* Bobby crossed the street, trotting with his shoulders hunched, his head down, and his hands in his pockets.

Across from the bar was an out-of-business restaurant with a tattered awning still overhanging its soaped windows. Bobby slipped into its shadow and kept going, shrinking back once when someone shouted and a bottle shattered. When he reached the next corner he re-crossed Nasty Gansett Street on the diagonal, getting back to the side The Corner Pocket was on.

As he went, he tried to tune his mind outward and pick up some sense of Ted, but there was nothing. Bobby wasn't all that surprised. If *he* had been Ted, he would have gone someplace like the Bridgeport Public Library where he could hang around without being noticed. Maybe after the library closed he'd get a bite to eat, kill a little more time that way. Eventually he'd call another cab and come to collect his money. Bobby didn't think he was anywhere close yet, but he kept listening for him. He was listening so hard that he walked into a guy without even seeing him.

"Hey, *cabrón!*" the guy said—laughing, but not in a nice way. Hands grabbed Bobby's shoulders and held him. "Where was you think you goin, *putino?*"

Bobby looked up and saw four young guys, what his mom would have called corner boys, standing in front of a place called BODEGA. They were Puerto Ricans, he thought, and all wearing sharp-creased slacks. Black boots with pointed toes poked out from beneath their pants cuffs. They were also wearing blue silk jackets with the word DIABLOS written on the back. The I was a devil's pitchfork. Something seemed familiar about the pitchfork, but Bobby had no time to think about that. He realized with a sinking heart that he had wandered into four members of some gang.

"I'm sorry," he said in a dry voice. "Really, I . . . 'scuse me."

He pulled back from the hands holding his shoulders and started around the guy. He made just a single step before one of the others grabbed him. "Where you goin, *tío?*" this one asked. "Where you goin, *tío mío?*"

Bobby pulled free, but the fourth guy pushed him back at the second. The second guy grabbed him again, not so gently this time. It was like being surrounded by Harry and his friends, only worse.

"You got any money, *tío?*" asked the third guy. "Cause this a toll-road, you know."

They all laughed and moved in closer. Bobby could smell their spicy aftershaves, their hair tonics, his own fear. He couldn't hear their mind-voices, but did he need to? They were probably going to beat him up and steal his money. If he was lucky that was all they'd do . . . but he might not be lucky.

"Little boy," the fourth guy almost sang. He reached out a hand, gripped the bristles of Bobby's crewcut, and pulled hard enough to make tears well up in Bobby's eyes. "Little *muchacho,* what you got for money, huh? How much of the good old *dinero?* You have something and we going to let you go. You have nothing and we going to bust your balls."

"Leave him alone, Juan."

They looked around—Bobby too—and here came a fifth guy, also wearing a Diablos jacket, also wearing slacks with a sharp crease; he had on loafers instead of pointy-toed boots, and Bobby recognized him at once. It was the young man who had been playing the Frontier Patrol game in The Corner Pocket when Ted was making his bet. No wonder that pitchfork shape had looked familiar—it was tattooed on the guy's hand. His jacket had been tied inside-out around his waist (*no club jacket in here,* he had told Bobby), but he wore the sign of the Diablos just the same.

Bobby tried to look into the newcomer's mind and saw only dim shapes. His ability was fading again, as it had on the day Mrs. Gerber took them to Savin Rock; shortly after they left McQuown's stand at the end of the midway, it had been gone. This time the winkle had lasted longer, but it was going now, all right.

"Hey Dee," said the boy who had pulled Bobby's hair. "We just gonna shake this little guy out a little. Make him pay his way across Diablo turf."

"Not this one," Dee said. "I know him. He's my *compadre.*"

"He look like a pansy uptown boy to me," said the one who had called Bobby *cabrón* and *putino.* "I teach im a little respect."

"He don't need no lesson from you," Dee said. "You want one from me, Moso?"

Moso stepped back, frowning, and took a cigarette out of his pocket. One of the others snapped him a light, and Dee drew Bobby a little farther down the street.

"What you doing down here, *amigo?*" he asked, gripping Bobby's shoulder with the tattooed hand. "You stupid to be down here alone and you fuckin *loco* to be down here at *night* alone."

"I can't help it," Bobby said. "I have to find the guy I was with yesterday. His name is Ted. He's old and thin and pretty tall. He walks kinda hunched over, like Boris Karloff—you know, the guy in the scary movies?"

"I know Boris Karloff but I don't know no fuckin Ted," Dee said. "I don't ever see him. Man, you ought to get outta here."

"I have to go to The Corner Pocket," Bobby said.

"I was just there," Dee said. "I didn't see no guy like Boris Karloff."

"It's still too early. I think he'll be there between nine-thirty and ten. I have to be there when he comes, because there's some men after him. They wear yellow coats and white shoes . . . they drive big flashy cars . . . one of them's a purple DeSoto, and—"

Dee grabbed him and spun him against the door of a pawnshop so hard that for a moment Bobby thought he had decided to go along with his corner-boy friends after all. Inside the pawnshop an old man with a pair of glasses pushed up on his bald head looked around, annoyed, then back down at the newspaper he was reading.

"The *jefes* in the long yellow coats," Dee breathed. "I seen those guys. Some of the others seen em, too. You don't want to mess with boys like that, *chico.* Something wrong with those boys. They don't look right. Make the bad boys hang around Mallory's Saloon look like good boys."

Something in Dee's expression reminded Bobby of Sully-John, and he remembered S-J saying he'd seen a couple of weird guys outside Commonwealth Park. When Bobby asked what was weird about them, Sully said he didn't exactly know. Bobby knew, though. Sully had seen the low men. Even then they had been sniffing around.

"When did you see them?" Bobby asked. "Today?"

"Cat, give me a break," Dee said. "I ain't been up but two hours, and most of that I been in the bathroom, makin myself pretty for the street. I seen em comin out of The Corner Pocket, a pair of em—day before yesterday, I think. And that place funny lately." He thought for a moment, then called, "Yo, Juan, get your ass over here."

The crewcut-puller came trotting over. Dee spoke to him in Spanish. Juan spoke back and Dee responded more briefly, pointing to Bobby. Juan leaned over Bobby, hands on the knees of his sharp pants.

"You seen 'ese guys, huh?"

Bobby nodded.

"One bunch in a big purple DeSoto? One bunch in a Cri'sler? One bunch in an Olds 98?"

Bobby only knew the DeSoto, but he nodded.

"Those cars ain't real cars," Juan said. He looked sideways at Dee to see if Dee was laughing. Dee wasn't; he only nodded for Juan to keep going. "They something else."

"I think they're alive," Bobby said.

Juan's eyes lit up. "Yeah! Like alive! And 'ose men—"

"What did they look like? I've seen one of their cars, but not *them*."

Juan tried but couldn't say, at least not in English. He lapsed into Spanish instead. Dee translated some of it, but in an absent fashion; more and more he was conversing with Juan and ignoring Bobby. The other corner boys—and boys were what they really were, Bobby saw—drew close and added their own contributions. Bobby couldn't understand their talk, but he thought they were scared, all of them. They were tough enough guys—down here you had to be tough just to make it through the day—but the low men had frightened them all the same. Bobby caught one final clear image: a tall striding figure in a calf-length mustard-colored coat, the kind of coat men sometimes wore in movies like *Gunfight at the O.K. Corral* and *The Magnificent Seven.*

"I see four of em comin out of that barber shop with the horse-parlor in the back," the one who seemed to be named Filio said. "That's what they do, those guys, go into places and ask questions. Always leave one of their big cars runnin at the curb. You'd think it'd be crazy to do that down here, leave a car runnin at the curb, but who'd steal one of *those* goddam things?"

No one, Bobby knew. If you tried, the steering wheel might turn into a snake and strangle you; the seat might turn into a quicksand pool and drown you.

"They come out all in a bunch," Filio went on, "all wearin 'ose long yellow coats even though the day's so hot you coulda fried a egg on the fuckin sidewalk. They was all wearin these nice white shoes—sharp, you know how I always notice what people got on their feet, I get hard for that shit—and I don't think . . . I don't think . . ." He paused, gathered himself, and said something to Dee in Spanish.

Bobby asked what he'd said.

"He sayin their shoes wasn' touchin the ground," Juan replied. His eyes were big. There was no scorn or disbelief in them. "He sayin they got this big red Cri'sler, and when they go back to it, their fuckin shoes ain't quite touchin the ground." Juan forked two fingers in front of his mouth, spat through them, then crossed himself.

No one said anything for a moment or two after that, and then Dee bent gravely over Bobby again. "These are the guys lookin for your frien'?"

"That's right," Bobby said. "I have to warn him."

He had a mad idea that Dee would offer to go with him to The Corner Pocket, and then the rest of the Diablos would join in; they would walk up the street snapping their fingers in unison like the Jets in *West Side Story.* They would be his friends now, gang guys who happened to have really good hearts.

Of course nothing of the sort happened. What happened was Moso wandered off, back toward the place where Bobby had walked into him. The others followed. Juan paused long enough to say, "You run into those *caballeros* and you gonna be one dead *putino, tío mío.*" Only Dee was left and Dee said, "He's right. You ought to go back to your own part of the worl', my frien'. Let your *amigo* take care of himself."

"I can't," Bobby said. And then, with genuine curiosity: "Could you?"

"Not against ordinary guys, maybe, but these ain't ordinary guys. Was you just lissen?"

"Yes," Bobby said. "But."

"You crazy, little boy. *Poco loco.*"

"I guess so." He *felt* crazy, all right. *Poco loco* and then some. Crazy as a shithouse mouse, his mother would have said.

Dee started away and Bobby felt his heart cramp. The big boy got to the corner—his buddies were waiting for him on the other side of the street—then wheeled back, made his finger into a gun, and pointed it at Bobby. Bobby grinned and pointed his own back.

"*Vaya con Dios, mi amigo loco,*" Dee said, then sauntered across the street with the collar of his gang jacket turned up against the back of his neck.

Bobby turned the other way and started walking again, detouring around the pools of light cast by fizzing neon signs and trying to keep in the shadows as much as he could.

Across the street from The Corner Pocket was a mortuary—DESPEGNI FUNERAL PARLOR, it said on the green awning. Hanging in the window was a clock whose face was outlined in a chilly circle of blue neon. Below the clock was a sign which read TIME AND TIDE WAIT FOR NO MAN. According to the clock it was twenty past eight. He was still in time, in plenty of time, and he could see an alley beyond the Pocket where he might wait in relative safety, but Bobby couldn't just park himself and wait, even though he knew that would be the smart thing to do. If he'd really been smart, he never would have come down here in the first place. He wasn't a wise old owl; he was a scared kid who needed help. He doubted if there was any in The Corner Pocket, but maybe he was wrong.

Bobby walked under the banner reading **COME IN IT'S KOOL INSIDE**. He had never felt less in need of air conditioning in his life; it was a hot night but he was cold all over.

God, if You're there, please help me now. Help me to be brave . . . and help me to be lucky.

Bobby opened the door and went in.

The smell of beer was much stronger and much fresher, and the room with the pinball machines in it banged and jangled with lights and noise. Where before only Dee had been playing pinball, there now seemed to be at least two dozen guys, all of them smoking, all of them wearing strap-style undershirts and Frank Sinatra hello-young-lovers hats, all of them with bottles of Bud parked on the glass tops of the Gottlieb machines.

The area by Len Files's desk was brighter than before because there were more lights on in the bar (where every stool was taken) as well as in the pinball room. The poolhall itself, which had been mostly dark on Wednesday, was now lit like an operating theater. There were men at every table bending and circling and making shots in a blue fog of cigarette smoke; the chairs along the walls were all taken. Bobby could see Old Gee with his feet up on the shoeshine posts, and—

"What the fuck are *you* doing here?"

Bobby turned, startled by the voice and shocked by the sound of that word coming out of a woman's mouth. It was Alanna Files. The door to the living-room area behind the desk was just swinging shut behind her. Tonight she was wearing a white silk blouse that showed her shoulders—pretty shoulders, creamy-white and as round as breasts—and the top of her prodigious bosom. Below the white blouse were the largest pair of red slacks Bobby had ever seen. Yesterday, Alanna had been kind, smiling . . . almost laughing at him, in fact, although in a way Bobby hadn't minded. Tonight she looked scared to death.

"I'm sorry . . . I know I'm not supposed to be in here, but I need to find my friend Ted and I thought . . . thought that . . ." He heard his voice shrinking like a balloon that's been let loose to fly around the room.

Something was horribly wrong. It was like a dream he sometimes had where he was at his desk studying spelling or science or just reading a story and everyone started laughing at him and he realized he had forgotten to put his pants on before coming to school, he was sitting at his desk with everything hanging out for everyone to look at, girls and teachers and just everyone.

The beat of the bells in the gameroom hadn't completely quit, but it had slowed down. The flood of conversation and laughter from the bar had dried up almost entirely. The click of pool and billiard balls had ceased. Bobby looked around, feeling those snakes in his stomach again.

They weren't all looking at him, but most were. Old Gee was staring with eyes that looked like holes burned in dirty paper. And although the window in Bobby's mind was almost opaque now—soaped over—he felt that a lot of the people in here had sort of been expecting him. He doubted if they knew it, and even if they did they wouldn't know why. They were kind of asleep, like the people of Midwich. The low men had been in. The low men had—

"Get out, Randy," Alanna said in a dry little whisper. In her distress she had called Bobby by his father's name. "Get out while you still can."

Old Gee had slid out of the shoeshine chair. His wrinkled seersucker jacket caught on one of the foot-pedestals and tore as he started forward, but he paid no attention as the silk lining floated down beside his knee like a toy parachute. His eyes looked more like burned holes than ever. "Get him," Old Gee said in a wavery voice. "Get that kid."

Bobby had seen enough. There was no help here. He scrambled for the door and tore it open. Behind him he had the sense of people starting to move, but slowly. Too slowly.

Bobby Garfield ran out into the night.

He ran almost two full blocks before a stitch in his side forced him to first slow down, then stop. No one was following and that was good, but if Ted went into The Corner Pocket to collect his money he was finished, done, *kaput.* It wasn't just the low men he had to worry about; now there was Old Gee and the rest of them to worry about, too, and Ted didn't know it. The question was, what could Bobby do about it?

He looked around and saw the storefronts were gone; he'd come to an area of warehouses. They loomed like giant faces from which most of the features had been erased. There was a smell of fish and sawdust and some vague rotted perfume that might have been old meat.

There was *nothing* he could do about it. He was just a kid and it was out of his hands. Bobby realized that, but he also realized he couldn't let Ted walk into The Corner Pocket without at least trying to warn him. There was nothing Hardy Boys–heroic about this, either; he simply couldn't leave without making the effort. And it was his mother who had put him in this position. *His own mother.*

"I hate you, Mom," he whispered. He was still cold, but sweat was pouring out of his body; every inch of his skin felt wet. "I don't care what Don Biderman and those other guys did to you, you're a bitch and I hate you."

Bobby turned and began to trot back the way he had come, keeping to the shadows. Twice he heard people coming and crouched in doorways, making himself small until they had passed by. Making himself small was easy. He had never felt smaller in his life.

This time he turned into the alley. There were garbage cans on one side and a stack of cartons on the other, full of returnable bottles that smelled of beer. This cardboard column was half a foot taller than Bobby, and when he stepped behind it he was perfectly concealed from the street. Once during his wait something hot and furry brushed against his ankle and Bobby started to scream. He stifled most of it before it could get out, looked down, and saw a scruffy alleycat looking back up at him with green headlamp eyes.

"Scat, Pat," Bobby whispered, and kicked at it. The cat revealed the needles of its teeth, hissed, then did a slow strut back down the alley, weaving around the clots of refuse and strews of broken glass, its tail lifted in what looked like disdain. Through the brick wall beside him Bobby could hear the dull throb of The Corner Pocket's juke. Mickey and Sylvia were singing "Love Is Strange." It was strange, all right. A big strange pain in the ass.

From his place of concealment Bobby could no longer see the mortuary clock and he'd lost any sense of how much or how little time was passing. Beyond the beer-and-garbage reek of the alley a summer streetlife opera was going on. People shouted out to each other, sometimes laughing, sometimes angry, sometimes in English, sometimes in one of a dozen other languages. There was a rattle of explosions that made him stiffen—gunshots was his first idea—and then he recognized the sound as firecrackers, probably ladyfingers, and relaxed a little again. Cars blasted by, many of them brightly painted railjobs and jackjobs with chrome pipes and glasspack mufflers. Once there was what sounded like a fistfight with people gathered around yelling encouragement to the scufflers. Once a lady who sounded both drunk and sad went by singing "Where the Boys Are" in a beautiful slurry voice. Once there were police sirens which approached and then faded away again.

Bobby didn't doze, exactly, but fell into a kind of daydream. He and Ted were living on a farm somewhere, maybe in Florida. They worked long hours, but Ted could work pretty hard for an old guy, especially now that he had quit smoking and had some of his wind back. Bobby went to school under another name—Ralph Sullivan—and at night they sat on the porch, eating Ted's cooking and drinking iced tea. Bobby read to him from the newspaper and when they went in to bed they slept deeply and their sleep was peaceful, interrupted by no bad dreams. When they went to the grocery store on Fridays, Bobby would check the bulletin board for lost-pet posters or upside-down file-cards advertising items for sale by owner, but he never found any. The low men had lost Ted's scent. Ted was no longer anyone's dog and they were safe on their farm. Not father and son or grandfather and grandson, but only friends.

Guys like us, Bobby thought drowsily. He was leaning against the brick wall now, his head slipping downward until his chin was almost on his chest. *Guys like us, why shouldn't there be a place for guys like us?*

Lights splashed down the alley. Each time this had happened Bobby had peered around the stack of cartons. This time he almost didn't—he wanted to close his eyes and think about the farm—but he forced himself to look, and what he saw was the stubby yellow tailfin of a Checker cab, just pulling up in front of The Corner Pocket.

Adrenaline flooded Bobby and turned on lights in his head he hadn't even known about. He dodged around the stack of boxes, spilling the top two off. His foot struck an empty garbage can and knocked it against the wall. He almost stepped on a hissing furry something—the cat again. Bobby kicked it aside and ran out of the alley. As he turned toward The Corner Pocket he slipped on some sort of greasy goo and went down on one knee. He saw the mortuary clock in its cool blue ring: 9:45. The cab was idling at the curb in front of The Corner Pocket's door. Ted Brautigan was standing beneath the banner reading **COME IN IT'S KOOL INSIDE**, paying the driver. Bent down to the driver's open window like that, Ted looked more like Boris Karloff than ever.

Across from the cab, parked in front of the mortuary, was a huge Oldsmobile as red as Alanna's pants. It hadn't been there earlier, Bobby was sure of that. Its shape wasn't quite solid. Looking at it didn't just make your eyes want to water; it made your *mind* want to water.

Ted! Bobby tried to yell, but no yell came out—all he could produce was a strawlike whisper. *Why doesn't he feel them?* Bobby thought. *How come he doesn't know?*

Maybe because the low men could block him out somehow. Or maybe the people inside The Corner Pocket were doing the blocking. Old Gee and all the rest. The low men had perhaps turned them into human sponges that could soak up the warning signals Ted usually felt.

More lights splashed the street. As Ted straightened and the Checker pulled away, the purple DeSoto sprang around the corner. The cab had to swerve to avoid it. Beneath the streetlights the DeSoto looked like a huge blood-clot decorated with chrome and glass. Its headlights were moving and shimmering like lights seen underwater . . . and then they *blinked.* They weren't headlights at all. They were eyes.

Ted! Still nothing but that dry whisper came out, and Bobby couldn't seem to get back on his feet. He was no longer sure he even *wanted* to get back on his feet. A terrible fear, as disorienting as the flu and as debilitating as a cataclysmic case of the squitters, was enveloping him. Passing the blood-clot DeSoto outside the William Penn Grille had been bad; to be caught in its oncoming eyelights was a thousand times worse. No—a *million* times.

He was aware that he had torn his pants and scraped blood out of his knee, he could hear Little Richard howling from someone's upstairs window, and he could still see the blue circle around the mortuary clock like a flashbulb afterimage tattooed on the retina, but none of that seemed real. Nasty Gansett Avenue suddenly seemed no more than a badly painted backdrop. Behind it was some unsuspected reality, and reality was *dark.*

The DeSoto's grille was moving. *Snarling. Those cars ain't real cars,* Juan had said. *They something else.*

They were something else, all right.

"Ted . . ." A little louder this time . . . and Ted heard. He turned toward Bobby, eyes widening, and then the DeSoto bounced up over the curb behind him, its blazing unsteady headlights pinning Ted and making his shadow grow as Bobby's and the Sigsby girls' shadows had grown when the pole-light came on in Spicer's little parking lot.

Ted wheeled back toward the DeSoto, raising one hand to shield his eyes from the glare. More light swept the street. This time it was a Cadillac coming up from the warehouse district, a snot-green Cadillac that looked at least a mile long, a Cadillac with fins like grins and sides that moved like the lobes of a lung. It thumped up over the curb just behind Bobby, stopping less than a foot from his back. Bobby heard a low panting sound. The Cadillac's motor, he realized, was breathing.

Doors were opening in all three cars. Men were getting out—or things that looked like men at first glance. Bobby counted six, counted eight, stopped counting. Each of them wore a long mustard-colored coat—the kind that was called a duster—and on the right front lapel of each was the staring crimson eye Bobby remembered from his dream. He supposed the red eyes were badges. The creatures wearing them were . . . what? Cops? No. A posse, like in a movie? That was a little closer. Vigilantes? Closer still but still not right. They were—

They're regulators. Like in that movie me and S-J saw at the Empire last year, the one with John Payne and Karen Steele.

That was it—oh yes. The regulators in the movie had turned out to be just a bunch of bad guys, but at first you thought they were ghosts or monsters or something. Bobby thought that these regulators really *were* monsters.

One of them grasped Bobby under the arm. Bobby cried out—the contact was quite the most horrible thing he had ever experienced in his life. It made being thrown against the wall by his mother seem like very small change indeed. The low man's touch was like being grasped by a hot-water bottle that had grown fingers . . . only the feel of them kept shifting. It would feel like fingers in his armpit, then like claws. Fingers . . . claws. Fingers . . . claws. That unspeakable touch buzzed into his flesh, reaching both up and down. *It's Jack's stick,* he thought crazily. *The one sharpened at both ends.*

Bobby was pulled toward Ted, who was surrounded by the others. He stumbled along on legs that were too weak to walk. Had he thought he would be able to warn Ted? That they would run away together down Narragansett Avenue, perhaps even skipping a little, the way Carol used to? That was quite funny, wasn't it?

Incredibly, Ted didn't seem afraid. He stood in the semicircle of low men and the only emotion on his face was concern for Bobby. The thing gripping Bobby—now with a hand, now with loathsome pulsing rubber fingers, now with a clutch of talons—suddenly let him go. Bobby staggered, reeled. One of the others uttered a high, barking cry and pushed him in the middle of the back. Bobby flew forward and Ted caught him.

Sobbing with terror, Bobby pressed his face against Ted's shirt. He could smell the comforting aromas of Ted's cigarettes and shaving soap, but they weren't strong enough to cover the stench that was coming from the low men—a meaty, garbagey smell—and a higher smell like burning whiskey that was coming from their cars.

Bobby looked up at Ted. "It was my mother," he said. "It was my mother who told."

"This isn't her fault, no matter what you may think," Ted replied. "I simply stayed too long."

"But was it a nice vacation, Ted?" one of the low men asked. His voice had a gruesome buzz, as if his vocal cords were packed with bugs—locusts or maybe crickets. He could have been the one Bobby spoke to on the phone, the one who'd said Ted was their dog . . . but maybe they all sounded the same. *If you don't want to be our dog, too, stay away,* the one on the phone had said, but he had come down here anyway, and now . . . oh now . . .

"Wasn't bad," Ted replied.

"I hope you at least got laid," another said, "because you probably won't get another chance."

Bobby looked around. The low men stood shoulder to shoulder, surrounding them, penning them in their smell of sweat and maggoty meat, blocking off any sight of the street with their yellow coats. They were dark-skinned, deep-eyed, red-lipped (as if they had been eating cherries) . . . but they weren't what they looked like. They weren't what they looked like at all. Their faces wouldn't stay in their faces, for one thing; their cheeks and chins and hair kept trying to spread outside the lines (it was the only way Bobby could interpret what he was seeing). Beneath their dark skins were skins as white as their pointed reet-petite shoes. *But their lips are still red,* Bobby thought, *their lips are always red.* As their eyes were always black, not really eyes at all but caves. *And they are so tall,* he realized. *So tall and so thin. There are no thoughts like our thoughts in their brains, no feelings like our feelings in their hearts.*

From across the street there came a thick slobbering grunt. Bobby looked in that direction and saw that one of the Oldsmobile's tires had turned into a blackish-gray tentacle. It reached out, snared a cigarette wrapper, and pulled it back. A moment later the tentacle was a tire again, but the cigarette wrapper was sticking out of it like something half swallowed.

"Ready to come back, hoss?" one of the low men asked Ted. He bent toward him, the folds of his yellow coat rustling stiffly, the red eye on the lapel staring. "Ready to come back and do your duty?"

"I'll come," Ted replied, "but the boy stays here."

More hands settled on Bobby, and something like a living branch caressed the nape of his neck. It set off that buzzing again, something that was both an alarm and a sickness. It rose into his head and hummed there like a hive. Within that lunatic hum he heard first one bell, tolling rapidly, then many. A world of bells in some terrible black night of hot hurricane winds. He supposed he was sensing wherever the low men had come from, an alien place trillions of miles from Connecticut and his mother. Villages were burning under unknown constellations, people were screaming, and that touch on his neck . . . that awful touch . . .

Bobby moaned and buried his head against Ted's chest again.

"He wants to be with you," an unspeakable voice crooned. "I think we'll bring him, Ted. He has no natural ability as a Breaker, but still . . . all things serve the King, you know." The unspeakable fingers caressed again.

"All things serve the *Beam,*" Ted said in a dry, correcting voice. His teacher's voice.

"Not for much longer," the low man said, and laughed. The sound of it loosened Bobby's bowels.

"Bring him," said another voice. It held a note of command. They *did* all sound sort of alike, but this was the one he had spoken to on the phone; Bobby was sure.

"No!" Ted said. His hands tightened on Bobby's back. "He stays here!"

"Who are you to give us orders?" the low man in charge asked. "How proud you have grown during your little time of freedom, Ted! How *haughty!* Yet soon you'll be back in the same room where you have spent so many years, with the others, and if I say the boy *comes,* then the boy *comes.*"

"If you bring him, you'll have to go on taking what you need from me," Ted said. His voice was very quiet but very strong. Bobby hugged him as tight as he could and shut his eyes. He didn't want to look at the low men, not ever again. The worst thing about them was that their touch was like Ted's, in a way: it opened a window. But who would want to look through such a window? Who would want to see the tall, red-lipped scissor-shapes as they really were? Who would want to see the owner of that red Eye?

"You're a Breaker, Ted. You were made for it, born to it. And if we tell you to break, you'll break, by God."

"You can force me, I'm not so foolish as to think you can't . . . but if you leave him here, I'll give what I have to you freely. And I have more to give than you could . . . well, perhaps you *could* imagine it."

"I want the boy," the low man in charge said, but now he sounded thoughtful. Perhaps even doubtful. "I want him as a pretty, something to give the King."

"I doubt if the Crimson King will thank you for a meaningless pretty if it interferes with his plans," Ted said. "There is a gunslinger—"

"Gunslinger, pah!"

"Yet he and his friends have reached the borderland of End-World," Ted said, and now he was the one who sounded thoughtful. "If I give you what you want instead of forcing you to take it, I may be able to speed things up by fifty years or more. As you say, I'm a Breaker, made for it and born to it. There aren't many of us. You need every one, and most of all you need me. Because I'm the best."

"You flatter yourself . . . and you overestimate your importance to the King."

"Do I? I wonder. Until the Beams break, the Dark Tower stands—surely I don't need to remind you of that. Is one boy worth the risk?"

Bobby hadn't the slightest idea what Ted was talking about and didn't care. All he knew was that the course of his life was being decided on the sidewalk outside a Bridgeport billiard parlor. He could hear the rustle of the low men's coats; he could smell them; now that Ted had touched him again he could feel them even more clearly. That horrible itching behind his eyes had begun again, too. In a weird way it harmonized with the buzzing in his head. The black specks drifted across his vision and he was suddenly sure what they meant, what they were for. In Clifford Simak's book *Ring Around the Sun,* it was a top that took you off into other worlds; you followed the rising spirals. In truth, Bobby suspected, it was the specks that did it. The black specks. They were alive . . .

And they were hungry.

"Let the boy decide," the leader of the low men said at last. His living branch of a finger caressed the back of Bobby's neck again. "He loves you so much, Teddy. You're his *te-ka.* Aren't you? That means destiny's friend, Bobby-O. Isn't that what this old smoky-smelling Teddy-bear is to you? Your destiny's friend?"

Bobby said nothing, only pressed his cold throbbing face against Ted's shirt. He now repented coming here with all his heart—would have stayed home hiding under his bed if he had known the truth of the low men—but yes, he supposed Ted was his *te-ka.* He didn't know about stuff like destiny, he was only a kid, but Ted was his friend. *Guys like us,* Bobby thought miserably. *Guys like us.*

"So how do you feel now that you see us?" the low man asked. "Would you like to come with us so you can be close to good old Ted? Perhaps see him on the odd weekend? Discuss *literature* with your dear old *te-ka?* Learn to eat what we eat and drink what we drink?" The awful fingers again, caressing. The buzzing in Bobby's head increased. The black specks fattened and now *they* looked like fingers—beckoning fingers. "We eat it hot, Bobby," the low man whispered. "And drink it hot as well. Hot . . . and sweet. Hot . . . and sweet."

"Stop it," Ted snapped.

"Or would you rather stay with your mother?" the crooning voice went on, ignoring Ted. "Surely not. Not a boy of your principles. Not a boy who has discovered the joys of friendship and *literature.* Surely you'll come with this wheezy old *ka-mai,* won't you? Or will you? Decide, Bobby. Do it now, and knowing that what you decide is what will bide. Now and forever."

Bobby had a delirious memory of the lobsterback cards blurring beneath McQuown's long white fingers: *Now they go, now they slow, now they rest, here's the test.*

I fail, Bobby thought. *I fail the test.*

"Let me go, mister," he said miserably. "Please don't take me with you."

"Even if it means your *te-ka* has to go on without your wonderful and revivifying company?" The voice was smiling, but Bobby could almost taste the knowing contempt under its cheery surface, and he shivered. With relief, because he understood he was probably going to be let free after all, with shame because he knew what he was doing—crawling, chintzing, chickening out. All the things the good guys in the movies and books he loved never did. But the good guys in the movies and books never had to face anything like the low men in the yellow coats or the horror of the black specks. And what Bobby saw of those things here, outside The Corner Pocket, was not the worst of it either. What if he saw the rest? What if the black specks drew him into a world where he saw the men in the yellow coats as they really were? What if he saw the shapes inside the ones they wore in this world?

"Yes," he said, and began to cry.

"Yes what?"

"Even if he has to go without me."

"Ah. And even if it means going back to your mother?"

"Yes."

"You perhaps understand your bitch of a mother a little better now, do you?"

"Yes," Bobby said for the third time. By now he was nearly moaning. "I guess I do."

"That's enough," Ted said. "Stop it."

But the voice wouldn't. Not yet. "You've learned how to be a coward, Bobby . . . haven't you?"

"*Yes!*" he cried, still with his face against Ted's shirt. "*A baby, a little chickenshit baby, yes yes yes! I don't care! Just let me go home!*" He drew in a great long unsteady breath and let it out in a scream. "*I WANT MY MOTHER!*" It was the howl of a terrified littlun who has finally glimpsed the beast from the water, the beast from the air.

"All right," the low man said. "Since you put it *that* way. Assuming your Teddy-bear confirms that he'll go to work with a will and not have to be chained to his oar as previously."

"I promise." Ted let go of Bobby. Bobby remained as he was,

clutching Ted with panicky tightness and pushing his face against Ted's chest, until Ted pushed him gently away.

"Go inside the poolhall, Bobby. Tell Files to give you a ride home. Tell him if he does that, my friends will leave *him* alone."

"I'm sorry, Ted. I wanted to come with you. I *meant* to come with you. But I can't. I'm so sorry."

"You shouldn't be hard on yourself." But Ted's look was heavy, as if he knew that from tonight on Bobby would be able to be nothing else.

Two of the yellowcoats grasped Ted's arms. Ted looked at the one standing behind Bobby—the one who had been caressing the nape of Bobby's neck with that horrible sticklike finger. "They don't need to do that, Cam. I'll walk."

"Let him go," Cam said. The low men holding Ted released his arms. Then, for the last time, Cam's finger touched the back of Bobby's neck. Bobby uttered a choked wail. He thought, *If he does it again I'll go crazy, I won't be able to help it. I'll start to scream and I won't be able to stop. Even if my head bursts open I'll go on screaming.* "Get inside there, little boy. Do it before I change my mind and take you anyway."

Bobby stumbled toward The Corner Pocket. The door stood open but empty. He climbed the single step, then turned back. Three of the low men were clustered around Ted, but Ted was walking toward the blood-clot DeSoto on his own.

"Ted!"

Ted turned, smiled, started to wave. Then the one called Cam leaped forward, seized him, whirled him, and thrust him into the car. As Cam swung the DeSoto's back door shut Bobby saw, for just an instant, an incredibly tall, incredibly scrawny being standing inside a long yellow coat, a thing with flesh as white as new snow and lips as red as fresh blood. Deep in its eyesockets were savage points of light and dancing flecks of darkness in pupils which swelled and contracted as Ted's had done. The red lips peeled back, revealing needly teeth that put the alleycat's to shame. A black tongue lolled out from between those teeth and wagged an obscene goodbye. Then the creature in the yellow coat sprinted around the hood of the purple DeSoto, thin legs gnashing, thin knees pumping, and plunged in behind the wheel. Across the street the Olds started up, its engine sounding like the roar of an awakening dragon. Perhaps it *was* a dragon. From its place skewed halfway across the sidewalk, the Cadillac's engine did the same. Living headlights flooded this part of Narragansett Avenue in a pulsing glare. The DeSoto skidded in a U-turn, one fenderskirt scraping up a brief train of sparks from the street, and for a moment Bobby saw Ted's face in the DeSoto's back window. Bobby raised his hand and waved. He thought Ted raised his own in return but could not be sure. Once more his head filled with a sound like hoofbeats.

He never saw Ted Brautigan again.

"Bug out, kid," Len Files said. His face was cheesy-white, seeming to hang off his skull the way the flesh hung off his sister's upper arms. Behind him the lights of the Gottlieb machines in the little arcade flashed and flickered with no one to watch them; the cool cats who made an evening specialty of Corner Pocket pinball were clustered behind Len Files like children. To Len's right were the pool and billiard players, many of them clutching cues like clubs. Old Gee stood off to one side by the cigarette machine. He didn't have a pool-cue; from one gnarled old hand there hung a small automatic pistol. It didn't scare Bobby. After Cam and his yellowcoat friends, he didn't think anything would have the power to scare him right now. For the time being he was all scared out.

"Put an egg in your shoe and beat it, kid. Now."

"Better do it, kiddo." That was Alanna, standing behind the desk. Bobby glanced at her and thought, *If I was older I bet I'd give you something. I bet I would.* She saw his glance—the quality of his glance—and looked away, flushed and frightened and confused.

Bobby looked back at her brother. "You want those guys back here?"

Len's hanging face grew even longer. "You kidding?"

"Okay then," Bobby said. "Give me what I want and I'll go away. You'll never see me again." He paused. "Or *them*."

"Whatchu want, kid?" Old Gee asked in his wavering voice.

Bobby was going to get whatever he asked for; it was flashing in Old Gee's mind like a big bright sign. That mind was as clear now as it had been when it had belonged to Young Gee, cold and calculating and unpleasant, but it seemed innocent after Cam and his regulators. Innocent as ice cream.

"A ride home," Bobby said. "That's number one." Then—speaking to Old Gee rather than Len—he gave them number two.

Len's car was a Buick: big, long, and new. Vulgar but not low. Just a car. The two of them rode to the sound of danceband music from the forties. Len spoke only once during the trip to Harwich. "Don't you go tuning that to no rock and roll. I have to listen to enough of that shit at work."

They drove past the Asher Empire, and Bobby saw there was a life-sized cardboard cutout of Brigitte Bardot standing to the left of the ticket booth. He glanced at it without very much interest. He felt too old for B.B. now.

They turned off Asher; the Buick slipped down Broad Street Hill like a whisper behind a cupped hand. Bobby pointed out his building. Now the apartment was lit up, all right; every light was blazing. Bobby looked at the clock on the Buick's dashboard and saw it was almost eleven P.M.

As the Buick pulled to the curb Len Files found his tongue again. "Who were they, kid? Who were those *gonifs?*"

Bobby almost grinned. It reminded him of how, at the end of almost every *Lone Ranger* episode, someone said *Who* was *that masked man?*

"Low men," he told Len. "Low men in yellow coats."

"I wouldn't want to be your pal right now."

"No," Bobby said. A shudder shook through him like a gust of wind. "Me neither. Thanks for the ride."

"Don't mention it. Just stay the fuck clear of my felts and greens from now on. You're banned for life."

The Buick—a boat, a Detroit cabin-cruiser, but not low—drew away. Bobby watched as it turned in a driveway across the street and then headed back up the hill past Carol's building. When it had disappeared around the corner, Bobby looked up at the stars—stacked billions, a spilled bridge of light. Stars and more stars beyond them, spinning in the black.

There is a Tower, he thought. *It holds everything together. There are Beams that protect it somehow. There is a Crimson King, and Breakers working to destroy the Beams . . . not because the Breakers want to but because* it *wants them to. The Crimson King.*

Was Ted back among the rest of the Breakers yet? Bobby wondered. Back and pulling his oar?

I'm sorry, he thought, starting up the walk to the porch. He remembered sitting there with Ted, reading to him from the newspaper. Just a couple of guys. *I wanted to go with you but I couldn't. In the end I couldn't.*

He stopped at the bottom of the porch steps, listening for Bowser around on Colony Street. There was nothing. Bowser had gone to sleep. It was a miracle. Smiling wanly, Bobby got moving again. His mother must have heard the creak of the second porch step—it was pretty loud—because she cried out his name and then there was the sound of her running footsteps. He was on the porch when the door flew open and she ran out, still dressed in the clothes she had been wearing when she came home from Providence. Her hair hung around her face in wild curls and tangles.

"Bobby!" she cried. "Bobby, oh Bobby! Thank God! Thank God!"

She swept him up, turning him around and around in a kind of dance, her tears wetting one side of his face.

"I wouldn't take their money," she babbled. "They called me back and asked for the address so they could send a check and I said never mind, it was a mistake, I was hurt and upset, I said no, Bobby, I said no, I said I didn't want their money."

Bobby saw she was lying. Someone had pushed an envelope with her name on it under the foyer door. Not a check, three hundred dollars in cash. Three hundred dollars for the return of their best Breaker; three hundred lousy rocks. They were even bigger cheapskates than she was.

"I said I didn't want it, did you hear me?"

Carrying him into the apartment now. He weighed almost a hundred pounds and was too heavy for her but she carried him anyway. As she babbled on, Bobby realized they wouldn't have the police to contend with, at least; she hadn't called them. Mostly she had just been sitting here, plücking at her wrinkled skirt and praying incoherently that he would come home. She loved him. That beat in her mind like the wings of a bird trapped in a barn. She loved him. It didn't help much . . . but it helped a little. Even if it was a trap, it helped a little.

"I said I didn't want it, we didn't need it, they could keep their money. I said . . . I told them . . ."

"That's good, Mom," he said. "That's good. Put me down."

"Where have you been? Are you all right? Are you hungry?"

He answered her questions back to front. "I'm hungry, yeah, but I'm fine. I went to Bridgeport. I got this."

He reached into his pants pocket and brought out the remains of the Bike Fund money. His ones and change were mixed into a messy green wad of tens and twenties and fifties. His mother stared at the money as it rained down on the endtable by the sofa, her good eye growing bigger and bigger until Bobby was afraid it might tumble right out of her face. The other eye remained squinched down in its thundercloud of blue-black flesh. She looked like a battered old pirate gloating over freshly unburied treasure, an image Bobby could have done without . . . and one which never entirely left him during the fifteen years between that night and the night of her death. Yet some new and not particularly pleasant part of him *enjoyed* that look—how it rendered her old and ugly and comic, a person who was stupid as well as avaricious. *That's my ma,* he thought in a Jimmy Durante voice. *That's my ma. We both gave him up, but I got paid better than you did, Ma, didn't I? Yeah! Hotcha!*

"Bobby," she whispered in a trembly voice. She looked like a pirate and sounded like a winning contestant on that Bill Cullen show, *The Price Is Right.* "Oh Bobby, so much *money!* Where did it come from?"

"Ted's bet," Bobby said. "This is the payout."

"But Ted . . . won't he—"

"He won't need it anymore."

Liz winced as if one of her bruises had suddenly twinged. Then she began sweeping the money together, sorting the bills even as she did so. "I'm going to get you that bike," she said. Her fingers moved with the speed of an experienced three-card monte dealer. *No one beats that shuffle,* Bobby thought. *No one has* ever *beaten that shuffle.* "First thing in the morning. Soon as the Western Auto opens. Then we'll—"

"I don't want a bike," he said. "Not from that. And not from you."

She froze with her hands full of money and he felt her rage bloom at once, something red and electrical. "No thanks from you, are there? I was a fool to ever expect any. God damn you if you're not the spitting image of your father!" She drew back her hand again with the fingers open. The difference this time was that he knew it was coming. She had blindsided him for the last time.

"How would you know?" Bobby asked. "You've told so many lies about him you don't remember the truth."

And this was so. He had looked into her and there was almost no Randall Garfield there, only a box with his name on it . . . his name and a faded image that could have been almost anyone. This was the box where she kept the things that hurt her. She didn't remember about how he liked that Jo Stafford song; didn't remember (if she had ever known) that Randy Garfield had been a real sweetie who'd give you the shirt right off his back. There was no room for things like that in the box she kept. Bobby thought it must be awful to need a box like that.

"He wouldn't buy a drunk a drink," he said. "Did you know that?"

"What are you *talking* about?"

"You can't make me hate him . . . and you can't make me into him." He turned his right hand into a fist and cocked it by the side of his head. "I won't be his ghost. Tell yourself as many lies as you want to about the bills he didn't pay and the insurance policy he lost out on and all the inside straights he tried to fill, but don't tell them to me. Not anymore."

"Don't raise your hand to me, Bobby-O. Don't you ever raise your hand to me."

In answer he held up his other hand, also fisted. "Come on. You want to hit me? I'll hit you back. You can have some more. Only this time you'll deserve it. Come on."

She faltered. He could feel her rage dissipating as fast as it had come, and what replaced it was a terrible blackness. In it, he saw, was fear. Fear of her son, fear that he might hurt her. Not tonight, no—not with those grimy little-boy fists. But little boys grew up.

And was he so much better than her that he could look down his nose and give her the old la-de-dah? Was he *any* better? In his mind he heard the unspeakable crooning voice asking if he wanted to go back home even though it meant Ted would have to go on without him. *Yes,* Bobby had said. Even if it meant going back to his bitch of a mother? *Yes,* Bobby had said. You understand her a little bit better now, do you? Cam had asked, and once again Bobby had said yes.

And when she recognized his step on the porch, there had at first been nothing in her mind but love and relief. Those things had been real.

Bobby unmade his fists. He reached up and took her hand, which was still held back to slap . . . although now without much conviction. It resisted at first, but Bobby at last soothed the tension from it. He kissed it. He looked at his mother's battered face and kissed her hand again. He knew her so well and he didn't want to. He longed for the window in his mind to close, longed for the opacity that made love not just possible but necessary. The less you knew, the more you could believe.

"It's just a bike I don't want," he said. "Okay? Just a bike."

"What *do* you want?" she asked. Her voice was uncertain, dreary. "What *do* you want from me, Bobby?"

"Pancakes," he said. "Lots." He tried a smile. "I am *so-ooo* hungry."

She made enough pancakes for both of them and they ate breakfast at midnight, sitting across from each other at the kitchen table. He insisted on helping her with the dishes even though it was going on toward one by then. Why not? he asked her. There was no school the next day, he could sleep as late as he wanted.

As she was letting the water out of the sink and Bobby was putting the last of their silverware away, Bowser began barking over on Colony

Street: *roop-roop-roop* into the dark of a new day. Bobby's eyes met his mother's, they laughed, and for a moment knowing was all right.

At first he lay in bed the old way, on his back with his heels spread to the lower corners of the mattress, but the old way no longer felt right. It felt exposed, as if anything that wanted to bag a boy could simply burst out of his closet and unzip his upturned belly with one claw. He rolled over on his side and wondered where Ted was now. He reached out, feeling for something that might be Ted, and there was nothing. Just as there had been nothing earlier, on Nasty Gansett Street. Bobby wished he could cry for Ted, but he couldn't. Not yet.

Outside, crossing the dark like a dream, came the sound of the clock in the town square: one single *bong*. Bobby looked at the luminous hands of the Big Ben on his desk and saw they were standing at one o'clock. That was good.

"They're gone," Bobby said. "The low men are gone."

But he slept on his side with his knees drawn up to his chest. His nights of sleeping wide open on his back were over.

XI. WOLVES AND LIONS. BOBBY AT BAT. OFFICER RAYMER. BOBBY AND CAROL. BAD TIMES. AN ENVELOPE.

Sully-John returned from camp with a tan, ten thousand healing mosquito bites, and a million tales to tell . . . only Bobby didn't hear many of them. That was the summer the old easy friendship among Bobby and Sully and Carol broke up. The three of them sometimes walked down to Sterling House together, but once they got there they went to different activities. Carol and her girlfriends were signed up for crafts and softball and badminton, Bobby and Sully for Junior Safaris and baseball.

Sully, whose skills were already maturing, moved up from the Wolves to the Lions. And while all the boys went on the swimming and hiking safaris together, sitting in the back of the battered old Sterling House panel truck with their bathing suits and their lunches in paper sacks, S-J more and more often sat with Ronnie Olmquist and Duke Wendell, boys with whom he had been at camp. They told the same old stories about short-sheeting beds and sending the little kids on snipe hunts until Bobby was bored with them. You'd think Sully had been at camp for fifty years.

On the Fourth of July the Wolves and Lions played their annual head-to-head game. In the decade and a half going back to the end of World War II the Wolves had never won one of these matches, but in the 1960 contest they at least made a game of it—mostly because of Bobby Garfield. He went three-for-three and even without his Alvin Dark glove made a spectacular diving catch in center field. (Getting up and hearing the applause, he wished only briefly for his mother, who hadn't come to the annual holiday outing at Lake Canton.)

Bobby's last hit came during the Wolves' final turn at bat. They were down by two with a runner at second. Bobby drove the ball deep to left field, and as he took off toward first he heard S-J grunt "Good hit, Bob!" from his catcher's position behind the plate. It *was* a good hit, but he was the potential tying run and should have stopped at second base. Instead he tried to stretch it. Kids under the age of thirteen were almost never able to get the ball back into the infield accurately, but this time Sully's Camp Winnie friend Duke Wendell threw a bullet from left field to Sully's *other* Camp Winnie friend, Ronnie Olmquist. Bobby slid but felt Ronnie's glove slap his ankle a split second before his sneaker touched the bag.

"*Yerrrrr*-ROUT!" cried the umpire, who had raced up from home plate to be on top of the play. On the sidelines, the friends and relatives of the Lions cheered hysterically.

Bobby got up glaring at the ump, a Sterling House counsellor of about twenty with a whistle and a white smear of zinc oxide on his nose. "I was safe!"

"Sorry, Bob," the kid said, dropping his ump impersonation and becoming a counsellor again. "It was a good hit and a great slide but you were out."

"Was not! You cheater! Why do you want to cheat?"

"Throw im out!" someone's dad called. "There's no call for guff like that!"

"Go sit down, Bobby," the counsellor said.

"I was *safe!*" Bobby shouted. "Safe by a mile!" He pointed at the man who had advised he be tossed from the game. "Did he pay you to make sure we lost? That fatso there?"

"Quit it, Bobby," the counsellor said. How stupid he looked with his little beanie hat from some nimrod college fraternity and his whistle! "I'm warning you."

Ronnie Olmquist turned away as if disgusted by the argument. Bobby hated him, too.

"You're nothing but a cheater," Bobby said. He could hold back the tears pricking the corners of his eyes but not the waver in his voice.

"That's the last I'll take," the counsellor said. "Go sit down and cool off. You—"

"Cheating *cocksucker.* That's what *you* are."

A woman close to third gasped and turned away.

"That's it," the counsellor said in a toneless voice. "Get off the field. Right now."

Bobby walked halfway down the baseline between third and home, his sneakers scuffling, then turned back. "By the way, a bird shit on your nose. I guess you're too dumb to figure that out. Better go wipe it off."

It sounded funny in his head but stupid when it came out and nobody laughed. Sully was straddling home plate, big as a house and serious as a heart attack in his ragtags of catching gear. His mask, mended all over with black tape, dangled from one hand. He looked flushed and angry. He also looked like a kid who would never be a Wolf again. S-J had been to Camp Winnie, had short-sheeted beds, had stayed up late telling ghost stories around a campfire. He would be a Lion forever and Bobby hated him.

"What's wrong with you?" Sully asked as Bobby plodded by. Both benches had fallen silent. All the kids were looking at him. All the parents were looking at him, too. Looking at him as though he was something disgusting. Bobby guessed he probably was. Just not for the reasons they thought.

Guess what, S-J, maybe you been to Camp Winnie, but I been down there. Way *down there.*

"Bobby?"

"Nothing's wrong with me," he said without looking up. "Who cares? I'm moving to Massachusetts. Maybe there's less twinkydink cheaters there."

"Listen, man—"

"Oh, shut up," Bobby said without looking at him. He looked at his sneakers instead. Just looked at his sneakers and kept on walking.

Liz Garfield didn't make friends ("I'm a plain brown moth, not a social butterfly," she sometimes told Bobby), but during her first couple of years at Home Town Real Estate she had been on good terms with a woman named Myra Calhoun. (In Liz-ese she and Myra saw eye to eye, marched to the same drummer, were tuned to the same wavelength, etc., etc.) In those days Myra had been Don Biderman's secretary and Liz had been the entire office pool, shuttling between agents, making their appointments and their coffee, typing their correspondence. Myra had left the agency abruptly, without much explanation, in 1955. Liz had moved up to her job as Mr. Biderman's secretary in early 1956.

Liz and Myra had remained in touch, exchanging holiday cards and the occasional letter. Myra—who was what Liz called "a maiden lady"—had moved to Massachusetts and opened her own little real-estate firm. In late June of 1960 Liz wrote her and asked if she could become a partner—a junior one to start with, of course—in Calhoun Real Estate Solutions. She had some capital she could bring with her; it wasn't a lot, but neither was thirty-five hundred dollars a spit in the ocean.

Maybe Miss Calhoun had been through the same wringer his mom had been through, maybe not. What mattered was that she said yes—she even sent his mom a bouquet of flowers, and Liz was happy for the first time in weeks. Perhaps truly happy for the first time in years. What mattered was they were moving from Harwich to Danvers, Massachusetts. They were going in August, so Liz would have plenty of time to get her Bobby-O, her newly quiet and often glum Bobby-O, enrolled in a new school.

What also mattered was that Liz Garfield's Bobby-O had a piece of business to take care of before leaving Harwich.

He was too young and small to do what needed doing in a straightforward way. He would have to be careful, and he'd have to be sneaky. Sneaky was all right with Bobby; he no longer had much interest in acting like Audie Murphy or Randolph Scott in the Saturday-matinee movies, and besides, some people needed ambushing, if only to find out what it felt like. The hiding-place he picked was the little copse of trees where Carol had taken him on the day he went all ushy-gushy and started crying; a fitting spot in which to wait for Harry Doolin, old Mr. Robin Hood, Robin Hood, riding through the glen.

Harry had gotten a part-time stockboy job at Total Grocery. Bobby had known that for weeks, had seen him there when he went shopping with his mom. Bobby had also seen Harry walking home after his shift ended at three o'clock. Harry was usually with one or more of his friends. Richie O'Meara was his most common sidekick; Willie Shearman seemed to have dropped out of old Robin Hood's life just as Sully had pretty much dropped out of Bobby's. But whether alone or in company, Harry Doolin always cut across Commonwealth Park on his way home.

Bobby started to drift down there in the afternoons. There was only morning baseball now that it was really hot and by three o'clock Fields A, B, and C were deserted. Sooner or later Harry would walk back from work and past those deserted fields without Richie or any of his other Merrie Men to keep him company. Meanwhile, Bobby spent the hour between three and four P.M. each day in the copse of trees where he had cried with his head in Carol's lap. Sometimes he read a book. The one about George and Lennie made him cry again. *Guys like us, that work on ranches, are the loneliest guys in the world.* That was how George saw it.

Guys like us got nothing to look ahead to. Lennie thought the two of them were going to get a farm and raise rabbits, but long before Bobby got to the end of the story he knew there would be no farms and no rabbits for George and Lennie. Why? Because people needed a beast to hunt. They found a Ralph or a Piggy or a big stupid hulk of a Lennie and then they turned into low men. They put on their yellow coats, they sharpened a stick at both ends, and then they went hunting.

But guys like us sometimes get a little of our own back, Bobby thought as he waited for the day when Harry would show up alone. *Sometimes we do.*

August sixth turned out to be the day. Harry strolled through the park toward the corner of Broad and Commonwealth still wearing his red Total Grocery apron—what a fucking nimrod—and singing "Mack the Knife" in a voice that could have melted screws. Careful not to rustle the branches of the close-growing trees, Bobby stepped out behind him and closed in, walking softly on the path and not cocking back his baseball bat until he was close enough to be sure. As he raised it he thought of Ted saying *Three boys against one little girl. They must have thought you were a lion.* But of course Carol wasn't a lion; neither was he. It was Sully who was the Lion and Sully hadn't been there, wasn't here now. The one creeping up behind Harry Doolin wasn't even a Wolf. He was just a hyena, but so what? Did Harry Doolin deserve any better?

Nope, Bobby thought, and swung the bat. It connected with the same satisfying thud he'd felt at Lake Canton when he'd gotten his third and best hit, the one to deep left. Connecting with the small of Harry Doolin's back was even better.

Harry screamed with pain and surprise and went sprawling. When he rolled over, Bobby brought the bat down on his leg at once, the blow this time landing just below the left knee. "*Owwwuuuu!*" Harry screamed. It was most satisfying to hear Harry Doolin scream; close to bliss, in fact. "*Owwwuuu, that hurts! That hurrrts!*"

Can't let him get up, Bobby thought, picking his next spot with a cold eye. *He's twice as big as me, if I miss once and let him get up, he'll tear me limb from limb. He'll fucking kill me.*

Harry was trying to retreat, digging at the gravel path with his sneakers, dragging a groove with his butt, paddling with his elbows. Bobby swung the bat and hit him in the stomach. Harry lost his air and his elbows and sprawled on his back. His eyes were dazed, filled with sunbright tears. His pimples stood out in big purple and red dots. His mouth—thin and mean on the day Rionda Hewson had rescued them—was now a big loose quiver. "*Owwwuuu, stop, I give, I give, oh Jeezis!*"

He doesn't recognize me, Bobby realized. *The sun's in his eyes and he doesn't even know who it is.*

That wasn't good enough. "Not satisfactory, boys!" was what the Camp Winnie counsellors said after a bad cabin inspection—Sully had told him that, not that Bobby cared; who gave a shit about cabin inspections and making bead wallets?

But he gave a shit about *this,* yes indeed, and he leaned close to Harry's agonized face. "Remember me, Robin Hood?" he asked. "You remember me, don't you? I'm the Maltex Baby."

Harry stopped screaming. He stared up at Bobby, finally recognizing him. "Get . . . you . . ." he managed.

"You won't get shit," Bobby said, and when Harry tried to grab his ankle Bobby kicked him in the ribs.

"*Ouuuuuu!*" Harry Doolin cried, reverting to his former scripture. What a creep! Nimrod Infants on Parade! *That probably hurt me more than it hurt you,* Bobby thought. *Kicking people when you're wearing sneakers is for dumbbells.*

Harry rolled over. As he scrambled for his feet Bobby uncoiled a home-run swing and drove the bat squarely across Harry's buttocks. The sound was like a carpet-beater hitting a heavy rug—a *wonderful* sound! The only thing that could have improved this moment would have been Mr. Biderman also sprawled on the path. Bobby knew exactly where he'd like to hit *him.*

Half a loaf was better than none, though. Or so his mother always said.

"That was for the Gerber Baby," Bobby said. Harry was lying flat on the path again, sobbing. Snot was running from his nose in thick green streams. With one hand he was feebly trying to rub some feeling back into his numb ass.

Bobby's hands tightened on the taped handle of the bat again. He wanted to lift it and bring it down one final time, not on Harry's shin or Harry's backside but on Harry's head. He wanted to hear the crunch of Harry's skull, and really, wouldn't the world be a better place without him? Little Irish shit. Low little—

Steady on, Bobby, Ted's voice spoke up. *Enough is enough, so just steady on. Control yourself.*

"Touch her again and I'll kill you," Bobby said. "Touch *me* again and I'll burn your house down. Fucking nimrod."

He had squatted by Harry to say this last. Now he got up, looked around, and walked away. By the time he met the Sigsby twins halfway up Broad Street Hill, he was whistling.

In the years which followed, Liz Garfield almost got used to seeing policemen at her door. The first to show up was Officer Raymer, the fat local cop who would sometimes buy the kids peanuts from the guy in the park. When he rang the doorbell of the ground-floor apartment at 149 Broad Street on the evening of August sixth, Officer Raymer didn't look happy. With him was Harry Doolin, who would not be able to sit in an uncushioned seat for a week or more, and his mother, Mary Doolin. Harry mounted the porch steps like an old man, with his hands planted in the small of his back.

When Liz opened the front door, Bobby was by her side. Mary Doolin pointed at him and cried: "That's him, that's the boy who beat up my Harry! Arrest him! Do your duty!"

"What's this about, George?" Liz asked.

For a moment Officer Raymer didn't reply. He looked from Bobby (five feet four inches tall, ninety-seven pounds) to Harry (six feet one inch tall, one hundred and seventy-five pounds), instead. His large moist eyes were doubtful.

Harry Doolin was stupid, but not so stupid he couldn't read that look. "He snuck up on me. Got me from behind."

Raymer bent down to Bobby with his chapped, red-knuckled

hands on the shiny knees of his uniform pants. "Harry Doolin here claims you beat im up in the park whilst he was on his way home from work." Raymer pronounced *work* as *rurrk*. Bobby never forgot that. "Says you hid and then lumped im up widda ball-bat before he could even turn around. What do you say, laddie? Is he telling the truth?"

Bobby, not stupid at all, had already considered this scene. He wished he could have told Harry in the park that paid was paid and done was done, that if Harry tattled to anyone about Bobby beating him up, then Bobby would tattle right back—would tell about Harry and his friends hurting Carol, which would look much worse. The trouble with that was that Harry's friends would deny it; it would be Carol's word against Harry's, Richie's, and Willie's. So Bobby had walked away without saying anything, hoping that Harry's humiliation—beat up by a little kid half his size—would keep his mouth shut. It hadn't, and looking at Mrs. Doolin's narrow face, pinched paintless lips, and furious eyes, Bobby knew why. She had gotten it out of him, that was all. Nagged it out of him, more than likely.

"I never touched him," Bobby told Raymer, and met Raymer's gaze firmly with his own as he said it.

Mary Doolin gasped, shocked. Even Harry, to whom lying must have been a way of life by the age of sixteen, looked surprised.

"Oh, the straight-out bare-facedness of it!" Mrs. Doolin cried. "You let me talk to him, Officer! I'll get the truth out of him, see if I don't!"

She started forward. Raymer swept her back with one hand, not rising or even taking his eyes from Bobby.

"Now, lad—why would a galoot the size of Harry Doolin say such a thing about a shrimp the size of you if it wasn't true?"

"Don't you be calling my boy a galoot!" Mrs. Doolin shrilled. "Ain't it enough he's been beat within an inch of his life by this coward? Why—"

"Shut up," Bobby's mom said. It was the first time she'd spoken since asking Officer Raymer what this was about, and her voice was deadly quiet. "Let him answer the question."

"He's still mad at me from last winter, that's why," Bobby told Raymer. "He and some other big kids from St. Gabe's chased me down the hill. Harry slipped on the ice and fell down and got all wet. He said he'd get me. I guess he thinks this is a good way to do it."

"You liar!" Harry shouted. "That wasn't me who chased you, that was Billy Donahue! That—"

He stopped, looked around. He'd put his foot in it somehow; a dim appreciation of the fact was dawning on his face.

"It wasn't me," Bobby said. He spoke quietly, holding Raymer's eyes. "If I tried to beat up a kid his size, he'd total me."

"Liars go to hell!" Mary Doolin shouted.

"Where were you around three-thirty this afternoon, Bobby?" Raymer asked. "Can you answer me that?"

"Here," Bobby said.

"Miz Garfield?"

"Oh yes," she said calmly. "Right here with me all afternoon. I washed the kitchen floor and Bobby cleaned the baseboards. We're getting ready to move, and I want the place to look nice when we do. Bobby complained a little—as boys will do—but he did his chore. And afterward we had iced tea."

"Liar!" Mrs. Doolin cried. Harry only looked stunned. "*Shocking* liar!" She lunged forward again, hands reaching in the general direction of Liz Garfield's neck. Once more Officer Raymer pushed her back without looking at her. A bit more roughly this time.

"You tell me on your oath that he was with you?" Officer Raymer asked Liz.

"On my oath."

"Bobby, you never touched him? On your oath?"

"On my oath."

"On your oath before God?"

"On my oath before God."

"I'm gonna get you, Garfield," Harry said. "I'm gonna fix your little red w—"

Raymer swung around so suddenly that if his mother hadn't seized him by one elbow, Harry might have tumbled down the porch steps, reinjuring himself in old places and opening fresh wounds in new ones.

"Shut your ugly stupid pot," Raymer said, and when Mrs. Doolin started to speak, Raymer pointed at her. "Shut yours as well, Mary Doolin. Maybe if you want to bring beatin charges against someone, you ought to start with yer own damned husband. There'd be more witnesses."

She gawped at him, furious and ashamed.

Raymer dropped the hand he'd been pointing with, as if it had suddenly gained weight. He gazed from Harry and Mary (neither full of grace) on the porch to Bobby and Liz in the foyer. Then he stepped back from all four, took off his uniform cap, scratched his sweaty head, and put his cap back on. "Something's rotten in the state of Denmark," he said at last. "Someone here's lyin faster'n a hoss can trot."

"He—" "You—" Harry and Bobby spoke together, but Officer George Raymer was interested in hearing from neither.

"*Shut up!*" he roared, loud enough to make an old couple strolling past on the other side of the street turn and look. "I'm declarin the case closed. But if there's any more trouble between the two of you"—pointing at the boys—"or *you*"—pointing at the mothers—"there's going to be woe for someone. A word to the wise is sufficient, they say. Harry, will you shake young Robert's hand and say all's well? Do the manly thing? . . . Ah, I thought not. The world's a sad goddamned place. Come on, Doolins. I'll see you home."

Bobby and his mother watched the three of them go down the steps, Harry's limp now exaggerated to the point of a sailor's stagger. At the foot of the walk Mrs. Doolin suddenly cuffed him on the back of the neck. "Don't make it worse'n it is, you little shite!" she said. Harry did better after that, but he still rolled from starboard to port. To Bobby the boy's residual limp looked like the goods. Probably *was* the goods. That last lick, the one across Harry's ass, had been a grand slam.

Back in the apartment, speaking in that same calm voice, Liz asked: "Was he one of the boys that hurt Carol?"

"Yes."

"Can you stay out of his way until we move?"

"I think so."

"Good," she said, and then kissed him. She hardly ever kissed him, and it was wonderful when she did.

Less than a week before they moved—the apartment had by then begun to fill up with cardboard boxes and to take on a strange denuded look—Bobby caught up to Carol Gerber in the park. She was walking along by herself for a change. He had seen her out walking with her girlfriends plenty of times, but that wasn't good enough, wasn't what he wanted. Now she was finally alone, and it wasn't until she looked over her shoulder at him and he saw the fear in her eyes that he knew she had been avoiding him.

"Bobby," she said. "How are you?"

"I don't know," he said. "Okay, I guess. I haven't seen you around."

"You haven't come up my house."

"No," he said. "No, I—" What? How was he supposed to finish? "I been pretty busy," he said lamely.

"Oh. Uh-huh." He could have handled her being cool to him. What he couldn't handle was the fear she was trying to hide. The fear of him. As if he was a dog that might bite her. Bobby had a crazy image of himself dropping down on all fours and starting to go *roop-roop-roop.*

"I'm moving away."

"Sully told me. But he didn't know exactly where. I guess you guys don't chum like you used to."

"No," Bobby said. "Not like we used to. But here." He reached into his back pocket and brought out a piece of folded-over paper from a school notebook. Carol looked at it doubtfully, reached for it, then pulled her hand back.

"It's just my address," he said. "We're going to Massachusetts. A town named Danvers."

Bobby held out the folded paper but she still wasn't taking it and he felt like crying. He remembered being at the top of the Ferris wheel with her and how it was like being at the top of the whole lighted world. He remembered a towel opening like wings, feet with tiny painted toes pivoting, and the smell of perfume. "She's dancin to the drag, the cha-cha rag-a-mop," Freddy Cannon sang from the radio in the other room, and it was Carol, it was Carol, it was Carol.

"I thought you might write," he said. "I'll probably be homesick, a new town and all."

Carol took the paper at last and put it into the pocket of her shorts without looking at it. *Probably throw it away when she gets home,* Bobby thought, but he didn't care. She had taken it, at least. That would be enough springboard for those times when he needed to take his mind away . . . and there didn't have to be any low men in the vicinity for you to need to do that, he had discovered.

"Sully says you're different now."

Bobby didn't reply.

"*Lots* of people say that, actually."

Bobby didn't reply.

"Did you beat Harry Doolin up?" she asked, and gripped Bobby's wrist with a cold hand. "Did you?"

Bobby slowly nodded his head.

Carol threw her arms around his neck and kissed him so hard their teeth clashed. Their mouths parted with an audible smack. Bobby didn't kiss another girl on the mouth for three years . . . and never in his life did he have one kiss *him* like that.

"Good!" she said in a low fierce voice. It was almost a growl. "*Good!*"

Then she ran toward Broad Street, her legs—browned with summer and scabbed by many games and many sidewalks—flashing.

"Carol!" he called after her. "Carol, wait!"

She ran.

"Carol, I love you!"

She stopped at that . . . or maybe it was just that she'd reached Commonwealth Avenue and had to look for traffic. In any case she paused a moment, head lowered, and then looked back. Her eyes were wide and her lips were parted.

"Carol!"

"I have to go home, I have to make the salad," she said, and ran away from him. She ran across the street and out of his life without looking back a second time. Perhaps that was just as well.

He and his mom moved to Danvers. Bobby went to Danvers Elementary, made some friends, made even more enemies. The fights started, and not long after, so did the truancies. On the **Comments** section of his first report card, Mrs. Rivers wrote: "*Robert is an extremely bright boy. He is also extremely troubled. Will you come and see me about him, Mrs. Garfield?*"

Mrs. Garfield went, and Mrs. Garfield helped as much as she could, but there were too many things about which she could not speak: Providence, a certain lost-pet poster, and how she'd come by the money she'd used to buy into a new business and a new life. The two women agreed that Bobby was suffering from growing pains; that he was missing his old town and old friends as well. He would eventually outlast his troubles. He was too bright and too full of potential not to.

Liz prospered in her new career as a real-estate agent. Bobby did well enough in English (he got an A-plus on a paper in which he compared Steinbeck's *Of Mice and Men* to Golding's *Lord of the Flies*) and did poorly in the rest of his classes. He began to smoke cigarettes.

Carol *did* write from time to time—hesitant, almost tentative notes in which she talked about school and friends and a weekend trip to New York City with Rionda. Appended to one that arrived in March of 1961 (her letters always came on deckle-edged paper with teddy bears dancing down the sides) was a stark P.S.: *I think my mom & dad are going to get a divorce. He signed up for another "hitch" and all she does is cry.* Mostly, however, she stuck to brighter things: she was learning to twirl, she had gotten new ice skates on her birthday, she still thought Fabian was cute even if Yvonne and Tina didn't, she had been to a twist party and danced every dance.

As he opened each of her letters and pulled it out Bobby would think, *This is the last. I won't hear from her again. Kids don't write letters for long even if they promise they will. There are too many new things coming along. Time goes by so fast. Too fast. She'll forget me.*

But he would not help her to do so. After each of her letters came he would sit down and write a response. He told her about the house in Brookline his mother sold for twenty-five thousand dollars—six months' salary at her old job in a single commission. He told her about the A-plus on his English theme. He told her about his friend Morrie, who was teaching him to play chess. He didn't tell her that sometimes he and Morrie went on window-breaking expeditions, riding their bikes (Bobby had finally saved up enough to buy one) as fast as they could past the scuzzy old apartment houses on Plymouth Street and throwing rocks out of their baskets as they went. He skipped the story of how he had told Mr. Hurley, the assistant principal at Danvers Elementary, to kiss his rosy red ass and how Mr. Hurley had responded by slapping him across the face and calling him an insolent, wearisome little boy. He didn't confide that he had begun shoplifting or that he had been drunk four or five times (once with Morrie, the other times by himself) or that sometimes he walked over to the train tracks and wondered if getting run over by the South Shore Express would be the quickest way to finish the job. Just a whiff of diesel fuel, a shadow falling over your face, and then blooey. Or maybe not that quick.

Each letter he wrote to Carol ended the same way:

You are sadly missed by
Your friend,
Bobby

Weeks would pass with no mail—not for him—and then there would be another envelope with hearts and teddy bears stuck to the back, another sheet of deckle-edged paper, more stuff about skating and baton twirling and new shoes and how she was still stuck on fractions. Each letter was like one more labored breath from a loved one whose death now seems inevitable. One more breath.

Even Sully-John wrote him a few letters. They stopped early in

1961, but Bobby was amazed and touched that Sully would try at all. In S-J's childishly big handwriting and painful misspellings Bobby could make out the approach of a good-hearted teenage boy who would play sports and lay cheerleaders with equal joy, a boy who would become lost in the thickets of punctuation as easily as he would weave through the defensive lines of opposing football teams. Bobby thought he could even see the man who was waiting for Sully up ahead in the seventies and eighties, waiting for him the way you'd wait for a taxi to arrive: a car salesman who'd eventually own his own dealership. Honest John's, of course; Honest John's Harwich Chevrolet. He'd have a big stomach hanging over his belt and lots of plaques on the wall of his office and he'd coach youth sports and start every peptalk with *Listen up guys* and go to church and march in parades and be on the city council and all that. It would be a good life, Bobby reckoned—the farm and the rabbits instead of the stick sharpened at both ends. Although for Sully the stick turned out to be waiting after all; it was waiting in Dong Ha Province along with the old *mamasan,* the one who would never completely go away.

Bobby was fourteen when the cop caught him coming out of the convenience store with two six-packs of beer (Narragansett) and three cartons of cigarettes (Chesterfields, naturally; twenty-one great tobaccos make twenty wonderful smokes). This was the blond *Village of the Damned* cop.

Bobby told the cop he hadn't broken in, that the back door was open and he'd just *walked* in, but when the cop shone his flashlight on the lock it hung askew in the old wood, half gouged out. *What about this?* the cop asked, and Bobby shrugged. Sitting in the car (the cop let Bobby sit in the front seat with him but wouldn't let him have a butt when Bobby asked), the cop began filling out a form on a clipboard. He asked the sullen, skinny kid beside him what his name was. Ralph, Bobby said. Ralph Garfield. But when they pulled up in front of the house where he now lived with his mom—a whole house, upstairs and downstairs both, times were good—he told the cop he had lied.

"My name's really Jack," he said.

"Oh yeah?" the blond *Village of the Damned* cop said.

"Yes," Bobby said, nodding. "Jack Merridew Garfield. That's me."

Carol Gerber's letters stopped coming in 1963, which happened to be the year of Bobby's first school expulsion and also the year of his first visit to Massachusetts Youth Correctional in Bedford. The cause of this visit was possession of five marijuana cigarettes, which Bobby and his friends called joysticks. Bobby was sentenced to ninety days, the last thirty forgiven for good behavior. He read a lot of books. Some of the other kids called him Professor. Bobby didn't mind.

When he got out of Bedbug Correctional, Officer Grandelle—the Danvers Juvenile Officer—came by and asked if Bobby was ready to straighten up and fly right. Bobby said he was, he had learned his lesson, and for awhile that seemed to be true. Then in the fall of 1964 he beat a boy so badly that the boy had to go to the hospital and there was some question of whether or not he would completely recover. The kid wouldn't give Bobby his guitar, so Bobby beat him up and took it. Bobby was playing the guitar (not very well) in his room when he was arrested. He had told Liz he'd bought the guitar, a Silvertone acoustic, in a pawnshop.

Liz stood weeping in the doorway as Officer Grandelle led Bobby to the police car parked at the curb. "I'm going to wash my hands of you if you don't stop!" she cried after him. "I mean it! I do!"

"Wash em," he said, getting in the back. "Go ahead, Ma, wash em now and save time."

Driving downtown, Officer Grandelle said, "I thought you was gonna straighten up and fly right, Bobby."

"Me too," Bobby said. That time he was in Bedbug for six months.

When he got out he cashed in his Trailways ticket and hitched home. When he let himself into the house, his mother didn't come out to greet him. "You got a letter," she said from her darkened bedroom. "It's on your desk."

Bobby's heart began to bang hard against his ribs as soon as he saw the envelope. The hearts and teddy bears were gone—she was too old for them now—but he recognized Carol's handwriting at once. He picked up the letter and tore it open. Inside was a single sheet of paper—deckle-edged—and another, smaller, envelope. Bobby read Carol's note, the last he ever received from her, quickly.

Dear Bobby,

How are you. I am fine. You got something from your old friend, the one who fixed my arm that time. It came to me because I guess he didn't know where you were. He put a note in asking me to send it along. So I am. Say hi to your mom.

Carol

No news of her adventures in twirling. No news of how she was doing with math. No news of boyfriends, either, but Bobby guessed she probably had had a few.

He picked up the sealed envelope with hands that were shaky and numb. His heart was pounding harder than ever. On the front, written in soft pencil, was a single word: his name. It was Ted's handwriting. He knew it at once. Dry-mouthed, unaware that his eyes had filled with tears, Bobby tore open the envelope, which was no bigger than the ones in which children send their first-grade valentines.

What came out first was the sweetest smell Bobby had ever experienced. It made him think of hugging his mother when he was small, the smell of her perfume and deodorant and the stuff she put on her hair; it made him think of how Commonwealth Park smelled in the summer; it made him think of how the Harwich Library stacks had smelled, spicy and dim and somehow explosive. The tears in his eyes overspilled and began to run down his cheeks. He'd gotten used to feeling old; feeling young again—knowing he *could* feel young again—was a terrible disorienting shock.

There was no letter, no note, no writing of any kind. When Bobby tilted the envelope, what showered down on the surface of his desk were rose petals of the deepest, darkest red he had ever seen.

Heart's blood, he thought, exalted without knowing why. All at once, and for the first time in years, he remembered how you could take your mind away, how you could just put it on parole. And even as he thought of it he felt his thoughts lifting. The rose petals gleamed on the scarred surface of his desk like rubies, like secret light spilled from the world's secret heart.

Not just one world, Bobby thought. *Not just one. There are other worlds than this, millions of worlds, all turning on the spindle of the Tower.*

And then he thought: *He got away from them again. He's free again.*

The petals left no room for doubt. They were all the yes anyone could ever need; all the you-may, all the you-can, all the it's-true.

Now they go, now they slow, Bobby thought, knowing he had heard those words before, not remembering where or knowing why they had recurred to him now. Not caring, either.

Ted was free. Not in this world and time, this time he had run in another direction . . . but in *some* world.

Bobby scooped up the petals, each one like a tiny silk coin. He cupped them like palmfuls of blood, then raised them to his face. He could have drowned in their sweet reek. Ted was in them, Ted clear as day with his funny stooped way of walking, his baby-fine white hair, and the yellow nicotine spots tattooed on the first two fingers of his right hand. Ted with his carryhandle shopping bags.

As on the day when he had punished Harry Doolin for hurting Carol, he heard Ted's voice. Then it had been mostly imagination. This time Bobby thought it was real, something which had been embedded in the rose petals and left for him.

Steady on, Bobby. Enough is enough, so just steady on. Control yourself.

He sat at his desk for a long time with the rose petals pressed to his face. At last, careful not to lose a single one, he put them back into the little envelope and folded down the torn top.

He's free. He's . . . somewhere. And he remembered.

"He remembered me," Bobby said. "He remembered *me.*"

He got up, went into the kitchen, and put on the tea kettle. Then he went into his mother's room. She was on her bed, lying there in her slip with her feet up, and he could see she had started to look old.

She turned her face away from him when he sat down next to her, a boy now almost as big as a man, but she let him take her hand. He held it and stroked it and waited for the kettle to whistle. After awhile she turned to look at him. "Oh Bobby," she said. "We've made such a mess of things, you and me. What are we going to do?"

"The best we can," he said, still stroking her hand. He raised it to his lips and kissed the palm where her lifeline and heartline tangled briefly before wandering away from each other again. "The best we can."

1966: Man, we just couldn't stop laughing.

1966
Hearts in Atlantis

1

When I came to the University of Maine in 1966, there was still a Goldwater sticker, tattered and faded but perfectly readable (AuH_2O-4-USA), on the old station wagon I inherited from my brother. When I left the University in 1970, I had no car. What I did have was a beard, hair down to my shoulders, and a backpack with a sticker on it reading RICHARD NIXON IS A WAR CRIMINAL. The button on the collar of my denim jacket read I AIN'T NO FORTUNATE SON. College is always a time of change, I guess, the last major convulsion of childhood, but I doubt there were ever changes of such magnitude as those faced by the students who came to their campuses in the late sixties.

Most of us don't say much about those years now, not because we don't remember them but because the language which we spoke back then has been lost. When I try to talk about the sixties—when I even try to *think* about them—I am overcome by horror and hilarity. I see bell-bottom pants and Earth Shoes. I smell pot and patchouli, incense and peppermints. And I hear Donovan Leitch singing his sweet and stupid song about the continent of Atlantis, lyrics that still seem profound to me in the watches of the night, when I can't sleep. The older I get, the harder it is to let go of that song's stupidity and hold onto its sweetness. I have to remind myself that we were smaller then, small enough to live our brightly hued lives under the mushrooms, all the time believing them to be trees, shelter from the sheltering sky. I know that doesn't make any real sense, but it's the best I can do: hail Atlantis.

2

I finished my senior year living off-campus in LSD Acres, the rotting cabins down by the Stillwater River, but when I came to U of M in 1966 I lived in Chamberlain Hall, which was part of a three-dorm complex: Chamberlain (men), King (men), and Franklin (women). There was also a dining hall, Holyoke Commons, which stood a little apart from the dorms—not far, perhaps only an eighth of a mile, but it seemed far on winter nights when the wind was strong and the temperature dipped below zero. Far enough so that Holyoke was known as the Palace on the Plains.

I learned a lot in college, the very least of it in the classrooms. I learned how to kiss a girl and put on a rubber at the same time (a necessary but often overlooked skill), how to chug a sixteen-ounce can of beer without throwing up, how to make extra cash in my spare time (writing term papers for kids with more money than I, which was most of them), how not to be a Republican even though I had sprung from a long line of them, how to go into the streets with a sign held up over my head, chanting *One two three four we won't fight your fucking war* and *Hey hey LBJ how many kids did you kill today.* I learned that you should try to get downwind of teargas and breathe slowly through a handkerchief or a bandanna if you couldn't do that. I learned that when the nightsticks come out, you want to fall on your side, draw your knees up to your chest, and cover the back of your head with your hands. In Chicago, in 1968, I learned that cops can beat the shit out of you no matter how well you cover up.

But before I learned any of those things, I learned about the pleasures and dangers of Hearts. There were sixteen rooms holding thirty-two boys on the third floor of Chamberlain Hall in the fall of 1966; by January of 1967, nineteen of those boys had either moved or flunked out, victims of Hearts. It swept through us that fall like a virulent strain of influenza. Only three of the young men on Three were completely immune, I think. One was my roommate, Nathan Hoppenstand. One was David "Dearie" Dearborn, the floor-proctor. The third was Stokely Jones III, soon to be known to the citizenry of Chamberlain Hall as Rip-Rip. Sometimes I think it's Rip-Rip I want to tell you about; sometimes I think it's Skip Kirk (later known as Captain Kirk, of course), who was my best friend during those years; sometimes I think it's Carol. Often I believe it's the sixties themselves I want to talk about, impossible as that has always seemed to me. But before I talk about any of those things, I better tell you about Hearts.

Skip once said that Whist is Bridge for dopes and Hearts is Bridge for *real* dopes. You'll get no argument from me, although that kind of misses the point. Hearts is fun, that's the point, and when you play it for money—a nickel a point was the going rate on Chamberlain Three—it quickly becomes compulsive. The ideal number of players is four. All the cards are dealt out and then played in tricks. Each hand amounts to twenty-six total points: thirteen hearts at a point each, and the queen of spades (which we called The Bitch), worth thirteen points all by herself. The game ends when one of the four players tops a hundred points. The winner is the player with the lowest score.

In our marathons, each of the other three players would cough up based on the difference between his score and the winner's score. If, for example, the difference between my score and Skip's was twenty points at the end of the game, I had to pay him a dollar at the going rate of a nickel a point. Chump-change, you'd say now, but this was 1966, and a dollar wasn't just change to the work-study chumps who lived on Chamberlain Three.

3

I recall quite clearly when the Hearts epidemic started: the first weekend in October. I remember because the semester's initial round of prelims had just ended and I had survived. Survival was an actual issue for most of the boys on Chamberlain Three; we were at college thanks to a variety of scholarships, loans (most, including my own, courtesy of the National Education Defense Act), and work-study jobs. It was like riding in a Soapbox Derby car which had been put together with paste instead of nails, and while our arrangements varied—mostly according to how crafty we were when it came to filling out forms and how diligently our high-school guidance counselors had worked for us—there was one hard fact of life. It was summed up by a sampler which hung in the third-floor lounge, where our marathon Hearts tournaments were played. Tony DeLucca's mother made it, told him to hang it someplace where he'd see it every day, and sent him off to college with it. As the fall of 1966 wore out and winter replaced it, Mrs. DeLucca's sampler seemed to glare bigger and brighter with each passing hand, each fall of The Bitch, each night I rolled into bed with my textbooks unopened, my notes unstudied, my papers unwritten. Once or twice I even dreamed about it:

2.5.

That's what the sampler said, in big red crocheted numerals. Mrs. DeLucca understood what it meant, and so did we. If you lived in one of the ordinary dorms—Jacklin or Dunn or Pease or Chadbourne—you could keep your place in the Class of 1970 with a 1.6 average . . . if, that was, Daddy and Mummy continued to pay the bills. This was the state land-grant college, remember; we are not talking about Harvard or Wellesley. For students trying to stagger through on scholarship-and-loan packages, however, 2.5 was the line drawn in the dust. Score below a 2.5—drop from a C average to a C-minus, in other words—and your little soapbox racer was almost certain to fall apart. "Be in touch, baby, seeya," as Skip Kirk used to say.

I did okay on that first round of prelims, especially for a boy who was almost ill with homesickness (I had never been away from home in my life except for a single week at basketball camp, from which I returned with a sprained wrist and an odd fungal growth between my toes and under my testes). I was carrying five subjects and got B's in everything except Freshman English. On that one I got an A. My instructor, who would later divorce his wife and wind up busking in

Sproul Plaza on the Berkeley campus, wrote "Your example of onomatopoeia is actually quite brilliant" beside one of my answers. I sent that test back home to my mother and father. My mother returned a postcard with one word—"Bravo!"—scrawled fervently across the back. Remembering that causes an unexpected pang, something actually close to physical pain. It was, I suppose, the last time I dragged home a school paper with a gold star pasted in the corner.

After that first round of prelims I complacently calculated my GPA-in-progress and came out with a 3.3. It never got near that again, and by late December I realized that the choices had become very simple: quit playing cards and maybe survive to the next semester with my fragile financial-aid package intact, or continue Bitch-hunting beneath Mrs. DeLucca's sampler in the third-floor lounge until Christmas and then head back to Gates Falls for good.

I'd be able to get a job at Gates Falls Mills and Weaving; my father had been there for twenty years, right up until the accident that cost him his sight, and he'd get me in. My mother would hate it, but she wouldn't stand in the way if I told her it was what I wanted. At the end of the day she was always the realist of the family. Even when her hopes and disappointments ran her half-mad, she was a realist. For awhile she'd be grief-stricken at my failure to make a go of it at the University, and for awhile I'd be guilt-ridden, but we'd both get over it. I wanted to be a writer, after all, not a damned English teacher, and I had an idea that only pompous writers needed college to do what they did.

Yet I didn't want to flunk out, either. It seemed the wrong way to start my life as a grownup. It smelled like failure, and all my Whitmanesque ruminations about how a writer should do his work among the people smelled like a rationalization for that failure. And still the third-floor lounge called to me—the snap of the cards, someone asking if this hand was pass left or pass right, someone else asking who had The Douche (a hand of Hearts begins by playing the two of clubs, a card known to us third-floor addicts as The Douche). I had dreams in which Ronnie Malenfant, the first true bred-in-the-bone asshole I had met since escaping the bullies of junior high, began to play spades one after another, screaming "Time to go Bitch-huntin! We chasin The Cunt!" in his high-pitched, reedy voice. We almost always see where our best interest lies, I think, but sometimes what we see means very little compared to what we feel. Tough but true.

4

My roommate didn't play Hearts. My roommate didn't have any use for the undeclared war in Vietnam. My roommate wrote home to his girlfriend, a senior at Wisdom Consolidated High School, every day. Put a glass of water next to Nate Hoppenstand and it was the water that looked vivacious.

He and I lived in Room 302, next to the stairwell, across from the Proctor's Suite (lair of the hideous Dearie) and all the way down the hall from the lounge with its card-tables, stand-up ashtrays, and its view of the Palace on the Plains. Our pairing suggested—to me, at least—that everyone's most macabre musings about the University Housing Office might well be true. On the questionnaire which I had returned to Housing in April of '66 (when my biggest concern was deciding where I should take Annmarie Soucie to eat after the Senior Prom), I had said that I was A. a smoker; B. a Young Republican; C. an aspiring folk guitarist; D. a night owl. In its dubious wisdom, the Housing Office paired me with Nate, a non-smoking dentist-in-progress whose folks were Aroostook County Democrats (the fact that Lyndon Johnson was a Democrat made Nate feel no better about U.S. soldiers running around South Vietnam). I had a poster of Humphrey Bogart above my bed; above his, Nate hung photos of his dog and his girl. The girl was a sallow creature dressed in a Wisdom High majorette's uniform and clutching a baton like a cudgel. She was Cindy. The dog was Rinty. Both the girl and the dog were sporting identical grins. It was fucking surreal.

Nate's worst failing, as far as Skip and I were concerned, was the collection of record albums he kept carefully shelved in alphabetical order below Cindy and Rinty and just above his nifty little RCA Swingline phonograph. He had three Mitch Miller records (*Sing Along with Mitch, More Sing Along with Mitch, Mitch and the Gang Sing John Henry and Other American Folk Favorites*), *Meet Trini Lopez,* a Dean Martin LP (*Dino Swings Vegas!*), a Gerry and the Pacemakers LP, the first Dave Clark Five album—perhaps the noisiest bad rock record ever made—and many others of the same ilk. I can't remember them all. It's probably a good thing.

"Nate, no," Skip said one evening. "Oh please, no." This was shortly before the onset of Hearts mania—perhaps only days.

"Oh please no what?" Nate asked without looking up from what he was doing at his desk. He seemed to spend all his waking hours either in class or at that desk. Sometimes I would catch him picking his nose and surreptitiously wiping the gleanings (after careful and thorough inspections) under the middle drawer. It was his only vice . . . if you excepted his horrible taste in music, that was.

Skip had been inspecting Nate's albums, something he did with absolutely no self-consciousness in every kid's room he visited. Now he was holding one up. He had the look of a doctor studying a bad X-ray . . . one that shows a juicy (and almost certainly malignant) tumor. He was standing between Nate's bed and mine, wearing his high-school letter jacket and a Dexter High School baseball cap. Never in college and rarely since have I met a man I thought so American Pie handsome as the Captain. Skip seemed unaware of his good looks, but he couldn't have been, not entirely, or he wouldn't have gotten laid as often as he did. It was a time when almost *anybody* could get laid, of course, but even by the standards of the time Skip was busy. None of that had started in the fall of '66, though; in the fall of '66 Skip's heart, like mine, would belong to Hearts.

"This is bad, little buddy," Skip said in a gentle, chiding voice. "Sorry, but this *bites.*"

I was sitting at my own desk, smoking a Pall Mall and looking for my meal ticket. I was always losing the fucking thing.

"What bites? Why are you looking at my records?" Nate's botany text was open in front of him. He was drawing a leaf on a piece of graph paper. His blue freshman beanie was cocked back on his head. Nate Hoppenstand was, I believe, the only member of the freshman class who actually wore that stupid blue dishrag until Maine's hapless football team finally scored a touchdown . . . a week or so before Thanksgiving, that was.

Skip went on studying the record album. "This sucks the rigid cock of Satan. It really does."

"I hate it when you talk that way!" Nate exclaimed, but still too stubborn to actually look up. Skip *knew* Nate hated him to talk that way, which was why he did it. "What are you talking *about,* anyway?"

"I'm sorry my language offends you, but I don't withdraw the comment. I can't. 'Cause this is bad. It hurts me, little buddy. It fuckin *hurts* me."

"*What?*" Nate finally looked up, irritated away from his leaf, which was marked as carefully as a map in a Rand McNally road atlas. "*WHAT?*"

"This."

On the album cover Skip was holding, a girl with a perky face and perky little breasts poking out the front of a middy blouse appeared to be dancing on the deck of a PT boat. One hand was raised, palm out, in a perky little wave. Cocked on her head was a perky little sailor's hat.

"I bet you're the only college student in America that brought *Diane Renay Sings Navy Blue* to school with him," Skip said. "It's wrong, Nate. This belongs back in your attic, along with the wiener pants I bet you wore to all the high-school pep rallies and church socials."

If wiener pants meant polyester Sansabelt slacks with that weird and purposeless little buckle in the back, I suspected Nate had brought most of his collection with him . . . was, in fact, wearing a pair at that very moment. I said nothing, though. I picked up a framed picture of my own girlfriend and spied my meal ticket behind it. I grabbed it and stuffed it in the pocket of my Levi's.

"That's a good record," Nate said with dignity. "That's a very good record. It . . . *swings.*"

"Swings, does it?" Skip asked, tossing it back onto Nate's bed. (He refused to reshelve Nate's records because he knew it drove Nate bugfuck.) " 'My steady boy said ship ahoy and joined the Nay-yay-vee'? If that fits your definition of good, remind me never to let you give me a fuckin physical."

"I'm going to be a dentist, not a doctor," Nate said, clipping off each word. Cords were beginning to stand out on his neck. So far as I know, Skip Kirk was the only person in Chamberlain Hall, maybe on the whole campus, who could get under my roomie's thick Yankee skin. "I'm in pre-dent, do you know what the dent in pre-dent means? It means *teeth,* Skip! It means—"

"Remind me to never let you fill one of my fuckin cavities."

"Why do you have to say that all the time?"

"What?" Skip asked, knowing but wanting Nate to say it. Nate eventually would, and his face always turned bright red when he finally did. This fascinated Skip. Everything about Nate fascinated Skip; the Captain once told me he was pretty sure Nate was an alien, beamed down from the planet Good Boy.

"Fuck," Nate Hoppenstand said, and immediately his cheeks became rosy. In a few moments he looked like a Dickens character, some earnest young man sketched by Boz. "*That.*"

"I had bad role models," Skip said. "I dread to think about your future, Nate. What if Paul Anka makes a fuckin comeback?"

"You've never heard this record," Nate said, snatching up *Diane Renay Sings Navy Blue* from the bed and putting it back between Mitch Miller and *Stella Stevens Is in Love!*

"Never fuckin want to, either," Skip said. "Come on, Pete, let's eat. I'm fuckin starving."

I picked up my geology text—there was a quiz coming up the following Tuesday. Skip took it out of my hand and slung it back onto the desk, knocking over the picture of my girlfriend, who wouldn't fuck but who would give a slow, excruciatingly pleasant handjob when she was in the mood. Nobody gives a handjob like a Catholic girl. I've changed my mind about a lot of things in the course of my life, but never about that.

"What did you do that for?" I asked.

"You don't read at the fuckin table," he said. "Not even when you're eating Commons slop. What kind of barn were you born in?"

"Actually, Skip, I was born into a family where people *do* read at the table. I know it's hard for you to believe there could be any way of doing things except for the Kirk way of doing them, but there is."

He looked unexpectedly grave. He took me by the forearms, looked into my eyes, and said, "At least don't study when you eat. Okay?"

"Okay." Mentally reserving the right to study whenever I fucking well pleased, or felt I needed to.

"Get into all that ram-drive behavior and you'll get ulcers. Ulcers are what killed my old man. He just couldn't stop ramming and driving."

"Oh," I said. "Sorry."

"Don't worry, it was a long time ago. Now come on. Before all the fucking tuna surprise is gone. Coming, Natebo?"

"I have to finish this leaf."

"Fuck the leaf."

If anyone else had said this to him, Nate would have looked at him as at something uncovered beneath a rotted log, and turned silently back to his work. In this case, Nate considered for a moment, then got up and took his jacket carefully off the back of the door, where he always hung it. He put it on. He adjusted the beanie on his head. Not even Skip dared to say much about Nate's stubborn refusal to stop wearing his freshman beanie. (When I asked Skip where his own had disappeared to—this was our third day at UM, and the day after I met him—he said, "Wiped my ass with it and threw the fucker up a tree." This was probably not the truth, but I never completely ruled it out, either.)

We clattered down the three flights of stairs and went out into the mild October dusk. From all three dorms students were headed toward Holyoke Commons, where I worked nine meals a week. I was a dishline boy, recently promoted from silverware boy; if I kept my nose clean, I'd be a stackboy before the Thanksgiving break. Chamberlain, King, and Franklin Halls were on high ground. So was the Palace on the Plains. To reach it, students took asphalt paths that dipped into a hollow like a long trough, then joined into one broad brick way and climbed again. Holyoke was the biggest of the four buildings, shining in the gloom like a cruise-ship on the ocean.

The dip where the asphalt paths met was known as Bennett's Run—if I ever knew why I have long since forgotten. Boys from King and Chamberlain came along two of these paths, girls from Franklin along the other. Where the paths joined, boys and girls did likewise, talking and laughing and exchanging looks both frank and shy. From there they moved together up the wide brick path known as Bennett's Walk to the Commons building.

Coming the other way, cutting back through the crowd with his head down and the usual closed-off expression on his pale, harsh face, was Stokely Jones III. He was tall, but you hardly realized it because he was always hunched over his crutches. His hair, a perfect glossy black with not so much as a single observable strand of anything lighter, spilled over his forehead in spikes, hid his ears, inked a few stray strands diagonally across his pale cheeks.

This was the heyday of the Beatle haircut, which for most boys consisted of no more than combing carefully down instead of carefully up, thus hiding the forehead (and a good crop of pimples, more often than not). Stoke Jones was capped off by nothing so prissy. His medium-length hair just went where it wanted to. His back was hunched in a way that would soon be permanent, if it wasn't already. His eyes were usually cast down, seeming to trace the arcs of his crutches. If those eyes happened to rise and meet your own, you were apt to be startled by their wild intelligence. He was a New England Heathcliff, only wasted away to a bare scrawn from the hips down. His legs, which were usually encased in huge metal braces when he went to class, could move, but only feebly, like the tentacles of a dying squid. His upper body was brawny by comparison. The combination was bizarre. Stoke Jones was a Charles Atlas ad in which BEFORE and AFTER had somehow been melted into the same body. He ate every meal as soon as Holyoke opened, and even three weeks into our first semester we all knew he did it not because he was one of the handicaps but because he wanted, like Greta Garbo, to be alone.

"Fuck him," Ronnie Malenfant said while we were on our way to breakfast one day—he'd just said hello to Jones and Jones had simply crutched his way past without even a nod. He'd been muttering under his breath, though; we all heard it. "Crippled-up hopping asshole." That was Ronnie, always sympathetic. I guess it was growing up amid the puke-in-the-corner beerjoints on lower Lisbon Street in Lewiston that gave him his grace and charm and *joie de vivre.*

"Stoke, what's up?" Skip asked on this particular evening as Jones plunged toward us on his crutches. Stoke went everywhere at that same controlled plunge, always with his Bluto Blutarsky upper half leaning forward so that he looked like a ship's figurehead, Stoke continually saying fuck you to whatever it was that had creamed his lower half, Stoke continually giving it the finger, Stoke looking at you with his smart wild eyes and saying fuck you too, stick it up your ass, sit on it and spin, eat me raw through a Flavr Straw.

He didn't respond but did raise his head for a moment and locked eyes with Skip. Then he dropped his chin and hurried on past us. Sweat was running out of his crazed hair and down the sides of his face. Under his breath he was muttering "Rip-*rip,* rip-*rip,* rip-*rip,*" as if keeping time . . . or articulating what he'd like to do to the whole walking bunch of us . . . or maybe both. You could smell him: the sour acrid tang of sweat, there was always that because he wouldn't go slow, it seemed to *offend* him to go slow, but there was something else, too. The sweat was pungent but not offensive. The undersmell was a lot less pleasant. I ran track in high school (forced as a college freshman to choose between Pall Malls and the four-forty, I chose the coffin-nails) and had smelled that particular combination before, usually when some kid with the flu or the grippe or a strep throat forced himself to run anyway. The only smell like it is an electric-train transformer that's been run too hard for too long.

Then he was past us. Stoke Jones, soon to be dubbed Rip-Rip by Ronnie Malenfant, free of his huge leg-braces for the evening and on his way back to the dorm.

"Hey, what's that?" Nate asked. He had stopped and was looking over his shoulder. Skip and I also stopped and looked back. I started to ask Nate what he meant, then saw. Jones was wearing a jeans jacket. On the back of it, drawn in what looked like black Magic Marker and just visible in the declining light of that early autumn evening, was a shape in a circle.

"Dunno," Skip said. "It looks like a sparrow-track."

The boy on the crutches merged into the crowds on their way to another Commons dinner on another Thursday night in another October. Most of the boys were clean-shaven; most of the girls wore skirts and Ship 'n' Shore blouses with Peter Pan collars. The moon was rising almost full, casting orange light on them. The full-blown Age of Freaks was still two years away, and none of the three of us realized we had seen the peace sign for the first time.

5

Saturday-morning breakfast was one of my meals to work the dish-line in Holyoke. It was a good meal to have because the Commons was never busy on Saturday mornings. Carol Gerber, the silverware girl, stood at the head of the conveyor belt. I was next; my job was to grab the plates as the trays came down the belt, rinse them, and stack them on the trolley beside me. If traffic on the conveyor belt was busy, as it was at most weekday evening meals, I just stacked the plates up, shit and all, and rinsed them later on when things slowed down. Next in line to me was the glassboy or -girl, who grabbed the glasses and cups and popped them into special dishwasher grids. Holyoke wasn't a bad place to work. Every now and then some wit of the Ronnie Malenfant sensibility would return an uneaten kielbasa or breakfast sausage with a Trojan fitted over the end or the oatmeal would come back with I GO TO FUCK U written in carefully torn-up strips of napkin (once, pasted on the surface of a soup-bowl filled with congealing meatloaf gravy, was the message HELP I AM BEING

HELD PRISONER IN A COW COLLEGE), and you wouldn't believe what pigs some kids can be—plates filled with ketchup, milk-glasses filled with mashed potatoes, splattered vegetables—but it really wasn't such a bad job, especially on Saturday mornings.

I looked out once past Carol (who was looking extraordinarily pretty for so early in the morning) and saw Stoke Jones. His back was to the pass-through window, but you couldn't miss the crutches leaning next to his place, or that peculiar shape drawn on the back of his jacket. Skip had been right; it looked like a sparrow-track (it was almost a year later when I first heard some guy on TV refer to it as "the track of the great American chicken").

"Do you know what that is?" I asked Carol, pointing.

She looked for a long time, then shook her head. "Nope. Must be some kind of in-joke."

"Stoke doesn't joke."

"Oh my, you're a poet and you don't know it."

"Quit it, Carol, you're killing me."

When our shift was over, I walked her back to her dorm (telling myself I was just being nice, that walking Carol Gerber back to Franklin Hall in no way made me unfaithful to Annmarie Soucie back in Gates Falls), then ambled toward Chamberlain, wondering who might know what that sparrow-track was. It occurs to me only at this late date that I never thought of asking Jones himself. And when I reached my floor, I saw something that changed the direction of my thoughts entirely. Since I'd gone out at six-thirty A.M. with one eye open to take my place behind Carol on the dishline, someone had shaving-creamed David Dearborn's door—all around the sides, on the doorknob, and with an extra-thick line along the bottom. In this lower deposit was a bare foot-track that made me smile. Dearie opens his door, clad only in a towel, on his way to the shower, and *poosh!,* howaya.

Still smiling, I went into 302. Nate was writing at his desk. Observing the way he kept one arm curled protectively around his notebook, I deduced it was that day's letter to Cindy.

"Someone shaving-creamed Dearie's door," I said, crossing to my shelves and grabbing my geology book. My plan was to head down to the third-floor lounge and do a little studying for the quiz on Tuesday.

Nate tried to look serious and disapproving, but couldn't help smiling himself. He was always trying for self-righteousness in those days and always falling just a little bit short. I suppose he's gotten better at it over the years, more's the pity.

"You should have heard him yell," Nate said. He snorted laughter, then put one small fist up to his mouth to stifle any further impropriety. "And *swear*—for a minute there he was in Skip's league."

"When it comes to swearing, I don't think anyone's in Skip's league."

Nate was looking at me with a worried furrow between his eyes. "You didn't do it, did you? Because I know you were up early—"

"If I was going to decorate Dearie's door, I would have used toilet paper," I said. "All my shaving cream goes on my own face. I'm a low-budget student, just like you. Remember?"

The worry-furrow smoothed out and Nate once more looked like a choirboy. For the first time I realized he was sitting there in nothing but his Jockey shorts and that stupid blue beanie. "That's good," he said, "because David was yelling that he'd get whoever did it and see that the guy was put on disciplinary pro."

"D.P. for creaming his fucking door? I doubt it, Nate."

"It's weird but I think he meant it," Nate said. "Sometimes David Dearborn reminds me of that movie about the crazy ship-captain. Humphrey Bogart was in it. Do you know the one I mean?"

"Yeah, *The Caine Mutiny.*"

"Uh-huh. And David . . . well, let's just say that for him, handing out D.P. is what being floor-proctor is all about."

In the University's code of rules and behavior, expulsion was the big gun, reserved for offenses like theft, assault, and possession/use of drugs. Disciplinary probation was a step below that, punishment for such offenses as having a girl in your room (having one in your room after Women's Curfew could tilt the penalty toward expulsion, hard as that is to believe now), having alcohol in your room, cheating on exams, plagiarism. Any of these latter offenses could theoretically result in expulsion, and in cheating cases often did (especially if the cases involved mid-term or final exams), but mostly it was disciplinary pro, which you carried with you for an entire semester. I didn't like to believe a dorm proctor would try to get a D.P. from Dean of Men Garretsen for a few harmless bursts of shaving cream . . . but this was Dearie, a prig who had so far insisted on weekly room inspections and carried a little stool with him so he could check the top shelves of the thirty-two closets which he seemed to feel were a part of his responsibility. This was probably an idea he got in ROTC, a program he loved as fervently as Nate loved Cindy and Rinty. Also he had gigged kids—this practice was still an official part of school policy, although it had been largely forgotten outside the ROTC program—who didn't keep up with their housework. Enough gigs and you landed on D.P. You could in theory flunk out of school, lose your deferment, get drafted, and wind up dodging bullets in Vietnam because you repeatedly forgot to empty the trash or sweep under the bed.

David Dearborn was a loan-and-scholarship boy himself, and his proctor's job was—also in theory—no different from my dishline job. That wasn't Dearie's theory, though. Dearie considered himself A Cut Above the Rest, one of the few, the proud, the brave. His family came from the coast, you see; from Falmouth, where in 1966 there were still over fifty Blue Laws inherited from the Puritans on the books. Something had happened to his family, had Brought Them Low like a family in an old stage melodrama, but Dearie still dressed like a Falmouth Prep School graduate, wearing a blazer to classes and a suit on Sundays. No one could have been more different from Ronnie Malenfant, with his gutter mouth, his prejudices, and his brilliance with numbers. When they passed in the hall you could almost see Dearie shrinking from Ronnie, whose red hair kinked over a face that seemed to run away from itself, bulging brow to almost nonexistent chin. In between were Ronnie's perpetually gum-caked eyes and perpetually dripping nose . . . not to mention lips so red he always seemed to be wearing something cheap and garish from the five-and-dime.

Dearie didn't like Ronnie, but Ronnie didn't have to face this disapproval alone; Dearie didn't seem to like *any* of the boys he was proctoring. We didn't like him, either, and Ronnie outright hated him. Skip Kirk's dislike was edged with contempt. He was in ROTC with Dearie (at least until November, when Skip dropped the course), and he said Dearie was bad at everything except kissing ass. Skip, who had narrowly missed being named to the All-State baseball team as a high-school senior, had one specific bitch about our floor-proctor—Dearie, Skip said, didn't put out. To Skip it was the worst sin. You had to put out. Even if you were just slopping the hogs, you had to fuckin put out.

I disliked Dearie as much as anyone. I can put up with a great many human failings, but I loathe a prig. Yet I harbored a bit of sympathy for him, as well. He had no sense of humor, for one thing, and I believe that is as much a crippling defect as whatever had gone wrong with Stoke Jones's bottom half. For another, I don't think Dearie liked himself much.

"D.P. won't be an issue if he never finds the culprit," I told Nate. "Even if he does, I doubt like hell if Dean Garretsen would agree to slap it on someone for creaming the proctor's door." Still, Dearie could be persuasive. He might have been Brought Low, but he had that something which said he was still upper crust. That was, of course, just one more thing the rest of us had to dislike about him. "Trotboy" was what Skip called him, because he wouldn't really run laps on the football field during ROTC workouts, but only go at a rapid jog.

"Just as long as you didn't do it," Nate said, and I almost laughed. Nate Hoppenstand sitting there in his underpants and beanie, his child's chest narrow, hairless, and dusted with freckles. Nate looking at me earnestly over his prominent case of slender ribs. Nate playing Dad.

Lowering his voice, he said: "Do you think Skip did it?"

"No. If I had to guess who on this floor would think shave-creaming the proctor's door was a real hoot, I'd say—"

"Ronnie Malenfant."

"Right." I pointed my finger at Nate like a gun and winked.

"I saw you walking back to Franklin with the blond girl," he said. "Carol. She's pretty."

"Just keeping her company," I said.

Nate sat there in his underpants and his beanie, smiling as if he knew better. Perhaps he did. I liked her, all right, although I didn't know much about her—only that she was from Connecticut. Not many work-study kids came from out of state.

I headed down the hall to the lounge, my geology book under my arm. Ronnie was there, wearing his beanie with the front pinned up so it looked sort of like a newspaper reporter's fedora. Sitting with him were two other guys from our floor, Hugh Brennan and Ashley Rice. None of them looked as if they were having the world's most exciting Saturday morning, but when Ronnie saw me, his eyes brightened.

"Pete Riley!" he said. "Just the man I was looking for! Do you know how to play Hearts?"

"Yes. Lucky for me, I also know how to study." I raised my geology book, already thinking that I'd probably end up in the second-floor lounge . . . if, that was, I really meant to get anything done. Because Ronnie never shut up. Was apparently *incapable* of shutting up. Ronnie Malenfant was the original motor-mouth.

"Come on, just one game to a hundred," he wheedled. "We're playing nickel a point, and these two guys play Hearts like old people fuck."

Hugh and Ashley grinned foolishly, as if they had just been complimented. Ronnie's insults were so raw and out front, so bulging with vitriol, that most guys took them as jokes, perhaps even as veiled compliments. They were neither. Ronnie meant every unkind word he ever said.

"Ronnie, I got a quiz Tuesday, and I don't really understand this geosyncline stuff."

"Shit on the geosyncline," Ronnie said, and Ashley Rice tittered. "You've still got the rest of today, all of tomorrow, and all of Monday for the geo-fuckin-syncline."

"I have classes Monday and tomorrow Skip and I were going to go up to Oldtown. They're having an open hoot at the Methodist church and we—"

"Stop it, quit it, spare my achin scrote and don't talk to me about that folkie shit. Michael can row his fuckin boat right up my ass, okay? Listen, Pete—"

"Ronnie, I really—"

"You two dimbulbs stay right the fuck there." Ronnie gave Ashley and Hugh a baleful look. Neither argued with him about it. They were probably eighteen like the rest of us, but anyone who's ever been to college will tell you that some very young eighteen-year-olds show up each September, especially in the rural states. It was the young ones with whom Ronnie succeeded. They were in awe of him. He borrowed their meal tickets, snapped them with towels in the shower, accused them of supporting the goals of the Reverend Martin Luther Coon (who, Ronnie would tell you, drove to protest rallies in his Jiguar), borrowed their money, and would respond to any request for a match with "My ass and your face, monkeymeat." They loved Ronnie in spite of it all . . . *because* of it all. They loved him because he was just so . . . *college.*

Ronnie grabbed me around the neck and tried to yank me out into the hall so he could talk to me in private. I, not at all in awe of him and a bit repelled by the jungle aroma drifting out of his armpits, clamped down on his fingers, bent them back, and removed his hand. "Don't do that, Ronnie."

"Ow, yow, ow, okay, okay, okay! Just come out here a minute, wouldja? And quit that, it hurts! Besides, it's the hand I jerk off with! Jesus! Fuck!"

I let go of his hand (wondering if he'd washed it since the last time he jerked off) but let him pull me out into the hall. Here he took hold of me by the arms, speaking to me earnestly, his gummy eyes wide.

"These guys can't play," he said in a breathless, confidential whisper. "They're a couple of afterbirths, Petesky, but they love the game. Fuckin love the game, you know? I don't love it, but unlike them, I can *play* it. Also I'm broke and there's a couple of Bogart movies tonight at Hauck. If I can squeeze em for two bucks—"

"Bogart movies? Is one of them *The Caine Mutiny*?"

"That's right, *The Caine Mutiny* and *The Maltese Falcon,* Bogie at his fuckin finest, here's lookin at *you,* shweetheart. If I can squeeze those two afterbirths for two bucks, I can go. Squeeze em for four, I call some scagola from Franklin, take her with me, maybe get a blowjob later." That was Ronnie, always the gosh-darned romantic. I had an image of him as Sam Spade in *The Maltese Falcon,* telling Mary Astor to drop and gobble. The idea was enough to make my sinuses swell shut.

"But there's a big problem, Pete. Three-handed Hearts is risky. Who dares shoot the moon when you got that one fucking leftover card to worry about?"

"How are you playing? Game over at a hundred, all losers pay the winner?"

"Yeah. And if you come in, I'll kick back half what I win. Plus *I give back what you lose.*" He sunned me with a saintlike smile.

"Suppose *I* beat *you?*"

Ronnie looked momentarily startled, then smiled wider than ever. "Not in this life, shweetheart. I'm a scientist at cards."

I glanced at my watch, then in at Ashley and Hugh. They really didn't look much like real competition, God love them. "Tell you what," I said. "One game straight up to a hundred. Nickel a point. Nobody kicks back anything. We play, then I study, and everyone has a nice weekend."

"You're on." As we went back into the lounge he added: "I like you, Pete, but business is business—your homo boyfriends back in high school never gave you a fucking like I'm going to give you this morning."

"I didn't have any homo boyfriends in high school," I said. "I spent most of my weekends hitching up to Lewiston to ass-bang your sister."

Ronnie smiled widely, sat down, picked up the deck of cards, began to shuffle. "I broke her in pretty good, didn't I?"

You couldn't get lower than Mrs. Malenfant's little boy, that was the thing. Many tried, but to the best of my knowledge no one ever actually succeeded.

6

Ronnie was a bigot with a foul mouth, a cringing personality, and that constant monkey-fungus stink, but he could play cards, I give him that. He wasn't the genius he claimed to be, at least not in Hearts, where luck is a big part of the game, but he was good. When he was concentrating full on he could remember almost every card that had been played . . . which was why, I suppose, he didn't like three-handed Hearts, with that extra card. With the kicker card gone, Ronnie was tough.

Still, I did all right that first morning. When Hugh Brennan went over a hundred in the first game we played, I had thirty-three points to Ronnie's twenty-eight. It had been two or three years since I'd played Hearts, it was the first time in my life I'd played it for money, and I thought two bits a small price to pay for such unexpected entertainment. That round cost Ashley two dollars and fifty cents; the unfortunate Hugh had to cough up three-sixty. It seemed Ronnie had won the price of a date after all, although I thought the girl would have to be a real Bogart fan to give him a blowjob. Or even a kiss goodnight, for that matter.

Ronnie puffed up like a crow guarding a fresh piece of roadkill. "I got it," he said. "I'm sorry for guys like you who don't, but I got it, Riley. It's like it says in the song, the men don't know but the little girls understand."

"You're ill, Ronnie," I said.

"I wanna go again," Hugh said. I think P. T. Barnum was right, there really *is* one like Hugh born every minute. "I wanna get my money back."

"Well," Ronnie said, revealing his dingy teeth in a big smile, "I'm willing to at least give you a chance." He looked my way. "What do you say, sporty?"

My geology text lay forgotten on the sofa behind me. I wanted my quarter back, and a few more to jingle beside it. What I wanted even more was to school Ronnie Malenfant. "Run em," I said, and then, for the first of at least a thousand times I'd speak the same words in the troubled weeks ahead: "Is this a pass left or pass right?"

"New game, pass right. What a dorkus." Ronnie cackled, stretched, and watched happily as the cards spun out of the deck. "God, I love this game!"

7

That second game was the one that really hooked me. This time it was Ashley instead of Hugh who went skyrocketing toward one hundred points, enthusiastically helped along by Ronnie, who dumped The Bitch on Ash's hapless head at every opportunity. I was dealt the queen only twice that game. The first time I held it for four consecutive tricks when I could have bombed Ashley with it. Finally, just as I was starting to think I'd end up eating it myself, Ashley lost the lead to Hugh Brennan, who promptly led a diamond. He should have known I was void in that suit, had been since the start of the hand, but the Hughs of the world know little. That is, I suppose, why the Ronnies of the world so love to play cards with them. I topped the trick with The Bitch, held my nose, and honked at Hugh. That was how we said "Booya!" in the quaint old days of the sixties.

Ronnie scowled. "Why'd you do that? You could have put that dicksnacker out!" He nodded at Ashley, who was looking at us rather vacantly.

"Yeah, but I'm not quite that stupid." I tapped the score sheet. Ronnie had taken thirty points as of then; I had taken thirty-four. The other two were far beyond that. The question wasn't which of Ronnie's marks would lose, but which of the two who knew how to play the game would win. "I wouldn't mind seeing those Bogie movies myself, you know. *Shweetheart.*"

Ronnie showed his questionable teeth in a grin. He was playing to a gallery by then; we had attracted about half a dozen spectators. Skip and Nate were among them. "Want to play it that way, do you? Okay. Spread your cheeks, moron; you're about to be corn-holed."

Two hands later, I cornholed him. Ashley, who started that last hand with ninety-eight points, went over the top in a hurry. The spectators were dead quiet, waiting to see whether I could actually hit Ronnie with six—the number of hearts he'd need to take for me to beat him by one.

Ronnie looked good at first, playing under everything that was led, staying away from the lead himself. When you have good low cards in Hearts, you're practically bulletproof. "Riley's cooked!" he informed the audience. "I mean fucking *toasty!*"

I thought so, too, but at least I had the queen of spades in my hand. If I could drop it on him, I'd still win. I wouldn't make much from Ronnie, but the other two would be coughing up blood: over five bucks between them. And I'd get to see Ronnie's face change. That's what I wanted most, to see the gloat go out and the goat come in. I wanted to shut him up.

It came down to the last three tricks. Ashley played the six of hearts. Hugh played the five. I played the three. I saw Ronnie's smile fade as he played the nine and took the trick. It dropped his edge to a mere three points. Better still, he finally had the lead. I had the jack of clubs and the queen of spades left in my hand. If Ronnie had a low club and played it, I was going to eat The Bitch and have to endure his crowing, which would be caustic. If, on the other hand . . .

He played the five of diamonds. Hugh played the two of diamonds, getting under, and Ashley, smiling in a puzzled way that suggested he didn't know just what the fuck he was doing, played void.

Dead silence in the room.

Then, smiling, I completed the trick—*Ronnie's* trick—by dropping the queen of spades on top of the other three cards. There was a soft sigh from around the card-table, and when I looked up I saw that the half-dozen spectators had become nearly a full dozen. David Dearborn leaned in the doorway, arms folded, frowning at us. Behind him, in the hall, was someone else. Someone leaning on a pair of crutches.

I suppose Dearie had already checked his well-thumbed book of rules—*Dormitory Regulations at the University of Maine, 1966–1967 Edition*—and had been disappointed to find there was none against playing cards, even when there was a stake involved. But you must believe me when I say his disappointment was nothing compared to Ronnie's.

There are good losers in this world, there are sore losers, sulky losers, defiant losers, weepy losers . . . and then there are your down-and-out fuckhead losers. Ronnie was of the down-and-out fuckhead type. His cheeks flushed pink on the skin and almost purple around his blemishes. His mouth thinned to a shadow, and I could see his jaws working as he chewed his lips.

"Oh gosh," Skip said. "Look who got hit with the shit."

"Why'd you do that?" Ronnie burst out, ignoring Skip—ignoring everyone in the room but me. "Why'd you do that, you numb fuck?"

I was bemused by the question and—let me admit this—absolutely delighted by his rage. "Well," I said, "according to Vince Lombardi, winning isn't everything, it's the only thing. Pay up, Ronnie."

"You're queer," he said. "You're a fucking homo majordomo. Who dealt that?"

"Ashley," I said. "And if you want to call me a cheater, say it right out loud. Then I'm going to come around this table, grab you before you can run, and beat the snot out of you."

"No one's beating the snot out of anyone on my floor!" Dearie said sharply from the doorway, but everyone ignored him. They were watching Ronnie and me.

"I didn't call you a cheater, I just asked who dealt," Ronnie said. I could almost see him making the effort to pull himself together, to swallow the lump I'd fed him and smile as he did it, but there were tears of rage standing in his eyes (big and bright green, those eyes were Ronnie's one redeeming feature), and beneath his earlobes the points of his jaw went on bulging and relaxing. It was like watching twin hearts beat in the sides of his face. "Who gives a shit, you beat me by ten points. That's fifty cents, big fucking deal."

I wasn't a big jock in high school like Skip Kirk—debate and track had been my only extracurricular activities—and I'd never told anyone in my life that I'd beat the snot out of them. Ronnie seemed like a good place to start, though, and God knows I meant it. I think everyone else knew it, too. There was a huge wallop of adolescent adrenaline in the room; you could smell it, almost taste it. Part of me—a big part—wanted him to give me some more grief. Part of me wanted to stick it to him, wanted to stick it right up his ass.

Money appeared on the table. Dearie took a step closer, frowning more ponderously than ever, but he said nothing . . . at least not about that. Instead he asked if anyone in the room had shaving-creamed his door, or knew who had. We all turned to look at him, and saw that Stoke Jones had moved into the doorway when Dearie stepped into the room. Stoke hung on his crutches, watching us all with his bright eyes.

There was a moment of silence and then Skip said, "You sure you didn't maybe go walking in your sleep and do it yourself, David?" A burst of laughter greeted this, and it was Dearie's turn to flush. The color started at his neck and worked its way up his cheeks and forehead to the roots of his flattop—no faggy Beatle haircut for Dearie, thank you very much.

"Pass the word that it better not happen again," Dearie said. Doing his own little Bogie imitation without realizing it. "I'm not going to have my authority mocked."

"Oh blow it out," Ronnie muttered. He had picked up the cards and was disconsolately shuffling them.

Dearie took three large steps into the room, grabbed Ronnie by the shoulders of his Ivy League shirt, and pulled him. Ronnie got up on his own so the shirt would not be torn. He didn't have a lot of good shirts; none of us did.

"What did you say to me, Malenfant?"

Ronnie looked around and saw what I imagine he'd been seeing for most of his life: no help, no sympathy. As usual, he was on his own. And he had no idea why.

"I didn't say anything. Don't be so fuckin paranoid, Dearborn."

"Apologize."

Ronnie wriggled in his grasp. "I didn't *say* nothing, why should I apologize for nothing?"

"Apologize anyway. And I want to hear true regret."

"Oh quit it," Stoke Jones said. "All of you. You should see yourselves. Stupidity to the nth power."

Dearie looked at him, surprised. We were all surprised, I think. Maybe Stoke was surprised himself.

"David, you're just pissed off that someone creamed your door," Skip said.

"You're right. I'm pissed off. And I want an apology from you, Malenfant."

"Let it go," Skip said. "Ronnie just got a little hot under the collar because he lost a close one. He didn't shaving-cream your fucking door."

I looked at Ronnie to see how he was taking the rare experience of having someone stand up for him and saw a telltale shift in his green eyes—almost a flinch. In that moment I was almost positive Ronnie *had* shaving-creamed Dearie's door. Who among my acquaintances was more likely?

If Dearie had noticed that guilty little blink, I believe he would have reached the same conclusion. But he was looking at Skip. Skip looked back at him calmly, and after a few more seconds to make it seem (to himself if not to the rest of us) like his own idea, Dearie let go of Ronnie's shirt. Ronnie shook himself, brushed at the wrinkles on his shoulders, then began digging in his pockets for small change to pay me with.

"I'm sorry," Ronnie said. "Whatever has got your panties in a bunch, I'm sorry. I'm sorry as hell, sorry as shit, I'm so sorry my ass hurts. Okay?"

Dearie took a step back. I had been able to feel the adrenaline; I suspected Dearie could feel the waves of dislike rolling in his direction just as clearly. Even Ashley Rice, who looked like a roly-poly bear in a kids' cartoon, was looking at Dearie in a flat-eyed, unfriendly way. It was a case of what the poet Gary Snyder might have called bad-karma baseball. Dearie was the proctor—strike one. He tried to run our floor as though it were an adjunct to his beloved ROTC program—strike two. And he was a jerkwad sophomore at a time when sophomores still believed that harassing freshmen was part of their bounden duty. Strike three, Dearie, you're out.

"Spread the word that I'm not going to put up with a lot of high-school crap on my floor," Dearie said (*his* floor, if you could dig it). He stood ramrod-straight in his U of M sweatshirt and khaki pants—*pressed* khaki pants, although it was Saturday. "This is *not* high school, gentlemen; this is Chamberlain Hall at the University of Maine. Your bra-snapping days are over. The time has come for you to behave like college men."

I guess there was a reason I was voted Class Clown in the '66 Gates Falls yearbook. I clicked my heels together and snapped off a pretty fair British-style salute, the kind with the palm turned mostly outward. "Yes *sir!*" I cried. There was nervous laughter from the gallery, a dirty guffaw from Ronnie, a grin from Skip. Skip gave Dearie a shrug, eyebrows lifted, hands up to the sky. *See what you get?* it said. *Act like an asshole and that's how people treat you.* Perfect eloquence is, I think, almost always mute.

Dearie looked at Skip, also mute. Then he looked at me. His face was expressionless, almost dead, but I wished I had for once forgone the smartass impulse. The trouble is, for the born smartass, the impulse has nine times out of ten been acted upon before the brain can even engage first gear. I bet that in days of old when knights were bold, more than one court jester was hung upside down by his balls. You don't read about it in the *Morte D'Arthur,* but I think it must be true—laugh *this* one off, ya motley motherfucker. In any case, I knew I had just made an enemy.

Dearie spun in a nearly perfect about-face and went marching out of the lounge. Ronnie's mouth drew down in a grimace that made his ugly face even uglier; the leer of the villain in a stage melodrama. He made a jacking-off gesture at Dearie's stiff retreating back. Hugh Brennan giggled a little, but no one really laughed. Stoke Jones had disappeared, apparently disgusted with the lot of us.

Ronnie looked around, eyes bright. "So," he said. "I'm still up for it. Nickel a point, who wants to play?"

"I will," Skip said.

"I will, too," I said, never once glancing in the direction of my geology book.

"Hearts?" Kirby McClendon asked. He was the tallest boy on the floor, maybe one of the tallest boys at school—six-seven at least, and possessed of a long, mournful bloodhound's face. "Sure. Good choice."

"What about us?" Ashley squeaked.

"Yeah!" Hugh said. Talk about your gluttons for punishment.

"You're outclassed at this table," Ronnie said, speaking with what was for him almost kindness. "Why don't you start up your own?"

Ashley and Hugh did just that. By four o'clock all of the lounge tables were occupied by quartets of third-floor freshmen, ragtag scholarship boys who had to buy their texts in the Used section of the bookstore playing Hearts at a nickel a point. In our dorm, the mad season had begun.

8

Saturday night was another of my meals on the Holyoke dishline. In spite of my awakening interest in Carol Gerber, I tried to get Brad Witherspoon to switch with me—Brad had Sunday breakfast and he hated to get up early almost as badly as Skip did—but Brad refused. By then he was playing, too, and two bucks out of pocket. He was crazy to catch up. He just shook his head at me and led a spade out of his hand. "Let's go Bitch-huntin!" he cried, sounding eerily like Ronnie Malenfant. The most insidious thing about Ronnie was that weak minds found him worth imitating.

I left my seat at the original table, where I had spent the balance of the day, and my place was immediately taken by a young man named Kenny Auster. I was nearly nine dollars ahead (mostly because Ronnie had moved to another table so I wouldn't cut into his profits) and should have been feeling good, but I wasn't. It wasn't the money, it was the game. I wanted to keep on playing.

I walked disconsolately down the hall, checked the room, and asked Nate if he wanted to eat early with the kitchen crew. He simply shook his head and waved me on without looking up from his history book. When people talk about student activism in the sixties, I have to remind myself that the majority of kids went through that mad season the way Nate did. They kept their heads down and their eyes on their history books while history happened all around them. Not that Nate was completely unaware, or completely dedicated to the study carrels on the sidelines, for that matter. You shall hear.

I walked toward the Palace on the Plains, zipping my jacket against the air, which had turned frosty. It was quarter past four. The Commons didn't officially open until five, so the paths which met in Bennett's Run were almost deserted. Stoke Jones was there, though, hunched over his crutches and brooding down at something on the path. I wasn't surprised to see him; if you had some sort of physical disability, you could chow an hour earlier than the rest of the students. As far as I remember, that was about the only special treatment the handicapped got. If you were physically fucked up, you got to eat with the kitchen help. That sparrow-track on the back of his coat was very clear and very black in the late light.

As I got closer to him I saw what he was looking down at—*Introduction to Sociology.* He had dropped it on the faded red bricks of Bennett's Walk and was trying to figure a way he could pick it up again without landing on his face. He kept poking at the book with the tip of one crutch. Stoke had two, maybe even three different pairs of crutches; these were the ones that fitted over his forearms in a series of ascending steel collars. I could hear him muttering "Rip-*rip,* rip-*rip*" under his breath as he prodded the book uselessly from place to place. When he was plunging along on his crutches, "Rip-*rip*" had a determined sound. In this situation it sounded frustrated. At the time I knew Stoke (I will not call him Rip-Rip, although many Ronnie-imitators had taken to doing so by the end of the semester), I was fascinated by how many different nuances there could be to any given "Rip-*rip.*" That was before I found out the Navajos have forty different ways of saying their word for *cloud.* That was before I found out a lot of things, actually.

He heard me coming and snapped his head around so fast he almost fell over anyway. I reached out to steady him. He jerked back, seeming to swim in the old army duffle coat he was wearing.

"Get away from me!" As if he expected me to give him a shove. I raised my hands to show him I was harmless and bent over. "And get your hands off my book!"

This I didn't dignify, only picked up the text and stuffed it under his arm like a newspaper.

"I don't need your help!"

I was about to reply sharply, but I noticed again how white his cheeks were around the patches of red in their centers, and how his hair was damp with perspiration. Once again I could smell him—that overworked-transformer aroma—and realized I could also *hear* him: his breathing had a raspy, snotty sound. If Stoke Jones hadn't found out where the infirmary was yet, I had an idea he would before long.

"I didn't offer you a piggyback, for God's sake." I tried to paste a smile on my puss and managed something or other. Hell, why shouldn't I smile? Didn't I have nine bucks in my pocket that I hadn't started the day with? By the standards of Chamberlain Three, I was rich.

Jones looked at me with those dark eyes of his. His lips thinned, but after a moment he nodded. "Okay. Point taken. Thanks." Then he resumed his breakneck pace up the hill. At first he was well ahead of me, but then the grade began to work on him and he slowed down. His snotty-sounding breathing got louder and quicker. I heard it clearly as I caught up to him.

"Why don't you take it easy?" I asked.

He gave me an impatient are-you-still-here glance. "Why don't you eat me?"

I pointed to his soash book. "That's sliding again."

He stopped, adjusted it under his arm, then fixed himself on his crutches again, hunched like a bad-tempered heron, glaring at me through his black tumbles of hair. "Go on," he said. "I don't need a minder."

I shrugged. "I wasn't babysitting you, just wanted some company."

"I don't."

I started on my way, nettled in spite of my nine bucks. Us class clowns aren't wild about making friends—two or three are apt to do us for a lifetime—but we don't react very well to the bum's rush, either. Our goal is vast numbers of acquaintances whom we can leave laughing.

"Riley," he said from behind me.

I turned. He'd decided to thaw a little after all, I thought. How wrong I was.

"There are gestures and gestures," he said. "Putting shaving cream on the proctor's door is about one step above wiping snot on the seat of Little Susie's desk because you can't think of another way to say you love her."

"*I* didn't shaving-cream Dearie's door," I said, more nettled than ever.

"Yeah, but you're playing cards with the asshole who did. Lending him credibility." I think it was the first time I heard that word, which went on to have an incredibly sleazy career in the seventies and coke-soaked eighties. Mostly in politics. I think *credibility* died of shame around 1986, just as all those sixties war protesters and fearless battlers for racial equality were discovering junk bonds, *Martha Stewart Living,* and the StairMaster. "Why do you waste your time?"

That was direct enough to rattle me, and I said what seems to me now, looking back, an incredibly stupid thing. "I've got plenty of time to waste."

Jones nodded as if he had expected no more and no better. He got going again and passed me at his accustomed plunge, head down, back humped, sweaty hair swinging, soash book clamped tight under his arm. I waited, expecting it to squirt free again. This time when it did, I'd leave him to poke it with his crutch.

But it didn't get away from him, and after I'd seen him reach the door of Holyoke, grapple with it, and finally lurch inside, I went on my own way. When I'd filled my tray I sat with Carol Gerber and the rest of the kids on the dishline crew. That was about as far from Stoke

Jones as it was possible to get, which suited me fine. He also sat apart from the other handicapped kids, I remember. Stoke Jones sat apart from everybody. Clint Eastwood on crutches.

9

The regular diners began to show up at five o'clock. By quarter past, the dishline crew was in full swing and stayed that way for an hour. Lots of dorm kids went home for the weekend, but those who stayed all showed up on Saturday night, which was beans and franks and cornbread. Dessert was Jell-O. At the Palace on the Plains, dessert was almost always Jell-O. If Cook was feeling frisky, you might get Jell-O with little pieces of fruit suspended in it.

Carol was doing silverware, and just as the rush began to subside, she wheeled away from the pass-through, shaking with laughter. Her cheeks were bright crimson. What came rolling along the belt was Skip's work. He admitted it later that night, but I knew right away. Although he was in the College of Education and probably destined to teach history and coach baseball at good old Dexter High until he dropped dead of a booze-fueled heart attack at the age of fifty-nine or so, Skip by rights should have been in fine arts . . . probably would have been if he hadn't come from five generations of farmers who said *ayuh* and *coss 'twill* and *sh'd smile n kiss a pig.* He was only the second or third in his sprawling family (their religion, Skip once said, was Irish Alcoholic) to ever go to college. Clan Kirk could visualize a teacher in the family—barely—but not a painter or a sculptor. And at eighteen, Skip could see no further than they could. He only knew he didn't quite fit the hole he was trying to slide into, and it made him restless. It made him wander into rooms other than his own, check the LPs, and criticize almost everyone's taste in music.

By 1969 he had a better idea of who and what he was. That was the year he constructed a *papier-mâché* Vietnamese family tableau that was set on fire at the end of a peace rally in front of the Fogler

Library while The Youngbloods played "Get Together" from a borrowed set of amps and part-time hippies worked out to the beat like tribal warriors after a hunt. You see how jumbled it all is in my mind? It was Atlantis, that's all I know for sure, way down below the ocean. The paper family burned, the hippie protesters chanted "Napalm! Napalm! Scum from the skies!" as they danced, and after awhile the jocks and the frat boys began to throw stuff. Eggs at first. Then stones.

It was no *papier-mâché* family that sent Carol laughing and reeling away from the dishline that night in the fall of 1966; it was a horny hotdog man standing atop a Matterhorn of Holyoke Commons baked beans. A pipe-cleaner wiener jutted jauntily from the appropriate spot. In his hand was a little University of Maine pennant, on his head a scrap of blue hanky folded to look like a freshman beanie. Along the front of the tray, carefully spelled out in crumbled cornbread, was the message EAT MORE MAINE BEANS!

A good deal of edible artwork came along the conveyor belt during my time on the Palace dishline, but I think that one was the all-time champ. Stoke Jones would no doubt have called it a waste of time, but I think in that case he would have been wrong. Anything with the power to make you laugh over thirty years later isn't a waste of time. I think something like that is very close to immortality.

10

I punched out at six-thirty, walked down the ramp behind the kitchen with one last bag of garbage, and dropped it into one of the four Dumpsters lined up behind the Commons like snubby steel boxcars.

When I turned around, I saw Carol Gerber and a couple of other kids standing by the corner of the building, smoking and watching the moon rise. The other two started away just as I walked over, pulling my Pall Malls out of my jacket pocket.

"Hey, Pete, eat more Maine beans," Carol said, and laughed.

"Yeah." I lit my cigarette. Then, without thinking about it much one way or the other, I said: "There's a couple of Bogart movies playing at Hauck tonight. They start at seven. We've got time to walk over. Want to go?"

She smoked, not answering me for a moment, but she was still smiling and I knew she was going to say yes. Earlier, all I'd wanted was to get back to the third-floor lounge and play Hearts. Now that I was away from the game, however, the game seemed a lot less important. Had I been hot enough to say something about beating the snot out of Ronnie Malenfant? It seemed I had—the memory was clear enough—but standing out here in the cool air with Carol, it was hard for me to understand why.

"I've got a boyfriend back home," she said at last.

"Is that a no?"

She shook her head, still with the little smile. The smoke from her cigarette drifted across her face. Her hair, free of the net the girls had to wear on the dishline, blew lightly across her brow. "That's information. Remember that show *The Prisoner*? 'Number Six, we want . . . *information.*' "

"I've got a girlfriend back home," I said. "More information."

"I've got another job, tutoring math. I promised to spend an hour tonight with this girl on the second floor. Calculus. Ag. She's hopeless and she whines, but it's six dollars an hour." Carol laughed. "This is getting good, we're exchanging information like mad."

"It doesn't look good for Bogie, though," I said. I wasn't worried. I knew we were going to see Bogie. I think I also knew there was romance in our future. It gave me an oddly light feeling, a lifting-off sensation in my midsection.

"I could call Esther from Hauck and tell her calc at ten o'clock instead of nine," Carol said. "Esther's a sad case. She never goes out. What she does mostly is sit around with her hair in curlers and write letters home about how hard college is. We could see the first movie, at least."

"That sounds good," I said.

We started walking toward Hauck. Those were the days, all right;

you didn't have to hire a babysitter, put out the dog, feed the cat, or set the burglar alarm. You just went.

"Is this like a date?" she asked after a little bit.

"Well," I said, "I guess it could be." We were walking past East Annex by then, and other kids were filling up the paths, heading toward the auditorium.

"Good," she said, "because I left my purse back in my room. I can't go dutch."

"Don't worry, I'm rich. Won big playing cards today."

"Poker?"

"Hearts. Do you know it?"

"Are you kidding? I spent three weeks at Camp Winiwinaia on Lake George the summer I was twelve. YMCA camp—poor kids' camp, my mom called it. It rained practically every day and all we did was play Hearts and hunt The Bitch." Her eyes had gone far away, the way people's eyes do when they trip over some memory like a shoe in the dark. "Find the lady in black. *Cherchez la femme noire.*"

"That's the game, all right," I said, knowing that for a moment I wasn't there for her at all. Then she came back, gave me a grin, and took her cigarettes out of her jeans pocket. We smoked a lot back then. All of us. Back then you could smoke in hospital waiting rooms. I told my daughter that and at first she didn't believe me.

I took out my own cigarettes and lit us both. It was a good moment, the two of us looking at each other in the Zippo's flame. Not as sweet as a kiss, but nice. I felt that lightness inside me again, that sense of lifting off. Sometimes your view widens and grows hopeful. Sometimes you think you can see around corners, and maybe you can. Those are good moments. I snapped my lighter shut and we walked on, smoking, the backs of our hands close but not quite brushing.

"How much money are we talking about?" she asked. "Enough to run away to California on, or maybe not quite that much?"

"Nine dollars."

She laughed and took my hand. "It's a date, all right," she said. "You can buy me popcorn, too."

"All right. Do you care which movie plays first?"

She shook her head. "Bogie's Bogie."

"That's true," I said, but I hoped it would be *The Maltese Falcon.*

It was. Halfway through it, while Peter Lorre was doing his rather ominous gay turn and Bogie was gazing at him with polite, amused incredulity, I looked at Carol. She was looking at me. I bent and kissed her popcorn-buttery mouth by the black-and-white moonlight of John Huston's inspired first film. Her lips were sweet and responsive. I pulled back a little. She was still looking at me. The little smile was back. Then she offered me her bag of popcorn, I reciprocated with my box of Dots, and we watched the rest of the movie.

11

Walking back to the Chamberlain-King-Franklin complex of dorms, I took her hand almost without thinking about it. She curled her fingers through mine naturally enough, but I thought I could feel a reserve now.

"Are you going to go back for *The Caine Mutiny*?" she asked. "You could, if you've still got your ticket stub. Or I could give you mine."

"Nah, I've got geology to study."

"Bet you wind up playing cards all night instead."

"I can't afford to," I said. And I meant it; I meant to go back and study. I really did.

"*Lonely Struggles,* or *A Scholarship Boy's Life,*" Carol said. "A heartbreaking novel by Charles Dickens. You'll weep as plucky Peter Riley throws himself into the river after finding that the Financial Aid Office has revoked his grant package."

I laughed. She was very sharp.

"I'm in the same boat, you know. If we screw up, maybe we can make it a double suicide. Into the Penobscot with us. Goodbye cruel world."

"What's a Connecticut girl doing at the University of Maine, anyway?" I asked.

"That's a little complicated. And if you ever plan on asking me out again, you should know you're robbing the cradle. I won't actually be eighteen until November. I skipped the seventh grade. That was the year my parents got divorced, and I was miserable. It was either study all the time or turn into one of the Harwich Junior High corner girls. They're the ones who major in French-kissing and usually wind up pregnant at sixteen. You know the kind I mean?"

"Sure." In Gates you saw them in giggling little groups outside Frank's Fountain or the Dairy Delish, waiting for the boys to come by in their dropped Fords and Plymouth hemis, fast cars with the fenderskirts and the decals saying FRAM and QUAKER STATE in the back windows. You could see those girls as women down at the other end of Main Street, ten years older and forty pounds heavier, drinking beers and shots in Chucky's Tavern.

"I turned into a study-grind. My father was in the Navy. He got out on a disability and moved here to Maine . . . Damariscotta, down on the coast?"

I nodded, thinking of Diane Renay's steady boy, the one who said ship ahoy and joined the Nay-yay-vee.

"I was living in Connecticut with my mother and going to Harwich High. I applied to sixteen different schools and got accepted by all but three . . . but . . ."

"But they expected you to pay your own way and you couldn't."

She nodded. "I think I missed the plum scholarships by maybe twenty SAT-points. An extracurricular activity or two probably wouldn't have hurt, either, but I was too busy grinding away at the books. And by then I was pretty hot and heavy with Sully-John . . ."

"The boyfriend, right?"

She nodded, but not as though this Sully-John interested her. "The only two schools offering realistic financial aid packages were Maine and UConn. I decided on Maine because by then I wasn't getting along very well with my mother. Lots of fights."

"You get along better with your father?"

"Hardly ever see him," she said in a dry, businesslike tone. "He lives with this woman who . . . well, they drink a lot and fight a lot, let's leave it at that. But he's a resident of the state, I'm his daughter, and this is a land-grant college. I didn't get everything I needed—UConn offered the better deal, frankly—but I'm not afraid of a little work. It's worth it, just to get away."

She took a deep breath of the night air and let it out, faintly white. We were almost back to Franklin. Inside the lobby I could see guys sitting in the hard plastic contour chairs, waiting for their girls to come down from upstairs. It looked like quite a rogues' gallery. *Worth it just to get away,* she had said. Did that mean the mother, the town, and the high school, or was the boyfriend included?

When we got to the wide double doors at the front of her dorm, I put my arms around her and bent to kiss her again. She put her hands on my chest, stopping me. Not pulling back, just stopping me. She looked up into my face, smiling that little smile of hers. I could get to love that smile, I thought—it was the kind of smile you might wake up thinking of in the middle of the night. The blue eyes and the blond hair too, but mostly the smile. The lips only curved a little, but the corners of the mouth deepened to dimples all the same.

"My boyfriend's real name is John Sullivan," she said. "Like the fighter. Now tell me the name of your girlfriend."

"Annmarie," I said, not much caring for the sound of it as it came out of my mouth. "Annmarie Soucie. She's a senior at Gates Falls High this year." I let Carol go. When I did, she took her hands off my chest and grabbed mine.

"This is information," she said. "Information, that's all. Still want to kiss me?"

I nodded. I wanted to more than ever.

"Okay." She tilted her face up, closed her eyes, opened her lips a little. She looked like a kid waiting at the foot of the stairs for her goodnight kiss from Papa. It was so cute I almost laughed. Instead I bent and kissed her. She kissed back with pleasure and enthusiasm. There were no tongues touching, but it was a thorough, searching kiss just the same. When she drew back, her cheeks were flushed and her eyes were bright. "Goodnight. Thanks for the movie."

"Want to do it again?"

"I have to think about that," she said. She was smiling but her eyes were serious. I suppose her boyfriend was on her mind; I know that Annmarie was on mine. "Maybe you better, too. I'll see you on the dishline Monday. What do you have?"

"Lunch and dinner."

"I have breakfast and lunch. So I'll see you at lunch."

"Eat more Maine beans," I said. That made her laugh. She went inside. I watched her go, standing outside with my collar turned up and my hands in my pockets and a cigarette between my lips, feeling like Bogie. I watched her say something to the girl on the reception desk and then hurry upstairs, still laughing.

I walked back to Chamberlain in the moonlight, determined to get serious about the geosyncline.

12

I only went into the third-floor lounge to get my geology book; I swear it's true. When I got there, every table—plus one or two which must have been hijacked from other floors—was occupied by a quartet of Hearts-playing fools. There was even a group in the corner, sitting cross-legged on the floor and staring intently at their cards. They looked like half-assed yogis. "We chasin The Cunt!" Ronnie Malenfant yelled to the room at large. "We gonna bust that bitch out, boys!"

I picked up my geology text from the sofa where it had lain all day and night (someone had sat on it, pushing it most of the way down between two cushions, but that baby was too big to hide entirely), and looked at it the way you might look at some artifact of unknown purpose. In Hauck Auditorium, sitting beside Carol Gerber, this crazy card-party had seemed like a dream. Now it was Carol who seemed dreamlike—Carol with her dimples and her boyfriend with the boxer's name. I still had six bucks in my pocket and it was absurd to feel disappointed just because there was no place for me in any of the games currently going on.

Study, that was what I had to do. Make friends with the geosyncline. I'd camp out in the second-floor lounge or maybe find a quiet corner in the basement rec.

Just as I was leaving with *Historical Geology* under my arm, Kirby McClendon tossed down his cards and cried, "Fuck this! I'm tapped! All because I keep getting hit with that fucking queen of spades! I'll give you guys IOUs, but I am honest-to-God tapped out." He went out past me without looking back, ducking his head as he went through the door—I've always thought that being that tall must be a kind of curse. A month later Kirby would be tapped out in a much larger sense, withdrawn from the University by his frightened parents after a mental breakdown and a half-assed suicide attempt. Not the first victim of Hearts-mania that fall, nor the last, but the only one to try and off himself by eating two bottles of orange-flavored baby aspirin.

Lennie Doria didn't even bother looking after him. He looked over at me instead. "You want to sit in, Riley?"

A brief but perfectly genuine struggle for my soul went on. I needed to study. I had *planned* on studying, and for a financial-aid boy like me, that was a good plan, certainly more sensible than sitting here in this smoky room and adding the effluent from my own Pall Malls to the general fug.

So I said "Yeah, why not?" and sat down and played Hearts until almost one in the morning. When I finally shambled back to my room, Nate was lying on his bed reading his Bible. That was the last thing he did every night before going to sleep. This was his third trip through what he always called The Word of God, he'd told me. He had reached the Book of Nehemiah. He looked up at me with an expression of calm enquiry—a look that never changed much. Now that I think about it, *Nate* never changed much. He was in pre-dent, and he stayed with it; tucked into his last Christmas card to me was a photo of his new office in Houlton. In the photo there are three Magi standing around a straw-filled cradle on the snowy office lawn. Behind Mary and Joseph you can read the sign on the door: NATHANIEL HOPPENSTAND, D.D.S. He married Cindy. They are still married, and their three children are mostly grown up. I imagine Rinty died and got replaced.

"Did you win?" Nate asked. He spoke in almost the same tone of voice my wife would use some years later, when I came home half-drunk after a Thursday-night poker game.

"Actually I did." I had gravitated to a table where Ronnie was playing and had lost three of my remaining six dollars, then drifted to another one where I won them back, and a couple of more besides. But I had never gotten around to the geosyncline or the mysteries of tectonic plates.

Nate was wearing red-and-white-striped pajamas. He was, I think, the only person I ever shared a room with in college, male or female, who wore pajamas. Of course he was also the only one who owned *Diane Renay Sings Navy Blue.* As I began undressing, Nate slipped between the covers of his bed and reached behind him to turn off the study lamp on his desk.

"Get your geology all studied up?" he asked as the shadows swallowed his half of the room.

"I'm in good shape with it," I said. Years later, when I came in from those late poker games and my wife would ask me how drunk I was, I'd say "I only had a couple" in that same chipper tone of voice.

I swung into my own bed, turned off my own light, and was asleep almost immediately. I dreamed I was playing Hearts. Ronnie Malenfant was dealing; Stoke Jones stood in the lounge doorway, hunched over his crutches and eyeing me—eyeing all of us—with the dour disapproval of a Massachusetts Bay Colony Puritan. In my dream there was an enormous amount of money lying on the table, hundreds of dollars in crumpled fives and ones, money orders, even a personal check or two. I looked at this, then back at the doorway. Carol Gerber was now standing on one side of Stokely. Nate, dressed in his candy-cane pajamas, was on the other side.

"We want information," Carol said.

"You won't get it," I replied—in the TV show, that was always Patrick McGoohan's reply to Number Two.

Nate said, "You left your window open, Pete. The room's cold and your papers blew everywhere."

I couldn't think of an adequate reply to this, so I picked up the hand I'd been dealt and fanned it open. Thirteen cards, and every one was the queen of spades. Every one was *la femme noire.* Every one was The Bitch.

13

In Vietnam the war was going well—Lyndon Johnson, on a swing through the South Pacific, said so. There *were* a few minor setbacks, however. The Viet Cong shot down three American Hueys practically in Saigon's back yard; a little farther out from Big S, an estimated one thousand Viet Cong soldiers kicked the shit out of at least twice that number of South Vietnamese regulars. In the Mekong Delta, U.S. gunships sank a hundred and twenty Viet Cong river patrol boats which turned out to contain—whoops—large numbers of refugee children. America lost its four hundredth plane of the war that October, an F-105 Thunderchief. The pilot parachuted to safety. In Manila, South Vietnam's Prime Minister, Nguyen Cao Ky, insisted that he was not a crook. Neither were the members of his cabinet, he said, and the fact that a dozen or so cabinet members resigned while Ky was in the Philippines was just coincidence.

In San Diego, Bob Hope did a show for Army boys headed in-country. "I wanted to call Bing and send him along with you," Bob said, "but that pipe-smoking son of a gun has unlisted his number." The Army boys roared with laughter.

? and the Mysterians ruled the radio. Their song, "96 Tears," was a monster hit. They never had another one.

In Honolulu hula-hula girls greeted President Johnson.

At the U.N., Secretary General U Thant was pleading with American representative Arthur Goldberg to stop, at least temporarily, the bombing of North Vietnam. Arthur Goldberg got in touch with the Great White Father in Hawaii to relay Thant's request. The Great White Father, perhaps still wearing his lei, said no way, we'd stop when the Viet Cong stopped, but in the meantime they were going to cry 96 tears. At *least* 96. (Johnson did a brief, clumsy shimmy with the hula-hula girls; I remember watching that on *The Huntley-Brinkley Report* and thinking he danced like every other white guy I knew . . . which was, incidentally, *all* the guys I knew.)

In Greenwich Village a peace march was broken up by the police. The marchers had no permit, the police said. In San Francisco war protesters carrying plastic skulls on sticks and wearing whiteface like a troupe of mimes were dispersed by teargas. In Denver police tore down thousands of posters advertising an antiwar rally at Chautauqua Park in Boulder. The police had discovered a statute forbidding the posting of such bills. The statute did not, the Denver Chief said, forbid posted bills which advertised movies, old clothes drives, VFW dances, or rewards for information leading to the recovery of lost pets. *Those* posters, the chief explained, were not political.

On our own little patch, there was a sit-in at East Annex, where Coleman Chemicals was holding job interviews. Coleman, like Dow, made napalm. Coleman also made Agent Orange, botulin compound, and anthrax, it turned out, although no one knew that until the company went bankrupt in 1980. In the Maine *Campus* there was a small picture of the protesters being led away. A larger photo showed one protester being pulled out of the East Annex doorway by a campus cop while another cop stood by, holding the protester's crutches—said protester was Stoke Jones, of course, wearing his duffle coat with the sparrow-track on the back. The cops were treating him kindly enough, I'm sure—at that point war protesters were still more novelty than nuisance—but the combination of the big cop and the staggering boy made the picture creepy, somehow. I thought of it many times between 1968 and 1971, years when, in the words of Bob Dylan, "the game got rough." The largest photo in that issue, the only one above the fold, showed ROTC guys in uniform marching on the sunny football field while large crowds watched. MANEUVERS DRAW RECORD CROWD, read the headline.

Closer to home still, one Peter Riley got a D on his Geology quiz and a D-plus on a Sociology quiz two days later. On Friday I got back a one-page "essay of opinion" I had scribbled just before Intro English

(Writing) on Monday morning. The subject was Ties **(Should/Should Not)** Be Required for Men in Restaurants. I had chosen Should Not. This little expository exercise had been marked with a big red C, the first C I'd gotten in English since arriving at U of M with my straight A's in high-school English and my 740 score on the SAT Verbals. That red hook shocked me in a way the quiz D's hadn't, and angered me as well. Across the top Mr. Babcock had written, "Your usual clarity is present, but in this case serves only to show what a meatless meal this is. Your humor, although facile, falls far short of wit. The C is actually something of a gift. Sloppy work."

I thought of approaching him after class, then rejected the idea. Mr. Babcock, who wore bowties and big hornrimmed glasses, had made it clear in just four weeks that he considered grade-grubbers the lowest form of academic life. Also, it was noon. If I grabbed a quick bite at the Palace on the Plains, I could be back on Chamberlain Three by one. All the tables in the lounge (and all four corners of the room) would be filled by three o'clock that afternoon, but at one I'd still be able to find a seat. I was almost twenty dollars to the good by then, and planned to spend a profitable late-October weekend lining my pockets. I was also planning on the Saturday-night dance in Lengyll Gym. Carol had agreed to go with me. The Cumberlands, a popular campus group, were playing. At some point (more likely at *several* points) they would do their version of "96 Tears."

The voice of conscience, already speaking in the tones of Nate Hoppenstand, suggested I'd do well to spend at least part of the weekend hitting the books. I had two chapters of geology to read, two chapters of sociology, forty pages of history (the Middle Ages at a gulp), plus a set of questions to answer concerning trade routes.

I'll get to it, don't worry, I'll get to it, I told that voice. Sunday's my day to study. You can count on it, you can take it to the bank. And for awhile on Sunday I actually did read about in-groups, out-groups, and group sanctions. Between hands of cards I read about them. Then things got interesting and my soash book ended up on the floor under the couch. Going to bed on Sunday night—*late* Sunday night—it occurred to me that not only had my winnings shrunk instead of grown (Ronnie now seemed actually to be seeking me out), but I hadn't really gotten very far with my studying. Also, I hadn't made a certain phone-call.

If you really want to put your hand there, Carol said, and she had been smiling that funny little smile when she said it, that smile which was mostly dimples and a look in the eyes. *If you really want to put your hand there.*

About halfway through the Saturday-night dance, she and I had gone out for a smoke. It was a mild night, and along Lengyll's brick north side maybe twenty couples were hugging and kissing by the light of the moon rising over Chadbourne Hall. Carol and I joined them. Before long I had my hand inside her sweater. I rubbed my thumb over the smooth cotton of her bra-cup, feeling the stiff little rise of her nipple. My temperature was also rising. I could feel hers rising, as well. She looked into my face with her arms still locked around my neck and said, "If you really want to put your hand there, I think you owe somebody a phone-call, don't you?"

There's time, I told myself as I drifted toward sleep. *There's plenty of time for studying, plenty of time for phone-calls. Plenty of time.*

14

Skip Kirk blew an Anthropology quiz—ended up guessing at half of the answers and getting a fifty-eight. He got a C-minus on an Advanced Calc quiz, and only did that well because his last math course in high school had covered some of the same concepts. We were in the same Sociology course and he got a D-minus on the quiz, scoring a bare seventy.

We weren't the only ones with problems. Ronnie was a winner at Hearts, better than fifty bucks up in ten days of play, if you believed him (no one completely did, although we knew he was winning), but a loser in his classes. He flunked a French quiz, blew off the little English paper in the class we shared ("Who gives a fuck about ties, I eat at McDonald's" he said), and scraped through a quiz in some other history division by scanning an admirer's notes just before class.

Kirby McClendon had quit shaving and began gnawing his fingernails between deals. He also began cutting significant numbers of classes. Jack Frady convinced his advisor to let him drop Statistics I even though add-drop was officially over. "I cried a little," he told me matter-of-factly one night in the lounge as we Bitch-hunted our way toward the wee hours. "It's something I learned to do in Dramatics Club." Lennie Doria tapped on my door a couple of nights later while I was cramming (Nate had been in the rack for an hour or more, sleeping the sleep of the just and the caught-up) and asked me if I had any interest in writing a paper about Crispus Atticus. He had heard I could do such things. He'd pay a fair price, Lennie said; he was currently ten bucks up in the game. I said I was sorry but I couldn't help him. I was behind a couple of papers myself. Lennie nodded and slipped out.

Ashley Rice broke out in horrible oozing acne all over his face, Mark St. Pierre had a sleepwalking interlude after losing almost twenty bucks in one catastrophic night, and Brad Witherspoon got into a fight with a guy on the first floor. The guy made some innocuous little crack—later on Brad himself admitted it had been innocuous—but Brad, who'd just been hit with The Bitch three times in four hands and only wanted a Coke out of the first-floor machine to soothe his butt-parched throat, wasn't in an innocuous mood. He turned, dropped his unopened soda into the sandwell of a nearby cigarette urn, and started punching. Broke the kid's glasses, loosened one of his teeth. So Brad Witherspoon, ordinarily about as dangerous as a library mimeograph, was the first of us to go on disciplinary pro.

I thought about calling Annmarie and telling her I had met someone and was dating, but it seemed like a lot of work—a lot of psychic effort—on top of everything else. I settled for hoping that she'd write me a letter saying she thought it was time we started seeing other people. Instead I got one saying how much she missed me and that she was making me "something special" for Christmas. Which probably meant a sweater, one with reindeer on it. Reindeer sweaters were an Annmarie specialty (those slow, stroking handjobs were another). She enclosed a picture of herself in a short skirt. Looking at it made me feel not horny but tired and guilty and put-upon. Carol also made me feel put-upon. I had wanted to cop a feel, that was all, not change my whole fucking life. Or hers, for that matter. But I liked her, that was true. A lot. That smile of hers, and her sharp wit. *This is getting good,* she had said, *we're exchanging information like mad.*

A week or so later I returned from Holyoke, where I'd worked lunch with her on the dishline, and saw Frank Stuart walking slowly down the third-floor hallway with his trunk hung from his hands. Frank was from western Maine, one of those little unincorporated townships that are practically all trees, and had a Yankee accent so thick you could slice it. He was just a so-so Hearts player, usually ducking in second or a close third when someone else went over the hundred-point mark, but a hell of a nice guy. He always had a smile on his face . . . at least until the afternoon I came upon him headed for the stairwell with his trunk.

"You moving rooms, Frank?" I asked, but even then I thought I knew better—it was in the look on his face, serious and pale and downcast.

He shook his head. "Goin back home. Got a letter from my ma. She says they need a caretaker at one of the big lake resorts we got over our way. I said sure. I'm just wastin my time here."

"You are not!" I said, a little shocked. "Christ, Frankie, you're getting a college education!"

"I ain't, though, that's the thing." The hall was gloomy and choked with shadows; it was raining outside. Still, I think I saw color come flushing into Frank's cheeks. I think he was ashamed. I think that was why he'd arranged to leave in the middle of a weekday, when the dorm was at its emptiest. "I ain't doin nothin but playin cards. Not very well, either. Also, I'm behind in all my classes."

"You can't be *that* far behind! It's only October twenty-fifth!"

Frank nodded. "I know. But I ain't quick like some. Wasn't quick in high school, either. I got to set my feet and bore in, like with an ice-auger. I ain't been doin it, and if you ain't got a hole in the ice you can't catch any perch. I'm goin, Pete. Gonna quit before they fire me in January."

He went on, plodding down the first of the three flights with his trunk held in front of him by the handles. His white tee-shirt floated in the gloom; when he passed a window running with rain his crew-cut glimmered like gold.

As he reached the second-floor landing and his footfalls began to take on an echoey beat, I rushed to the stairwell and looked down. "Frankie! Hey, Frank!"

The footfalls stopped. In the shadows I could see his round face looking up at me and the dim held shape of his trunk.

"Frank, what about the draft? If you drop out of school the draft'll get you!"

A long pause, as if he was thinking how to answer. He never did, not with his mouth. He answered with his feet. Their echoey sound resumed. I never saw Frank again.

I remember standing by the stairwell, scared, thinking *That could happen to me . . . maybe* is *happening to me,* then pushing the thought away.

Seeing Frank with his trunk was a warning, I decided, and I would heed it. I would do better. I had been coasting, and it was time to turn on the jets again. But from down the hall I could hear Ronnie yelling gleefully that he was Bitch-hunting, that he meant to have that whore out of hiding, and I decided I would do better starting tonight. Tonight would be time enough to re-light those fabled jets. This afternoon I'd play my farewell game of Hearts. Or two. Or forty.

15

It was years before I isolated the key part of my final conversation with Frank Stuart. I had told him he couldn't be so far behind so soon, and he had replied that it happened because he wasn't a quick study. We were both wrong. It *was* possible to fall catastrophically behind in a short period of time, and it happened to the quick studies like me and Skip and Mark St. Pierre as well as to the plodders. In the backs of our minds we must have been holding onto the idea that we'd be able to loaf and then spurt, loaf and then spurt, which was the way most of us had gone through our dozy hometown high schools. But as Dearie Dearborn had pointed out, this wasn't high school.

I told you that of the thirty-two students who began the fall semester on our floor of Chamberlain (thirty-three, if you also count Dearie . . . but he was immune to the charms of Hearts), only fifteen remained to start the spring semester. That doesn't mean the nineteen who left were all dopes, though; not by any means. In fact, the smartest fellows on Chamberlain Three in the fall of 1966 were probably the ones who transferred before flunking out became a real possibility. Steve Ogg and Jack Frady, who had the room just up the hall from Nate and me, went to Chadbourne the first week in November, citing "distractions" on their joint application. When the Housing Officer asked what sort of distractions, they said it was the usual—all-night bull sessions, toothpaste ambushes in the head, abrasive relations with a couple of the guys. As an afterthought, both added they were probably playing cards in the lounge a little too much. They'd heard Chad was a quieter environment, one of the campus's two or three "brain dorms."

The Housing Officer's question had been anticipated, the answer as carefully rehearsed as an oral presentation in a speech class. Neither Steve nor Jack wanted the nearly endless Hearts game shut down; that might cause them all sorts of grief from people who believed folks should mind their own business. All they wanted was to get the fuck off Chamberlain Three while there was still time to salvage their scholarships.

16

The bad quizzes and unsuccessful little papers were nothing but unpleasant skirmishes. For Skip and me and too many of our card-playing buddies, our second round of prelims was a full-fledged disaster. I got an A-minus on my in-class English theme and a D in European History, but flunked the Sociology multiple-choicer and the Geology multiple-choicer—soash by a little and geo by a lot. Skip flunked his Anthropology prelim, his Colonial History prelim, and the soash prelim. He got a C on the Calculus test (but the ice was getting pretty thin there, too, he told me) and a B on his in-class essay. We agreed that life would be much simpler if it were all a matter of in-class essays, writing assignments which necessarily took place far from the third-floor lounge. We were wishing for high school, in other words, without even knowing it.

"Okay, that's enough," Skip said to me that Friday night. "I'm buckling down, Peter. I don't give a shit about being a college man or having a diploma to hang over the mantel in my rumpus room, but I'll be fucked if I want to go back to Dexter and hang around fuckin Bowlarama with the rest of the retards until Uncle Sam calls me."

He was sitting on Nate's bed. Nate was across the way at the Palace on the Plains, chowing down on Friday-night fish. It was nice to know somebody on Chamberlain Three had an appetite. This was a conversation we couldn't have around Nate in any case; my country-mouse roommate thought he'd done pretty well on the latest round of prelims, all C's and B's. He wouldn't have *said* anything if he'd heard us talking, but would have looked at us in a way that said we lacked gumption. That, although it might not be our fault, we were morally weak.

"I'm with you," I said, and then, from down the hall, came an agonized cry ("*Ohhhhhh. . . . FUCK ME!*") that we recognized instantly: someone had just taken The Bitch. Our eyes met. I can't say about Skip, not for sure (even though he was my best friend in college), but I was still thinking that there was time . . . and why wouldn't I think that? For me there always had been.

Skip began to grin. I began to grin. Skip began to giggle. I began to giggle right along with him.

"What the fuck," he said.

"Just tonight," I said. "We'll go over to the library together tomorrow."

"Hit the books."

"All day. But right now . . ."

He stood up. "Let's go Bitch-hunting."

We did. And we weren't the only ones. That's no explanation, I know; it's only what happened.

At breakfast the next morning, as we worked side by side on the dishline, Carol said: "I'm hearing there's some kind of big card-game going on in your dorm. Is that true?"

"I guess it is," I said.

She looked at me over her shoulder, giving me that smile—the one I always thought about when I thought about Carol. The one I think about still. "Hearts? Hunting The Bitch?"

"Hearts," I agreed. "Hunting The Bitch."

"I heard that some of the guys are getting in over their heads. Getting in grades trouble."

"I guess that might be," I said. Nothing was coming down the conveyor belt, not so much as a single tray. There's never a rush when you need one, I've noticed.

"How are *your* grades?" she asked. "I know it's none of my business, but I want—"

"Information, yeah, I know. I'm doing okay. Besides, I'm getting out of the game."

She just gave me the smile, and sure I still think about it sometimes; you would, too. The dimples, the slightly curved lower lip that knew so many nice things about kissing, the dancing blue eyes. Those were days when no girl saw further into a boys' dorm than the lobby . . . and vice-versa, of course. Still, I have an idea that for a little while in October and November of 1966 Carol saw plenty, more than I did. But of course, she wasn't insane—at least not then. The war in Vietnam became *her* insanity. Mine as well. And Skip's. And Nate's. Hearts were nothing, really, only a few tremors in the earth, the kind that flap the screen door on its hinges and rattle the glasses on the shelves. The killer earthquake, the apocalyptic continent-drowner, was still on its way.

17

Barry Margeaux and Brad Witherspoon both got the Derry *News* delivered to their rooms, and the two copies had usually made the rounds of the third floor by the end of the day—we'd find the remnants in the lounge when we took our seats for the evening session of Hearts, the pages torn and out of order, the crossword filled in by three or four different hands. There would be mustaches inked on the photodot faces of Lyndon Johnson and Ramsey Clark and Martin Luther King (someone, I never found out who, would invariably put large smoking horns on Vice President Humphrey and print HUBERT THE DEVIL underneath in tiny anal capital letters). The *News* was hawkish on the war, putting the most positive spin on each day's military events and relegating any protest news to the depths . . . usually beneath the Community Calendar.

Yet more and more we found ourselves discussing not movies or dates or classes as the cards were shuffled and dealt; more and more it was Vietnam. No matter how good the news or how high the Cong body count, there always seemed to be at least one picture of agonized U.S. soldiers after an ambush or crying Vietnamese children watching their village go up in smoke. There was always some unsettling detail tucked away near the bottom of what Skip called "the daily kill-column," like the thing about the kids who got wasted when we hit the Cong PT boats in the Delta.

Nate, of course, didn't play cards. He wouldn't debate the pros and cons of the war, either—I doubt if he knew, any more than I did, that Vietnam had once been under the French, or what had happened to the *monsieurs* unlucky enough to have been in the fortress city of Dien Bien Phu in 1954, let alone who might've decided it was time for President Diem to go to that big rice-paddy in the sky so Nguyen Cao Ky and the generals could take over. Nate only knew that he had no quarrel with those Congs, that they weren't going to be in Mars Hill or Presque Isle in the immediate future.

"Haven't you ever heard about the domino theory, shitbird?" a banty little freshman named Nicholas Prouty asked Nate one afternoon. My roommate rarely came down to the third-floor lounge now, preferring the quieter one on Two, but that day he had dropped in for a few moments.

Nate looked at Nick Prouty, a lobsterman's son who had become a devout disciple of Ronnie Malenfant, and sighed. "When the dominoes come out, I leave the room. I think it's a boring game. That's *my* domino theory." He shot me a glance. I got my eyes away as fast as I could, but not quite in time to avoid the message: what in hell's *wrong* with you? Then he left, scuffing back down to Room 302 in his fuzzy slippers to do some more studying—to resume his charted course from pre-dent to dent, in other words.

"Riley, your roommate's fucked, you know that?" Ronnie said. He had a cigarette tucked in the corner of his mouth. Now he scratched a match one-handed, a specialty of his—college guys too ugly and abrasive to get girls have all sorts of specialties—and lit up.

No, man, I thought, *Nate's doing fine. We're the ones who are fucked up.* For a second I felt real despair. In that second I realized I was in a terrible jam and had no idea at all of how to extricate myself. I was aware of Skip looking at me, and it occurred to me that if I snatched up the cards, sprayed them in Ronnie's face, and walked out of the room, Skip would join me. Likely with relief. Then the feeling passed. It passed as rapidly as it had come.

"Nate's okay," I said. "He's got some funny ideas, that's all."

"Some funny *communist* ideas is what he's got," Hugh Brennan said. His older brother was in the Navy and was most recently heard from in the South China Sea. Hugh had no use for peaceniks. As a Goldwater Republican I should have felt the same, but Nate had started getting to me. I had all sorts of canned knowledge, but no real arguments in favor of the war . . . nor time to work any up. I was too busy to study my sociology, let alone to bone up on U.S. foreign policy.

I'm pretty sure that was the night I almost called Annmarie Soucie. The phone-booth across from the lounge was empty, I had a pocketful of change from my latest victory in the Hearts wars, and I suddenly decided The Time Had Come. I dialed her number from memory (although I had to think for a moment about the last four digits—were they 8146 or 8164?) and plugged in three quarters when the operator asked for them. I let the phone ring a single time, then racked the receiver with a bang and retrieved my quarters when I heard them rattle into the return.

18

A day or two later—shortly before Halloween—Nate got an album by a guy I'd only vaguely heard of: Phil Ochs. A folkie, but not the blunk-blunk banjo kind who used to show up on *Hootenanny.* The album cover, which showed a rumpled troubadour sitting on a curb in New York City, went oddly with the covers of Nate's other records—Dean Martin looking tipsy in a tux, Mitch Miller with his sing-along smile, Diane Renay in her middy blouse and perky sailor cap. The Ochs record was called *I Ain't Marchin' Anymore,* and Nate played it a lot as the days shortened and turned chilly. I took to playing it myself, and Nate didn't seem to mind.

There was a kind of baffled anger in Ochs's voice. I suppose I liked it because most of the time I felt pretty baffled myself. He was like Dylan, but less complicated in his expression and clearer in his rage. The best song on the album—also the most troubling—was the title song. In that song Ochs didn't just suggest but came right out and said that war wasn't worth it, war was never worth it. Even when it was worth it, it wasn't worth it. This idea, coupled with the image of young men just walking away from Lyndon and his Vietnam obsession by the thousands and tens of thousands, excited my imagination in a way that had nothing to do with history or policy or rational thought. I must have killed a million men and now they want me back again but I ain't marchin anymore, Phil Ochs sang through the speaker of Nate's nifty little Swingline phono. Just quit it, in other words. Quit doing what they say, quit doing what they want, quit playing their game. It's an old game, and in this one The Bitch is hunting *you.*

And maybe to show you mean it, you start wearing a symbol of your resistance—something others will first wonder about and then perhaps rally to. It was a couple of days after Halloween that Nate Hoppenstand showed us what the symbol was going to be. Finding out started with one of those crumpled leftover newspapers in the third-floor lounge.

19

"Son of a bitch, look at this," Billy Marchant said.

Harvey Twiller was shuffling the cards at Billy's table, Lennie Doria was adding up the current score, and Billy was taking the opportunity to do a quick scan-through of the *News*'s Local section. Kirby McClendon—unshaven, tall n twitchy, well on his way to his date with all those baby aspirins—leaned in to take a look.

Billy drew back from him, fluttering a hand in front of his face. "Jesus, Kirb, when did you take your last shower? Columbus Day? Fourth of July?"

"Let me see," Kirby said, ignoring him. He snatched the paper away. "Fuck, that's Rip-Rip!"

Ronnie Malenfant got up so fast his chair fell over, entranced by the idea that Stoke had made the paper. When college kids showed up in the Derry *News* (except on the sports page, of course) it was always because they were in trouble. Others gathered around Kirby, Skip and me among them. It was Stokely Jones III, all right, and not just him. Standing in the background, their faces almost but not quite lost in the clusters of dots . . .

"Christ," Skip said, "I think that's Nate." He sounded amused and astonished.

"And that's Carol Gerber just up ahead of him," I said in a funny, shocked voice. I knew the jacket with HARWICH HIGH SCHOOL on the back; knew the blond hair hanging over the jacket's collar in a ponytail; knew the faded jeans. And I knew the face. Even half-turned away and shadowed by a sign reading U.S. OUT OF VIETNAM NOW!, I knew the face. "That's my girlfriend." It was the first time the word *girlfriend* had come out of my mouth tied to Carol's name, although I had been thinking of her that way for a couple of weeks at least.

POLICE BREAK UP DRAFT PROTEST, the photo caption read. No names were given. According to the accompanying story, a dozen or so protesters from the University of Maine had gathered in front of the Federal Building in downtown Derry. They had carried signs and marched around the entrance to the Selective Service office for about an hour, singing songs and "chanting slogans, some obscene." Police had been called and had at first only stood by, intending to allow the demonstration to run its course, but then an opposing group of demonstrators had turned up—mostly construction workers on their lunch break. They had begun chanting their own slogans, and although the *News* didn't mention if they were obscene or not, I could guess there had been invitations to go back to Russia, suggestions as to where the demonstrators could store their signs while not in use, and directions to the nearest barber shop.

When the protesters began to shout back at the construction workers and the construction workers began firing pieces of fruit from their dinner-buckets at the protesters, the police had stepped in. Citing the protesters' lack of a permit (the Derry cops had apparently never heard about the right of Americans to assemble peaceably), they rounded up the kids and took them to the police substation on Witcham Street. There they were simply released. "We only wanted to get them out of a bad atmosphere," one cop was quoted as saying. "If they go back down there, they're even dumber than they look."

The photo really wasn't much different from the one taken at East Annex during the Coleman Chemicals protest. It showed the cops leading the protesters away while construction workers (a year or so later they would all be sporting small American flags on their hardhats) jeered and grinned and shook their fists. One cop was frozen in the act of reaching out toward Carol's arm; Nate, standing behind her, had not attracted their attention, it seemed. Two more cops were escorting Stoke Jones, who was back to the camera but unmistakable on his crutches. If any further aid to identification was needed, there was that hand-drawn sparrow-track on his jacket.

"Look at that dumb fuck!" Ronnie crowed. (Ronnie, who had flunked two of four on the last round of prelims, had a nerve calling anyone a dumb fuck.) "Like he didn't have anything better to do!"

Skip ignored him. So did I. For us Ronnie's bluster was already fading into insignificance no matter what the subject. We were fascinated by the sight of Carol . . . and of Nate Hoppenstand behind her, watching as the demonstrators were led away. Nate as neat as ever in an Ivy League shirt and jeans with cuffs and creases, Nate standing near the jeering, fist-shaking construction workers but totally ignored by them. Ignored by the cops, too. Neither group knew my roommate had lately become a fan of the subversive Mr. Phil Ochs.

I slipped out to the telephone booth and called Franklin Hall, second floor. Someone from the lounge answered and when I asked for Carol, the girl said Carol wasn't there, she'd gone over to the library to study with Libby Sexton. "Is this Pete?"

"Yeah," I said.

"There's a note here for you. She left it on the glass." This was common practice in the dorms at that time. "It says she'll call you later."

"Okay. Thanks."

Skip was outside the telephone booth, motioning impatiently for me to come. We walked down the hall to see Nate, even though we knew we'd both lose our places at the tables where we'd been playing. In this case, curiosity outweighed obsession.

Nate's face didn't change much when we showed him the paper and asked him about the demonstration the day before, but his face never changed much. All the same, I sensed that he was unhappy, perhaps even miserable. I couldn't understand why that would be—everything had ended well, after all; no one had gone to jail or even been named in the paper.

I'd just about decided I was reading too much into his usual quietness when Skip said, "What's eating you?"

There was a kind of rough concern in his voice. Nate's lower lip trembled and then firmed at the sound of it. He leaned over the neat surface of his desk (my own was already covered in about nineteen layers of junk) and snagged a Kleenex from the box he kept by his record-player. He blew his nose long and hard. When he was finished he was under control again, but I could see the baffled unhappiness in his eyes. Part of me—a mean part—was glad to see it. Glad to know that you didn't have to turn into a Hearts junkie to have problems. Human nature can be so shitty sometimes.

"I rode up with Stoke and Harry Swidrowski and a few other guys," Nate said.

"Was Carol with you?" I asked.

Nate shook his head. "I think she was with George Gilman's bunch. There were five carloads of us in all." I didn't know George Gilman from Adam, but that did not prevent me from directing a dart of fairly sick jealousy at him. "Harry and Stoke are on the Committee of Resistance. Gilman, too. Anyway, we—"

"Committee of Resistance?" Skip asked. "What's that?"

"A club," Nate said, and sighed. "They think it's something more—especially Harry and George, they're real firebrands—but it's just another club, really, like the Maine Masque or the pep squad."

Nate said he himself had gone along because it was a Tuesday and he didn't have any classes on Tuesday afternoons. No one gave orders; no one passed around loyalty oaths or even sign-up sheets; there was no real pressure to march and none of the paramilitary beret-wearing fervor that crept into the antiwar movement later on. Carol and the kids with her had been laughing and bopping each other with their signs when they left the gym parking lot, according to Nate. (Laughing. Laughing with George Gilman. I threw another one of those germ-laden jealousy-darts.)

When they got to the Federal Building, some people demonstrated, marching around in circles in front of the Selective Service office door, and some people didn't. Nate was one of those who didn't. As he told us that, his usually smooth face tightened in another brief cramp of something that might have been real misery in a less settled boy.

"I *meant* to march with them," he said. "All the way up I expected to march with them. It was exciting, six of us crammed into Harry Swidrowski's Saab. A real trip. Hunter McPhail . . . do you guys know him?"

Skip and I shook our heads. I think both of us were a little awestruck to discover the owner of *Meet Trini Lopez* and *Diane Renay Sings Navy Blue* had what amounted to a secret life, including connections to the sort of people who attracted both cops and newspaper coverage.

"He and George Gilman started the Committee. Anyway, Hunter was holding Stoke's crutches out the window of the Saab because we couldn't fit them inside and we sang 'I Ain't Marchin' Anymore' and talked about how maybe we could really stop the war if enough of us got together—that is, all of us talked about stuff like that except Stoke. He keeps pretty quiet."

So, I thought. Even with them he keeps quite . . . except, presumably, when he decides a little credibility lecture is in order. But Nate wasn't thinking about Stoke; Nate was thinking about Nate. Brooding over his feet's inexplicable refusal to carry his heart where it had clearly wanted to go.

"All the way up I'm thinking, 'I'll march with them, I'll march with them because it's right . . . at least *I* think it's right . . . and if someone takes a swing at me I'll be nonviolent, just like the guys in the lunchroom sit-ins. Those guys won, maybe we can win, too.' " He looked at us. "I mean, it was never a question in my mind. You know?"

"Yeah," Skip said. "I know."

"But when we got there, I couldn't do it. I helped hand out signs saying STOP THE WAR and U.S. OUT OF VIETNAM NOW and BRING THE BOYS HOME . . . Carol and I helped Stoke fix his so he could march with it and still use his crutches . . . but I couldn't take one myself. I stood on the sidewalk with Bill Shadwick and Kerry Morin and a girl named Lorlie McGinnis . . . she's my partner in Botany Lab . . ." He took the sheet of newspaper out of Skip's hand and studied it, as if to confirm again that yes, it had all really happened; the master of Rinty and the boyfriend of Cindy had actually gone to an antiwar demonstration. He sighed and then let the piece of newspaper drift to the floor. This was so unlike him it kind of hurt my head.

"I thought I would march with them. I mean, why else did I come? All the way down from Orono it was never, you know, a question in my mind."

He looked at me, kind of pleading. I nodded as if I understood.

"But then I didn't. I don't know why."

Skip sat down next to him on his bed. I found the Phil Ochs album and put it on the turntable. Nate looked at Skip, then looked away. Nate's hands were as small and neat as the rest of him, except for the nails. The nails were ragged, bitten right down to the quick.

"Okay," he said as if Skip had asked out loud. "I *do* know why. I was afraid they'd get arrested and I'd get arrested with them. That my picture would be in the paper getting arrested and my folks would see it." There was a long pause. Poor old Nate was trying to say the rest. I held the needle over the first groove of the spinning record, waiting to see if he could. At last he did. "That my *mother* would see it."

"It's okay, Nate," Skip said.

"I don't think so," Nate replied in a trembling voice. "I really don't." He wouldn't meet Skip's eyes, only sat there on his bed with his prominent chicken-ribs and bare white Yankee skin between his pajama bottoms and his freshman beanie, looking down at his gnawed cuticles. "I don't like to argue about the war. Harry does . . . and Lorlie . . . George Gilman, gosh, you can't get George to shut up about it, and most of the others on the Committee are the same. But when it comes to talking, I'm more like Stoke than them."

"No one's like Stoke," I said. I remembered the day I met him on Bennett's Walk. *Why don't you take it easy?* I'd asked. *Why don't you eat me?* Mr. Credibility had replied.

Nate was still studying his cuticles. "What I *think* is that Johnson is sending American boys over there to die for no reason. It isn't imperialism or colonialism, like Harry Swidrowski believes, it's not any *ism* at all. Johnson's got it all mixed up in his mind with Davy Crockett and Daniel Boone and the New York Yankees, that's all.

And if I think that, I ought to *say* that. I ought to try to stop it. That's what I learned in church, in school, even in the darned *Boy Scouts of America.* You're supposed to stand up. If you see something happening that's wrong, like a big guy beating up a little guy, you're supposed to stand up and at least try to stop it. But I was afraid my mother'd see a picture of me getting arrested and cry."

Nate raised his head and we saw he was crying himself. Just a little; wet lids and lashes, no more than that. For him that was a big deal, though.

"I found out one thing," he said. "What that is on the back of Stoke Jones's jacket."

"What?" Skip asked.

"A combination of two British Navy semaphore letters. Look." Nate stood up with his bare heels together. He lifted his left arm straight up toward the ceiling and dropped his right down to the floor, making a straight line. "That's N." Next he held his arms out at forty-five-degree angles to his body. I could see how the two shapes, when superimposed, would make the shape Stoke had inked on the back of his old duffle coat. "This one's D."

"N-D," Skip said. "So?"

"The letters stand for nuclear disarmament. Bertrand Russell invented the symbol in the fifties." He drew it on the back of his notebook: ☮ "He called it a peace sign."

"Cool," Skip said.

Nate smiled and wiped under his eyes with his fingers. "That's what I thought," he agreed. "It's a groove thing."

I dropped the needle on the record and we listened to Phil Ochs sing. Grooved to it, as we Atlanteans used to say.

20

The lounge in the middle of Chamberlain Three had become my Jupiter—a scary planet with a huge gravitational pull. Still, I resisted it that night, slipping back into the phone-booth instead and calling Franklin again. This time I got Carol.

"I'm all right," she said, laughing a little. "I'm fine. One of the cops even called me little lady. Sheesh, Pete, such concern."

How much concern did this guy Gilman show you? I felt like asking, but even at eighteen I knew that wasn't the way to go.

"You should have given me a call," I said. "Maybe I would have gone with you. We could have taken my car."

Carol began to giggle, a sweet sound but puzzling.

"What?"

"I was thinking about riding to an antiwar demonstration in a station wagon with a Goldwater sticker on the bumper."

I guessed that *was* sort of funny.

"Besides," she said, "I imagine you had other things to do."

"What's that supposed to mean?" As if I didn't know. Through the glass of the phone-booth and that of the lounge, I could see most of my floor-mates playing cards in a fume of cigarette smoke. And even in here with the door closed I could hear Ronnie Malenfant's high-pitched cackle. We're chasing The Bitch, boys, we are *cherchez*-ing *la* cunt *noire,* and we're going to have her out of the bushes.

"Studying or Hearts," she said. "Studying, I hope. One of the girls on my floor goes out with Lennie Doria—or did, when he still had the time to go out. She calls it the card-game from hell. Am I being a nag yet?"

"No," I said, not knowing if she was or not. Maybe I needed to be nagged. "Carol, are you okay?"

There was a long pause. "Yeah," she said at last. "Sure I am."

"The construction workers who showed up—"

"Mostly mouth," she said. "Don't worry. Really."

But she didn't sound right to me, not quite right . . . and there was George Gilman to worry about. I worried about him in a way I didn't about Sully, the boyfriend back home.

"Are you on this Committee Nate told me about?" I asked her. "This Committee of Resistance whatsit?"

"No," she said. "Not yet, at least. George has asked me to join. He's this guy from my Polysci course. George Gilman. Do you know him?"

"Heard of him," I said. I was clutching the phone too tightly and couldn't seem to loosen up.

"He was the one who told me about the demonstration. I rode up with him and some others. I . . ." She broke off for a moment, then said with honest curiosity: "You're not jealous of him, are you?"

"Well," I said carefully, "he got to spend an afternoon with you. I'm jealous of *that,* I guess."

"Don't be. He's got brains, plenty of them, but he's also got a wiffle haircut and great big shifty eyes. He shaves, but it seems like he always misses a big patch. *He's* not the attraction, believe me."

"Then what is?"

"Can I see you? I want to show you something. It won't take long. But it might help if I could just *explain* . . ." Her voice wavered on the word and I realized she was close to tears.

"What's wrong?"

"You mean other than that my father probably won't let me back into his house once he's seen me in the *News*? He'll have the locks changed by this weekend, I bet. That's if he hasn't changed them already."

I thought of Nate saying he was afraid his mother would see a picture of him getting arrested. Mommy's good little pre-dent pinched down in Derry for parading in front of the Federal Building without a permit. Ah, the shame, the shame. And Carol's dad? Not quite the same deal, but close. Carol's dad was a steady boy who said ship ahoy and joined the Nay-yay-vee, after all.

"He may not see the story," I said. "Even if he does, the paper didn't use any names."

"The *picture.*" She spoke patiently, as if to someone who can't help being dense. "Didn't you see the picture?"

I started to say that her face was mostly turned away from the camera and what you could see was in shadow. Then I remembered her high-school jacket with HARWICH HIGH SCHOOL blaring across the back. Also, he was her *father,* for Christ's sake. Even half-turned away from the camera, her father would know her.

"He may not see the picture, either," I said lamely. "Damariscotta's at the far edge of the *News*'s area."

"Is that how you want to live your life, Pete?" She still sounded patient, but now it was patience with an edge. "Doing stuff and then hoping people won't find out?"

"No," I said. And could I get mad at her for saying that, considering that Annmarie Soucie still didn't have the slightest idea that Carol Gerber was alive? I didn't think so. Carol and I weren't married or anything, but marriage wasn't the issue. "No, I don't. But Carol . . . you don't have to shove the damned newspaper under his nose for him, do you?"

She laughed. The sound had none of the brightness I had heard in her earlier giggle, but I thought even a rueful laugh was better than none at all. "I won't have to. He'll find it. That's just the way he is. But I had to go, Pete. And I'll probably join the Committee of Resistance even though George Gilman always looks like a little kid who just got caught eating boogers and Harry Swidrowski has the world's worst breath. Because it's . . . the thing of it is . . . you see . . ." She blew a frustrated I-can't-explain sigh into my ear. "Listen, you know where we go out for smoke-breaks?"

"At Holyoke? By the Dumpsters, sure."

"Meet me there," Carol said. "In fifteen minutes. Can you?"

"Yes."

"I have a lot more studying to do so I can't stay long, but I . . . I just . . ."

"I'll be there."

I hung up the phone and stepped out of the booth. Ashley Rice was standing in the doorway of the lounge, smoking and doing a little shuffle-step. I deduced that he was between games. His face was too pale, the black stubble on his cheeks standing out like pencil-marks, and his shirt had gone beyond simply soiled; it looked lived-in. He had a wide-eyed Danger High Voltage look that I later came to associate with heavy cocaine users. And that's what the game really was; a kind of drug. Not the kind that mellowed you out, either.

"What do you say, Pete?" he asked. "Want to play a few hands?"

"Maybe later," I said, and started down the hall. Stoke Jones was thumping back from the bathroom in a frayed old robe. His crutches left round wet tracks on the dark red linoleum. His long, crazy hair was wet. I wondered how he did in the shower; certainly there were none of the railings and grab-handles that later became standard in public washing facilities. He didn't look as though he would much enjoy discussing the subject, however. That or any other subject.

"How you doing, Stoke?" I asked.

He went by without answering, head down, dripping hair plastered to his cheeks, soap and towel clamped under one arm, muttering "Rip-*rip,* rip-*rip*" under his breath. He never even looked up at me. Say whatever you wanted about Stoke Jones, you could depend on him to put a little fuck-you into your day.

21

Carol was already at Holyoke when I got there. She had brought a couple of milk-boxes from the area where the Dumpsters were lined up and was sitting on one of them, legs crossed, smoking a cigarette. I sat down on the other one, put my arm around her, and kissed her. She put her head on my shoulder for a moment, not saying anything. This wasn't much like her, but it was nice. I kept my arm around her and looked up at the stars. The night was mild for so late in the season, and lots of people—couples, mostly—were out walking, taking advantage of the weather. I could hear their murmured conversations. From above us, in the Commons dining room, a radio was playing "Hang On, Sloopy." One of the janitors, I suppose.

Carol raised her head at last and moved away from me a little—just enough to let me know I could take my arm back. That was more like her, actually. "Thanks," she said. "I needed a hug."

"My pleasure."

"I'm a little scared about facing my dad. Not real scared, but a little."

"It'll be all right." Not saying it because I really thought it would be—I couldn't know a thing like that—but because it's what you say, isn't it? Just what you say.

"My dad's not the reason I went with Harry and George and the rest. It's no big Freudian rebellion, or anything like that."

She flicked her cigarette away and we watched it fountain sparks when it struck the bricks of Bennett's Walk. Then she took her little clutch purse out of her lap, opened it, found her wallet, opened *that,* and thumbed through a selection of snapshots stuck in those small celluloid windows. She stopped, slipped one out, and handed it to me. I leaned forward so I could see it by the light falling through the dining-hall windows, where the janitors were probably doing the floors.

The picture showed three kids of eleven or twelve, a girl and two boys. They were all wearing blue tee-shirts with the words STERLING HOUSE on them in red block letters. They were standing in a parking lot somewhere and had their arms around each other—an easy pals-forever pose that was sort of beautiful. The girl was in the middle. The girl was Carol, of course.

"Which one is Sully-John?" I asked. She looked at me, a little surprised . . . but with the smile. In any case, I thought I already knew. Sully-John would be the one with the broad shoulders, the wide grin, and the tumbled black hair. It reminded me of Stoke's hair, although the boy had obviously run a comb through his thatch. I tapped him. "This one, right?"

"That's Sully," she agreed, then touched the face of the other boy with her fingernail. He had a sunburn rather than a tan. His face was narrower, the eyes a little closer together, the hair a carroty red and mowed in a crewcut that made him look like a kid on a Norman Rockwell *Saturday Evening Post* cover. There was a faint frown-line on his brow. Sully's arms were already muscular for a kid's; this other boy had thin arms, thin stick arms. They were probably still thin stick arms. On the hand not slung around Carol's shoulders he was wearing a big brown baseball glove.

"This one's Bobby," she said. Her voice had changed, somehow. There was something in it I'd never heard before. Sorrow? But she was still smiling. If it was sorrow she felt, why was she smiling? "Bobby Garfield. He was my first boyfriend. My first love, I guess you could say. He and Sully and I were best friends back then. Not so long ago, 1960, but it *seems* long ago."

"What happened to him?" I was somehow sure she was going to tell me he had died, this boy with the narrow face and the crewcut carrot-top.

"He and his mom moved away. We wrote back and forth for awhile, and then we lost touch. You know how kids are."

"Nice baseball glove."

Carol still with the smile. I could see the tears that had come into her eyes as we sat looking down at the snapshot, but still with the smile. In the white light of the fluorescents from the dining hall, her tears looked silver—the tears of a princess in a fairy-tale.

"That was Bobby's favorite thing. There's a baseball player named Alvin Dark, right?"

"There was."

"That's what kind of a glove Bobby had. An Alvin Dark model."

"Mine was a Ted Williams. I think my mom rummage-saled it a couple of years ago."

"Bobby's got stolen," Carol said. I'm not sure she knew I was there anymore. She kept touching that narrow, slightly frowning face with her fingertip. It was as if she had regressed into her own past. I've heard that hypnotists can do that with good subjects. "Willie took it."

"Willie?"

"Willie Shearman. I saw him playing ball with it a year later, down at Sterling House. I was so mad. My mom and dad were always fighting then, working up to the divorce, I guess, and I was mad all the time. Mad at them, mad at my math teacher, mad at the whole world. I was still scared of Willie, but mostly I was mad at him . . . and besides, I wasn't by myself, not that day. So I marched right up to him and said I knew that was Bobby's glove and he ought to give it to me. I said I had Bobby's address in Massachusetts and I'd send it to him. Willie said I was crazy, it was *his* glove, and he showed me his name on the side. He'd erased Bobby's—best as he could, anyway—and printed his own over where it had been. But I could still see the *bby,* from Bobby."

A creepy sort of indignation had crept into her voice. It made her sound younger. And *look* younger. I suppose my memory could be wrong about that, but I don't think it is. Sitting there on the edge of the white light from the dining hall, I think she looked about twelve. Thirteen at the most.

"He couldn't erase the Alvin Dark signature in the pocket, though, or write over it . . . and he blushed. Dark red. Red as roses. Then—do you know what?—he apologized for what he and his two friends did to me. He was the only one who ever did, and I think he meant it. But he lied about the glove. I don't think he wanted it, it was old and the webbing was all broken out and it looked all wrong on his hand, but he lied so he could keep it. I don't understand why. I never have."

"I'm not following this," I said.

"Why should you? It's all jumbled up in *my* mind and I was *there.* My mother told me once that happens to people who are in accidents or fights. I remember some of it pretty well—mostly the parts with Bobby in them—but almost everything else comes from what people told me later on.

"I was in the park down the street from my house, and these three boys came along—Harry Doolin, Willie Shearman, and another one. I can't remember the other one's name. It doesn't matter, anyway. They beat me up. I was only eleven but that didn't stop them. Harry Doolin hit me with a baseball bat. Willie and the other one held me so I couldn't run away."

"A baseball bat? Are you shitting me?"

She shook her head. "At first they were joking, I think, and then . . . they weren't. My arm got dislocated. I screamed and I guess they ran away. I sat there, holding my arm, too hurt and too . . . too shocked I guess . . . to know what to do. Or maybe I tried to get up and get help for myself and couldn't. Then Bobby came along. He walked me out of the park and then he picked me up and carried me back to his apartment. All the way up Broad Street Hill on one of the hottest days of the year. He carried me in his arms."

I took the snapshot from her, held it in the light, and bent over it, looking at the boy with the crewcut. Looking at his thin stick arms, then looking at the girl. She was an inch or two taller than he was, and broader in the shoulders. I looked at the other boy, Sully. He of the tumbled black hair and the All-American grin. Stoke Jones's hair; Skip Kirk's grin. I could see Sully carrying her in his arms, yeah, but the other kid—

"I know," she said. "He doesn't look big enough, does he? But he carried me. I started to faint and he carried me." She took the picture back.

"And while he was doing that, this kid Willie who helped beat you up came back and stole his glove?"

She nodded. "Bobby took me to his apartment. There was this old guy who lived in a room upstairs, Ted, who seemed to know a little bit about everything. He popped my arm back into its socket. I remember he gave me his belt to bite on when he did it. Or maybe it was Bobby's belt. He said I could catch the pain, and I did. After that . . . after that, something bad happened."

"Worse than getting lumped up with a baseball bat?"

"In a way. I don't want to talk about it." She wiped her tears away with one hand, first one side and then the other, still looking at the snapshot. "Later on, before he and his mother left Harwich, Bobby beat up the boy who actually used the bat. Harry Doolin."

Carol put her photograph back in its little compartment.

"What I remember best about that day—the only thing about it *worth* remembering—is that Bobby Garfield stood up for me. Sully was bigger, and Sully *might* have stood up for me if he'd been there, but he wasn't. Bobby was there, and he carried me all the way up the hill. He did what was right. It's the best thing, the most important thing, anyone has ever done for me in my life. Do you see that, Pete?"

"Yeah. I do."

I saw something else, too: she was saying almost exactly what Nate had said not an hour before . . . only she *had* marched. Had taken one of the signs and marched with it. Of course Nate Hoppenstand had never been beaten up by three boys who started out joking and then decided they were serious. And maybe that was the difference.

"He carried me up that hill," she said. "I always wanted to tell him how much I loved him for that, and how much I loved him for showing Harry Doolin that there's a price to pay for hurting people, especially people who are smaller than you and don't mean you any harm."

"So you marched."

"I marched. I wanted to tell someone why. I wanted to tell someone who'd understand. My father won't and my mother can't. Her friend Rionda called me and said . . ." She didn't finish, only sat there on the milk-box, fidgeting with her little bag.

"Said what?"

"Nothing." She sounded exhausted, forlorn. I wanted to kiss her, at least put my arm around her, but I was afraid doing either would spoil what had just happened. Because something *had* happened. There was magic in her story. Not in the middle, but somewhere out around the edges. I felt it.

"I marched, and I guess I'll join the Committee of Resistance. My roommate says I'm crazy, I'll never get a job if a commie student group's part of my college records, but I think I'm going to do it."

"And your father? What about him?"

"Fuck him."

There was a semi-shocked moment when we considered what she had just said, and then Carol giggled. "Now *that's* Freudian." She stood up. "I have to go back and study. Thanks for coming out, Pete. I haven't ever shown that picture to anyone. I haven't looked at it myself in who knows how long. I feel better. Lots."

"Good." I got up myself. "Before you go in, will you help *me* do something?"

"Sure, what?"

"I'll show you. It won't take long."

I walked her down the side of Holyoke and then we started up the hill behind it. About two hundred yards away was the Steam Plant parking lot, where undergrads ineligible for parking stickers (freshmen, sophomores, and most juniors) had to keep their cars. It was the prime makeout spot on campus once it got cold, but making out in my car wasn't on my mind that night.

"Did you ever tell Bobby about who got his baseball glove?" I asked. "You said you wrote to him."

"I didn't see the point."

We walked in silence for a little while. Then I said: "I'm going to call it off with Annmarie over Thanksgiving. I started to phone her, then didn't. If I'm going to do it, I guess I better find the guts to do it face to face." I hadn't been aware of coming to any such decision, not consciously, but it seemed I had. Certainly it wasn't something I was saying just to please Carol.

She nodded, scuffing through the leaves in her sneakers, holding her little bag in one hand, not looking at me. "I had to use the phone. Called S-J and told him I was seeing a guy."

I stopped. "When?"

"Last week." Now she looked up at me. Dimples; slightly curved lower lip; the smile.

"Last *week?* And you didn't tell me?"

"It was my business," she said. "Mine and Sully's. I mean, it isn't like he's going to come after you with a . . ." She paused long enough for both of us to think *with a baseball bat* and then went on, "That he's going to come after you, or anything. Come on, Pete. If we're going to do something, let's do it. I'm not going riding with you, though. I really have to study."

"No rides."

We got walking again. The Steam Plant lot seemed huge to me in those days—hundreds of cars parked in dozens of moonlit rows. I could hardly ever remember where I left my brother's old Ford wagon. The last time I was back at UM, the lot was three, maybe even four times as big, with space for a thousand cars or more. Time passes and everything gets bigger except us.

"Hey Pete?" Walking. Looking down at her sneakers again even though we were on the asphalt now and there were no more leaves to scuff.

"Uh-huh."

"I don't want you to go breaking up with Annmarie because of me. Because I have an idea we're . . . temporary. All right?"

"Yeah." What she said made me unhappy—it was what the citizens of Atlantis referred to as *a bummer*—but it didn't really surprise me. "I guess it'll have to be."

"I like you, and I like being with you now, but it's just liking you, that's all it is, and it's best to be honest. So if you want to keep your mouth shut when you go home for the holiday—"

"Kind of keep her around at home? Sort of like a spare tire in case we get a flat here at school?"

She looked startled, then laughed. "*Touché,*" she said.

"*Touché* for what?"

"I don't even know, Pete . . . but I *do* like you."

She stopped, turned to me, slipped her arms around my neck. We kissed for a little while between two rows of cars, kissed until I got a pretty decent bone on, one I'm sure she could feel. Then she gave me a final peck on the lips and we started walking again.

"What did Sully say when you told him? I don't know if I'm supposed to ask, but—"

"—but you want *information,*" she said in a brusque Number Two voice. Then she laughed. It was the rueful one. "I was expecting he'd be angry, or that he might even cry. Sully's big and he scares the devil out of the football players he matches up against, but his feelings are always close to the skin. What I *didn't* expect was relief."

"Relief?"

"Relief. He's been seeing this girl in Bridgeport for a month or more . . . except my mom's friend Rionda told me she's actually a woman, maybe twenty-four or -five."

"Sounds like a recipe for disaster," I said, hoping I sounded measured and thoughtful. I was actually delighted. Of course I was. And if pore ole gosh-darned tender-hearted John Sullivan stumbled into the plot of a country-western Merle Haggard song, well, four hundred million Red Chinese wouldn't give a shit, and that went double for me.

We had almost arrived at my car. It was just one more old heap among all the others, but, courtesy of my brother, it was mine. "He's got more on his mind than his new love interest," Carol said. "He's going into the Army when he finishes high school next June. He's already talked to the recruiter and got it arranged. He can't wait to get over there in Vietnam and start making the world safe for democracy."

"Did you have a fight with him about the war?"

"Nope. What would be the use? For that matter, what would I tell him? That for me it's all about Bobby Garfield? That all the stuff Harry Swidrowski and George Gilman and Hunter McPhail say seems like smoke and mirrors compared to Bobby carrying me up Broad Street Hill? Sully would think I was crazy. Or say it's because I'm too smart. Sully feels sorry for people who are too smart. He says being too smart is a disease. And maybe he's right. I kind of love him, you know. He's sweet. He's also the kind of guy who needs someone to take care of him."

And I hope he finds someone, I thought. Just as long as it's not you.

She looked judiciously at my car. "Okay," she said. "It's ugly, it *desperately* needs a wash, but it's transportation. The question is, what're we doing here when I should be reading a Flannery O'Connor story?"

I took out my pocket-knife and opened it. "Got a nail-file in your bag?"

"As a matter of fact, I do. Are we going to fight? Number Two and Number Six go at it in the Steam Plant parking lot?"

"Don't be a smartass. Just get it out and follow me."

By the time we got around to the back of the station wagon, she was laughing—not the rueful laugh but the full-out guffaw I'd first heard when Skip's horny hotdog man came down the dishline conveyor belt. She finally understood why we were here.

Carol took one side of the bumper sticker; I took the other; we met in the middle. Then we watched the shreds blow away across the macadam. *Au revoir,* AuH_2O-4-USA. Bye-bye, Barry. And we laughed. Man, we just couldn't stop laughing.

22

A couple of days later my friend Skip, who'd come to college with the political awareness of a mollusk, put up a poster on his side of the room he shared with Brad Witherspoon. It showed a smiling businessman in a three-piece suit. One hand was extended to shake. The other was hidden behind his back, but something clutched in it was dripping blood between his shoes. WAR IS GOOD BUSINESS, the poster said. INVEST YOUR SON.

Dearie was horrified.

"So you're against Vietnam now?" he asked when he saw it. Below his chin-out truculence I think our beloved floor-proctor was badly shocked by that poster. Skip, after all, had been a first-class high-school baseball player. Was expected to play college ball, too. Had been courted by both Delta Tau Delta and Phi Gam, the jock frats. Skip was no sickly cripple like Stoke Jones (Dearie Dearborn had also taken to calling Stoke Rip-Rip), no frog-eyed weirdo like George Gilman.

"Hey, all this poster means is that a lot of people are making money out of a big bloody mess," Skip said. "McDonnell-Douglas. Boeing. GE. Dow Chemical and Coleman Chemicals. Pepsi Fuckin Cola. Lots more."

Dearie's gimlet gaze conveyed (or tried to) the idea that he had thought about such issues more deeply than Skip Kirk ever could. "Let me ask you something—do you think we should just stand back and let Uncle Ho take over down there?"

"I don't know *what* I think," Skip said, "not yet. I only started getting interested in the subject a couple of weeks ago. I'm still playing catch-up."

This was at seven-thirty in the morning, and a little group outbound for eight o'clock classes had gathered around Skip's door. I saw Ronnie (plus Nick Prouty; by this point the two of them had become inseparable), Ashley Rice, Lennie Doria, Billy Marchant, maybe four or five others. Nate was leaning in the doorway of 302, wearing a tee-shirt and his pj bottoms. In the stairwell, Stoke Jones leaned on his crutches. He had apparently been on his way out and had turned back to monitor the discussion.

Dearie said, "When the Viet Cong come into a South Viet 'ville, the first thing they look for are people wearing crucifixes, St. Christopher medals, Mary medals, anything of that nature. Catholics are killed. People who believe in *God* are killed. Do you think we should stand back while the commies kill people who believe in God?"

"Why not?" Stoke said from the stairwell. "We stood back and let the Nazis kill the Jews for six years. Jews believe in God, or so I'm told."

"Fucking Rip-Rip!" Ronnie shouted. "Who the fuck asked you to play the piano?"

But by then Stoke Jones, aka Rip-Rip, was making his way down the stairs. The echoey sound of his crutches made me think of the recently departed Frank Stuart.

Dearie turned back to Skip. His hands were fisted on his hips. Lying against the front of his white tee-shirt was a set of dogtags. His father had worn them in France and Germany, he told us; had been wearing them as he lay behind a tree, hiding from the machine-gun fire that had killed two men in his company and wounded four more. What this had to do with the Vietnam conflict none of us quite knew, but it was clearly a big deal to Dearie, so none of us asked. Even Ronnie had sense enough to keep his trap shut.

"If we let them take South Vietnam, they'll take Cambodia." Dearie's eyes moved from Skip to me to Ronnie . . . to all of us. "Then Laos. Then the Philippines. One after the other."

"If they can do that, maybe they deserve to win," I said.

Dearie looked at me, shocked. I was sort of shocked myself, but I didn't take it back.

23

There was one more round of prelims before the Thanksgiving break, and for the young scholars of Chamberlain Three, it was a disaster. By then most of us understood that *we* were a disaster, that we were committing a kind of group suicide. Kirby McClendon did his freak-out thing and disappeared like a rabbit in a magic trick. Kenny Auster, who usually sat in the corner during the marathon games and picked his nose when he couldn't decide what card to play next, simply bugged out one day. He left a queen of spades with the words "I quit" written across it on his pillow. George Lessard joined Steve Ogg and Jack Frady in Chad, the brain dorm.

Six down, thirteen to go.

It should have been enough. Hell, just what happened to poor old Kirby should have been enough; in the last three or four days before he freaked, his hands were trembling so badly he had trouble picking up his cards and he jumped in his seat if someone slammed a door in the hall. Kirby should have been enough but he wasn't. Nor was my time with Carol the answer. When I was actually with her, yes, I was fine. When I was with her all I wanted was information (and maybe to ball her socks off). When I was in the dorm, though, especially in that goddamned third-floor lounge, I became another version of Peter Riley. In the third-floor lounge I was a stranger to myself.

As Thanksgiving approached, a kind of blind fatalism set in. None of us talked about it, though. We talked about the movies, or sex ("I get more ass than a merry-go-round pony!" Ronnie used to crow, usually with no warning or conversational lead-in of any kind), but mostly we talked about Vietnam . . . and Hearts. Our Hearts discussions were about who was ahead, who was behind, and who couldn't seem to master the few simple strategic ploys of the game: void yourself in at least one suit; pass midrange hearts to someone who likes to shoot the moon; if you have to take a trick, always take it high.

Our only real response to the looming third round of prelims was to organize the game into a kind of endless, revolving tournament.

We were still playing nickel-a-point, but we were now also playing for "match points." The system for awarding match points was quite complex, but Randy Echolls and Hugh Brennan worked out a good formula in two feverish late-night sessions. Both of them, incidentally, were flunking their introductory math courses; neither was invited back at the conclusion of the fall semester.

Thirty-three years have passed since that pre-Thanksgiving round of exams, and the man that boy became still winces at the memory of them. I flunked everything but Sociology and Intro English. I didn't have to see the grades to know it, either. Skip said he'd flagged the board except for Calc, and there he barely squeaked by. I was taking Carol out to a movie that night, our one pre-break date (and our last, although I didn't know that then), and saw Ronnie Malenfant on my way to get my car. I asked him how he thought he'd done on his tests; Ronnie smiled and winked and said, "Aced everything, champ. Just like on fuckin *College Bowl.* I'm not worried." But in the light of the parking lot I could see his smile wavering minutely at the corners. His skin was too pale, and his acne, bad when we started school in September, was worse than ever. "How 'bout you?"

"They're going to make me Dean of Arts and Sciences," I said. "That tell you anything?"

Ronnie burst out laughing. "You fuckin pisspot!" He clapped me on the shoulder. The cocky look in his eyes had been replaced by fright that made him look younger. "Goin out?"

"Yeah."

"Carol?"

"Yeah."

"Good for you. She's a great-lookin chick." For Ronnie, this was nearly heartrending sincerity. "And if I don't see you in the lounge later on, have a great turkey-day."

"You too, Ronnie."

"Yeah. Sure." Looking at me from the corners of his eyes rather than straight on. Trying to hold the smile. "One way or another, I guess we're both gonna eat the bird, wouldn't you say?"

"Yeah. I guess that pretty well sums it up."

24

It was hot, even with the engine off and the heater off it was hot, we had warmed up the whole inside of the car with our bodies, the windows steamed so that the light from the parking lot came in all diffused, like light through a pebbled-glass bathroom window, and the radio was on, Mighty John Marshall making with the oldies, The Humble Yet Nonetheless Mighty playing The Four Seasons and The Dovells and Jack Scott and Little Richard and Freddie "Boom Boom" Cannon, all those oldies, and her sweater was open and her bra was draped over the seat with one strap hanging down, a thick white strap, bra-technology in those days hadn't yet taken that next great leap forward, and oh man her skin was warm, her nipple rough in my mouth, and she still had her panties on but only sort of, they were all pushed and bunched to one side and I had first one finger in her and then two fingers, Chuck Berry singing "Johnny B. Goode" and The Royal Teens singing "Short Shorts," and her hand was inside my fly, fingers pulling at the elastic of my own short-shorts, and I could smell her, the perfume on her neck and the sweat on her temples just below where her hair started, and I could hear her, hear the live pulse of her breath, wordless whispers in my mouth as we kissed, all of this with the front seat of my car pushed back as far as it would go, me not thinking of flunked prelims or the war in Vietnam or LBJ wearing a lei or Hearts or anything, only wanting her, wanting her right here and right now, and then suddenly she was straightening up and straightening *me* up, both hands planted on my chest, splayed fingers pushing me back toward the steering wheel. I moved toward her again, slipping one of my own hands up her thigh, and she said "Pete, *no!*" in a sharp voice and closed her legs, the knees coming together loud enough so I could hear the sound they made, that locking sound that means you're done making out, like it or not. I didn't like it but I stopped.

I leaned my head back against the fogged-up window on the driver's side, breathing hard. My cock was an iron bar stuffed down the front of my underwear, so hard it hurt. That would go away soon enough—

no hardon lasts forever, I think Benjamin Disraeli said that—but even after the erection's gone, the blue balls linger on. It's just a fact of guy life.

We had left the movie—some really terrible good-ole-boy thang with Burt Reynolds in it—early and had come back to the Steam Plant parking lot with the same thing on our minds . . . or so I'd hoped. I guess it *was* the same thing, except I had been hoping for a little more of it than I'd gotten.

Carol had pulled the sides of her sweater together but her bra still hung over the back of the seat and she looked madly desirable with her breasts trying to tumble out through the gap and half an areola visible in the dim light. She had her purse open and was fumbling her cigarettes out with shaky hands.

"Whooo," she said. Her voice was as shaky as her hands. "I mean holy cow."

"You look like Brigitte Bardot with your sweater open like that," I told her.

She looked up, surprised and—I thought—pleased. "Do you really think so? Or is it just the blond hair?"

"The hair? Shit, no. Mostly it's . . ." I gestured toward her front. She looked down at herself and laughed. She didn't do the buttons, though, or try to pull the sides any more closely together. I'm not sure she could have, anyway—as I remember, that sweater was a wonderfully tight fit.

"There was a theater up the street from us when I was a kid, the Asher Empire. It's torn down now, but when we were kids—Bobby and Sully-John and me—it seemed they were always showing her pictures. I think that one of them, *And God Created Woman,* must have played there for about a thousand years."

I burst out laughing and took my own cigarettes off the dashboard. "That was always the third feature at the Gates Falls Drive-In on Friday and Saturday nights."

"Did you ever see it?"

"Are you kidding? I wasn't even *allowed* to go to the drive-in unless it was a Disney double feature. I think I must have seen *Tonka* with

Sal Mineo at least seven times. But I remember the previews. Brigitte in her towel."

"I'm not coming back to school," she said, and lit her cigarette. She spoke so calmly that at first I thought we were still talking about old movies, or midnight in Calcutta, or whatever it took to persuade our bodies that it was time to go back to sleep, the action was over. Then it clicked in my head.

"You . . . did you say . . . ?"

"I said I'm not coming back after break. And it's not going to be much of a Thanksgiving at home, as far as that goes, but what the hell."

"Your father?"

She shook her head, drawing on her cigarette. In the light of its coal her face was all orange highlights and crescents of gray shadow. She looked older. Still beautiful, but older. On the radio Paul Anka was singing "Diana." I snapped it off.

"My father's got nothing to do with it. I'm going back to Harwich. Do you remember me mentioning my mother's friend Rionda?"

I sort of did, so I nodded.

"Rionda took the picture I showed you, the one of me with Bobby and S-J. She says . . ." Carol looked down at her skirt, which was still hiked most of the way to her waist, and began plucking at it. You can never tell what's going to embarrass people; sometimes it's toilet functions, sometimes it's the sexual hijinks of relatives, sometimes it's show-off behavior. And sometimes, of course, it's drink.

"Let's put it this way, my dad's not the only one in the Gerber family with a booze problem. He taught my mother how to tip her elbow, and she was a good student. For a long time she laid off—she went to AA meetings, I think—but Rionda says she's started again. So I'm going home. I don't know if I can take care of her or not, but I'm going to try. For my brother as much as my mother. Rionda says Ian doesn't know if he's coming or going. Of course he never did." She smiled.

"Carol, that's maybe not such a good idea. To shoot your education that way—"

She looked up angrily. "You want to talk about shooting *my* education? You know what I'm hearing about that fucking Hearts game on Chamberlain Three these days? That *everyone on the floor* is going to flunk out by Christmas, including you. Penny Lang says that by the start of spring semester there won't be anyone left up there but that shithead proctor of yours."

"Nah," I said, "that's an exaggeration. Nate'll be left. Stokely Jones, too, if he doesn't break his neck going downstairs some night."

"You act as though it's funny," she said.

"It's not funny," I said. No, it wasn't funny.

"Then why don't you quit it?"

Now *I* was the one starting to feel angry. She had pushed me away and clapped her knees shut, had told me she was going away just when I was starting to not only want her around but need her around, she had left me with what was soon going to be a world-class case of blue balls . . . and now it was all about me. Now it was all about cards.

"I don't *know* why I don't quit it," I said. "Why don't you find someone else to take care of your mother? Why doesn't this friend of hers, Rawanda—"

"Ri-*on*-da."

"—take care of her? I mean, is it your fault your mother's a lush?"

"*My mother is not a lush! Don't you call her that!*"

"Well, she's sure something, if you're going to drop out of college on her account. If it's that serious, Carol, it's sure something."

"Rionda has a job and a mother of her own to worry about," Carol said. The anger had gone out of her. She sounded deflated, dispirited. I could remember the laughing girl who had stood beside me, watching the shreds of Goldwater bumper sticker blow away across the macadam, but this didn't seem like the same one. "My mother is my mother. There's only Ian and me to take care of her, and Ian's barely making it in high school. Besides, there's always UConn."

"You want some *information?*" I asked her. My voice was trembling, thickening. "I'll give you some whether you want it or not. Okay? You're breaking my heart here. That's the *information.* You're breaking my goddam heart."

"I'm not, though," she said. "Hearts are tough, Pete. Most times they don't break. Most times they only bend."

Yeah, yeah, and Confucius say woman who fly upside down have crackup. I began to cry. Not a lot, but they were tears, all right. Mostly I think it was being caught so utterly unprepared. And okay, maybe I was crying for myself, as well. Because I was scared. I was now flunking or in danger of flunking all but a single subject, one of my friends was planning to push the EJECT button, and I couldn't seem to stop playing cards. Nothing was going the way I had expected it would once I got to college, and I was terrified.

"I don't want you to go," I said. "I love you." Then I tried to smile. "Just a little more information, okay?"

She looked at me with an expression I couldn't read, then cranked down her window and tossed out her cigarette. She rolled the window back up and held out her arms to me. "Come here."

I put out my own cigarette in the overflowing ashtray and slipped across to her side of the seat. Into her arms. She kissed me, then looked into my eyes. "Maybe you love me and maybe you don't. I'd never try to talk anyone out of loving me, I can tell you that much, because there's never enough loving to go around. But you're confused, Pete. About school, about Hearts, about Annmarie, and about me, too."

I started to say I wasn't, but of course I was.

"I can go to UConn," she said. "If my mother shapes up, I *will* go to UConn. If that doesn't work out, I can take courses part-time at Pennington in Bridgeport, or even CED courses at night in Stratford or Harwich. I can do those things, I have the luxury of doing those things, because I'm a girl. This is a good time to be a girl, believe me. Lyndon Johnson has seen to that."

"Carol—"

She put her hand gently against my mouth. "If you flunk out this December, you're apt to be in the jungle next December. You need to think about that, Pete. It's one thing for Sully. He thinks it's right and he *wants* to go. You don't know what you want or what you think, and you won't as long as you keep running those cards."

"Hey, I took the Goldwater sticker off my car, didn't I?" It sounded foolish to my own ears.

She said nothing.

"When are you going?"

"Tomorrow afternoon. I have a ticket on the four o'clock Trailways bus to New York. The Harwich stop isn't more than three blocks from my front door."

"Are you leaving from Derry?"

"Yes."

"Can I drive you to the depot? I could pick you up at your dorm around three."

She considered it, then nodded . . . but I saw a shaded look in her eyes. It was hard to miss, because those eyes were usually so wide and guileless. "That would be good," she said. "Thank you. And I didn't lie to you, did I? I told you we might be temporary."

I sighed. "Yeah." Only this was a lot more temporary than I had been expecting.

"Now, Number Six: We want . . . *information.*"

"You won't get it." It was hard to sound as tough as Patrick McGoohan in *The Prisoner* when you still felt like crying, but I did my best.

"Even if I ask pretty please?" She took my hand, slipped it inside her sweater, placed it on her left breast. The part of me which had begun to swoon snapped immediately back to attention.

"Well . . ."

"Have you ever done it before? I mean, all the way? That's the information I want."

I hesitated. It's a question most boys find difficult, I imagine, and one most lie about. I didn't want to lie to Carol. "No," I said.

She slipped daintily out of her panties, tossed them over into the back seat, and laced her fingers together behind my neck. "I have. Twice. With Sully. I don't think he was very good at it . . . but he'd never been to college. You have."

My mouth felt very dry, but that must have been an illusion, because when I kissed her our mouths were wet; they slipped all around, tongues and lips and nipping teeth. When I could talk I said, "I'll do my best to share my college education."

"Put on the radio," she said, unbuckling my belt and unsnapping my jeans. "Put on the radio, Pete, I like the oldies."

So I put on the radio and I kissed her and there was a spot, a certain spot, her fingers guided me to it and there was a moment when I was the same old same old and then there was a new place to be. She was very warm in there. Very warm and very tight. She whispered in my ear, her lips tickling against the skin: "Slow. Eat every one of your vegetables and maybe you'll get dessert."

Jackie Wilson sang "Lonely Teardrops" and I went slow. Roy Orbison sang "Only the Lonely" and I went slow. Wanda Jackson sang "Let's Have a Party" and I went slow. Mighty John did an ad for Brannigan's, Derry's hottest bottle club, and I went slow. Then she began to moan and it wasn't her fingers on my neck but her nails digging into it, and when she began to move her hips up against me in short hard thrusts I couldn't go slow and then The Platters were on the radio, The Platters were singing "Twilight Time" and she began to moan that she hadn't known, hadn't had a *clue,* oh gee, oh Pete, oh *gee,* oh *Jesus,* Jesus *Christ,* Pete, and her lips were all over my mouth and my chin and my jaw, she was frantic with kisses. I could hear the seat creaking, I could smell cigarette smoke and the pine air-freshener hanging from the rearview mirror, and by then *I* was moaning, too, I don't know what, The Platters were singing "Each day I pray for evening just to be with you," and then it started to happen. The pump turns on in ecstasy. I closed my eyes, I held her with my eyes closed and went into her that way, that way you do, shaking all over, hearing the heel of my shoe drumming against the driver's-side door in a spastic tattoo, thinking that I could do this even if I was dying, even if I was dying, even if I was dying; thinking also that it was information. The pump turns on in ecstasy, the cards fall where they fall, the world never misses a beat, the queen hides, the queen is found, and it was all information.

25

The next morning I had a brief meeting with my Geology instructor, who told me I was "edging into a grave situation." *That is not exactly new information, Number Six,* I thought of telling him, but didn't. The world looked different this morning—both better and worse.

When I got back to Chamberlain I found Nate getting ready to leave for home. He had his suitcase in one hand. There was a sticker on it that said I CLIMBED MT. WASHINGTON. Slung over his shoulder was a duffel full of dirty clothes. Like everything else, Nate looked different now.

"Have a good Thanksgiving, Nate," I said, opening my closet and starting to yank out pants and shirts at random. "Eat lots of stuffing. You're too fuckin skinny."

"I will. Cranberry dressing, too. When I was at my most homesick that first week, my mom's dressing was practically all I could think about."

I filled my own suitcase, thinking that I could take Carol to the bus depot in Derry and then just keep on going. If the traffic on Route 136 wasn't too heavy, I could be home before dark. Maybe even stop in Frank's Fountain for a mug of rootbeer before heading up Sabbatus Road to the house. Suddenly being out of this place—away from Chamberlain Hall and Holyoke Commons, away from the whole damned University—was my number-one priority. *You're confused, Pete,* Carol had said in the car last night. *You don't know what you want or what you think, and you won't as long as you keep running those cards.*

Well, this was my chance to get away from the cards. It hurt to know Carol was leaving, but I'd be lying if I said that was foremost in my mind right then. At that moment, getting away from the third-floor lounge was. Getting away from The Bitch. *If you flunk out this December, you're apt to be in the jungle next December.* Be in touch, baby, seeya, as Skip Kirk usually put it.

When I latched the suitcase shut and looked around, Nate was still standing in the doorway. I jumped and let out a little squeak of surprise. It was like being visited by Banquo's fucking ghost.

"Hey, go on, bug out," I said. "Time and tide wait for no man, not even one in pre-dent."

Nate only stood there, looking at me. "You're going to flunk out," he said.

Again I thought of how weirdly alike Nate and Carol were, almost male and female sides of the same coin. I tried to smile, but Nate didn't smile back. His face was small and white and pinched. The perfect Yankee face. You see a skinny guy who always burns instead of tanning, whose idea of dressing up includes a string tie and a liberal application of Vitalis, a guy who looks like he hasn't had a decent shit in three years, and that guy was most likely born and raised north of White River, New Hampshire. And on his deathbed his last words are apt to be "Cranberry dressing."

"Nah," I said. "Don't sweat it, Natie. All's cool."

"You're going to flunk out," he repeated. Dull, bricky color was rising in his cheeks. "You and Skip are the best guys I know, there wasn't anybody in high school like you guys, not in *my* high school at least, and you're going to flunk out and it's so *stupid.*"

"I'm *not* going to flunk out," I said . . . but since last night I had found myself accepting the idea that I *could.* I wasn't just *edging* into a grave situation; man, I was there. "Skip, either. It's under control."

"The world's falling down and you two are flunking out of school over Hearts! Over a *stupid fuckin card-game!*"

Before I could say anything else he was gone, headed back up the county for turkey and his mom's stuffing. Maybe even a through-the-pants handjob from Cindy. Hey, why not? It was Thanksgiving.

26

I don't read my horoscope, have rarely watched *The X-Files,* have *never* called the Psychic Friends Hotline, but I nevertheless believe that we all get glimpses of the future from time to time. I got one that afternoon, when I pulled up in front of Franklin Hall in my brother's old station wagon: she was already gone.

I went inside. The lobby, where there were usually eight or nine gentlemen callers sitting in the plastic chairs, looked oddly empty. A housekeeper in a blue uniform was vacuuming the industrial-strength rug. The girl behind the counter was reading a copy of *McCall's* and listening to the radio. ? and The Mysterians, as a matter of fact. Cry cry cry, baby, 96 tears.

"Pete Riley for Carol Gerber," I said. "Can you buzz her?"

She looked up, put her magazine aside, and gave me a sweet, sympathetic look. It was the look of a doctor who has to tell you gee, sorry, the tumor's inoperable. Bad luck, man, better make friends with Jesus. "Carol said she had to leave early. She took the Black Bear Shuttle to Derry. But she told me you'd be by and asked me to give you this."

She handed me an envelope with my name written across the front. I thanked her and left Franklin with it in my hand. I went down the walk and stood for a moment by my car, looking across toward Holyoke Commons, fabled Palace on the Plains and home of the horny hotdog man. Below it, in Bennett's Run, leaves flew before the wind in rattling drifts. The bright colors had gone out of them; only November's dark brown was left. It was the day before Thanksgiving, the doorstep of winter in New England. The world was all wind and cold sunshine. I had started crying again. I could tell by the warmth on my cheeks. 96 tears, baby; cry cry cry.

I got into the car where I had lost my virginity the night before and opened the envelope. There was a single sheet of paper inside. Brevity is the soul of wit, according to Shakespeare. If it's true, then Carol's letter was witty as hell.

Dear Pete,

I think we ought to let last night be our goodbye—how could we do any better? I may write to you at school or I may not, right now I'm so confused I just don't know (hey, I may even change my mind and come back!). But please let me be the one to get in touch, okay? You said you loved me. If you do, let me be the one to get in touch. I will, I promise.

Carol

P.S. Last night was the sweetest thing that's ever happened to me. If it gets any better than that, I don't see how people can live thru it.
P.P.S. Get out of that stupid card-game.

She said it was the sweetest thing that had ever happened to her, but she hadn't put "love" at the bottom of the note, only her signature. Still . . . *If it gets any better than that, I don't see how people can live thru it.* I knew what she meant. I reached over and touched the side of the seat where she had lain. Where we had lain together.

Put on the radio, Pete, I like the oldies.

I looked at my watch. I had gotten to the dorm early (that half-conscious premonition at work, maybe), and it had just gone three now. I could easily get to the Trailways depot before she left for Connecticut . . . but I wasn't going to do it. She was right, we had said a brilliant goodbye in my old station wagon; anything more would be a step down. At best we would find ourselves going over the same ground; at worst, we'd splash mud over last night with an argument.

We want information.

Yes. And we had gotten it. God knew we had.

I folded her letter, stuck it into the back pocket of my jeans, and drove home to Gates Falls. At first my eyes kept blurring and I had to keep wiping at them. Then I turned on the radio and the music made things a little better. The music always does. I'm past fifty now, and the music still makes things better; it's the fabled automatic.

27

I got back to Gates around five-thirty, slowed as I drove past Frank's, then kept on going. By then I wanted to get home a lot more than I wanted a draft Hires and a gossip with Frank Parmeleau. Mom's way of saying welcome home was to tell me I was too skinny, my hair was too long, and I hadn't been "standing close enough to the razor." Then she sat in her rocking chair and had a little weep over the return of the prodigal son. My dad put a kiss on my cheek, hugged me with one arm, and then shuffled to the fridge for a glass of Mom's red tea, his head poking forward out of the neck of his old brown sweater like the head of a curious turtle.

We—my mom and me, that is—thought he had twenty per cent of his eyesight left, maybe a bit more. It was hard to tell, because he so rarely talked. It was a bagging-room accident that did for him, a terrible two-story fall. He had scars on the left side of his face and his neck; there was a dented-in patch of skull where the hair never grew back. The accident pretty much blacked out his vision, and it did something to his mind, as well. But he was not a "total ijit," as I once heard some asshole down at Gendron's Barber Shop say, nor was he mute, as some people seemed to think. He was in a coma for nineteen days. After he woke up he became mostly silent, that much is true, and he was often terribly confused in his mind, but sometimes he was still there, all present and accounted for. He was there enough when I came home to give me a kiss and that strong one-armed hug, his way of hugging for as long as I could remember. I loved my old man a lot . . . and after a semester of playing cards with Ronnie Malenfant, I had learned that talking is a wildly overrated skill.

I sat with them for awhile, telling them some of my college stories (not about chasing The Bitch, though), then went outside. I raked fallen leaves in the twilight—the frosty air on my cheeks felt like a blessing—waved at the passing neighbors, and ate three of my mom's hamburgers for supper. After, she told me she was going down to the church, where the Ladies' Aid was preparing Thanksgiving meals for shut-ins. She didn't think I'd want to spend my first evening home with a bunch of old hens, but I was welcome to attend the cluckfest if I wanted. I thanked her and said I thought I'd give Annmarie a call instead.

"Now why doesn't that surprise me?" she said, and went out. I heard the car start and then, with no great joy, I dragged myself to the telephone and called Annmarie Soucie. An hour later she drove over in her father's pickup, smiling, her hair down on her shoulders, mouth radiant with lipstick. The smile didn't last long, as I guess you can probably figure out for yourself, and fifteen minutes after she came in, Annmarie was out of the house and out of my life. Be in touch, baby, seeya. Right around the time of Woodstock, she married an insurance agent from Lewiston and became Annmarie Jalbert. They had three kids, and they're still married. I guess that's good, isn't it? Even if it isn't, you have to admit it's pretty goddam American.

I stood at the window over the kitchen sink, watching the taillights of Mr. Soucie's truck disappear down the road. I felt ashamed of myself—Christ, the way her eyes had widened, the way her smile had faded and begun to tremble—but I also felt shittily happy, disgustingly relieved; light enough to dance up the walls and across the ceiling like Fred Astaire.

There were shuffling steps from behind me. I turned and there was my dad, doing his slow turtle-walk across the linoleum in his slippers. He went with one hand held out before him. The skin on it was beginning to look like a big loose glove.

"Did I just hear a young lady call a young gentleman a fucking jerk?" he asked in a mild just-passing-the-time voice.

"Well . . . yeah." I shuffled my feet. "I guess maybe you did."

He opened the fridge, groped, and brought out the jug of red tea. He drank it without sugar. I have taken it that same way on occasion, and can tell you it tastes like almost nothing at all. My theory is that my dad always went for the red tea because it was the brightest thing in the icebox, and he always knew what it was.

"Soucie girl, wasn't it?"

"Yeah, Dad. Annmarie."

"All them Soucies have the distemper, Pete. Slammed the door, didn't she?"

I was smiling. I couldn't help it. It was a wonder the glass was still in that poor old door. "I guess she did."

"You trade her in for a newer model up there t'the college, did you?"

That was a fairly complicated question. The simple answer—and maybe the truest, in the end—was no I hadn't. That was the answer I gave.

He nodded, set out the biggest glass in the cabinet next to the fridge, and then looked like he was getting ready to pour the tea all over the counter and his own feet, anyway.

"Let me do that for you," I said. "Okay?"

He made no reply but stood back and let me pour the tea. I put the three-quarters-full glass into his hands and the jug back in the fridge.

"Is it good, Dad?"

Nothing. He only stood there with the glass in both hands, the way a child holds a glass, drinking in little sips. I waited, decided he wasn't going to reply, and fetched my suitcase out of the corner. I'd thrown my textbooks in on top of my clothes and now took them out.

"Studying on the first night of break," Dad said, startling me—I'd almost forgotten he was there. "Gorry."

"Well, I'm a little behind in a couple of classes. The teachers move a lot faster than the ones in high school."

"College," he said. A long pause. "You're in college."

It seemed almost to be a question, so I said, "That's right, Dad."

He stood there awhile longer, seeming to watch me as I stacked my books and notebooks. Maybe he was watching. Or maybe he was just standing there. You couldn't tell, not for sure. At last he began to shuffle toward the door, neck stretched out, that defensive hand slightly raised, his other hand—the one with the glass of red tea in it—now curled against his chest. At the door he stopped. Without looking around, he said: "You're well shut of that Soucie girl. All Soucies has got bad tempers. You can dress em up but you can't take em out. You can do better."

He went out, holding his glass of tea curled to his chest.

28

Until my brother and his wife showed up from New Gloucester, I actually did study, half caught up on my sociology, and slogged through forty pages of geology, all in three brain-busting hours. By the time I stopped to make coffee, I'd begun to feel faint stirrings of hope. I was behind, disastrously behind, but maybe not quite *fatally* behind. I felt like an outfielder who has tracked a ball back and back to the left-field wall; he stands there looking up but not *giving* up, knowing that the ball's going to carry over but also knowing that if he times his leap just right, he can catch it as it does. I could do that.

If, that was, I could stay out of the third-floor lounge in the future.

At quarter of ten my brother, who arrives nowhere while the sun is still up if he can help it, drove in. His wife of eight months, glamorous in a coat with a real mink collar, was carrying a bread pudding; Dave had a bowl of butter-beans. Only my brother of all people on earth would think of transporting butter-beans across county lines for Thanksgiving purposes. He's a good guy, Dave, my elder by six years and in 1966 an accountant for a small hamburger chain with half a dozen "shoppes" in Maine and New Hampshire. By 1996 there were eighty "shoppes" and my brother, along with three partners, owned the company. He's worth three million dollars—on paper, at least—and has had a triple bypass. One bypass for each million, I guess you could say.

Hard on Dave and Katie's heels came Mom from the Ladies' Aid, dusted with flour, exhilarated from good works, and overjoyed to have both of her sons in the house. There was a lot of cheerful babble. Our dad sat in the corner listening to it without adding anything . . . but he was smiling, his odd, big-pupiled eyes going from Dave's face to mine and then back to Dave's. It was actually our voices his eyes were responding to, I suppose. Dave wanted to know where Annmarie was. I said Annmarie and I had decided to cool it for awhile. Dave started to ask if that meant we were—

Before he could finish the question, both his mother and his wife gave him those sharp little female pokes that mean *not now, buddy, not now.* Looking at Mom's wide eyes, I guessed she would have her own questions for me later on. Probably quite a few of them. Mom wanted *information.* Moms always do.

Other than being called a fucking jerk by Annmarie and wondering from time to time how Carol Gerber was doing (mostly if she had changed her mind about coming back to school and if she was sharing her Thanksgiving with old Army-bound Sully-John), that was a pretty great holiday. The whole family showed up at one time or another on Thursday or Friday, it seemed, wandering through the house and gnawing on turkey-legs, watching football games on TV and roaring at the big plays, chopping wood for the kitchen stove (by Sunday night Mom had enough stovelengths to heat the house all winter with just the Franklin, if she'd wanted). After supper we ate pie and played Scrabble. Most entertaining of all, Dave and Katie had a huge fight over the house they were planning to buy, and Katie hucked a Tupperware dish of leftovers at my brother. I had taken a few lumps at Dave's hands over the years, and I liked watching that plastic container of squash bounce off the side of his head. Man, that was fun.

But underneath all the good stuff, the ordinary joy you feel when your whole family's there, was my fear of what was going to happen when I went back to school. I found an hour to study late Thursday night, after the fridge had been stuffed full of leftovers and everyone else had gone to bed, and two more hours on Friday afternoon, when there was a lull in the flow of relatives and Dave and Katie, their differences temporarily resolved, retired for what I thought was an extremely noisy "nap."

I still felt I could catch up—knew it, actually—but I also knew I couldn't do it alone, or with Nate. I had to buddy up with someone who understood the suicidal pull of that third-floor lounge, and how the blood surged when someone started playing spades in an effort to force The Bitch. Someone who understood the primitive joy of managing to sock Ronnie with *la femme noire.*

It would have to be Skip, I thought. Even if Carol were to come back, she would never be able to understand in the same way. It had to be Skip and me, swimming out of deep water and in toward the shore. I thought if we stuck together, we could both pull through. Not that I cared so much about him. Admitting that feels scuzzy, but it's the truth. By Saturday of Thanksgiving break I'd done lots of soul-searching and understood I was mostly concerned about myself, mostly looking out for Number Six. If Skip wanted to use me, that was fine. Because I sure wanted to use him.

By noon Saturday I'd read enough geology to know I needed help on some of the concepts, and fast. There were only two more big test-periods in the semester: a set of prelims and then final exams. I would have to do really well on both to keep my scholarships.

Dave and Katie left at around seven on Saturday night, still bickering (but more good-naturedly) about the house they planned to buy in Pownal. I settled down at the kitchen table and started reading about out-group sanctions in my soash book. What it seemed to amount to was that even nerds have to have someone to shit on. A depressing concept.

At some point I became aware I wasn't alone. I looked up and saw my mother standing there in her old pink housecoat, her face ghostly with Pond's Cold Cream. I wasn't surprised that I hadn't heard her; after twenty-five years in the same little house, she knew where all the creaks and groans were. I thought she had finally gotten around to her questions about Annmarie, but it turned out that my love-life was the last thing on her mind.

"How much trouble are you in, Peter?" she asked.

I thought of about a hundred different answers, then settled for the truth. "I don't really know."

"Is it any one thing in particular?"

This time I didn't tell the truth, and looking back on it I realize how telling that lie was: some part of me, alien to my best interests but very powerful, still reserved the right to frog-march me to the cliff . . . and over the edge.

Yeah, Mom, the third-floor lounge is the problem, cards are the problem—just a few hands is what I tell myself every time, and when I look up at the clock it's quarter of midnight and I'm too tired to study. Hell, too wired *to study. Other than play Hearts, all I've really managed to do this fall is lose my virginity.*

If I could have said at least the first part of that, I think it would have been like guessing Rumpelstiltskin's name and then speaking it out loud. But I didn't say any of it. I told her it was just the pace of college; I had to redefine what studying meant, learn some new habits. But I could do it. I was sure I could.

She stood there a moment longer, her arms crossed and her hands deep in her housecoat sleeves—she looked sort of like a Chinese Mandarin when she stood that way—and then she said, "I'll always love you, Pete. Your father, too. He doesn't say it, but he feels it. We both do. You know that."

"Yeah," I said. "I know that." I got up and hugged her. Pancreatic cancer was what got her. That one's quick, at least, but it wasn't quick enough. I guess none of them are when it's someone you love.

"But you have to work hard at your studies. Boys who don't work hard at them have been dying." She smiled. There wasn't much humor in it. "Probably you knew that."

"I heard a rumor."

"You're still growing," she said, tilting her head up.

"I don't think so."

"Yes. At least an inch since summer. And your hair! Why don't you cut your hair?"

"I like it the way it is."

"It's as long as a girl's. Take my advice, Pete, cut your hair. Look decent. You're not one of those Rolling Stones or a Herman's Hermit, after all."

I burst out laughing. I couldn't help it. "I'll think about it, Mom, okay?"

"You do that." She gave me another hard hug, then let me go. She looked tired, but I thought she also looked rather beautiful. "They're killing boys across the sea," she said. "At first I thought there was a good reason for it, but your father says it's crazy and I'm not so sure he isn't right. You study hard. If you need a little extra for books—or a tutor—we'll scrape it up."

"Thanks, Mom. You're a peach."

"Nope," she said. "Just an old mare with tired feet. I'm going to bed."

I studied another hour, then all the words started to double and triple in front of my eyes. I went to bed myself but couldn't sleep. Every time I started to drift I saw myself picking up a Hearts hand and beginning to arrange it in suits. Finally I let my eyes roll open and just stared up at the ceiling. *Boys who don't work hard at their studies have been dying,* my mother had said. And Carol telling me that this was a good time to be a girl, Lyndon Johnson had seen to that.

We chasin The Bitch!

Pass left or right?

Jesus Christ, fuckin Riley's shootin the moon!

Voices in my head. Voices seeming to seep out of the very air.

Quitting the game was the only sane solution to my problems, but even with the third-floor lounge a hundred and thirty miles north of where I was lying, it had a hold on me, one which had little to do with sanity or rationality. I'd amassed twelve points in the *uber tourney;* only Ronnie, with fifteen, was now ahead of me. I didn't see how I could give those twelve points up, just walk away and leave that windbag Malenfant with a clear field. Carol had helped me keep Ronnie in some sort of perspective, allowed me to see him for the creepy, small-minded, bad-complexioned gnome that he was. Now that she was gone—

Ronnie's also going to be gone before long, the voice of reason interposed. *If he lasts to the end of the semester it'll be a blue-eyed miracle. You know that.*

True. And in the meantime, Ronnie had nothing else but Hearts, did he? He was clumsy, potbellied, and thin-armed, an old man waiting to happen. He wore a chip on his shoulder to at least partially hide his massive feelings of inferiority. His boasting about girls was ludicrous. Also, he wasn't really smart, like some of the kids currently in danger of flunking out (Skip Kirk, for instance). Hearts and empty brag were the only things Ronnie was good at, so far as I'd been able to tell, so why not just stand back and let him run the cards and run his mouth while he still could?

Because I didn't want to, that was why. Because I wanted to wipe the smirk off his hollow, pimply face and silence his grating blare of a laugh. It was mean but it was true. I liked Ronnie best when he was sulking, when he was glowering at me with his greasy hair tumbled down over his forehead and his lower lip pushed out.

Also, there was the game itself. I loved playing. I couldn't even stop thinking about it here, in my childhood bed, so how was I supposed to stay away from the lounge when I got back? How was I supposed to ignore Mark St. Pierre yelling at me to hurry up, there was a seat empty, everyone stood at zero on the scorepad and the game was about to commence? Christ!

I was still awake when the cuckoo clock in the parlor below me sang two o'clock. I got up, threw on my old tartan robe over my skivvies, and went downstairs. I got myself a glass of milk and sat at the kitchen table to drink it. There were no lights on except for the fluorescent bar over the stove, no sounds except for the sough of the furnace through the floor-grates and my father's soft snores from the back bedroom. I felt a little nutso, as if the combination of turkey and cramming had set off a minor earthquake in my head. And as if I might next fall asleep around, oh, say St. Patrick's Day.

I happened to glance into the entry. There, hung on one of the hooks above the woodbox, was my high-school jacket, the one with the big white GF entwined on the breast. Nothing else but the initials; I hadn't been much of a jock. When Skip asked me, shortly after we met at the University, if I'd lettered in anything, I'd told him I had the big M for masturbation—first team, the short overhand stroke my specialty. Skip had laughed until he cried, and maybe that was when we'd started being friends. Actually, I guess I could have gotten a D for debate or dramatics, but they don't give letters in those things, do they? Not then and not now.

High school seemed far in the past to me on that night, almost in another planetary system . . . but there was the jacket, a birthday present from my folks the year I turned sixteen. I crossed to the entry and took it off the hook. I put it up to my face and smelled it and thought of Period 5 study-hall with Mr. Mezensik—the bitter aroma of pencil-shavings, the girls whispering and giggling under their breath, faint shouts from outside as the phys ed kids played what the jocks called Remedial Volleyball. I saw that the place where the jacket had hung on the hook continued to stick up in a kind of dimple; the damned thing probably hadn't been worn, even by my mother to go out to grab the mail in her nightgown, since the previous April or May.

I thought of seeing Carol frozen in newsprint dots, her face shadowed by a sign reading U.S. OUT OF VIETNAM NOW!, her ponytail lying against the collar of her own high-school jacket . . . and I had an idea.

Our telephone, a Bakelite dinosaur with a rotary dial, was on a table in the front hall. In the drawer beneath it was the Gates Falls phonebook, my mom's address book, and a litter of writing implements. One was a black laundry-marker. I took it back to the kitchen table and sat down again. I spread my high-school jacket over my knees, then used the marker to make a large sparrow-track on the back. As I worked I felt the nervous tension draining out of my muscles. It occurred to me that I could award myself my own letter if I wanted, and that was sort of what I was doing.

When I was done I held the jacket up and took a look. In the faint white light of the fluorescent bar, what I'd drawn looked harsh and declamatory and somehow childish:

But I liked it. I liked that motherfucker. I wasn't sure what I thought about the war even then, but I liked that sparrow-track quite a lot. And I felt as if I could finally go to sleep; drawing it had done that much for me, anyway. I rinsed out my milk-glass and went upstairs with my jacket under my arm. I stuck it in the closet and then lay down. I thought of Carol putting my hand inside her sweater and the taste of her breath in my mouth. I thought of how we had been only ourselves behind the fogged-up windows of my old station wagon, maybe our best selves. And I thought of how we had laughed as we stood watching the tatters of my Goldwater sticker blow away across the Steam Plant parking lot. I was thinking about that when I fell asleep.

I took my modified high-school jacket back to school on Sunday packed into my suitcase—despite her freshly voiced doubts about Mr. Johnson's and Mr. McNamara's war, my mom would have had lots of questions about the sparrow-track, and I didn't have answers to give, not yet.

I felt equipped to wear the jacket, though, and I did. I spilled beer and cigarette ashes on it, puked on it, bled on it, got teargassed in Chicago while wearing it and screaming "The whole world is watching!" at the top of my lungs. Girls cried on the entwined GF on the left breast (by my senior year those letters were dingy gray instead of white), and one girl lay on it while we made love. We did it with no protection, so probably there's a trace of semen on the quilted lining, too. By the time I packed up and left LSD Acres in 1970, the peace sign I drew on the back in my mother's kitchen was only a shadow. But the shadow remained. Others might not see it, but I always knew what it was.

29

We came back to school on the Sunday after Thanksgiving in this order: Skip at five (he lived in Dexter, the closest of the three of us), me at seven, Nate at around nine.

I called Franklin Hall even before I unpacked my suitcase. No, the girl on the desk said, Carol Gerber wasn't back. She was plainly reluctant to say more, but I badgered her. There were two pink LEFT SCHOOL cards on the desk, she said. One of them had Carol's name and room number on it.

I thanked her and hung up. I stood there a minute, fogging up the booth with my cigarette smoke, then turned around. Across the hall I could see Skip sitting at one of the card-tables, just picking up a spilled trick.

I sometimes wonder if things might have been different if Carol *had* come back, or even if I'd beaten Skip back, had a chance to get to him before the third-floor lounge got to him. I didn't, though.

I stood there in the phone-booth, smoking a Pall Mall and feeling sorry for myself. Then, from across the way, someone screamed: "*Oh shit no! I don't fuckin* BELIEVE IT!"

To which Ronnie Malenfant (from where I stood in the phone-booth he was out of my view, but his voice was as unmistakable as the sound of a saw ripping through a knot in a pine-branch) hollered gleefully back: "Whoa, look at this—*Randy Echolls takes the first Bitch of the post-Thanksgiving era!*"

Don't go in there, I told myself. *You are absolutely fucked if you do, fucked once and for all.*

But of course I did. The tables were all taken, but there were three other guys—Billy Marchant, Tony DeLucca, and Hugh Brennan—standing around. We could snag a corner, if we so chose.

Skip looked up from his hand and shot me a high five in the smoky air. "Welcome back to the loonybin, Pete."

"Hey!" Ronnie said, looking around. "Look who's here! The only asshole in the place who can almost play the game! Where you been, Chuckles?"

"Lewiston," I said, "fucking your grandmother."

Ronnie cackled, his pimply cheeks turning red.

Skip was looking at me seriously, and maybe there was something in his eyes. I can't say for sure. Time goes by, Atlantis sinks deeper and deeper into the ocean, and you have a tendency to romanticize. To mythologize. Maybe I saw that he had given up, that he intended to stay here and play cards and then go on to whatever was next; maybe he was giving me permission to go in my own direction. But I was eighteen, and more like Nate in many ways than I liked to admit. I had also never had a friend like Skip. Skip was fearless, Skip said fuck every other word, when Skip was eating at the Palace the girls couldn't keep their eyes off him. He was the kind of babe magnet Ronnie could be only in his dampest dreams. But Skip also had something adrift inside of him, something like a bit of bone which may, after years of harmless wandering, pierce the heart or clog the brain. He knew it, too. Even then, with high school still sticking all over him like afterbirth, even then when he still thought he'd somehow wind up teaching school and coaching baseball, he knew it. And I loved him. The look of him, the smile of him, the walk and talk of him. I loved him and I would not leave him.

"So," I said to Billy, Tony, and Hugh. "You guys want a lesson?"

"Nickel a point!" Hugh said, laughing like a loon. Shit, he *was* a loon. "Let's go! Wheel em and deal em!"

Pretty soon we were in the corner, all four of us smoking furiously and the cards flying. I remembered the desperate cramming I'd done over the holiday weekend; remembered my mother saying that boys who didn't work hard in school were dying these days. I remembered those things, but they seemed as distant as making love to Carol in my car while The Platters sang "Twilight Time."

I looked up once and saw Stoke Jones in the doorway, leaning on his crutches and looking at us with his usual distant contempt. His black hair was thicker than ever, the corkscrews crazier over his ears and heavier against the collar of his sweatshirt. He sniffed steadily, his nose dripped and his eyes were running, but otherwise he didn't seem any sicker than before the break.

"Stoke!" I said. "How are you doing?"

"Oh well, who knows," he said. "Better than you, maybe."

"Come on in, Rip-Rip, drag up a milking-stool," Ronnie said. "We'll teach you the game."

"You know nothing I want to learn," Stoke said, and went thumping away. We listened to his receding crutches and a brief coughing fit.

"That crippled-up queer loves me," Ronnie said. "He just can't show it."

"I'll show you something if you don't deal some fuckin cards," Skip said.

"I'm bewwy, bewwy scared," Ronnie said in an Elmer Fudd voice which only he found amusing. He laid his head on Mark St. Pierre's arm to show how terrified he was.

Mark lifted the arm, hard. "The fuck off me. This is a new shirt, Malenfant, I don't want your pimple-pus all over it."

Before Ronnie's face lit with amusement and he cawed laughter, I saw a moment of desperate hurt there. It left me unmoved. Ronnie's problems might be genuine, but they didn't make him any easier to like. To me he was just a blowhard who could play cards.

"Come on," I said to Billy Marchant. "Hurry up and deal. I want to get some studying done later." But of course there was no studying done by any of us that night. Instead of burning out over the holiday, the fever was stronger and hotter than ever.

I went down the hall around quarter of ten to get a fresh pack of smokes and knew Nate was back while I was still six doors away. "Love Grows Where My Rosemary Goes" was coming from the room Nick Prouty shared with Barry Margeaux, but from farther down I could hear Phil Ochs singing "The Draft Dodger Rag."

Nate was deep in his closet, hanging up his clothes. Not only was he the only person I ever knew in college who wore pajamas, he was the only one who ever used the hangers. The only thing I myself had hung up was my high-school jacket. Now I took it out and began to rummage in the pockets for my cigarettes.

"Hey, Nate, how you doing? Get enough of that cranberry dressing to hold you?"

"I'm—" he began, then saw what was on the back of my jacket and burst out laughing.

"What?" I asked. "Is it *that* funny?"

"In a way," he said, and leaned deeper into his closet. "Look." He reappeared with an old Navy pea coat in his hands. He turned it around so I could see the back. On it, much neater than my freehand work, was the sparrow-track. Nate had rendered his in bright silver duct tape. This time we both laughed.

"Ike and Mike, they think alike," I said.

"Nonsense. Great minds run in the same channel."

"Is that what it is?"

"Well . . . what I like to think, anyway. Does this mean you've changed your mind about the war, Pete?"

"What mind?" I asked.

30

Andy White and Ashley Rice never came back to college at all—eight down, now. For the rest of us, there was an obvious change for the worse in the three days before that winter's first storm. Obvious, that was, to anyone else. If you were inside the thing, burning with the fever, it all seemed just a step or two north of normal.

Before Thanksgiving break, the card quartets in the lounge had a tendency to break up and re-form during the school-week; sometimes they died out altogether for awhile as kids went off to classes. Now the groups became almost static, the only changes occurring when someone staggered off to bed or table-hopped to escape Ronnie's skills and constant abrasive chatter. This settling occurred because most of the third-floor players hadn't returned to continue furthering their educations; Barry, Nick, Mark, Harvey, and I don't know how many others had pretty much given up on the education part. They had returned in order to resume the quest for totally valueless "match points." Many of the boys on Chamberlain Three were in fact now majoring in Hearts. Skip Kirk and I, sad to say, were among them. I made a couple of classes on Monday, then said fuck it and cut the rest. I cut everything on Tuesday, played Hearts in my dreams on Tuesday night (in one fragment I remember dropping The Bitch and seeing that her face was Carol's), then spent all day Wednesday playing it for real. Geology, sociology, history . . . all concepts without meaning.

In Vietnam, a fleet of B-52s hit a Viet Cong staging area outside Dong Ha. They also managed to hit a company of U.S. Marines, killing twelve and wounding forty—whoops, shit. And the forecast for Thursday was heavy snow turning to rain and freezing rain in the afternoon. Very few of us took note of this; certainly I had no reason to think that storm would change the course of my life.

I went to bed at midnight on Wednesday and slept heavily. If I had dreams of Hearts or Carol Gerber, I don't remember them. When I woke up at eight o'clock on Thursday morning, it was snowing so heavily I could barely see the lights of Franklin Hall across the way. I showered, then padded down the hall to see if the game had started yet. There was one table going—Lennie Doria, Randy Echolls, Billy Marchant, and Skip. They looked pale and stubbly and tired, as if they had been there all night. Probably had been. I leaned in the doorway, watching the game. Outside in the snow, something quite a bit more interesting than cards was going on, but none of us knew it until later.

31

Tom Huckabee lived in King, the other boys' dorm in our complex. Becka Aubert lived in Franklin. They had become quite cozy in the last three or four weeks, and that included taking their meals together. They were coming back from breakfast on that snowy late-November morning when they saw something printed on the north side of Chamberlain Hall. That was the side which faced the rest of the campus . . . which faced East Annex in particular, where the big corporations held their job interviews.

They walked closer, stepping off the path and into the new snow—by then about four inches had fallen.

"Look," Becka said, pointing down at the snow. There were queer tracks there—not footprints but drag-marks, almost, and deep punched holes running in lines outside them. Tom Huckabee said they reminded him of tracks made by a person wearing skis and wielding ski-poles. Neither of them thought that someone using crutches might have made such tracks. Not then.

They drew closer to the side of the dorm. The letters there were big and black, but by then the snow was so heavy that they had to get within ten feet of the wall before they could read the words, which had been posted by someone with a can of spray-paint . . . and in a state of total piss-off, from the jagged look of the message. (Again, neither of them considered that someone trying to spray-paint a message while at the same time maintaining his balance on a set of crutches might not be able to manage much in the way of neatness.)

The message read:

☮ FUCK JOHNSON! KILLER PRESIDENT
U.S. OUT OF VIETNAM **NOW!** ☮

32

I've read that some criminals—perhaps a great many criminals—actually want to be caught. I think that was the case with Stoke Jones. Whatever he had come to the University of Maine looking for, he wasn't finding it. I believe he'd decided it was time to leave . . . and if he was going, he would make the grandest gesture a guy on crutches could manage before he did.

Tom Huckabee told dozens of kids about what was spray-painted on our dorm; so did Becka Aubert. One of the people she told was Franklin's second-floor proctor, a skinny self-righteous girl named Marjorie Stuttenheimer. Marjorie became quite a figure on campus by 1969, as founder and president of Christians for College America. The CCA supported the war in Vietnam and at their booth in the Memorial Union sold the little lapel flag-pins which Richard Nixon made so popular.

I was scheduled to work Thursday lunch at the Palace on the Plains, and while I might cut classes, it never crossed my mind to cut my job—I wasn't made that way. I gave my seat in the lounge to

Tony DeLucca and started over to Holyoke at about eleven o'clock to do my dishly duty. I saw a fairly large group of students gathered in the snow, looking at something on the north side of my dorm. I walked over, read the message, and knew at once who'd put it there.

On Bennett Road, a blue University of Maine sedan and one of the University's two police cars were drawn up by the path leading to Chamberlain's side door. Margie Stuttenheimer was there, part of a little group that consisted of four campus cops, the Dean of Men, and Charles Ebersole, the University's Disciplinary Officer.

There were perhaps fifty people in the crowd when I joined it at the rear; in the five minutes I stood there rubbernecking, it swelled to seventy-five. By the time I finished wipedown-shutdown at one-fifteen and headed back to Chamberlain, there were probably two hundred people gawping in little clusters. I suppose it's hard to believe now that any graffiti could have such a draw, especially on a shitty day like that one, but we are talking about a far different world, one where no magazine in America (except, very occasionally, *Popular Photography*) would show a nude so nude that the subject's pubic hair was on view, where no newspaper would dare so much as a whisper about any political figure's sex-life. This was before Atlantis sank; this was long ago and far away in a world where at least one comedian was jailed for uttering "fuck" in public and another observed that on *The Ed Sullivan Show* you could prick your finger but not finger your prick. It was a world where some words were still shocking.

Yes, we knew fuck. Of course we did. We *said* fuck all the time: fuck you, fuck your dog, go take a flying fuck at a rolling doughnut, fuck a duck, hey, go fuck your sister, the rest of us did. But there, written in black letters five feet high, were the words FUCK *JOHNSON*. Fuck *the President of the United States!* And KILLER PRESIDENT! Someone had called *the President of the United States of America* a murderer! We couldn't believe it.

When I came back from Holyoke, the other campus police car had arrived, and there were six campus cops—almost the whole damned force, I calculated—trying to put up a big rectangle of yellow canvas over the message. The crowd muttered, then started booing. The cops looked at them, annoyed. One shouted for them to break it up, go on, they all had places to go. That might have been true, but apparently most of them liked it right there, because the crowd didn't thin out much.

The cop holding the far left end of the canvas dropcloth slipped in the snow and nearly fell. A few onlookers applauded. The cop who had slipped looked toward the sound with an expression of blackest hate momentarily congesting his face, and for me that's when things really started to change, when the generations really started to gap.

The cop who'd slipped turned away and began to struggle with the piece of canvas again. In the end they settled for covering the first peace sign and the FUCK of FUCK JOHNSON! And once the Really Bad Word was hidden, the crowd *did* begin to break up. The snow was changing to sleet and standing around had become uncomfortable.

"Better not let the cops see the back of your jacket," Skip said, and I looked around. He was standing beside me in a hooded sweatshirt, his hands plunged deep into the pouch in front. His breath came out of his mouth in frozen plumes; his eyes never left the campus cops and the part of the message which still remained: JOHNSON! KILLER PRESIDENT! U.S. OUT OF VIETNAM NOW! "They'll think you did it. Or me."

Smiling a little, Skip turned around. On the back of his sweatshirt, drawn in bright red ink, was another of those sparrow-tracks.

"Jesus," I said. "When did you do that?"

"This morning," he said. "I saw Nate's." He shrugged. "It was too cool not to copy."

"They won't think it was us. Not for a minute."

"No, I suppose not."

The only question was why they weren't questioning Stoke already . . . not that they'd have to ask many questions to get the truth out of him. But if Ebersole, the Disciplinary Officer, and Garretsen, the Dean of Men, *weren't* talking to him, it was only because they hadn't yet talked to—

"Where's Dearie?" I asked. "Do you know?" The sleet was falling hard now, rattling through the trees and pinging every inch of exposed skin.

"The young and heroic Mr. Dearborn is out sanding sidewalks and paths with a dozen or so of his ROTC buddies," Skip said. "We saw them from the lounge. They're driving around in a real army truck. Malenfant said their pricks are probably so hard they won't be able to sleep on their stomachs for a week. I thought that was pretty good, for Ronnie."

"When Dearie comes back—"

"Yeah, when he comes back." Skip shrugged, as if to say all that was beyond our control. "Meantime, let's get out of this slop and play some cards, what do you say?"

I wanted to say a lot of stuff about a lot of things . . . but then again I didn't. We went back inside, and by mid-afternoon the game was in full swing once more. There were five four-handed "sub-games" going on, the room was blue with smoke, and someone had dragged in a phonograph so we could listen to the Beatles and the Stones. Someone else produced a scratched-up Cameo forty-five of "96 Tears" and that spun for at least an hour non-stop: cry cry cry. The windows gave a good view on Bennett's Run and Bennett's Walk, and I kept looking out there, expecting to see David Dearborn and some of his khaki buddies staring at the north side of the dorm, perhaps discussing if they should go after Stoke Jones with their carbines or just chase him with their bayonets. Of course they wouldn't do anything of the sort. They might chant "Kill Cong! Go U.S.!" while drilling on the football field, but Stoke was a cripple. They would happily settle for seeing his commie-loving ass busted out of the University of Maine.

I didn't want that to happen, but I didn't see any way it wouldn't. Stoke had had a sparrow-track on the back of his coat since the beginning of school, long before the rest of us were hip to what it meant, and Dearie knew it. Plus, Stoke *would* admit it. He'd deal with the Dean and the Disciplinary Officer's questions the same way he dealt with his crutches—at a full-out plunge.

And anyway, the whole thing began to seem distant, okay? The way classes did. The way Carol did, now that I understood she was really gone. The way the concept of being drafted and sent away to die in the jungle did. What seemed real and immediate was hunting out that bad Bitch, or shooting the moon and hitting everyone else at your table with twenty-six points at a whack. What seemed real was Hearts.

But then something happened.

33

Around four o'clock the sleet changed to rain, and by four-thirty, when it began to get dark, we could see that Bennett's Run was under three or four inches of water. Most of the Walk looked like a canal. Below the water was an icy, melting slush Jell-O.

The pace of the games slowed as we watched those unfortunates who were working the dishline cross from the dorms to the Palace on the Plains. Some of them—the wiser ones—cut across the slope of the hillside, making their way through the rapidly melting snow. The others came down the paths, slipping and sliding on their treacherous, icy surfaces. A thick mist had begun to rise from the wet ground, making it even harder for people to see where they were going. One guy from King met a girl from Franklin at the place where the paths converged. When they started up Bennett's Walk together the guy slipped and grabbed the girl. They almost went down together, but managed to keep their combined balance. We all applauded.

At my table we began a hold hand. Ronnie's weaselly little friend Nick dealt me an incredible thirteen cards, maybe the best pat hand I'd ever gotten. It was a shoot-the-moon opportunity if ever I had one: six high hearts and no really low ones, the king and queen of spades, plus court-cards in the other two suits, as well. I had the seven of hearts, a borderline card, but you can catch people napping in a hold hand; no one expects you to shoot the moon in a situation where you can't improve your original draw.

Lennie Doria played The Douche to start us off. Ronnie immediately played void, ridding himself of the ace of spades. He thought that was great. So did I; my two court spades were now both winners. The queen was thirteen points, but if I got all the hearts, I wouldn't eat those points; Ronnie, Nick, and Lennie would.

I let Nick take the trick. We spilled three more tricks uneventfully—first Nick and then Lennie mined for diamonds—and then I took the ten of hearts mixed into a club trick.

"Hearts have been broken and Riley eats the first one!" Ronnie bugled gleefully. "You're goin down, country boy!"

"Maybe," I said. And maybe, I thought, Ronnie Malenfant would soon be smiling on the other side of his face. With a successful shoot, I could put the idiotic Nick Prouty over a hundred and cost Ronnie a game he'd been on his way to winning.

Three tricks later what I was doing became almost obvious. As I'd hoped, Ronnie's smirk became the expression I most enjoyed seeing on his face—the disgruntled pout.

"You can't," he said. "I don't believe it. Not in a hold hand. You ain't got the fuckin horses." Yet he knew it was possible. It was in his voice.

"Well, let's see," I said, and played the ace of hearts. I was running in the open now, but why not? If the hearts were spread evenly, I could win the game right here. "Let's just see what we—"

"Look!" Skip called from the table nearest the window. His voice held disbelief and a kind of awe. "Jesus Christ, it's fuckin Stokely!"

Play stopped. We all swivelled in our chairs to look out the window at the darkening, dripping world below us. The quartet of boys in the corner stood up to see. The old wrought-iron lamps on Bennett's Walk cast weak electric beams through the groundmist, making me think of London and Tyne Street and Jack the Ripper. From its place on the hill, Holyoke Commons looked more like an ocean liner than ever. Its shape wavered as rain streamed down the lounge windows.

"Fuckin Rip-Rip, out in *this* crap—I don't believe it," Ronnie breathed.

Stoke came rapidly down the path which led from the north entrance of Chamberlain to the place where all the asphalt paths joined in the lowest part of Bennett's Run. He was wearing his old duffle coat, and it was clear he hadn't just come from the dorm; the coat was soaked through. Even through the streaming glass we could see the peace sign on his back, as black as the words which were now partly covered by a rectangle of yellow canvas (if it was still up). His wild hair was soaked into submission.

Stoke never looked toward his KILLER PRESIDENT graffiti, just thumped on toward Bennett's Walk. He was going faster than I'd ever seen him, paying no heed to the driving rain, the rising mist, or the slop under his crutches. Did he want to fall? Was he daring the slushy crap to take him down? I don't know. Maybe he was just too deep in his own thoughts to have any idea of how fast he was moving or how bad the conditions were. Either way, he wasn't going to get far if he didn't cool it.

Ronnie began to giggle, and the sound spread the way a little flame spreads through dry tinder. I didn't want to join in but was helpless to stop. So, I saw, was Skip. Partly because giggling is contagious, but also because it really was funny. I know how unkind that sounds, of course I do, but I've come too far not to tell the truth about that day . . . and *this* day, almost half a lifetime later. Because it still seems funny to me, I still smile when I think back to how he looked, a frantic clockwork toy in a duffle coat thudding along through the pouring rain, his crutches splashing up water as he went. You knew what was going to happen, you just *knew* it, and that was the funniest part of all—the question of just how far he could make it before the inevitable wipeout.

Lennie was roaring with one hand clutched to his face, staring out between his splayed fingers, his eyes streaming. Hugh Brennan was holding his not inconsiderable gut and braying like a donkey stuck in a mudhole. Mark St. Pierre was howling uncontrollably and saying he was gonna piss himself, he'd drunk too many Cokes and he was gonna spray his fuckin jeans. I was laughing so hard I couldn't hold my cards; the nerves in my right hand went dead, my fingers relaxed, and those last few winning tricks fluttered into my lap. My head was pounding and my sinuses were full.

Stoke made the bottom of the dip, where the Walk started. There he paused and for some reason did a crazed three-sixty spin, seeming to balance on one crutch. The other crutch he held out like a machine-gun, as if in his mind he was spraying the whole campus—Kill Cong! Slaughter proctors! Bayonet those upperclassmen!

"*Annnd . . . the Olympic judges give him . . . ALL TENS!*" Tony DeLucca called in a perfect sports announcer's voice. It was the final touch; the place turned into bedlam on the spot. Cards flew everywhere. Ashtrays spilled, and one of the glass ones (most were just those little aluminum Table Talk pie-dishes) broke. Someone fell out of his chair and began to roll around, bellowing and kicking his legs. Man, we just couldn't stop laughing.

"That's it!" Mark was howling. "I just drowned my Jockeys! I couldn't help it!" Behind him Nick Prouty was crawling toward the window on his knees with tears coursing down his burning face and his hands held out, the wordless begging gesture of a man who wants to say make it stop, make it stop before I burst a fuckin blood-vessel in the middle of my brain and die right here.

Skip got up, overturning his chair. I got up. Laughing our brains out, we groped for one another and staggered toward the window with our arms slung around each other's back. Below, unaware that he was being watched and laughed at by two dozen or so freaked-out cardplayers, Stoke Jones was still, amazingly, on his feet.

"Go Rip-Rip!" Ronnie began to chant. "Go Rip-Rip!" Nick joined in. He had reached the window and was leaning his forehead against it, still laughing.

"Go, Rip-Rip!"

"Go, baby!"

"Go!"

"On, Rip-Rip! Mush those huskies!"

"Work those crutches, big boy!"

"*Go you fuckin Rip-Rip!*"

It was like the last play of a close football game, except everyone was chanting *Go Rip-Rip* instead of *Hold that line* or *Block that kick. Almost* everyone; I wasn't chanting, and I don't think Skip was, either, but we were laughing. We were laughing just as hard as the rest.

Suddenly I thought of the night Carol and I had sat on the milk-boxes beside Holyoke, the night she had shown me the snapshot of herself and her childhood friends . . . and then told me the story of what those other boys had done to her. What they had done with a baseball bat. *At first they were joking, I think,* Carol had said. And had they been laughing? Probably, yeah. Because that's what you did when you were joking around, having a good time, you laughed.

Stoke stood where he was for a moment, hanging from his crutches with his head down . . . and then he attacked the hill like the Marines going ashore at Tarawa. He went tearing up Bennett's Walk, spraying water everywhere with his flying crutches; it was like watching a duck with rabies.

The chant became deafening: "*GO RIP-RIP! GO RIP-RIP! GO RIP-RIP!*"

At first they were joking, she had said as we sat there on the milk-boxes, smoking our cigarettes. By then she was crying, her tears silver in the white light from the dining hall above us. *At first they were joking and then . . . they weren't.*

That thought ended the joke of Stoke for me—I swear to you that it did. And still I couldn't stop laughing.

Stokely made it about a third of the way up the hill toward Holyoke, almost back to the visible bricks, before the slippery-slop finally got him. He planted his crutches far in advance of his body—too far for even dry conditions—and when he swung forward, both sticks flew out from under him. His legs flipped up like the legs of a gymnast doing some fabulous trick on the balance beam, and he went down on his back with a tremendous splash. We could hear it even from the third-floor lounge. It was the final perfect touch.

The lounge looked like a lunatic asylum where the inmates had all come down with food-poisoning at the same time. We staggered aimlessly about, laughing and clutching at our throats, our eyes spouting tears. I was hanging onto Skip because my legs would no longer support me; my knees felt like noodles. I was laughing harder than I ever had in my life, harder than I ever have since, I think, and still I kept thinking about Carol sitting there on the milk-box beside me, legs crossed, cigarette in one hand, snapshot in the other, Carol saying *Harry Doolin hit me . . . Willie and the other one held me so I couldn't run away . . . at first they were joking, I think, and then . . . they weren't.*

Out on Bennett's Walk, Stoke tried to sit up. He got his upper body partway out of the water . . . and then lay back, full length, as if that icy, slushy water were a bed. He lifted both arms skyward in a gesture which was almost invocatory, then let them fall again. It was every surrender ever given summed up in three motions: the lying back, the lifting of the arms, the double splash as they fell back wide to either side. It was the ultimate fuck it, do what you want, I quit.

"Come on," Skip said. He was still laughing but he was also completely serious. I could hear the seriousness in his laughing voice and see it in his hysterically contorted face. I was glad it was there, God I was glad. "Come on, before the stupid motherfuck drowns."

Skip and I crammed through the doorway of the lounge shoulder to shoulder and sprinted down the third-floor hall, bouncing off each other like pinballs, reeling, almost as out of control as Stoke had been on the path. Most of the others followed us. The only one I know for sure who didn't was Mark; he went down to his room to change out of his soaked jeans.

We met Nate on the second-floor landing—damned near ran him down. He was standing there with an armload of books in a plastic sack, looking at us with some alarm.

"Good grief," he said. That was Nate at his strongest, *good grief.* "What's wrong with *you?*"

"Come on," Skip said. His throat was so choked the words came out in a growl. If I hadn't been with him earlier, I'd have thought he'd just finished a fit of weeping. "It's not us, it's fuckin Jones. He fell down. He needs—" Skip broke off as laughter—great big belly-gusts of it—overtook him and shook him once again. He fell back against the wall, rolling his eyes in a kind of hilarious exhaustion. He shook his head as if to deny it, but of course you can't deny laughter; when it comes, it plops down in your favorite chair and stays as long as it wants. Above us, the stairs began to thunder with descending third-floor cardplayers. "He needs help," Skip finished, wiping his eyes.

Nate looked at me in growing bewilderment. "If he needs help, why are you guys laughing?"

I couldn't explain it to him. Hell, I couldn't explain it to myself. I grabbed Skip by the arm and yanked. We started down the steps to the first floor. Nate followed us. So did the rest.

34

The first thing I saw when we banged out through the north door was that rectangle of yellow canvas. It was lying on the ground, full of water and floating lumps of slush. Then the water on the path started pouring in through my sneakers and I forgot all about sight-seeing. It was freezing. The rain drove down on my exposed skin in needles that were not quite ice.

In Bennett's Run the water was ankle-deep, and my feet went from cold to numb. Skip slipped and I grabbed his arm. Nate steadied us both from behind and kept us from tumbling over backward. Ahead of us I could hear a nasty sound that was half coughing and half choking. Stoke lay in the water like a sodden log, his duffle coat floating around his body and those masses of black hair floating around his face. The cough was deep and bronchial. Fine droplets sprayed from his lips with each gagging, choking outburst. One of his crutches lay next to him, caught between his arm and his side. The other was floating away in the direction of Bennett Hall.

Water slopped over Stoke's pale face. His coughing took on a strangled, gargling quality. His eyes stared straight up into the rain and fog. He gave no sign that he heard us coming, but when I knelt on one side of him and Skip on the other, he tried to beat us away with his hands. Water ran into his mouth and he began to thrash. He was drowning in front of us. I no longer felt like laughing, but I might still have been doing it. At first they were joking, Carol said. At first they were joking. Put on the radio, Pete, I like the oldies.

"Pick him up," Skip said, and grabbed one of Stoke's shoulders. Stoke slapped at him weakly with one wax-dummy hand. Skip ignored this, might not even have felt it. "Hurry, for Christ's sake."

I grabbed Stoke's other shoulder. He splashed water in my face as though we were fucking around in someone's backyard pool. I had thought he'd be as cold as I was, but there was a sickish heat coming off his skin. I looked across his waterlogged body to Skip.

Skip nodded back at me. "Ready . . . set . . . *now.*"

We heaved. Stoke came partly out of the water—from the waist up—but that was all. I was astounded by the weight of him. His shirt had come untucked from his pants and floated around his middle like a ballerina's tutu. Below it I could see his white skin and the black bullethole of his navel. There were scars there, too, healed scars wavering every whichway like snarls of knotted string.

"Help out, Natie!" Skip grunted. "Prop him up, for fuck's sake!"

Nate dropped to his knees, splashing all three of us, and grabbed Stoke in a kind of backwards hug. We struggled to get him all the way up and out of the soup, but the slush on the bricks kept us off-balance, made it impossible for us to work together. And Stoke, although still coughing and half-drowned, was also working against us, struggling as best he could to be free of us. Stoke wanted to go back in the water.

The others arrived, Ronnie in the lead. "Fucking Rip-Rip," he breathed. He was still giggling, but he looked slightly awestruck. "You screwed up big this time, Rip. No doubt."

"Don't just stand there, you numb tool!" Skip cried. "Help us!"

Ronnie paused a moment longer, not angry, just assessing how this might best be done, then turned to see who else was there. He slipped on the slush and Tony DeLucca—also still giggling—grabbed him and steadied him. They were crowded together on the drowned Walk, all my cardplaying buddies from the third-floor lounge, and most of them still couldn't stop laughing. They looked like something, but I didn't know what. I might never have known, if not for Carol's Christmas present . . . but of course that came later.

"You, Tony," Ronnie said. "Brad, Lennie, Barry. Let's get his legs."

"What about me, Ronnie?" Nick asked. "What about me?"

"You're too small to help lift him," Ronnie said, "but it might cheer him up to get his dick sucked."

Nick stood back.

Ronnie, Tony, Brad, Lennie, and Barry Margeaux slipped past us on either side. Ronnie and Tony got Stoke by the calves.

"Christ Jesus!" Tony cried, disgusted and still half-laughing. "Nothing to him! Legs like on a scarecrow!"

" 'Legs like on a scarecrow, legs like on a scarecrow!' " Ronnie cried, viciously mimicking. "Pick him the fuck up, you wop nimrod, this isn't art appreciation! Lennie and Barry, get under his deprived ass when they do. Then you come up—"

"—when the rest of you guys lift him," Lennie finished. "Got it. And don't call my *paisan* a wop."

"Leave me alone," Stoke coughed. "Stop it, get away from me . . . fucking losers . . ." The coughing overtook him again. He began to make gruesome retching sounds. In the lamplight his lips looked gray and slick.

"Look who's talkin about being a loser," Ronnie said. "Fuckin half-drowned crippled-up Jerry's Kid homo." He looked at Skip, water running out of his wavy hair and over his pimply face. "Count us off, Kirk."

"One . . . two . . . three . . . *now!*"

We lifted. Stoke Jones came out of the water like a salvaged ship. We staggered back and forth with him. One of his arms flopped in front of me; it hung there for a moment and then the hand attached to the end of it arced up and slapped me hard across the face. Whacko! I started laughing again.

"*Put me down! Motherfuckers, put me* DOWN!"

We staggered, dancing on the slush, water pouring off him, water pouring off us. "Echolls!" Ronnie bawled. "Marchant! Brennan! *Jesus Christ, little help here you fuckin brain-dead ringmeats, what do you say?*"

Randy and Billy splashed forward. Others—three or four drawn by the shouts and splashing, most still from the third-floor Hearts group—took hold of Stoke as well. We turned him awkwardly, probably looking like the world's most spastic cheerleading squad, for some reason out practicing in the downpour. Stoke had quit struggling. He lay in our grip, arms hanging out to either side, palms up and filling with little cups of rain. Diminishing waterfalls ran out of his sodden jacket and from the seat of his pants. *He picked me up and carried me,* Carol had said. Talking about the boy with the crewcut, the boy who had been her first love. *All the way up Broad Street on one of the hottest days of the year. He carried me in his arms.* I couldn't get her voice out of my head. In a way I never have.

"The dorm?" Ronnie asked Skip. "We takin him into the dorm?"

"Jeepers, no," Nate said. "The infirmary."

Since we'd managed to get him out of the water—that was the hardest part and it was behind us—the infirmary made sense. It was a small brick building just beyond Bennett Hall, no more than three or four hundred yards away. Once we got off the path and onto the road, the footing would be good.

So we carried him to the infirmary—bore him up at shoulder height like a slain hero being ceremonially removed from the field of battle. Some of us were still laughing in little snorts and giggles. I was one of them. Once I saw Nate looking at me as if I was a thing almost below contempt, and I tried to stop the sounds that were coming out of me. I'd do okay for a little while, then I'd think of him spinning on the pivot of his crutch ("*The Olympic judges give him . . . ALL TENS!*") and I'd start in again.

Stoke only spoke once as we carried him up the walk to the infirmary door. "Let me die," he said. "For once in your stupid greedy-me-me lives do something worthwhile. Put me down and let me die."

35

The waiting room was empty, the television in the corner showing an old episode of *Bonanza* to no one at all. In those days they hadn't really found the handle on color TV yet, and Pa Cartwright's face was the color of a fresh avocado. We must have sounded like a herd of hippopotami just out of the watering-hole, and the duty-nurse came on the run. Following her was a candystriper (probably a work-study kid like me) and a little guy in a white coat. He had a stethoscope hung around his neck and a cigarette poked in the corner of his mouth. In Atlantis even the doctors smoked.

"What's the trouble with him?" The doc asked Ronnie, either because Ronnie had an in-charge look or because he was the closest at hand.

"Took a header in Bennett's Run while he was on his way to Holyoke," Ronnie said. "Damned near drowned himself." He paused, then added: "He's a cripple."

As if to underline this point, Billy Marchant waved one of Stoke's crutches. Apparently no one had bothered to salvage the other one.

"Put that thing down, you want to fuckin bonk my brains out?" Nick Prouty asked waspishly, ducking.

"What brains?" Brad responded, and we all laughed so hard we nearly dropped Stoke.

"Suck me sideways, ass-breath," Nick said, but he was laughing, too.

The doctor was frowning. "Bring him in here, and save that language for your bull sessions." Stoke began coughing again, a deep, ratcheting sound. You expected to see blood and filaments of tissue come popping out of his mouth, that cough was so heavy.

We carried Stoke down the infirmary hallway in a conga-line, but we couldn't get him through the door that way. "Let me," Skip said.

"You'll drop him," Nate said.

"No," Skip said. "I won't. Just let me get a good hold."

He stepped up beside Stoke, then nodded first to me on his right, then to Ronnie on his left.

"Lower him down," Ronnie said. We did. Skip grunted once as he took Stoke's weight, and I saw the veins pop out in his neck. Then we stood back and Skip carried Stoke into the room and laid him on the exam table. The thin sheet of paper covering the leather was immediately soaked. Skip stepped back. Stoke was staring up at him, his face dead pale except for two red patches high on his cheekbones—red as rouge, those patches were. Water ran out of his hair in rivulets.

"Sorry, man," Skip said.

Stoke turned his head away and closed his eyes.

"Out," the doctor told Skip. He had ditched the cigarette somewhere. He looked around at us, a gaggle of perhaps a dozen boys, most still grinning, all dripping on the hall's tile floor. "Does anyone know the nature of his disability? It can make a difference in how we treat him."

I thought of the scars I'd seen, those tangles of knotted string, but said nothing. I didn't really know anything. And now that the uncontrollable urge to laugh had passed, I felt too ashamed of myself to speak up.

"It's just one of those cripple things, isn't it?" Ronnie asked. Actually faced with an adult, he had lost his shrill cockiness. He sounded unsure, perhaps even uneasy. "Muscular palsy or cerebral dystrophy?"

"You clown," Lennie said. "It's muscular dystrophy and cerebral—"

"He was in a car accident," Nate said. We all looked around at him. Nate still looked neat and totally put together in spite of the soaking he'd taken. This afternoon he was wearing a Fort Kent High School ski-hat. The Maine football team had finally scored a touchdown and freed Nate from his beanie; go you Black Bears. "Four years ago. His father, mother, and older sister were killed. He was the only family survivor."

There was silence. I looked between Skip and Tony's shoulders and into the examination room. Stoke still lay streaming on the table, his head turned to the side, his eyes shut. The nurse was taking his blood pressure. His pants clung to his legs and I thought of the Fourth of July parade they used to have back home in Gates Falls when I was just a little kid. Uncle Sam would come striding along between the school band and the Anah Temple Shrine guys on their midget motorcycles, looking at least ten feet tall in his starry blue hat, but when the wind blew his pants against his legs you could see the trick.

That's what Stoke Jones's legs looked like inside his wet pants: a trick, a bad joke, sawed-off stilts with sneakers poked onto the ends of them.

"How do you know that?" Skip asked. "Did he tell you, Natie?"

"No." Nate looked ashamed. "He told Harry Swidrowski, after a Committee of Resistance meeting. They—we—were in the Bear's Den. Harry asked him right out what happened to his legs and Stoke told him."

I thought I understood the look on Nate's face. After the meeting, he had said. *After.* Nate didn't know what had been said *at* the meeting, because Nate hadn't been there. Nate wasn't a member of the Committee of Resistance; Nate was strictly a sidelines boy. He might agree with the C.R.'s goals and tactics . . . but he had his mother to think about. And his future as a dentist.

"Spinal injury?" the doctor asked. Brisker than ever.

"I think so, yeah," Nate said.

"All right." Doc began to make shooing gestures with his hands as if we were a flock of geese. "Go on back to your dorms. We'll take good care of him."

We began to back up toward the reception area.

"Why were you boys laughing when you brought him in?" the nurse asked suddenly. She stood by the doctor with the blood-pressure cuff in her hands. "Why are you grinning now?" She sounded angry. Hell, she sounded *furious.* "What was so funny about this boy's misfortune that it made you laugh?"

I didn't think anyone would answer. We'd just stand there and look down at our shuffling feet, realizing that we were still a lot closer to the fourth grade than we had perhaps thought. But someone *did* answer. Skip answered. He even managed to look at her as he did.

"His misfortune, ma'am," he said. "That was what it was, you're right. It was his misfortune that was funny."

"How terrible," she said. There were tears of rage standing in the corners of her eyes. "How terrible you are."

"Yes, ma'am," Skip said. "I guess you're right about that, too." He turned away from her.

We followed him back to the reception area in a wet and beaten little group. I can't say that being called terrible was the low point of my college career ("If you can remember much of the sixties, you weren't there," the hippie known as Wavy Gravy once said), but it may have been. The waiting room was still empty. Little Joe Cartwright was on the tube now, and just as green as his dad. Pancreatic cancer was what got Michael Landon, too—he and my mother had that in common.

Skip stopped. Ronnie, head down, pushed past him toward the door, followed by Nick, Billy, Lennie, and the rest.

"Hold it," Skip said, and they turned. "I want to talk to you guys about something."

We gathered around him. Skip glanced once toward the door leading back to the exam area, verified that we were alone, then began to talk.

36

Ten minutes later Skip and I walked back to the dorm by ourselves. The others had gone ahead. Nate hung with us for a little bit, then must have picked up a vibe that I wanted to talk privately to Skip. Nate was always good at picking up the vibe. I bet he's a good dentist, that the children in particular like him.

"I'm done playing Hearts," I said.

Skip said nothing.

"I don't know if it's too late to pull up my grades enough to keep my scholarship or not, but I'm going to try. And I don't care much, one way or the other. The fucking scholarship's not the point."

"No. *They're* the point, right? Ronnie and the rest of them."

"I think they're only part of it." It was so cold out there as that day turned to dark—cold and damp and evil. It seemed that it would never be summer again. "Man, I miss Carol. Why'd she have to go?"

"I don't know."

"When he fell over it sounded like a nuthouse up there," I said. "Not a college dorm, a fucking *nuthouse.*"

"You laughed too, Pete. So did I."

"I know," I said. I might not have if I'd been alone, and Skip and I might not have if it had just been the two of us, but how could you tell? You were stuck with the way things played out. I kept thinking of Carol and those boys with their baseball bat. And I thought of the way Nate had looked at me, as if I were a thing below contempt. "I know."

We walked in silence for awhile.

"I can live with laughing at him, I guess," I said, "but I don't want to wake up forty with my kids asking me what college was like and not be able to remember anything but Ronnie Malenfant telling Polish jokes and that poor fucked-up asshole McClendon trying to kill himself with baby aspirin." I thought about Stoke Jones twirling on his crutch and felt like laughing; thought of him lying beached on the exam table in the infirmary and felt like crying. And you know what? It was, as far as I could tell, exactly the same feeling. "I just feel bad about it. I feel like shit."

"So do I," Skip said. The rain poured down around us, soaking and cold. The lights of Chamberlain Hall were bright but not particularly comforting. I could see the yellow canvas the cops had put up lying on the grass, and above it the dim shapes of the spray-painted letters. They were running in the rain; by the following day they would be all but unreadable.

"When I was a little kid, I always pretended I was the hero," Skip said.

"Fuck yeah, me too. What little kid ever pretended to be part of the lynch-mob?"

Skip looked down at his soaked shoes, then up at me. "Could I study with you for the next couple of weeks?"

"Any time you want."

"You really don't mind?"

"Why would I fuckin mind?" I made myself sound irritated because I didn't want him to hear how relieved I was, how almost thrilled I was. Because it might work. I paused, then said, "This other . . . do you think we can pull it off?"

"I don't know. Maybe."

We had almost reached the north entrance, and I pointed to the running letters just before we went in. "Maybe Dean Garretsen and that guy Ebersole will let the whole thing drop. The paint Stoke used didn't get a chance to set. It'll be gone by morning."

Skip shook his head. "They won't let it drop."

"Why not? How can you be so sure?"

"Because Dearie won't let them."

And of course he was right.

37

For the first time in weeks the third-floor lounge was empty for awhile as drenched cardplayers dried themselves off and put on fresh clothes. Many of them also took care of some stuff Skip Kirk had suggested in the infirmary waiting room. When Nate and Skip and I came back from dinner, however, it was business as usual in the lounge—three tables were up and going.

"Hey, Riley," Ronnie said. "Twiller here says he's got a study date. If you want his seat, I'll teach you how to play the game."

"Not tonight," I said. "Got studying to do myself."

"Yeah," Randy Echolls said. "The Art of Self-Abuse."

"That's right, honey, a couple more weeks of hard work and I'll be able to switch hands without missing a stroke, just like you."

As I started away, Ronnie said, "I had you stopped, Riley."

I turned around. Ronnie was leaning back in his chair, smiling that unpleasant smile of his. For a short period of time, out there in the rain, I had glimpsed a different Ronnie, but that young man had gone back into hiding.

"No," I said, "you didn't. It was a done deal."

"No one shoots the moon on a hold hand," Ronnie said, leaning back farther than ever. He scratched one cheek, busting the heads off a couple of pimples. They oozed tendrils of yellow-white cream. "Not at my table they don't. I had you stopped in clubs."

"You were *void* in clubs, unless you reneged on the first trick. You played the ace of spades when Lennie played The Douche. And in hearts I had the whole court."

Ronnie's smile faltered for just a moment, then came back strong. He waved a hand at the floor, from which all the spilled cards had been picked up (the butty remains of the overturned ashtrays still remained; most of us had been raised in homes where moms cleaned up such messes). "All the high hearts, huh? Too bad we can't check and see."

"Yeah. Too bad." I started away again.

"You're going to fall behind on match points!" he called after me. "You know that, don't you?"

"You can have mine, Ronnie. I don't want them anymore."

I never played another hand of Hearts in college. Many years later I taught my kids the game, and they took to it like ducks to water. We have a tournament at the summer cottage every August. There are no match points, but there's a trophy from Atlantic Awards—a loving cup. I won it one year, and kept it on my desk where I could see it. I shot the moon twice in the championship round, but neither was a hold hand. Like my old school buddy Ronnie Malenfant once said, no one shoots the moon on a hold hand. You might as well expect Atlantis to rise from the ocean, palm trees waving.

38

At eight o'clock that night, Skip Kirk was at my desk and deep in his anthro text. His hands were plunged into his hair, as if he had a bad headache. Nate was at his desk, doing a botany paper. I was sprawled on my bed, struggling with my old friend geology. On the stereo Bob Dylan sang: "She was the funniest woman I ever seen, the great-grandmother of Mr. Clean."

There was a hard double rap on the door: *pow-pow.* So must the Gestapo have rapped on the doors of Jews in 1938 and 1939. "Floor meeting!" Dearie called. "Floor meeting in the rec at nine o'clock! Attendance mandatory!"

"Oh Christ," I said. "Burn the secret papers and eat the radio."

Nate turned down Dylan, and we heard Dearie going on up the hall, rapping that *pow-pow* on every door and yelling about the floor meeting in the rec. Most of the rooms he was hailing were probably empty, but no problem; he'd find the occupants down in the lounge, chasing The Bitch.

Skip was looking at me. "Told you," he said.

39

Each dorm in our complex had been built at the same time, and each had a big common area in the basement as well as the lounges in the center of each floor. There was a TV alcove which filled up mostly for weekend sports events and a vampire soap opera called *Dark Shadows* during the week; a canteen corner with half a dozen vending machines; a Ping-Pong table and a number of chess- and checker-boards. There was also a meeting area with a podium standing before several rows of folding wooden chairs. We'd had a floor-meeting there at the beginning of the year, at which Dearie had explained the dorm rules and the dire consequences of unsatisfactory room inspections. I'd have to say that room inspections were Dearie's big thing. That and ROTC, of course.

He stood behind the little wooden podium, upon which he had laid a thin file-folder. I supposed it contained his notes. He was still dressed in his damp and muddy ROTC fatigues. He looked exhausted from his day of shovelling and sanding, but he also looked excited . . . "turned on" is how we'd put it a year or two later.

Dearie had been on his own at the first floor-meeting; this time he had backup. Sitting against the green cinderblock wall, hands folded in his lap and knees primly together, was Sven Garretsen, the Dean of Men. He said almost nothing during that meeting, and looked benign even when the air grew stormy. Standing beside Dearie, wearing a black topcoat over a charcoal-gray suit and looking very can-do, was Ebersole, the Disciplinary Officer.

After we had settled in the chairs and those of us who smoked had lit up, Dearie looked first over his shoulder at Garretsen, then at Ebersole. Ebersole gave him a little smile. "Go ahead, David. Please. They're your boys."

I felt a rankle of irritation. I might be a lot of things, including a creep who laughed at cripples when they fell down in the pouring rain, but I was not Dearie Dearborn's boy.

Dearie gripped the podium and looked at us solemnly, perhaps thinking (far back in the part of his mind reserved expressly for dreamy dreams) that a day would come when he would address his staff officers this way, setting some great tide of Hanoi-bound troops into motion.

"Jones is missing," he said finally. It came out sounding portentous and corny, like a line in a Charles Bronson movie.

"He's in the infirmary," I said, and enjoyed the surprise on Dearie's face. Ebersole looked surprised, too. Garretsen just went on gazing benignly into the middle distance, like a man on a three-pipe high.

"What happened to him?" Dearie asked. This wasn't in the script—either the one he had worked out or the one he and Ebersole had prepared together—and Dearie began to frown. He was also gripping the podium more tightly, as if afraid it might fly away.

"Faw down go boom," Ronnie said, and puffed up when the people around him laughed. "Also, I think he's got pneumonia or double bronchitis or something like that." He caught Skip's eye and I thought Skip nodded slightly. This was Skip's show, not Dearie's, but if we were lucky—if *Stoke* was lucky—the three at the front of the room would never know it.

"Tell me this from the beginning," Dearie said. The frown was becoming a glower. It was the way he'd looked after discovering his door had been shaving-creamed.

Skip told Dearie and Dearie's new friends how we'd seen Stoke heading toward the Palace on the Plains from the third-floor lounge windows, how he'd fallen into the water, how we'd rescued him and taken him to the infirmary, how the doctor had said Stoke was one sick puppy. The doc hadn't said any such thing, but he didn't need to. Those of us who had touched Stoke's skin knew that he was running a fever, and all of us had heard that horrible deep cough. Skip said nothing about how fast Stoke had been moving, as if he wanted to kill the whole world and then die himself, and he said nothing about how we'd laughed, Mark St. Pierre so hard he'd wet his pants.

When Skip finished, Dearie glanced uncertainly at Ebersole. Ebersole looked back blandly. Behind them, Dean Garretsen continued to smile his little Buddha smile. The implication was clear. It was Dearie's show. He'd better have a show to put on.

Dearie took a deep breath and looked back at us. "We believe Stokely Jones was responsible for the act of vandalism and public obscenity which was perpetrated on the north end of Chamberlain Hall at a time we don't know when this morning."

I'm telling you exactly what he said, not making a single word of it up. Other than "It became necessary to destroy the village in order to save it," that was perhaps the most sublime example of honcho-speak I ever heard in my life.

I believe Dearie expected us to ooh and aah like the extras in a *Perry Mason* courtroom finale, where the revelations start coming thick and fast. Instead we were silent. Skip watched closely, and when he saw Dearie draw in another deep breath for the next pronouncement, he said: "What makes you think it was him, Dearie?"

Although I'm not completely sure—I never asked him—I believe Skip used the nickname purposely, to throw Dearie even further off his stride. In any case it worked. Dearie started to go off, looked at Ebersole, and recalculated his options. A red line was rising out of his collar. I watched it climb, fascinated. It was a little like watching a Disney cartoon where Donald Duck is trying to control his temper. You know he can't possibly do it; the suspense comes from not knowing how long he can maintain even a semblance of reason.

"I think you know the answer to that, Skip," Dearie finally said. "Stokely Jones wears a coat with a very particular symbol on the back." He picked up the folder he had carried in, removed a sheet of paper, looked at it, then turned it around so we could look at it, too. None of us was very surprised by what was there. "*This* symbol. It was invented by the Communist Party shortly after the end of the Second World War. It means 'victory through infiltration' and is commonly called the Broken Cross by subversives. It has also become popular with such inner-city radical groups as the Black Muslims and the Black Panthers. Since this symbol was visible on Stoke Jones's coat long before it appeared on the side of our dorm, I hardly think it takes a rocket scientist to—"

"David, that is such bullshit!" Nate said, standing up. He was pale and trembling, but with anger rather than fear. Had I ever heard him say the word *bullshit* in public before? I don't think so.

Garretsen smiled his benign smile at my roommate. Ebersole raised his eyebrows, expressing polite interest. Dearie looked stunned. I suppose the last person he expected trouble from was Nate Hoppenstand.

"That symbol is based on British semaphore and stands for nuclear disarmament. It was invented by a famous British philosopher. I think he might even be a knight. To say the Russians made it up! Goodness' sake! Is that what they teach you in ROTC? Bullshit like that?"

Nate was staring at Dearie angrily, his hands planted on his hips. Dearie gaped at him, now completely knocked off his stride. Yes, they had taught him that in ROTC, and he had swallowed it hook, line, and sinker. It made you wonder what else the ROTC kids were swallowing.

"I'm sure these facts about the Broken Cross are very interesting," Ebersole cut in smoothly, "and it's certainly information worth having—if it's true, of course—"

"It's true," Skip said. "Bert Russell, not Joe Stalin. British kids were wearing it five years ago when they marched to protest U.S. nuclear subs operating out of ports in the British Isles."

"Fuckin A!" Ronnie cried, and pumped his fist in the air. A year or so later the Panthers—who never had much use for Bertrand Russell's peace sign, so far as I know—were doing that same thing at their rallies. And, of course, twenty years or so further on down the line, all us cleaned-up sixties babies were doing it at rock concerts. *Broooo-oooooce! Broooo-oooooce!*

"Go, baby!" Hugh Brennan chimed in, laughing. "Go, Skip! Go, big Nate!"

"Watch your language while the Dean's here!" Dearie shouted at Ronnie.

Ebersole ignored the profanity and the cross-talk from the peanut gallery. He kept his interested, skeptical gaze trained on my roommate and on Skip.

"Even if all that's true," he said, "we still have a problem, don't we? I think so. We have an act of vandalism and public obscenity. This comes at a time when the tax-paying public is looking at University youth with an ever more critical eye. And this institution depends upon the tax-paying public, gentlemen. I think it behooves us all—"

"To think about this!" Dearie suddenly shouted. His cheeks were now almost purple; his forehead swarmed with weird red spots like brands, and right between his eyes a big vein was pulsing rapidly.

Before Dearie could say more—and he clearly had a lot to say—Ebersole put a hand out to his chest, shushing him. Dearie seemed to deflate. He'd had his chance and fluffed it. Later he'd perhaps tell himself it was because he was tired; while we'd spent the day in the nice warm lounge, playing cards and shooting holes in our future, Dearie had been outside shovelling snow and sanding walks so brittle old psychology professors wouldn't fall down and break their hips. He was tired, a little slow on the draw, and in any case, that prick Ebersole hadn't given him a fair chance to prove himself. All of which probably didn't help much with what was happening right then: he had been set aside. The grownup was back in charge. Poppa would fix.

"I think it behooves us all to identify the fellow who did this and see he's punished with some severity," Ebersole continued. Mostly it was Nate he was looking at; amazing as it seemed to me at the time, he had identified Nate Hoppenstand as the center of the resistance he felt in the room.

Nate, God bless his molars and wisdom teeth, was more than up to the likes of Ebersole. He remained standing with his hands on his hips and his eyes never wavered, let alone dropped from Ebersole's. "How do you propose doing that?" Nate asked.

"What is your name, young man? Please."

"Nathan Hoppenstand."

"Well, Nathan, I think the perpetrator has already been singled out, don't you?" Ebersole spoke in a patient, teacherly way. "Or rather singled himself out. I'm told this unfortunate fellow Stokely Jones has been a walking billboard for the Broken Cross symbol since—"

"Quit calling it that!" Skip said, and I jumped a little at the raw anger in his voice. "It's not a broken anything! It's a damn *peace* sign!"

"What is *your* name, sir?"

"Stanley Kirk. Skip to my friends. You can call me Stanley." There was a tense little titter at this, which Ebersole seemed not to hear.

"Well, Mr. Kirk, your semantic quibble is noted, but it doesn't change the fact that Stokely Jones—and Stokely Jones *alone*—has been displaying that particular symbol all over campus since the first day of the semester. Mr. Dearborn tells me—"

Nate said, " 'Mr. Dearborn' doesn't even know what the peace sign is or where it came from, so I think you'd be sort of unwise to trust what he tells you very far. It just so happens I've got a peace sign on the back of my own jacket, Mr. Ebersole. So how do you know *I* wasn't the one with the spray-paint?"

Ebersole's mouth dropped open. Not much, but enough to spoil his sympathetic smile and magazine-ad good looks. And Dean Garretsen frowned, as if presented with some concept he couldn't understand. One very rarely sees a good politician or college administrator caught completely by surprise. They are moments to treasure. I treasured that one then, and find I still do today.

"That's a lie!" Dearie said. He sounded more wounded than angry.

"Why would you lie that way, Nate? You're the last person on Three I'd expect to—"

"It's *not* a lie," Nate said. "Go on up to my room and pull the pea coat out of my closet if you don't believe me. Check."

"Yeah, and check mine while you're at it," I said, standing up next to Nate. "My old high-school jacket. You can't miss it. It's the one with the peace sign on the back."

Ebersole studied us through slightly narrowed eyes. Then he asked, "Exactly when did you put this so-called peace sign on the backs of your jackets, young fellows?"

This time Nate did lie. I knew him well enough by then to know it must have hurt . . . but he did it like a champ. "September."

That was it for Dearie. *He went nuclear* is how my own kids might express it, only that wouldn't be accurate. Dearie went Donald Duck. He didn't quite jump up and down, flapping his arms and going *wak-wak-waugh-wak* like Donald does when he's mad, but he *did* give a howl of outrage and smacked his mottled forehead with the heels of his palms. Ebersole stilled him again, this time by gripping his arm.

"Who are you?" Ebersole asked me. More curt than courteous by now.

"Pete Riley. I put a peace sign on the back of my jacket because I liked the look of Stoke's. Also to show I've got some big questions about what we're doing over there in Vietnam."

Dearie pulled away from Ebersole. His chin was thrust out, his lips pulled back enough to show a complete set of teeth. "*Helping our allies is what we're doing, you doofus!*" he shouted. "If you're too stupid to see that on your own, I suggest you take Colonel Anderson's Intro Military History Class! Or maybe you're just another chickenguts who won't—"

"Hush, Mr. Dearborn," Dean Garretsen said. His quiet was somehow louder than Dearie's shouting. "This is not the place for a foreign policy debate, nor is it the time for personal aspersions. Quite the contrary."

Dearie dropped his burning face, studied the floor, and began to gnaw at his own lips.

"And when, Mr. Riley, did you put the peace sign symbol on *your* jacket?" Ebersole asked. His voice remained courteous, but there was an ugly look in his eyes. He knew by then, I think, that Stoke was going to squiggle away, and Ebersole was *very* unhappy about that. Dearie was small change next to this guy, who was in 1966 a new type on the college campuses of America. Times call the men, Lao-tzu said, and the late sixties called Charles Ebersole. He wasn't an educator; he was an enforcer minoring in public relations.

Don't lie to me, his eyes said. *Don't lie to me, Riley. Because if you do and I find out, I'll turn you into salad.*

But what the hell. I'd probably be gone come January 15th, anyway; by Christmas of 1967 I might be in Phu Bai, keeping the place warm for Dearie.

"October," I said. "Put it on my jacket right around Columbus Day."

"I've got it on my jacket and some sweatshirts," Skip said. "All that stuff's in my room. I'll show it to you, if you want."

Dearie, still looking down at the floor and red to the roots of his hair, was shaking his head monotonously back and forth.

"I've got it on a couple of my sweatshirts, too," Ronnie said. "I'm no peacenik, but it's a cool sign. I like it."

Tony DeLucca said he also had one on the back of a sweatshirt.

Lennie Doria told Ebersole and Garretsen he had doodled it on the endpapers of several different textbooks; it was on the front of his general assignments notebook as well. He'd show them, if they wanted to see.

Billy Marchant had it on his jacket.

Brad Witherspoon had inked it on his freshman beanie. The beanie was in the back of his closet somewhere, probably beneath the underwear he'd forgotten to take home for his mom to wash.

Nick Prouty said he'd drawn peace signs on his favorite record albums: *Meet the Beatles* and *Wayne Fontana and the Mindbenders.* "You ain't got any mind to bend, dinkleballs," Ronnie muttered, and there was laughter from behind cupped hands.

Several others reported having the peace sign on books or items of clothing. All claimed to have done this long before the discovery of the graffiti on the north end of Chamberlain Hall. In a final surreal touch, Hugh stood up, stepped into the aisle, and hiked the legs of his jeans so we could see the yellowing athletic socks climbing his hairy shins. A peace sign had been drawn on both with the laundry-marker Mrs. Brennan had sent to school with her baby boy—it was probably the first time the fuckin thing had been used all semester.

"So you see," Skip said when show-and-tell was over, "it could have been any of us."

Dearie slowly raised his head. All that remained of his flush was a single red patch over his left eye. It looked like a blister.

"Why are you lying for him?" he asked. He waited, but no one answered. "Not one of you had a peace sign on a single thing before Thanksgiving break, I'd swear to it, and I bet most of you never had one on anything before tonight. Why are you lying for him?"

No one answered. The silence spun out. In it there grew a sense of power, an unmistakable force we all felt. But who did it belong to? Them or us? There was no way of saying. All these years later there's still no real way of saying.

Then Dean Garretsen stepped to the podium. Dearie moved aside without even seeming to see him. The Dean looked at us with a small and cheerful smile. "This is foolishness," he said. "What Mr. Jones wrote on the wall was foolishness, and this lying is more foolishness. Tell the truth, men. 'Fess up."

No one said anything.

"We'll be speaking to Mr. Jones in the morning," Ebersole said. "Perhaps after we do, some of you fellows may want to change your stories a bit."

"Oh man, I wouldn't put too much trust in anything Stoke might tell you," Skip said.

"Right, old Rip-Rip's crazy as a shithouse rat," Ronnie said.

There was strangely affectionate laughter at this. "Shithouse rat!" Nick cried, eyes shining. He was as joyful as a poet who has finally found *le mot juste.* "Shithouse rat, yeah, that's Old Rip!" And, in what was probably that day's final triumph of lunacy over rational discourse, Nick Prouty fell into an eerily perfect Foghorn Leghorn imitation: "Ah say, Ah say the boy's *craizy!* Missin a wheel off his *baiby*-carriage! Lost two-three *cahds* out'n his *deck!* Fella's a beer shote of a *six*-pack! He's . . ."

Nick gradually realized that Ebersole and Garretsen were looking at him, Ebersole with contempt, Garretsen almost with interest, as at a new bacterium glimpsed through the lens of a microscope.

". . . you know, a little sick in the head," Nick finished, losing the imitation as self-consciousness, that bane of all great artists, set in. He quickly sat down.

"That's not the kind of sick I meant, exactly," Skip said. "I'm not talking about him being a cripple, either. He's been sneezing, coughing, and running at the nose ever since he got here. Even you must have noticed that, Dearie."

Dearie didn't reply, didn't even react to the use of the nickname this time. He must have been pretty tired, all right.

"All I'm saying is that he might claim a whole lot of stuff," Skip said. "He might even believe some of it. But he's out of it."

Ebersole's smile had resurfaced, no humor in it now. "I believe I grasp the thrust of your argument, Mr. Kirk. You want us to believe that Mr. Jones was not responsible for the writing on the wall, but if he does confess to having done it, we should not credit his statement."

Skip also smiled—the thousand-watt smile that made the girls' hearts go giddyup. "That's it," he said, "that's the thrust of my argument, all right."

There was a moment's silence, and then Dean Garretsen spoke what could have been the epitaph of our brief age. "You fellows have disappointed me," he said. "Come on, Charles, we have no further business here." Garretsen hoisted his briefcase, turned on his heel, and headed for the door.

Ebersole looked surprised but hurried after him. Which left Dearie and his third-floor charges to stare at each other with mingled expressions of distrust and reproach.

"Thanks, guys." David was almost crying. "Thanks a fucking

pantload." He stalked out with his head down and his folder clutched in one hand. The following semester he left Chamberlain and joined a frat. All things considered, that was probably for the best. As Stoke might have said, Dearie had lost his credibility.

40

"So you stole that, too," Stoke Jones said from his bed in the infirmary when he could finally talk. I had just told him that almost everyone in Chamberlain Hall was now wearing the sparrow-track on at least one article of clothing, thinking this news would cheer him up. I had been wrong.

"Settle down, man," Skip said, patting his shoulder. "Don't have a hemorrhage."

Stoke never so much as glanced at him. His black, accusing eyes remained on me. "You took the credit, then you took the peace sign. Did any of you check my wallet? I think there were nine or ten dollars in there. You could have had that, too. Made it a clean sweep." He turned his head aside and began to cough weakly. On that cold day in early December of '66 he looked one fuck of a lot older than eighteen.

This was four days after Stoke went swimming in Bennett's Run. The doctor—Carbury, his name was—seemed by the second of those days to accept that most of us were Stoke's friends no matter how oddly we'd acted when we brought him in, because we kept stopping by to ask after him. Carbury had been at the college infirmary, prescribing for strep throats and splinting wrists dislocated in softball games, for donkey's years and probably knew there was no accounting for the behavior of young men and women homing in on their majority; they might look like adults, but most retained plenty of their childhood weirdnesses, as well. Nick Prouty auditioning Foghorn Leghorn for the Dean of Men, for instance—I rest my case.

Carbury never told us how bad things had been with Stoke. One of the candystripers (half in love with Skip by the second time she saw him, I believe) gave us a clearer picture, not that we really needed one. The fact that Carbury stuck him in a private room instead of on Men's Side told us something; the fact that we weren't allowed to so much as peek in on him for the first forty-eight hours of his stay told us more; the fact that he hadn't been moved to Eastern Maine, which was only ten miles up the road, told us most of all. Carbury hadn't *dared* move him, not even in the University ambulance. Stoke Jones had been in bad straits indeed. According to the candystriper, he had pneumonia, incipient hypothermia from his dunk, and a temperature which crested at a hundred and five degrees. She'd overheard Carbury talking with someone on the phone and saying that if Jones's lung capacity had been any further reduced by his disability—or if he'd been in his thirties or forties instead of his late teens—he almost certainly would have died.

Skip and I were the first visitors he was allowed. Any other kid in the dorm probably would have been visited by at least one parent, but that wasn't going to happen in Stoke's case, we knew that now. And if there were other relatives, they hadn't bothered to put in an appearance.

We told him everything that had happened that night, with one exception: the laugh-in which had begun in the lounge when we saw him spraying his way through Bennett's Run and continued until we delivered him, semi-conscious, to the infirmary. He listened silently as I told him about Skip's idea to put peace signs on our books and clothes so Stoke couldn't be hung out all by himself. Even Ronnie Malenfant had gone along, I said, and without a single quibble. We told him so he could jibe his story with ours; we also told him so he'd understand that by trying to take the blame/credit for the graffiti now, he'd get us in trouble as well as himself. And we told him without ever coming right out and telling him. We didn't need to. His legs didn't work, but the stuff between his ears was just fine.

"Get your hand off me, Kirk." Stoke hunched as far away from us as his narrow bed would allow, then began to cough again. I remember thinking he looked like he had about four months to live, but I was wrong about that; Atlantis sank but Stoke Jones is still in the swim, practicing law in San Francisco. His black hair has gone silver and is prettier than ever. He's got a red wheelchair. It looks great on CNN.

Skip sat back and folded his arms. "I didn't expect wild gratitude, but this is too much," he said. "You've outdone yourself this time, Rip-Rip."

His eyes flashed. "Don't call me that!"

"Then don't call us thieves just because we tried to save your scrawny ass. Hell, we *did* save your scrawny ass!"

"No one asked you to."

"No," I said. "You don't ask anyone for anything, do you? I think you're going to need bigger crutches to haul around the chip on your shoulder before long."

"That chip's what I've got, shithead. What have you got?"

A lot of catching-up to do, that's what I had. But I didn't tell Stoke that. Somehow I didn't think he'd exactly melt with sympathy. "How much of that day do you remember?" I asked him.

"I remember putting the FUCK JOHNSON thing on the dorm—I'd been planning that for a couple of weeks—and I remember going to my one o'clock class. I spent most of it thinking about what I was going to say in the Dean's office when he called me in. What kind of a *statement* I was going to make. After that, everything fades into little fragments." He uttered a sardonic laugh and rolled his eyes in their bruised-looking sockets. He'd been in bed for the best part of a week and still looked unutterably tired. "I think I remember telling you guys I wanted to die. Did I say that?"

I didn't answer. He gave me all the time in the world, but I stood on my right to remain silent.

At last Stoke shrugged, the kind of shrug that says okay, let's drop it. It pulled the johnny he was wearing off one bony shoulder. He tugged it back into place, using his hand carefully—there was an I.V. drip in it. "So you guys discovered the peace sign, huh? Great. You can wear it when you go to see Neil Diamond or fucking Petula Clark at Winter Carnival. Me, I'm out of here. This is over for me."

"If you go to school on the other side of the country, do you think you'll be able to throw the crutches away?" Skip asked. "Maybe run track?"

I was a little shocked, but Stoke smiled. It was a real smile, too, sunny and unaffected. "The crutches aren't relevant," he said. "Time's too short to waste, *that's* relevant. People around here don't know what's happening, and they don't care. They're gray people. Just-getting-by people. In Orono, Maine, buying a Rolling Stones record passes for a revolutionary act."

"Some people know more than they did," I said . . . but I was troubled by thoughts of Nate, who had been worried his mother might see a picture of him getting arrested and had stayed on the curb in consequence. A face in the background, the face of a gray boy on the road to dentistry in the twentieth century.

Dr. Carbury stuck his head in the door. "Time you were on your way, men. Mr. Jones has a lot of rest to catch up on."

We stood. "When Dean Garretsen comes to talk to you," I said, "or that guy Ebersole . . ."

"As far as they'll ever know, that whole day is a blank," Stoke said. "Carbury can tell them I had bronchitis since October and pneumonia since Thanksgiving, so they'll have to accept it. I'll say I could have done anything that day. Except, you know, drop the old crutches and run the four-forty."

"We really didn't steal your sign, you know," Skip said. "We just borrowed it."

Stoke appeared to think this over, then sighed. "It's not my sign," he said.

"No," I agreed. "Not anymore. So long, Stoke. We'll come back and see you."

"Don't make it a priority," he said, and I guess we took him at his word, because we never did. I saw him back at the dorm a few times, but only a few, and I was in class when he moved out without bothering to finish the semester. The next time I saw him was on the TV news almost twenty years later, speaking at a Greenpeace rally just after the French blew up the *Rainbow Warrior,* 1984 or '85, that would've been. Since then I've seen him on the tube quite a lot. He raises money for environmental causes, speaks on college campuses from that snazzy red wheelchair, defends the eco-activists in court when they need defending. I've heard him called a tree-hugger, and I bet he sort of enjoys that. He's still carrying the chip. I'm glad. Like he said, it's what he's got.

As we reached the door he called, "Hey?"

We looked back at a narrow white face on a white pillow above a white sheet, the only real color about him those masses of black hair. The shapes of his legs under the sheet again made me think of Uncle Sam in the Fourth of July parade back home. And again I thought that he looked like a kid with about four months to live. But add some white teeth to the picture, as well, because Stoke was smiling.

"Hey what?" Skip said.

"You two were so concerned with what I was going to say to Garretsen and Ebersole . . . maybe I've got an inferiority complex or something, but I have trouble believing all that concern is for me. Have you two decided to actually try going to school for a change?"

"If we did, do you think we'd make it?" Skip asked.

"You might," Stoke said. "There is one thing I remember about that night. Pretty clearly, too."

I thought he'd say he remembered us laughing at him—Skip thought so, too, he told me later—but that wasn't it.

"You carried me through the doorway of the exam room by yourself," he said to Skip. "Didn't drop me, either."

"No chance of that. You don't weigh much."

"Still . . . dying's one thing, but no one likes the idea of being dropped on the floor. It's undignified. Because you didn't, I'll give you some good advice. Get out of the sports programs, Kirk. Unless, that is, you've got some kind of athletic scholarship you can't do without."

"Why?"

"Because they'll turn you into someone else. It may take a little longer than it took ROTC to turn David Dearborn into Dearie, but they'll get you there in the end."

"What do you know about sports?" Skip asked gently. "What do you know about being on a team?"

"I know it's a bad time for boys in uniforms," Stoke said, then lay back on his pillow and closed his eyes. But a good time to be a girl, Carol had said. 1966 was a good time to be a girl.

We returned to the dorm and went to my room to study. Down the hall Ronnie and Nick and Lennie and most of the others were chasing The Bitch. After awhile Skip shut the door to block the sound of them out, and when that didn't entirely work I turned on Nate's little RCA Swingline and we listened to Phil Ochs. Ochs is dead now—as dead as my mother and Michael Landon. He hanged himself with his belt. The suicide rate among surviving Atlanteans has been pretty high. No surprise there, I guess; when your continent sinks right out from under your feet, it does a number on your head.

41

A day or two after that visit to Stoke in the infirmary, I called my mother and said that if she could really afford to send a little extra cash my way, I'd like to take her up on her idea about getting a tutor. She didn't ask many questions and didn't scold—you knew you were in serious trouble with my mom when she didn't scold—but three days later I had a money order for three hundred dollars. To this I added my Hearts winnings—I was astonished to find they came to almost eighty bucks. That's a lot of nickels.

I never told my mom, but I actually hired *two* tutors with her three hundred, one a grad student who helped me with the mysteries of tectonic plates and continental drift, the other a pot-smoking senior from King Hall who helped Skip with his anthropology (and might have written a paper or two for him, although I don't know that for sure). This second fellow's name was Harvey Brundage, and he was the first person to ever say "Wow, man, bummer!" in my presence.

Together Skip and I went to the Dean of Arts and Sciences—

there was no way we were going to go to Garretsen, not after that November meeting in the Chamberlain rec—and laid out the problems we were facing. Technically neither of us belonged to A and S; as freshmen we weren't yet eligible to declare majors, but Dean Randle listened to us. He recommended that we go around to each of our instructors and explain the problem . . . more or less throw ourselves on their mercy.

We did it, loathing every minute of the process; one of the factors that made us powerful friends in those years was being raised with the same Yankee ideas, one of which was that you didn't ask for help unless you absolutely had to, and maybe not even then. The only thing that got us through that embarrassing round of calls was the buddy system. When Skip was in with his teachers I waited for him out in the hall, smoking one cigarette after another. When it was my turn, he waited for me.

As a group, the instructors were a lot more sympathetic than I ever would have guessed; most bent over backwards to help us not only pass, but pass high enough to hold onto our scholarships. Only Skip's calculus teacher was completely unreceptive, and Skip was doing well enough there to skate by without any special help. Years later I realized that for many of the instructors it was a moral issue rather than an academic one: they didn't want to read their ex-students' names in a casualty list and have to wonder if they had been partially responsible; that the difference between a D and a C-minus had also been the difference between a kid who could see and hear and one sitting senseless in a V.A. hospital somewhere.

42

After one of these meetings, and with the end-of-semester exams looming, Skip went to the Bear's Den to meet his Anthro tutor for a coffee-fueled cram session. I had dishline at Holyoke. When the conveyor finally shut down for the afternoon, I went back to the dorm to resume my own studies. I stopped in the lobby to check my mailbox, and there was a pink package-slip in it.

The package was brown paper and string, but livened up with some stick-on Christmas bells and holly. The return address hit me in the stomach like an unexpected sucker-punch: Carol Gerber, 172 Broad Street, Harwich, Connecticut.

I hadn't tried to call her, and not just because I was busy trying to save my ass. I don't think I realized the real reason until I saw her name on that package. I'd been convinced she'd gone back to Sully-John. That the night we'd made love in my car while the oldies played was ancient history to her now. That *I* was ancient history.

Phil Ochs was playing on Nate's record-player, but Nate himself was snoozing on his bed with a copy of *Newsweek* lying open on his face. General William Westmoreland was on the cover. I sat down at my desk, put the package in front of me, reached for the string, then paused. My fingers were trembling. *Hearts are tough,* she had said. *Most times they don't break. Most times they only bend.* She was right, of course . . . but mine hurt as I sat there looking at the Christmas package she had sent me; it hurt plenty. Phil Ochs was on the record-player, but in my mind I was hearing older, sweeter music. In my mind I was hearing The Platters.

I snapped the string, tore the tape, removed the brown paper, and eventually liberated a small white department-store box. Inside was a gift wrapped in shiny red paper and white satin ribbon. There was also a square envelope with my name written on it in her familiar hand. I opened the envelope and pulled out a Hallmark card—when you care enough to send the very best, and all that. There were foil snowflakes and foil angels blowing foil trumpets. When I opened the card, a newspaper clipping fell out onto the present she'd sent me. It was from a newspaper called the Harwich *Journal.* In the top margin, above the headline, Carol had written: *This time I made it—Purple Heart! Don't worry, 5 stitches at the Emerg. Room & I was home for supper.*

The story's headline read: 6 INJURED, 14 ARRESTED AS DRAFT OFFICE PROTEST TURNS INTO MELEE. The photo was in stark contrast to the one in the Derry *News* where everyone, even the cops and the construction workers who had started their own impromptu counter-protest, looked sort of relaxed. In the Harwich *Journal* photo, folks looked raw-nerved, confused, and about two thousand light-years from relaxed. There were hardhat types with tattoos on their bulging arms and hateful grimaces on their faces; there were long-haired kids staring back at them with angry defiance. One of the latter was holding his arms out to a jeering trio of men as if to say *Come on, you want a piece of me?* There were cops between the two groups, looking strained and tense.

To the left (Carol had drawn an arrow to this part of the photo, as if I might have missed it otherwise) was a familiar jacket with HARWICH HIGH SCHOOL printed on the back. Once more her head was turned, but this time toward the camera instead of away from it. I could see the blood running down her cheek much more clearly than I wanted to. She could draw joke arrows and write all the breezy comments she wanted to in the margin; I was not amused. That was not chocolate syrup on her face. A cop had her by one arm. The girl in the news photo didn't seem to mind either that or the fact that her head was bleeding (if she even *knew* her head was bleeding at that point). The girl in the news photo was smiling. In one of her hands was a sign reading STOP THE MURDER. The other was held out toward the camera, the first two fingers making a V. V-for-victory, I thought then, but of course it wasn't. By 1969, that V went with the sparrow-track the way ham went with eggs.

I scanned the text of the clipping, but there was nothing there of any particular interest. Protest . . . counter-protest . . . epithets . . . thrown rocks . . . a few fistfights . . . police arrive on the scene. The story's tone was lofty and disgusted and patronizing all at the same time; it reminded me of how Ebersole and Garretsen had looked that night in the rec. *You fellows have disappointed me.* All but three of the protesters who had been arrested were released later that day and none were named, so presumably they were all under twenty-one.

Blood on her face. And yet she was smiling . . . triumphant, in fact. I became aware Phil Ochs was still singing—I must have killed a million men and now they want me back again—and a shake of gooseflesh went up my back.

I turned to the card. It bore the typical rhymed sentiments; they always come to about the same, don't they? Merry Christmas, sure hope you don't die in the New Year. I barely read them. On the blank side facing the verse, she had written me a note. It was long enough to use up most of the white space.

Dear Number Six,

I just wanted to wish you the merriest of merry Christmases, and to tell you I'm okay. I'm not back in school, although I have been associating with certain school types (see enclosed clipping) and expect I will return eventually, probably fall semester next year. My mom is not doing too well, but she is trying, and my brother is getting his act back together. Rionda helps, too. I've seen Sully a couple of times, but it's not the same. He came over to watch TV one night and we are like strangers . . . or maybe what I really mean is that we're like old acquaintances on trains going in different directions.

I miss you, Pete. I think our trains are going in different directions, too, but I'll never forget the time we spent together. It was the sweetest and the best (especially the last night). You can write me if you want, but I sort of wish you wouldn't. It might not be good for either of us. This doesn't mean I don't care or remember but that I do.

Remember the night I showed you that picture and told you about how I got beaten up? How my friend Bobby took care of me? He had a book that summer. The man upstairs gave it to him. Bobby said it was the best book he ever read. Not saying much when you're just eleven, I know, but I saw it again in the high-school library when I was a senior and read it, just to see what it was like. And I thought it was pretty great. Not the best book I ever read, but pretty great. I thought you might like a copy. Although it was written twelve years ago, I sort of think it's about Vietnam. Even if it's not, it's full of information.

I love you, Pete. Merry Christmas.

Carol

P.S. Get out of that stupid card-game.

I read it twice, then folded the clipping carefully and put it back in the card, my hands still shaking. Somewhere I think I still have that card . . . as I'm sure that somewhere "Red Carol" Gerber has still got her little snapshot of her childhood friends. If she's still alive, that is. Not exactly a sure thing; a lot of her last-known bunch of friends are not.

I opened the package. Inside it—and in jarring contrast to the cheery Christmas paper and white satin ribbon—was a paperback copy of *Lord of the Flies,* by William Golding. I had somehow missed it in high school, opting for *A Separate Peace* in Senior Lit instead because *Peace* looked a little shorter.

I opened it, thinking there might be an inscription. There was, but not the sort I had expected, not at all. This was what I found in the white space on the title page:

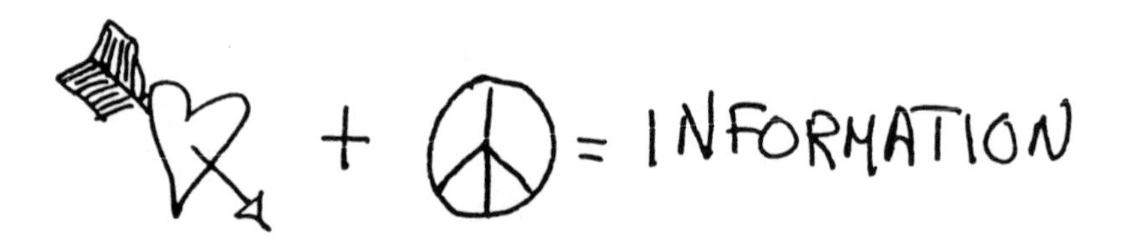

My eyes filled with sudden unexpected tears. I put my hands over my mouth to hold in the sob that wanted to come out. I didn't want to wake Nate up, didn't want him to see me crying. But I cried, all right. I sat there at my desk and cried for her, for me, for both of us, for all of us. I can't remember hurting any more ever in my life than I did then. Hearts are tough, she said, most times hearts don't break, and I'm sure that's right . . . but what about then? What about who we were then? What about hearts in Atlantis?

43

In any case, Skip and I survived. We did the makeup work, squeaked through the finals, and returned to Chamberlain Hall in mid-January. Skip told me he'd written a letter to John Winkin, the baseball coach, over the holiday, saying he'd changed his mind about coming out for the team.

Nate was back on Chamberlain Three. So, amazingly, was Lennie Doria—on academic pro but there. His *paisan* Tony DeLucca was gone, though. So were Mark St. Pierre, Barry Margeaux, Nick Prouty, Brad Witherspoon, Harvey Twiller, Randy Echolls . . . and Ronnie, of course. We got a card from him in March. It was postmarked Lewiston and simply addressed to The Yo-Yo's Of Chamberlain Three. We taped it up in the lounge, over the chair where Ronnie had most often sat during the games. On the front was Alfred E. Neuman, the *Mad* magazine cover-boy. On the back Ronnie had written: "Uncle Sam calls and I gotta go. Palm trees in my future and who gives a f—k. What me worry. I finished with 21 match points. That makes me the winner." It was signed "RON." Skip and I had a laugh at that. As far as we were concerned, Mrs. Malenfant's foulmouthed little boy was going to be a Ronnie until the day he died.

Stoke Jones, aka Rip-Rip, was also gone. I didn't think of him much for awhile, but his face and memory came back to me with startling (if brief) vividness a year and a half later. I was in jail at the time, in Chicago. I don't know how many of us the cops swept up outside the convention center on the night Hubert Humphrey was nominated, but there were a lot, and a lot of us were hurt—a blue-ribbon commission would a year later designate the event a "police riot" in its report.

I ended up in a holding cell meant for fifteen prisoners—twenty, max—with about sixty gassed-out, punched-out, drugged-out, beat-up, messed-up, worked-over, fucked-over, blood-all-over hippies, some smoking joints, some crying, some puking, some singing protest songs (from far over in the corner, issuing from some guy I never even saw, came a stoned-out version of "I'm Not Marchin' Anymore"). It was like some weird penal version of telephone-booth cramming.

I was jammed up against the bars, trying to protect my shirt pocket (Pall Malls), and my hip pocket (the copy of *Lord of the Flies* Carol had given me, now very battered, missing half its front cover, and falling out of its binding), when all at once Stoke's face flashed into my mind as bright and complete as a high-resolution photograph. It came from nowhere, it seemed, perhaps the product of a dormant memory circuit which had gone momentarily hot, joggled by either a nightstick to the head or a revivifying whiff of teargas. And a question came with it.

"What the *fuck* was a cripple doing on the third floor?" I asked out loud.

A little guy with a huge mass of golden hair—a kind of Peter Frampton dwarf, if you could dig that—looked around. His face was pale and pimply. Blood was drying beneath his nose and on one cheek. "What, man?" he asked.

"What the fuck was a cripple doing on the third floor of a college dorm? One with no elevator? Wouldn't they have put him on the first floor?" Then I remembered Stoke plunging toward Holyoke with his head down and his hair hanging in his eyes, Stoke muttering "Rip-*rip,* rip-*rip,* rip-*rip*" under his breath. Stoke going everywhere as if everything was his enemy; give him a quarter and he'd try to shoot down the whole world.

"Man, I'm not following you. What—"

"Unless he asked them to," I said. "Unless he maybe right out *demanded* it."

"Bingo," said the little guy with the Peter Frampton hair. "Got a joint, man? I want to get high. This place sucks. I want to go to Hobbiton."

44

Skip became an artist, and he's famous in his own way. Not like Norman Rockwell, and you'll never see a reproduction of one of *Skip's* sculptures on a plate offered by the Franklin Mint, but he's had plenty of shows—London, Rome, New York, last year in Paris—and he's reviewed regularly. There are plenty of critics who call him jejune, the flavor of the month (some have been calling him the flavor of the month for twenty-five years), a trite mind communicating via low imagery with other trite minds. Other critics have praised him for his honesty and energy. I tend in this direction, but I suppose I would; I knew him back in the day, we escaped the great sinking continent together, and he has remained my friend; in a distant way he has remained my *paisan.*

There are also critics who have commented on the rage his work so often expresses, the rage I first saw clearly in the *papier-mâché* Vietnamese family tableau he set afire in front of the school library to the amplified pulse of The Youngbloods back in 1969. And yeah. Yeah, there's something to that. Some of Skip's stuff is funny and some of it's sad and some of it's bizarre, but most of it looks angry, most of his stiff-shouldered plaster and paper and clay people seem to whisper *Light me, oh light me and listen to me scream, it's really still 1969, it's still the Mekong and always will be.* "It is Stanley Kirk's anger which makes his work worthy," a critic wrote during an exhibition in Boston, and I suppose it was that same anger which contributed to his heart attack two months ago.

His wife called and said Skip wanted to see me. The doctors believed it hadn't been a serious cardiac event, but the Captain begged to disagree. My old *paisan* Captain Kirk thought he was dying.

I flew down to Palm Beach, and when I saw him—white face below mostly white hair on a white pillow—it called up a memory I could not at first pin down.

"You're thinking of Jones," he said in a husky voice, and of course he was right. I grinned, and at the same moment a cold chill traced a finger down the middle of my back. Sometimes things come back to you, that's all. Sometimes they come back.

I came in and sat down beside him. "Not bad, O swami."

"Not hard, either," he said. "It's that day at the infirmary all over again, except that Carbury's probably dead and this time I'm the one with a tube in the back of my hand." He raised one of his talented hands, showed me the tube, then lowered it again. "I don't think I'm going to die anymore. At least not yet."

"Good."

"You still smoking?"

"I've retired. As of last year."

He nodded. "My wife says she'll divorce me if I don't do the same . . . so I guess I better try."

"It's the worst habit."

"Actually, I think living's the worst habit."

"Save the phrase-making shit for the *Reader's Digest,* Cap."

He laughed, then asked if I'd heard from Natie.

"A Christmas card, like always. With a photo."

"Fuckin Nate!" Skip was delighted. "Was it his office?"

"Yeah. He's got a Nativity scene out front this year. The Magi all look like they need dental work."

We looked at each other and began to giggle. Before Skip could really get going, he began to cough. It was eerily like Stoke—for a moment he even *looked* like Stoke—and I felt that shiver slide down my back again. If Stoke had been dead I'd have thought he was haunting us, but he wasn't. And in his own way Stoke Jones was as much of a sellout as every retired hippie who progressed from selling cocaine to selling junk bonds over the phone. He loves his TV coverage, does Stoke; when O.J. Simpson was on trial you could catch Stoke somewhere on the dial every night, just another vulture circling the carrion.

Carol was the one who didn't sell out, I guess. Carol and her friends, and what about the chem students they killed with their bomb? It was a mistake, I believe that with all my heart—the Carol Gerber I knew would have no patience with the idea that all power comes out of the barrel of a gun. The Carol I knew would have understood that was just another fucked-up way of saying we had to destroy the village in order to save it. But do you think the relatives of those kids care that it was a mistake, the bomb didn't go off when it was supposed to, sorry? Do you think questions of who sold out and who didn't matter to the mothers, fathers, brothers, sisters, lovers, friends? Do you think it matters to the people who have to pick up the pieces and somehow go on? Hearts can break. Yes. Hearts can break. Sometimes I think it would be better if we died when they did, but we don't.

Skip worked on getting his breath back. The monitor beside his bed was beeping in a worried way. A nurse looked in and Skip waved her off. The beeps were settling back to their previous rhythm, so she went. When she was gone, Skip said: "Why did we laugh so hard when he fell down that day? That question has never entirely left me."

"No," I said. "Me either."

"So what's the answer? Why did we laugh?"

"Because we're human. For awhile, I think it was between Woodstock and Kent State, we thought we were something else, but we weren't."

"We thought we were stardust," Skip said. Almost with a straight face.

"We thought we were golden," I agreed, laughing. "And we've got to get ourselves back to the garden."

"Lean over, hippie-boy," Skip said, and I did. I saw that my old friend, who had outfoxed Dearie and Ebersole and the Dean of Men, who had gone around and begged his teachers to help him, who had taught me to drink beer by the pitcher and say fuck in a dozen different intonations, was crying a little bit. He reached up his arms to me. They had gotten thin over the years, and now the muscles hung rather than bunched. I bent down and hugged him.

"We tried," he said in my ear. "Don't you ever forget that, Pete. *We tried.*"

I suppose we did. In her way, Carol tried harder than any of us and paid the highest price . . . except, that is, for the ones who died. And although we've forgotten the language we spoke in those years—it is as lost as the bell-bottom jeans, home-tie-dyed shirts, Nehru jackets, and signs that said KILLING FOR PEACE IS LIKE FUCKING FOR CHASTITY—sometimes a word or two comes back. Information, you know. Information. And sometimes, in my dreams and memories (the older I get the more they seem to be the same), I smell the place where I spoke that language with such easy authority: a whiff of earth, a scent of oranges, and the fading smell of flowers.

1983: Gobless us every one.

1983

Blind Willie

6:15 A.M.

He wakes to music, always to music; the shrill *beep-beep-beep* of the clock-radio's alarm is too much for his mind to cope with during those first blurry moments of the day. It sounds like a dump truck backing up. The radio is bad enough at this time of year, though; the easy-listening station he keeps the clock-radio tuned to is wall-to-wall Christmas carols, and this morning he wakes up to one of the two or three on his Most Hated List, something full of breathy voices and phony wonder. The Hare Krishna Chorale or the Andy Williams Singers or some such. Do you hear what I hear, the breathy voices sing as he sits up in bed, blinking groggily, hair sticking out in every direction. Do you see what I see, they sing as he swings his legs out, grimaces his way across the cold floor to the radio, and bangs the button that turns it off. When he turns around, Sharon has assumed her customary defensive posture—pillow folded over her head, nothing showing but the creamy curve of one shoulder, a lacy nightgown strap, and a fluff of blond hair.

He goes into the bathroom, closes the door, slips off the pajama bottoms he sleeps in, drops them into the hamper, clicks on his electric razor. As he runs it over his face he thinks, *Why not run through the rest of the sensory catalogue while you're at it, boys? Do you smell what I smell, do you taste what I taste, do you feel what I feel, I mean, hey, go for it.*

"Humbug," he says as he turns on the shower. "All humbug."

Twenty minutes later, while he's dressing (the dark gray suit from Paul Stuart this morning, plus his favorite Sulka tie), Sharon wakes up a little. Not enough for him to fully understand what she's telling him, though.

"Come again?" he asks. "I got eggnog, but the rest was just ugga-wugga."

"I asked if you'd pick up two quarts of eggnog on your way home," she says. "We've got the Allens and the Dubrays coming over tonight, remember?"

"Christmas," he says, checking his hair carefully in the mirror. He no longer looks like the glaring, bewildered man who sits up in bed to the sound of music five mornings a week—sometimes six. Now he looks like all the other people who will ride into New York with him on the seven-forty, and that is just what he wants.

"What about Christmas?" she asks with a sleepy smile. "Humbug, right?"

"Right," he agrees.

"If you remember, get some cinnamon, too—"

"Okay."

"—but if you forget the eggnog, I'll *slaughter* you, Bill."

"I'll remember."

"I know. You're very dependable. Look nice, too."

"Thanks."

She flops back down, then props herself up on one elbow as he makes a final minute adjustment to the tie, which is a dark blue. He has never worn a red tie in his life, and hopes he can go to his grave untouched by that particular virus. "I got the tinsel you wanted," she says.

"Mmmm?"

"The *tinsel,*" she says. "It's on the kitchen table."

"Oh." Now he remembers. "Thanks."

"Sure." She's back down and already starting to drift off again. He doesn't envy the fact that she can stay in bed until nine—hell, until eleven, if she wants—but he envies that ability of hers to wake up, talk, then drift off again. He had that when he was in the bush—most guys did—but the bush was a long time ago. *In country* was what the new guys and the correspondents always said; if you'd been there awhile it was just the bush, or sometimes the green.

In the green, yeah.

She says something else, but now she's back to ugga-wugga. He knows what it is just the same, though: have a good day, hon.

"Thanks," he says, kissing her cheek. "I will."

"Look very nice," she mumbles again, although her eyes are closed. "Love you, Bill."

"Love you, too," he says and goes out.

His briefcase—Mark Cross, not quite top-of-the-line but close—is standing in the front hall, by the coat tree where his topcoat (from Tager's, on Madison) hangs. He snags the case on his way by and takes it into the kitchen. The coffee is all made—God bless Mr. Coffee—and he pours himself a cup. He opens the briefcase, which is entirely empty, and picks up the ball of tinsel on the kitchen table. He holds it up for a moment, watching the way it sparkles under the light of the kitchen fluorescents, then puts it in his briefcase.

"Do you hear what I hear," he says to no one at all and snaps the briefcase shut.

8:15 A.M.

Outside the dirty window to his left, he can see the city drawing closer. The grime on the glass makes it look like some filthy, gargantuan ruin—dead Atlantis, maybe, just heaved back to the surface to glare at the gray sky. The day's got a load of snow caught in its throat, but that doesn't worry him much; it is just eight days until Christmas, and business will be good.

The train-car reeks of morning coffee, morning deodorant, morning aftershave, morning perfume, and morning stomachs. There is a tie in almost every seat—even some of the women wear them these days. The faces have that puffy eight o'clock look, the eyes both introspective and defenseless, the conversations half-hearted. This is the hour at which even people who don't drink look hungover. Most folks just stick to their newspapers. Why not? Reagan is king of

America, stocks and bonds have turned to gold, the death penalty is back in vogue. Life is good.

He himself has the *Times* crossword open in front of him, and although he's filled in a few squares, it's mostly a defensive measure. He doesn't like to talk to people on the train, doesn't like loose conversation of any sort, and the last thing in the world he wants is a commuter buddy. When he starts seeing the same faces in any given car, when people start to nod to him or say "How you doin today?" as they go to their seats, he changes cars. It's not that hard to remain unknown, just another commuter from suburban Connecticut, a man conspicuous only in his adamant refusal to wear a red tie. Maybe he was once a parochial-school boy, maybe once he held a weeping little girl while one of his friends struck her repeatedly with a baseball bat, and maybe he once spent time in the green. Nobody on the train has to know these things. That's the good thing about trains.

"All ready for Christmas?" the man in the aisle seat asks him.

He looks up, almost frowning, then decides it's not a substantive remark, only the sort of empty time-passer some people seem to feel compelled to make. The man beside him is fat and will undoubtedly stink by noon no matter how much Speed Stick he used this morning . . . but he's hardly even looking at Bill, so that's all right.

"Yes, well, you know," he says, looking down at the briefcase between his shoes—the briefcase that contains a ball of tinsel and nothing else. "I'm getting in the spirit, little by little."

8:40 A.M.

He comes out of Grand Central with a thousand other topcoated men and women, mid-level executives for the most part, sleek gerbils who will be running full tilt on their exercise wheels by noon. He stands still for a moment, breathing deep of the cold gray air. Lexington Avenue is dressed in its Christmas lights, and a little distance away a Santa Claus who looks Puerto Rican is ringing a bell. He's got a pot for contributions with an easel set up beside it. HELP THE HOMELESS THIS CHRISTMAS, the sign on the easel says, and the man in the blue tie thinks, *How about a little truth in advertising, Santa? How about a sign that says HELP ME SUPPORT MY COKE HABIT THIS CHRISTMAS?* Nevertheless, he drops a couple of dollar bills into the pot as he walks past. He has a good feeling about today. He's glad Sharon reminded him of the tinsel—he would have forgotten to bring it, probably; in the end he always forgets stuff like that, the grace notes.

A walk of ten minutes takes him to his building. Standing outside the door is a black youth, maybe seventeen, wearing black jeans and a dirty red hooded sweatshirt. He jives from foot to foot, blowing puffs of steam out of his mouth, smiling frequently, showing a gold tooth. In one hand he holds a partly crushed styrofoam coffee cup. There's some change in it, which he rattles constantly.

"Spare a lil?" he asks the passersby as they stream toward the revolving doors. "Spare me a lil, sir? Spare just a lil, ma'am? Just trying to get a spot of breffus. Thank you, gobless you, merry Christmas. Spare a lil, my man? Quarter, maybe? Thank you. Spare a lil, ma'am?"

As he passes, Bill drops a nickel and two dimes into the young black man's cup.

"Thank you, sir, gobless, merry Christmas."

"You, too," he says.

The woman next to him frowns. "You shouldn't encourage them," she says.

He gives her a shrug and a small, shamefaced smile. "It's hard for me to say no to anyone at Christmas," he tells her.

He enters the lobby with a stream of others, stares briefly after the opinionated bitch as she heads for the newsstand, then goes to the elevators with their old-fashioned floor dials and their art deco numbers. Here several people nod to him, and he exchanges a few words with a couple of them as they wait—it's not like the train, after all, where you can change cars. Plus, the building is an old one; the elevators are slow and cranky.

"How's the wife, Bill?" a scrawny, constantly grinning man from the fifth floor asks.

"Carol's fine."

"Kids?"

"Both good." He has no kids and his wife's name isn't Carol. His wife is the former Sharon Anne Donahue, St. Gabriel the Steadfast Secondary Parochial School, Class of 1964, but that's something the scrawny, constantly grinning man will never know.

"Bet they can't wait for the big day," the scrawny man says, his grin widening and becoming something unspeakable. To Bill Shearman he looks like an editorial cartoonist's conception of Death, all big eyes and huge teeth and stretched shiny skin. That grin makes him think of Tam Boi, in the A Shau Valley. Those guys from 2nd Battalion went in looking like the kings of the world and came out looking like singed escapees from hell's half acre. They came out with those big eyes and huge teeth. They still looked like that in Dong Ha, where they all got kind of mixed together a few days later. A lot of mixing-together went on in the bush. A lot of shake-and-bake, too.

"Absolutely can't wait," he agrees, "but I think Sarah's getting kind of suspicious about the guy in the red suit." Hurry up, elevator, he thinks, Jesus, save me from these stupidities.

"Yeah, yeah, it happens," the scrawny man says. His grin fades for a moment, as if they were discussing cancer instead of Santa. "How old's Sarah now?"

"Eight."

"Seems like she was just born a year or two ago. Boy, the time sure flies when you're havin fun, doesn't it?"

"You can say that again," he says, fervently hoping the scrawny man *won't* say it again. At that moment one of the four elevators finally gasps open its doors and they herd themselves inside.

Bill and the scrawny man walk a little way down the fifth-floor hall together, and then the scrawny man stops in front of a set of old-fashioned double doors with the words CONSOLIDATED INSURANCE written on one frosted-glass panel and ADJUSTORS OF AMERICA on the other. From behind these doors comes the muted clickety-click of keyboards and the slightly louder sound of ringing phones.

"Have a good day, Bill."

"You too."

The scrawny man lets himself into his office, and for a moment Bill sees a big wreath hung on the far side of the room. Also, the windows have been decorated with the kind of snow that comes in a spray can. He shudders and thinks, *God save us, every one.*

9:05 A.M.

His office—one of two he keeps in this building—is at the far end of the hall. The two offices closest to it are dark and vacant, a situation that has held for the last six months and one he likes just fine. Printed on the frosted glass of his own office door are the words WESTERN STATES LAND ANALYSTS. There are three locks on the door: the one that was on when he moved into the building, plus two he has put on himself. He lets himself in, closes the door, turns the bolt, then engages the police lock.

A desk stands in the center of the room, and it is cluttered with papers, but none of them mean anything; they are simply window dressing for the cleaning service. Every so often he throws them all out and redistributes a fresh batch. In the center of the desk is a telephone on which he makes occasional random calls so that the phone company won't register the line as totally inactive. Last year he purchased a copier, and it looks very businesslike over in its corner by the door to the office's little second room, but it has never been used.

"Do you hear what I hear, do you smell what I smell, do you taste what I taste," he murmurs, and crosses to the door leading to the second room. Inside are shelves stacked high with more meaningless paper, two large file-cabinets (there is a Walkman on top of one, his excuse on the few occasions when someone knocks on the locked door and gets no answer), a chair, and a stepladder.

Bill takes the stepladder back to the main room and unfolds it to the left of the desk. He puts his briefcase on top of it. Then he mounts the first three steps of the ladder, reaches up (the bottom half of his coat bells out and around his legs as he does), and carefully moves aside one of the suspended ceiling panels.

Above is a dark area which cannot quite be called a utility space, although a few pipes and wires do run through it. There's no dust up here, at least not in this immediate area, and no rodent droppings, either—he uses D-Con Mouse-Prufe once a month. He wants to keep his clothes nice as he goes back and forth, of course, but that's not really the important part. The important part is to respect your work and your field. This he learned in the Army, during his time in the green, and he sometimes thinks it is the second most important thing he's ever learned in his life. The most important is that only penance replaces confession, and only penance defines identity. This is a lesson he began learning in 1960, when he was fourteen. That was the last year he could go into the booth and say "Bless me father for I have sinned" and then tell everything.

Penance is important to him.

Gobless, he thinks there in the stale-smelling darkness of the utility space. *Gobless you, gobless me, gobless us every one.*

Above this narrow space (a ghostly, gentle wind hoots endlessly through it, bringing a smell of dust and the groan of the elevators) is the bottom of the sixth floor, and here is a square trapdoor about thirty inches on a side. Bill installed it himself; he's handy with tools, which is one of the things Sharon appreciates about him.

He flips the trapdoor up, letting in muted light from above, then grabs his briefcase by the handle. As he sticks his head into the space between floors, water rushes gustily down the fat bathroom conduit twenty or thirty feet north of his present position. An hour from now, when the people in the building start their coffee breaks, that sound will be as constant and as rhythmic as waves breaking on a beach. Bill hardly notices this or any of the other interfloor sounds; he's used to them.

He climbs carefully to the top of the stepladder, then boosts himself through into his sixth-floor office, leaving Bill down on Five. Up here he is Willie again, just as he was in high school. Just as he was in Vietnam, where he was sometimes known as Baseball Willie.

This upper office has a sturdy workshop look, with coils and motors and vents stacked neatly on metal shelves and what looks like a filter of some kind squatting on one corner of the desk. It *is* an office, however; there's a typewriter, a Dictaphone, an IN/OUT basket full of papers (also window dressing, which he periodically rotates like a farmer rotating crops), and file-cabinets. Lots of file-cabinets.

On one wall is a Norman Rockwell painting of a family praying over Thanksgiving dinner. Behind the desk is a framed studio portrait of Willie in his first lieutenant's uniform (taken in Saigon shortly before he won his Silver Star for action at the site of the helicopter crash outside of Dong Ha) and next to it is a blow-up of his honorable discharge, also framed; the name on the sheet is William Shearman, and here his decorations are duly noted. He saved Sullivan's life on the trail outside the 'ville. The citation accompanying the Silver Star says so, the men who survived Dong Ha said so, and more important than either of those, Sullivan said so. It's the first thing he said when they wound up in San Francisco together at the hospital known as the Pussy Palace: *You saved my life, man.* Willie sitting on Sullivan's bed, Willie with one arm still bandaged and salve all around his eyes, but really okay, yeah, he was cruisin, it was Sullivan who had been badly hurt. That was the day the AP photographer took their picture, the photo that appeared in newspapers all over the country . . . including the Harwich *Journal.*

He took my hand, Willie thinks as he stands there in his sixth-floor office with Bill Shearman now a floor down. Above the studio portrait and his discharge is a poster from the sixties. This item, not framed and starting to yellow at the edges, shows the peace sign. Below it, in red, white, and blue, is this punchline: TRACK OF THE GREAT AMERICAN CHICKEN.

He took my hand, he thinks again. Yes, Sullivan had done that, and Willie had come within an ace of leaping to his feet and running back down the ward, screaming. He had been positive that Sullivan would say *I know what you did, you and your friends Doolin and O'Meara. Did you think she wouldn't tell me?*

Sullivan had said nothing like that. What he'd said was, *You saved my life, man, from the old home town and you saved my life. Shit, what are the odds? And we used to be so scared of the boys from St. Gabe's.* When he said that, Willie had known for sure that Sullivan had no idea of what Doolin, O'Meara, and he had done to Carol Gerber. There was no relief in knowing he was safe, however. None. And as he smiled and squeezed Sullivan's hand, he had thought: *You were right to be scared, Sully. You were right to be.*

Willie puts Bill's briefcase on the desk, then lies down on his stomach. He pokes his head and arms into the windy, oil-smelling darkness between floors and replaces the ceiling panel of the fifth-floor office. It's locked up tight; he doesn't expect anyone anyway (he never does; Western States Land Analysts has never had a single customer), but it's better to be safe. Always safe, never sorry.

With his fifth-floor office set to rights, Willie lowers the trapdoor in this one. Up here the trap is hidden by a small rug which is Super-Glued to the wood, so it can go up and down without too much flopping or sliding around.

He gets to his feet, dusts off his hands, then turns to the briefcase and opens it. He takes out the ball of tinsel and puts it on top of the Dictaphone which stands on the desk.

"Good one," he says, thinking again that Sharon can be a real peach when she sets her mind to it . . . and she often does. He relatches the briefcase and then begins to undress, doing it carefully and methodically, reversing the steps he took at six-thirty, running the film backward. He strips off everything, even his undershorts and his black knee-high socks. Naked, he hangs his topcoat, suit jacket, and shirt carefully in the closet where only one other item hangs—a heavy red jacket, not quite thick enough to be termed a parka. Below it is a boxlike thing, a little too bulky to be termed a briefcase. Willie puts his Mark Cross case next to it, then places his slacks in the pants press, taking pains with the crease. The tie goes on the rack screwed to the back of the closet door, where it hangs all by itself like a long blue tongue.

He pads barefoot-naked across to one of the file-cabinet stacks. On top of it is an ashtray embossed with a pissed-off-looking eagle and the words IF I DIE IN A COMBAT ZONE. In the ashtray are a pair of dogtags on a chain. Willie slips the chain over his head, then slides out the bottom drawer of the cabinet stack. Inside are underclothes. Neatly folded on top are a pair of khaki boxer shorts. He slips them on. Next come white athletic socks, followed by a white cotton tee-shirt—roundneck, not strappy. The shapes of his dogtags stand out against it, as do his biceps and quads. They aren't as good as they were in A Shau and Dong Ha, but they aren't bad for a guy who is closing in on forty.

Now, before he finishes dressing, it is time for penance.

He goes to another stack of cabinets and rolls out the second drawer. He thumbs rapidly through the bound ledgers there, passing those for late 1982, then thumbing through those from this year: Jan–April, May–June, July, August (he always feels compelled to write more in the summer), September–October, and at last the current volume: November–December. He sits at his desk, opens the ledger, and flicks rapidly through pages of densely packed writing. There are small variations in the writing, but the essence is always the same: *I am heartily sorry.*

He only writes for ten minutes or so this morning, pen scratching busily, sticking to the basic fact of the matter: *I am heartily sorry.* He has, to the best of his reckoning, written this over two million times . . . and is just getting started. Confession would be quicker, but he is willing to take the long way around.

He finishes—no, he never finishes, but he finishes for today—and puts the current ledger back between those finished and all those yet to be filled. Then he returns to the stack of file-cabinets which serve as his chest of drawers. As he opens the one above his socks and skivvies, he begins to hum under his breath—not "Do You Hear What I Hear" but The Doors, the one about how the day destroys the night, the night divides the day.

He slips on a plain blue chambray shirt, then a pair of fatigue pants. He rolls this middle drawer back in and opens the top one. Here there is a scrapbook and a pair of boots. He takes the scrapbook out and looks at its red leather cover for a moment. The word MEMORIES is stamped on the front in flaking gold. It's a cheap thing, this book. He could afford better, but you don't always have a right to what you can afford.

In the summer he writes more sorries but memory seems to sleep. It is in winter, especially around Christmas, that memory awakens. Then he wants to look in this book, which is full of clippings and photos where everyone looks impossibly young.

Today he puts the scrapbook back into the drawer unopened and takes out the boots. They are polished to a high sheen and look as if they might last until the trump of judgment. Maybe even longer. They aren't standard Army issue, not these—these are jumpboots, 101st Airborne stuff. But that's all right. He isn't actually trying to dress like a soldier. If he wanted to dress like a soldier, he would.

Still, there is no more reason to look sloppy than there is to allow dust to collect in the pass-through, and he's careful about the way he dresses. He does not tuck his pants into his boots, of course—he's headed for Fifth Avenue in December, not the Mekong in August, snakes and poppy-bugs are not apt to be a problem—but he intends to look squared away. Looking good is as important to him as it is to Bill, maybe even more important. Respecting one's work and one's field begins, after all, with respecting one's self.

The last two items are in the back of the top drawer of his bureau stack: a tube of makeup and a jar of hair gel. He squeezes some of the makeup into the palm of his left hand, then begins applying it, working from forehead to the base of his neck. He moves with the unconcerned speed of long experience, giving himself a moderate tan. With that done, he works some of the gel into his hair and then recombs it, getting rid of the part and sweeping it straight back from his forehead. It is the last touch, the smallest touch, and perhaps the most telling touch. There is no trace of the commuter who walked out of Grand Central an hour ago; the man in the mirror mounted on the back of the door to the small storage annex looks like a washed-up mercenary. There is a kind of silent, half-humbled pride in the tanned face, something people won't look at too long. It hurts them if they do. Willie knows this is so; he has seen it. He doesn't ask why it should be so. He has made himself a life pretty much without questions, and that's the way he likes it.

"All *right,*" he says, closing the door to the storage room. "Lookin good, trooper."

He goes back to the closet for the red jacket, which is the reversible type, and the boxy case. He slips the jacket over his desk chair for the time being and puts the case on the desk. He unlatches it and swings the top up on sturdy hinges; now it looks a little like the cases street salesmen use to display their knockoff watches and questionable gold chains. There are only a few items in Willie's, one of them broken down into two pieces so it will fit. There is a sign. There is a pair of gloves, the kind you wear in cold weather, and a third glove which he used to wear when it was warm. He takes out the pair (he will want them today, no doubt about that), and then the sign on its length of stout cord. The cord has been knotted through holes in the cardboard at either side, so Willie can hang the sign around his neck. He closes the case again, not bothering to latch it, and puts the sign on top of it—the desk is so cluttery, it's the only good surface he has to work on.

Humming (we chased our pleasures here, dug our treasures there), he opens the wide drawer above the kneehole, paws past the pencils and Chap Sticks and paperclips and memo pads, and finally finds his stapler. He then unrolls the ball of tinsel, placing it carefully around the rectangle of his sign. He snips off the extra and staples the shiny stuff firmly into place. He holds it up for a moment, first assessing the effect, then admiring it.

"Perfect!" he says.

The telephone rings and he stiffens, turning to look at it with eyes which are suddenly very small and hard and totally alert. One ring. Two. Three. On the fourth, the machine kicks in, answering in his voice—the version of it that goes with this office, anyway.

"Hi, you've reached Midtown Heating and Cooling," Willie Shearman says. "No one can take your call right now, so leave a message at the beep."

Bee-eep.

He listens tensely, standing over his just-decorated sign with his hands balled into fists.

"Hi, this is Ed, from the NYNEX Yellow Pages," the voice from the machine says, and Willie lets out a breath he hasn't known he was holding. His hands begin to loosen. "Please have your company rep call me at 1-800-555-1000 for information on how you can increase your ad space in both versions of the Yellow Pages, and at the same time save big money on your yearly bill. Happy holidays to all! Thanks."

Click.

Willie looks at the answering machine a moment longer, almost as if he expects it to speak again—to threaten him, perhaps to accuse him of all the crimes of which he accuses himself—but nothing happens.

"Squared away," he murmurs, putting the decorated sign back into the case. This time when he closes it, he latches it. Across the front is a bumper sticker, its message flanked by small American flags. I WAS PROUD TO SERVE, it reads.

"Squared away, baby, you better believe it."

He leaves the office, closing the door with MIDTOWN HEATING AND COOLING printed on the frosted-glass panel behind him, and turning all three of the locks.

9:45 A.M.

Halfway down the hall, he sees Ralph Williamson, one of the tubby accountants from Garowicz Financial Planning (all the accountants at Garowicz are tubby, from what Willie has been able to observe). There's a key chained to an old wooden paddle in one of Ralph's pink hands, and from this Willie deduces that he is looking at an accountant in need of a wee. Key on a paddle! If a fuckin key on a fuckin paddle won't make you remember the joys of parochial school, remember all those hairy-chin nuns and all those knuckle-whacking wooden rulers, then nothing will, he thinks. And you know what? Ralph Williamson probably likes having that key on a paddle, just like he likes having a soap on a rope in the shape of a bunny rabbit or a circus clown hanging from the HOT faucet in his shower at home. And so what if he does? Judge not, lest ye be fuckin judged.

"Hey, Ralphie, what's doin?"

Ralph turns, sees Willie, brightens. "Hey, hi, merry Christmas!"

Willie grins at the look in Ralph's eyes. Tubby little fucker worships him, and why not? Ralph is looking at a guy so squared away it hurts. Gotta like it, sweetheart, *gotta* like that.

"Same to you, bro." He holds out his hand (now gloved, so he doesn't have to worry about it being too white, not matching his face), palm up. "Gimme five!"

Smiling shyly, Ralph does.

"Gimme ten!"

Ralph turns his pink, pudgy hand over and allows Willie to slap it.

"So goddam good I gotta do it again!" Willie exclaims, and gives Ralph five more. "Got your Christmas shopping done, Ralphie?"

"Almost," Ralph says, grinning and jingling the bathroom key. "Yes, almost. How about you, Willie?"

Willie tips him a wink. "Oh, you know how it is, brother-man; I got two-three women, and I just let each of em buy me a little keepsake."

Ralph's admiring smile suggests he does not, in fact, know how it is, but rather wishes he did. "Got a service call?"

"A whole day's worth. 'Tis the season, you know."

"Seems like it's always the season for you. Business must be good. You're hardly ever in your office."

"That's why God gave us answering machines, Ralphie. You better go on, now, or you're gonna be dealin with a wet spot on your best gabardine slacks."

Laughing (blushing a little, too), Ralph heads for the men's room.

Willie goes on down to the elevators, carrying his case in hand and checking to make sure his glasses are still in his jacket pocket with the other. They are. The envelope is in there, too, thick and crackling with twenty-dollar bills. Fifteen of them. It's time for a little visit from Officer Wheelock; Willie expected him yesterday. Maybe he won't show until tomorrow, but Willie is betting on today . . . not that he likes it. He knows it's the way of the world, you have to grease the wheels if you want your wagon to roll, but he still has a resentment. There are lots of days when he thinks about how pleasant it would be to put a bullet in Jasper Wheelock's head. It was the way things happened in the green, sometimes. The way things *had* to happen. That thing with Malenfant, for instance. That crazy motherfucker, him with his pimples and his deck of cards.

Oh yes, in the bush things were different. In the bush you sometimes had to do something wrong to prevent an even greater wrong. Behavior like that shows that you're in the wrong place to start with, no doubt, but once you're in the soup, you just have to swim. He and his men from Bravo Company were only with the Delta Company boys a few days, so Willie didn't have much experience with Malenfant, but his shrill, grating voice is hard to forget, and he remembers something Malenfant would yell during his endless Hearts games if someone tried to take back a card after it was laid down: *No way, fuckwad! Once it's laid, it's played!*

Malenfant might have been an asshole, but he had been right about that. In life as well as in cards, once it's laid, it's played.

The elevator doesn't stop on Five, but the thought of that happening no longer makes him nervous. He has ridden down to the lobby many times with people who work on the same floor as Bill Shearman—including the scrawny drink of water from Consolidated Insurance—and they don't recognize him. They should, he knows they *should,* but they don't. He used to think it was the change of clothes and the makeup, then he decided it was the hair, but in his heart he knows that none of those things can account for it. Not even their numb-hearted insensitivity to the world they live in can account for it. What he's doing just isn't that radical—fatigue pants, billyhop boots, and a little brown makeup don't make a disguise. No way do they make a disguise. He doesn't know exactly how to explain it, and so mostly leaves it alone. He learned this technique, as he learned so many others, in Vietnam.

The young black man is still standing outside the lobby door (he's flipped up the hood of his grungy old sweatshirt now), and he shakes his crumpled styrofoam cup at Willie. He sees that the dude carrying the Mr. Repairman case in one hand is smiling, and so his own smile widens.

"Spare a lil?" he asks Mr. Repairman. "What do you say, my man?"

"Get the fuck out of my way, you lazy dickhead, that's what I say," Willie tells him, still smiling. The young man falls back a step, looking at Willie with wide shocked eyes. Before he can think of anything to say, Mr. Repairman is halfway down the block and almost lost in the throngs of shoppers, his big blocky case swinging from one gloved hand.

10:00 A.M.

He goes into the Whitmore Hotel, crosses the lobby, and takes the escalator up to the mezzanine, where the public restrooms are. This is the only part of the day he ever feels nervous about, and he can't say why; certainly nothing has ever happened before, during, or after one of his hotel bathroom stops (he rotates among roughly two dozen of them in the midtown area). Still, he is somehow certain that if things *do* turn dinky-dau on him, it will happen in a hotel shithouse. Because what happens next is not like transforming from Bill Shearman to Willie Shearman; Bill and Willie are brothers, perhaps even fraternal twins, and the switch from one to the other feels clean and perfectly normal. The workday's final transformation, however—from Willie Shearman to Blind Willie Garfield—has never felt that way. The last change always feels murky, furtive, almost werewolfy. Until it's done and he's on the street again, tapping his white cane in front of him, he feels as a snake must after it's shed its old skin and before the new one works in and grows tough.

He looks around and sees the men's bathroom is empty except for a pair of feet under the door of the second stall in a long row of them—there must be a dozen in all. A throat clears softly. A newspaper rattles. There is the *ffft* sound of a polite little midtown fart.

Willie goes all the way to the last stall in line. He puts down his case, latches the door shut, and takes off his red jacket. He turns it inside-out as he does so, reversing it. The other side is olive green. It has become an old soldier's field jacket with a single pull of the arms. Sharon, who really does have a touch of genius, bought this side of his coat in an army surplus store and tore out the lining so she could sew it easily into the red jacket. Before sewing, however, she put a first lieutenant's badge on it, plus black strips of cloth where the name-and-unit slugs would have gone. She then washed the garment thirty times or so. The badge and the unit markings are gone, now, of course, but the places where they were stand out clearly—the cloth is greener on the sleeves and the left breast, fresher in patterns any veteran of the armed services must recognize at once.

Willie hangs the coat on the hook, drops trou, sits, then picks up his case and settles it on his thighs. He opens it, takes out the disassembled cane, and quickly screws the two pieces together. Holding it far down the shaft, he reaches up from his sitting position and hooks the handle over the top of his jacket. Then he relatches the case, pulls a little paper off the roll in order to create the proper business-is-finished sound effect (probably unnecessary, but always safe, never sorry), and flushes the john.

Before stepping out of the stall he takes the glasses from the jacket pocket which also holds the payoff envelope. They're big wraparounds; retro shades he associates with lava lamps and outlaw-biker movies starring Peter Fonda. They're good for business, though, partly because they somehow say veteran to people, and partly because no one can peek in at his eyes, even from the sides.

Willie Shearman stays behind in the mezzanine restroom of the Whitmore just as Bill Shearman stays behind in the fifth-floor office of Western States Land Analysts. The man who comes out—a man wearing an old fatigue jacket, shades, and tapping a white cane lightly before him—is Blind Willie, a Fifth Avenue fixture since the days of Gerald Ford.

As he crosses the small mezzanine lobby toward the stairs (unaccompanied blind men never use escalators), he sees a woman in a red blazer coming toward him. With the heavily tinted lenses between them, she looks like some sort of exotic fish swimming in muddy water. And of course it is not just the glasses; by two this afternoon he really *will* be blind, just as he kept screaming he was when he and John Sullivan and God knows how many others were medevacked out of Dong Ha Province back in '70. *I'm blind,* he was yelling it even as he picked Sullivan up off the path, but he hadn't been, exactly; through the throbbing post-flash whiteness he had seen Sullivan rolling around and trying to hold his bulging guts in. He had picked Sullivan up and ran with him clasped clumsily over one shoulder. Sullivan was bigger than Willie, a lot bigger, and Willie had no idea how he could possibly have carried such a weight but somehow he had, all the way to the clearing where Hueys like God's mercy had taken them off—gobless you Hueys, gobless, oh gobless you every one. He had run to the clearing and the copters with bullets whicking all around him and body-parts made in America lying on the trail where the mine or the booby-trap or whatever the fuck it was had gone off.

I'm blind, he had screamed, carrying Sullivan, feeling Sullivan's blood drenching his uniform, and Sullivan had been screaming, too. If Sullivan had stopped screaming, would Willie have simply rolled the man off his shoulder and gone on alone, trying to outrun the ambush? Probably not. Because by then he knew who Sullivan was, exactly who he was, he was Sully from the old home town, Sully who had gone out with Carol Gerber from the old home town.

I'm blind, I'm blind, I'm blind! That's what Willie Shearman was screaming as he toted Sullivan, and it's true that much of the world was blast-white, but he still remembers seeing bullets twitch through leaves and thud into the trunks of trees; remembers seeing one of the men who had been in the 'ville earlier that day clap his hand to his throat. He remembers seeing the blood come bursting through that man's fingers in a flood, drenching his uniform. One of the other men from Delta Company two-two—Pagano, his name had been—grabbed this fellow around the middle and hustled him past the staggering Willie Shearman, who really *couldn't* see very much. Screaming *I'm blind I'm blind I'm blind* and smelling Sullivan's blood, the stink of it. And in the copter that whiteness had started to come on strong. His face was burned, his hair was burned, his scalp was burned, the world was white. He was scorched and smoking, just one more escapee from hell's half acre. He had believed he would never see again, and that had actually been a relief. But of course he had.

In time, he had.

The woman in the red blazer has reached him. "Can I help you, sir?" she asks.

"No, ma'am," Blind Willie says. The ceaselessly moving cane stops tapping floor and quests over emptiness. It pendulums back and forth, mapping the sides of the staircase. Blind Willie nods, then moves carefully but confidently forward until he can touch the railing with the hand which holds the bulky case. He switches the case to his cane-hand so he can grasp the railing, then turns toward the woman. He's careful not to smile directly at her but a little to her left. "No, thank you—I'm fine. Merry Christmas."

He starts downstairs tapping ahead of him as he goes, big case held easily in spite of the cane—it's light, almost empty. Later, of course, it will be a different story.

10:15 A.M.

Fifth Avenue is decked out for the holiday season—glitter and finery he can barely see. Streetlamps wear garlands of holly. The big stores have become garish Christmas packages, complete with gigantic red bows. A wreath which must be forty feet across graces the staid beige facade of Brooks Brothers. Lights twinkle everywhere. In Saks' show-window, a high-fashion mannequin (haughty fuck-you-Jack expression, almost no tits or hips) sits astride a Harley-Davidson motorcycle. She is wearing a Santa hat, a fur-trimmed motorcycle jacket, thigh-high boots, and nothing else. Silver bells hang from the cycle's handlebars. Somewhere nearby, carolers are singing "Silent Night," not exactly Blind Willie's favorite tune, but a good deal better than "Do You Hear What I Hear."

He stops where he always stops, in front of St. Patrick's, across the street from Saks, allowing the package-laden shoppers to flood past in front of him. His movements now are simple and dignified. His discomfort in the men's room—that feeling of gawky nakedness about to be exposed—has passed. He never feels more Catholic than when he arrives on this spot. He was a St. Gabe's boy, after all; wore the cross, wore the surplice and took his turn as altar-boy, knelt in the booth, ate the hated haddock on Fridays. He is in many ways still a St. Gabe's boy, all three versions of him have that in common, that part crossed the years and got over, as they used to say. Only these days he does penance instead of confession, and his certainty of heaven is gone. These days all he can do is hope.

He squats, unlatches the case, and turns it so those approaching from uptown will be able to read the sticker on the top. Next he takes out the third glove, the baseball glove he has had since the summer of 1960. He puts the glove beside the case. Nothing breaks more hearts than a blind man with a baseball glove, he has found; gobless America.

Last but not least, he takes out the sign with its brave skirting of tinsel, and ducks under the string. The sign comes to rest against the front of his field jacket.

FORMER 1 LT. WILLIAM J. GARFIELD, U.S. ARMY

SERVED QUANG TRI, THUA THIEN, TAM BOI, A SHAU

LOST MY SIGHT DONG HA PROVINCE 1970

ROBBED OF BENEFITS BY A GRATEFUL GOVERNMENT 1973

LOST HOME 1975

ASHAMED TO BEG BUT HAVE A SON IN SCHOOL

THINK WELL OF ME IF YOU CAN

He raises his head so that the white light of this cold, almost-ready-to-snow day slides across the blind bulbs of his dark glasses. Now the work begins, and it is harder work than anyone will ever know. There is a way to stand, not quite the military posture which is called parade rest, but close to it. The head must stay up, looking both at and through the people who pass back and forth in their thousands and tens of thousands. The hands must hang straight down in their black gloves, never fiddling with the sign or with the fabric of his pants or with each other. He must continue to project that sense of hurt, humbled pride. There must be no sense of shame or shaming, and most of all no taint of insanity. He never speaks unless spoken to, and only then when he is spoken to in kindness. He does not respond to people who ask him angrily why he doesn't get a real job, or what he means about being robbed of his benefits. He does not argue with those who accuse him of fakery or speak scornfully of a son who would allow his father to put him through school by begging on a streetcorner. He remembers breaking this ironclad rule only once, on a sweltering summer afternoon in 1981. What school does your son go to? a woman asked him angrily. He doesn't know what she looked like, by then it was four o'clock and he had been as blind as a bat for at least two hours, but he had felt anger exploding out of her in all directions, like bedbugs exiting an old mattress. In a way she had reminded him of Malenfant with his shrill you-can't-not-hear-it voice. Tell me which one, I want to mail him a dog turd. Don't bother, he replied, turning toward the sound of her voice. If you've got a dog turd you want to mail somewhere, send it to LBJ. Federal Express must deliver to hell, they deliver everyplace else.

"God bless you, man," a guy in a cashmere overcoat says, and his voice trembles with surprising emotion. Except Blind Willie Garfield isn't surprised. He's heard it all, he reckons, and a bit more. A surprising number of his customers put their money carefully and reverently in the pocket of the baseball glove. The guy in the cashmere coat drops his contribution into the open case, however, where it properly belongs. A five. The workday has begun.

10:45 A.M.

So far, so good. He lays his cane down carefully, drops to one knee, and dumps the contents of the baseball glove into the box. Then he sweeps a hand back and forth through the bills, although he can still see them pretty well. He picks them up—there's four or five hundred dollars in all, which puts him on the way to a three-thousand-dollar day, not great for this time of year, but not bad, either—then rolls them up and slips a rubber band around them. He then pushes a button on the inside of the case, and the false floor drops down on springs, dumping the load of change all the way to the bottom. He adds the roll of bills, making no attempt to hide what he's doing, but feeling no qualms about it, either; in all the years he has been doing this, no one has ever taken him off. God help the asshole who ever tries.

He lets go of the button, allowing the false floor to snap back into place, and stands up. A hand immediately presses into the small of his back.

"Merry Christmas, Willie," the owner of the hand says. Blind Willie recognizes him by the smell of his cologne.

"Merry Christmas, Officer Wheelock," Willie responds. His head remains tilted upward in a faintly questioning posture; his hands hang at his sides; his feet in their brightly polished boots remain apart in a stance not quite wide enough to be parade rest but nowhere near tight enough to pass as attention. "How are you today, sir?"

"In the pink, motherfucker," Wheelock says. "You know me, always in the pink."

Here comes a man in a topcoat hanging open over a bright red ski sweater. His hair is short, black on top, gray on the sides. His face has a stern, carved look Blind Willie recognizes at once. He's got a couple of handle-top bags—one from Saks, one from Bally—in his hands. He stops and reads the sign.

"Dong Ha?" he asks suddenly, speaking not as a man does when naming a place but as one does when recognizing an old acquaintance on a busy street.

"Yes, sir," Blind Willie says.

"Who was your CO?"

"Captain Bob Brissum—with a *u,* not an *o*—and above him, Colonel Andrew Shelf, sir."

"I heard of Shelf," says the man in the open coat. His face suddenly looks different. As he walked toward the man on the corner, it looked as if it belonged on Fifth Avenue. Now it doesn't. "Never met him, though."

"Toward the end of my run, we didn't see anyone with much rank, sir."

"If you came out of the A Shau Valley, I'm not surprised. Are we on the same page here, soldier?"

"Yes, sir. There wasn't much command structure left by the time we hit Dong Ha. I pretty much rolled things along with another lieutenant. His name was Dieffenbaker."

The man in the red ski sweater is nodding slowly. "You boys were there when those helicopters came down, if I've got this placed right."

"That's affirmative, sir."

"Then you must have been there later, when . . ."

Blind Willie does not help him finish. He can smell Wheelock's cologne, though, stronger than ever, and the man is practically panting in his ear, sounding like a horny kid at the end of a hot date. Wheelock has never bought his act, and although Blind Willie pays for the privilege of being left alone on this corner, and quite handsomely by going rates, he knows that part of Wheelock is still cop enough to hope he'll fuck up. Part of Wheelock is actively rooting for that. But the Wheelocks of the world never understand that what looks fake isn't always fake. Sometimes the issues are a little more complicated than they appear at first glance. That was something else Vietnam had to teach him, back in the years before it became a political joke and a crutch for hack filmwriters.

"Sixty-nine and seventy were the hard years," the graying man says. He speaks in a slow, heavy voice. "I was at Hamburger Hill with the 3/187, so I know the A Shau and Tam Boi. Do you remember Route 922?"

"Ah, yes, sir, Glory Road," Blind Willie says. "I lost two friends there."

"Glory Road," the man in the open coat says, and all at once he looks a thousand years old, the bright red ski sweater an obscenity, like something hung on a museum mummy by cutup kids who believe they are exhibiting a sense of humor. His eyes are off over a hundred horizons. Then they come back here, to this street where a nearby carillon is playing the one that goes I hear those sleighbells jingling, ring-ting-tingling too. He sets his bags down between his expensive shoes and takes a pigskin wallet out from an inner pocket. He opens it, riffles through a neat thickness of bills.

"Son all right, Garfield?" he asks. "Making good grades?"

"Yes, sir."

"How old?"

"Fifteen, sir."

"Public school?"

"Parochial, sir."

"Excellent. And God willing, he'll never see Glory Fuckin Road." The man in the open topcoat takes a bill out of his wallet. Blind Willie feels as well as hears Wheelock's little gasp and hardly has to look at the bill to know it is a hundred.

"Yes, sir, that's affirmative, God willing."

The man in the topcoat touches Willie's hand with the bill, looks surprised when the gloved hand pulls back, as if it were bare and had been touched by something hot.

"Put it in my case or my ball-glove, sir, if you would," Blind Willie says.

The man in the topcoat looks at him for a moment, eyebrows raised, frowning slightly, then seems to understand. He stoops, puts the bill in the ancient oiled pocket of the glove with GARFIELD printed in blue ink on the side, then reaches into his front pocket and brings out a small handful of change. This he scatters across the face of old Ben Franklin, in order to hold the bill down. Then he stands up. His eyes are wet and bloodshot.

"Do you any good to give you my card?" he asks Blind Willie. "I can put you in touch with several veterans' organizations."

"Thank you, sir, I'm sure you could, but I must respectfully decline."

"Tried most of them?"

"Tried some, yes, sir."

"Where'd you V.A.?"

"San Francisco, sir." He hesitates, then adds, "The Pussy Palace, sir."

The man in the topcoat laughs heartily at this, and when his face crinkles, the tears which have been standing in his eyes run down his weathered cheeks. "Pussy Palace!" he cries. "I haven't heard that in ten years! Christ! A bedpan under every bed and a naked nurse between every set of sheets, right? Naked except for the lovebeads, which they left on."

"Yes, sir, that about covers it, sir."

"Or uncovers it. Merry Christmas, soldier." The man in the topcoat ticks off a little one-finger salute.

"Merry Christmas to you, sir."

The man in the topcoat picks up his bags again and walks off. He doesn't look back. Blind Willie would not have seen him do so if he had; his vision is now down to ghosts and shadows.

"That was beautiful," Wheelock murmurs. The feeling of Wheelock's freshly used air puffing into the cup of his ear is hateful to Blind Willie—gruesome, in fact—but he will not give the man the pleasure of moving his head so much as an inch. "The old fuck was actually *crying.* As I'm sure you saw. But you can talk the talk, Willie, I'll give you that much."

Willie says nothing.

"Some V.A. hospital called the Pussy Palace, huh?" Wheelock asks. "Sounds like my kind of place. Where'd you read about it, *Soldier of Fortune*?"

The shadow of a woman, a dark shape in a darkening day, bends over the open case and drops something in. A gloved hand touches Willie's gloved hand and squeezes briefly. "God bless you, my friend," she says.

"Thank you, ma'am."

The shadow moves off. The little puffs of breath in Blind Willie's ear do not.

"You got something for me, pal?" Wheelock asks.

Blind Willie reaches into his jacket pocket. He produces the envelope and holds it out, jabbing the chilly air with it. It is snatched from his fingers as soon as Wheelock can track it down and get hold of it.

"You asshole!" There's fear as well as anger in the cop's voice. "How many times have I told you, palm it, *palm* it!"

Blind Willie says nothing. He is thinking of the baseball glove, how he erased BOBBY GARFIELD—as well as you could erase ink from leather, anyway—and then printed Willie Shearman's name in its place. Later, after Vietnam and just as he was starting his new career, he erased a second time and printed a single name, GARFIELD, in big block letters. The place on the side of the old Alvin Dark glove where all these changes have been made looks flayed and raw. If he thinks of the glove, if he concentrates on that scuffed place and its layer of names, he can probably keep from doing something stupid. That's what Wheelock wants, of course, what he wants a lot more than his shitty little payoff: for Willie to do something stupid, to give himself away.

"How much?" Wheelock asks after a moment.

"Three hundred," Blind Willie says. "Three hundred dollars, Officer Wheelock."

This is greeted by a little thinking silence, but Wheelock takes a step back from Blind Willie, and the puffs of breath in his ear diffuse a little. Blind Willie is grateful for small favors.

"That's okay," Wheelock says at last. "*This* time. But a new year's coming, pal, and your friend Jasper the Police-Smurf has a piece of land in upstate New York that he wants to build a little cabana on. You capeesh? The price of poker is going up."

Blind Willie says nothing, but he is listening very, very carefully now. If this were all, all would be well. But Wheelock's voice suggests it isn't all.

"Actually, the cabana isn't the important part," Wheelock goes on. "The important thing is I need a little better compensation if I have to deal with a lowlife fuck like you." Genuine anger is creeping into his voice. "How you can do this every day—even at *Christmas*—man, I don't know. People who beg, that's one thing, but a guy like you . . . you're no more blind than I am."

Oh, you're *lots* blinder than me, Blind Willie thinks, but still he holds his peace.

"And you're doing okay, aren't you? Probably not as good as those PTL fucks on the tube, but you must clear . . . what? A grand a day, this time a year? Two grand?"

He is way low, but the miscalculation is music to Blind Willie Garfield's ears. It means that his silent partner is not watching him too closely or too frequently . . . not yet, anyway. But he doesn't like the anger in Wheelock's voice. Anger is like a wild card in a poker game.

"You're no more blind than I am," Wheelock repeats. Apparently this is the part that really gets him. "Hey, pal, you know what? I ought to follow you some night when you get off work, you know? See what you do." He pauses. "Who you turn into."

For a moment Blind Willie actually stops breathing . . . then he starts again.

"You wouldn't want to do that, Officer Wheelock," he says.

"I wouldn't, huh? Why not, Willie? Why not? You lookin out for my welfare, is that it? Afraid I might kill the shitass who lays the golden eggs? Hey, what I get from you in the course of a year ain't all that much when you weigh it against a commendation, maybe a promotion." He pauses. When he speaks again, his voice has a dreamy quality which Willie finds especially alarming. "I could be in the *Post.* HERO COP BUSTS HEARTLESS SCAM ARTIST ON FIFTH AVENUE."

Jesus, Willie thinks. *Good Jesus, he sounds serious.*

"Says Garfield on your glove there, but I'd bet Garfield ain't your name. I'd bet dollars to doughnuts."

"That's a bet you'd lose."

"Says you . . . but the side of that glove looks like it's seen more than one name written there."

"It was stolen when I was a kid." Is he talking too much? It's hard to say. Wheelock has managed to catch him by surprise, the bastard. First the phone rings while he's in his office—good old Ed from NYNEX—and now this. "The boy who stole it from me wrote his name in it while he had it. When I got it back, I erased his and put mine on again."

"And it went to Vietnam with you?"

"Yes." It's the truth. If Sullivan had seen that battered Alvin Dark fielder's mitt, would he have recognized it as his old friend Bobby's? Unlikely, but who could know? Sullivan never *had* seen it, not in the green, at least, which made the whole question moot. Officer Jasper Wheelock, on the other hand, was posing all sorts of questions, and *none* of them were moot.

"Went to this Achoo Valley with you, did it?"

Blind Willie doesn't reply. Wheelock is trying to lead him on now, and there's noplace Wheelock can lead that Willie Garfield wants to go.

"Went to this Tomboy place with you?"

Willie says nothing.

"Man, I thought a tomboy was a chick that liked to climb trees."

Willie continues to say nothing.

"The *Post,*" Wheelock says, and Willie dimly sees the asshole raise his hands slightly apart, as if framing a picture. "HERO COP." He might just be teasing . . . but Willie can't tell.

"You'd be in the *Post,* all right, but there wouldn't be any commendation," Blind Willie says. "No promotion, either. In fact, you'd be out on the street, Officer Wheelock, looking for a job. You could skip applying for one with security companies, though—a man who'll take a payoff can't be bonded."

It is Wheelock's turn to stop breathing. When he starts again, the puffs of breath in Blind Willie's ear have become a hurricane; the cop's moving mouth is almost on his skin. "What do you mean?" he whispers. A hand settles on the arm of Blind Willie's field jacket. "You just tell me what the fuck you mean."

But Blind Willie continues silent, hands at his sides, head slightly raised, looking attentively into the darkness that will not clear until daylight is almost gone, and on his face is that lack of expression which so many passersby read as ruined pride, courage brought low but somehow still intact.

Better be careful, Officer Wheelock, he thinks. *The ice under you is getting thin. I may be blind, but you must be deaf if you can't hear the sound of it cracking under your feet.*

The hand on his arm shakes him slightly. Wheelock's fingers are digging in. "You got a friend? Is that it, you son of a bitch? Is that why you hold the envelope out that way half the damned time? You got a friend taking my picture? Is that it?"

Blind Willie goes on saying nothing; to Jasper the Police-Smurf he is now giving a sermon of silence. People like Officer Wheelock will always think the worst if you let them. You only have to give them time to do it.

"You don't want to fuck with me, pal," Wheelock says viciously, but there is a subtle undertone of worry in his voice, and the hand on Blind Willie's jacket loosens. "We're going up to four hundred a month starting in January, and if you try playing any games with me, I'm going to show you where the real playground is. You understand me?"

Blind Willie says nothing. The puffs of air stop hitting his ear, and he knows Wheelock is getting ready to go. But not yet, alas; the nasty little puffs come back.

"You'll burn in hell for what you're doing," Wheelock tells him. He speaks with great, almost fervent, sincerity. "What I'm doing when I take your dirty money is a venial sin—I asked the priest, so I'm sure—but yours is mortal. You're going to hell, see how many handouts you get down there."

Blind Willie thinks of a jacket Willie and Bill Shearman sometimes see on the street. There is a map of Vietnam on the back, usually the years the wearer of the jacket spent there, and this message: WHEN I DIE I'M GOING STRAIGHT TO HEAVEN, BECAUSE I SPENT MY TIME IN HELL. He could mention this sentiment to Officer Wheelock, but it would do no good. Silence is better.

Wheelock walks away, and Willie's thought—that he's glad to see him go—causes a rare smile to touch his face. It comes and goes like an errant ray of sunshine on a cloudy day.

1:40 P.M.

Three times he has banded the bills into rolls and dumped the change into the bottom of the case (this is really a storage function, and not an effort at concealment), now working completely by touch. He can no longer see the money, doesn't know a one from a hundred, but he senses he is having a very good day indeed. There is no pleasure in the knowledge, however. There's never much, pleasure is not what Blind Willie is about, but even the sense of accomplishment he might have felt on another day has been muted by his conversation with Officer Wheelock.

At quarter to twelve, a young woman with a pretty voice (to Blind Willie she sounds like Diana Ross) comes out of Saks and gives him a cup of hot coffee, as she does most days at this time. At quarter past, another woman—this one not so young, and probably white—brings him a cup of steaming chicken noodle soup. He thanks them both. The white lady kisses his cheek with soft lips and wishes him the merriest of merry Christmases.

There is a counterbalancing side to the day, though; there almost always is. Around one o'clock a teenage boy with his unseen gang of buddies laughing and joking and skylarking all around him speaks out of the darkness to Blind Willie's left, says he is one ugly motherfuck, then asks if he wears those gloves because he burned his fingers off trying to read the waffle iron. He and his friends charge off, howling with laughter at this ancient jape. Fifteen minutes or so later someone kicks him, although that might have been an accident. Every time he bends over to the case, however, the case is right there. It is a city of hustlers, muggers, and thieves, but the case is right there, just as it has always been right there.

And through it all, he thinks about Wheelock.

The cop before Wheelock was easy; the one who comes when Wheelock either quits the force or gets moved out of Midtown may also be easy. Wheelock will shake, bake, or flake eventually, that's something else he learned in the bush, and in the meantime, he,

Blind Willie, must bend like a reed in a windstorm. Except even the limberest reed breaks if the wind blows hard enough.

Wheelock wants more money, but that isn't what bothers the man in the dark glasses and the army coat; sooner or later they all want more money. When he started on this corner, he paid Officer Hanratty a hundred and a quarter. Hanratty was a live-and-let-live type of guy who smelled of Old Spice and whiskey just like George Raymer, the neighborhood beat-cop of Willie Shearman's childhood, but easygoing Eric Hanratty'd still had Blind Willie up to two hundred a month by the time he retired in 1978. And the thing is—dig it, my brothers—Wheelock was angry this morning, *angry,* and Wheelock talked about having consulted a priest. These things worry him, but what worries him most of all is what Wheelock said about following him. *See what you do. Who you turn into. Garfield ain't your name. I'd bet dollars to doughnuts.*

It's a mistake to fuck with the truly penitential, Officer Wheelock, Blind Willie thinks. *You'd be safer fucking with my wife than with my name, believe me. Safer by far.*

Wheelock could do it, though—what could be simpler than shadowing a blind man, or even one who can see little more than shadows? Simpler than watching him turn into some hotel and enter the public men's room? Watching him go into a stall as Blind Willie Garfield and come out as Willie Shearman? Suppose Wheelock was even able to backtrail him from Willie to Bill?

Thinking this brings back his morning jitters, his feeling of being a snake between skins. The fear that he has been photographed taking a bribe will hold Wheelock for awhile, but if he is angry enough, there is no predicting what he may do. And that is scary.

"God love you, soldier," says a voice out of the darkness. "I wish I could do more."

"Not necessary, sir," Blind Willie says, but his mind is still on Jasper Wheelock, who smells of cheap cologne and talked to a priest about the blind man with the sign, the blind man who is not, in Wheelock's opinion, blind at all. What had he said? *You're going to hell, see how many handouts you get down there.* "Have a very merry Christmas, sir, thank you for helping me."

And the day goes on.

4:25 P.M.

His sight has started to re-surface—dim, distant, but there. It is his cue to pack up and go.

He kneels, back ramrod-stiff, and lays his cane behind the case again. He bands the last of the bills, dumps them and the last coins into the bottom of the case, then puts the baseball glove and the tinsel-decorated sign inside. He latches the case and stands up, holding his cane in the other hand. Now the case is heavy, dragging at his arm with the dead weight of all that well-meant metal. There is a heavy rattling crunch as the coins avalanche into a new position, and then they are as still as ore plugged deep in the ground.

He sets off down Fifth, dangling the case at the end of his left arm like an anchor (after all these years he's used to the weight of it, could carry it much farther than he'll need to this afternoon, if circumstances demanded), holding the cane in his right hand and tapping it delicately on the paving in front of him. The cane is magic, opening a pocket of empty space before him on the crowded, jostling sidewalk in a teardrop-shaped wave. By the time he gets to Fifth and Forty-third, he can actually see this space. He can also see the DON'T WALK sign at Forty-second stop flashing and hold solid, but he keeps walking anyway, letting a well-dressed man with long hair and gold chains reach out and grasp his shoulder to stop him.

"Watch it, my man," the longhair says. "Traffic's on the way."

"Thank you, sir," Blind Willie says.

"Don't mention it—merry Christmas."

Blind Willie crosses, passes the lions standing sentry at the Public Library, and goes down two more blocks, where he turns toward

Sixth Avenue. No one accosts him; no one has loitered, watching him collect all day long, and then followed, waiting for the opportunity to bag the case and run (not that many thieves *could* run with it, not *this* case). Once, back in the summer of '79, two or three young guys, maybe black (he couldn't say for sure; they *sounded* black, but his vision had been slow returning that day, it was always slower in warm weather, when the days stayed bright longer), had accosted him and begun talking to him in a way he didn't quite like. It wasn't like the kids this afternoon, with their jokes about reading the waffle iron and what does a *Playboy* centerfold look like in Braille. It was softer than that, and in some weird fashion almost kind—questions about how much he took in by St. Pat's back there, and would he perchance be generous enough to make a contribution to something called the Polo Recreational League, and did he want a little protection getting to his bus stop or train station or whatever. One, perhaps a budding sexologist, had asked if he liked a little young pussy once in awhile. "It pep you up," the voice on his left said softly, almost longingly. "Yessir, you must believe *that* shit."

He had felt the way he imagined a mouse must feel when the cat is just pawing at it, claws not out yet, curious about what the mouse will do, and how fast it can run, and what sorts of noises it will make as its terror grows. Blind Willie had not been terrified, however. Scared, yes indeed, you could fairly say he had been scared, but he has not been out-and-out terrified since his last week in the green, the week that had begun in the A Shau Valley and ended in Dong Ha, the week the Viet Cong had harried them steadily west at what was not quite a full retreat, at the same time pinching them on both sides, driving them like cattle down a chute, always yelling from the trees, sometimes laughing from the jungle, sometimes shooting, sometimes screaming in the night. The little men who ain't there, Sullivan called them. There is nothing like them here, and his blindest day in Manhattan is not as dark as those nights after they lost the Captain. Knowing this had been his advantage and those young fellows' mistake. He had simply raised his voice, speaking as a man might speak to a large room filled with old friends. "Say!" he had exclaimed to the shadowy phantoms drifting slowly around him on the sidewalk. "Say, does anyone see a policeman? I believe these young fellows here mean to take me off." And that did it, easy as pulling a segment from a peeled orange; the young fellows bracketing him were suddenly gone like a cool breeze.

He only wishes he could solve the problem of Officer Wheelock that easily.

4:40 P.M.

The Sheraton Gotham, at Fortieth and Broadway, is one of the largest first-class hotels in the world, and in the cave of its lobby thousands of people school back and forth beneath the gigantic chandelier. They chase their pleasures here and dig their treasures there, oblivious to the Christmas music flowing from the speakers, to the chatter from three different restaurants and five bars, to the scenic elevators sliding up and down in their notched shafts like pistons powering some exotic glass engine . . . and to the blind man who taps among them, working his way toward a sarcophagal public men's room almost the size of a subway station. He walks with the sticker on the case turned inward now, and he is as anonymous as a blind man can be. In this city, that's very anonymous.

Still, he thinks as he enters one of the stalls and takes off his jacket, turning it inside-out as he does so, *how is it that in all these years no one has* ever *followed me? No one has* ever *noticed that the blind man who goes in and the sighted man who comes out are the same size, and carrying the same case?*

Well, in New York, hardly anyone notices anything that isn't his or her own business—in their own way, they are all as blind as Blind Willie. Out of their offices, flooding down the sidewalks, thronging in the subway stations and cheap restaurants, there is something both repulsive and sad about them; they are like nests of moles turned up by a farmer's harrow. He has seen this blindness over and over again, and he knows that it is one reason for his success . . . but surely not the only reason. They are not *all* moles, and he has been rolling the dice for a long time now. He takes precautions, of course he does, many of them, but there are still those moments (like now, sitting here with his pants down, unscrewing the white cane and stowing it back in his case) when he would be easy to catch, easy to rob, easy to expose. Wheelock is right about the *Post;* they would love him. They would hang him higher than Haman. They would never understand, never even *want* to understand, or hear his side of it. *What* side? And why has none of this ever happened?

Because of God, he believes. Because God is good. God is hard but God is good. He cannot bring himself to confess, but God seems to understand. Atonement and penance take time, but he has been given time. God has gone with him every step of the way.

In the stall, still between identities, he closes his eyes and prays—first giving his thanks, then making a request for guidance, then giving more thanks. He finishes as he always does, in a whisper only he and God can hear: "If I die in a combat zone, bag me up and ship me home. If I die in a state of sin, close Your eyes and take me in. Yeah. Amen."

He leaves the stall, leaves the bathroom, leaves the echoing confusion of the Sheraton Gotham, and no one walks up to him and says, "Excuse me, sir, but weren't you just blind?" No one looks at him twice as he walks out into the street, carrying the bulky case as if it weighed twenty pounds instead of a hundred. God takes care of him.

It has started to snow. He walks slowly through it, Willie Shearman again now, switching the case frequently from hand to hand, just one more tired guy at the end of the day. He continues to think about his inexplicable success as he goes. There's a verse from the Book of Matthew which he has committed to memory. *They be blind leaders of the blind,* it goes. *And if the blind lead the blind, both shall fall into the ditch.* Then there's the old saw that says in the kingdom of the blind, the one-eyed man is king. Is *he* the one-eyed man? God aside, has that been the *practical* secret of his success all these years?

Perhaps so, perhaps not. In any case, he *has* been protected . . . and in no case does he believe he can put God aside. God is in the picture.

God marked him in 1960, when he first helped Harry Doolin tease Carol and then helped Harry beat her. That occasion of sin has never left his mind. What happened in the grove of trees near Field B stands for everything else. He even has Bobby Garfield's glove to help him remember. Willie doesn't know where Bobby is these days and doesn't care. He kept track of Carol as long as he could, but Bobby doesn't matter. Bobby ceased to matter when he helped her. Willie saw him help her. He didn't dare come out and help her himself—he was afraid of what Harry might do to him, afraid of all the kids Harry might tell, afraid of being marked—but *Bobby* dared. Bobby helped her then, Bobby punished Harry Doolin later that summer, and by doing these things (probably just for doing the first of them), Bobby got well, Bobby got over. He did what Willie didn't dare to do, he rolled with it and got over, got well, and now Willie has to do all the rest. And that's a lot to do. Sorry is a full-time job and more. Why, even with three of him working at it, he can barely keep up.

Still, he can't say he lives in regret. Sometimes he thinks of the good thief, the one who joined Christ in Paradise that very night. Friday afternoon you're bleeding on Golgotha's stony hill; Friday night you're having tea and crumpets with the King. Sometimes someone kicks him, sometimes someone pushes him, sometimes he worries about being taken off. So what? Doesn't he stand for all those who can only stand in the shadows, watching while the damage is done? Doesn't he beg for them? Didn't he take Bobby's Alvin Dark–model baseball glove for them in 1960? He did. Gobless him, he did. And now they put their money in it as he stands eyeless outside the cathedral. He begs for them.

Sharon knows . . . exactly what *does* Sharon know? Some of it, yes. Just how much he can't say. Certainly enough to provide the tinsel; enough to tell him he looks nice in his Paul Stuart suit and blue Sulka tie; enough to wish him a good day and remind him to get the eggnog. It is enough. All is well in Willie's world except for Jasper Wheelock. What is he going to do about Jasper Wheelock?

Maybe I ought to follow you some night, Wheelock whispers in his ear as Willie shifts the increasingly heavy case from one hand to the other. Both arms ache now; he will be glad to reach his building. *See what you do. See who you turn into.*

What, exactly, is he going to do about Jasper the Police-Smurf? What *can* he do?

He doesn't know.

5:15 P.M.

The young panhandler in the dirty red sweatshirt is long gone, his place taken by yet another streetcorner Santa. Willie has no trouble recognizing the tubby young fellow currently dropping a dollar into Santa's pot.

"Hey, Ralphie!" he cries.

Ralph Williamson turns, his face lights up when he recognizes Willie, and he raises one gloved hand. It's snowing harder now; with the bright lights around him and Santa Claus beside him, Ralph looks like the central figure in a holiday greeting card. Or maybe a modern-day Bob Cratchit.

"Hey, Willie! How's it goin?"

"Like a house afire," Willie says, approaching Ralph with an easy grin on his face. He sets his case down with a grunt, feels in his pants pocket, finds a buck for Santa's pot. Probably just another crook, and his hat's a moth-eaten piece of shit, but what the hell.

"What you got in there?" Ralph asks, looking down at Willie's case as he fiddles with his scarf. "Sounds like you busted open some little kid's piggy bank."

"Nah, just heatin coils," Willie says. " 'Bout a damn thousand of em."

"You working right up until Christmas?"

"Yeah," he says, and suddenly has a glimmer of an idea about Wheelock. Just a twinkle, here and gone, but hey, it's a start. "Yeah, right up until Christmas. No rest for the wicked, you know."

Ralph's wide and pleasant face creases in a smile. "I doubt if you're very wicked."

Willie smiles back. "You don't know what evil lurks in the heart of the heatin-n-coolin man, Ralphie. I'll probably take a few days off after Christmas, though. I'm thinkin that might be a really good idea."

"Go south? Florida, maybe?"

"South?" Willie looks startled, then laughs. "Oh, no," he says. "Not *this* kid. I've got plenty to do around the house. A person's got to keep their house in order. Else it might come right down around their ears someday when the wind blows."

"I suppose." Ralph bundles the scarf higher around his ears. "See you tomorrow?"

"You bet," Willie says and holds out his gloved hand. "Gimme five."

Ralphie gives him five, then turns his hand over. His smile is shy but eager. "Give me ten, Willie."

Willie gives him ten. "How good is that, Ralphie-baby?"

The man's shy smile becomes a gleeful boy's grin. "So goddam good I gotta do it again!" he cries, and slaps Willie's hand with real authority.

Willie laughs. "You the man, Ralph. You get *over.*"

"You the man, too, Willie," Ralph replies, speaking with a prissy earnestness that's sort of funny. "Merry Christmas."

"Right back atcha."

He stands where he is for a moment, watching Ralph trudge off into the snow. Beside him, the streetcorner Santa rings his bell monotonously. Willie picks up his case and starts for the door of his building. Then something catches his eye, and he pauses.

"Your beard's on crooked," he says to the Santa. "If you want people to believe in you, fix your fuckin beard."

He goes inside.

5:25 P.M.

There's a big carton in the storage annex of Midtown Heating and Cooling. It's full of cloth bags, the sort banks use to hold loose coins.

Such bags usually have various banks' names printed on them, but these don't—Willie orders them direct from the company in Moundsville, West Virginia, that makes them.

He opens his case, quickly sets aside the rolls of bills (these he will carry home in his Mark Cross briefcase), then fills four bags with coins. In a far corner of the storage room is a battered old metal cabinet simply marked PARTS. Willie swings it open—there is no lock to contend with—and reveals another hundred or so coin-stuffed bags. A dozen times a year he and Sharon tour the midtown churches, pushing these bags through the contribution slots or hinged package-delivery doors when they will fit, simply leaving them by the door when they won't. The lion's share always goes to St. Pat's, where he spends his days wearing dark glasses and a sign.

But not *every* day, he thinks, now undressing. I don't have to be there *every* day, and he thinks again that maybe Bill, Willie, and Blind Willie Garfield will take the week after Christmas off. In that week there might be a way to handle Officer Wheelock. To make him go away. Except . . .

"I can't kill him," he says in a low, nagging voice. "I'll be fucked if I kill him." Only fucked isn't what he's worried about. *Damned* is what he's worried about. Killing was different in Vietnam, or seemed different, but this isn't Vietnam, isn't the green. Has he built these years of penance just to tear them down again? God is testing him, testing him, testing him. There is an answer here. He knows there is, there must be. He is just—ha-ha, pardon the pun—too blind to see it.

Can he even *find* the self-righteous son of a bitch? Shit yeah, that's not the problem. He can find Jasper the Police-Smurf, all right. Just about any old time he wants. Trail him right to wherever it is that he takes off his gun and his shoes and puts his feet up on the hassock. But then what?

He worries at this as he uses cold cream to remove his makeup, and then he puts his worries away. He takes the Nov–Dec ledger out of its drawer, sits at his desk, and for twenty minutes he writes *I am heartily sorry for hurting Carol.* He fills an entire page, top to bottom and margin to margin. He puts it back, then dresses in Bill Shearman's clothes. As he is putting away Blind Willie's boots, his eye falls on the scrapbook with its red leather cover. He takes it out, puts it on top of the file-cabinet, and flips back the cover with its single word—MEMORIES—stamped in gold.

On the first page is the certificate of a live birth—William Robert Shearman, born January 4th, 1946—and his tiny footprints. On the following pages are pictures of him with his mother, pictures of him with his father (Pat Shearman smiling as if he had never pushed his son over in his high chair or hit his wife with a beer bottle), pictures of him with his friends. Harry Doolin is particularly well represented. In one snapshot eight-year-old Harry is trying to eat a piece of Willie's birthday cake with a blindfold on (a forfeit in some game, no doubt). Harry's got chocolate smeared all over his cheeks, he's laughing and looks as if he doesn't have a mean thought in his head. Willie shivers at the sight of that laughing, smeary, blindfolded face. It almost always makes him shiver.

He flips away from it, toward the back of the book, where he's put the pictures and clippings of Carol Gerber he has collected over the years: Carol with her mother, Carol holding her brand-new baby brother and smiling nervously, Carol and her father (him in Navy dress blue and smoking a cigarette, her looking up at him with big wonderstruck eyes), Carol on the j.v. cheering squad at Harwich High her freshman year, caught in midleap with one hand waving a pom-pom and the other holding down her pleated skirt, Carol and John Sullivan on tinfoil thrones at Harwich High in 1965, the year they were elected Snow Queen and Snow King at the Junior-Senior prom. They look like a couple on a wedding cake, Willie thinks this every time he looks at the old yellow newsprint. Her gown is strapless, her shoulders flawless. There is no sign that for a little while, once upon a time, the left one was hideously deformed, sticking up in a witchlike double hump. She had cried before that last hit, cried plenty, but mere crying hadn't been enough for Harry Doolin. That last time he had swung from the heels, and the smack of the bat hitting her had been like the sound of a mallet hitting a half-thawed roast, and *then* she had screamed, screamed so loud that Harry had fled without even looking back to see if Willie and Richie O'Meara were following him. Took to his heels, had old Harry Doolin, ran like a jackrabbit. But if he hadn't? Suppose that, instead of running, Harry had said *Hold her, guys, I ain't listening to that, I'm going to shut her up,* meaning to swing from the heels again, this time at her head? *Would* they have held her? Would they have held her for him even then?

You know you would have, he thinks dully. *You do penance as much for what you were spared as for what you actually did. Don't you?*

Here's Carol Gerber in her graduation gown; *Spring 1966,* it's marked. On the next page is a news clipping from the Harwich *Journal* marked *Fall 1966.* The accompanying picture is her again, but this version of Carol seems a million years removed from the young lady in the graduation gown, the young lady with the diploma in her hand, the white pumps on her feet, and her eyes demurely downcast. This girl is fiery and smiling, these eyes look straight into the camera. She seems unaware of the blood coursing down her left cheek. She is flashing the peace sign. This girl is on her way to Danbury already, this girl has got her Danbury dancing shoes on. People died in Danbury, the guts flew, baby, and Willie does not doubt that he is partly responsible. He touches the fiery smiling bleeding girl with her sign that says STOP THE MURDER (only instead of stopping it she became a part of it) and knows that in the end her face is the only one that matters, her face is the spirit of the age. 1960 is smoke; here is fire. Here is Death with blood on her cheek and a smile on her lips and a sign in her hand. Here is that good old Danbury dementia.

The next clipping is the entire front page of the Danbury paper. He has folded it three times so it will fit in the book. The biggest of four photos shows a screaming woman standing in the middle of a street and holding up her bloody hands. Behind her is a brick building which has been cracked open like an egg. *Summer 1970,* he has written beside it.

6 DEAD, 14 INJURED IN DANBURY BOMB ATTACK

Radical Group Claims Responsibility

"No One Meant to Be Hurt," Female Caller Tells Police

The group—Militant Students for Peace, they called themselves—planted the bomb in a lecture hall on the Danbury UConn campus. On the day of the explosion, Coleman Chemicals was holding job interviews there between ten A.M. and four P.M. The bomb was apparently supposed to go off at six in the morning, when the building was empty. It failed to do so. At eight o'clock, then again at nine, someone (presumably someone from the MSP) called Campus Security and reported the presence of a bomb in the first-floor lecture hall. There were cursory searches and no evacuation. "This was our eighty-third bomb-threat of the year," an unidentified Campus Security officer was quoted as saying. No bomb was found, although the MSP later claimed vehemently that the exact location—the air-conditioning duct on the left side of the hall—had been given. There was evidence (persuasive evidence, to Willie Shearman if to no one else) that at quarter past noon, while the job interviews were in recess for lunch, a young woman made an effort—at considerable risk to her own life and limb—to retrieve the UXB herself. She spent perhaps ten minutes in the then-vacant lecture hall before being led away, protesting, by a young man with long black hair. The janitor who saw them later identified the man as Raymond Fiegler, head of the MSP. He identified the young woman as Carol Gerber.

At ten minutes to two that afternoon, the bomb finally went off. Gobless the living; gobless the dead.

Willie turns the page. Here is a headline from the Oklahoma City *Oklahoman*. April of 1971.

3 RADICALS KILLED IN ROADBLOCK SHOOTOUT
"Big Fish" May Have Escaped by Minutes,
Says FBI SAC Thurman

The big fish were John and Sally McBride, Charlie "Duck" Golden, the elusive Raymond Fiegler . . . and Carol. The remaining members of the MSP, in other words. The McBrides and Golden died in Los Angeles six months later, someone in the house still shooting and tossing grenades even as the place burned down. Neither Fiegler nor Carol was in the burned-out shell, but the police techs found large quantities of spilled blood which had been typed AB Positive. A rare blood-type. Carol Gerber's blood-type.

Dead or alive? Alive or dead? Not a day goes by that Willie doesn't ask himself this question.

He turns to the next page of the scrapbook, knowing he should stop, he should get home, Sharon will worry if he doesn't at least call (he *will* call, from downstairs he will call, she's right, he's very dependable), but he doesn't stop just yet.

The headline over the photo showing the charred skull of the house on Benefit Street is from the Los Angeles *Times:*

3 OF "DANBURY 12" DIE IN EAST L.A.
Police Speculate Murder-Suicide Pact
Only Fiegler, Gerber Unaccounted For

Except the cops believed Carol, at least, was dead. The piece made that clear. At the time, Willie had also been convinced it was so. All that blood. Now, however . . .

Dead or alive? Alive or dead? Sometimes his heart whispers to him that the blood doesn't matter, that she got away from that small frame house long before the final acts of insanity were committed there. At other times he believes what the police believe—that she and Fiegler slipped away from the others only after the first shootout, before the house was surrounded; that she either died of wounds suffered in that shootout or was murdered by Fiegler because she was slowing him down. According to this scenario the fiery girl with the blood on her face and the sign in her hand is probably now just a bag of bones cooking in the desert someplace east of the sun and west of Tonopah.

Willie touches the photo of the burned-out house on Benefit Street . . . and suddenly a name comes to him, the name of the man who maybe stopped Dong Ha from becoming another My Lai or My Khe. Slocum. That was his name, all right. It's as if the blackened beams and broken windows have whispered it to him.

Willie closes the scrapbook and puts it away, feeling at peace. He finishes squaring up what needs to be squared up in the offices of Midtown Heating and Cooling, then steps carefully through the trapdoor and finds his footing on top of the stepladder below. He takes the handle of his briefcase and pulls it through. He descends to the third step, then lowers the trapdoor into place and slides the ceiling panel back where it belongs.

He cannot do anything . . . anything *permanent* . . . to Officer Jasper Wheelock . . . but Slocum could. Yes indeed, *Slocum* could. Of course Slocum was black, but what of that? In the dark, all cats are gray . . . and to the blind, they're no color at all. Is it really much of a reach from Blind Willie Garfield to Blind Willie Slocum? Of course not. Easy as breathing, really.

"Do you hear what I hear," he sings softly as he folds the stepladder and puts it back, "do you smell what I smell, do you taste what I taste?"

Five minutes later he closes the door of Western States Land Analysts firmly behind him and triple-locks it. Then he goes down the hallway. When the elevator comes and he steps in, he thinks, *Eggnog. Don't forget. The Allens and the Dubrays.*

"Also cinnamon," he says out loud. The three people in the elevator car with him look around, and Bill grins self-consciously.

Outside, he turns toward Grand Central, registering only one thought as the snow beats full into his face and he flips up his coat collar: the Santa outside the building has fixed his beard.

MIDNIGHT

"Share?"

"Hmmmm?"

Her voice is sleepy, distant. They have made long, slow love after the Dubrays finally left at eleven o'clock, and now she is drifting away. That's all right; he is drifting too. He has a feeling that all of his problems are solving themselves . . . or that God is solving them.

"I may take a week or so off after Christmas. Do some inventory. Poke around some new sites. I'm thinking about changing locations." There is no need for her to know about what Willie Slocum may be doing in the week before New Year's; she couldn't do anything but worry and—perhaps, perhaps not, he sees no reason to find out for sure—feel guilty.

"Good," she says. "See a few movies while you're at it, why don't you?" Her hand gropes out of the dark and touches his arm briefly. "You work so hard." Pause. "Also, you remembered the eggnog. I really didn't think you would. I'm very pleased with you, sweetheart."

He grins in the dark at that, helpless not to. It is so perfectly Sharon.

"The Allens are all right, but the Dubrays are boring, aren't they?" she asks.

"A little," he allows.

"If that dress of hers had been cut any lower, she could have gotten a job in a topless bar."

He says nothing to that, but grins again.

"It was good tonight, wasn't it?" she asks him. It's not their little party that she's talking about.

"Yes, excellent."

"Did you have a good day? I didn't have a chance to ask."

"Fine day, Share."

"I love you, Bill."

"Love you, too."

"Goodnight."

"Goodnight."

As he drifts toward sleep he thinks about the man in the bright red ski sweater. He crosses over without knowing it, thought melting effortlessly into dream. "Sixty-nine and seventy were the hard years," the man in the red sweater says. "I was at Hamburger Hill with the 3/187. We lost a lot of good men." Then he brightens. "But I got this." From the lefthand pocket of his topcoat he takes a white beard hanging on a string. "And this." From the righthand pocket he takes a crumpled styrofoam cup, which he shakes. A few loose coins rattle in the bottom like teeth. "So you see," he says, fading now, "there are compensations for even the blindest life."

Then the dream itself fades and Bill Shearman sleeps deeply until six-fifteen the next morning, when the clock-radio wakes him to the sound of "The Little Drummer Boy."

1999: When someone dies, you think about the past.

1999

Why We're in Vietnam

When someone dies, you think about the past. Sully had probably known this for years, but it was only on the day of Pags's funeral that it formed in his mind as a conscious postulate.

It was twenty-six years since the helicopters took their last loads of refugees (some dangling photogenically from the landing skids) off the roof of the U.S. embassy in Saigon and almost thirty since a Huey evacked John Sullivan, Willie Shearman, and maybe a dozen others out of Dong Ha Province. Sully-John and his magically refound childhood acquaintance had been heroes that morning when the choppers fell out of the sky; they'd been something else come afternoon. Sully could remember lying there on the Huey's throbbing floor and screaming for someone to kill him. He could remember Willie screaming as well. *I'm blind* was what Willie had been screaming. *Ah Jesus-fuck, I'm blind!*

Eventually it had become clear to him—even with some of his guts hanging out of his belly in gray ropes and most of his balls blown off—that no one was going to do what he asked and he wasn't going to be able to do the job on his own. Not soon enough to suit him, anyway. So he asked someone to get rid of the *mamasan,* they could do that much, couldn't they? Land her or just dump her the fuck out, why not? Wasn't she dead already? Thing was, she wouldn't stop *looking* at him, and enough was enough.

By the time they swapped him and Shearman and half a dozen others—the worst ones—to a Medevac at the rally-point everyone called Peepee City (the chopper-jockeys were probably damned glad to see them go, all that screaming), Sully had started to realize none of the others could see old *mamasan* squatting there in the cockpit, old white-haired *mamasan* in the green pants and orange top and those weird bright Chinese sneakers, the ones that looked like Chuck

Taylor hightops, bright red, wow. Old *mamasan* had been Malenfant's date, old Mr. Card-Shark's big date. Earlier that day Malenfant had run into the clearing along with Sully and Dieffenbaker and Sly Slocum and the others, never mind the gooks firing at them out of the bush, never mind the terrible week of mortars and snipers and ambushes, Malenfant had been hero-bound and Sully had been hero-bound too, and now oh hey look at this, Ronnie Malenfant was a murderer, the kid Sully had been so afraid of back in the old days had saved his life and been blinded, and Sully himself was lying on the floor of a helicopter with his guts waving in the breeze. As Art Linkletter always said, it just proved that people are funny.

Somebody kill me, he had screamed on that bright and terrible afternoon. *Somebody shoot me, for the love of God just let me die.*

But he hadn't died, the doctors had managed to save one of his mangled testicles, and now there were even days when he felt more or less glad to be alive. Sunsets made him feel that way. He liked to go out to the back of the lot, where the cars they'd taken in trade but hadn't yet fixed up were stored, and stand there watching the sun go down. Corny shit, granted, but it was still the good part.

In San Francisco Willie was on the same ward and visited him a lot until the Army in its wisdom sent First Lieutenant Shearman somewhere else; they had talked for hours about the old days in Harwich and people they knew in common. Once they'd even gotten their picture taken by an AP news photographer—Willie sitting on Sully's bed, both of them laughing. Willie's eyes had been better by then but still not right; Willie had confided to Sully that he was afraid they never *would* be right. The story that went with the picture had been pretty dopey, but had it brought them letters? Holy Christ! More than either of them could read! Sully had even gotten the crazy idea that he might hear from Carol, but of course he never did. It was the spring of 1970 and Carol Gerber was undoubtedly busy smoking pot and giving blowjobs to end-the-war hippies while her old high-school boyfriend was getting his balls blown off on the other side of the world. That's right, Art, people are funny. Also, kids say the darndest things.

When Willie shipped out, old *mamasan* stayed. Old *mamasan* hung right in there. During the seven months Sully spent in San Francisco's Veterans Hospital she had come every day and every night, his most constant visitor in that endless time when the whole world seemed to smell of piss and his heart hurt like a headache. Sometimes she showed up in a *muumuu* like the hostess at some nutty *luau,* sometimes she came wearing one of those grisly green golf-skirts and a sleeveless top that showed off her scrawny arms . . . but mostly she wore what she had been wearing on the day Malenfant killed her—the green pants, the orange smock, the red sneakers with the Chinese symbols on them.

One day that summer he unfolded the San Francisco *Chronicle* and saw his old girlfriend had made the front page. His old girlfriend and her hippie pals had killed a bunch of kids and job-recruiters back in Danbury. His old girlfriend was now "Red Carol." His old girlfriend was a celebrity. "You cunt," he had said as the paper first doubled, then trebled, then broke up into prisms. "You stupid fucked-up *cunt.*" He had balled the paper up, meaning to throw it across the room, and there was his *new* girlfriend, there was old *mamasan* sitting on the next bed, looking at Sully with her black eyes, and Sully had broken down completely at the sight of her. When the nurse came Sully either couldn't or wouldn't tell her what he was crying about. All he knew was that the world had gone insane and he wanted a shot and eventually the nurse found a doctor to give him one and the last thing he saw before he passed out was *mamasan,* old fuckin *mamasan* sitting there on the next bed with her yellow hands in her green polyester lap, sitting there and watching him.

She made the trip across the country with him, too, had come all the way back to Connecticut with him, deadheading across the aisle in the tourist cabin of a United Airlines 747. She sat next to a businessman who saw her no more than the crew of the Huey had, or Willie Shearman, or the staff at the Pussy Palace. She had been Malenfant's date in Dong Ha, but she was John Sullivan's date now and never took her black eyes off him. Her yellow, wrinkled fingers always stayed folded in her lap and her eyes always stayed on him.

Thirty years. Man, that was a long time.

But as those years went by, Sully had seen her less and less. When he returned to Harwich in the fall of '70, he still saw old *mamasan* just about every day—eating a hotdog in Commonwealth Park by Field B, or standing at the foot of the iron steps leading up to the railway station where the commuters ebbed and flowed, or just walking down Main Street. Always looking at him.

Once, not long after he'd gotten his first post-Vietnam job (selling cars, of course; it was the only thing he really knew how to do) he had seen old *mamasan* sitting in the passenger seat of a 1968 Ford LTD with PRICED TO SELL! soaped on the windshield.

You'll start to understand her in time, the headshrinker in San Francisco had told him, and refused to say much more no matter how hard Sully pressed him. The shrink wanted to hear about the helicopters that had collided and fell out of the sky; the headshrinker wanted to know why Sully so often referred to Malenfant as "that cardplaying bastard" (Sully wouldn't tell him); the headshrinker wanted to know if Sully still had sexual fantasies, and if so, had they become noticeably violent. Sully had sort of liked the guy—Conroy, his name was—but that didn't change the fact that he was an asshole. Once, near the end of his time in San Francisco, he had come close to telling Dr. Conroy about Carol. On the whole he was glad he hadn't. He didn't know how to *think* about his old girlfriend, let alone talk about her (*conflicted* was Conroy's word for this state). He had called her a stupid fucked-up cunt, but the whole damn world was sort of fucked-up these days, wasn't it? And if anyone knew how easily violent behavior could break its leash and just run away, John Sullivan did. All he was sure of was that he hoped the police wouldn't kill her when they finally caught up to her and her friends.

Asshole or not, Dr. Conroy hadn't been entirely wrong about Sully coming to understand old *mamasan* as time went by. The most important thing was understanding—on a gut level—that old *mamasan* wasn't there. Head-knowledge of that basic fact was easy, but his gut was slower to learn, possibly because his gut had been torn open in Dong Ha and a thing like that just had to slow the understanding process down.

He had borrowed some of Dr. Conroy's books, and the hospital librarian had gotten him a couple of others on inter-library loan. According to the books, old *mamasan* in her green pants and orange top was "an externalized fantasy" which served as a "coping mechanism" to help him deal with his "survivor guilt" and "post-traumatic stress syndrome." She was a daydream, in other words.

Whatever the reasons, his attitude about her changed as her appearances became less frequent. Instead of feeling revulsion or a kind of superstitious dread when she turned up, he began to feel almost happy when he saw her. The way you felt when you saw an old friend who had left town but sometimes came back for a little visit.

He lived in Milford now, a town about twenty miles north of Harwich on I-95 and light-years away in most other senses. Harwich had been a pleasant, tree-filled suburb when Sully lived there as a kid, chumming with Bobby Garfield and Carol Gerber. Now his old home town was one of those places you didn't go at night, just a grimy adjunct to Bridgeport. He still spent most of his days there, on the lot or in his office (Sullivan Chevrolet had been a Gold Star dealership four years running now), but he was gone by six o'clock most evenings, seven for sure, tooling north to Milford in his Caprice demonstrator. He usually went with an unacknowledged but very real sense of gratitude.

On this particular summer day he had gone south from Milford on I-95 as usual, but at a later hour and without getting off at Exit 9, ASHER AVENUE HARWICH. Today he had kept the new demo pointed south (it was blue with blackwall tires, and watching people's brakelights go on when they saw him in their rearview mirrors never failed to amuse him—they thought he was a cop) and drove all the way into New York City.

He left the car at Arnie Mossberg's dealership on the West Side (when you were a Chevy dealer there was never a parking problem; that was one of the nice things about it), did some window-shopping on his way across town, had a steak at Palm Too, then went to Pagano's funeral.

Pags had been one of the guys at the chopper crash-site that morning, one of the guys in the 'ville that afternoon. Also one of the guys caught in the final ambush on the trail, the ambush which had begun when Sully himself either stepped on a mine or broke a wire and popped a satchel-charge strapped to a tree. The little men in the black pajamas had been in the high toolies and man, they had opened up. On the trail, Pags had grabbed Wollensky when Wollensky got shot in the throat. He got Wollensky into the clearing, but by then Wollensky was dead. Pags would have been covered with Wollensky's blood (Sullivan didn't actually remember seeing that; he had been in his own hell by then), but that was probably something of a relief to the man because it covered up the other blood, still not entirely dry. Pagano had been standing close enough to get splattered when Slocum shot Malenfant's buddy. Splattered with Clemson's blood, splattered with Clemson's brains.

Sully had never said a word about what happened to Clemson in the 'ville, not to Dr. Conroy or anyone else. He had dummied up. All of them had dummied up.

Pags had died of cancer. Whenever one of Sully's old Nam buddies died (well okay, they weren't *buddies,* exactly, most of them dumb as stone boats and not what Sully would really call *buddies,* but it was the word they used because there was no word invented for what they had really been to each other), it always seemed to be cancer or drugs or suicide. Usually the cancer started in the lung or the brain and then just ran everywhere, as if these men had left their immune systems back in the green. With Dick Pagano it had been pancreatic cancer—him and Michael Landon. It was the disease of the stars. The coffin was open and old Pags didn't look too shabby. His wife had had the undertaker dress him in an ordinary business suit, not a uniform. She probably hadn't even considered the uniform option, despite the decorations Pagano had won. Pags had worn a uniform for only two or three years, those years like an aberration, like time spent in some county joint because you did something entirely out of character on one bad-luck occasion, probably while you were drunk. Killed a guy in a barroom fight, say, or took it into your head to burn down the church where your ex-wife taught Sunday school. Sully couldn't think of a single man he'd served with, including himself, who would want to be buried in an Army uniform.

Dieffenbaker—Sully still thought of him as the new lieutenant—came to the funeral. Sully hadn't seen Dieffenbaker in a long time, and they had had themselves quite a talk . . . although Dieffenbaker actually did most of the talking. Sully wasn't sure talking ever made a difference, but he kept thinking about the stuff Dieffenbaker said. How *mad* Dieffenbaker had sounded, mostly. All the way back to Connecticut he kept thinking about it.

He was on the Triborough Bridge heading north again by two o'clock, in plenty of time to beat the rush-hour traffic. "Smooth movement across the Triborough and at key points along the LIE," was how the traffic-reporter in the WINS copter put it. That's what copters were for these days; gauging the flow of traffic in and out of America's cities.

When the traffic started to slow just north of Bridgeport, Sully didn't notice. He had switched from news to oldies and had fallen to thinking about Pags and his harmonicas. It was a war-movie cliché, the grizzled G.I. with the mouth-harp, but Pagano, dear God, Pagano could drive you out of your ever-fuckin mind. Night and day he had played em, until one of the guys—it might have been Hexley or even Garrett Slocum—told him that if he didn't quit it, he was apt to wake up one morning with the world's first whistling rectal implant.

The more he considered it, the more Sully thought Sly Slocum had been the one to threaten the rectal implant. Big black man from Tulsa, thought Sly and the Family Stone was the best group on earth, hence the nickname, and refused to believe that another group he admired, Rare Earth, was white. Sully remembered Deef (this was before Dieffenbaker became the new lieutenant and gave Slocum that nod, probably the most important gesture Dieffenbaker had ever made or ever would make in his life) telling Slocum that those guys were just as white as fuckin Bob Dylan ("the folksingin honky" was what Slocum called Dylan). Slocum thought this over, then replied with what was for him rare gravity. *The fuck you say. Rare*

Earth, man, those guys black. They record on fuckin Motown, and all Motown groups are black, everyone know that. Supremes, fuckin Temps, Smokey Robinson and the Miracles. I respect you, Deef, you bad and you nationwide, without a doubt, man, but if you persist in your bullshit, I going to knock you down.

Slocum hated harmonica music. Harmonica music made him think of the folksingin honky. If you tried to tell him that Dylan cared about the war, Slocum asked then how come the mulebray muthafucka didn't come on over here with Bob Hope one time. *I tell you why,* Slocum said. *He scared, that's why. Fuckin candyass harmonica-blowin mulebray muthafucka!*

Musing on Dieffenbaker rapping about the sixties. Thinking of those old names and old faces and old days. Not noticing as the Caprice's speedometer dropped from sixty to fifty to forty, the traffic starting to stack up in all four northbound lanes. He remembered how Pags had been over there in the green—skinny, black-haired, his cheeks still dotted with the last of his post-adolescent acne, a rifle in his hands and two Hohner harmonicas (one key of C, one key of G) stuffed into the waistband of his camo trousers. Thirty years ago, that had been. Roll back ten more and Sully was a kid growing up in Harwich, palling with Bobby Garfield and wishing that Carol Gerber would look at him, John Sullivan, just once the way she always looked at Bobby.

In time she *had* looked at him of course, but never in quite the same way. Was it because she was no longer eleven or because he wasn't Bobby? Sully didn't know. The look itself had been a mystery. It seemed to say that Bobby was killing her and she was glad, she would die that way until the stars fell from the sky and the rivers ran uphill and all the words to "Louie Louie" were known.

What had happened to Bobby Garfield? Had he gone to Vietnam? Joined the flower children? Married, fathered children, died of pancreatic cancer? Sully didn't know. All he knew for sure was that Bobby had changed somehow in the summer of 1960—the summer Sully had won a free week at the YMCA camp on Lake George—and had left town with his mother. Carol had stayed through high school, and even if she had never looked at him quite the way she had looked at Bobby, he had been her first, and she his. One night out in the country behind some Newburg dairy-farmer's barnful of lowing cattle. Sully remembered smelling sweet perfume on her throat as he came.

Why that odd cross-connection between Pagano in his coffin and the friends of his childhood? Perhaps because Pags had looked a little bit like Bobby had looked in those bygone days. Bobby's hair had been dark red instead of black, but he'd had that same skinny build and angular face . . . and the same freckles. Yeah! Both Pags and Bobby with that Opie Taylor spray of freckles across the cheeks and the bridge of the nose! Or maybe it was just because when someone dies, you think about the past, the past, the fuckin past.

Now the Caprice was down to twenty miles an hour and the traffic stopped dead farther up, just shy of Exit 9, but Sully still didn't notice. On WKND, the oldies station, ? and The Mysterians were singing "96 Tears" and he was thinking about walking down the center aisle of the chapel with Dieffenbaker in front of him, walking up to the coffin for his first look at Pagano while the canned hymns played. "Abide with Me" was the current ditty wafting through the air above Pagano's corpse—Pags, who had been perfectly happy to sit for hours with the .50-caliber propped up beside him and his pack on his lap and a deck of Winstons parked in the strap of his helmet, playing "Goin' Up the Country" over and over again.

Any resemblance to Bobby Garfield was long gone, Sully saw as he looked into the coffin. The mortician had done a job good enough to justify the open coffin, but Pags still had the loose-skinned, sharp-chinned look of a fat man who has spent his final months on the Cancer Diet, the one they never write up in the *National Enquirer,* the one that consists of radiation, injected chemical poisons, and all the potato chips you want.

"Remember the harmonicas?" Dieffenbaker asked.

"I remember," Sully said. "I remember everything." It came out sounding weird, and Dieffenbaker glanced at him.

Sully had a clear, fierce flash of how Deef had looked on that day in the 'ville when Malenfant, Clemson, and those other nimrods had all of a sudden started paying off the morning's terror . . . the whole last week's terror. They wanted to put it somewhere, the howls in the night and the sudden mortar-shots and finally the burning copters that had fallen with their rotors still turning, dispersing the smoke of their own deaths as they dropped. Down they came, whacko! And the little men in the black pajamas were shooting at Delta two-two and Bravo two-one from the bush just as soon as the Americans ran out into the clearing. Sully had run with Willie Shearman beside him on the right and Lieutenant Packer in front of him; then Lieutenant Packer took a round in the face and no one was in front of him. Ronnie Malenfant was on his left and Malenfant had been yelling in his high-pitched voice, on and on and on, he was like some mad high-pressure telephone salesman gourded out on amphetamines: *Come on, you fuckin ringmeats! Come on, you slopey Joes! Shoot me, ya fucks! You fuckin fucks! Can't shoot fa shit!* Pagano was behind them, and Slocum was beside Pags. Some Bravo guys but mostly Delta boys, that was his memory. Willie Shearman yelled for his own guys, but a lot of them hung back. Delta two-two didn't hang back. Clemson was there, and Wollensky, and Hackermeyer, and it was amazing how he could remember their names; their names and the smell of that day. The smell of the green and the smell of the kerosene. The sight of the sky, blue on green, and oh man how they would shoot, how those little fuckers would *shoot,* you never forgot how they would shoot or the feel of a round passing close beside you, and Malenfant was screaming *Shoot me, ya deadass ringmeats! Can't! Fuckin blind! Come on, I'm right here! Fuckin blindeye homo slopehead assholes, I'm right here!* And the men in the downed helicopters were screaming, so they pulled them out, got the foam on the fire and pulled them out, only they weren't men anymore, not what you'd call men, they were screaming TV dinners for the most part, TV dinners with eyes and belt-buckles and these clittery reaching fingers with smoke rising from the melted nails, yeah, like that, not stuff you could tell people like Dr. Conroy, how when you pulled them parts of them came off, kind of *slid* off the way the baked skin of a freshly cooked turkey will slide along the hot liquefied fat just beneath, like that, and all the time you're smelling the green and the kerosene, it's all happening, it's a rilly rilly big shew, as

Ed Sullivan used to say, and it's all happening on *our* stage, and all you can do is roll with it, try to get over.

That was the morning, that was the helicopters, and something like that had to go *somewhere.* When they got to the shitty little 'ville that afternoon they still had the stink of charred helicopter crewmembers in their noses, the old lieutenant was dead, and some of the men—Ronnie Malenfant and his friends, if you wanted to get right down to particulars—had gone a little bughouse. Dieffenbaker was the new lieutenant, and all at once he had found himself in charge of crazy men who wanted to kill everyone they saw—children, old men, old *mamasans* in red Chinese sneakers.

The copters crashed at ten. At approximately two-oh-five, Ronnie Malenfant first stuck his bayonet into the old woman's stomach and then announced his intention of cutting off the fuckin pig's head. At approximately four-fifteen, less than four klicks away, the world blew up in John Sullivan's face. That had been his big day in Dong Ha Province, his rilly big shew.

Standing there between two shacks at the head of the 'ville's single street, Dieffenbaker had looked like a scared sixteen-year-old kid. But he hadn't been sixteen, he'd been twenty-five, years older than Sully and most of the others. The only other man there of Deef's age and rank was Willie Shearman, and Willie seemed reluctant to step in. Perhaps the rescue operation that morning had exhausted him. Or perhaps he had noticed that once again it was the Delta two-two boys who were leading the charge. Malenfant was screaming that when the fuckin slopehead Cong saw a few dozen heads up on sticks, they'd think twice about fucking with Delta Lightning. On and on in that shrill, drilling phone salesman's voice of his. The cardplayer. Mr. Card-Shark. Pags had his harmonicas; Malenfant had his deck of fuckin Bikes. Hearts, that was Malenfant's game. A dime a point if he could get it, nickel a point if he couldn't. *Come on, boys!* he'd yell in that shrill voice of his, a voice Sully swore could cause nosebleeds and kill locusts on the wing. *Come on, pony up, we huntin The Bitch!*

Sully remembered standing in the street and looking at the new lieutenant's pale, exhausted, confused face. He remembered thinking, *He can't do it. Whatever needs to be done to stop this before it really gets going, he can't do it.* But then Dieffenbaker got it together and gave Sly Slocum the nod. Slocum didn't hesitate a moment. Slocum, standing there in the street beside an overturned kitchen chair with chrome legs and a red seat, had shouldered his rifle, sighted in, and blown Ralph Clemson's head clean off. Pagano, standing nearby and gaping at Malenfant, hardly seemed aware that he had been splattered pretty much from head to toe. Clemson fell dead in the street and that stopped the party. Game over, baby.

These days Dieffenbaker had a substantial golf-gut and wore bifocals. Also, he'd lost most of his hair. Sully was amazed at this, because Deef had had a pretty full head of it five years ago, at the unit's reunion on the Jersey shore. That was the last time, Sully had vowed to himself, that he would party with those guys. They didn't get better. They didn't fuckin mellow. Each reunion was more like the cast of *Seinfeld* on a really mean batch of crank.

"Want to come outside and have a smoke?" the new lieutenant asked. "Or did you give that up when everyone else did?"

"Gave it up like everyone else, that's affirmative." They had been standing a little to the left of the coffin by then so the rest of the mourners could get a look and then get past them. Talking in low tones, the taped music rolling easily over their voices, the draggy salvation soundtrack. The current tune was "The Old Rugged Cross," Sully believed.

He said, "I think Pags would've preferred—"

"'Goin' Up the Country' or 'Let's Work Together,'" Dieffenbaker finished, grinning.

Sully grinned back. It was one of those unexpected moments, like a brief sunny break in a day-long spell of rain, when it was okay to remember something—one of those moments when you were, amazingly, almost glad you had been there. "Or maybe 'Boom Boom,' that one by The Animals," he said.

"Remember Sly Slocum telling Pags he'd stuff that harmonica up his ass if Pags didn't give it a rest?"

Sully had nodded, still grinning. "Said if he shoved it up there far enough, Pags could play 'Red River Valley' when he farted." He had glanced fondly back at the coffin, as if expecting Pagano would also be grinning at the memory. Pagano wasn't. Pagano was just lying there with makeup on his face. Pagano had gotten over. "Tell you what—I'll come outside and watch *you* smoke."

"Done deal." Dieffenbaker, who had once given the okay for one of his soldiers to kill another of his soldiers, had started up the chapel's side aisle, his bald head lighting up with mixed colors as he passed beneath each stained-glass window. Limping after him—he had been limping over half his life now and never noticed anymore—came John Sullivan, Gold Star Chevrolet dealer.

The traffic on I-95 slowed to a crawl and then came to a complete stop, except for the occasional forward twitch in one of the lanes. On the radio ? and The Mysterians had given way to Sly and the Family Stone—"Dance to the Music." Fuckin Slocum would have been seat-bopping for sure, seat-bopping to the max. Sully put the Caprice demonstrator in Park and tapped in time on the steering wheel.

As the song began to wind down he looked to his right and there was old *mamasan* in the shotgun seat, not seat-bopping but just sitting there with her yellow hands folded in her lap and her crazy-bright sneakers, those Chuck Taylor knockoffs, planted on the disposable plastic floormat with SULLIVAN CHEVROLET APPRECIATES YOUR BUSINESS printed on it.

"Hello, you old bitch," Sully said, pleased rather than disturbed. When was the last time she'd shown her face? The Tacklins' New Year's Eve party, perhaps, the last time Sully had gotten really drunk. "Why weren't you at Pags's funeral? The new lieutenant asked after you."

She made no reply, but hey, when did she ever? She only sat there with her hands folded and her black eyes on him, a Halloween vision in green and orange and red. Old *mamasan* was like no ghost in a Hollywood movie, though; you couldn't see through her, she never changed her shape, never faded away. She wore a woven piece of twine on one scrawny yellow wrist like a junior-high-school kid's friendship bracelet. And although you could see every twist of the twine and every wrinkle on her ancient face, you couldn't smell her and the one time Sully tried to touch her she had disappeared on him. She was a ghost and his head was the haunted house she lived in. Only every now and then (usually without pain and always without warning), his head would vomit her out where he had to look at her.

She didn't change. She never went bald or got gallstones or needed bifocals. She didn't die as Clemson and Pags and Packer and the guys in the crashed helicopters had died (even the two they had taken from the clearing covered in foam like snowmen had died, they were too badly burned to live and it had all been for nothing). She didn't disappear as Carol had done, either. No, old *mamasan* continued to pop in for the occasional visit, and she hadn't changed a bit since the days when "Instant Karma" was a top-ten hit. She had to die once, that was true, had to lie there in the mud while Malenfant first drove his bayonet into her belly and then announced his intention of removing her head, but since then she had been absolutely cruisin.

"Where you been, darlin?" If anyone in another car happened to look over (his Caprice was surrounded on all four sides now, boxed in) and saw his lips moving, they'd just assume he was singing along with the radio. Even if they thought anything else, who gave a fuck? Who gave a fuck what any of them thought? He had seen things, *terrible* things, not the least of them a roll of his own intestines lying in the bloody mat of his pubic hair, and if he sometimes saw this old ghost (and talked to her), so fuckin what? Whose business was it but his own?

Sully looked up the road, trying to spy what had plugged the traffic (he couldn't, you never could, you just had to wait and creep forward a little when the guy in front of you crept forward), and then looked back. Sometimes when he did that she was gone. Not this time; this time she had just changed her clothes. The red sneaks were the same but now she was wearing a nurse's uniform: white nylon pants, white blouse (with a small gold watch pinned to it, what a nice touch), white cap with a little black stripe. Her hands were still folded in her lap, though, and she was still looking at him.

"Where you been, Mama? I missed you. I know that's weird but it's true. Mama, you been on my mind. You should have seen the new lieutenant. Really, it's amazing. He's entered the solar sex-panel phase. Totally bald on top, I mean *shiny.*"

Old *mamasan* said nothing. Sully wasn't surprised.

There was an alley beside the funeral parlor with a green-painted bench placed against one side. At either end of the bench was a butt-studded bucket of sand. Dieffenbaker sat beside one of the buckets, stuck a cigarette in his mouth (it was a Dunhill, Sully observed, pretty impressive), then offered the pack to Sully.

"No, I really quit."

"Excellent." Dieffenbaker lit up with a Zippo, and Sully realized an odd thing: he had never seen anyone who'd been in Vietnam light his cigarette with matches or those disposable butane lighters; Nam vets all seemed to carry Zippos. Of course that couldn't really be true. Could it?

"You've still got quite a limp on you," Dieffenbaker said.

"Yeah."

"On the whole, I'd call it an improvement. The last time I saw you it was almost a lurch. Especially after you got a couple of drinks down the hatch."

"You still go to the reunions? Do they still *have* them, the picnics and shit?"

"I think they still have them, but I haven't been in three years. Got too depressing."

"Yeah. The ones who don't have cancer are raving alcoholics. The ones who have managed to kick the booze are on Prozac."

"You noticed."

"Fucking yeah I noticed."

"I guess I'm not surprised. You were never the smartest guy in the world, Sully-John, but you were a perceptive son of a bitch. Even back then. Anyway, you nailed it—booze, cancer, and depression, those're the main problems, it seems like. Oh, and teeth. I never met a Vietnam vet who wasn't having the veriest shitpull with his teeth

. . . if he has any left, that is. What about you, Sully? How's the old toofers?"

Sully, who'd had six out since Vietnam (plus root canals almost beyond numbering), wiggled his hand from side to side in a *comme ci, comme ça* gesture.

"And the other problem?" Dieffenbaker asked. "How's that?"

"Depends," Sully said.

"On what?"

"On what I described as my problem. We were at three of those fuckin reunion picnics together—"

"Four. There was also at least one I went to that you didn't. The year after the one on the Jersey shore? That was the one where Andy Hackermeyer said he was going to kill himself by jumping from the top of the Statue of Liberty."

"Did he ever do it?"

Dieffenbaker dragged deeply on his cigarette and gave Sully what was still a Lieutenant Look. Even after all these years he could muster that up. Sort of amazing. "If he'd done it, you would have read about it in the *Post.* Don't you read the *Post*?"

"Religiously."

Dieffenbaker nodded. "Vietnam vets all have trouble with their teeth and they all read the *Post.* If they're in the *Post*'s fallout area, that is. What do you suppose they do if they're not?"

"Listen to Paul Harvey," Sully said promptly, and Dieffenbaker laughed.

Sully was remembering Hack, who'd also been there the day of the helicopters and the 'ville and the ambush. Blond kid with an infectious laugh. Had a picture of his girlfriend laminated so it wouldn't rot in the damp and then wore it around his neck on a little silver chain. Hackermeyer had been right next to Sully when they came into the 'ville and the shooting started. Both of them watching as the old *mamasan* came running out of her hooch with her hands raised, jabbering six licks to the dozen, jabbering at Malenfant and Clemson and Peasley and Mims and the other ones who were shooting the place up. Mims had put a round through a little boy's calf, maybe by accident. The boy was lying in the dirt outside one of the shitty little shacks, screaming. Old *mamasan* decided Malenfant was the one in charge—why not? Malenfant was the one doing all the yelling—and ran up to him, still waving her hands in the air. Sully could have told her that was a bad mistake, old Mr. Card-Shark had had himself a morning and a half, they all had, but Sully never opened his mouth. He and Hack stood there watching as Malenfant raised the butt of his rifle and drove it down into her face, knocking her flat and stopping her jabber. Willie Shearman had been standing twenty yards or so away, Willie Shearman from the old home town, one of the Catholic boys he and Bobby had been sort of scared of, and there was nothing readable on Willie's face. Willie Baseball, some of his men called him, and always affectionately.

"So what about your problem, Sully-John?"

Sully came back from the 'ville in Dong Ha to the alley beside the funeral parlor in New York . . . but slowly. Some memories were like the Tar-Baby in that old story about Brer Fox and Brer Rabbit; you got stuck on them. "I guess it all depends. What problem did I say I had?"

"You said you got your balls blown off when they hit us outside the 'ville. You said it was God punishing you for not stopping Malenfant before he went all dinky-dau and killed the old lady."

Dinky-dau didn't begin to cover it, Malenfant standing with his legs planted on either side of the old lady, bringing the bayonet down and still running his mouth the whole time. When the blood started to come out it made her orange top look like tie-dye.

"I exaggerated a trifle," Sully said, "as drunks tend to do. Part of the old scrotal sack is still present and accounted for and sometimes the pump still turns on. Especially since Viagra. God bless that shit."

"Have you quit the booze as well as the cigarettes?"

"I take the occasional beer," Sully said.

"Prozac?"

"Not yet."

"Divorced?"

Sully nodded. "You?"

"Twice. Thinking about taking the plunge again, though. Mary

Theresa Charlton, how sweet she is. Third time lucky, that's my motto."

"You know something, Loot?" Sully asked. "We've uncovered some clear legacies of the Vietnam experience here." He popped up a finger. "Vietnam vets get cancer, usually of the lung or the brain, but other places, too."

"Like Pags. Pags was the pancreas, wasn't it?"

"Right."

"All that cancer's because of the Orange," Dieffenbaker said. "Nobody can prove it but we all know it. Agent Orange, the gift that keeps on giving."

Sully popped up a second finger—yer fuckfinger, Ronnie Malenfant would undoubtedly have called it. "Vietnam vets get depressed, get drunk at parties, threaten to jump off national landmarks." Out with the third finger. "Vietnam vets have bad teeth." Pinky finger. "Vietnam vets get divorced."

Sully had paused at that point, vaguely hearing canned organ music coming through a partially opened window, looking at his four popped fingers and then at the thumb still tucked against his palm. Vets were drug addicts. Vets were bad loan risks, by and large; any bank officer would tell you so (in the years when Sully had been getting the dealership up and running a number of bankers had told *him* so). Vets maxed out their credit cards, got thrown out of gambling casinos, wept over songs by George Strait and Patty Loveless, knifed each other over shuffleboard bowling games in bars, bought muscle cars on credit and then wrecked them, beat their wives, beat their kids, beat their fuckin *dogs,* and probably cut themselves shaving more often than people who had never been closer to the green than *Apocalypse Now* or that fucking piece of shit *The Deer Hunter.*

"What's the thumb?" Dieffenbaker asked. "Come on, Sully, you're killing me here."

Sully looked at his folded thumb. Looked at Dieffenbaker, who now wore bifocals and carried a potbelly (what Vietnam vets usually called "the house that Bud built") but who still might have that skinny young man with the wax-candle complexion somewhere inside of him. Then he looked back at his thumb and popped it out like a guy trying to hitch a ride.

"Vietnam vets carry Zippos," he said. "At least until they stop smoking."

"Or until they get cancer," Dieffenbaker said. "At which point their wives no doubt pry em out of their weakening palsied hands."

"Except for all the ones who're divorced," Sully said, and they both laughed. It had been good outside the funeral parlor. Well, maybe not *good,* exactly, but better than inside. The organ music in there was bad, the sticky smell of the flowers was worse. The smell of the flowers made Sully think of the Mekong Delta. "In country," people said now, but he didn't remember ever having heard that particular phrase back then.

"So you didn't entirely lose your balls after all," Dieffenbaker said.

"Nope, never quite made it into Jake Barnes country."

"Who?"

"Doesn't matter." Sully wasn't much of a book-reader, never had been (his friend Bobby had been the book-reader), but the rehab librarian had given him *The Sun Also Rises* and Sully had read it avidly, not once but three times. Back then it had seemed very important—as important as that book *Lord of the Flies* had been to Bobby when they were kids. Now Jake Barnes seemed remote, a tin man with fake problems. Just one more made-up thing.

"No?"

"No. I can have a woman if I really want to have one—not kids, but I can have a woman. There's a fair amount of preparation involved, though, and mostly it seems like too much trouble."

Dieffenbaker said nothing for several moments. He sat looking at his hands. When he looked up, Sully thought he'd say something about how he had to get moving, a quick goodbye to the widow and then back to the wars (Sully thought that in the new lieutenant's case the wars these days involved selling computers with something magical called Pentium inside them), but Dieffenbaker didn't say that. He asked, "And what about the old lady? Do you still see her, or is she gone?"

Sully had felt dread—unformed but vast—stir at the back of his mind. "What old lady?" He couldn't remember telling Dieffenbaker, couldn't remember telling *anybody,* but of course he must have. Shit, he could have told Dieffenbaker anything at those reunion picnics; they were nothing but liquor-smelling black holes in his memory, every one of them.

"Old *mamasan,*" Dieffenbaker said, and brought out his cigarettes again. "The one Malenfant killed. You said you used to see her. 'Sometimes she wears different clothes, but it's always her,' you said. Do you still see her?"

"Can I have one of those?" Sully asked. "I never had a Dunhill."

On WKND Donna Summer was singing about a bad girl, bad girl, you're such a naughty bad girl, beep-beep. Sully turned to old *mamasan,* who was in her orange top and her green pants again, and said: "Malenfant was never obviously crazy. No crazier than anyone else, anyway . . . except maybe about Hearts. He was always looking for three guys to play Hearts with him, and that isn't really crazy, would you say? No crazier than Pags with his harmonicas and a lot less than the guys who spent their nights snorting heroin. Also, Ronnie helped yank those guys out of the choppers. There must've been a dozen gooks in the bush, maybe two dozen, all of them shooting away like mad, they wasted Lieutenant Packer and Malenfant must have seen it happen, he was right there, but he never hesitated." Nor had Fowler or Hack or Slocum or Peasley or Sully himself. Even after Packer went down they had kept going. They were brave kids. And if their bravery had been wasted in a war made by pigheaded old men, did that mean the bravery was of no account? For that matter, was Carol Gerber's cause wrong because a bomb had gone off at the wrong time? Shit, lots of bombs had gone off at the wrong time in Vietnam. What was Ronnie Malenfant, when you got right down to it, but a bomb that had gone off at the wrong time?

Old *mamasan* went on looking at him, his ancient white-haired date sitting there in the passenger seat with her hands in her lap—yellow hands folded where the orange smock met the green polyester pants.

"They'd been shooting at us for almost two weeks," Sully said. "Ever since we left the A Shau Valley. We won at Tam Boi and when you win you're supposed to roll, at least that's what I always thought, but what we were doing was a retreat, not a roll. Shit, one step from a rout is what it was, and we sure didn't feel like winners for long. There was no support, we were just hung out to dry. Fuckin Vietnamization! What a joke that was!"

He fell silent for a moment or two, looking at her while she looked calmly back. Beyond them, the halted traffic glittered like a fever. Some impatient trucker hit his airhorn and Sully jumped like a man suddenly awakened from a doze.

"That's when I met Willie Shearman, you know—falling back from the A Shau Valley. I knew he looked familiar and I was sure I'd met him someplace, but I couldn't think where. People change a hell of a lot between fourteen and twenty-four, you know. Then one afternoon he and a bunch of the other Bravo Company guys were sitting around and bullshitting, talking about girls, and Willie said that the first time he ever got French-kissed, it was at a St. Theresa of Avila Sodality dance. And I think, 'Holy shit, those were the St. Gabe's girls.' I walked up to him and said, 'You Steadfast guys might have been the kings of Asher Avenue, but we whipped your pansy asses every time you came down to Harwich High to play football.' Hey, you talk about a gotcha! Fuckin Willie jumped up so fast I thought he was gonna run away like the Gingerbread Man. It was like he'd seen a ghost, or something. Then he laughed and stuck out his hand and I saw he was still wearing his St. Gabe's high-school ring! And you know what it all goes to prove?"

Old *mamasan* didn't say anything, she never did, but Sully could see in her eyes that she *did* know what it all went to prove: people were funny, kids say the darndest things, winners never quit and quitters never win. Also God bless America.

"Anyway, that whole week they chased us, and it started to get obvious that they were bearing down . . . squeezing the sides . . . our casualties kept going up and you couldn't get any sleep because of the flares and the choppers and the howling they'd do at night, back there in the toolies. And then they'd come at you, see . . . twenty of them, three dozen of them . . . poke and pull back, poke and pull back, like that . . . and they had this thing they'd do . . ."

Sully licked his lips, aware that his mouth had gone dry. Now he wished he hadn't gone to Pags's funeral. Pags had been a good guy, but not good enough to justify the return of such memories.

"They'd set up four or five mortars in the bush . . . on one of our flanks, you know . . . and beside each mortar they'd line up eight or nine guys, each one with a shell. The little men in the black pajamas, all lined up like kids at the drinking fountain back in grammar school. And when the order came, each guy would drop his shell into the mortar-tube and then run forward just as fast as he could. Running that way, they'd engage the enemy—us—at about the same time their shells came down. It always made me think of something the guy who lived upstairs from Bobby Garfield told us once when we were playing pass on Bobby's front lawn. It was about some baseball player the Dodgers used to have. Ted said this guy was so fuckin fast he could hit a fungo pop fly at home plate, then run out to shortstop and catch it himself. It was . . . sort of unnerving."

Yes. The way he was sort of unnerved right now, sort of freaked out, like a kid who makes the mistake of telling himself ghost stories in the dark.

"The fire they poured into that clearing where the choppers went down was only more of the same, believe you me." Except that wasn't exactly true. The Cong had let it all hang out that morning; turned the volume up to eleven and then pulled the knobs off, as Mims liked to say. The shooting from the bush around the burning choppers had been like a steady downpour instead of a shower.

There were cigarettes in the Caprice's glove compartment, an old pack of Winstons Sully kept for emergencies, transferring from one car to the next whenever he switched rides. That one cigarette he'd bummed from Dieffenbaker had awakened the tiger and now he reached past old *mamasan,* opened the glove-box, pawed past all the paperwork, and found the pack. The cigarette would taste stale and hot in his throat, but that was okay. That was sort of what he wanted.

"Two weeks of shooting and squeezing," he told her, pushing in the lighter. "Shake and bake and don't look for the fuckin ARVN, baby, because they always seemed to have better things to do. Bitches, barbecues, and bowling tournaments, Malenfant used to say. We kept taking casualties, the air cover was never there when it was supposed to be, no one was getting any sleep, and it seemed like the more other guys from the A Shau linked up with us the worse it got. I remember one of Willie's guys—Havers or Haber, something like that—got it right in the head. Got it in the fuckin head and then just lay there on the path with his eyes open, trying to talk. Blood pouring out of this hole right here . . ." Sully tapped a finger against his skull just over his ear. ". . . and we couldn't believe he was still alive, let alone trying to talk. Then the thing with the choppers . . . *that* was like something out of a movie, all the smoke and shooting, *bup-bup-bup-bup.* That was the lead-in for us—you know, into your 'ville. We came up on it and boy . . . there was this one chair, like a kitchen chair with a red seat and steel legs pointing up at the sky, in the street. It just looked *crapass,* I'm sorry but it did, not worth living in, let alone dying for. Your guys, the ARVN, *they* didn't want to die for places like that, why would we? The place stank, it smelled like shit, but they all did. That's how it seemed. I didn't care so much about the smell, anyway. Mostly I think it was the chair that got to me. That one chair said it all."

Sully pulled out the lighter, started to apply the cherry-red coil to the tip of his cigarette, and then remembered he was in a demonstrator. He could smoke in a demo—hell, it was off his own lot—but if one of the salesmen smelled the smoke and concluded that the boss was doing what was a firing offense for anyone else, it wouldn't be good. You had to walk the walk as well as talk the talk . . . at least you did if you wanted to get a little respect.

"*Excusez-moi,*" he told the old *mamasan.* He got out of the car, which was still running, lit his cigarette, then bent in the window to slide the lighter back into its dashboard receptacle. The day was hot, and the four-lane sea of idling cars made it seem even hotter. Sully could sense the impatience all around him, but his was the only radio he could hear; everyone else was under glass, buttoned into their little air-conditioned cocoons, listening to a hundred different kinds of music, from Liz Phair to William Ackerman. He guessed that any vets caught in the jam who didn't have the Allman Brothers on CD or Big Brother and the Holding Company on tape were probably also listening to WKND, where the past had never died and the future never came. Toot-toot, beep-beep.

Sully hitch-stepped to the hood of his car and stood on tiptoe, shading his eyes against the glare of sun on chrome and looking for the problem. He couldn't see it, of course.

Bitches, barbecues, and bowling tournaments, he thought, and the thought came in Malenfant's squealing, drilling voice. That nightmare voice under the blue and out of the green. *Come on, boys, who's got The Douche? I'm down to ninety and a wakeup, time's short, let's get this fuckin show on the fuckin road!*

He took a deep drag on the Winston, then coughed out stale hot smoke. Black dots began a sudden dance in the afternoon brightness, and he looked down at the cigarette between his fingers with an expression of nearly comic horror. What was he doing, starting up with this shit again? Was he crazy? Well yes, of *course* he was crazy, anyone who saw dead old ladies sitting beside them in their cars *had* to be crazy, but that didn't mean he had to start up with this shit again. Cigarettes were Agent Orange that you paid for. Sully threw the Winston away. It felt like the right decision, but it didn't slow the accelerating beat of his heart or his sense—so well remembered from the patrols he'd been on—that the inside of his mouth was drying out and pulling together, puckering and crinkling like burned skin. Some people were afraid of crowds—agoraphobia, it was called, fear of the marketplace—but the only time Sully ever had that sense of *too much* and *too many* was at times like this. He was okay in elevators and crowded lobbies at intermission and on rush-hour train platforms, but when traffic clogged to a stop all around him, he got dinky-dau. There was, after all, nowhere to run, baby, nowhere to hide.

A few other folks were emerging from their air-conditioned lifepods. A woman in a severe brown business suit standing by a severe brown BMW, a gold bracelet and silver earrings summarizing the summer sunlight, all but tapping one cordovan high heel with impatience. She caught Sully's eye, rolled her own heavenward as if to say *Isn't this typical,* and glanced at her wristwatch (also gold, also gleaming). A man astride a green Yamaha crotchrocket killed his bike's raving engine, put the bike on its kickstand, removed his helmet, and placed it on the oilstained pavement next to one footpedal. He was wearing black bike-shorts and a sleeveless shirt with PROPERTY OF THE NEW YORK KNICKS printed on the front. Sully estimated this gentleman would lose approximately seventy per cent of his skin if he happened to dump the crotchrocket at a speed greater than five miles an hour while wearing such an outfit.

"Bummer, man," the crotchrocket guy said. "Must be an accident. Hope it's nothing radioactive." And laughed to show he was joking.

Up ahead in the far left lane—what would be the fast lane when traffic was actually moving on this stretch of highway—a woman in tennis whites was standing beside a Toyota with a NO NUKES bumper sticker on the left side of the license plate and one reading HOUSECAT: THE OTHER WHITE MEAT on the right. Her skirt was very short, her thighs were very long and brown, and when she pushed her sunglasses up, propping them in her blond-streaked hair, Sully got a look at her eyes. They were wide and blue and somehow alarmed. It was a look that made you want to stroke her cheek (or perhaps give her a one-armed brother-hug) and tell her not to worry, everything was going to be all right. It was a look Sully remembered well. It was the one that had turned him inside out. It was Carol Gerber up there, Carol Gerber in sneakers and a tennis dress. He hadn't seen her since one night in late 1966 when he'd gone over to her house and they'd sat on the sofa (along with Carol's mother, who had smelled strongly of wine) watching TV. They had ended up arguing about the war and he had left. *I'll go back and see her again when I'm sure I can stay cool,* he remembered thinking as he drove away in his old Chevrolet (even back then he'd been a Chevrolet man). But he never had. By late '66 she was already up to her ass in antiwar shit—that much she'd learned during her semester in Maine, if nothing else—and just thinking about her was enough to make him furious. Fucking little empty-headed idiot was what she was, she'd swallowed all that communist antiwar propaganda hook, line, and sinker. Then, of course, she'd joined that nutty group, that MSP, and had high-sided it completely.

"Carol!" he called, starting toward her. He passed the snot-green crotchrocket, cut between the rear bumper of a van and a sedan, temporarily lost sight of her as he hurried along the side of a rumbling sixteen-wheeler, then saw her again. "Carol! Hey Carol!" Yet when she turned toward him he wondered what the hell was wrong with him, what had possessed him. If Carol was still alive she had to be pushing fifty now, just as he was. This woman looked maybe thirty-five.

Sully stopped, still a lane away. Cars and trucks rumbling everywhere. And an odd whickering sound in the air, which he at first thought was the wind, although the afternoon was hot and perfectly still.

"Carol? Carol Gerber?"

The whicker was louder, a sound like someone flicking his tongue repeatedly through his pursed lips, a sound like a helicopter five klicks away. Sully looked up and saw a lampshade tumbling out of the hazy blue sky, directly at him. He dodged backward in an instinctive startle reflex, but he had spent his entire school career playing athletic sports of one kind or another, and even as he was pulling back his head he was reaching with his hand. He caught the lampshade quite deftly. On it was a paddleboat churning downriver against a lurid red sunset. WE'RE DOING FINE ON THE MISSISSIPPI was written above the boat in scrolly, old-fashioned letters. Below it, in the same scrolly caps: HOW'S BAYOU?

Where the fuck did this come from? Sully thought, and then the woman who looked like an all-grown-up version of Carol Gerber screamed. Her hands rose as if to adjust the sunglasses propped in her hair and then just hung beside her shoulders, shaking like the hands of a distraught symphony conductor. It was how old *mamasan* had looked as she came running out of her shitty fucked-up hooch and into the shitty fucked-up street of that shitty fucked-up little 'ville in Dong Ha Province. Blood spilled down over the shoulders of the tennis woman's white dress, first in spatters, then in a flood. It ran down her tanned upper arms and dripped from her elbows.

"Carol?" Sully asked stupidly. He was standing between a Dodge Ram pickup and a Mack semi, dressed in a dark blue suit, the one he wore to funerals, holding a lampshade souvenir of the Mississippi River (how's bayou) and looking at a woman who now had something sticking out of her head. As she staggered a step forward, blue eyes still wide, hands still shaking in the air, Sully realized it was a cordless phone. He could tell by the stub of aerial, which jiggled with each step she took. A cordless phone had fallen out of the sky, had fallen God knew how many thousands of feet, and now it was in her head.

She took another step, struck the hood of a dark green Buick, and began to sink slowly behind it as her knees buckled. It was like watching a submarine go down, Sully thought, only instead of a periscope all that would be sticking up after she was out of sight would be the stubby antenna of that cordless phone.

"Carol?" he whispered, but it couldn't be her; no one he'd known as a kid, no one he'd ever slept with, had been destined to die from injuries inflicted by a falling telephone, surely.

People were starting to scream and yell and shout. Mostly the shouts seemed to be questions. Horns were honking. Engines were revving, just as if there were someplace to go. Beside Sully, the driver of the Mack sixteen-wheeler was goosing his power-plant in big, rhythmic snorts. A car alarm began to wibble-wobble. Someone howled in either pain or surprise.

A single trembling white hand clutched at the hood of the dark green Buick. There was a tennis bracelet on the wrist. Slowly the hand and the bracelet slid away from Sully. The fingers of the woman who had looked like Carol gripped at the edge of the hood for a moment, then disappeared. Something else fell, whistling, out of the sky.

"*Get down!*" Sully screamed. "*Ah fuck, get down!*"

The whistling rose to a shrill, earsplitting pitch, then stopped as the falling object struck the hood of the Buick, bashing it downward like a fist and popping it up from beneath the windshield. The thing poking out of the Buick's engine compartment appeared to be a microwave oven.

From all around him there now came the sound of falling objects. It was like being caught in an earthquake that was somehow going on above the ground instead of in it. A harmless shower of magazines fell past him—*Seventeen* and *GQ* and *Rolling Stone* and *Stereo Review.* With their open fluttering pages they looked like shot birds. To his right an office chair dropped out of the blue, spinning on its base as it came. It struck the roof of a Ford station wagon. The wagon's windshield blew out in milky chunks. The chair rebounded into the air, tilted, and came to rest on the station wagon's hood. Beyond that a portable TV, a plastic clothes basket, what looked like a clutch of cameras with the straps all tangled together, and a rubber home plate fell on the slow lane and into the breakdown lane. The home plate was followed by what looked like a Louisville Slugger baseball bat. A theater-size popcorn popper shattered into glittering shards when it hit the road.

The guy in the Knicks shirt, the one with the snot-green crotchrocket, had seen enough. He started running up the narrow corridor between the traffic stalled in the third lane and the traffic stalled in the fast lane, twisting like a slalom skier to avoid the jutting side mirrors, holding one hand over his head like a man crossing the street during a spring shower. Sully, still clutching the lampshade, thought the guy would have done a lot better to have grabbed his helmet and put it back on, but of course when things started falling all around you you got forgetful and the first thing you were apt to forget was where your best interests lay.

Something else was coming down now, falling close and falling big—bigger than the microwave oven that had bashed in the Buick's hood, certainly. This time the sound wasn't a whistle, like a bomb or a mortar-shell, but the sound of a falling plane or helicopter or even a house. In Vietnam Sully had been around when all those things fell out of the sky (the house had been in pieces, granted), and yet this sound was different in one crucial way: it was also *musical,* like the world's biggest windchime.

It was a grand piano, white with gold chasing, the sort of piano on which you'd expect a long cool woman in a black dress to tinkle out "Night and Day"—in the traffic's boom, in the silence of my lonely room, toot-toot, beep-beep. A white grand piano falling out of the Connecticut sky, turning over and over, making a shadow like a jellyfish on the jammed-up cars, making windy music in its cables as air blew through its rolling chest, its keys rippling like the keys of a player piano, the hazy sun winking on the pedals.

It fell in lazy revolutions, and the fattening sound of its drop was like the sound of something vibrating endlessly in a tin tunnel. It fell toward Sully, its uneasy shadow now starting to focus and shrink, his upturned face its seeming target.

"*INCOMING!*" Sully screamed, and began to run. "*INNCOMMING!*"

The piano plummeted toward the turnpike, the white bench falling right behind it, and behind the bench came a comet's tail of sheet music, 45-rpm records with fat holes in the middle, small appliances, a flapping yellow coat that looked like a duster, a Goodyear Wide Oval tire, a barbecue grill, a weathervane, a file-cabinet, and a teacup with WORLD'S GREATEST GRANDMA printed on the side.

"Can I have one of those?" Sully had asked Dieffenbaker outside the funeral parlor where Pags was lying in his silk-lined box. "I never had a Dunhill."

"Whatever floats your boat." Dieffenbaker sounded amused, as if he had never been shit-scared in his life.

Sully could still remember Dieffenbaker standing in the street by that overturned kitchen chair: how pale he had been, how his lips had trembled, how his clothes still smelled of smoke and spilled copter fuel. Dieffenbaker looking around from Malenfant and the old woman to the others who were starting to pour fire into the hooches to the howling kid Mims had shot; he could remember Deef looking at Lieutenant Shearman but there was no help there. No help from Sully himself, for that matter. He could also remember how Slocum was staring at Deef, Deef the lieutenant now that Packer was dead. And finally Deef had looked back at Slocum. Sly

Slocum was no officer—not even one of those bigmouth bush generals who were always second-guessing everything—and never would be. Slocum was just your basic E-3 or E-4 who thought that a group who sounded like Rare Earth had to be black. Just a grunt, in other words, but one prepared to do what the rest of them weren't. Never losing hold of the new lieutenant's distraught eye, Slocum had turned his head back the other way just a little, toward Malenfant and Clemson and Peasley and Mims and the rest, self-appointed regulators whose names Sully no longer remembered. Then Slocum was back to total eye-contact with Dieffenbaker again. There were six or eight men in all who had gone loco, trotting down the muddy street past the screaming bleeding kid and into that scurgy little 'ville, shouting as they went—football cheers, basic-training cadences, the chorus to "Hang On Sloopy," shit like that—and Slocum was saying with his eyes *Hey, what you want? You the boss now, what you want?*

And Dieffenbaker had nodded.

Sully wondered if he could have given that nod himself. He thought not. He thought if it had come down to him, Clemson and Malenfant and those other fuckheads would have killed until their ammo ran out—wasn't that pretty much what the men under Calley and Medina had done? But Dieffenbaker was no William Calley, give him that. Dieffenbaker had given the little nod. Slocum nodded back, then raised his rifle and blew off Ralph Clemson's head.

At the time Sully had thought Clemson got the bullet because Slocum knew Malenfant too well, Slocum and Malenfant had smoked more than a few loco-leaves together and Slocum had also been known to spend at least some of his spare time hunting The Bitch with the other Hearts players. But as he sat here rolling Dieffenbaker's Dunhill cigarette between his fingers, it occurred to Sully that Slocum didn't give a shit about Malenfant and his loco-leaves; Malenfant's favorite card-game, either. There was no shortage of *bhang* or card-games in Vietnam. Slocum picked Clemson because shooting Malenfant wouldn't have worked. Malenfant, screaming all his bullshit about putting heads up on sticks to show the Cong what happened to people who fucked with Delta Lightning, was too far away to get the attention of the men splashing and squashing and shooting their way down that muddy street. Plus old *mamasan* was already dead, so what the fuck, let him carve on her.

Now Deef was Dieffenbaker, a bald computer salesman who had quit going to the reunions. He gave Sully a light with his Zippo, then watched as Sully drew the smoke deep and coughed it back out.

"Been awhile, hasn't it?" Dieffenbaker asked.

"Two years, give or take."

"You want to know the scary thing? How fast you get back into practice."

"I told you about the old lady, huh?"

"Yeah."

"When?"

"I think it was the last reunion you came to . . . the one on the Jersey shore, the one when Durgin ripped that waitress's top off. That was an ugly scene, man."

"Was it? I don't remember."

"You were shitfaced by then."

Of course he had been, that part was always the same. Come to think of it, all parts of the reunions were always the same. There was a dj who usually left early because someone wanted to beat him up for playing the wrong records. Until that happened the speakers blasted out stuff like "Bad Moon Rising" and "Light My Fire" and "Gimme Some Lovin' " and "My Girl," songs from the soundtracks of all those Vietnam movies that were made in the Philippines. The truth about the music was that most of the grunts Sully remembered used to get choked up over The Carpenters or "Angel of the Morning." That stuff was the real bush soundtrack, always playing as the men passed around fatties and pictures of their girlfriends, getting stoned and all weepy-goopy over "One Tin Soldier," popularly known in the green as "The Theme from Fuckin *Billy Jack*." Sully couldn't remember hearing The Doors once in Vietnam; it was always The Strawberry Alarm Clock singing "Incense and Peppermints." On some level he had known the war was lost the first time he heard that fuckin piece of shit on the commissary jukebox.

The reunions started with music and the smell of barbecues (a smell that always vaguely reminded Sully of burning helicopter fuel) and with cans of beer in pails of chipped ice and that part was all right, that part was actually pretty nice, but then all at once it was the next morning and the light burned your eyes and your head felt like a tumor and your stomach was full of poison. On one of those mornings-after Sully had had a vague sick memory of making the dj play "Oh! Carol" by Neil Sedaka over and over again, threatening to kill him if he stopped. On another Sully awoke next to Frank Peasley's ex-wife. She was snoring because her nose was broken. Her pillow was covered with blood, her cheeks covered with blood too, and Sully couldn't remember if he had broken her nose or if fuckin Peasley had done it. Sully wanted it to be Peasley but knew it could have been him; sometimes, especially in those days B.V. (Before Viagra) when he failed at sex almost as often as he succeeded, he got mad. Fortunately, when the lady awoke, she couldn't remember, either. She remembered what he'd looked like with his underwear off, though. "How come you only have one?" she'd asked him.

"I'm lucky to have that," Sully had replied. His headache had been bigger than the world.

"What'd I say about the old lady?" he asked Dieffenbaker as they sat smoking in the alley beside the chapel.

Dieffenbaker shrugged. "Just that you used to see her. You said sometimes she put on different clothes but it was always her, the old *mamasan* Malenfant wasted. I had to shush you up."

"Fuck," Sully said, and put the hand not holding the cigarette in his hair.

"You also said it was better once you got back to the East Coast," Dieffenbaker said. "And look, what's so bad about seeing an old lady once in awhile? Some people see flying saucers."

"Not people who owe two banks almost a million dollars," Sully said. "If they knew . . ."

"If they knew, what? I'll tell you what. Nothing. As long as you keep making the payments, Sully-John, keep bringing them that fabled monthly cashew, no one cares what you see when you turn out the light . . . or what you see when you leave it on, for that matter. They don't care if you dress in ladies' underwear or if you beat your wife and hump the Labrador. Besides, don't you think there are guys in those banks who spent time in the green?"

Sully took a drag on the Dunhill and looked at Dieffenbaker. The truth was that he never *had* considered such a thing. He dealt with two loan officers who were the right age, but they never talked about it. Of course, neither did he. *Next time I see them,* he thought, *I'll have to ask if they carry Zippos. You know, be subtle.*

"What are you smiling about?" Dieffenbaker asked.

"Nothing. What about you, Deef? Do you have an old lady? I don't mean your girlfriend, I mean an old lady. A *mamasan.*"

"Hey man, don't call me Deef. Nobody calls me that now. I never liked it."

"Do you have one?"

"Ronnie Malenfant's my *mamasan,*" Dieffenbaker said. "Sometimes I see him. Not the way you said you see yours, like she's really there, but memory's real too, isn't it?"

"Yeah."

Dieffenbaker shook his head slowly. "If memory was all. You know? If memory was *all.*"

Sully sat silent. In the chapel the organ was now playing something that didn't sound like a hymn but just music. The recessional, he thought they called it. A musical way of telling the mourners to get lost. Get back, Jo-Jo. Your mama's waitin.

Dieffenbaker said: "There's memory and then there's what you actually see in your mind. Like when you read a book by a really good author and he describes a room and you see that room. I'll be mowing the lawn or sitting at our conference table listening to a presentation or reading a story to my grandson before putting him in bed or maybe even smooching with Mary on the sofa, and boom, there's Malenfant, goddam little acne-head with that wavy hair. Remember how his hair used to wave?"

"Yeah."

"Ronnie Malenfant, always talking about the fuckin this and the fuckin that and the fuckin other thing. Ethnic jokes for every occasion. And the poke. You remember that?"

"Sure. Little leather poke he wore on his belt. He kept his cards in it. Two decks of Bikes. 'Hey, we're goin Bitch-huntin, boys! Nickel a point! Who's up for it?' And out they'd come."

"Yeah. You remember. *Remember.* But I *see* him, Sully, right down to the whiteheads on his chin. I hear him, I can smell the fucking *dope* he smoked . . . but mostly I see him, how he knocked her over and she was lying there on the ground, still shaking her fists at him, still running her mouth—"

"Stop it."

"—and I couldn't believe it was going to happen. At first I don't think Malenfant could believe it, either. He just jabbed the bayonet at her a couple of times to begin with, pricking her with the tip of it like the whole thing was a goof . . . but then he went and did it, he stuck it in her. Fuckin A, Sully; I mean *fuck*-in-A. She screamed and started jerking all around and he had his feet, remember, on either side of her, and the rest of them were running, Ralph Clemson and Mims and I don't know who else. I always hated that little fuck Clemson, even worse than Malenfant because at least Ronnie wasn't sneaky, with him what you saw was what you got. Clemson was crazy *and* sneaky. I was scared to death, Sully, scared to fucking death. I knew I was supposed to put a stop to it, but I was afraid they'd scrag me if I tried, all of them, all of *you,* because at that precise moment there was all you guys and then there was me. Shearman . . . nothing against him, he went into that clearing where the copters came down like there was no tomorrow, but in that 'ville . . . I looked at him and there was nothing there."

"He saved my life later on, when we got ambushed," Sully said quietly.

"I know. Picked you up and carried you like fucking Superman. He had it in the clearing, he got it back on the trail, but in between, in the 'ville . . . nothing. In the 'ville it was down to me. It was like I was the only grownup, only I didn't feel like a grownup."

Sully didn't bother telling him to stop again. Dieffenbaker meant to have his say. Nothing short of a punch in the mouth would stop him from having it.

"You remember how she screamed when he stuck it in? That old lady? And Malenfant standing over her and running his mouth, slopehead this and gook that and slant the other thing. Thank God for Slocum. He looked at me and that made me do something . . . except all I did was tell him to shoot."

No, Sully thought, *you didn't even do that, Deef. You just nodded your head. If you're in court they don't let you get away with shit like that; they make you speak out loud. They make you state it for the record.*

"I think Slocum saved our souls that day," Dieffenbaker said. "You knew he offed himself, didn't you? Yeah. In '86."

"I thought it was a car accident."

"If driving into a bridge abutment at seventy miles an hour on a clear evening is an accident, it was an accident."

"What about Malenfant? Any idea?"

"Well, he never came to any of the reunions, of course, but he was alive the last I knew. Andy Brannigan saw him in southern California."

"Hedgehog saw him?"

"Yeah, Hedgehog. You know where it was?"

"No, course not."

"It's going to kill you, Sully-John, it's going to blow your mind. Brannigan's in Alcoholics Anonymous. It's his religion. He says it saved his life, and I suppose it did. He used to drink fiercer than any of us, maybe fiercer than all of us put together. So now he's addicted to AA instead of tequila. He goes to about a dozen meetings a week, he's a GSR—don't ask me, it's some sort of political position in the group—he mans a hotline telephone. And every year he goes to the National Convention. Five years or so ago the drunks got together in San Diego. Fifty thousand alkies all standing in the San Diego Convention Center, chanting the Serenity Prayer. Can you picture it?"

"Sort of," Sully said.

"Fucking Brannigan looks to his left and who does he see but Ronnie Malenfant. He can hardly believe it, but it's Malenfant, all right. After the big meeting, he grabs Malenfant and the two of them go out for a drink." Dieffenbaker paused. "Alcoholics do that too, I guess. Lemonades and Cokes and such. And Malenfant tells Hedgehog he's almost two years clean and sober, he's found a higher power he chooses to call God, he's had a rebirth, everything is five by fucking five, he's living life on life's terms, he's letting go and letting God, all that stuff they talk. And Brannigan, he can't help it. He asks Malenfant if he's taken the Fifth Step, which is confessing the stuff you've done wrong and becoming entirely ready to make amends. Malenfant doesn't bat an eyelash, just says he took the Fifth a year ago and he feels a lot better."

"Hot damn," Sully said, surprised at the depth of his anger. "Old *mamasan* would certainly be glad to know that Ronnie's gotten past it. I'll tell her the next time I see her." Not knowing he would see her later that day, of course.

"You do that."

They sat without talking much for a little while. Sully asked Dieffenbaker for another cigarette and Dieffenbaker gave him one, also another flick of the old Zippo. From around the corner came tangles of conversation and some low laughter. Pags's funeral was over. And somewhere in California Ronnie Malenfant was perhaps reading his AA Big Book and getting in touch with that fabled higher power he chose to call God. Maybe Ronnie was also a GSR, whatever the fuck that was. Sully wished Ronnie was dead. Sully wished Ronnie Malenfant had died in a Viet Cong spiderhole, his nose full of sores and the smell of ratshit, bleeding internally and puking up chunks of his own stomach lining. Malenfant with his poke and his cards, Malenfant with his bayonet, Malenfant with his feet planted on either side of the old *mamasan* in her green pants and orange top and red sneakers.

"Why were we in Vietnam to begin with?" Sully asked. "Not to get all philosophical or anything, but have you ever figured that out?"

"Who said 'He who does not learn from the past is condemned to repeat it'?"

"Richard Dawson, the host of *Family Feud.*"

"Fuck you, Sullivan."

"I don't know who said it. Does it matter?"

"Fuckin yeah," Dieffenbaker said. "Because we never got out. We never got out of the green. Our generation died there."

"That sounds a little—"

"A little what? A little pretentious? You bet. A little silly? You bet. A little self-regarding? Yes sir. But that's us. That's us all over. What have we done since Nam, Sully? Those of us who went, those of us who marched and protested, those of us who just sat home watching the Dallas Cowboys and drinking beer and farting into the sofa cushions?"

Color was seeping into the new lieutenant's cheeks. He had the look of a man who has found his hobby-horse and is now climbing on, helpless to do anything but ride. He held up his hands and began popping fingers the way Sully had when talking about the legacies of the Vietnam experience.

"Well, let's see. We're the generation that invented Super Mario Brothers, the ATV, laser missile-guidance systems, and crack cocaine. We discovered Richard Simmons, Scott Peck, and *Martha Stewart Living.* Our idea of a major lifestyle change is buying a dog. The girls who burned their bras now buy their lingerie from Victoria's Secret and the boys who fucked fearlessly for peace are now fat guys who sit in front of their computer screens late at night, pulling their puddings while they look at pictures of naked eighteen-year-olds on the Internet. That's us, brother, we like to watch. Movies, video games, live car-chase footage, fistfights on *The Jerry Springer Show,* Mark McGwire, World Federation Wrestling, impeachment hearings, we don't care, we just like to watch. But there was a time . . . don't laugh, but there was a time when it was really all in our hands. Do you know that?"

Sully nodded, thinking of Carol. Not the version of her sitting on the sofa with him and her wine-smelling mother, not the one flipping the peace sign at the camera while the blood ran down the side of her face, either—that one was already too late and too crazy, you could see it in her smile, read it in the sign, where screaming words forbade all discussion. Rather he thought of Carol on the day her mother had taken all of them to Savin Rock. His friend Bobby had won some money from a three-card monte dealer that day and Carol had worn her blue bathing suit on the beach and sometimes she'd give Bobby that look, the one that said he was killing her and death was sweet. It *had* been in their hands then; he was quite sure of it. But kids lose everything, kids have slippery fingers and holes in their pockets and they lose everything.

"We filled up our wallets on the stock market and went to the gym and booked therapy sessions to get in touch with ourselves. South America is burning, Malaysia's burning, fucking *Vietnam* is burning, but we finally got past that self-hating thing, finally got to like ourselves, so *that's* okay."

Sully thought of Malenfant getting in touch with himself, learning to like the inner Ronnie, and suppressed a shudder.

All of Dieffenbaker's fingers were held up in front of his face and poked out; to Sully he looked like Al Jolson getting ready to sing "Mammy." Dieffenbaker seemed to become aware of this at the same moment Sully did, and lowered his hands. He looked tired and distracted and unhappy.

"I like lots of people our age when they're one by one," he said, "but I loathe and despise my generation, Sully. We had an opportunity to change everything. We actually did. Instead we settled for designer jeans, two tickets to Mariah Carey at Radio City Music Hall, frequent-flier miles, James Cameron's *Titanic,* and retirement portfolios. The only generation even close to us in pure, selfish self-indulgence is the so-called Lost Generation of the twenties, and at least most of them had the decency to stay drunk. We couldn't even do that. Man, we suck."

The new lieutenant was close to tears, Sully saw. "Deef—"

"You know the price of selling out the future, Sully-John? You can never really leave the past. You can never get over. My thesis is that you're really not in New York at all. You're in the Delta, leaning back against a tree, stoned and rubbing bug-dope on the back of your neck. Packer's still the man because it's still 1969. Everything you think of as 'your later life' is a big fucking pot-bubble. And it's better that way. Vietnam is better. That's why we stay there."

"You think?"

"Absolutely."

A dark-haired, brown-eyed woman in a blue dress peeked around the corner and said, "So there you are."

Dieffenbaker stood up as she came toward them, walking slow and pretty on her high heels. Sully stood up, too.

"Mary, this is John Sullivan. He served with me and Pags. Sully, this is my good friend Mary Theresa Charlton."

"Pleased to meet you," Sully said, and put out his hand.

Her grip was firm and sure, long cool fingers in his own, but she was looking at Dieffenbaker. "Mrs. Pagano wants to see you, hon. Please?"

"You bet," Dieffenbaker said. He started toward the front of the building, then turned back to Sully. "Hang in a little bit," he said. "We'll go for a drink. I promise not to preach." But his eyes shifted from Sully's when he said this, as if they knew it was a promise he couldn't keep.

"Thanks, Loot, but I really ought to get back. I want to beat the rush-hour traffic."

But he hadn't beaten the traffic after all and now a piano was falling toward him, gleaming in the sun and humming to itself as it came. Sully fell flat on his stomach and rolled under a car. The piano came down less than five feet away, detonating and throwing up rows of keys like teeth.

Sully slid back out from beneath the car, burning his back on the hot tailpipe, and struggled to his feet. He looked north along the turnpike, eyes wide and unbelieving. A vast rummage sale was falling out of the sky: tape recorders and rugs and a riding lawn-mower with the grass-caked blade whirling in its housing and a black lawn-jockey and an aquarium with the fish still swimming in it. He saw an old man with a lot of theatrical gray hair running up the breakdown lane and then a flight of steps fell on him, tearing off his left arm and sending him to his knees. There were clocks and desks and coffee tables and a plummeting elevator with its cable uncoiling into the air behind it like a greasy severed umbilicus. A squall of ledgers fell in the parking lot of a nearby industrial complex; their clapping covers sounded like applause. A fur coat fell on a running woman, trapping her, and then a sofa landed on her, crushing her. The air filled with a storm of light as large panes of greenhouse glass dropped out of the blue. A statue of a Civil War soldier smashed through a panel truck. An ironing board hit the railing of the overpass up ahead and then fell into the stalled traffic below like a spinning propeller. A stuffed lion dropped into the back of a pickup truck. Everywhere were running, screaming people. Everywhere were cars with dented roofs and smashed windows; Sully saw a Mercedes with the unnaturally pink legs of a department-store mannequin sticking up from the sunroof. The air shook with whines and whistles.

Another shadow fell on him and even as he ducked and raised his hand he knew it was too late, if it was an iron or a toaster or something like that it would fracture his skull. If it was something bigger he'd be nothing but a grease-spot on the highway.

The falling object struck his hand without hurting it in the slightest, bounced, and landed at his feet. He looked down at it first with surprise, then with dawning wonder. "Holy shit," he said.

Sully bent over and picked up the baseball glove which had fallen from the sky, recognizing it at once even after all these years: the deep scratch down the last finger and the comically tangled knots in the rawhide laces of the webbing were as good as fingerprints. He looked on the side, where Bobby had printed his name. It was still there, but the letters looked fresher than they should have, and the leather here looked frayed and faded and whipsawed, as if other names had been inked in the same spot and then erased.

Closer to his face, the smell of the glove was both intoxicating and irresistible. Sully slipped it onto his hand, and when he did something crackled beneath his little finger—a piece of paper shoved in there. He paid no attention. Instead he put the glove over his face, closed his eyes, and inhaled. Leather and neat's-foot oil and sweat and grass. All the summers that were. The summer of 1960, for instance, when he had had come back from his week at camp to find everything changed—Bobby sullen, Carol distant and palely thoughtful (at least for awhile), and the cool old guy who'd lived on the third floor of Bobby's building—Ted—gone. Everything had changed . . . but it was still summer, he had still been eleven, and everything had still seemed . . .

"Eternal," he murmured into the glove, and inhaled deeply of its aroma again as, nearby, a glass case filled with butterflies shattered on the roof of a bread-van and a stop-sign stuck, quivering, into the breakdown lane like a thrown spear. Sully remembered his Bo-lo Bouncer and his black Keds and the taste of Pez straight out of the gun, how the pieces of candy would hit the roof of your mouth and then ricochet onto your tongue; he remembered the way his catcher's mask felt when it sat on his face just right and the *hisha-hisha-hisha* of the lawn-sprinklers on Broad Street and how mad Mrs. Conlan got if you walked too close to her precious flowers and Mrs. Godlow at the Asher Empire wanting to see your birth certificate if she thought you were too big to be still under twelve and the poster of Brigitte Bardot

(*if she's trash I'd love to be the trashman*)

in her towel and playing guns and playing pass and playing Careers and making arm-farts in the back of Mrs. Sweetser's fourth-grade classroom and—

"Hey, American." Only she said it *Amellican* and Sully knew who he was going to see even before he raised his head from Bobby's Alvin Dark–model glove. It was old *mamasan,* standing there between the crotchrocket, which had been crushed by a freezer (wrapped meat was spilling out of its shattered door in frosty blocks), and a Subaru with a lawn-flamingo punched through its roof. Old *mamasan* in her green pants and orange smock and red sneakers, old *mamasan* lit up like a bar-sign in hell.

"Hey, American, you come me, I keep safe." And she held out her arms.

Sully walked toward her through the noisy hail of falling televisions and backyard pools and cartons of cigarettes and high-heeled shoes and a great big pole hairdryer and a pay telephone that hit and vomited a jackpot of quarters. He walked toward her with a feeling of relief, that feeling you get only when you are coming home.

"I keep safe." Holding out her arms now. "Poor boy, I keep safe." Sully stepped into the dead circle of her embrace as people screamed and ran and all things American fell out of the sky, blitzing I-95 north of Bridgeport with their falling glitter. She put her arms around him.

"I keep safe," she said, and Sully was in his car. Traffic was stopped all around him, four lanes of it. The radio was on, tuned to WKND. The Platters were singing "Twilight Time" and Sully couldn't breathe. Nothing appeared to have fallen out of the sky, except for the traffic tie-up everything seemed to be in good order, but how could that be? How could it be when he still had Bobby Garfield's old baseball glove on his hand?

"I keep safe," old *mamasan* was saying. "Poor boy, poor American boy, I keep safe."

Sully couldn't breathe. He wanted to smile at her. He wanted to tell her he was sorry, that some of them had at least meant well, but he had no air and he was very tired. He closed his eyes and tried to raise Bobby's glove one final time, get one final shallow whiff of that oily, summery smell, but it was too heavy.

Dieffenbaker was standing at the kitchen counter the next morning, wearing a pair of jeans and nothing else, pouring himself a cup of coffee, when Mary came in from the living room. She was wearing her PROPERTY OF THE DENVER BRONCOS sweatshirt and had the New York *Post* in her hand.

"I think I have some bad news for you," she said, then seemed to reconsider. "*Moderately* bad news."

He turned to her warily. Bad news should always come after lunch, he thought. At least a person was halfway prepared for bad news after lunch. First thing in the morning everything left a bruise. "What is it?"

"The man you introduced me to yesterday at your buddy's funeral—you said he was a car dealer in Connecticut, right?"

"Right."

"I wanted to be sure because John Sullivan isn't, you know, the world's most striking and uncommon—"

"What are you talking about, Mary?"

She handed him the paper, which was folded open to a page about halfway into the tabloid. "They say it happened while he was on his way home. I'm sorry, hon."

She had to be wrong, that was his first thought; people couldn't die just after you'd seen them and talked to them, it seemed like a basic rule, somehow.

But it was him, all right, and in triplicate: Sully in a high-school baseball uniform with a catcher's mask pushed back to the top of his head, Sully in an Army uniform with sergeant's stripes on the sleeve, and Sully in a business suit that had to hail from the late seventies. Beneath the row of pictures was the sort of headline you found only in the *Post:*

JAMBO!

SILVER STAR VIET VET DIES IN CONN. TRAFFIC JAM

Dieffenbaker scanned the story quickly, feeling the sense of unease and betrayal he always felt these days when he read the death-notice of someone his own age, someone he knew. *We are still too young for natural deaths,* he always thought, knowing that it was a foolish idea.

Sully had died of an apparent heart attack while stuck in a traffic tie-up caused by a jackknifed tractor-trailer truck. He might well have died within sight of his own dealership's Chevrolet sign, the article lamented. Like the JAMBO! headline, such epiphanies could be found only in the *Post.* The *Times* was a good paper if you were smart; the *Post* was the newspaper of drunks and poets.

Sully had left an ex-wife and no children. Funeral arrangements were being made by Norman Oliver, of First Connecticut Bank and Trust.

Buried by his bank! Dieffenbaker thought, his hands beginning to shake. He had no idea why this thought filled him with such horror, but it did. *By his fucking* bank! *Oh man!*

"Honey?" Mary was looking at him a little nervously. "Are you all right?"

"Yes," he said. "He died in a traffic jam. Maybe they couldn't even get an ambulance to him. Maybe they never even found him until the traffic started moving again. Christ."

"Don't," she said, and took the paper away from him again.

Sully had won the Silver Star for the rescue, of course—the helicopter rescue. The gooks had been shooting but Packer and Shearman had led in a bunch of American soldiers, mostly Delta two-twos, just the same. Ten or twelve of the Bravo Company soldiers had laid down a confused and probably not very effective covering fire as the rescue operation took place . . . and for a wonder two of the men from the tangled copters had actually been alive, at least when they came out of the clearing. John Sullivan had carried one of them to cover all by himself, the chopper guy shrieking in his arms and covered with fire-retardant foam.

Malenfant had gone running into the clearing, too—Malenfant clutching one of the extinguisher cannisters like a big red baby and screaming at the Cong in the bush to shoot him if they could, except they couldn't, he knew they couldn't, they were just a bunch of blind slopehead syphilitic fucks and they couldn't hit him, couldn't hit the broad side of a fuckin barn. Malenfant had also been put up for the Silver Star, and although Dieffenbaker couldn't say for sure, he supposed the pimply little murdering asshole had probably won one. Had Sully known or guessed? Wouldn't he have mentioned it while they were sitting together outside the funeral parlor? Maybe; maybe not. Medals had a way of seeming less important as time passed, more and more like the award you got in junior high for memorizing a poem or the letter you got in high school for running track and blocking home plate when the throw came home. Just something you kept on a shelf. They were the things old men used to jazz the kids. The things they held out to make you jump higher, run faster, fling yourself forward. Dieffenbaker thought the world would probably be a better place without old men (this revelation coming just as he was getting ready to be one himself). Let the old women live, old women never hurt anyone as a rule, but old men were more dangerous than rabid dogs. Shoot all of them, then douse their bodies with gasoline, then light them on fire. Let the children join hands and dance around the blaze, singing corny old Crosby, Stills and Nash songs.

"Are you really okay?" Mary asked.

"About Sully? Sure. I hadn't seen him in years."

He sipped his coffee and thought about the old lady in the red sneakers, the one Malenfant had killed, the one who came to visit Sully. She wouldn't be visiting Sully anymore; there was that much, at least. Old *mamasan*'s visiting days were done. It was how wars really ended, Dieffenbaker supposed—not at truce tables but in cancer wards and office cafeterias and traffic jams. Wars died one tiny piece at a time, each piece something that fell like a memory, each lost like an echo that fades in winding hills. In the end even war ran up the white flag. Or so he hoped. He hoped that in the end even war surrendered.

1999: Come on, you bastard, come on home.

Heavenly Shades of Night Are Falling

1999

On an afternoon in the last summer before the year 2000, Bobby Garfield came back to Harwich, Connecticut. He went to West Side Cemetery first, where the actual memorial service took place at the Sullivan family plot. Old Sully-John got a good crowd; the *Post* story had brought them out in droves. Several small children were startled into tears when the American Legion honor-guard fired their guns. After the graveside service there was a reception at the local Amvets Hall. Bobby made a token appearance—long enough to have a slice of cake and a cup of coffee and say hello to Mr. Oliver—but he saw no one he knew, and there were places he wanted to go while there was still plenty of good daylight. He hadn't been back to Harwich in almost forty years.

The Nutmeg Mall stood where St. Gabriel the Steadfast Upper and Secondary Schools had been. The old post office was now a vacant lot. The railway station continued to overlook the Square, but the stone overpass support-posts were covered with graffiti and Mr. Burton's newsstand kiosk was boarded up. There were still grassy swards between River Avenue and the Housatonic, but the ducks were gone. Bobby remembered throwing one of those ducks at a man in a tan suit—improbable but true. *I'll give you two bucks to let me blow you,* the man had said, and Bobby had hucked a duck at him. He could grin about it now, but that nimrod had scared the hell out of him, and for all sorts of reasons.

There was a great beige UPS warehouse where the Asher Empire had stood. Farther along toward Bridgeport, where Asher Avenue emptied into Puritan Square, the William Penn Grille was also gone, replaced by a Pizza Uno. Bobby thought about going in there, but not very seriously. His stomach was fifty, just like the rest of him, and it didn't do so well with pizza anymore.

Except that wasn't really the reason. It would be too easy to imagine things, that was the real reason—too easy to envision big vulgar cars out front, the paintjobs so bright they seemed to howl.

So he had driven back to Harwich proper, and damned if the Colony Diner wasn't still where it had always been, and damned if there weren't still grilled hotdogs on the menu. Hotdogs were as bad as fuckin pizza, maybe worse, but what the hell was Prilosec for, if not the occasional gastronomic ramble down memory lane? He had swallowed one, and chased it with two hotdogs. They still came in those little grease-spotted cardboard sleeves, and they still tasted like heaven.

He tamped the hotdogs down with pie à la mode, then went out and stood by his car for a moment. He decided to leave it where it was—there were only two more stops he wanted to make, and both were within walking distance. He took the gym bag off the passenger seat and walked slowly past Spicer's, which had evolved into a 7-Eleven store with gas-pumps out front. Voices came to him as he passed, 1960 ghost-voices, voices of the Sigsby twins.

Mumma-Daddy havin a fight.

Mumma said stay out.

Why'd you do that, stupid old Bobby Garfield?

Stupid old Bobby Garfield, yes, that had been him. He might have gotten a little smarter over the years, but probably not that much.

Halfway up Broad Street Hill he spied a faded hopscotch grid on the sidewalk. He dropped to one knee and looked at it closely in the latening light, brushing at the squares with the tips of his fingers.

"Mister? You all right?" It was a young woman with a 7-Eleven bag in her arms. She was looking at Bobby with equal parts concern and mistrust.

"I'm fine," he said, getting to his feet and dusting off his hands. He was, too. Not a single moon or star beside the grid, let alone a comet. Nor had he seen any lost-pet posters in his rambles around town. "I'm fine."

"Well, good for you," the young woman said, and hurried on her way. She did not smile. Bobby watched her go and then started walking again himself, wondering what had happened to the Sigsby twins, where they were now. He remembered Ted Brautigan talking about time once, calling it the old bald cheater.

Until he actually saw 149 Broad Street, Bobby hadn't realized how sure he'd been that it would have become a video-rental store or a sandwich shop or maybe a condominium. Instead it was exactly the same except for the trim, now cream instead of green. There was a bike on the porch, and he thought of how desperately he had wanted a bike that last summer in Harwich. He'd even had a jar to save money in, with a label on it that said Bike Account, or something.

More ghost-voices as he stood there with his shadow lengthening into the street.

If we were the Gotrocks, you wouldn't have to borrow from your bike-jar if you wanted to take your little girlfriend on the Loop-the-Loop.

She's not my girlfriend! She is not my little girlfriend!

In his memory he had said that out loud to his mother, *screamed* it at her, in fact . . . but he doubted the accuracy of that memory. He hadn't had the kind of mother you could scream at. Not if you wanted to keep your scalp.

And besides. Carol *had* been his little girlfriend, hadn't she? She *had* been.

He had one more stop to make before returning to his car, and after a final long look at the house where he had lived with his mother until August of 1960, Bobby started back down Broad Street Hill, swinging the gym bag in one hand.

There had been magic that summer, even at the age of fifty he did not question that, but he no longer knew of what sort it had been. Perhaps he had experienced only the Ray Bradbury kind of childhood so many smalltown kids had, or at least remembered having; the kind where the real world and that of dreams sometimes overlapped, creating a kind of magic.

Yes, but . . . well . . .

There were the rose petals, of course, the ones which had come by way of Carol . . . but had they meant anything? Once it had seemed so—to the lonely, almost lost boy he had been, it had seemed so—

but the rose petals were long gone. He had lost them right around the time he'd seen the photograph of that burned-out house in Los Angeles and realized that Carol Gerber was dead.

Her death cancelled not only the idea of magic but, it seemed to Bobby, the very purpose of childhood. What good was it if it brought you to such things? Bad eyes and bad blood-pressure were one thing; bad ideas, bad dreams, and bad ends were another. After awhile you wanted to say to God, ah, come on, Big Boy, *quit* it. You lost your innocence when you grew up, all right, everyone knew that, but did you have to lose your hope, as well? What good was it to kiss a girl on the Ferris wheel when you were eleven if you were to open the paper eleven years later and learn that she had burned to death in a slummy little house on a slummy little dead-end street? What good was it to remember her beautiful alarmed eyes or the way the sun had shone in her hair?

He would have said all of this and more a week ago, but then a tendril of that old magic had reached out and touched him. *Come on,* it had whispered. *Come on, Bobby, come on, you bastard, come home.* So here he was, back in Harwich. He had honored his old friend, he had had himself a little sightseeing tour of the old town (and without misting up a single time), and now it was almost time to go. He had, however, one more stop to make before he did.

It was the supper hour and Commonwealth Park was nearly empty. Bobby walked to the wire backstop behind the Field B home plate as three dawdling players went past him in the other direction. Two were carrying equipment in big red duffel bags; the third had a boombox from which The Offspring blasted at top volume. All three boys gave him mistrustful looks, which Bobby found unsurprising. He was an adult in the land of children, living in a time when all such as he were suspect. He avoided making things worse by giving them a nod or a wave or saying something stupid like *How was the game, fellas?* They passed on their way.

He stood with his fingers hooked into the wire diamonds of the backstop, watching the late red light slant across the outfield grass, reflecting from the scoreboard and the signs reading STAY IN SCHOOL and WHY DO YOU THINK THEY CALL IT DOPE. And again he felt that breathless sense of magic, that sense of the world as a thin veneer stretched over something else, something both brighter and darker. The voices were everywhere now, spinning like the lines on a top.

Don't you call me stupid, Bobby-O.

You shouldn't hit Bobby, he's not like those men.

A real sweetie, kid, he'd play that song by Jo Stafford.

It's ka . . . *and* ka *is destiny.*

I love you, Ted . . .

"I love you, Ted." Bobby spoke the words, not declaiming them but not whispering them, either. Trying them on for size. He couldn't even remember what Ted Brautigan had looked like, not with any real clarity (only the Chesterfields, and the endless bottles of rootbeer), but saying it still made him feel warm.

There was another voice here, too. When it spoke, Bobby felt tears sting the corners of his eyes for the first time since coming back.

I wouldn't mind being a magician when I grow up, Bobby, you know it? Travel around with a carnival or a circus, wear a black suit and a top hat . . .

"And pull rabbits and shit out of the hat," Bobby said, turning away from Field B. He laughed, wiped his eyes, then ran one hand over the top of his head. No hair up there; he'd lost the last of it right on schedule, about fifteen years ago. He crossed one of the paths (gravel in 1960, now asphalt and marked with little signs reading BIKES ONLY **NO ROLLERBLADES!**) and sat down on one of the benches, possibly the same one where he'd sat on the day Sully had asked him to come to the movies and Bobby had turned him down, wanting to finish *Lord of the Flies* instead. He put his gym bag on the bench next to him.

Directly ahead was a grove of trees. Bobby was pretty sure it was the one where Carol had taken him when he started to cry. She did it so no one would see him bawling like a baby. No one but her. Had she taken him in her arms until it was cried out of him? He wasn't sure, but he thought she had. What he remembered more clearly was how the three St. Gabe's boys had almost beaten them up later. Carol's mother's friend had saved them. He couldn't remember her name, but she'd come along just in the nick of time . . . the way the

Navy guy came along just in time to save Ralph's bacon at the end of *Lord of the Flies.*

Rionda, that was her name. She told them she'd tell the priest, and the priest would tell their folks.

But Rionda hadn't been around when those boys found Carol again. Would Carol have burned to death in Los Angeles if Harry Doolin and his friends had left her alone? You couldn't say for sure, of course, but Bobby thought the answer was probably no. And even now he felt his hands clenching as he thought: *But I got you, Harry, didn't I? Yes indeed.*

Too late by then, though. By then everything had changed.

He unzipped the gym bag, rummaged, and brought out a battery radio. It was nowhere as big as the boombox which had just gone past him toward the equipment sheds, but big enough for his purposes. All he had to do was turn it on; it was already tuned to WKND, Southern Connecticut's Home of the Oldies. Troy Shondell was singing "This Time." That was fine with Bobby.

"Sully," he said, looking into the grove of trees, "you were one cool bastard."

From behind him, very prim, a woman said: "If you swear, I won't walk with you."

Bobby swivelled around so rapidly that the radio fell out of his lap and tumbled into the grass. He couldn't see the woman's face; she was nothing but a silhouette with red sky spread out on either side of her like wings. He tried to speak and couldn't. His breathing had come to a dead stop and his tongue was stuck to the roof of his mouth. Far back in his brain a voice mused: *So this is what seeing a ghost is like.*

"Bobby, are you all right?"

She moved fast, coming around the bench, and the red setting sun smacked him full in the eyes when she did. Bobby gasped, raised a hand, shut his eyes. He smelled perfume . . . or was it summer grass? He didn't know. And when he opened his eyes again, he could still see nothing but the woman's shape; there was a hanging green afterimage of the sun where her face belonged.

"Carol?" he asked. His voice was hoarse and uneven. "Dear God, is it really you?"

"Carol?" the woman asked. "I don't know any Carol. My name is Denise Schoonover."

Yet it was her. She'd only been eleven the last time he had seen her, but he knew. He rubbed his eyes frantically. From the radio on the grass the dj said, "This is WKND, where your past is always present. Here's Clyde McPhatter. He's got 'A Lover's Question.' "

You knew if she was alive she'd come. You knew *that.*

Of course; wasn't that why he had come himself? Surely not for Sully, or not just for Sully. And yet at the same time he had been so sure she was dead. From the instant he'd seen the picture of that burned-out house in Los Angeles, he had been positive. And how that had hurt his heart, not as if he had last seen her forty years before, running across Commonwealth Avenue, but as if she had always remained his friend, as close as a phone-call or a trip up the street.

While he was still trying to blink away the floating sunspot afterimage hanging before his eyes, the woman kissed him firmly on the mouth, and then whispered in his ear: "I have to go home. I have to make the salad. What's that?"

"The last thing you ever said to me when we were kids," he replied, and turned to her. "You came. You're alive and you came."

The sunset light fell on her face, and the afterimage had diminished enough for him to see her. She was beautiful in spite of the scar which began at the corner of her right eye and ran down to her chin in a cruel fishhook . . . or perhaps because of it. There were tiny sprays of crow's-feet beside her eyes, but no lines on her forehead or bracketing her paintless mouth.

Her hair, Bobby saw with wonder, was almost entirely gray.

As if reading his mind, she reached out and touched his head. "I'm so sorry," she said . . . but he thought he saw her old merriness dancing in her eyes. "You had the most gorgeous hair. Rionda used to say that was half of what I was in love with."

"Carol—"

She reached out and put her fingers over his lips. There were scars on her hand, as well, Bobby saw, and her little finger was misshapen, almost melted. These were burn scars.

"I told you, I don't know anyone named Carol. My name is Denise. Like in the old Randy and The Rainbows song?" She hummed a snatch of it. Bobby knew it well. He knew all the oldies. "If you were to check my ID, you'd see Denise Schoonover all up and down the line. I saw you at the service."

"I didn't see you."

"I'm good at not being seen," she said. "It's a trick someone taught me a long time ago. The trick of being *dim.*" She shuddered a little. Bobby had read of people shuddering—mostly in bad novels—but had never actually seen it done. "And when it comes to crowd scenes, I'm good at standing all the way at the back. Poor old Sully-John. Do you remember his Bo-lo Bouncer?"

Bobby nodded, starting to smile. "I remember one time when he tried to get extra-cool with it, hit it between his legs as well as between his arms and behind his back? He bopped himself a good one in the balls and we all just about killed ourselves laughing. A bunch of girls ran over—you were one of them, I'm pretty sure—wanting to know what happened, and we wouldn't tell you. You were pretty mad."

She smiled, a hand going to her mouth, and in that old gesture Bobby could see the child she had been with complete clarity.

"How did you know he died?" Bobby asked.

"Read it in the New York *Post.* There was one of those horrible headlines that are their specialty—JAMBO!, it said—and pictures of him. I live in Poughkeepsie, where the *Post* is regularly available." She paused. "I teach at Vassar."

"You teach at Vassar and you read the *Post*?"

She shrugged, smiling. "Everyone has their vices. How about you, Bobby? Did you read it in the *Post*?"

"I don't get the *Post.* Ted told me. Ted Brautigan."

She only sat there looking at him, her smile fading.

"You remember Ted?"

"I thought I'd never be able to use my arm again and Ted fixed it like magic. Of course I remember him. But Bobby—"

"He knew you'd be here. I thought that as soon as I opened the package, but I don't think I believed it until I saw you." He reached out to her and with the unself-consciousness of a child traced the course of the scar on her face. "You got this in L.A., didn't you? What happened? How did you get out?"

She shook her head. "I don't talk about any of that. I've never talked about what went on in that house. I never will. That was a different life. That was a different girl. That girl died. She was very young, very idealistic, and she was tricked. Do you remember the Monte Man at Savin Rock?"

He nodded, smiling a little. He took her hand and she gripped his own tightly. "Now they go, now they slow, now they rest, here's the test. His name was McCann or McCausland or something like that."

"The name doesn't matter. What matters is that he always let you think you knew where the queen was. He always let you think you could win. Right?"

"Right."

"This girl got involved with a man like that. A man who could always move the cards just a little faster than you thought he could. He was looking for some confused, angry kids, and he found them."

"Did he have a yellow coat?" Bobby asked. He didn't know if he was joking or not.

She looked at him, frowning a little, and he understood she didn't remember that part. Had he even told her about the low men? He thought so, he thought he had told her just about everything, but she didn't remember. Perhaps what had happened to her in L.A. had burned a few holes in her memory. Bobby could see how a thing like that might happen. And it wouldn't exactly make her unique, would it? A lot of people their age had worked very hard to forget who they had been and what they had believed during those years between the murder of John Kennedy in Dallas and the murder of John Lennon in New York City.

"Never mind," he said. "Go on."

She shook her head. "I've said all I'm going to about that part. All I can. Carol Gerber died on Benefit Street in Los Angeles. Denise

Schoonover lives in Poughkeepsie. Carol hated math, couldn't even get fractions, but Denise *teaches* math. How could they be the same person? It's a ridiculous idea. Case closed. I want to know what you mean about Ted. He *can't* still be alive, Bobby. He'd be over a hundred. Well over."

"I don't think time means much if you're a Breaker," Bobby said. Nor did it mean much on WKND, where Jimmy Gilmer was now singing about the Sugar Shack to the tooting accompaniment of what sounded like a sweet potato.

"A Breaker? What's—"

"I don't know and it doesn't matter," Bobby said. "This part might, so listen closely. Okay?"

"Okay."

"I live in Philadelphia. I've got a lovely wife who's a professional photographer, three lovely grown children, a lovely old dog with bad hips and a good disposition, and an old house which is always in desperate need of repairs. My wife says that's because the shoemaker's kids always go barefoot and the carpenter's house always has a leaky roof."

"Is that what you are? A carpenter?"

He nodded. "I live in Redmont Hills, and when I remember to get a paper, the Philly *Inquirer* is the one I buy."

"A carpenter," she mused. "I always thought you'd wind up a writer, or something."

"I did, too. But I also went through a period when I thought I'd wind up in Connecticut State Prison and *that* never happened, so I guess things have a way of balancing out."

"What was in the package you mentioned? And what does it have to do with Ted?"

"The package came FedEx, from a guy named Norman Oliver. A banker. He was Sully-John's executor. This was inside."

He reached into the gym bag again and brought out a battered old baseball glove. He laid it in the lap of the woman sitting next to him on the bench. She tipped it at once and looked at the name inked on the side.

"My God," she said. Her voice was flat, shocked.

"I haven't seen this baby since the day I found you over there in those trees with your arm dislocated. I suppose some kid came along, saw it lying on the grass, and just gleeped it. Although it wasn't in very good shape, even then."

"Willie stole it," she said, almost inaudibly. "Willie Shearman. I thought he was nice. You see what a fool I was about people? Even back then."

He looked at her in silent surprise, but she didn't see his look; she was gazing down at the old Alvin Dark–model glove, plucking at the tangle of rawhide strings somehow still holding the webbing in place. And then she delighted and touched him by doing what he had done as soon as he opened the box and saw what was there: she lifted the baseball glove to her face and smelled the sweet oil-and-leather aroma of the pocket. Only he had slipped it on his hand first, without even thinking about it. It was a baseball-player thing to do, a kid-thing, automatic as breathing. Norman Oliver must have been a kid at some point, but he'd apparently never been a ballplayer, because he hadn't found the piece of paper poked deep into the last finger of the glove—the finger with the deep scratch in the old cowhide. Bobby was the one who found the paper. The nail of his little finger poked against it and made it crackle.

Carol put the glove down again. Gray hair or no gray hair, she looked young again, and fully alive. "Tell me."

"It was on Sully's hand when they found him sitting dead in his car."

Her eyes went huge and round. In that instant she did not just look like the little girl who had ridden the Ferris wheel with him at Savin Rock; she *was* that little girl.

"Look on the heel of the glove, there by Alvin Dark's signature. Do you see?"

The light was fading fast now, but she saw, all right.

B.G.
1464 Dupont Circle Road
Redmont Hills, Pennsylvania
Zone 11

"Your address," she murmured. "Your address *now.*"

"Yes, but look at this." He tapped the words *Zone 11.* "The post office quit zoning mail in the sixties. I checked. Ted either didn't know or forgot."

"Maybe he put it that way on purpose."

Bobby nodded. "It's possible. In any case, Oliver read the address and sent me the glove—said he saw no need to put an old fielder's mitt through probate. He mostly wanted me to know that Sully had died, if I didn't know already, and that there was going to be a memorial service in Harwich. I believe he wanted me to come so he could hear the story of the glove. I couldn't help him much with that, though. Carol, are you sure Willie—"

"I saw him wearing it. I told him to give it back so I could send it to you, but he wouldn't."

"Do you suppose he gave it to Sully-John later?"

"He must have." Yet it did not ring true to her, somehow; she felt the truth must be stranger than that. Willie's attitude to the glove itself had been strange, although she could no longer exactly remember how.

"Anyway," he said, tapping the address on the heel of the glove, "that's Ted's printing. I'm sure it is. Then I put my hand up inside the glove, and I found something. It's really why I came."

He reached into the gym bag a third time. The redness was going out of the light now; the remains of the day were a fading pink, the color of wild roses. The radio, still lying in the grass, played "Don'tcha Just Know It," by Huey "Piano" Smith and The Clowns.

Bobby brought out a crumpled piece of paper. It had been stained in a couple of places by the glove's sweaty innards, but otherwise it looked remarkably white and fresh. He handed it to Carol.

She held it up to the light and slightly away from her face—her eyes, Bobby saw, were not as good as they once had been. "It's the title-page from a book," she said, and then laughed. "*Lord of the Flies,* Bobby! Your favorite!"

"Look at the bottom," he said. "Read what's there."

"Faber and Faber, Limited . . . 24 Russell Square . . . London." She looked at him questioningly.

"It's from the Faber paperback edition published in 1960," Bobby said. "That's on the back. But look at it, Carol! It looks brand-new. I think the book this page came from might have been in 1960 only *weeks* ago. Not the glove, that's a *lot* more beat-up than when I found it, but the title-page."

"Bobby, not all old books turn yellow if they're kept well. Even an old paperback might—"

"Turn it over," he said. "Take a look at the other side."

Carol did. Printed below the line reading *All rights reserved* was this: *Tell her she was as brave as a lion.*

"That's when I knew I had to come because *he* thought you'd be here, that you were still alive. I couldn't believe that, it was easier to believe in him than it was to believe—Carol? What's wrong? Is it the thing at the very bottom? What *is* that thing at the very bottom?"

She was crying now, and crying hard, holding the torn-out title-page in her hand and looking at what had been placed there on the back, squeezed into the scant white space below the conditions of sale:

+ = INFORMATION

"What does it mean? Do you know? You do, don't you?"

Carol shook her head. "It doesn't matter. It's special to me, that's all. Special to me the way the glove is special to you. For an old guy, he sure knows how to push the right buttons, doesn't he?"

"I guess so. Maybe that's what a Breaker does."

She looked at him. She was still weeping but was not, Bobby thought, truly unhappy. "Bobby, why would he do this? And how did he know we'd come? Forty years is a long time. People grow up, they grow up and leave the kids they were behind."

"Do they?"

She continued to look at him in the darkening day. Beyond them, the shadows of the grove deepened. In there—in the trees where he had wept on one day and found her, hurt and alone, the next—dark had almost come.

"Sometimes a little of the magic sticks around," Bobby said. "That's what I think. We came because we still hear some of the right voices. Do you hear them? The voices?"

"Sometimes," she said, almost reluctantly. "Sometimes I do."

Bobby took the glove from her. "Will you excuse me for a second?"

"Sure."

Bobby went to the grove of trees, dropped down on one knee to get beneath a low-hanging branch, and placed his old baseball glove on the grass with the pocket up to the darkening sky. Then he came back to the bench and sat down beside Carol again. "That's where it belongs," he said.

"Some kid'll just come along tomorrow and pick it up, you know that, don't you?" She laughed and wiped her eyes.

"Maybe," he agreed. "Or maybe it'll be gone. Back to wherever it came from."

As the day's last pink faded to ash, Carol put her head on Bobby's shoulder and he put an arm around her. They sat that way without speaking, and from the radio at their feet, The Platters began to sing.

AUTHOR'S NOTE

There is a University of Maine in Orono, of course. I know because I went there from 1966 to 1970. The characters in this story are completely fictional, however, and a good deal of the campus geography I have described never existed. Harwich is similarly fictional, and although Bridgeport is real, my version of it is not. Although it is difficult to believe, the sixties are not fictional; they actually happened.

I've also taken chronological liberties, the most noticable being my use of "The Prisoner" two years before it actually telecast in the United States—but I have tried to remain true to the spirit of the age. Is that really possible? I don't know, but I have tried.

An earlier and very different version of "Blind Willie" appeared in the magazine *Antaeus*. It was published in 1994.

I want to thank Chuck Verrill, Susan Moldow, and Nan Graham for helping me find the courage to write this book. I also want to thank my wife. Without her, I never would have gotten over.

S.K.

December 22, 1998

♥ + ☮ = INFORMATION